A Graphic Novel Adaptation by Damian Duffy and John Jennings

OCTAVIA E. BUTLER'S

KINDRED

Introduction by Nnedi Okorafor

ABRAMS COMICARTS • NEW YORK

Editor: Sheila Keenan
Project Manager: Charles Kochman
Designer: Pamela Notarantonio
Managing Editor: Michael Clark
Production Manager: Kathy Lovisolo

Library of Congress Control Number: 2016940630

ISBN: 978-1-4197-0947-0

Published in 2017 by Abrams ComicArts®, an imprint of ABRAMS.

Printed and bound in the U.S.A.
10 9 8 7 6 5 4 3

ABRAMS The Art of Books
115 West 18th Street, New York, NY 10011
abramsbooks.com

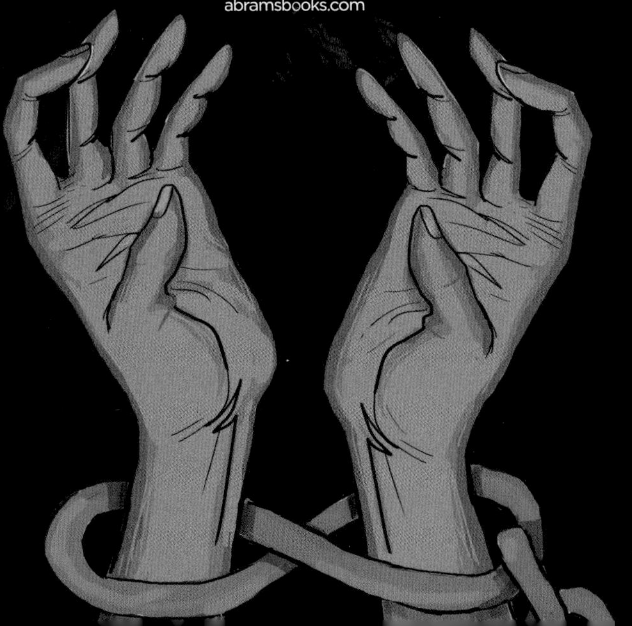

CONTENTS

INTRODUCTION

Finally.

A graphic-novel adaptation of Octavia E. Butler's mold-smashing science fiction book, *Kindred*. Can you believe it? And created by visual mad scientists John Jennings and Damian Duffy to boot? Fantastic. To see Butler's work presented in this way is deliciously harrowing. The very medium of the graphic novel already electrifies words and images. Tell one of Octavia's most immersive, relatable tales through this medium and you have fire. This is an exciting moment in storytelling. Octavia Butler, Level 2.

I first came across Octavia's work around 2001, when I was well on my way to identifying as a black female writer of speculative fiction. I was attending the Clarion Science Fiction and Fantasy Writers' Workshop at Michigan State University, and the organizers had brought my group to the local bookstore. As I strolled through the aisles, something extraordinary caught my eye, something I'd only ever seen once before in the science fiction and fantasy section of a bookstore: a cover featuring a dark-skinned black woman.

I was staring at *Wild Seed* by Octavia Estelle Butler.

There was only one copy of the book there on that fateful day. I grabbed it, clasped it to my chest as if someone was going to snatch it from me, quickly bought it, and ran to my dorm room to start reading.

That was the beginning of my bingeing on Octavia Butler's works.

In the previous weeks at Clarion, I had just begun writing about an angry Nigerian woman in pre-colonial Nigeria who'd been run out of her village because she'd developed the ability to fly. I was one of only two people of color in the writing group, and I was uncomfortable about workshopping my story. Plus, I'd never read a purely speculative story set anywhere on the continent of Africa that addressed womanhood and patriarchy bluntly.

When I look back, it's clear to me that I discovered Octavia right when I needed her. Reading *Wild Seed*, a story that featured an ageless shape-shifting Nigerian woman, blew my mind. And there is nothing like seeing a story in print that is similar to what you are trying to write. In many ways, reading *Wild*

Seed proved that what I was writing was okay, that people like me could be a part of this canon. This was a *very* big deal to me.

Sometime during those few weeks at the Clarion workshop, I learned that Octavia had once taught there, which meant that the organizers could reach her. I immediately asked if they could track her down. Within a day, I was on the phone with the great Octavia Butler, babbling my way through a conversation I don't remember; I was so starstruck. What I do remember was that Octavia was incredibly kind and liked to crack jokes.

That wasn't the last time we spoke to each other. When the 9/11 attacks happened, I found myself having a surreal email exchange with her. I kept those emails. What she said about terrorists still applies (and was an important theme in *Kindred*):

> One of my favorite quotes—so sadly true—is from Steve Biko: "The most potent weapon in the hands of the oppressor is the mind of the oppressed."

> There is also the sad reality that it takes very little to set off young men who want to feel powerful and important, but who are either unwilling or unable to find constructive outlets for their energies. Testosterone poisoning. And men have the nerve to complain about women's hormonal mood swings.

In 2005, I had a long conversation with Octavia when I interviewed her about her vampire novel *Fledgling*; later that year, I met her in person (for the first and only time) when she came to Chicago State University.

Octavia's email address was butler8star@qwest.net. For a long time after her shocking, sudden passing on February 24, 2006, I continued to send emails to that address, consoling myself by talking to her. Then one sad day, the emails started bouncing back. Thankfully, she left us with so many questions to ponder. Like, *what would you do if you were suddenly pulled into the past and had to find a way to survive?*

Kindred, a story about a modern African-American woman who mysteriously gets dragged into slave times and situations to save *herself*, is Octavia's most popular book. If one of her works is taught in a literature class, nine times out of ten it's this one. That is because *Kindred* is her most accessible book. It is a narrative that deftly connects America's past, present, and future through the use of mysterious time travel. It's a most unique slave narrative that is no less relevant and "realistic" than *Incidents in the Life of a Slave Girl*, *Beloved*, and *12 Years a Slave*.

And now, here is that story powerfully told in graphic-novel form. Buckle your seat belt. Still your mind. *Kindred* makes the old new, and in doing so brings back the sting. If you've read *Kindred* before, the graphic-novel format will renew the story. If you have not read Octavia Butler before, prepare yourself for an experience. You've chosen the perfect introduction to her work. *Kindred* will pull you right in.

Welcome.

Nnedi Okorafor
Flossmoor, Illinois
January 2017

Nnedi Okorafor is an acclaimed Nigerian-American author of science fiction, fantasy, and magic realism whose work has won the World Fantasy Award for Best Novel and the Wole Soyinka Prize for African Literature, among others. She teaches creative writing and literature at the University of Buffalo.

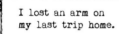

I lost an arm on my last trip home.

THE RIVER

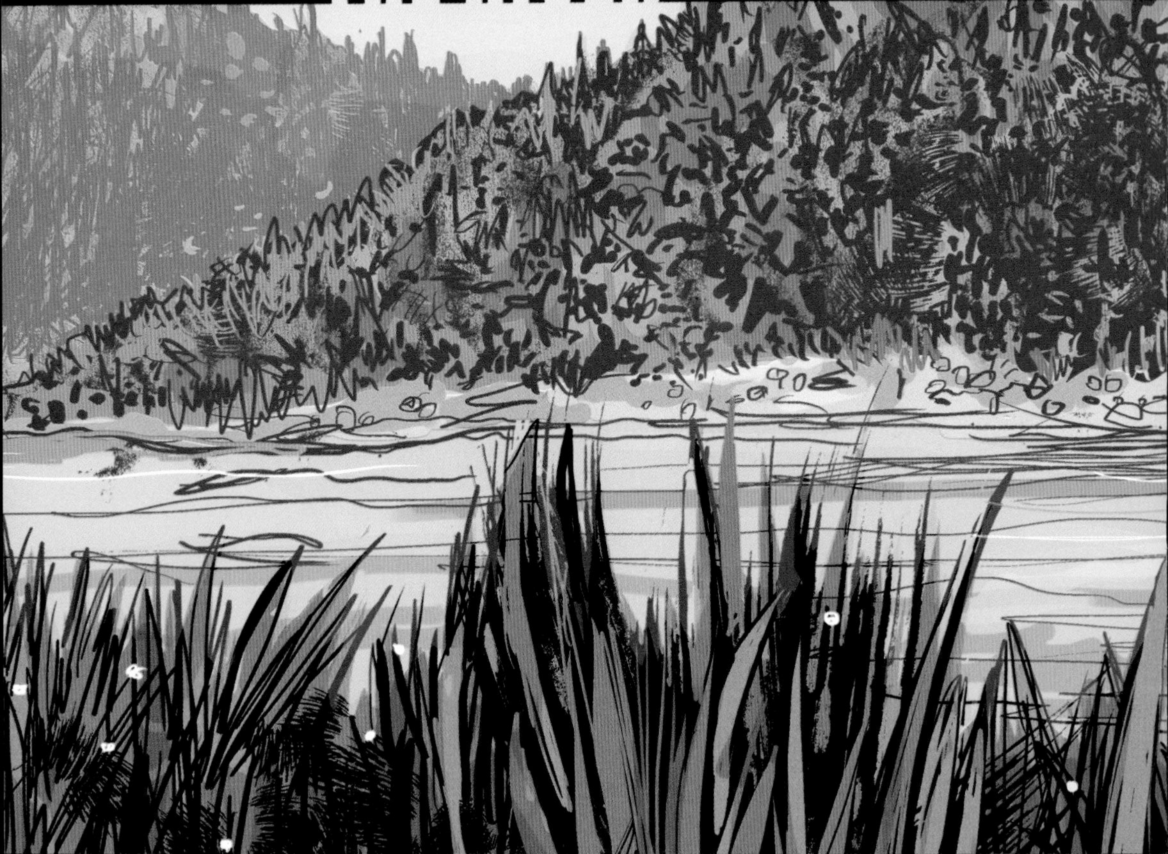

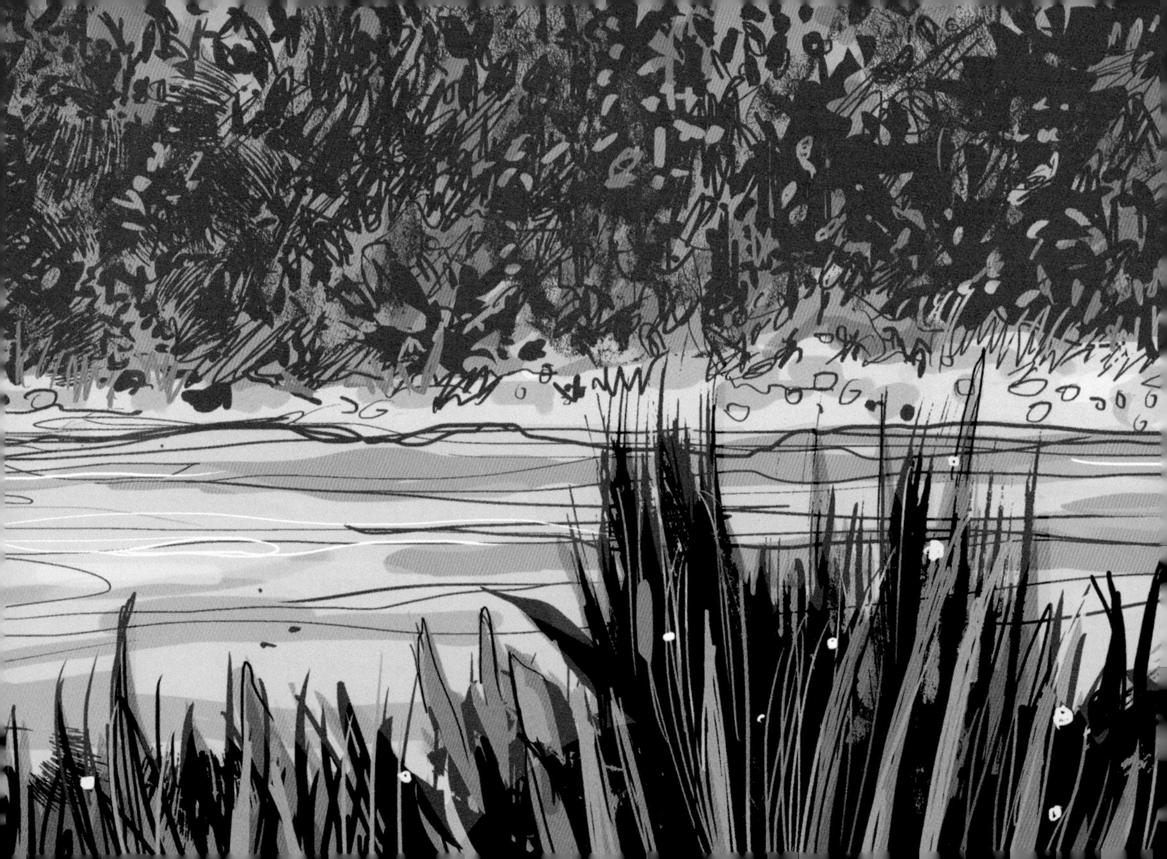

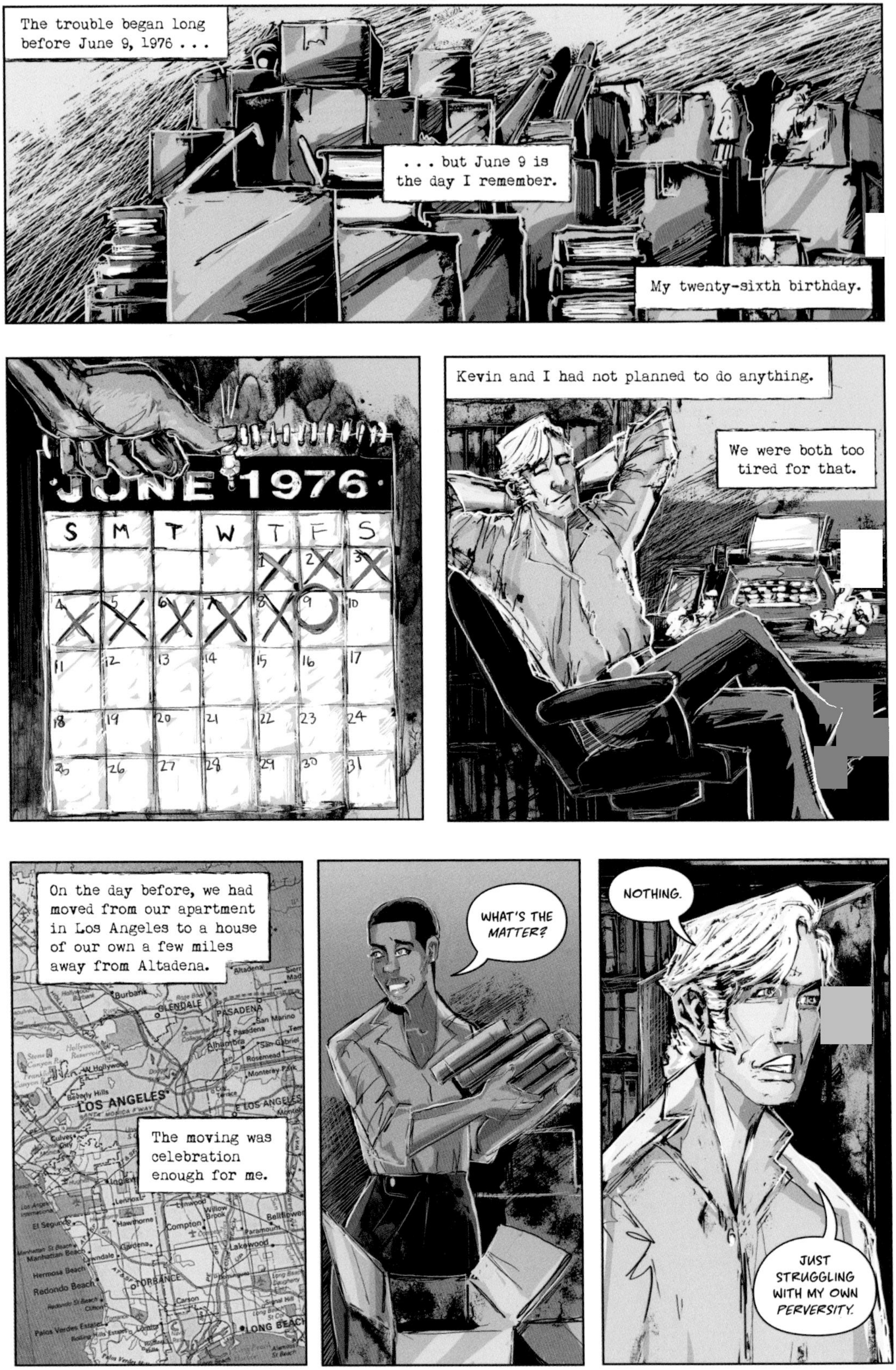
The trouble began long before June 9, 1976 . . .
. . . but June 9 is the day I remember.
My twenty-sixth birthday.
JUNE 1976
S M T W T F S
Kevin and I had not planned to do anything.
We were both too tired for that.
On the day before, we had moved from our apartment in Los Angeles to a house of our own a few miles away from Altadena.
The moving was celebration enough for me.
LOS ANGELES
PASADENA
GLENDALE
WHAT'S THE MATTER?
NOTHING.
JUST STRUGGLING WITH MY OWN PERVERSITY.

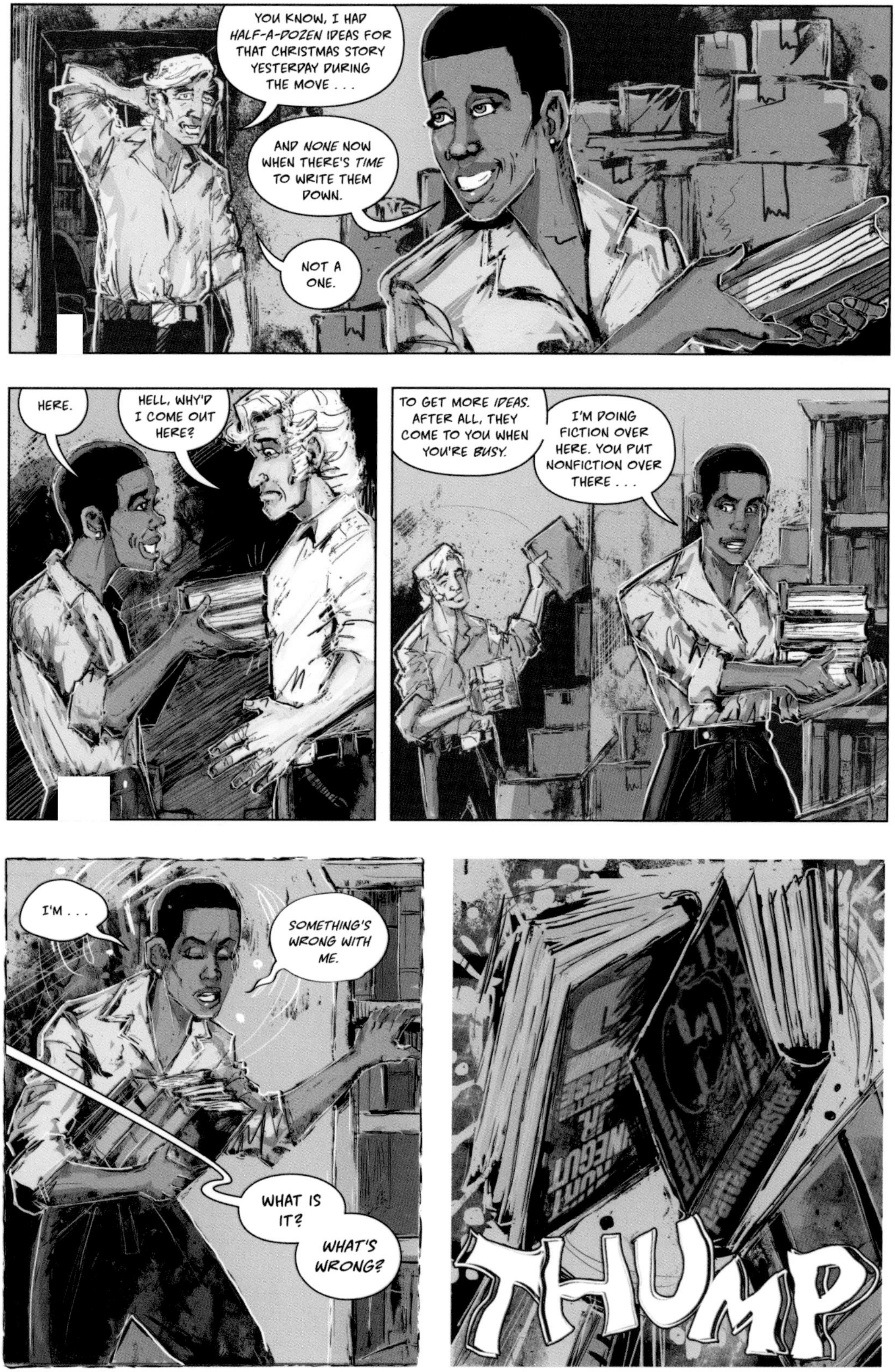
YOU KNOW, I HAD HALF-A-DOZEN IDEAS FOR THAT CHRISTMAS STORY YESTERDAY DURING THE MOVE . . .
AND NONE NOW WHEN THERE'S TIME TO WRITE THEM DOWN.
NOT A ONE.
HERE.
HELL, WHY'D I COME OUT HERE?
TO GET MORE IDEAS. AFTER ALL, THEY COME TO YOU WHEN YOU'RE BUSY.
I'M DOING FICTION OVER HERE. YOU PUT NONFICTION OVER THERE . . .
I'M . . .
SOMETHING'S WRONG WITH ME.
WHAT IS IT?
WHAT'S WRONG?
THUMP

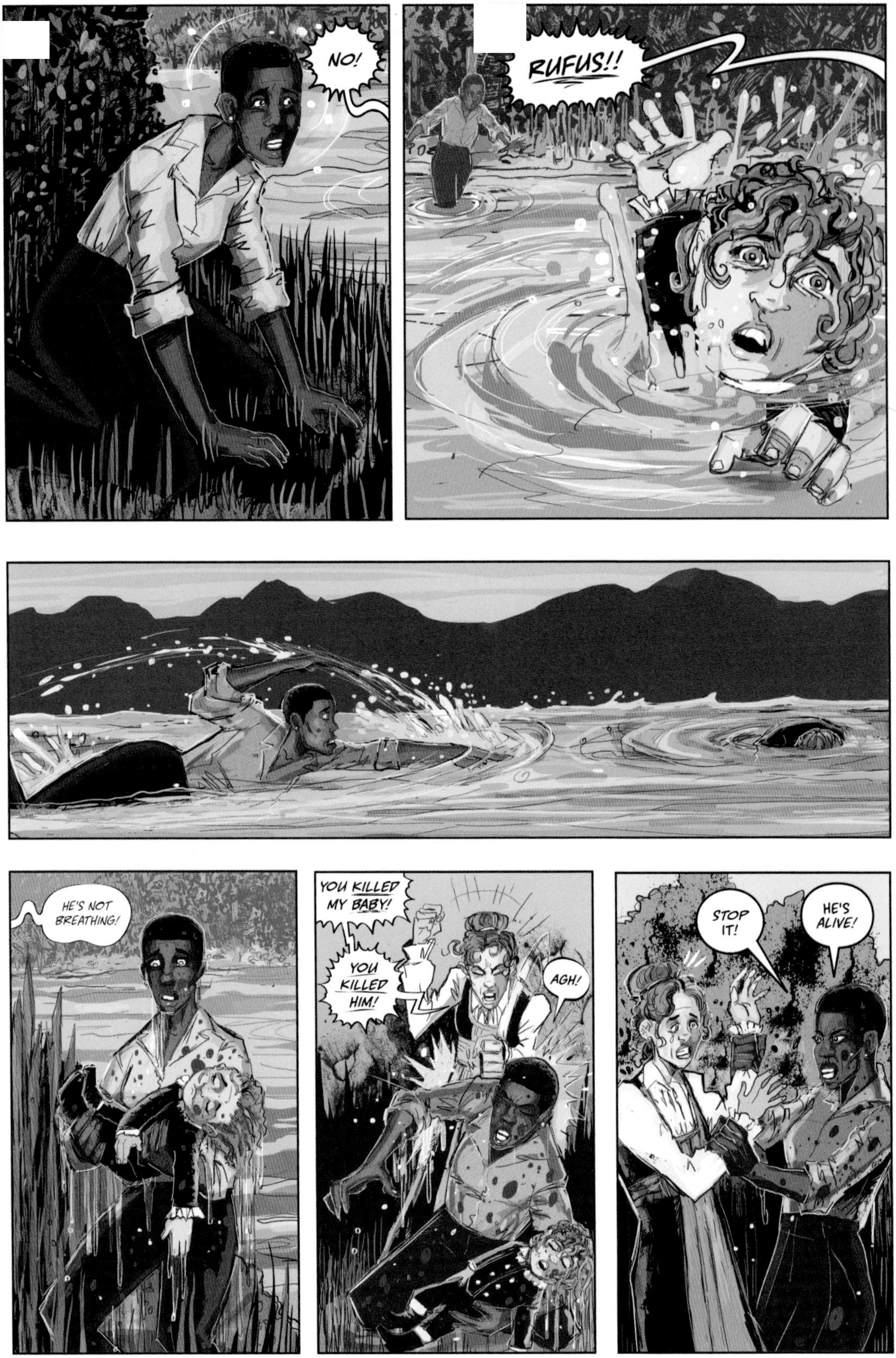
NO!
RUFUS!!
HE'S NOT BREATHING!
YOU KILLED MY BABY!
YOU KILLED HIM!
AGH!
STOP IT!
HE'S ALIVE!

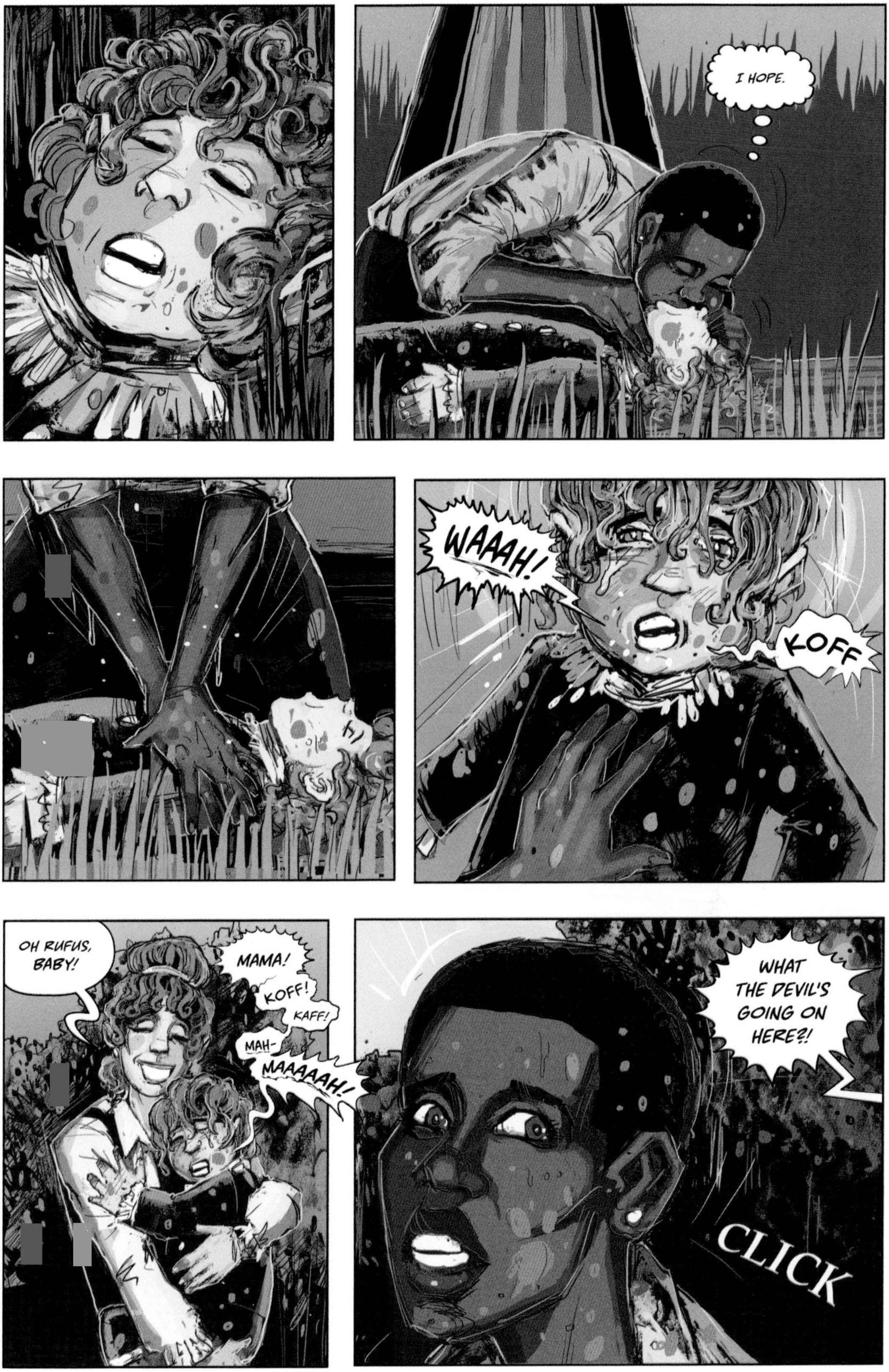
I HOPE.
WAAAH!
KOFF
OH RUFUS, BABY!
MAMA!
KOFF!
KAFF!
MAH-
MAAAAAH!
WHAT THE DEVIL'S GOING ON HERE?!
CLICK

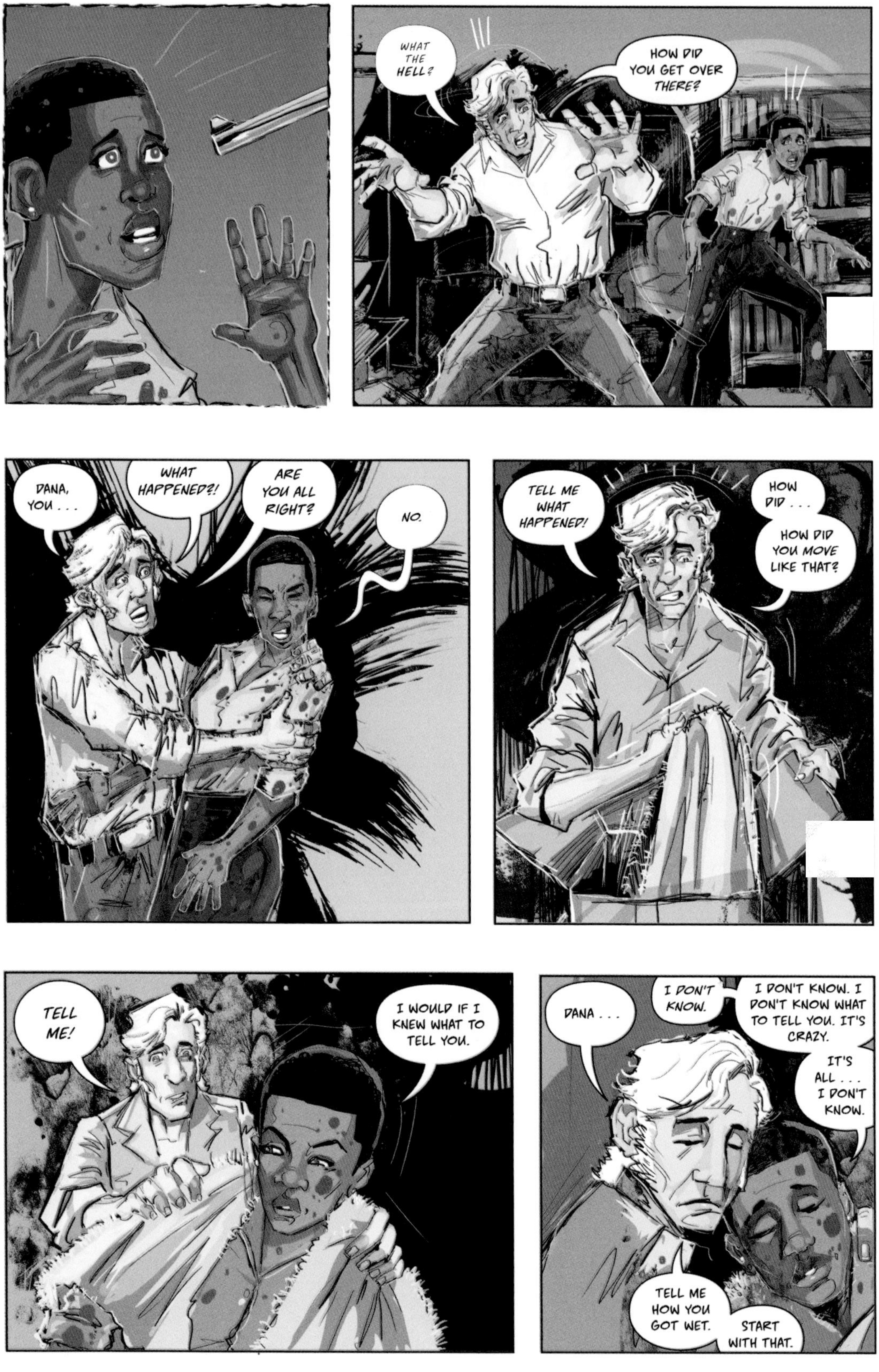
WHAT THE HELL?
HOW DID YOU GET OVER THERE?
DANA, YOU . . .
WHAT HAPPENED?!
ARE YOU ALL RIGHT?
NO.
TELL ME WHAT HAPPENED!
HOW DID . . .
HOW DID YOU MOVE LIKE THAT?
TELL ME!
I WOULD IF I KNEW WHAT TO TELL YOU.
DANA . . .
I DON'T KNOW.
I DON'T KNOW. I DON'T KNOW WHAT TO TELL YOU. IT'S CRAZY.
IT'S ALL . . . I DON'T KNOW.
TELL ME HOW YOU GOT WET.
START WITH THAT.

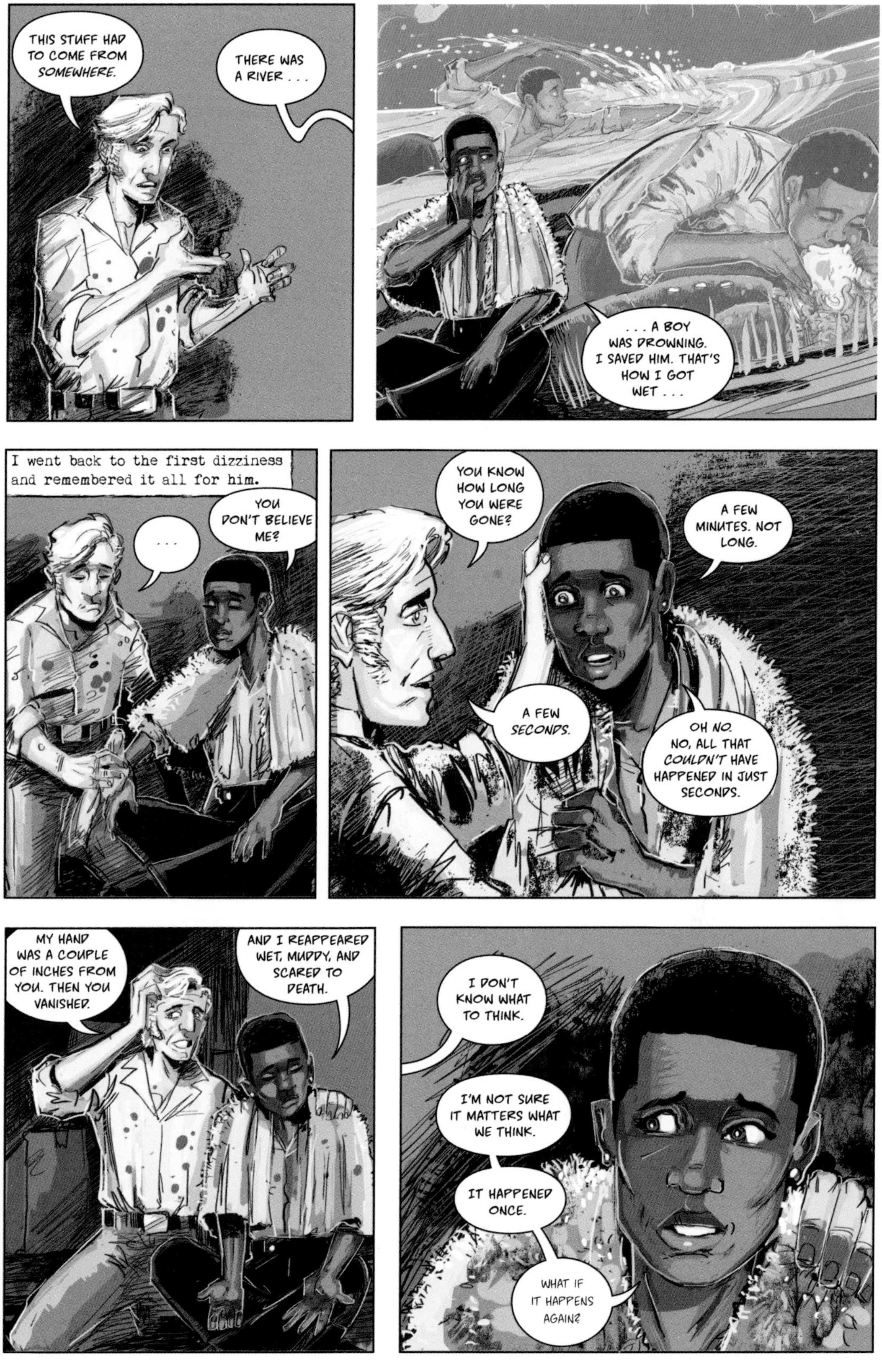
THIS STUFF HAD TO COME FROM SOMEWHERE.
THERE WAS A RIVER . . .
. . . A BOY WAS DROWNING. I SAVED HIM. THAT'S HOW I GOT WET . . .
I went back to the first dizziness and remembered it all for him.
. . .
YOU DON'T BELIEVE ME?
YOU KNOW HOW LONG YOU WERE GONE?
A FEW MINUTES. NOT LONG.
A FEW SECONDS.
OH NO. NO, ALL THAT COULDN'T HAVE HAPPENED IN JUST SECONDS.
MY HAND WAS A COUPLE OF INCHES FROM YOU. THEN YOU VANISHED.
AND I REAPPEARED WET, MUDDY, AND SCARED TO DEATH.
I DON'T KNOW WHAT TO THINK.
I'M NOT SURE IT MATTERS WHAT WE THINK.
IT HAPPENED ONCE.
WHAT IF IT HAPPENS AGAIN?

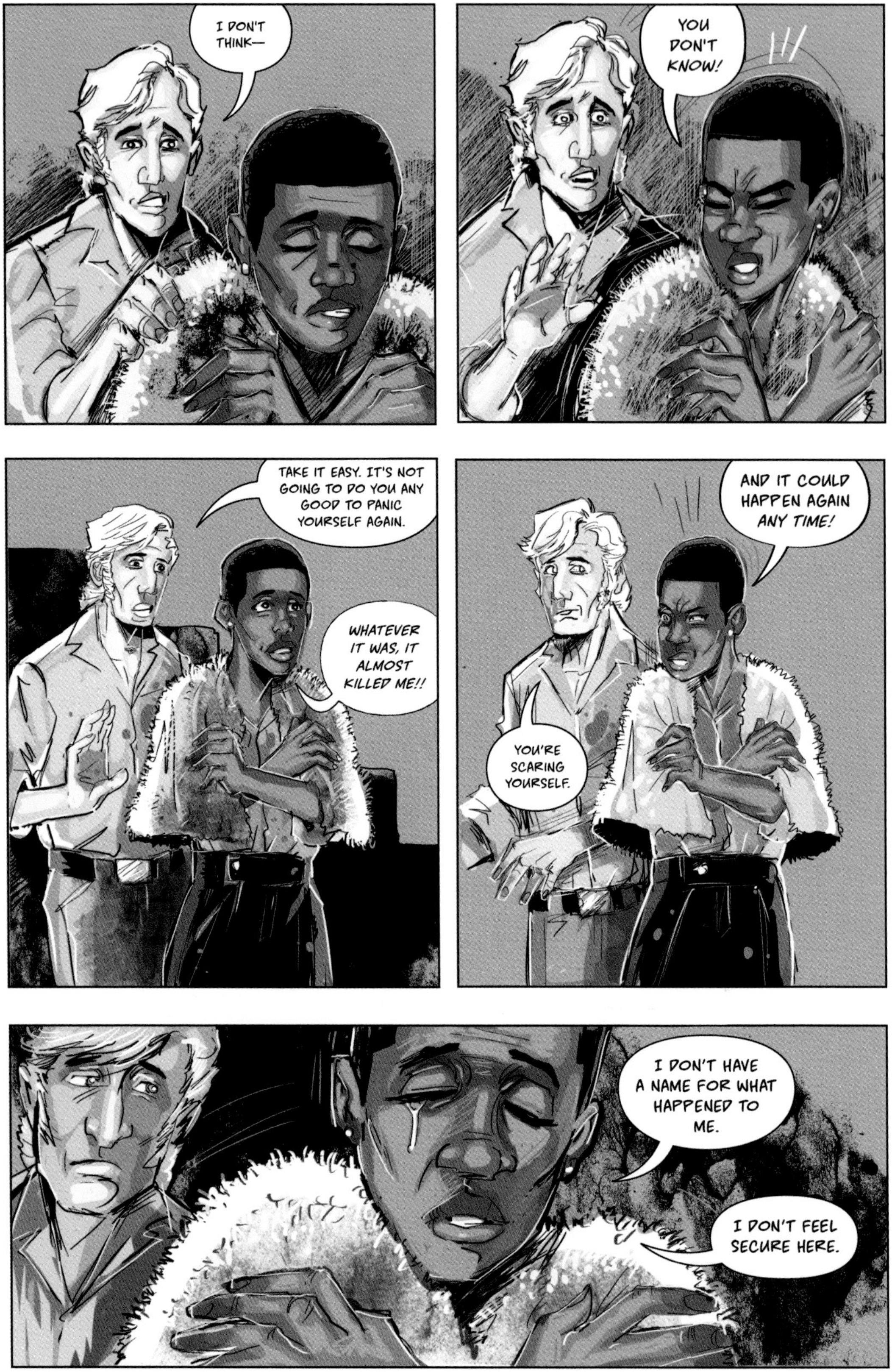
I DON'T THINK—
YOU DON'T KNOW!
TAKE IT EASY. IT'S NOT GOING TO DO YOU ANY GOOD TO PANIC YOURSELF AGAIN.
WHATEVER IT WAS, IT ALMOST KILLED ME!!
AND IT COULD HAPPEN AGAIN ANY TIME!
YOU'RE SCARING YOURSELF.
I DON'T HAVE A NAME FOR WHAT HAPPENED TO ME.
I DON'T FEEL SECURE HERE.

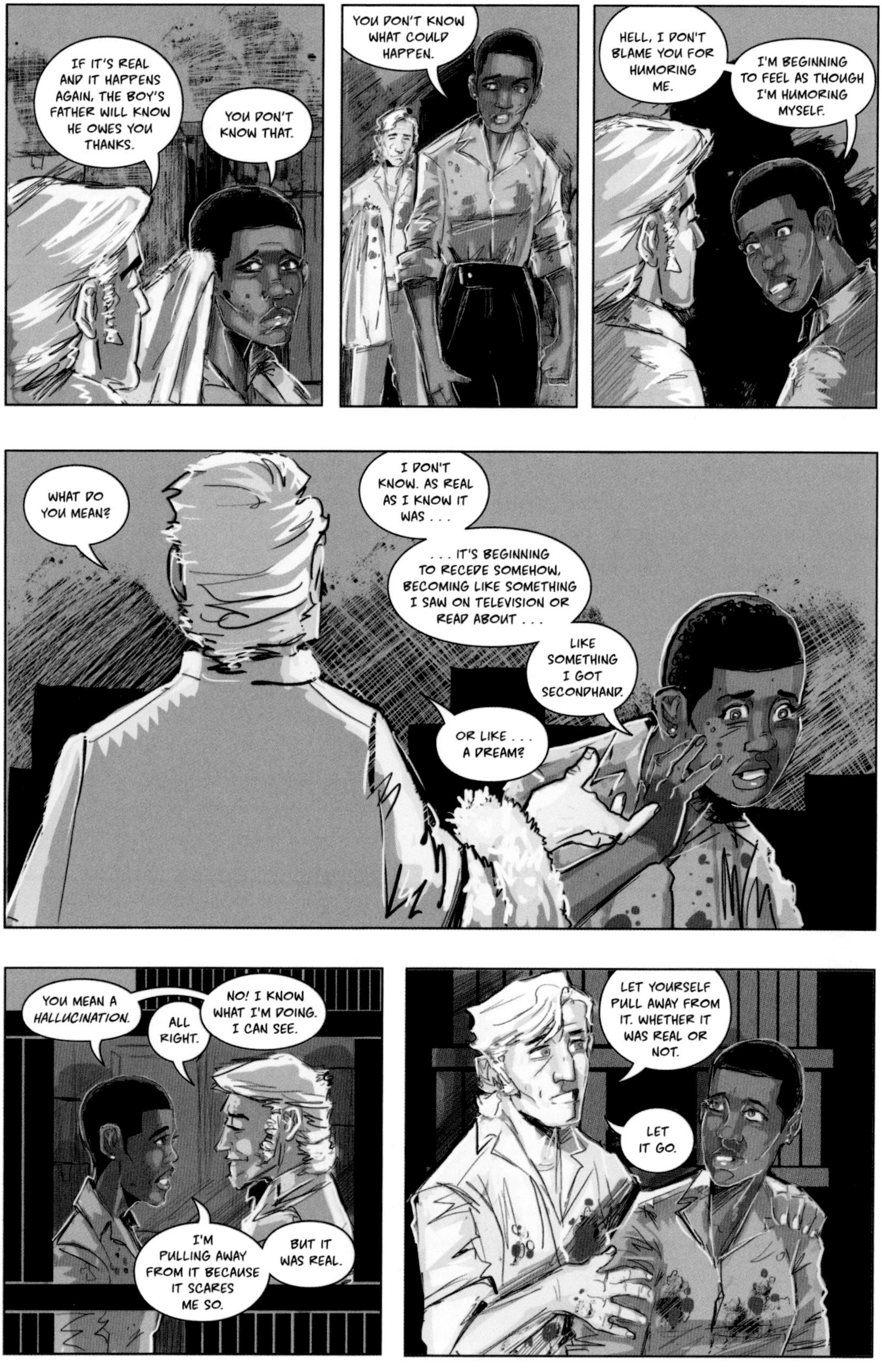
IF IT'S REAL AND IT HAPPENS AGAIN, THE BOY'S FATHER WILL KNOW HE OWES YOU THANKS.
YOU DON'T KNOW THAT.
YOU DON'T KNOW WHAT COULD HAPPEN.
HELL, I DON'T BLAME YOU FOR HUMORING ME.
I'M BEGINNING TO FEEL AS THOUGH I'M HUMORING MYSELF.
WHAT DO YOU MEAN?
I DON'T KNOW. AS REAL AS I KNOW IT WAS . . .
. . . IT'S BEGINNING TO RECEDE SOMEHOW, BECOMING LIKE SOMETHING I SAW ON TELEVISION OR READ ABOUT . . .
LIKE SOMETHING I GOT SECONDHAND.
OR LIKE . . . A DREAM?
YOU MEAN A HALLUCINATION.
NO! I KNOW WHAT I'M DOING. I CAN SEE.
ALL RIGHT.
I'M PULLING AWAY FROM IT BECAUSE IT SCARES ME SO.
BUT IT WAS REAL.
LET YOURSELF PULL AWAY FROM IT. WHETHER IT WAS REAL OR NOT.
LET IT GO.

THE FIRE

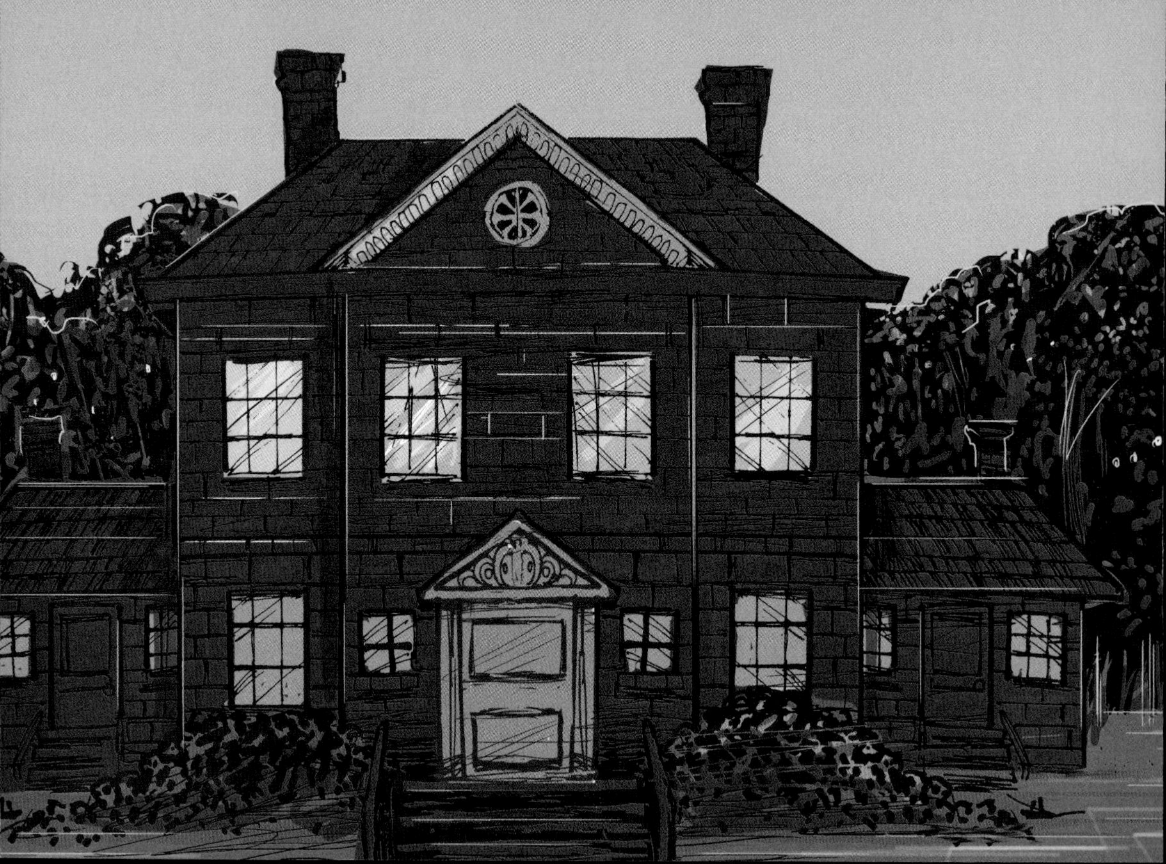

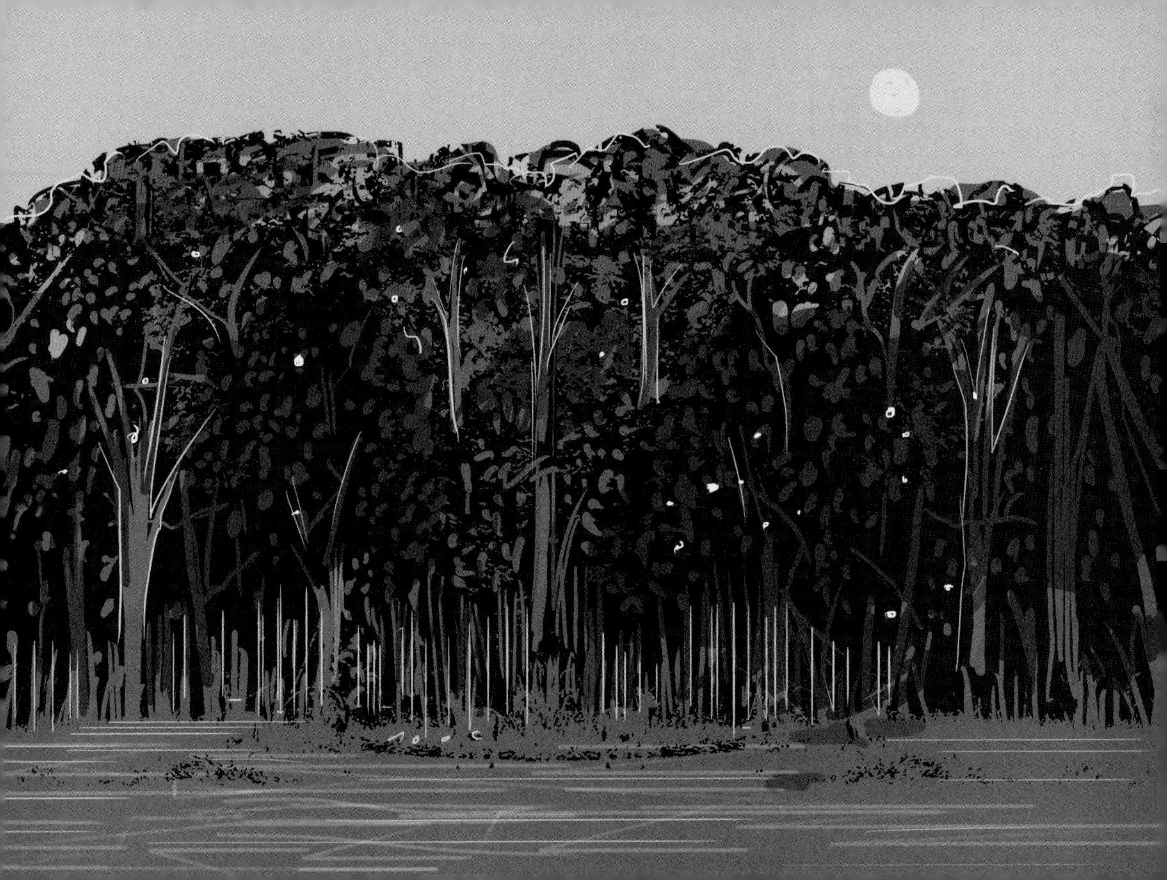

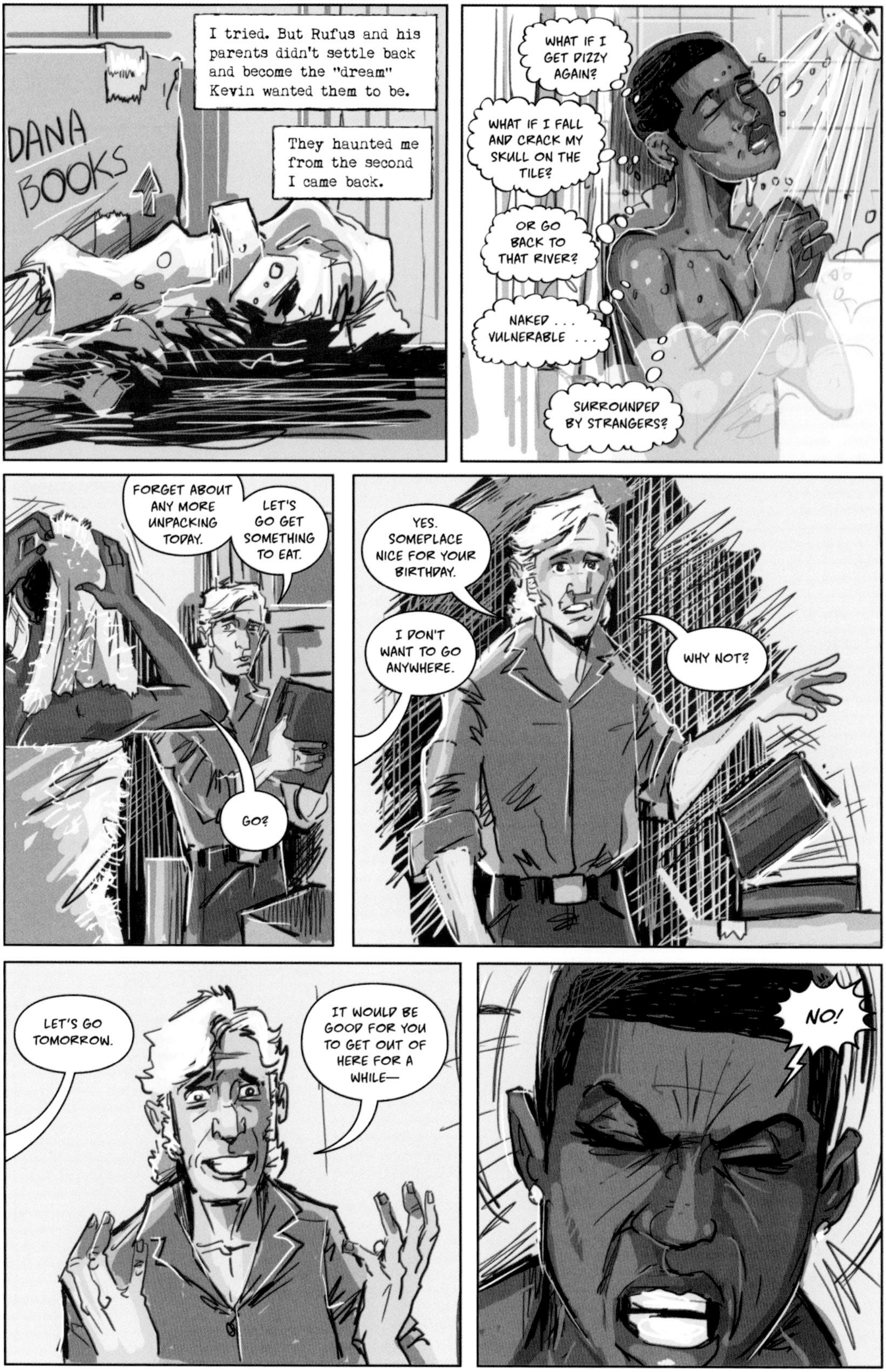
I tried. But Rufus and his parents didn't settle back and become the "dream" Kevin wanted them to be.
DANA BOOKS
They haunted me from the second I came back.
WHAT IF I GET DIZZY AGAIN?
WHAT IF I FALL AND CRACK MY SKULL ON THE TILE?
OR GO BACK TO THAT RIVER?
NAKED . . . VULNERABLE . . .
SURROUNDED BY STRANGERS?
FORGET ABOUT ANY MORE UNPACKING TODAY.
LET'S GO GET SOMETHING TO EAT.
GO?
YES. SOMEPLACE NICE FOR YOUR BIRTHDAY.
I DON'T WANT TO GO ANYWHERE.
WHY NOT?
LET'S GO TOMORROW.
IT WOULD BE GOOD FOR YOU TO GET OUT OF HERE FOR A WHILE—
NO!

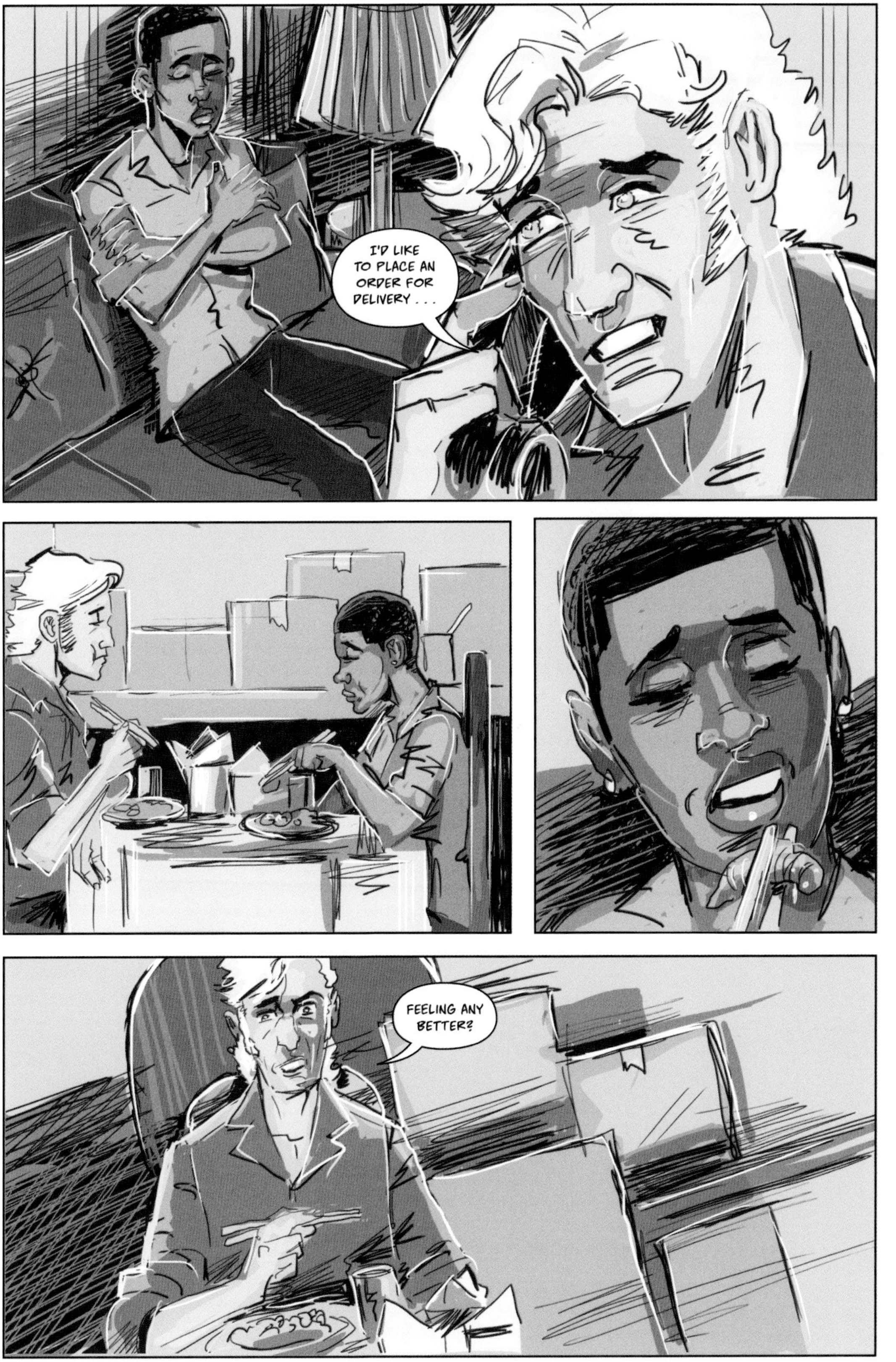
I'D LIKE TO PLACE AN ORDER FOR DELIVERY . . .
FEELING ANY BETTER?

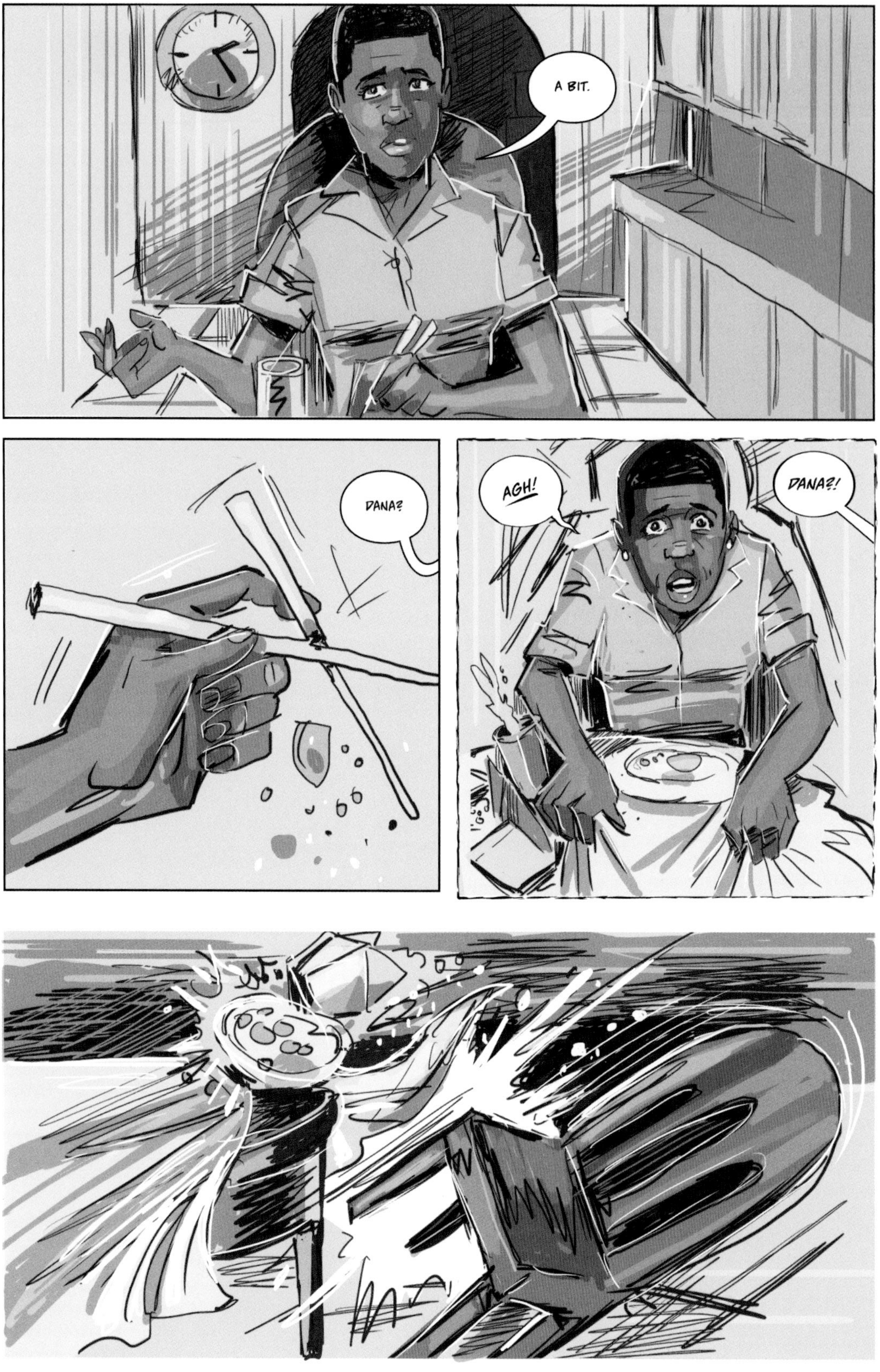
A BIT.
DANA?
AGH!
DANA?!

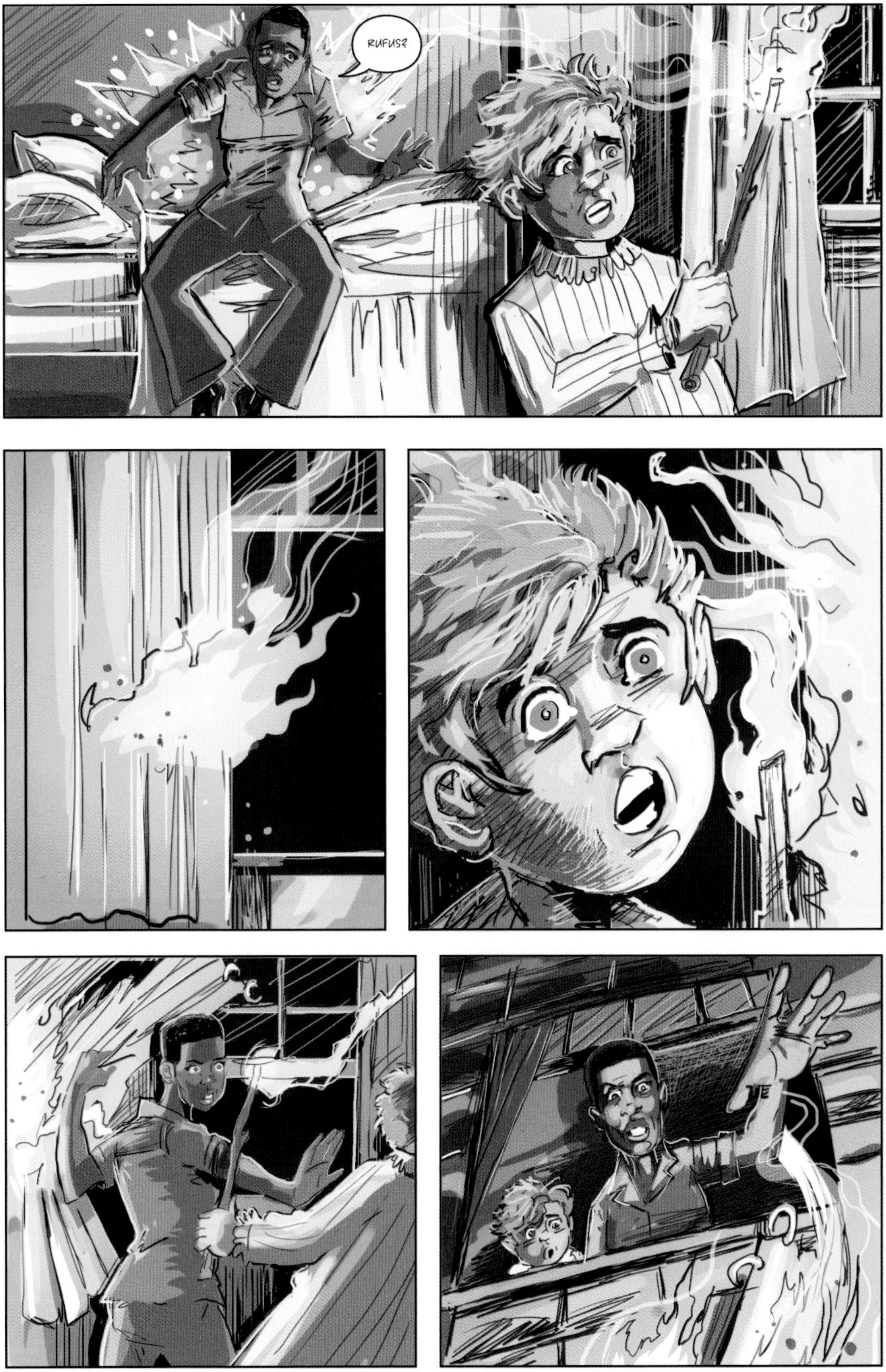
RUFUS?

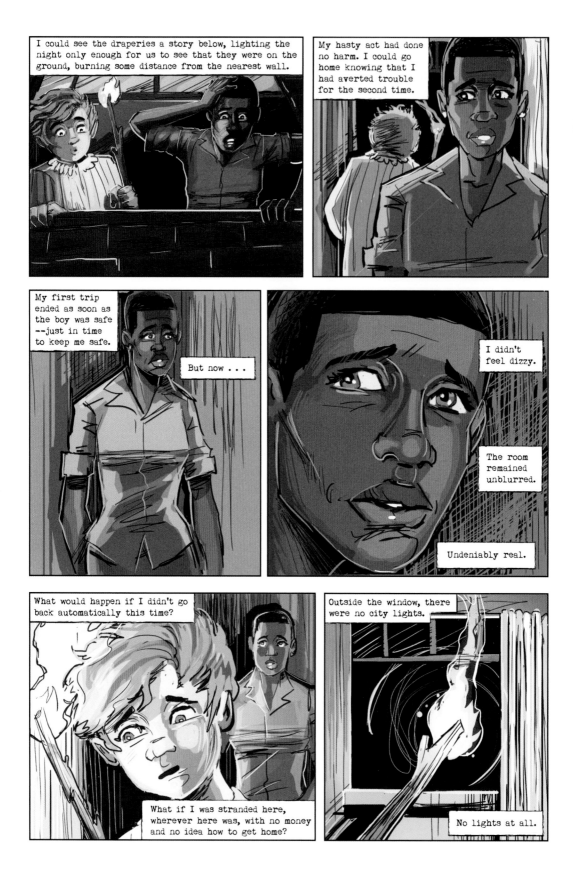

I could see the draperies a story below, lighting the night only enough for us to see that they were on the ground, burning some distance from the nearest wall.

My hasty act had done no harm. I could go home knowing that I had averted trouble for the second time.

My first trip ended as soon as the boy was safe—just in time to keep me safe.

But now . . .

I didn't feel dizzy.

The room remained unblurred.

Undeniably real.

What would happen if I didn't go back automatically this time?

What if I was stranded here, wherever here was, with no money and no idea how to get home?

Outside the window, there were no city lights.

No lights at all.

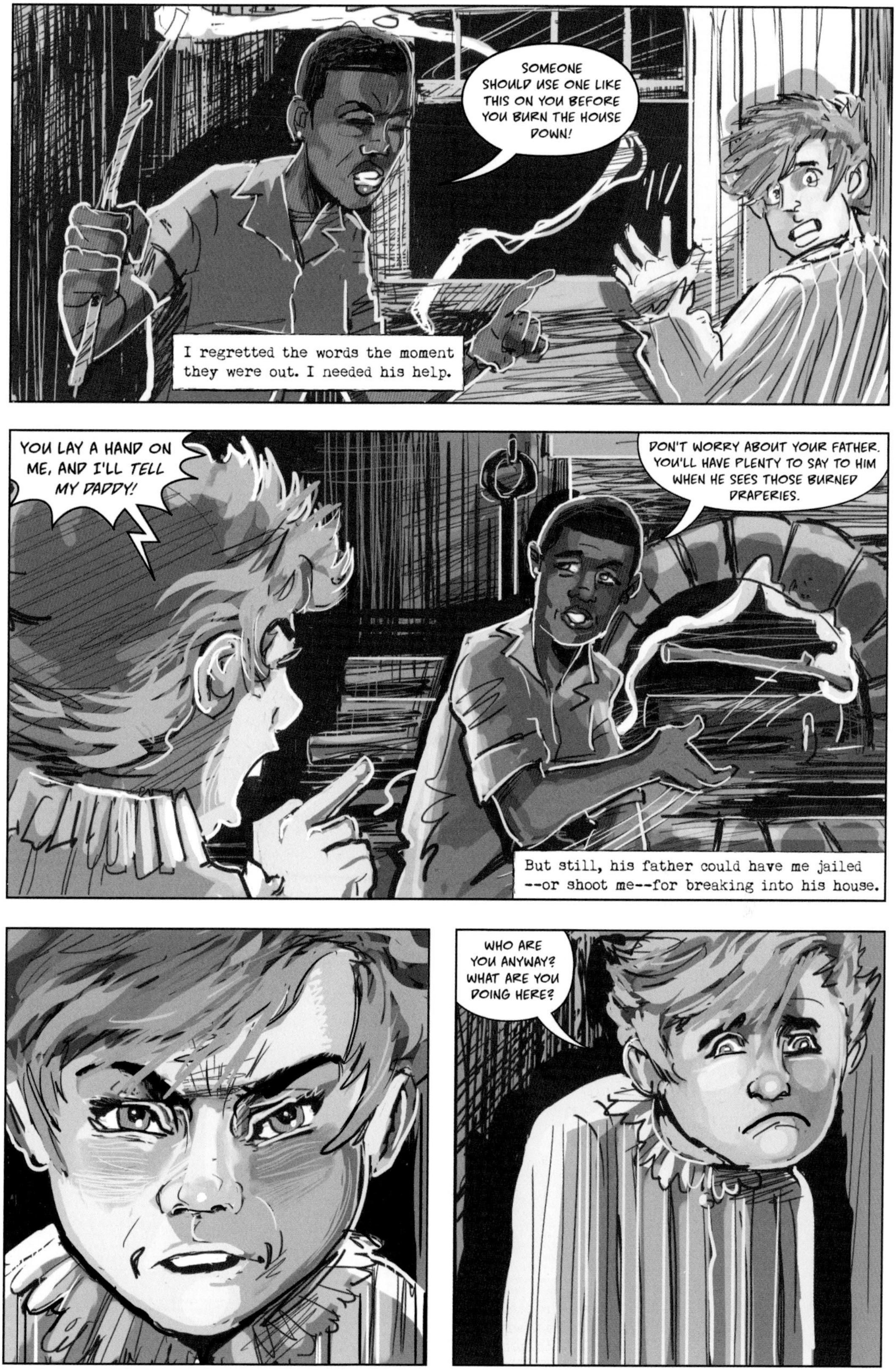
SOMEONE SHOULD USE ONE LIKE THIS ON YOU BEFORE YOU BURN THE HOUSE DOWN!
I regretted the words the moment they were out. I needed his help.
YOU LAY A HAND ON ME, AND I'LL *TELL* MY DADDY!
DON'T WORRY ABOUT YOUR FATHER. YOU'LL HAVE PLENTY TO SAY TO HIM WHEN HE SEES THOSE BURNED DRAPERIES.
But still, his father could have me jailed --or shoot me--for breaking into his house.
WHO ARE YOU ANYWAY? WHAT ARE YOU DOING HERE?

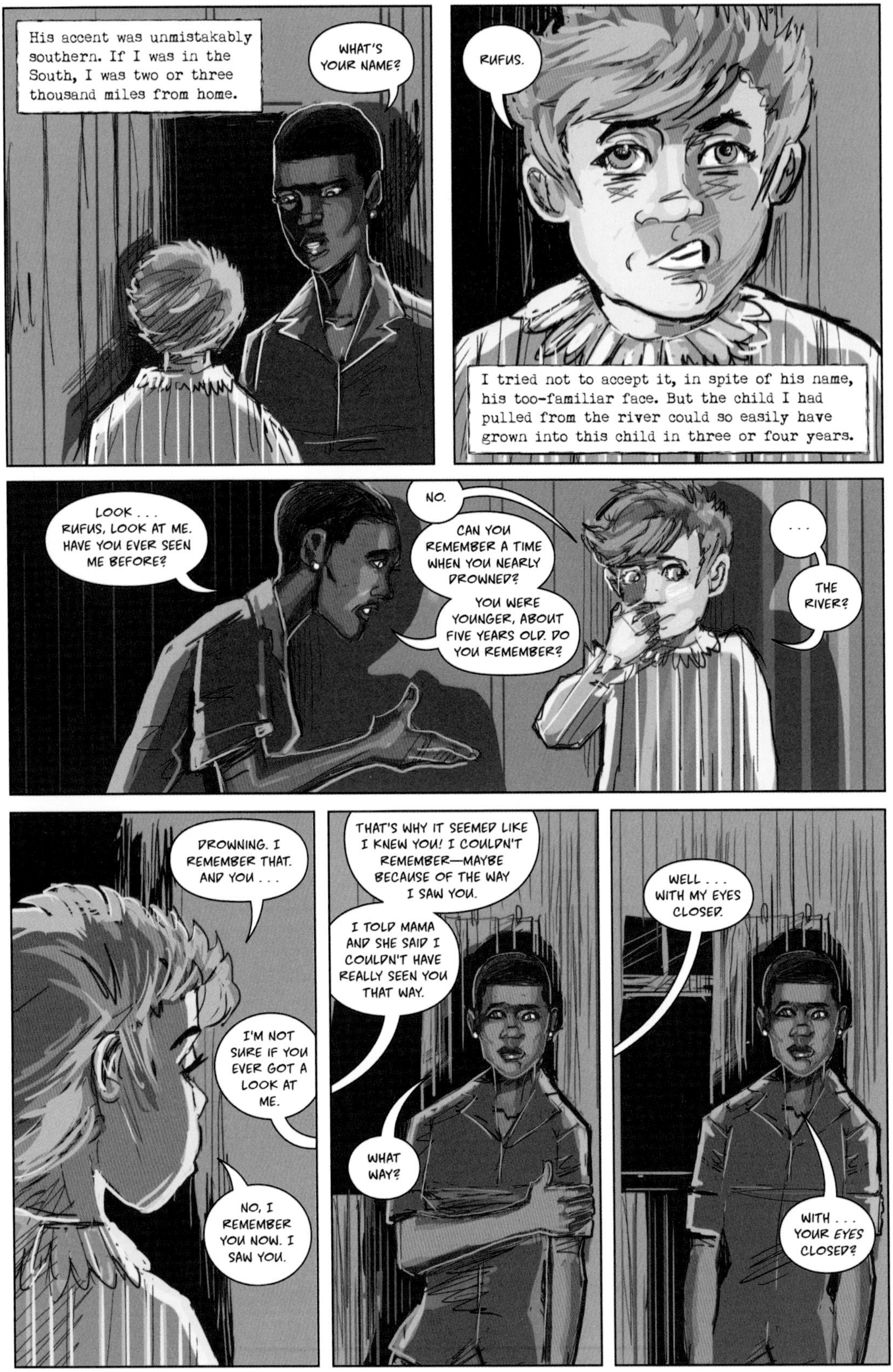
His accent was unmistakably southern. If I was in the South, I was two or three thousand miles from home.
WHAT'S YOUR NAME?
RUFUS.
I tried not to accept it, in spite of his name, his too-familiar face. But the child I had pulled from the river could so easily have grown into this child in three or four years.
LOOK . . . RUFUS, LOOK AT ME. HAVE YOU EVER SEEN ME BEFORE?
NO.
CAN YOU REMEMBER A TIME WHEN YOU NEARLY DROWNED?
YOU WERE YOUNGER, ABOUT FIVE YEARS OLD. DO YOU REMEMBER?
. . .
THE RIVER?
DROWNING. I REMEMBER THAT. AND YOU . . .
I'M NOT SURE IF YOU EVER GOT A LOOK AT ME.
NO, I REMEMBER YOU NOW. I SAW YOU.
THAT'S WHY IT SEEMED LIKE I KNEW YOU! I COULDN'T REMEMBER—MAYBE BECAUSE OF THE WAY I SAW YOU.
I TOLD MAMA AND SHE SAID I COULDN'T HAVE REALLY SEEN YOU THAT WAY.
WHAT WAY?
WELL . . . WITH MY EYES CLOSED.
WITH . . . YOUR EYES CLOSED?

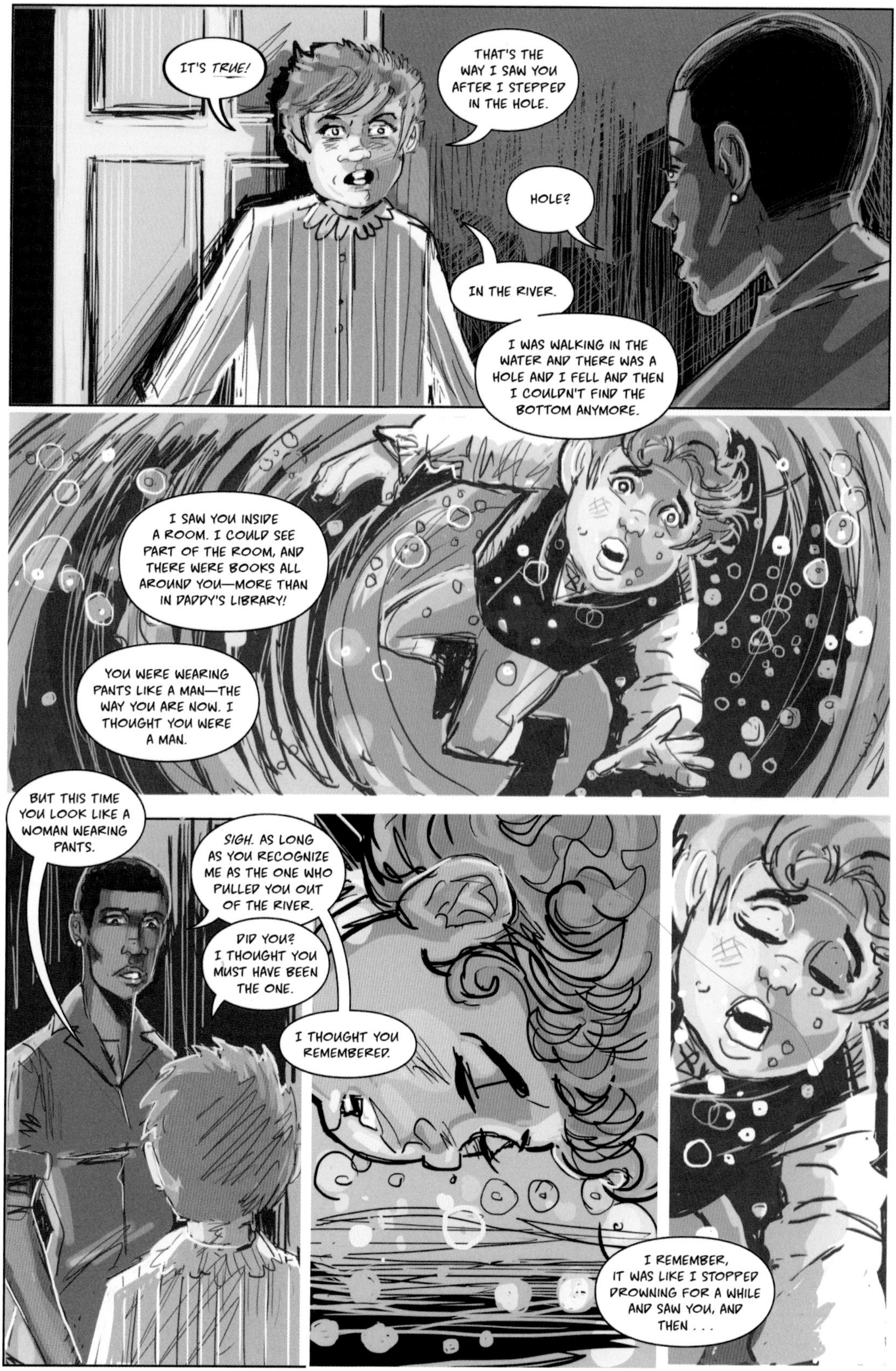

IT'S TRUE!
THAT'S THE WAY I SAW YOU AFTER I STEPPED IN THE HOLE.
HOLE?
IN THE RIVER.
I WAS WALKING IN THE WATER AND THERE WAS A HOLE AND I FELL AND THEN I COULDN'T FIND THE BOTTOM ANYMORE.
I SAW YOU INSIDE A ROOM. I COULD SEE PART OF THE ROOM, AND THERE WERE BOOKS ALL AROUND YOU—MORE THAN IN DADDY'S LIBRARY!
YOU WERE WEARING PANTS LIKE A MAN—THE WAY YOU ARE NOW. I THOUGHT YOU WERE A MAN.
BUT THIS TIME YOU LOOK LIKE A WOMAN WEARING PANTS.
SIGH. AS LONG AS YOU RECOGNIZE ME AS THE ONE WHO PULLED YOU OUT OF THE RIVER.
DID YOU? I THOUGHT YOU MUST HAVE BEEN THE ONE.
I THOUGHT YOU REMEMBERED.
I REMEMBER, IT WAS LIKE I STOPPED DROWNING FOR A WHILE AND SAW YOU, AND THEN . . .

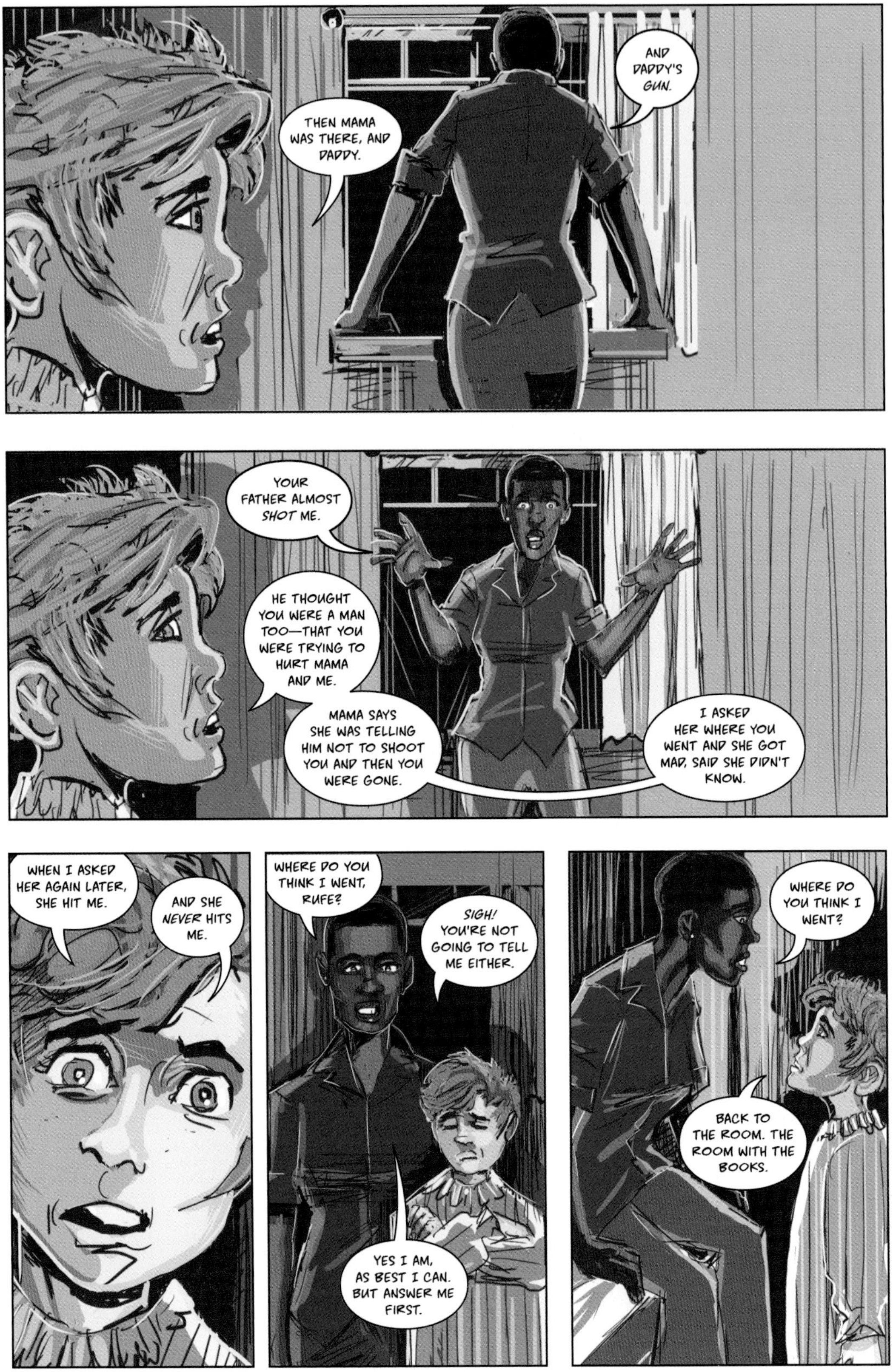
THEN MAMA WAS THERE, AND DADDY.
AND DADDY'S GUN.
YOUR FATHER ALMOST SHOT ME.
HE THOUGHT YOU WERE A MAN TOO—THAT YOU WERE TRYING TO HURT MAMA AND ME.
MAMA SAYS SHE WAS TELLING HIM NOT TO SHOOT YOU AND THEN YOU WERE GONE.
I ASKED HER WHERE YOU WENT AND SHE GOT MAD, SAID SHE DIDN'T KNOW.
WHEN I ASKED HER AGAIN LATER, SHE HIT ME.
AND SHE NEVER HITS ME.
WHERE DO YOU THINK I WENT, RUFE?
SIGH! YOU'RE NOT GOING TO TELL ME EITHER.
YES I AM, AS BEST I CAN. BUT ANSWER ME FIRST.
WHERE DO YOU THINK I WENT?
BACK TO THE ROOM. THE ROOM WITH THE BOOKS.

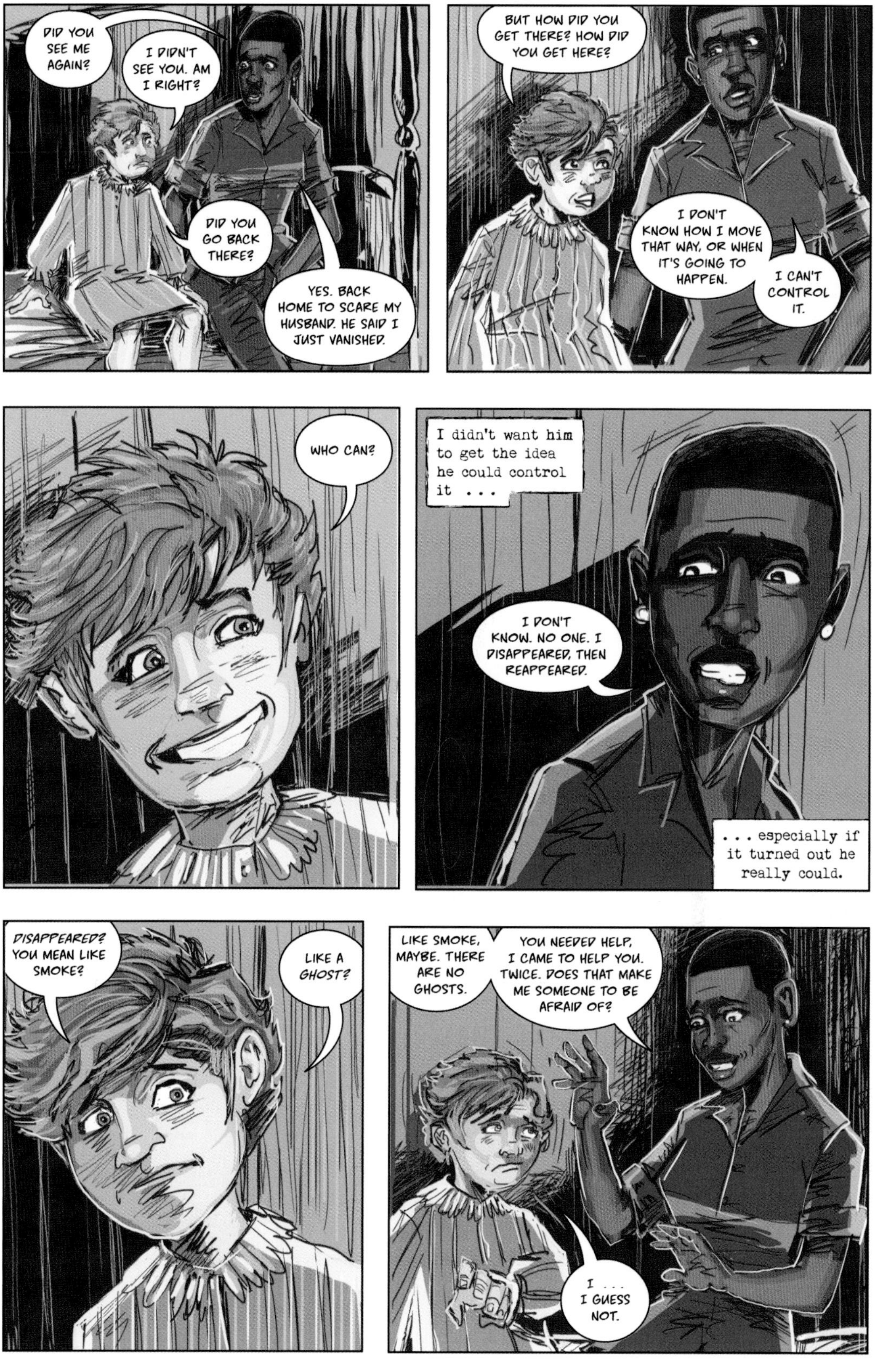
DID YOU SEE ME AGAIN?
I DIDN'T SEE YOU. AM I RIGHT?
DID YOU GO BACK THERE?
YES. BACK HOME TO SCARE MY HUSBAND. HE SAID I JUST VANISHED.
BUT HOW DID YOU GET THERE? HOW DID YOU GET HERE?
I DON'T KNOW HOW I MOVE THAT WAY, OR WHEN IT'S GOING TO HAPPEN.
I CAN'T CONTROL IT.
WHO CAN?
I didn't want him to get the idea he could control it . . .
I DON'T KNOW. NO ONE. I DISAPPEARED, THEN REAPPEARED.
. . . especially if it turned out he really could.
DISAPPEARED? YOU MEAN LIKE SMOKE?
LIKE A GHOST?
LIKE SMOKE, MAYBE. THERE ARE NO GHOSTS.
YOU NEEDED HELP, I CAME TO HELP YOU. TWICE. DOES THAT MAKE ME SOMEONE TO BE AFRAID OF?
I . . . I GUESS NOT.

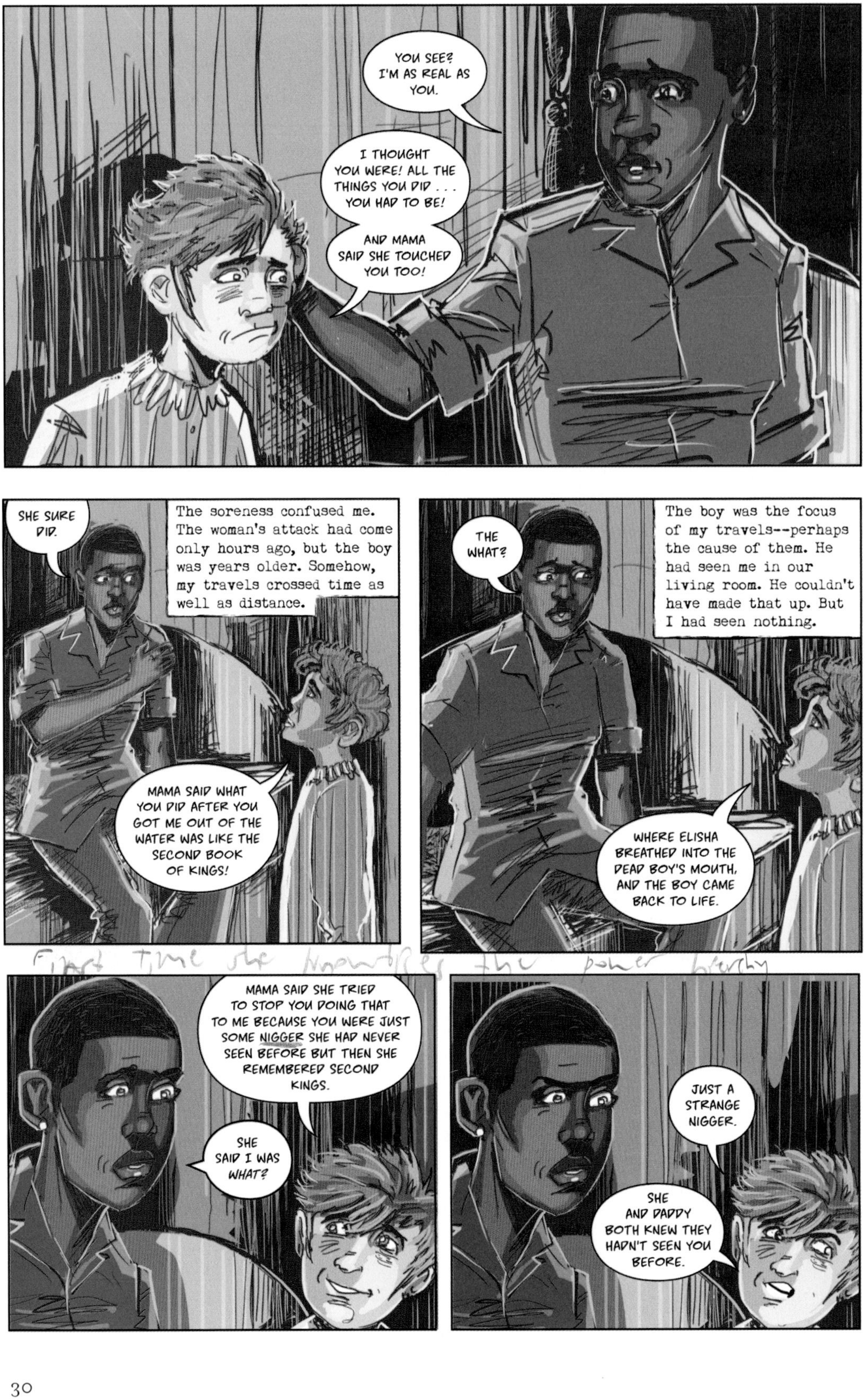
YOU SEE? I'M AS REAL AS YOU.
I THOUGHT YOU WERE! ALL THE THINGS YOU DID . . . YOU HAD TO BE!
AND MAMA SAID SHE TOUCHED YOU TOO!
SHE SURE DID.
The soreness confused me. The woman's attack had come only hours ago, but the boy was years older. Somehow, my travels crossed time as well as distance.
MAMA SAID WHAT YOU DID AFTER YOU GOT ME OUT OF THE WATER WAS LIKE THE SECOND BOOK OF KINGS!
THE WHAT?
The boy was the focus of my travels--perhaps the cause of them. He had seen me in our living room. He couldn't have made that up. But I had seen nothing.
WHERE ELISHA BREATHED INTO THE DEAD BOY'S MOUTH, AND THE BOY CAME BACK TO LIFE.
MAMA SAID SHE TRIED TO STOP YOU DOING THAT TO ME BECAUSE YOU WERE JUST SOME NIGGER SHE HAD NEVER SEEN BEFORE BUT THEN SHE REMEMBERED SECOND KINGS.
SHE SAID I WAS WHAT?
JUST A STRANGE NIGGER.
SHE AND DADDY BOTH KNEW THEY HADN'T SEEN YOU BEFORE.

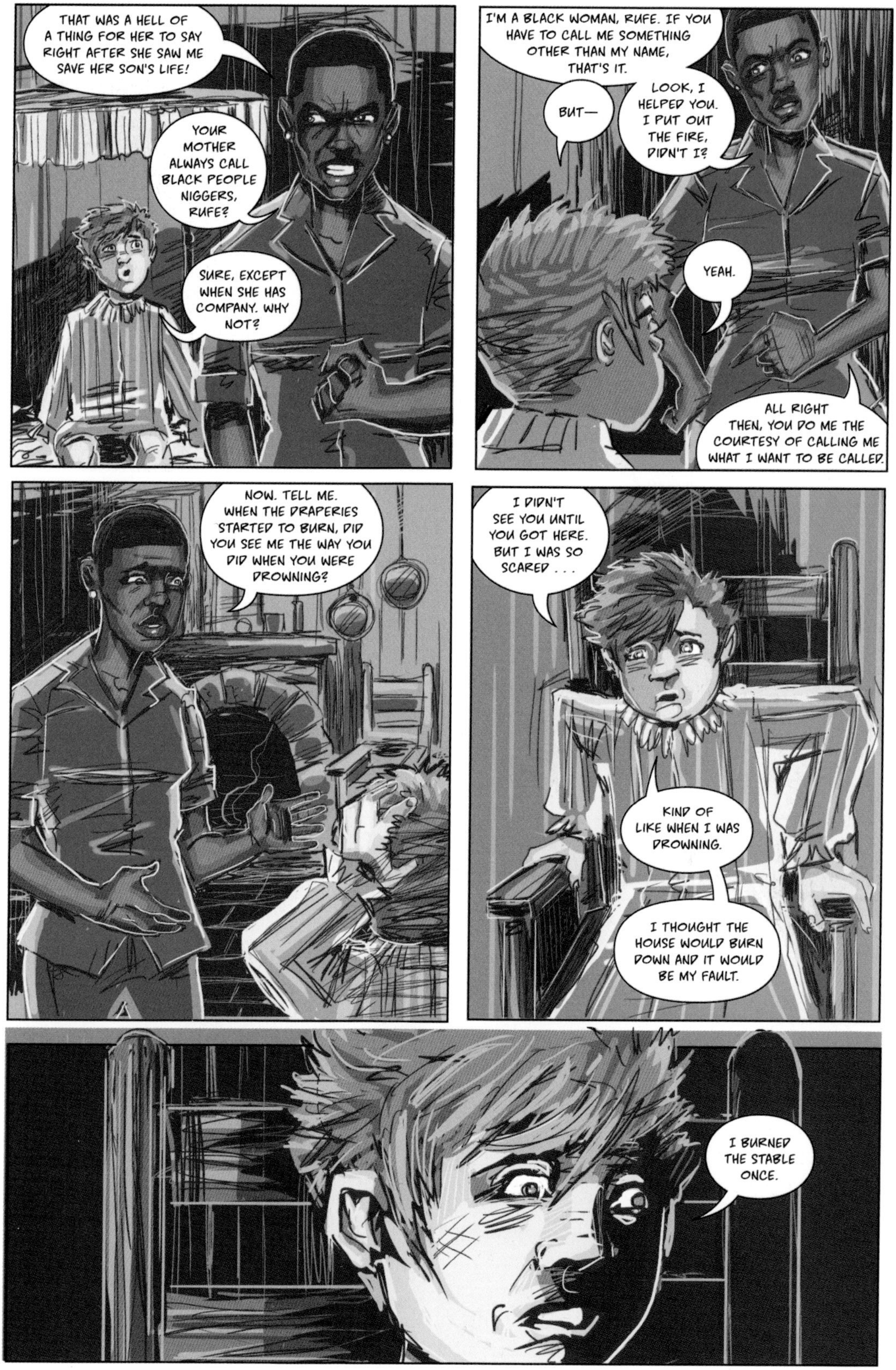
THAT WAS A HELL OF A THING FOR HER TO SAY RIGHT AFTER SHE SAW ME SAVE HER SON'S LIFE!
YOUR MOTHER ALWAYS CALL BLACK PEOPLE NIGGERS, RUFE?
SURE, EXCEPT WHEN SHE HAS COMPANY. WHY NOT?
I'M A BLACK WOMAN, RUFE. IF YOU HAVE TO CALL ME SOMETHING OTHER THAN MY NAME, THAT'S IT.
BUT—
LOOK, I HELPED YOU. I PUT OUT THE FIRE, DIDN'T I?
YEAH.
ALL RIGHT THEN, YOU DO ME THE COURTESY OF CALLING ME WHAT I WANT TO BE CALLED.
NOW. TELL ME. WHEN THE DRAPERIES STARTED TO BURN, DID YOU SEE ME THE WAY YOU DID WHEN YOU WERE DROWNING?
I DIDN'T SEE YOU UNTIL YOU GOT HERE. BUT I WAS SO SCARED . . .
KIND OF LIKE WHEN I WAS DROWNING.
I THOUGHT THE HOUSE WOULD BURN DOWN AND IT WOULD BE MY FAULT.
I BURNED THE STABLE ONCE.

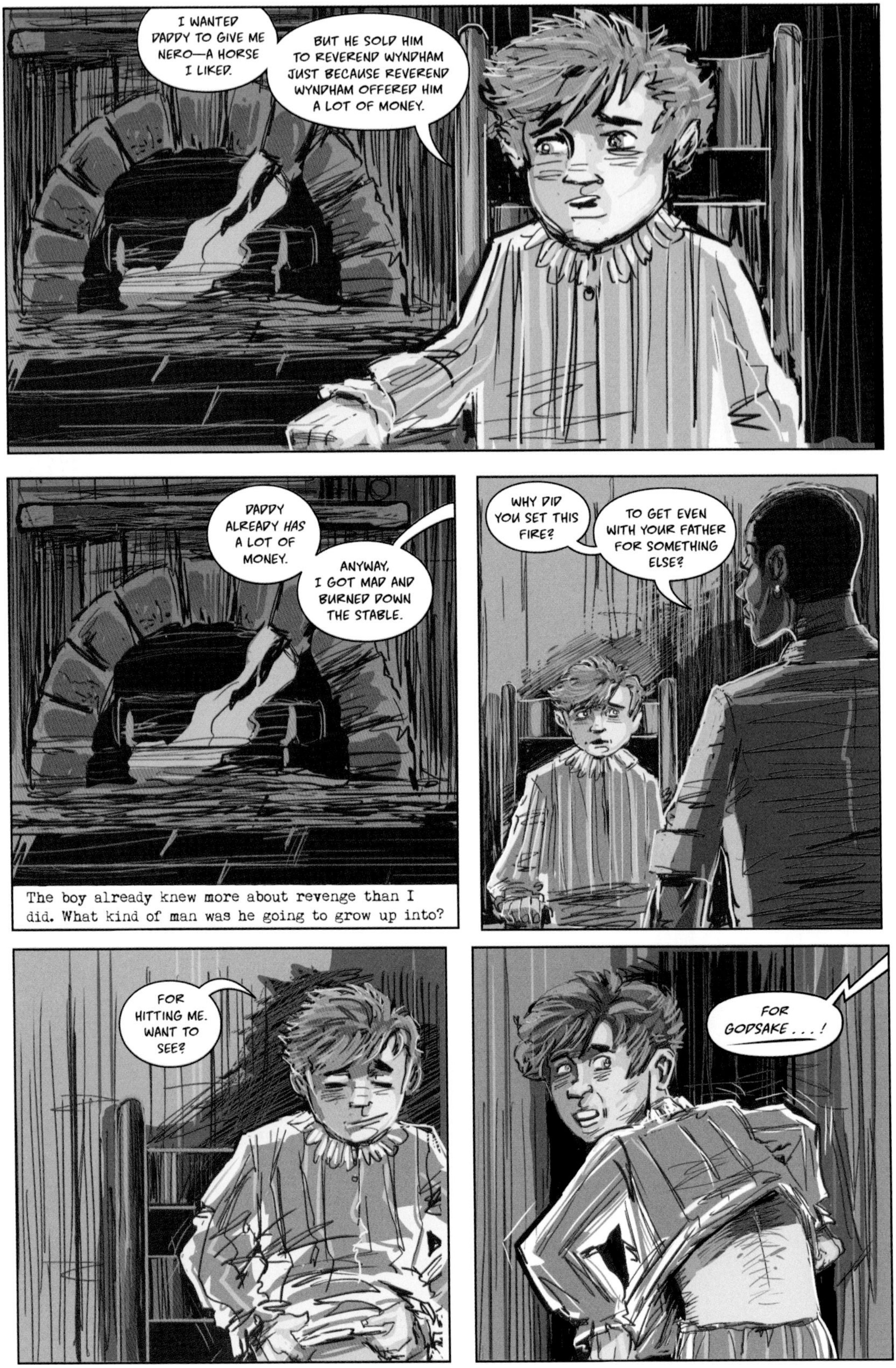
I WANTED DADDY TO GIVE ME NERO—A HORSE I LIKED.
BUT HE SOLD HIM TO REVEREND WYNDHAM JUST BECAUSE REVEREND WYNDHAM OFFERED HIM A LOT OF MONEY.
DADDY ALREADY HAS A LOT OF MONEY.
ANYWAY, I GOT MAD AND BURNED DOWN THE STABLE.
The boy already knew more about revenge than I did. What kind of man was he going to grow up into?
WHY DID YOU SET THIS FIRE?
TO GET EVEN WITH YOUR FATHER FOR SOMETHING ELSE?
FOR HITTING ME. WANT TO SEE?
FOR GODSAKE . . . !

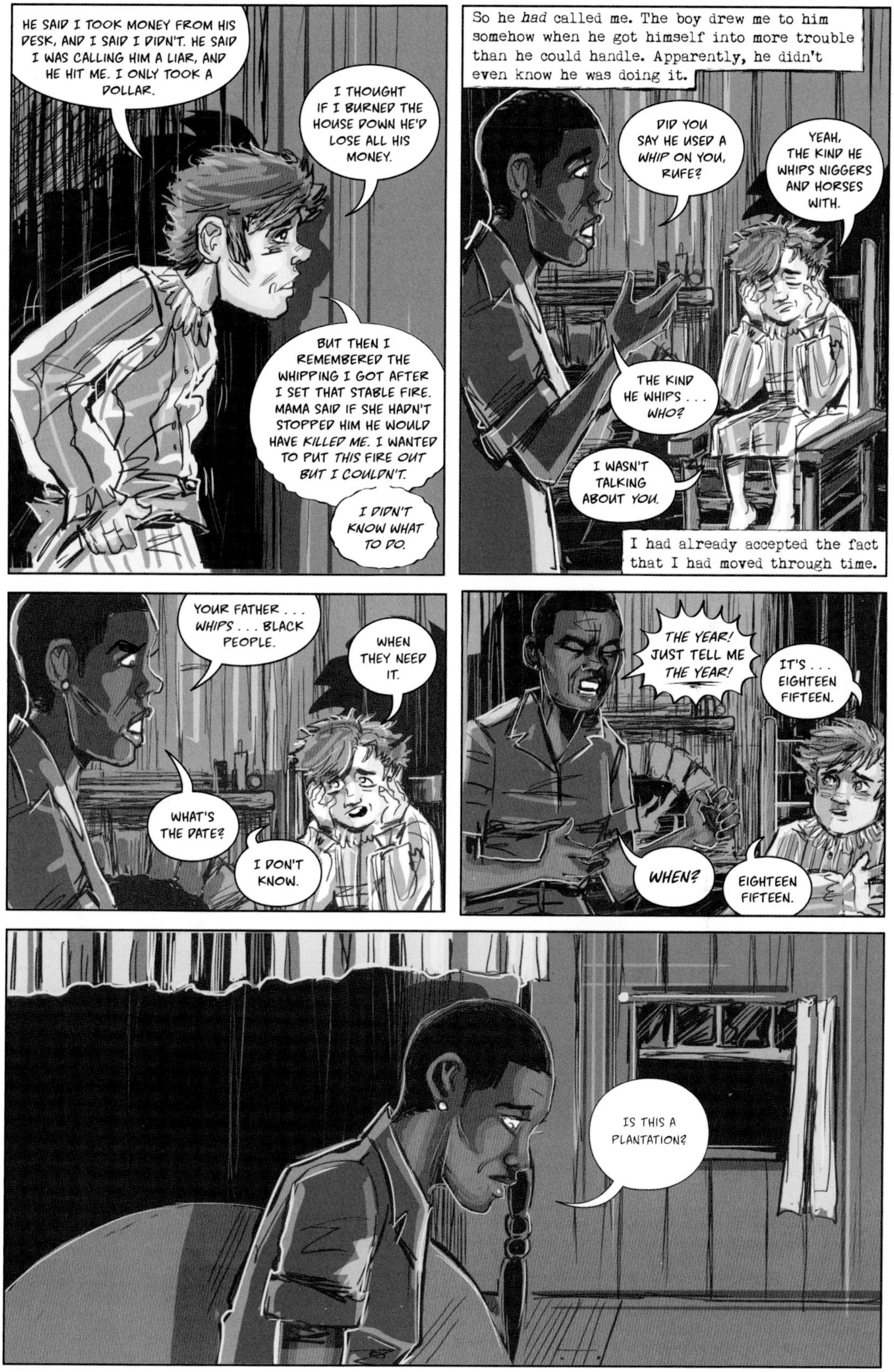
HE SAID I TOOK MONEY FROM HIS DESK, AND I SAID I DIDN'T. HE SAID I WAS CALLING HIM A LIAR, AND HE HIT ME. I ONLY TOOK A DOLLAR.
I THOUGHT IF I BURNED THE HOUSE DOWN HE'D LOSE ALL HIS MONEY.
BUT THEN I REMEMBERED THE WHIPPING I GOT AFTER I SET THAT STABLE FIRE. MAMA SAID IF SHE HADN'T STOPPED HIM HE WOULD HAVE KILLED ME. I WANTED TO PUT THIS FIRE OUT BUT I COULDN'T.
I DIDN'T KNOW WHAT TO DO.
So he had called me. The boy drew me to him somehow when he got himself into more trouble than he could handle. Apparently, he didn't even know he was doing it.
DID YOU SAY HE USED A WHIP ON YOU, RUFE?
YEAH, THE KIND HE WHIPS NIGGERS AND HORSES WITH.
THE KIND HE WHIPS . . . WHO?
I WASN'T TALKING ABOUT YOU.
I had already accepted the fact that I had moved through time.
YOUR FATHER . . . WHIPS . . . BLACK PEOPLE.
WHEN THEY NEED IT.
WHAT'S THE DATE?
I DON'T KNOW.
THE YEAR! JUST TELL ME THE YEAR!
IT'S . . . EIGHTEEN FIFTEEN.
WHEN?
EIGHTEEN FIFTEEN.
IS THIS A PLANTATION?

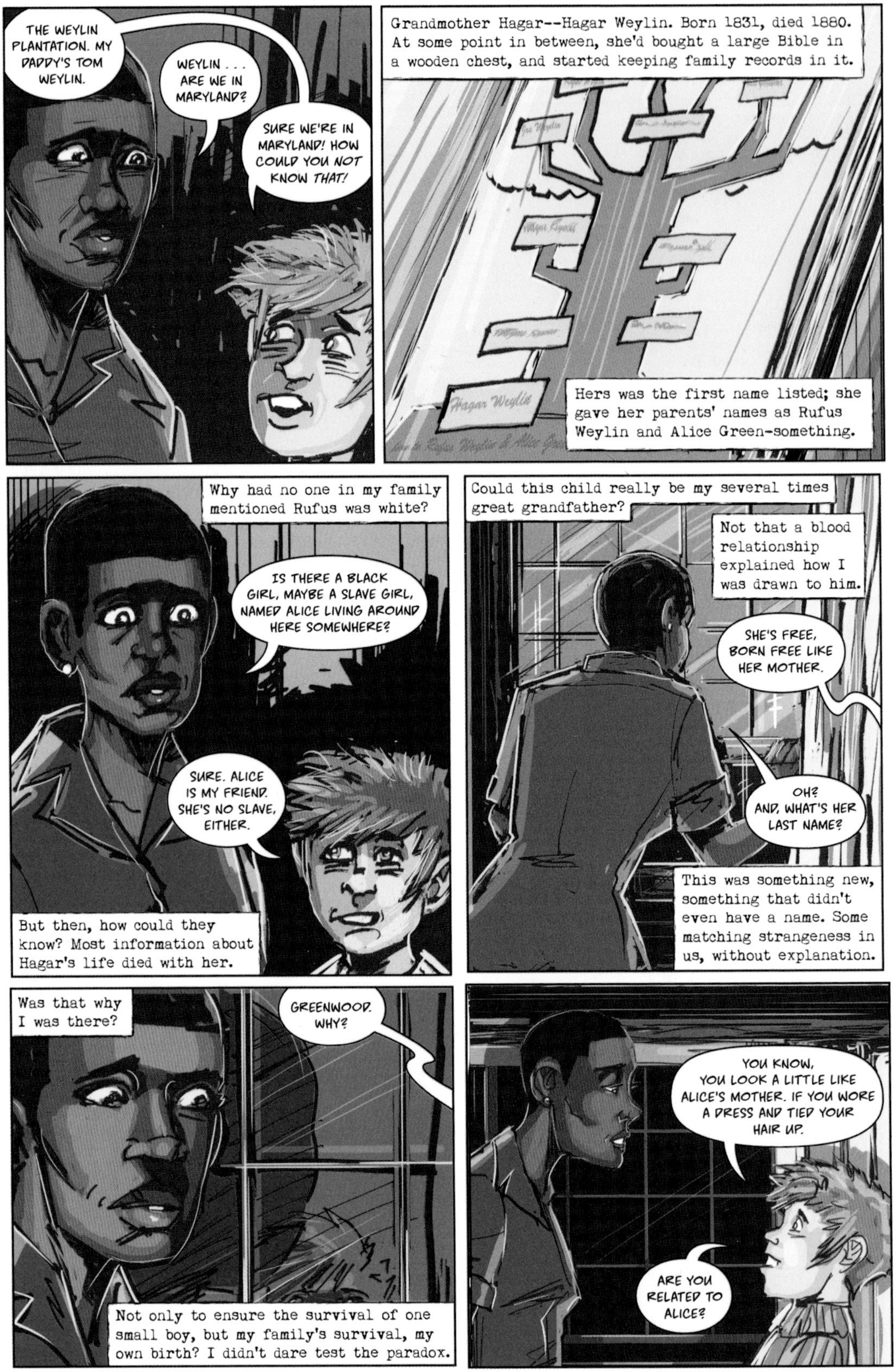

THE WEYLIN PLANTATION. MY DADDY'S TOM WEYLIN.
WEYLIN . . . ARE WE IN MARYLAND?
SURE WE'RE IN MARYLAND! HOW COULD YOU NOT KNOW THAT!
Grandmother Hagar--Hagar Weylin. Born 1831, died 1880. At some point in between, she'd bought a large Bible in a wooden chest, and started keeping family records in it.
Hagar Weylin
Hers was the first name listed; she gave her parents' names as Rufus Weylin and Alice Green-something.
Why had no one in my family mentioned Rufus was white?
IS THERE A BLACK GIRL, MAYBE A SLAVE GIRL, NAMED ALICE LIVING AROUND HERE SOMEWHERE?
SURE. ALICE IS MY FRIEND. SHE'S NO SLAVE, EITHER.
But then, how could they know? Most information about Hagar's life died with her.
Could this child really be my several times great grandfather?
Not that a blood relationship explained how I was drawn to him.
SHE'S FREE, BORN FREE LIKE HER MOTHER.
OH? AND, WHAT'S HER LAST NAME?
This was something new, something that didn't even have a name. Some matching strangeness in us, without explanation.
Was that why I was there?
GREENWOOD. WHY?
Not only to ensure the survival of one small boy, but my family's survival, my own birth? I didn't dare test the paradox.
YOU KNOW, YOU LOOK A LITTLE LIKE ALICE'S MOTHER. IF YOU WORE A DRESS AND TIED YOUR HAIR UP.
ARE YOU RELATED TO ALICE?

NOT THAT I KNOW OF.

ARE THERE SLAVES HERE?

THIRTY-EIGHT, DADDY SAID.

YOU'RE NOT A SLAVE, ARE YOU?

NO.

I DIDN'T THINK SO. YOU DON'T TALK RIGHT OR DRESS RIGHT OR ACT RIGHT.

NOT EVEN LIKE A RUNAWAY. AND YOU DON'T CALL ME MASTER.

WHA— MASTER?!

see her identity is being stripped, pwr of new paw- biling

YOU'LL GET INTO TROUBLE IF YOU DON'T.

IF DADDY HEARS YOU.

ALL RIGHT. IF ANYONE COMES, I'LL CALL YOU MISTER RUFUS. WILL THAT DO?

YES. WHAT'S YOUR NAME? YOU NEVER SAID.

EDANA. MOST PEOPLE CALL ME DANA.

OH NO!

WHAT'S WRONG?

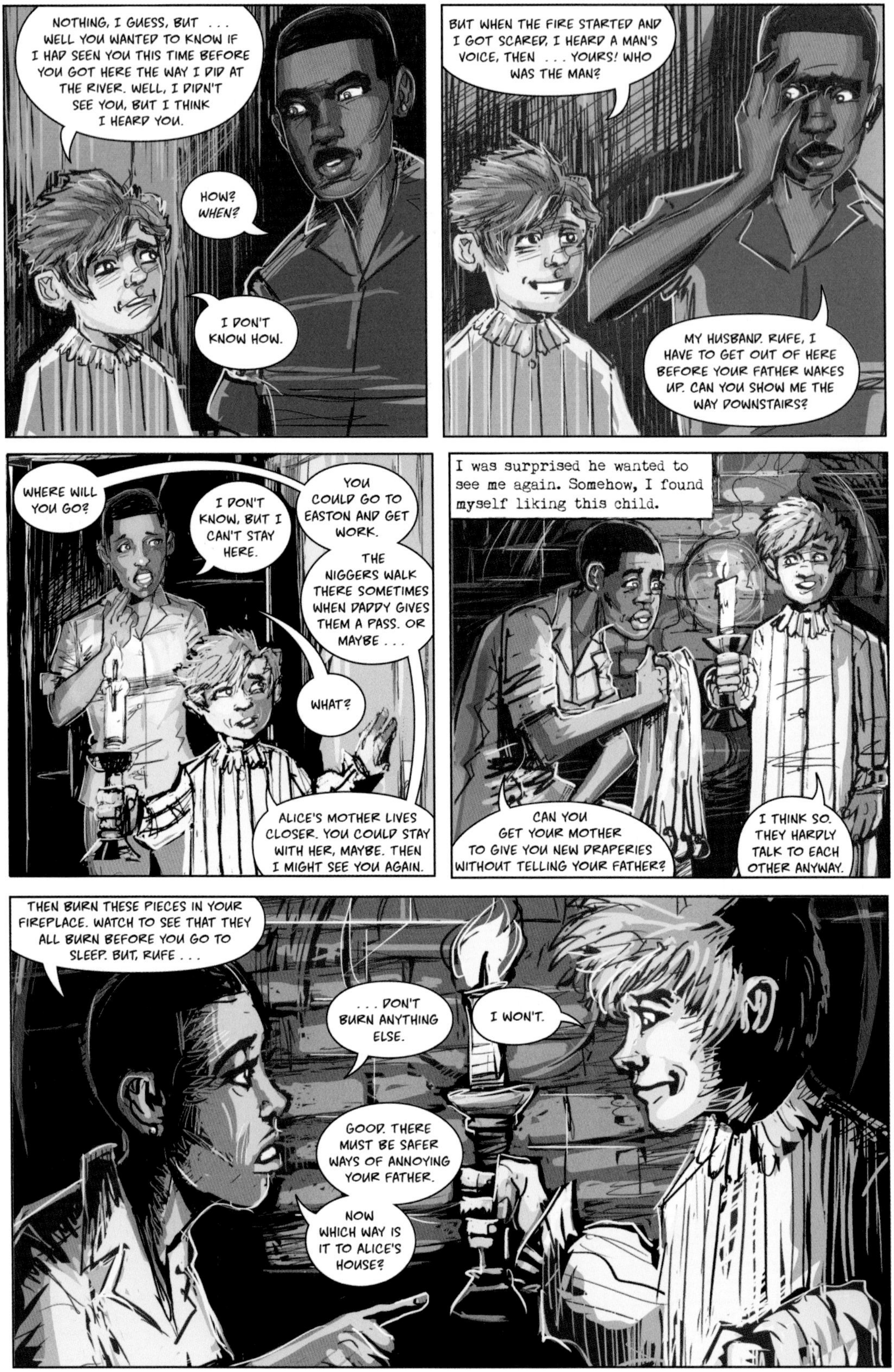
NOTHING, I GUESS, BUT . . . WELL YOU WANTED TO KNOW IF I HAD SEEN YOU THIS TIME BEFORE YOU GOT HERE THE WAY I DID AT THE RIVER. WELL, I DIDN'T SEE YOU, BUT I THINK I HEARD YOU.
HOW? WHEN?
I DON'T KNOW HOW.
BUT WHEN THE FIRE STARTED AND I GOT SCARED, I HEARD A MAN'S VOICE, THEN . . . YOURS! WHO WAS THE MAN?
MY HUSBAND. RUFE, I HAVE TO GET OUT OF HERE BEFORE YOUR FATHER WAKES UP. CAN YOU SHOW ME THE WAY DOWNSTAIRS?
WHERE WILL YOU GO?
I DON'T KNOW, BUT I CAN'T STAY HERE.
YOU COULD GO TO EASTON AND GET WORK.
THE NIGGERS WALK THERE SOMETIMES WHEN DADDY GIVES THEM A PASS. OR MAYBE . . .
WHAT?
ALICE'S MOTHER LIVES CLOSER. YOU COULD STAY WITH HER, MAYBE. THEN I MIGHT SEE YOU AGAIN.
I was surprised he wanted to see me again. Somehow, I found myself liking this child.
CAN YOU GET YOUR MOTHER TO GIVE YOU NEW DRAPERIES WITHOUT TELLING YOUR FATHER?
I THINK SO. THEY HARDLY TALK TO EACH OTHER ANYWAY.
THEN BURN THESE PIECES IN YOUR FIREPLACE. WATCH TO SEE THAT THEY ALL BURN BEFORE YOU GO TO SLEEP. BUT, RUFE . . .
. . . DON'T BURN ANYTHING ELSE.
I WON'T.
GOOD. THERE MUST BE SAFER WAYS OF ANNOYING YOUR FATHER.
NOW WHICH WAY IS IT TO ALICE'S HOUSE?

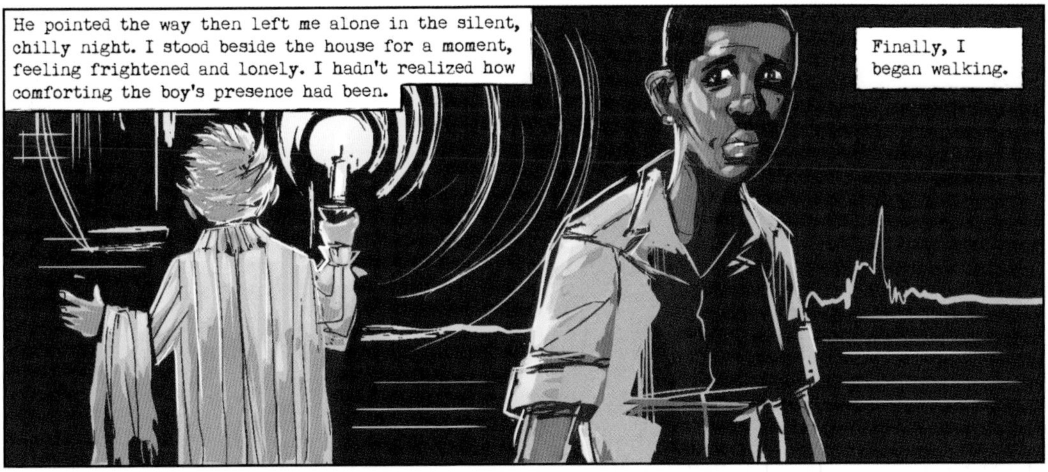
He pointed the way then left me alone in the silent, chilly night. I stood beside the house for a moment, feeling frightened and lonely. I hadn't realized how comforting the boy's presence had been.
Finally, I began walking.

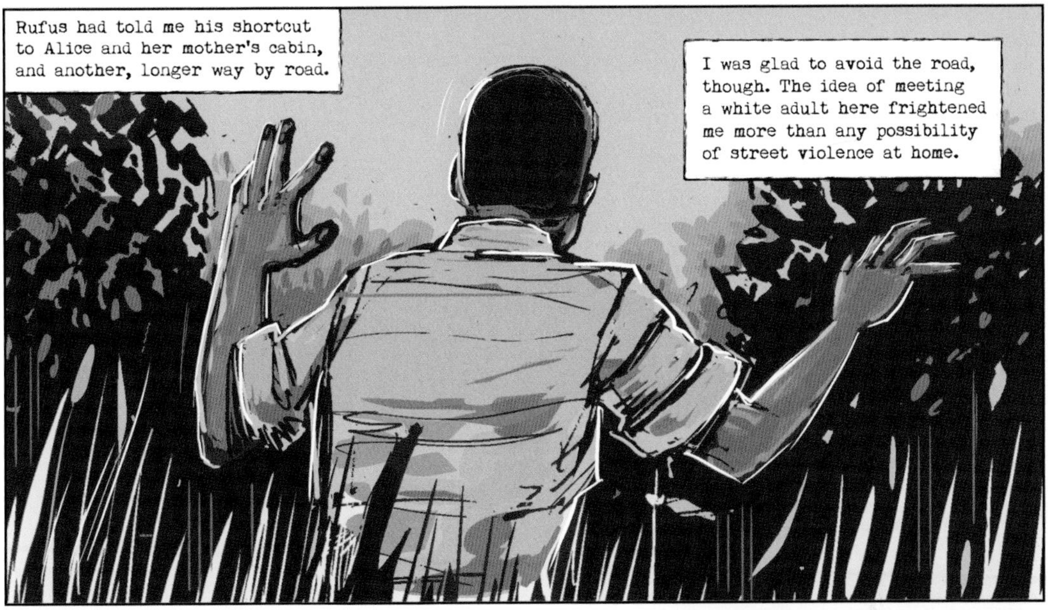
Rufus had told me his shortcut to Alice and her mother's cabin, and another, longer way by road.
I was glad to avoid the road, though. The idea of meeting a white adult here frightened me more than any possibility of street violence at home.

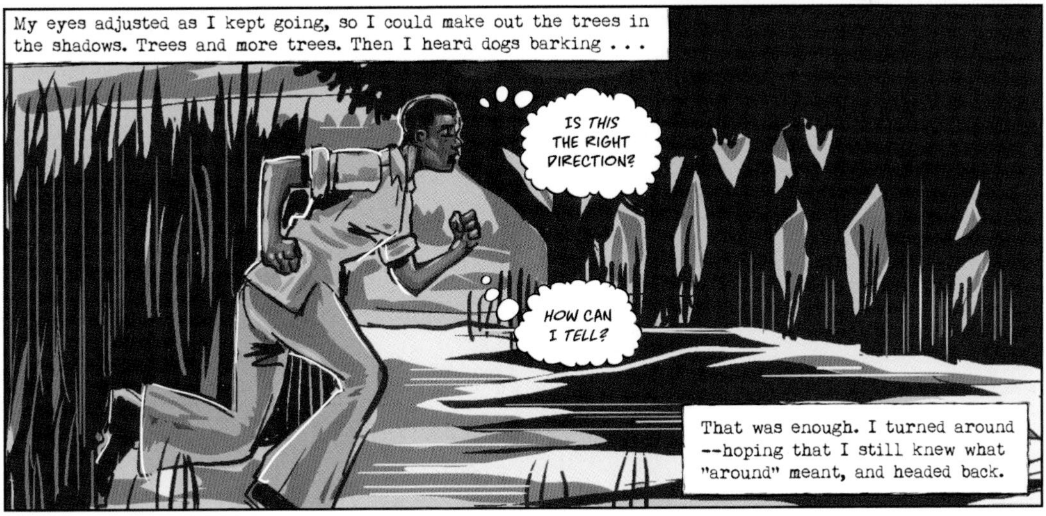
My eyes adjusted as I kept going, so I could make out the trees in the shadows. Trees and more trees. Then I heard dogs barking . . .
IS THIS THE RIGHT DIRECTION?
HOW CAN I TELL?
That was enough. I turned around --hoping that I still knew what "around" meant, and headed back.

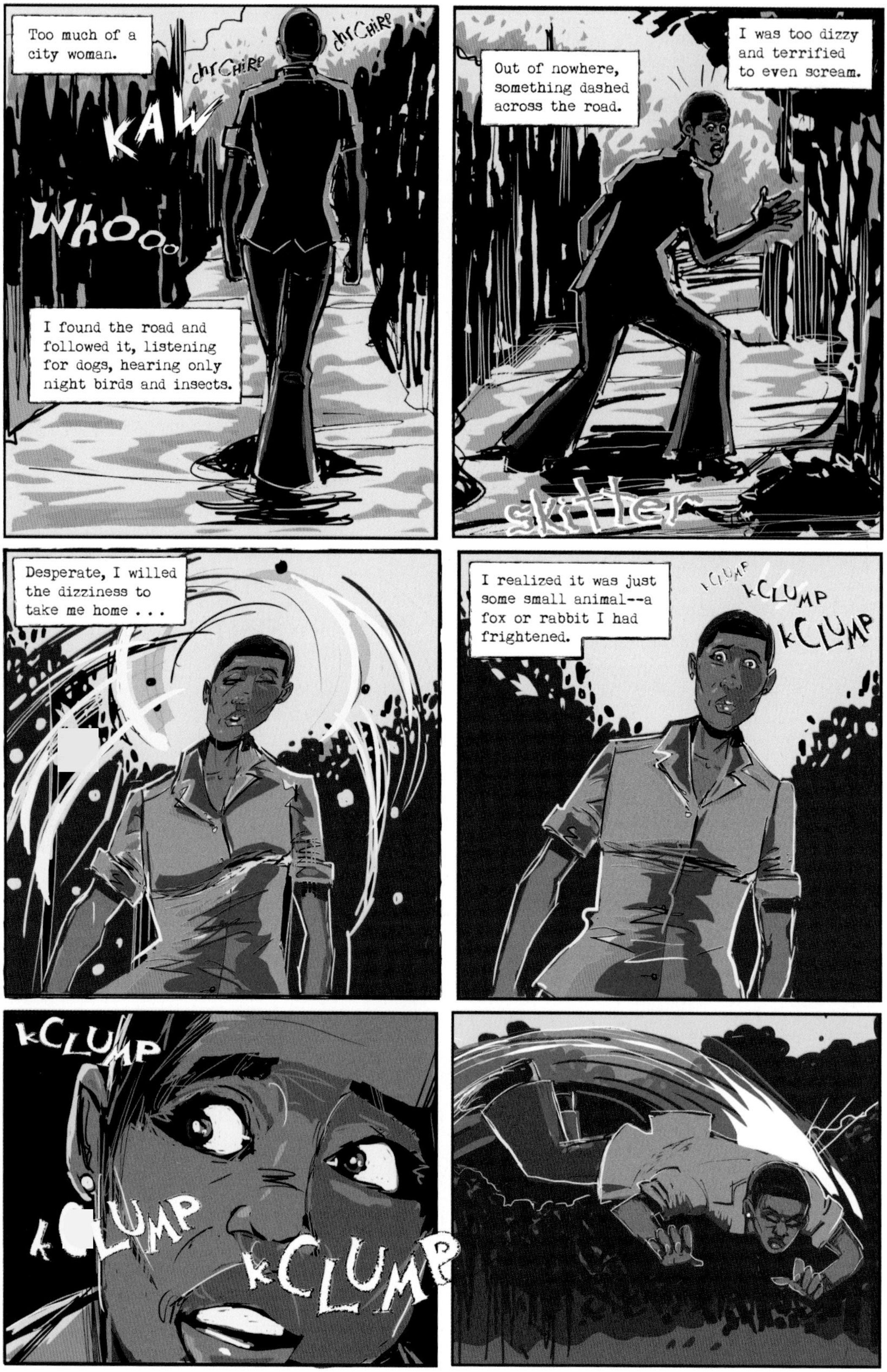
Too much of a city woman.
chrCHIRP
chrCHIRP
KAW
WhOoo
I found the road and followed it, listening for dogs, hearing only night birds and insects.
Out of nowhere, something dashed across the road.
I was too dizzy and terrified to even scream.
skitter
Desperate, I willed the dizziness to take me home . . .
I realized it was just some small animal--a fox or rabbit I had frightened.
kCLUMP
kCLUMP
kCLUMP
kCLUMP
k LUMP
kCLUMP

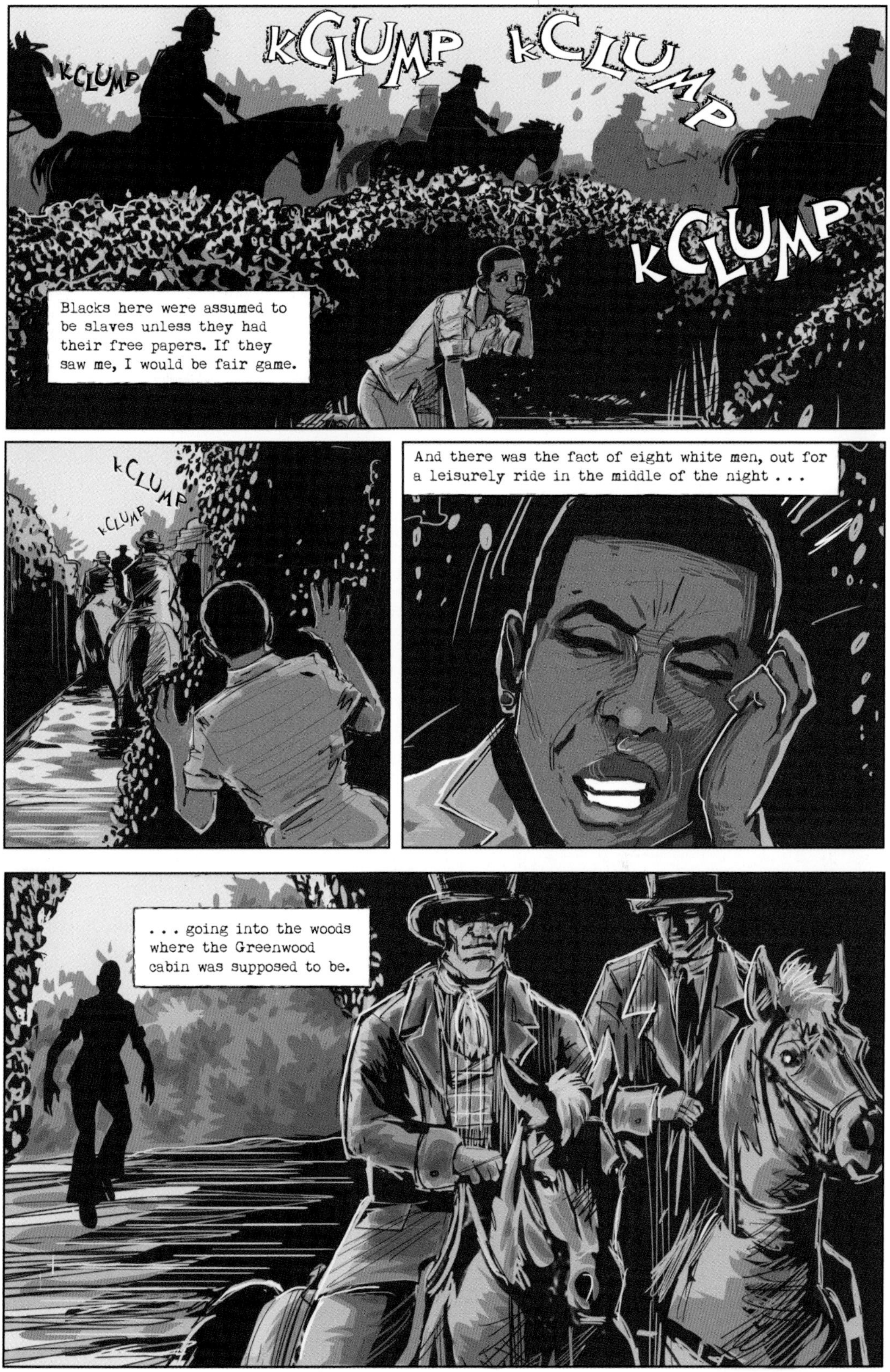
KCLUMP
KCLUMP KCLUMP
KCLUMP
Blacks here were assumed to be slaves unless they had their free papers. If they saw me, I would be fair game.
KCLUMP
KCLUMP
And there was the fact of eight white men, out for a leisurely ride in the middle of the night . . .
. . . going into the woods where the Greenwood cabin was supposed to be.

Mark of the power hierarchy

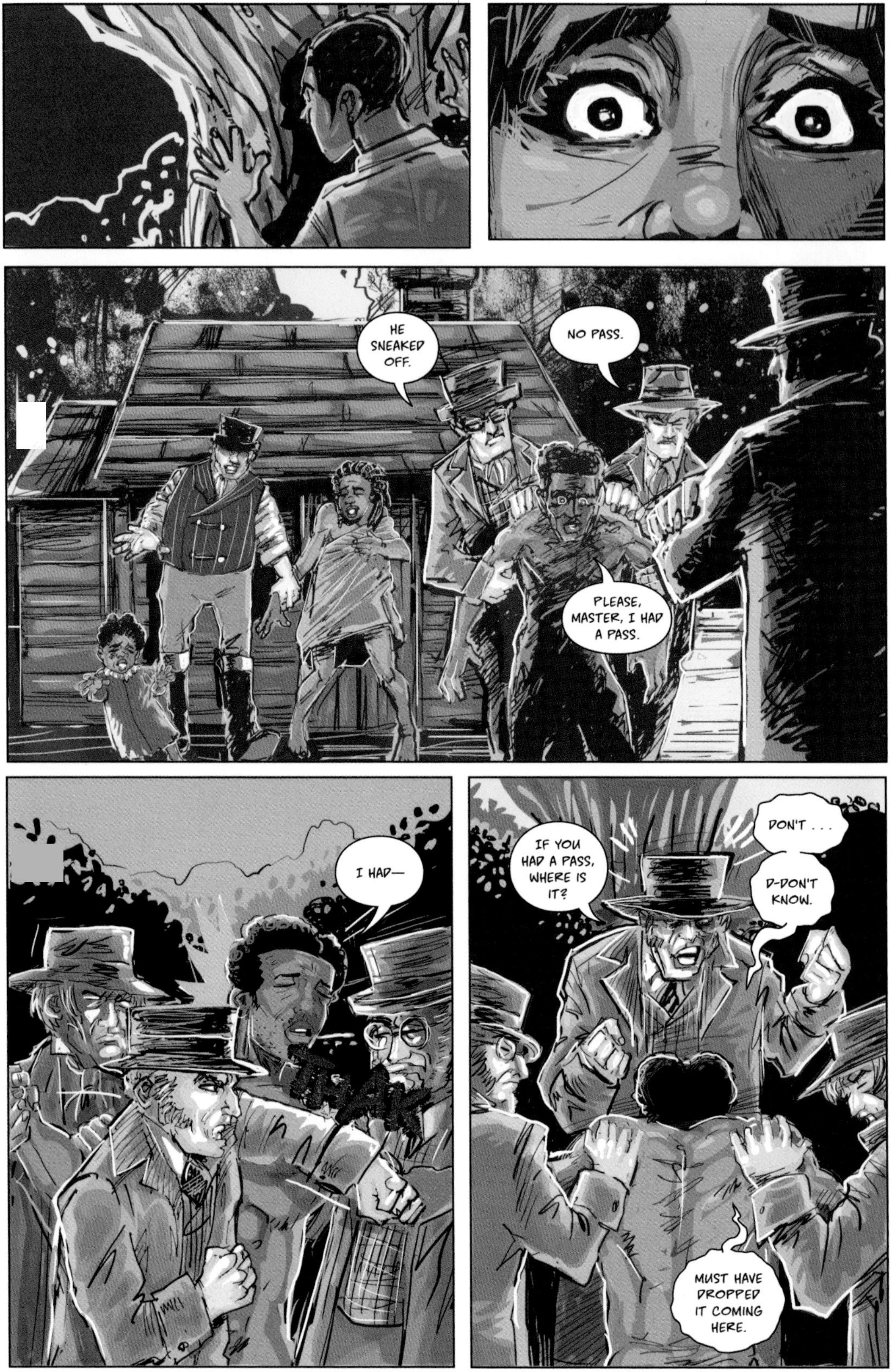
HE SNEAKED OFF.
NO PASS.
PLEASE, MASTER, I HAD A PASS.
I HAD—
IF YOU HAD A PASS, WHERE IS IT?
DON'T . . .
D-DON'T KNOW.
MUST HAVE DROPPED IT COMING HERE.

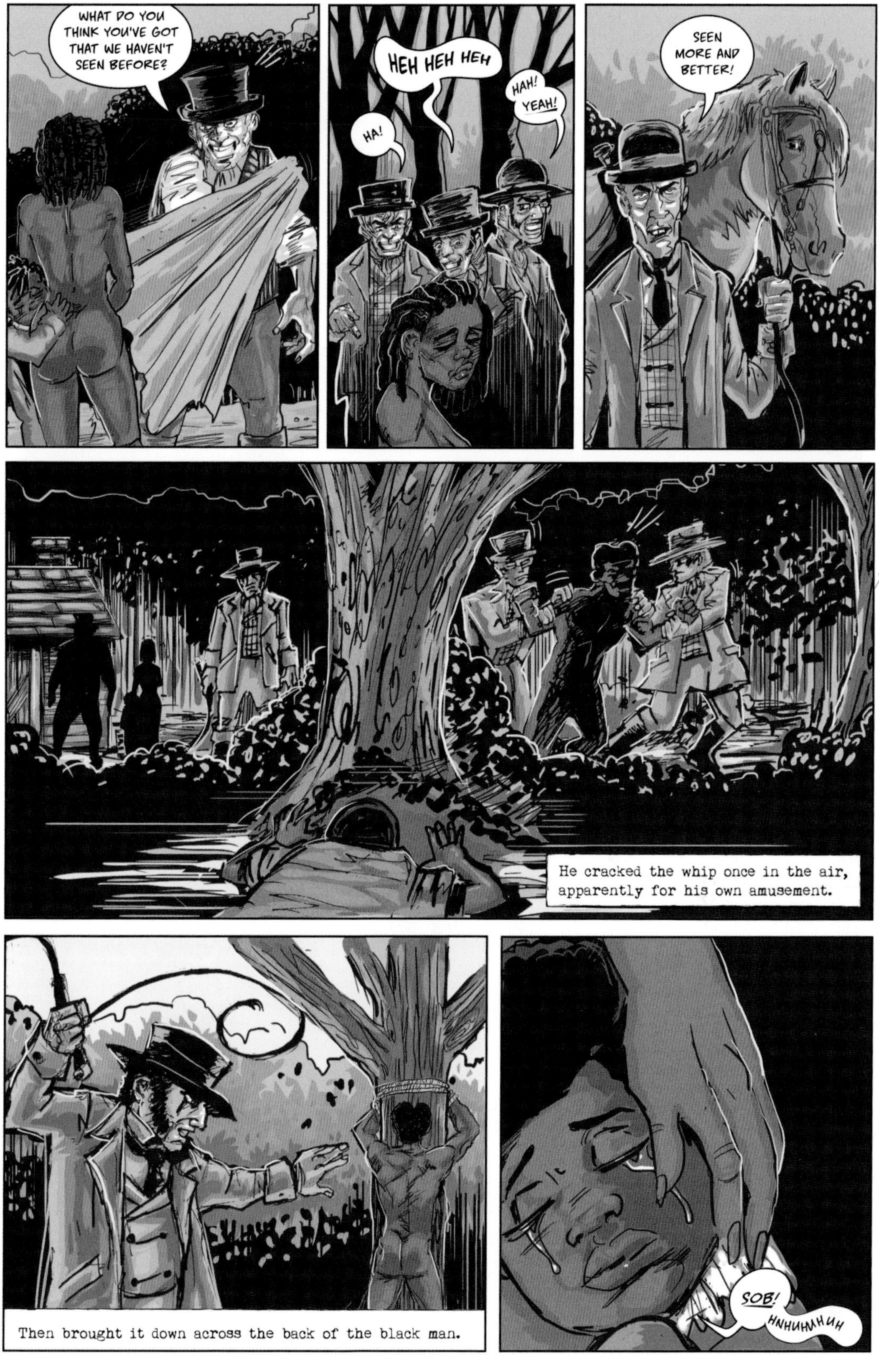
WHAT DO YOU THINK YOU'VE GOT THAT WE HAVEN'T SEEN BEFORE?
HEH HEH HEH
HA!
HAH! YEAH!
SEEN MORE AND BETTER!
He cracked the whip once in the air, apparently for his own amusement.
Then brought it down across the back of the black man.
SOB!
HNHUHNHUH

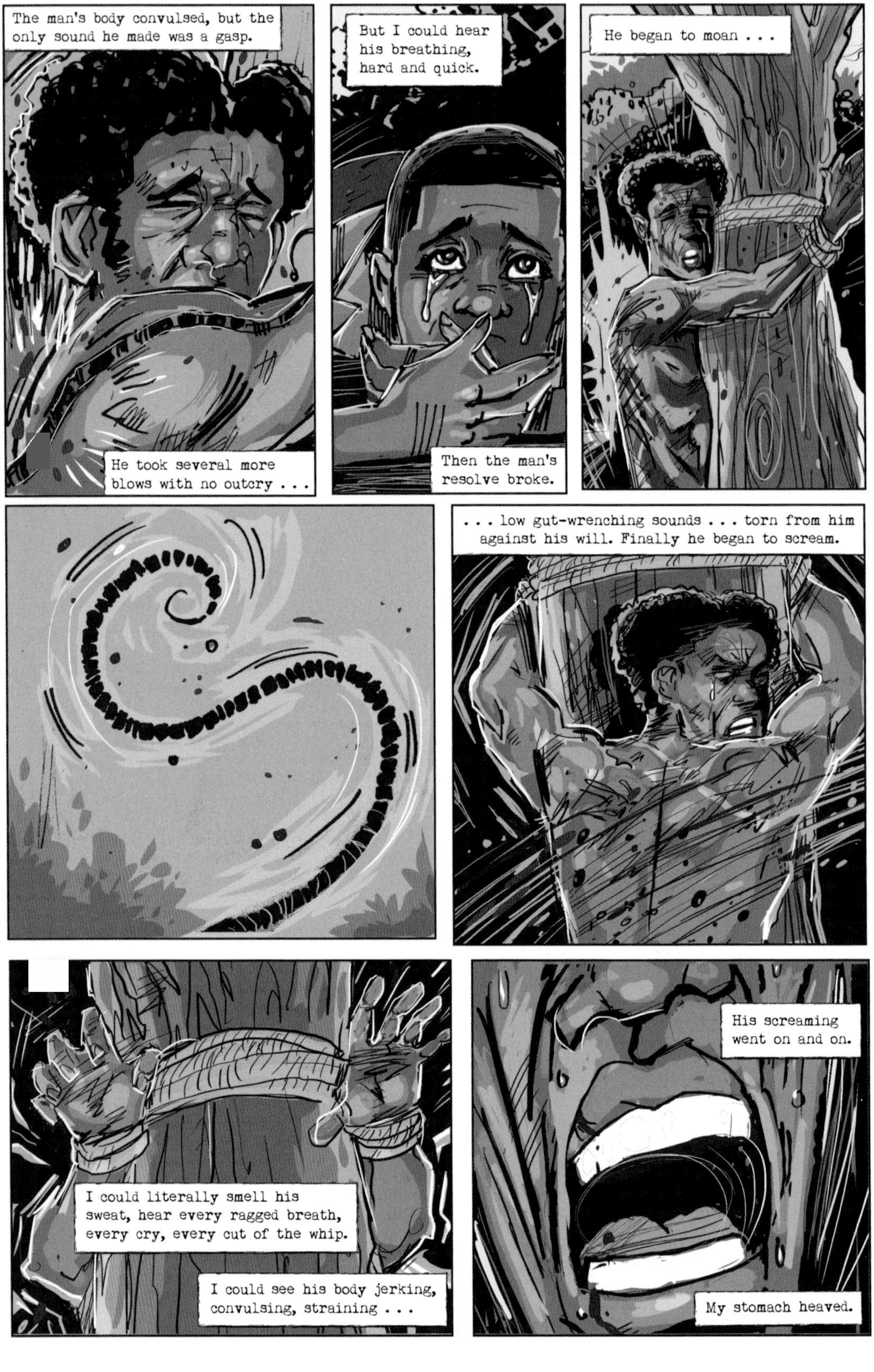
The man's body convulsed, but the only sound he made was a gasp.
He took several more blows with no outcry . . .
But I could hear his breathing, hard and quick.
Then the man's resolve broke.
He began to moan . . .
. . . low gut-wrenching sounds . . . torn from him against his will. Finally he began to scream.
I could literally smell his sweat, hear every ragged breath, every cry, every cut of the whip.
I could see his body jerking, convulsing, straining . . .
His screaming went on and on.
My stomach heaved.

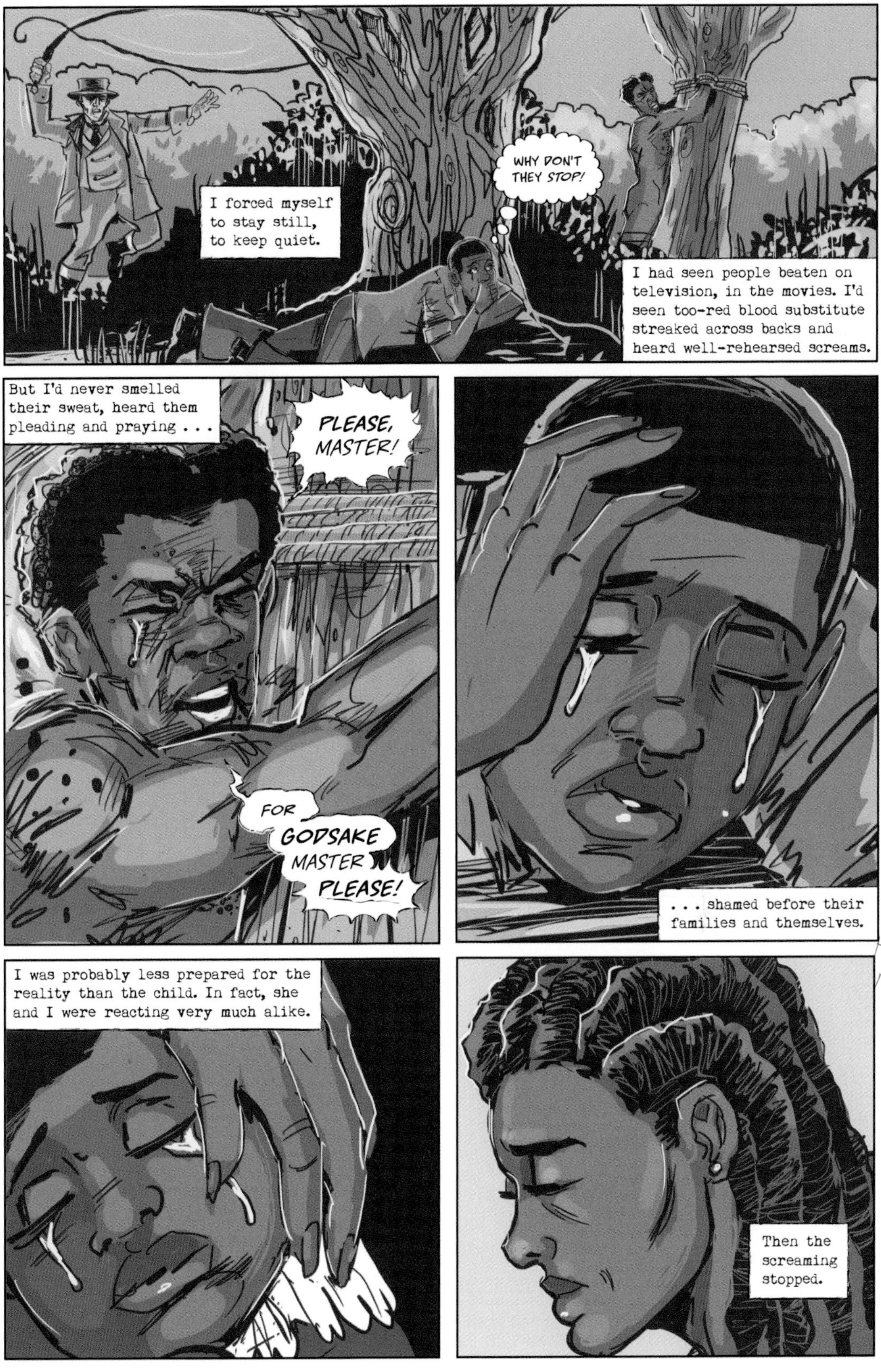
I forced myself to stay still, to keep quiet.
WHY DON'T THEY STOP!
I had seen people beaten on television, in the movies. I'd seen too-red blood substitute streaked across backs and heard well-rehearsed screams.
But I'd never smelled their sweat, heard them pleading and praying . . .
PLEASE, MASTER!
FOR GODSAKE MASTER PLEASE!
. . . shamed before their families and themselves.
I was probably less prepared for the reality than the child. In fact, she and I were reacting very much alike.
Then the screaming stopped.

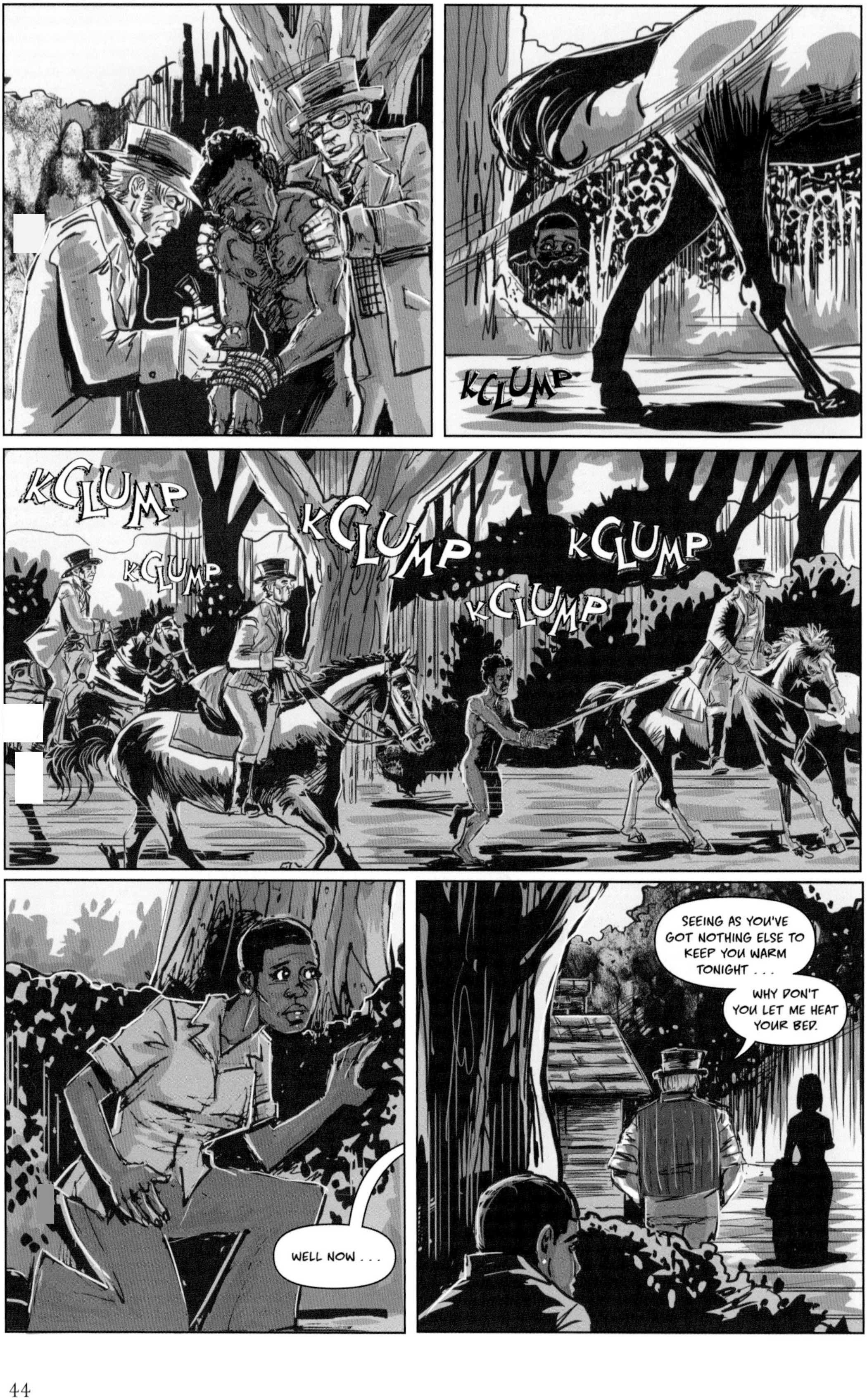
KCLUMP
KCLUMP
KCLUMP
KCLUMP
KCLUMP
KCLUMP
WELL NOW . . .
SEEING AS YOU'VE GOT NOTHING ELSE TO KEEP YOU WARM TONIGHT . . .
WHY DON'T YOU LET ME HEAT YOUR BED.

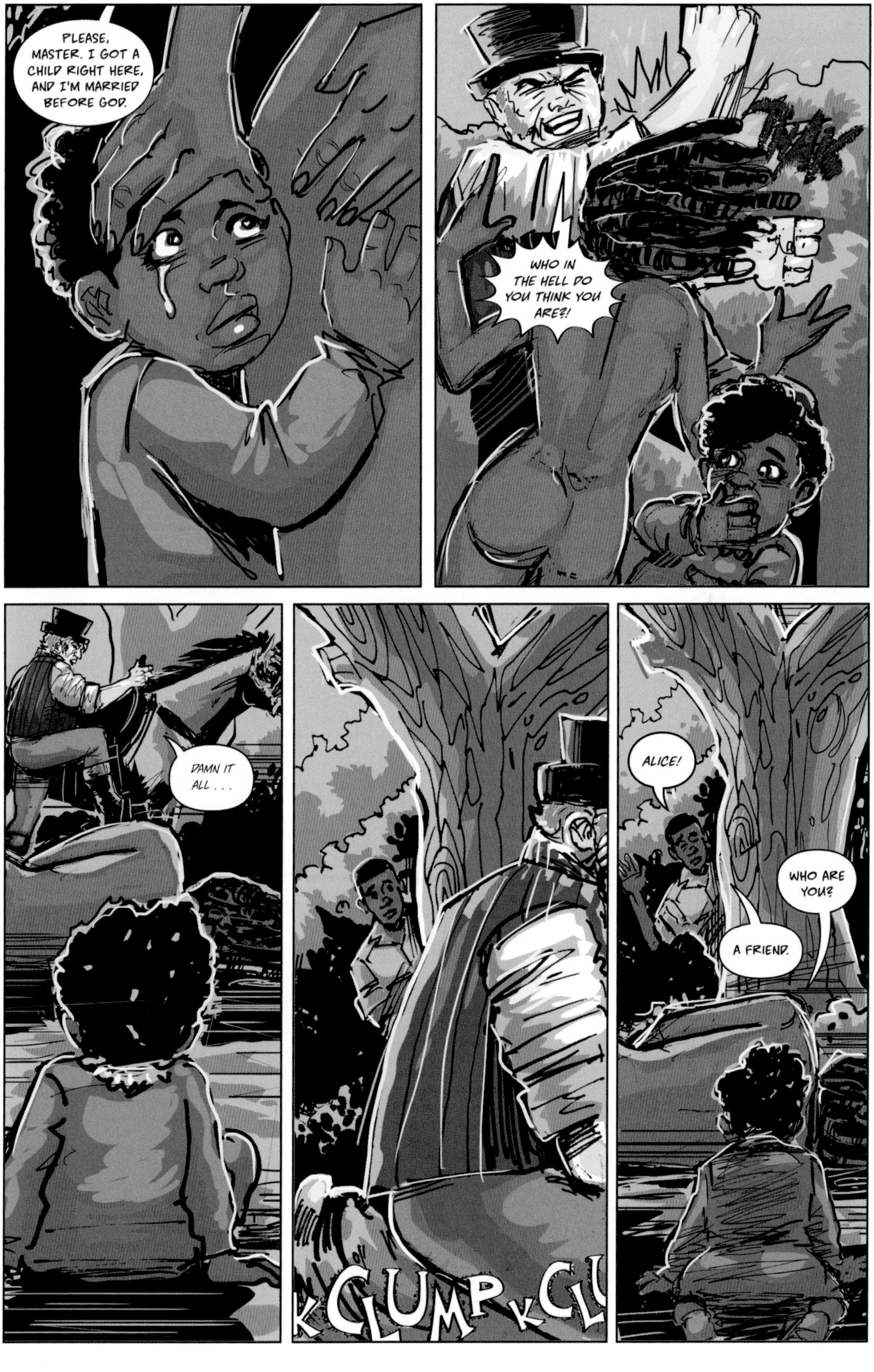
PLEASE, MASTER. I GOT A CHILD RIGHT HERE, AND I'M MARRIED BEFORE GOD.
WHO IN THE HELL DO YOU THINK YOU ARE?!
DAMN IT ALL . . .
KCLUMP KCLU
ALICE!
WHO ARE YOU?
A FRIEND.

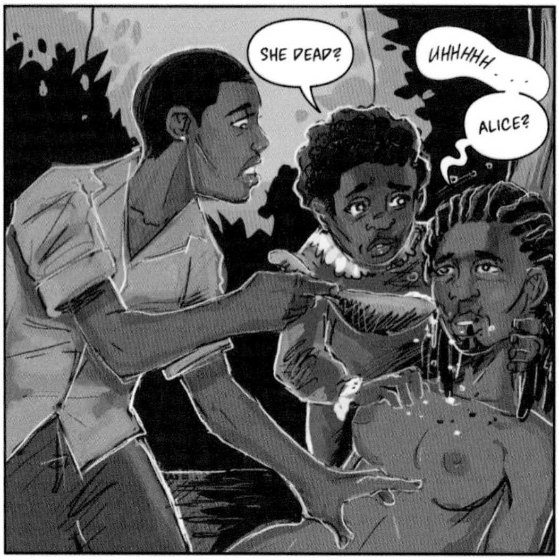
SHE DEAD?
UHHHHH . . .
ALICE?

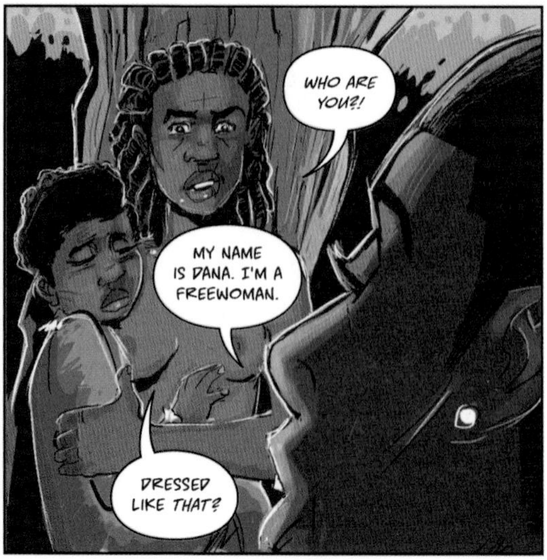
WHO ARE YOU?!
MY NAME IS DANA. I'M A FREEWOMAN.
DRESSED LIKE THAT?

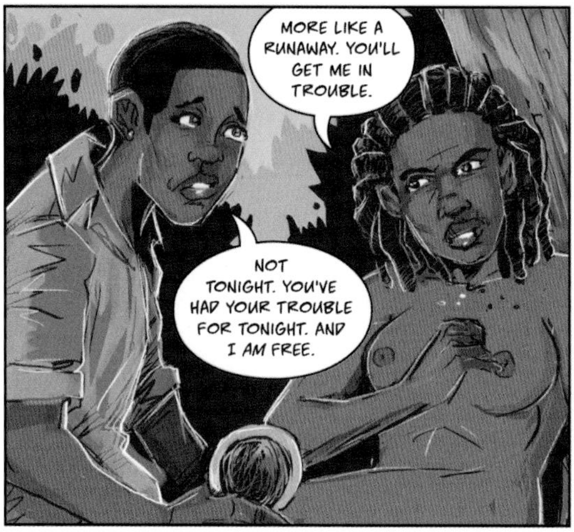
MORE LIKE A RUNAWAY. YOU'LL GET ME IN TROUBLE.
NOT TONIGHT. YOU'VE HAD YOUR TROUBLE FOR TONIGHT. AND I AM FREE.

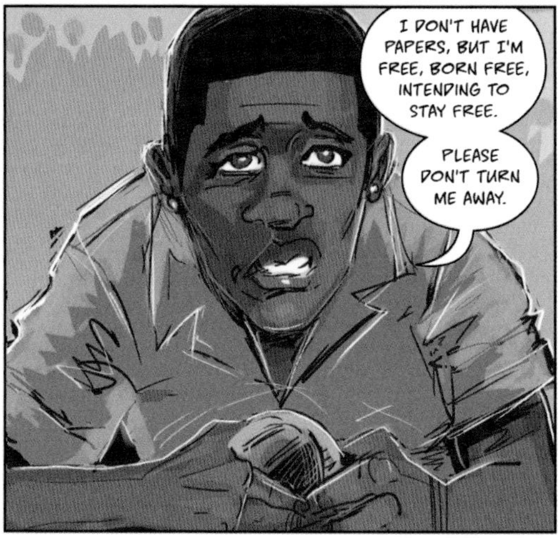
I DON'T HAVE PAPERS, BUT I'M FREE, BORN FREE, INTENDING TO STAY FREE.
PLEASE DON'T TURN ME AWAY.

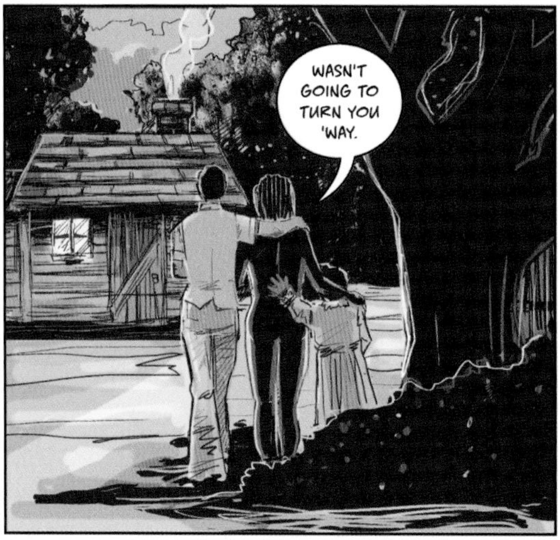
WASN'T GOING TO TURN YOU 'WAY.

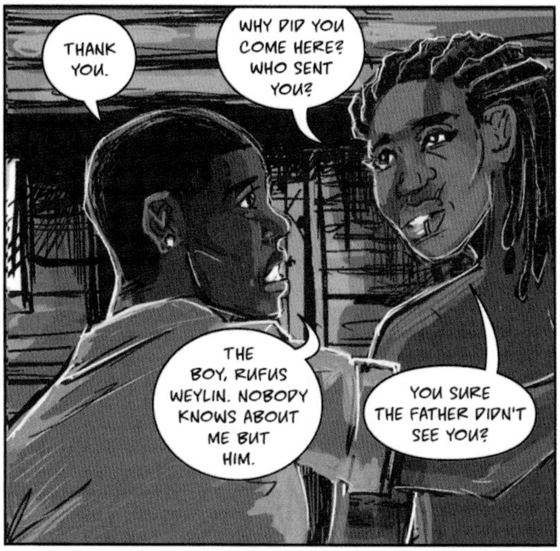
THANK YOU.
WHY DID YOU COME HERE? WHO SENT YOU?
THE BOY, RUFUS WEYLIN. NOBODY KNOWS ABOUT ME BUT HIM.
YOU SURE THE FATHER DIDN'T SEE YOU?

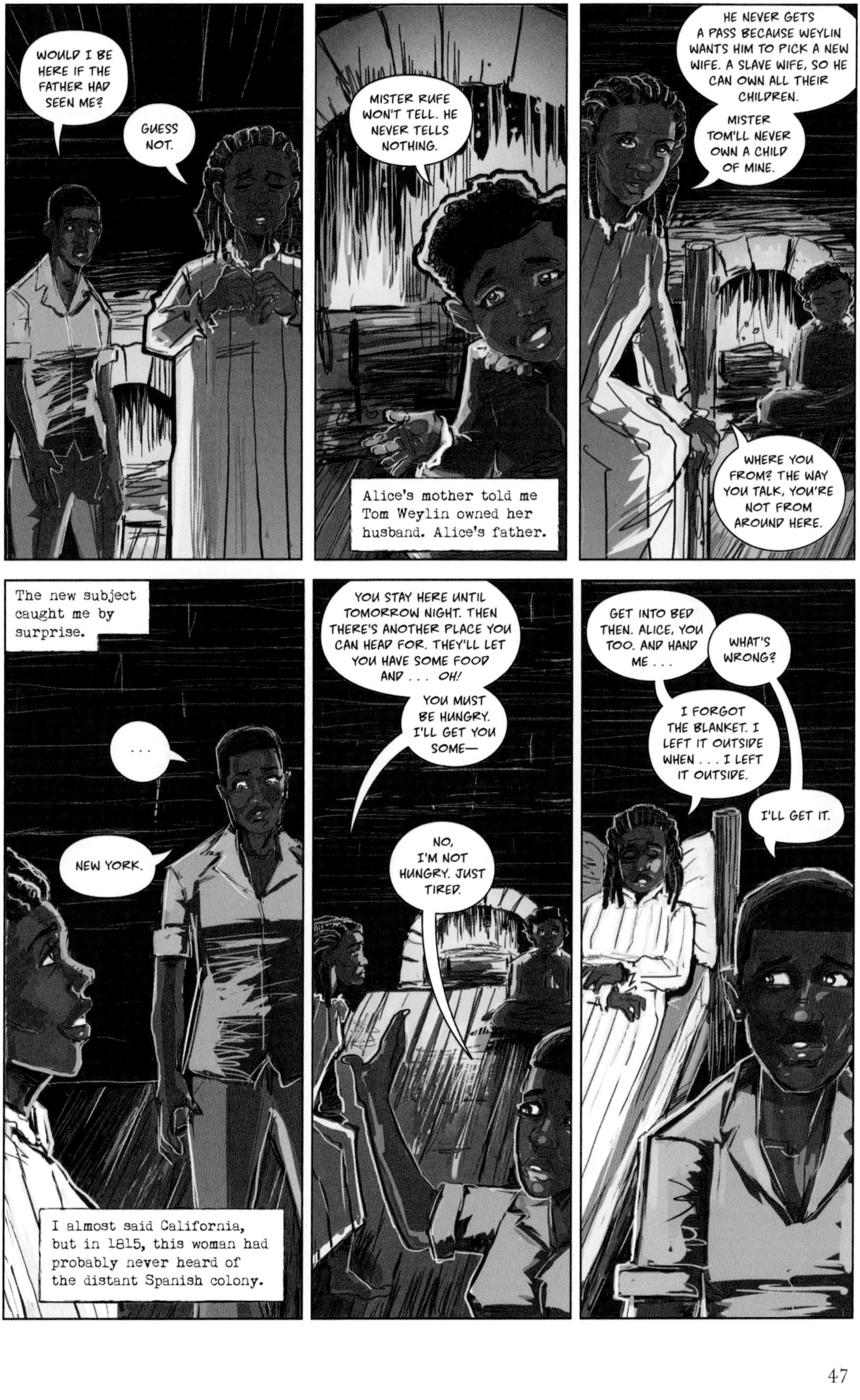
WOULD I BE HERE IF THE FATHER HAD SEEN ME?
GUESS NOT.
MISTER RUFE WON'T TELL. HE NEVER TELLS NOTHING.
Alice's mother told me Tom Weylin owned her husband. Alice's father.
HE NEVER GETS A PASS BECAUSE WEYLIN WANTS HIM TO PICK A NEW WIFE. A SLAVE WIFE, SO HE CAN OWN ALL THEIR CHILDREN.
MISTER TOM'LL NEVER OWN A CHILD OF MINE.
WHERE YOU FROM? THE WAY YOU TALK, YOU'RE NOT FROM AROUND HERE.
The new subject caught me by surprise.
. . .
NEW YORK.
I almost said California, but in 1815, this woman had probably never heard of the distant Spanish colony.
YOU STAY HERE UNTIL TOMORROW NIGHT. THEN THERE'S ANOTHER PLACE YOU CAN HEAD FOR. THEY'LL LET YOU HAVE SOME FOOD AND . . . OH!
YOU MUST BE HUNGRY. I'LL GET YOU SOME—
NO, I'M NOT HUNGRY. JUST TIRED.
GET INTO BED THEN. ALICE, YOU TOO. AND HAND ME . . .
WHAT'S WRONG?
I FORGOT THE BLANKET. I LEFT IT OUTSIDE WHEN . . . I LEFT IT OUTSIDE.
I'LL GET IT.

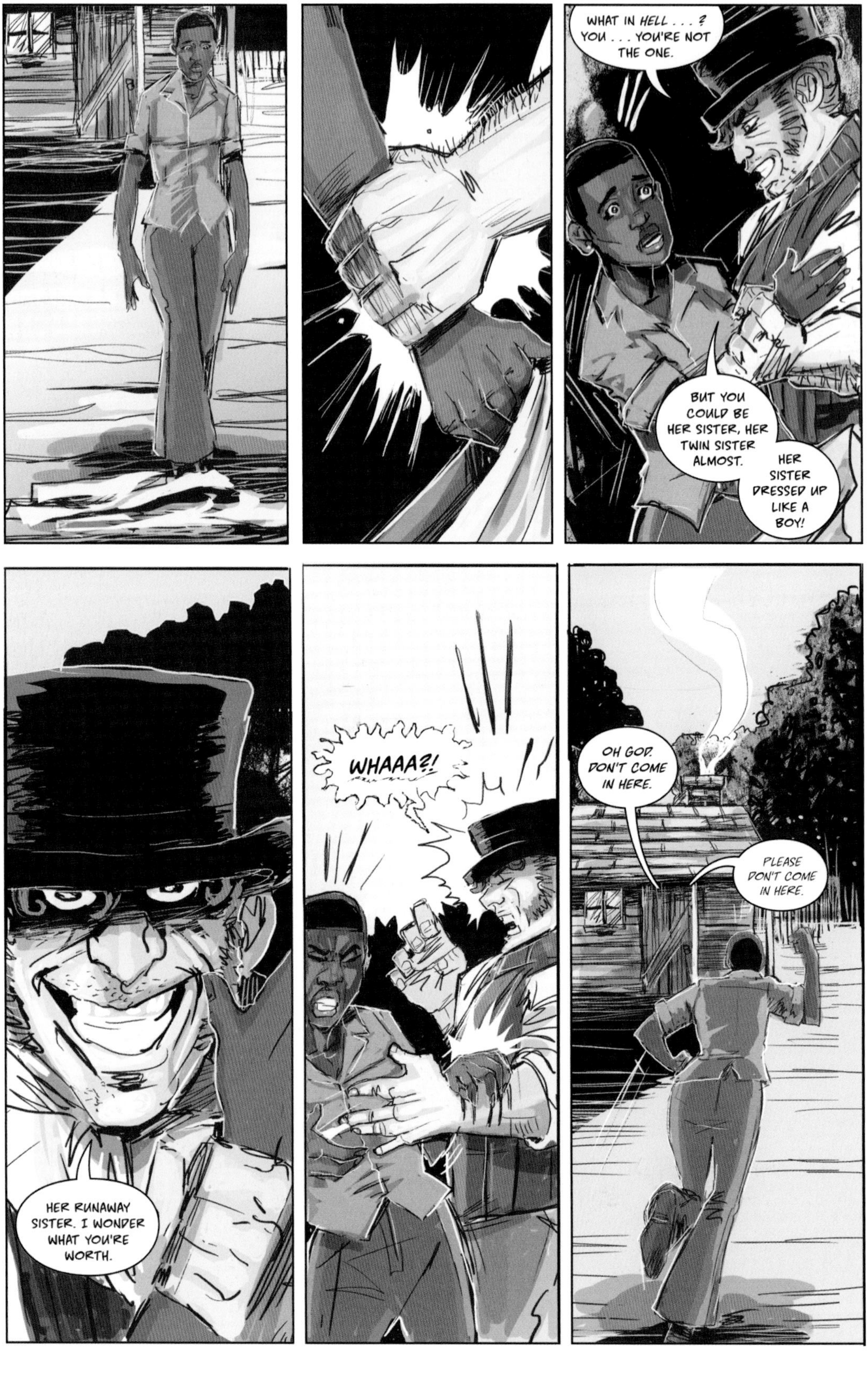
WHAT IN HELL . . . ? YOU . . . YOU'RE NOT THE ONE.
BUT YOU COULD BE HER SISTER, HER TWIN SISTER ALMOST.
HER SISTER DRESSED UP LIKE A BOY!
HER RUNAWAY SISTER. I WONDER WHAT YOU'RE WORTH.
WHAAA?!
OH GOD. DON'T COME IN HERE.
PLEASE DON'T COME IN HERE.

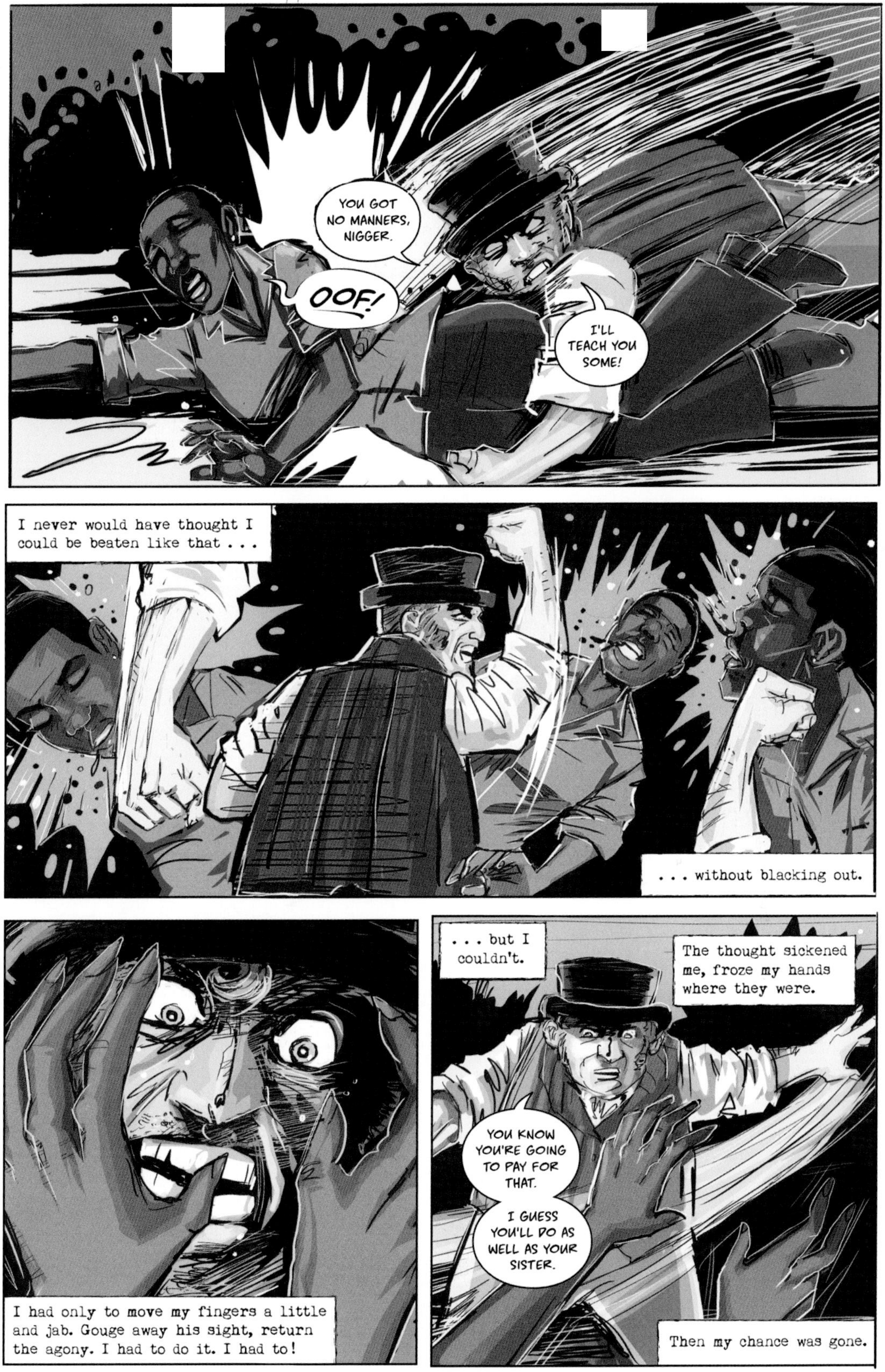
YOU GOT NO MANNERS, NIGGER.
OOF!
I'LL TEACH YOU SOME!
I never would have thought I could be beaten like that . . .
. . . without blacking out.
I had only to move my fingers a little and jab. Gouge away his sight, return the agony. I had to do it. I had to!
. . . but I couldn't.
The thought sickened me, froze my hands where they were.
YOU KNOW YOU'RE GOING TO PAY FOR THAT.
I GUESS YOU'LL DO AS WELL AS YOUR SISTER.
Then my chance was gone.

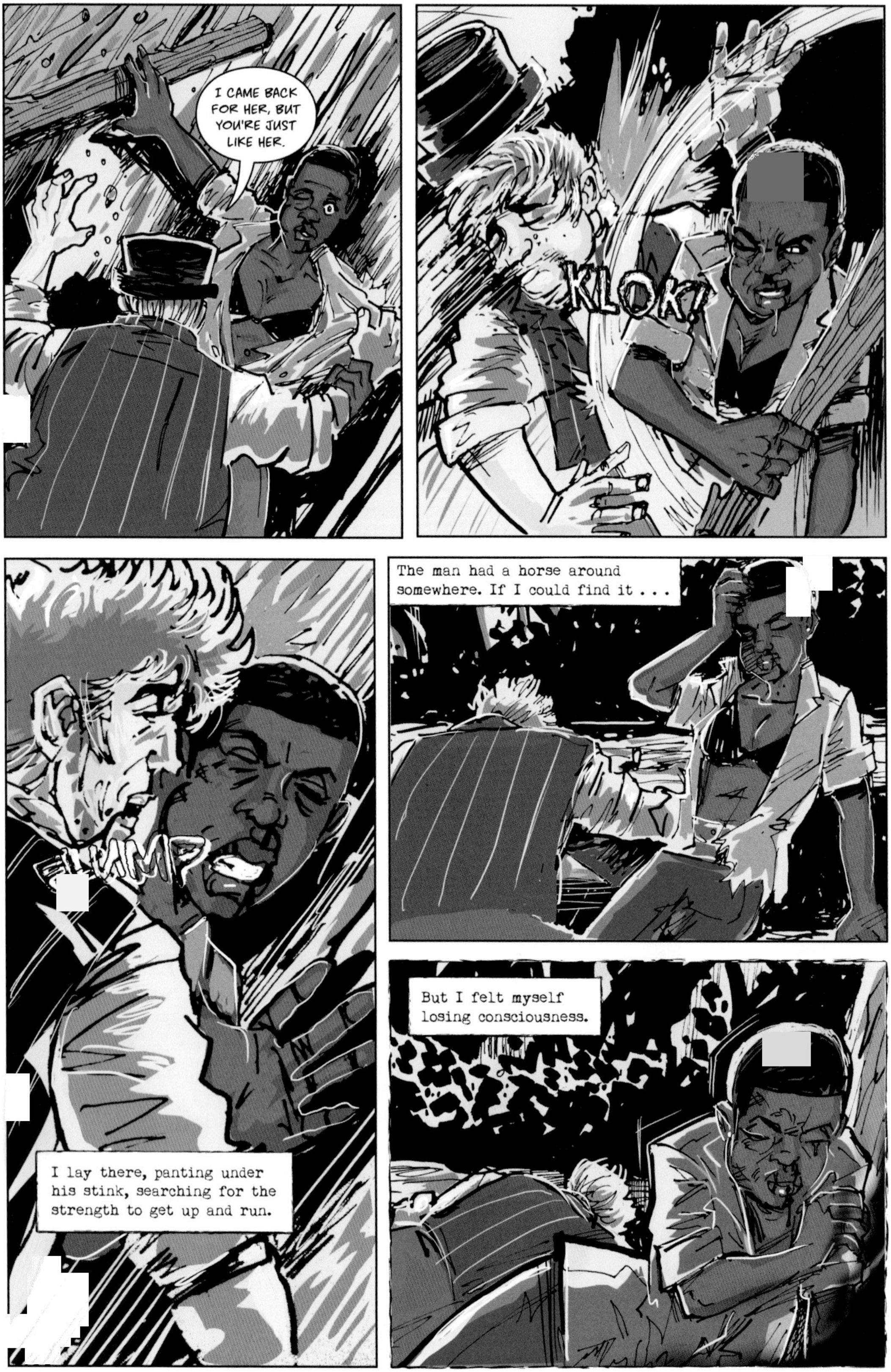
I CAME BACK FOR HER, BUT YOU'RE JUST LIKE HER.
KLOK!
The man had a horse around somewhere. If I could find it . . .
I lay there, panting under his stink, searching for the strength to get up and run.
But I felt myself losing consciousness.

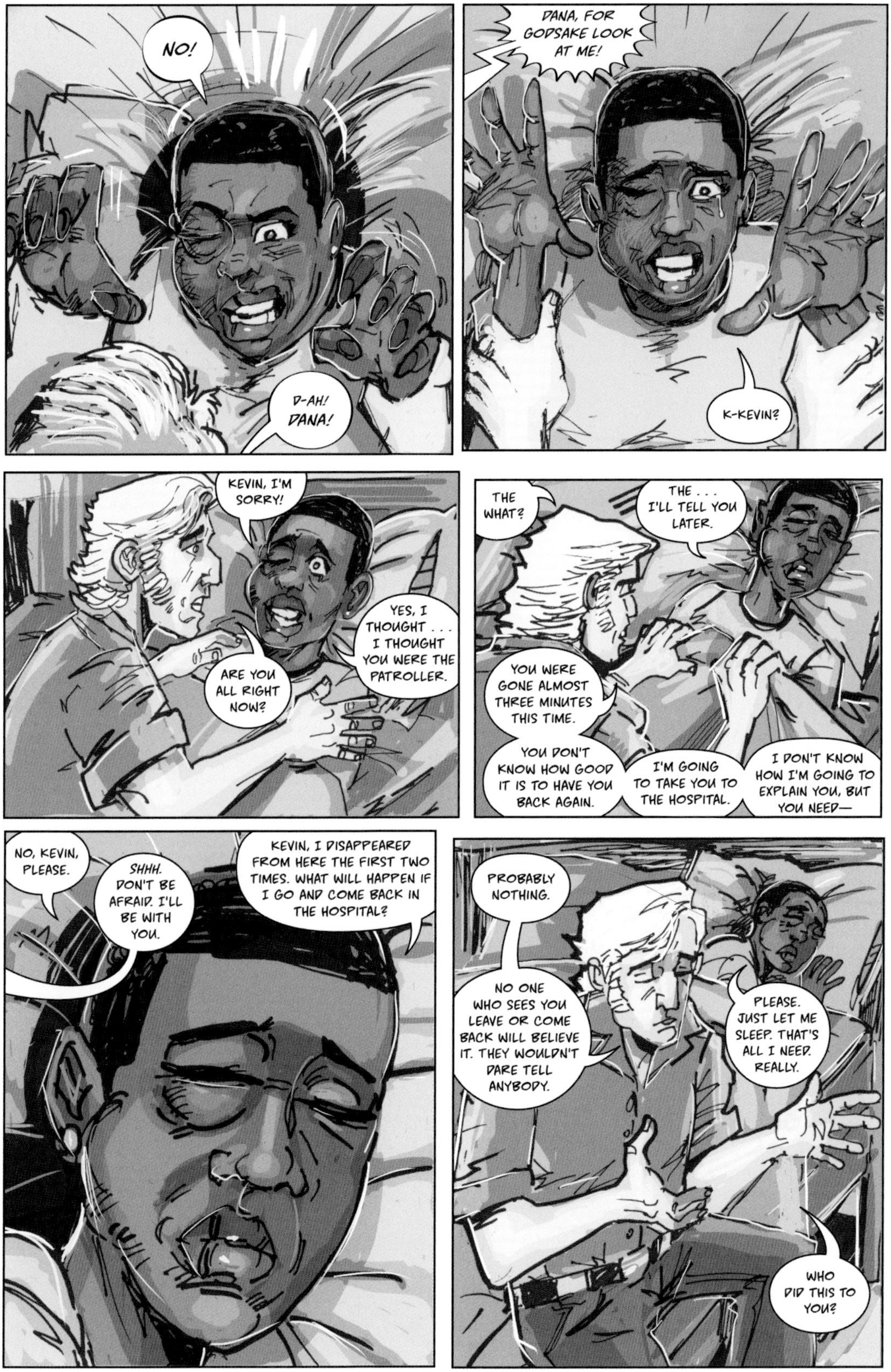
NO!
D-AH! DANA!
DANA, FOR GODSAKE LOOK AT ME!
K-KEVIN?
KEVIN, I'M SORRY!
ARE YOU ALL RIGHT NOW?
YES, I THOUGHT . . . I THOUGHT YOU WERE THE PATROLLER.
THE WHAT?
THE . . . I'LL TELL YOU LATER.
YOU WERE GONE ALMOST THREE MINUTES THIS TIME.
YOU DON'T KNOW HOW GOOD IT IS TO HAVE YOU BACK AGAIN.
I'M GOING TO TAKE YOU TO THE HOSPITAL.
I DON'T KNOW HOW I'M GOING TO EXPLAIN YOU, BUT YOU NEED—
NO, KEVIN, PLEASE.
SHHH. DON'T BE AFRAID. I'LL BE WITH YOU.
KEVIN, I DISAPPEARED FROM HERE THE FIRST TWO TIMES. WHAT WILL HAPPEN IF I GO AND COME BACK IN THE HOSPITAL?
PROBABLY NOTHING.
NO ONE WHO SEES YOU LEAVE OR COME BACK WILL BELIEVE IT. THEY WOULDN'T DARE TELL ANYBODY.
PLEASE. JUST LET ME SLEEP. THAT'S ALL I NEED. REALLY.
WHO DID THIS TO YOU?

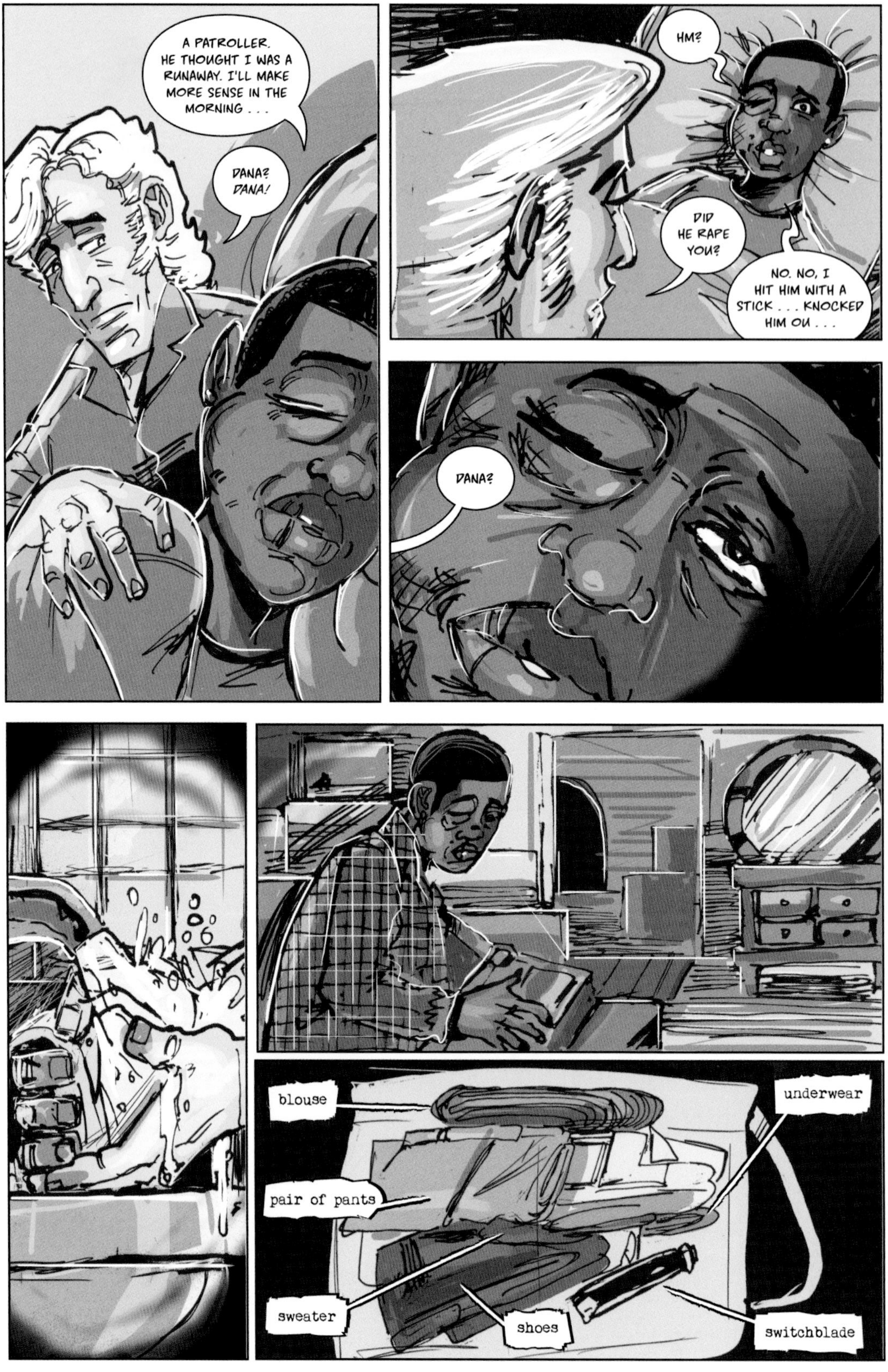
A PATROLLER. HE THOUGHT I WAS A RUNAWAY. I'LL MAKE MORE SENSE IN THE MORNING . . .
DANA? DANA!
HM?
DID HE RAPE YOU?
NO. NO, I HIT HIM WITH A STICK . . . KNOCKED HIM OU . . .
DANA?
blouse
underwear
pair of pants
sweater
shoes
switchblade

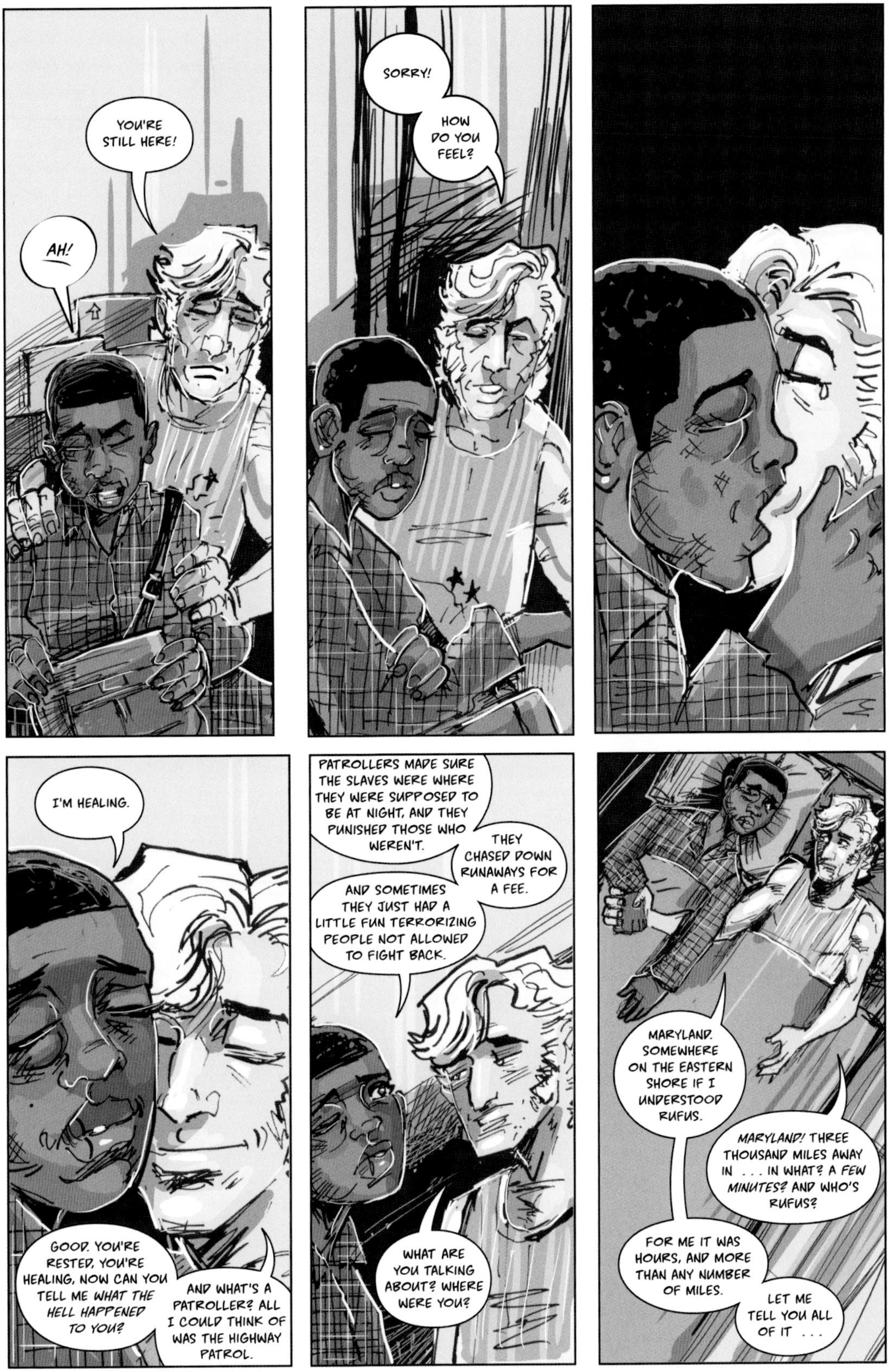
YOU'RE STILL HERE!
AH!
SORRY!
HOW DO YOU FEEL?
I'M HEALING.
GOOD. YOU'RE RESTED, YOU'RE HEALING, NOW CAN YOU TELL ME WHAT THE HELL HAPPENED TO YOU?
AND WHAT'S A PATROLLER? ALL I COULD THINK OF WAS THE HIGHWAY PATROL.
PATROLLERS MADE SURE THE SLAVES WERE WHERE THEY WERE SUPPOSED TO BE AT NIGHT, AND THEY PUNISHED THOSE WHO WEREN'T.
THEY CHASED DOWN RUNAWAYS FOR A FEE.
AND SOMETIMES THEY JUST HAD A LITTLE FUN TERRORIZING PEOPLE NOT ALLOWED TO FIGHT BACK.
WHAT ARE YOU TALKING ABOUT? WHERE WERE YOU?
MARYLAND. SOMEWHERE ON THE EASTERN SHORE IF I UNDERSTOOD RUFUS.
MARYLAND! THREE THOUSAND MILES AWAY IN . . . IN WHAT? A FEW MINUTES? AND WHO'S RUFUS?
FOR ME IT WAS HOURS, AND MORE THAN ANY NUMBER OF MILES.
LET ME TELL YOU ALL OF IT . . .

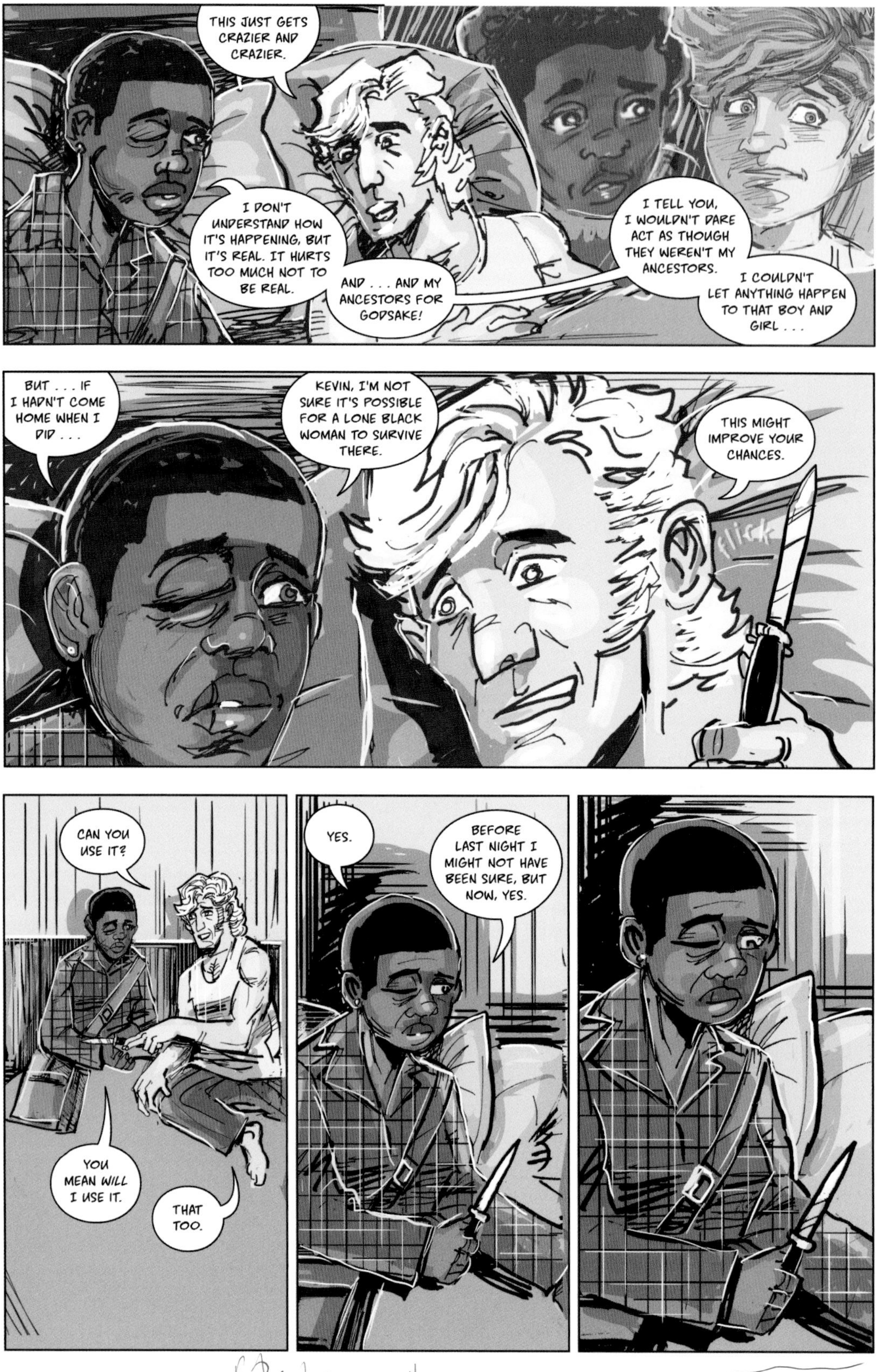
THIS JUST GETS CRAZIER AND CRAZIER.
I DON'T UNDERSTAND HOW IT'S HAPPENING, BUT IT'S REAL. IT HURTS TOO MUCH NOT TO BE REAL.
AND . . . AND MY ANCESTORS FOR GODSAKE!
I TELL YOU, I WOULDN'T DARE ACT AS THOUGH THEY WEREN'T MY ANCESTORS.
I COULDN'T LET ANYTHING HAPPEN TO THAT BOY AND GIRL . . .
BUT . . . IF I HADN'T COME HOME WHEN I DID . . .
KEVIN, I'M NOT SURE IT'S POSSIBLE FOR A LONE BLACK WOMAN TO SURVIVE THERE.
THIS MIGHT IMPROVE YOUR CHANCES.
flick
CAN YOU USE IT?
YOU MEAN WILL I USE IT.
THAT TOO.
YES.
BEFORE LAST NIGHT I MIGHT NOT HAVE BEEN SURE, BUT NOW, YES.

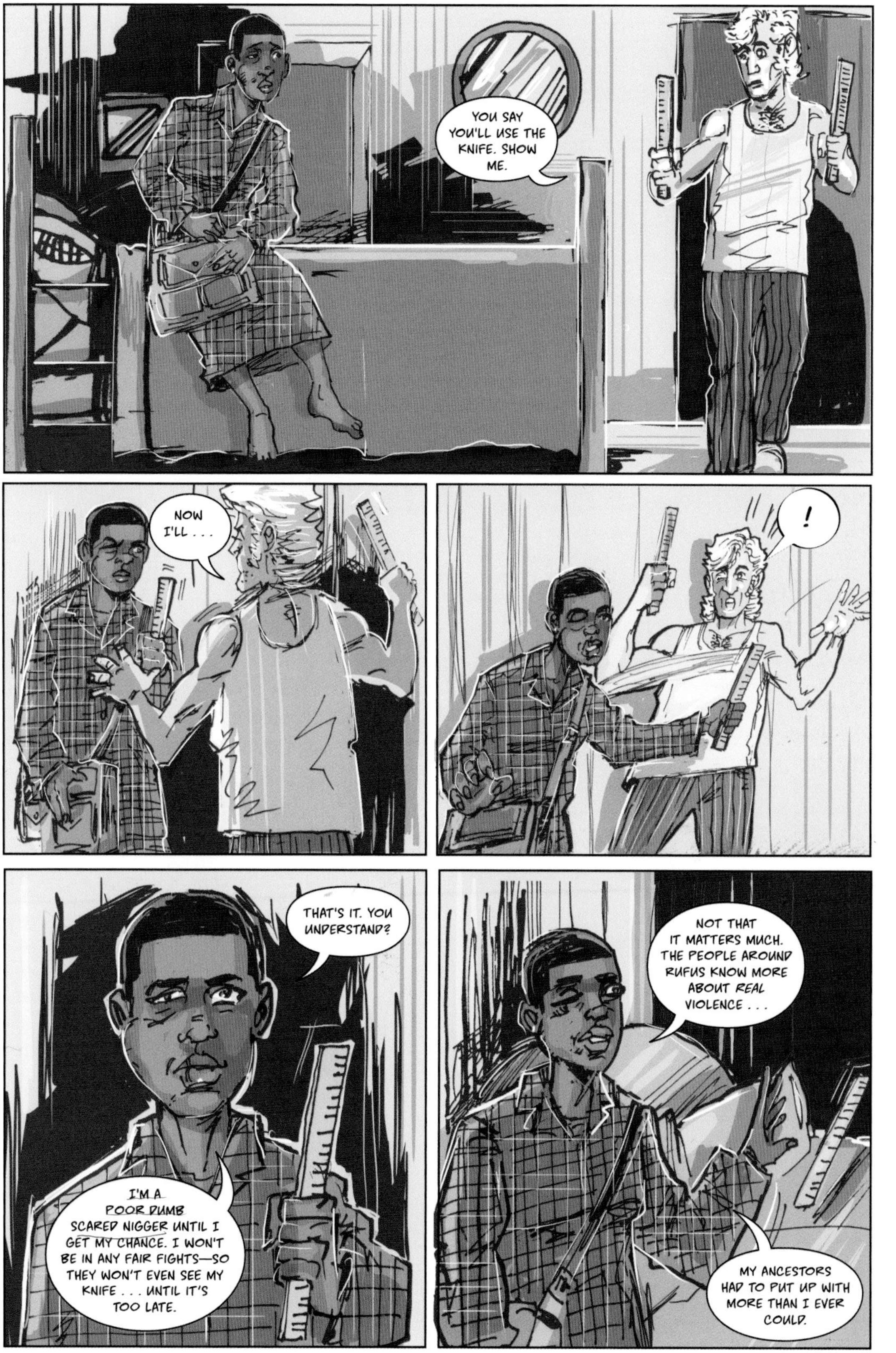
YOU SAY YOU'LL USE THE KNIFE. SHOW ME.
NOW I'LL . . .
!
THAT'S IT. YOU UNDERSTAND?
I'M A POOR DUMB SCARED NIGGER UNTIL I GET MY CHANCE. I WON'T BE IN ANY FAIR FIGHTS—SO THEY WON'T EVEN SEE MY KNIFE . . . UNTIL IT'S TOO LATE.
NOT THAT IT MATTERS MUCH. THE PEOPLE AROUND RUFUS KNOW MORE ABOUT *REAL* VIOLENCE . . .
MY ANCESTORS HAD TO PUT UP WITH MORE THAN I EVER COULD.

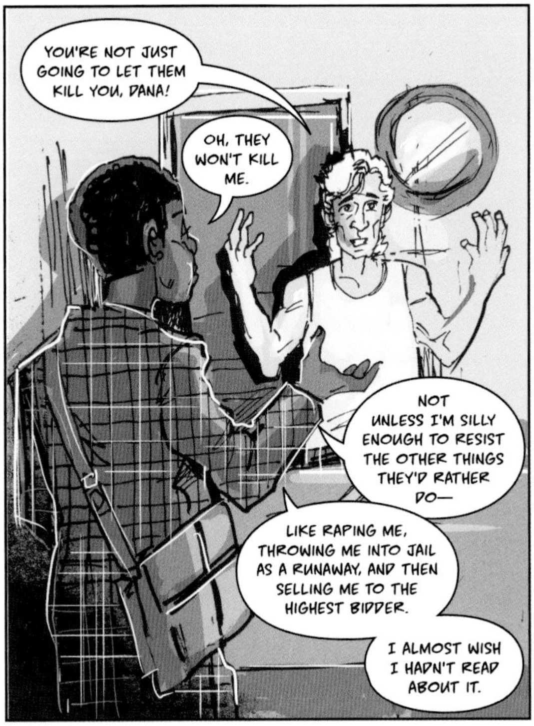
YOU'RE NOT JUST GOING TO LET THEM KILL YOU, DANA!
OH, THEY WON'T KILL ME.
NOT UNLESS I'M SILLY ENOUGH TO RESIST THE OTHER THINGS THEY'D RATHER DO—
LIKE RAPING ME, THROWING ME INTO JAIL AS A RUNAWAY, AND THEN SELLING ME TO THE HIGHEST BIDDER.
I ALMOST WISH I HADN'T READ ABOUT IT.

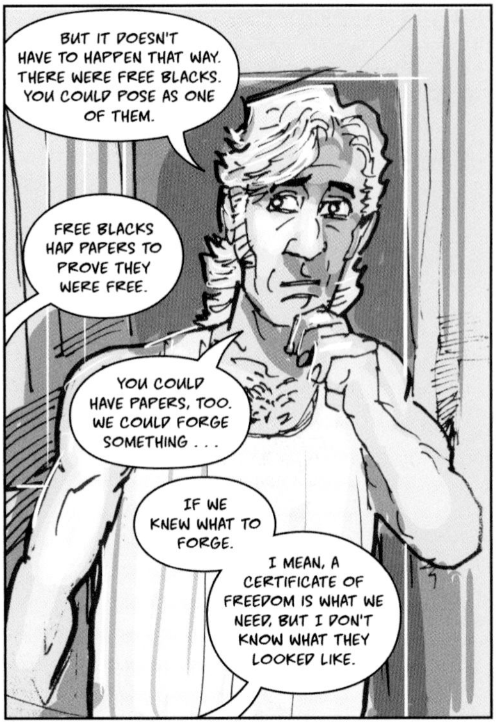
BUT IT DOESN'T HAVE TO HAPPEN THAT WAY. THERE WERE FREE BLACKS. YOU COULD POSE AS ONE OF THEM.
FREE BLACKS HAD PAPERS TO PROVE THEY WERE FREE.
YOU COULD HAVE PAPERS, TOO. WE COULD FORGE SOMETHING . . .
IF WE KNEW WHAT TO FORGE.
I MEAN, A CERTIFICATE OF FREEDOM IS WHAT WE NEED, BUT I DON'T KNOW WHAT THEY LOOKED LIKE.

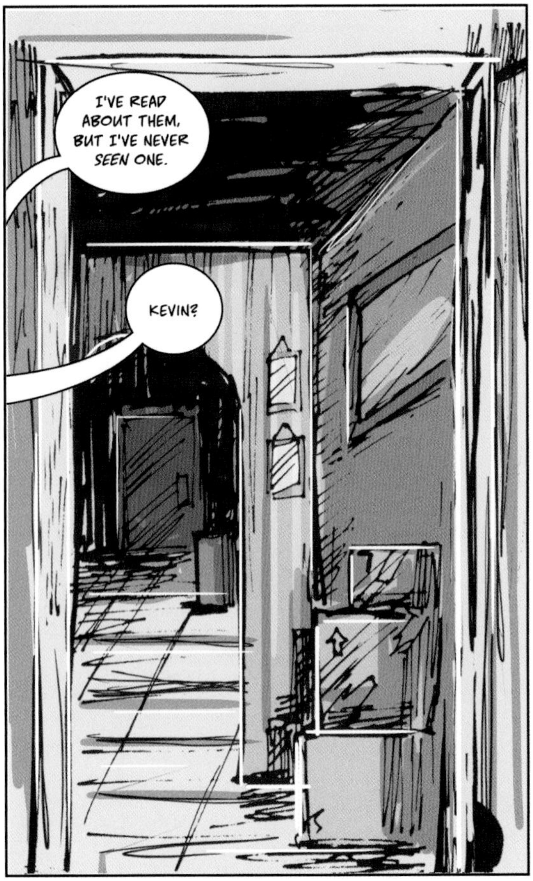
I'VE READ ABOUT THEM, BUT I'VE NEVER *SEEN* ONE.
KEVIN?

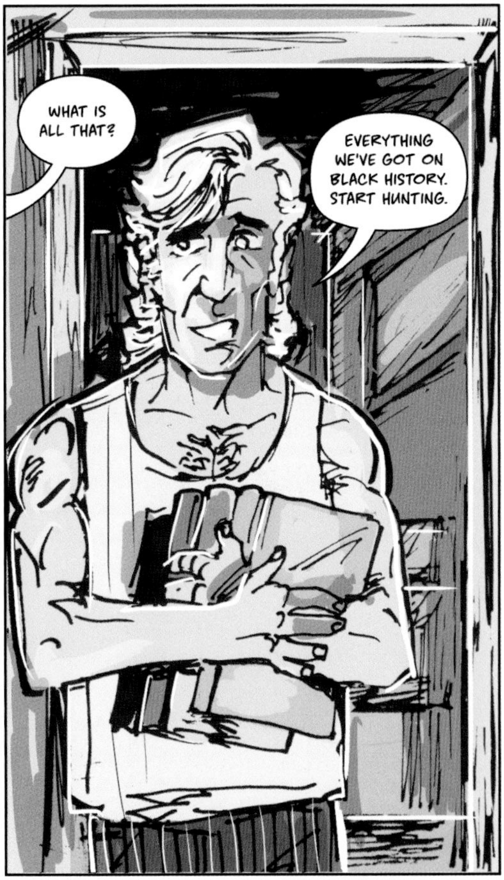
WHAT IS ALL THAT?
EVERYTHING WE'VE GOT ON BLACK HISTORY. START HUNTING.

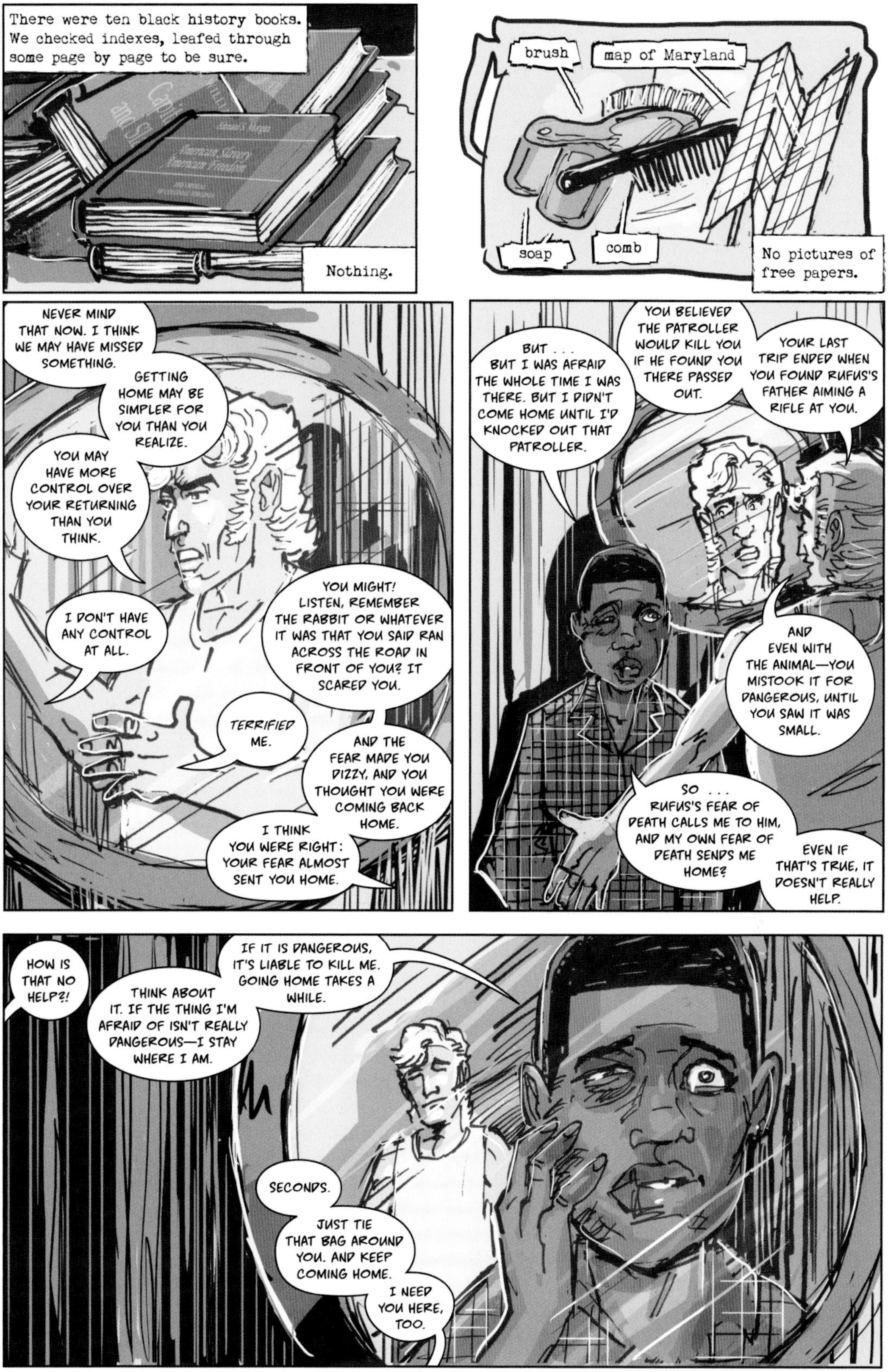
There were ten black history books. We checked indexes, leafed through some page by page to be sure.
Nothing.
brush
map of Maryland
soap
comb
No pictures of free papers.
NEVER MIND THAT NOW. I THINK WE MAY HAVE MISSED SOMETHING.
GETTING HOME MAY BE SIMPLER FOR YOU THAN YOU REALIZE.
YOU MAY HAVE MORE CONTROL OVER YOUR RETURNING THAN YOU THINK.
I DON'T HAVE ANY CONTROL AT ALL.
YOU MIGHT! LISTEN, REMEMBER THE RABBIT OR WHATEVER IT WAS THAT YOU SAID RAN ACROSS THE ROAD IN FRONT OF YOU? IT SCARED YOU.
TERRIFIED ME.
AND THE FEAR MADE YOU DIZZY, AND YOU THOUGHT YOU WERE COMING BACK HOME.
I THINK YOU WERE RIGHT: YOUR FEAR ALMOST SENT YOU HOME.
BUT . . . BUT I WAS AFRAID THE WHOLE TIME I WAS THERE. BUT I DIDN'T COME HOME UNTIL I'D KNOCKED OUT THAT PATROLLER.
YOU BELIEVED THE PATROLLER WOULD KILL YOU IF HE FOUND YOU THERE PASSED OUT.
YOUR LAST TRIP ENDED WHEN YOU FOUND RUFUS'S FATHER AIMING A RIFLE AT YOU.
AND EVEN WITH THE ANIMAL—YOU MISTOOK IT FOR DANGEROUS, UNTIL YOU SAW IT WAS SMALL.
SO . . . RUFUS'S FEAR OF DEATH CALLS ME TO HIM, AND MY OWN FEAR OF DEATH SENDS ME HOME?
EVEN IF THAT'S TRUE, IT DOESN'T REALLY HELP.
HOW IS THAT NO HELP?!
THINK ABOUT IT. IF THE THING I'M AFRAID OF ISN'T REALLY DANGEROUS—I STAY WHERE I AM.
IF IT IS DANGEROUS, IT'S LIABLE TO KILL ME. GOING HOME TAKES A WHILE.
SECONDS.
JUST TIE THAT BAG AROUND YOU. AND KEEP COMING HOME.
I NEED YOU HERE, TOO.

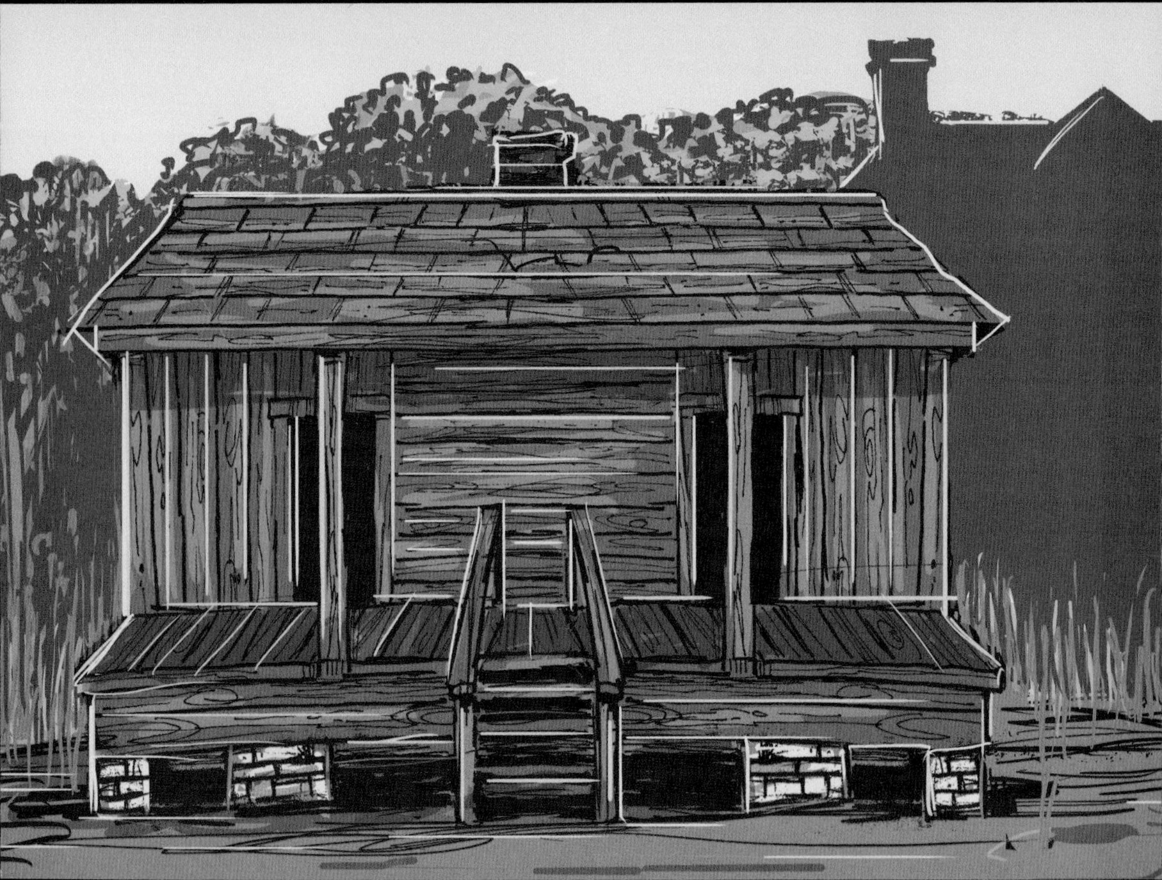

THE FALL

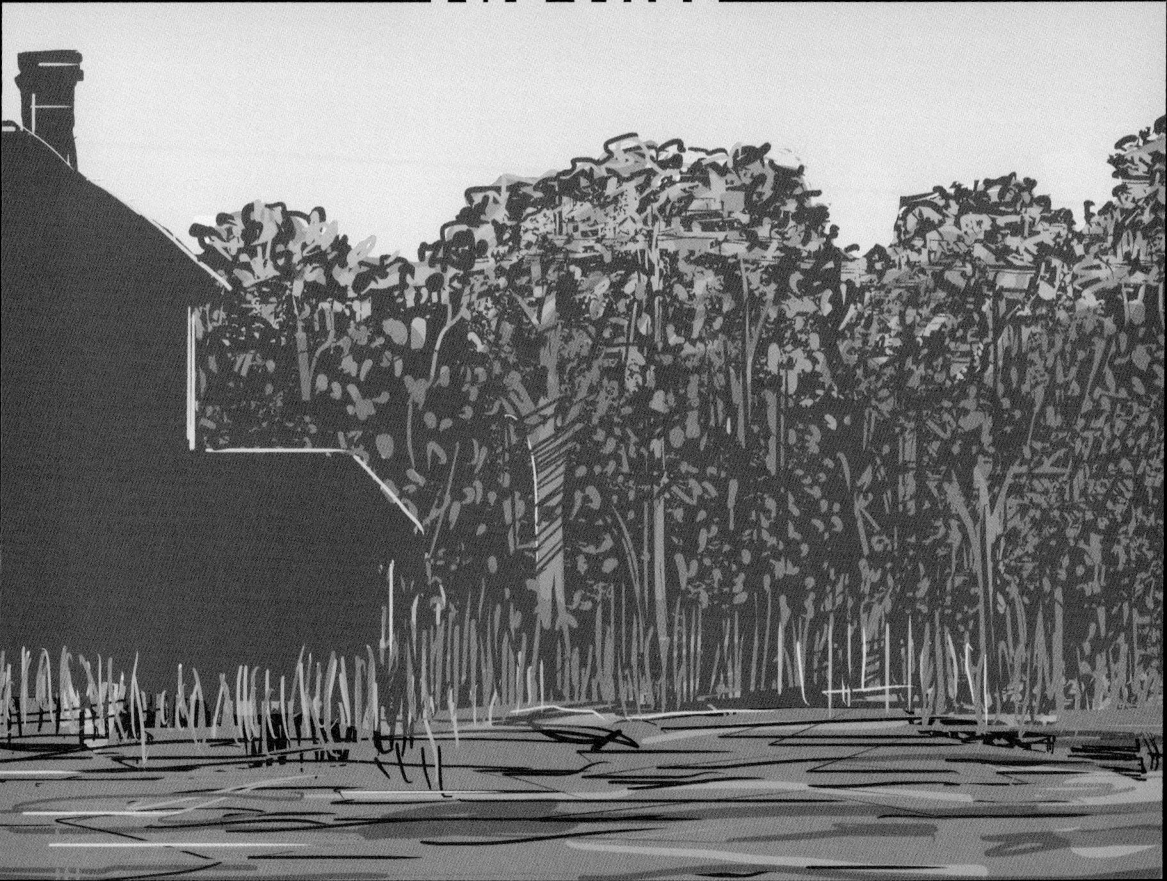

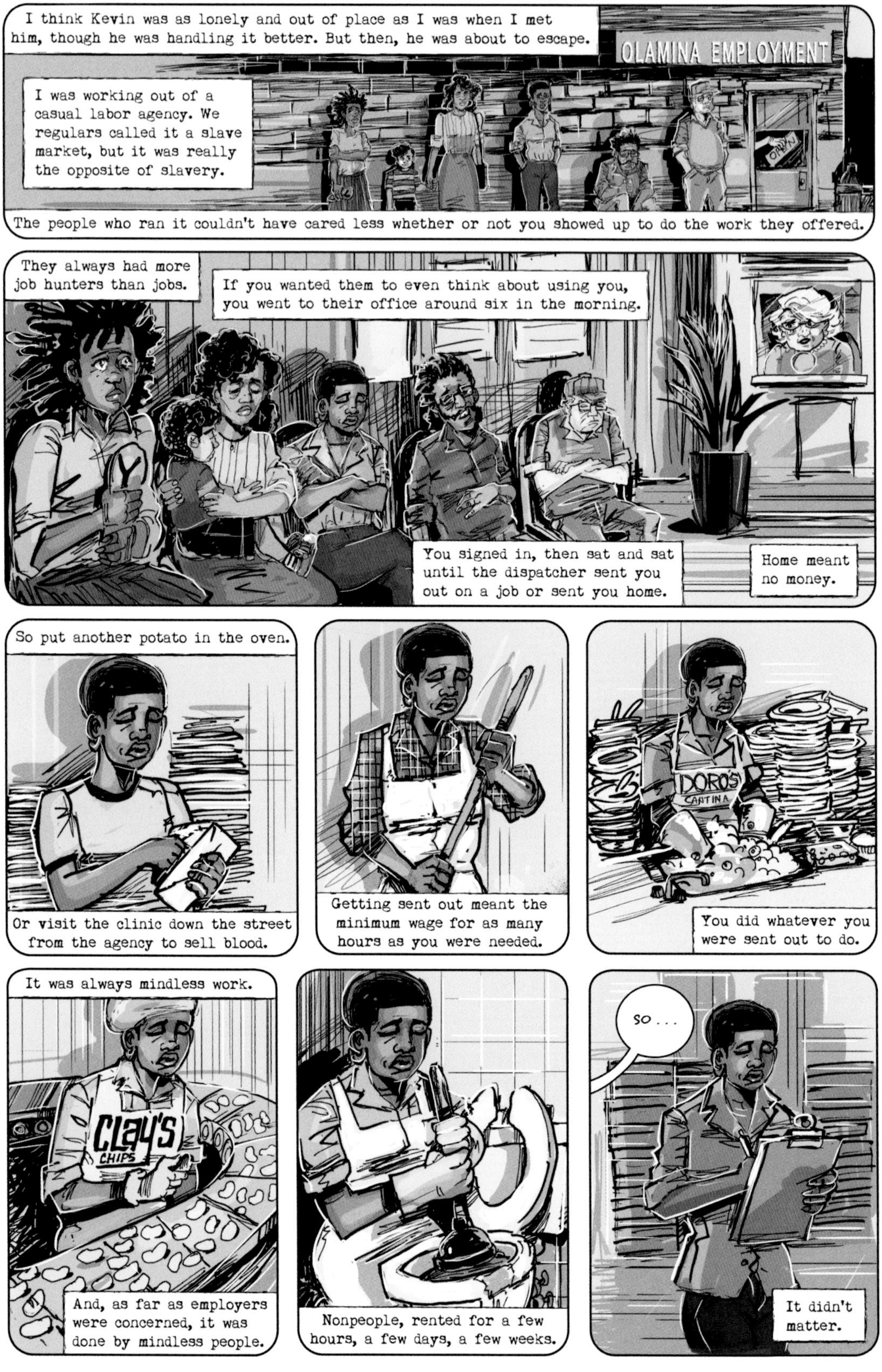
I think Kevin was as lonely and out of place as I was when I met him, though he was handling it better. But then, he was about to escape.
OLAMINA EMPLOYMENT
I was working out of a casual labor agency. We regulars called it a slave market, but it was really the opposite of slavery.
OPEN
The people who ran it couldn't have cared less whether or not you showed up to do the work they offered.
They always had more job hunters than jobs.
If you wanted them to even think about using you, you went to their office around six in the morning.
You signed in, then sat and sat until the dispatcher sent you out on a job or sent you home.
Home meant no money.
So put another potato in the oven.
Or visit the clinic down the street from the agency to sell blood.
Getting sent out meant the minimum wage for as many hours as you were needed.
DORO'S
CANTINA
You did whatever you were sent out to do.
It was always mindless work.
CLAY'S
CHIPS
And, as far as employers were concerned, it was done by mindless people.
Nonpeople, rented for a few hours, a few days, a few weeks.
So . . .
It didn't matter.

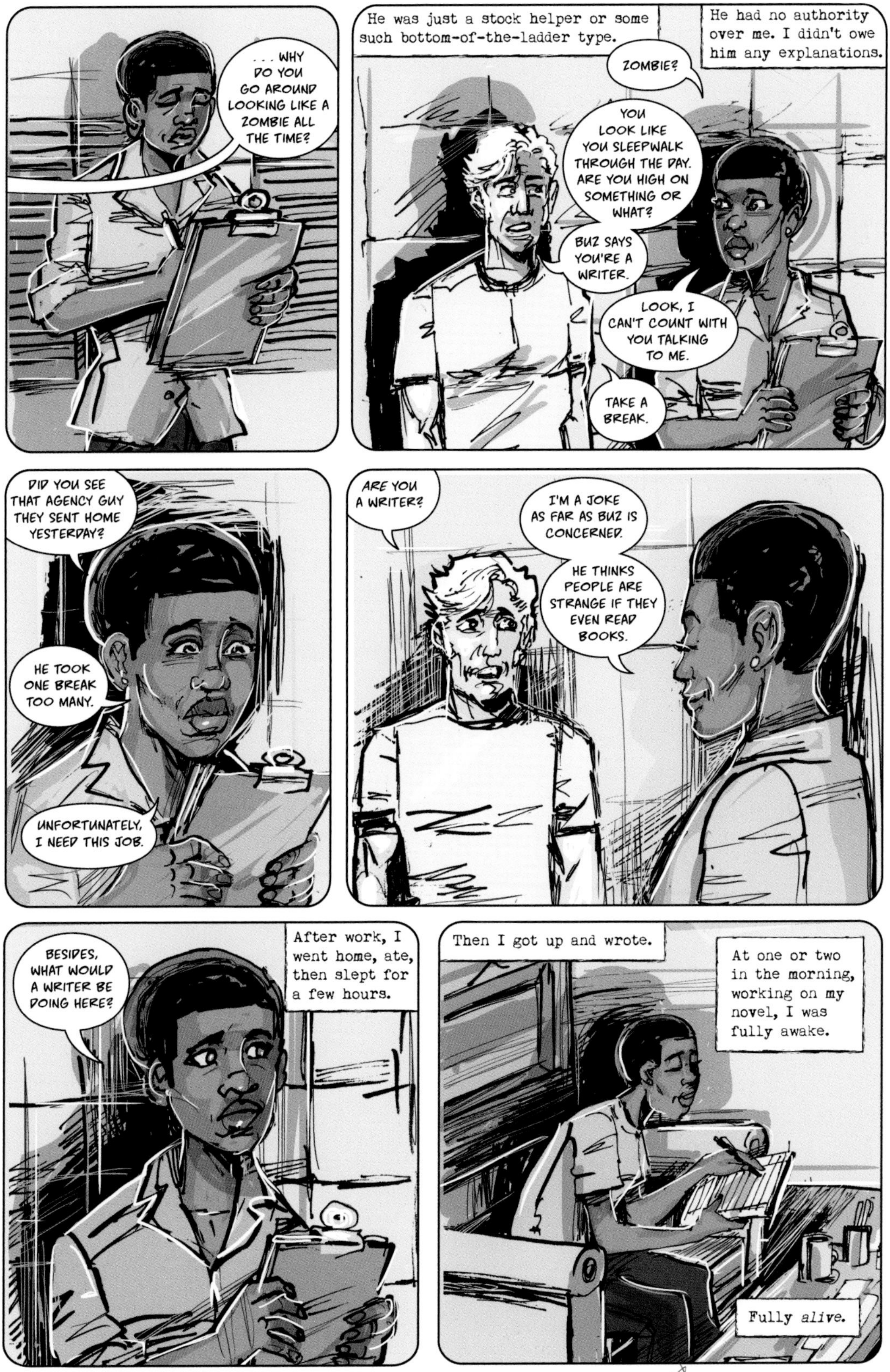
. . . WHY DO YOU GO AROUND LOOKING LIKE A ZOMBIE ALL THE TIME?
He was just a stock helper or some such bottom-of-the-ladder type.
He had no authority over me. I didn't owe him any explanations.
ZOMBIE?
YOU LOOK LIKE YOU SLEEPWALK THROUGH THE DAY. ARE YOU HIGH ON SOMETHING OR WHAT?
BUZ SAYS YOU'RE A WRITER.
LOOK, I CAN'T COUNT WITH YOU TALKING TO ME.
TAKE A BREAK.
DID YOU SEE THAT AGENCY GUY THEY SENT HOME YESTERDAY?
HE TOOK ONE BREAK TOO MANY.
UNFORTUNATELY, I NEED THIS JOB.
ARE YOU A WRITER?
I'M A JOKE AS FAR AS BUZ IS CONCERNED.
HE THINKS PEOPLE ARE STRANGE IF THEY EVEN READ BOOKS.
BESIDES, WHAT WOULD A WRITER BE DOING HERE?
After work, I went home, ate, then slept for a few hours.
Then I got up and wrote.
At one or two in the morning, working on my novel, I was fully awake.
Fully *alive.*

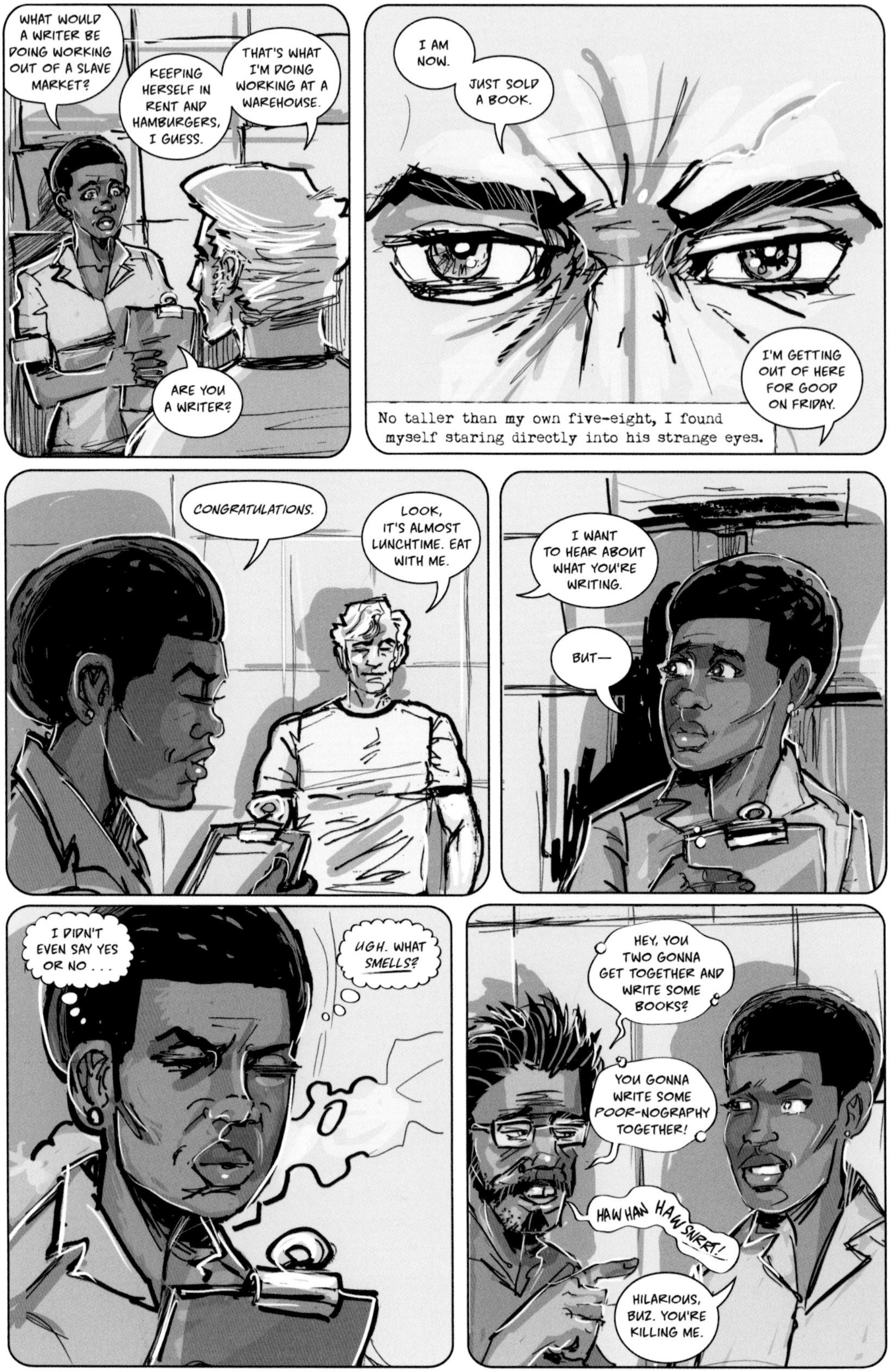
WHAT WOULD A WRITER BE DOING WORKING OUT OF A SLAVE MARKET?
KEEPING HERSELF IN RENT AND HAMBURGERS, I GUESS.
THAT'S WHAT I'M DOING WORKING AT A WAREHOUSE.
ARE YOU A WRITER?
I AM NOW.
JUST SOLD A BOOK.
No taller than my own five-eight, I found myself staring directly into his strange eyes.
I'M GETTING OUT OF HERE FOR GOOD ON FRIDAY.
CONGRATULATIONS.
LOOK, IT'S ALMOST LUNCHTIME. EAT WITH ME.
I WANT TO HEAR ABOUT WHAT YOU'RE WRITING.
BUT—
I DIDN'T EVEN SAY YES OR NO . . .
UGH. WHAT SMELLS?
HEY, YOU TWO GONNA GET TOGETHER AND WRITE SOME BOOKS?
YOU GONNA WRITE SOME POOR-NOGRAPHY TOGETHER!
HAW HAW HAW SNRRT!
HILARIOUS, BUZ. YOU'RE KILLING ME.

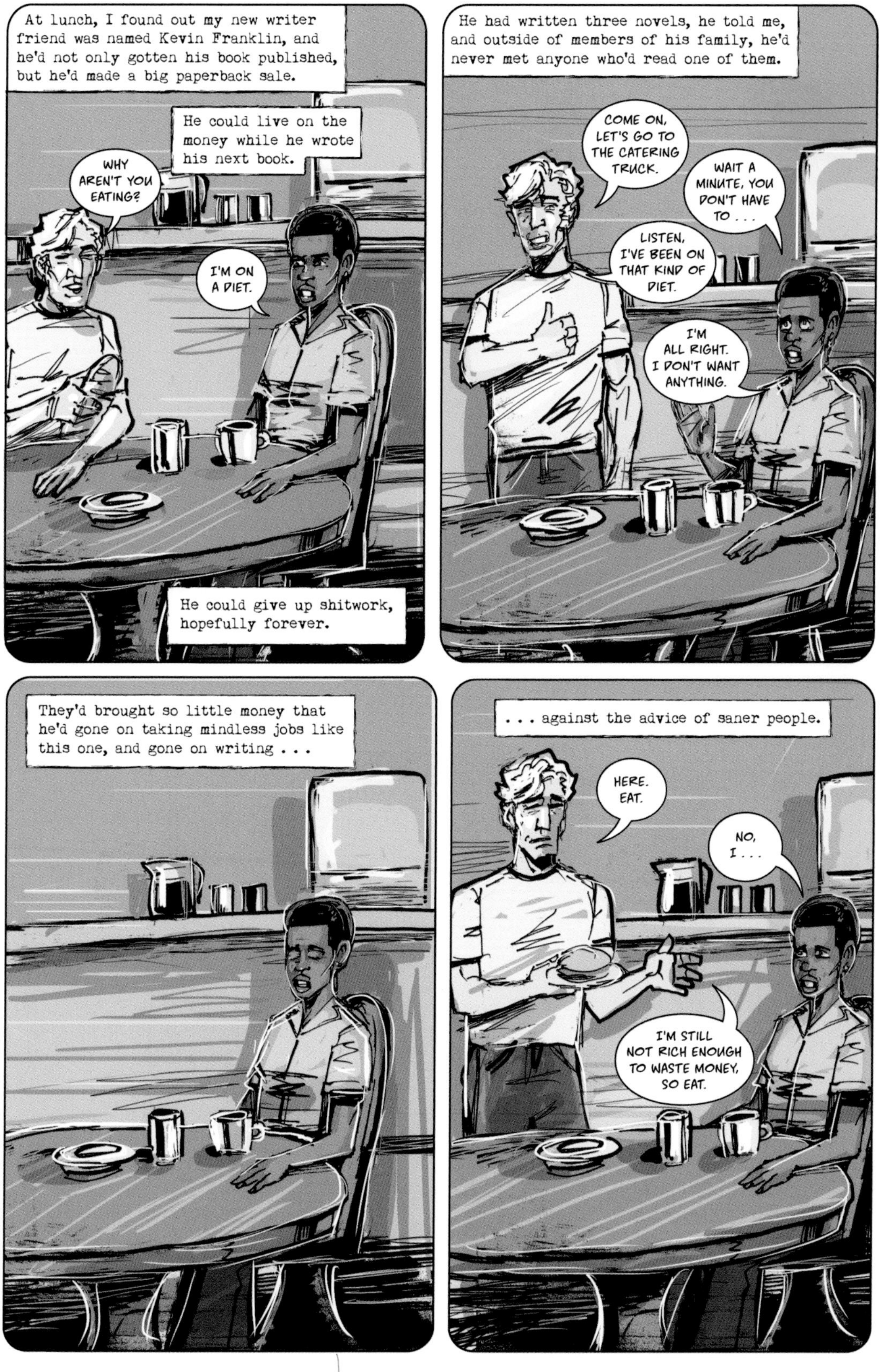
At lunch, I found out my new writer friend was named Kevin Franklin, and he'd not only gotten his book published, but he'd made a big paperback sale.
He could live on the money while he wrote his next book.
WHY AREN'T YOU EATING?
I'M ON A DIET.
He could give up shitwork, hopefully forever.
He had written three novels, he told me, and outside of members of his family, he'd never met anyone who'd read one of them.
COME ON, LET'S GO TO THE CATERING TRUCK.
WAIT A MINUTE, YOU DON'T HAVE TO . . .
LISTEN, I'VE BEEN ON THAT KIND OF DIET.
I'M ALL RIGHT. I DON'T WANT ANYTHING.
They'd brought so little money that he'd gone on taking mindless jobs like this one, and gone on writing . . .
. . . against the advice of saner people.
HERE. EAT.
NO, I . . .
I'M STILL NOT RICH ENOUGH TO WASTE MONEY, SO EAT.

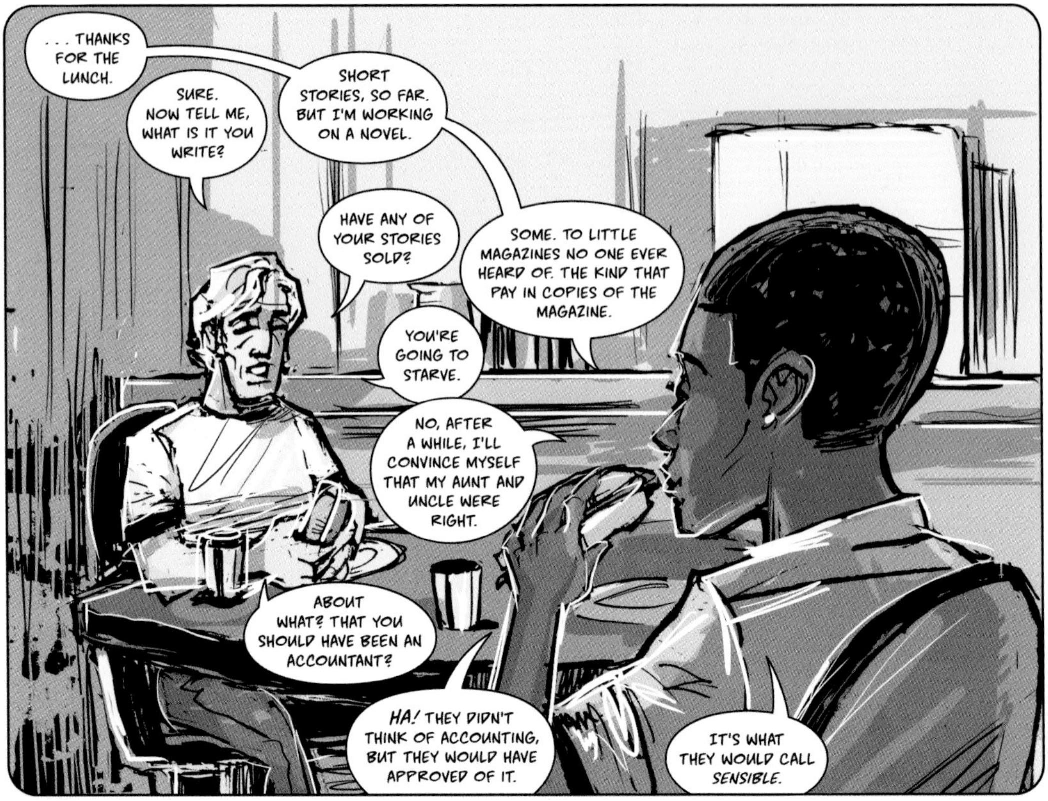
. . . THANKS FOR THE LUNCH.
SURE. NOW TELL ME, WHAT IS IT YOU WRITE?
SHORT STORIES, SO FAR. BUT I'M WORKING ON A NOVEL.
HAVE ANY OF YOUR STORIES SOLD?
SOME. TO LITTLE MAGAZINES NO ONE EVER HEARD OF. THE KIND THAT PAY IN COPIES OF THE MAGAZINE.
YOU'RE GOING TO STARVE.
NO, AFTER A WHILE, I'LL CONVINCE MYSELF THAT MY AUNT AND UNCLE WERE RIGHT.
ABOUT WHAT? THAT YOU SHOULD HAVE BEEN AN ACCOUNTANT?
HA! THEY DIDN'T THINK OF ACCOUNTING, BUT THEY WOULD HAVE APPROVED OF IT.
IT'S WHAT THEY WOULD CALL SENSIBLE.

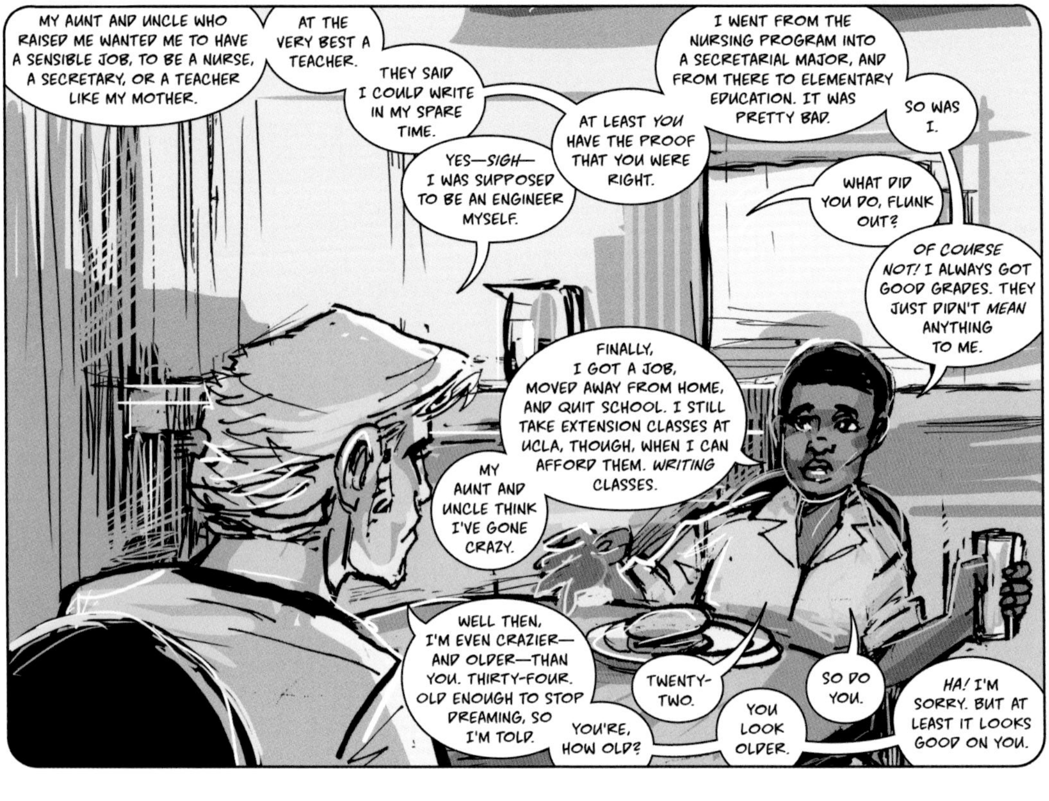
MY AUNT AND UNCLE WHO RAISED ME WANTED ME TO HAVE A SENSIBLE JOB, TO BE A NURSE, A SECRETARY, OR A TEACHER LIKE MY MOTHER.
AT THE VERY BEST A TEACHER.
THEY SAID I COULD WRITE IN MY SPARE TIME.
YES—SIGH—I WAS SUPPOSED TO BE AN ENGINEER MYSELF.
AT LEAST YOU HAVE THE PROOF THAT YOU WERE RIGHT.
I WENT FROM THE NURSING PROGRAM INTO A SECRETARIAL MAJOR, AND FROM THERE TO ELEMENTARY EDUCATION. IT WAS PRETTY BAD.
SO WAS I.
WHAT DID YOU DO, FLUNK OUT?
OF COURSE NOT! I ALWAYS GOT GOOD GRADES. THEY JUST DIDN'T MEAN ANYTHING TO ME.
FINALLY, I GOT A JOB, MOVED AWAY FROM HOME, AND QUIT SCHOOL. I STILL TAKE EXTENSION CLASSES AT UCLA, THOUGH, WHEN I CAN AFFORD THEM. WRITING CLASSES.
MY AUNT AND UNCLE THINK I'VE GONE CRAZY.
WELL THEN, I'M EVEN CRAZIER—AND OLDER—THAN YOU. THIRTY-FOUR. OLD ENOUGH TO STOP DREAMING, SO I'M TOLD.
YOU'RE, HOW OLD?
TWENTY-TWO.
YOU LOOK OLDER.
SO DO YOU.
HA! I'M SORRY. BUT AT LEAST IT LOOKS GOOD ON YOU.

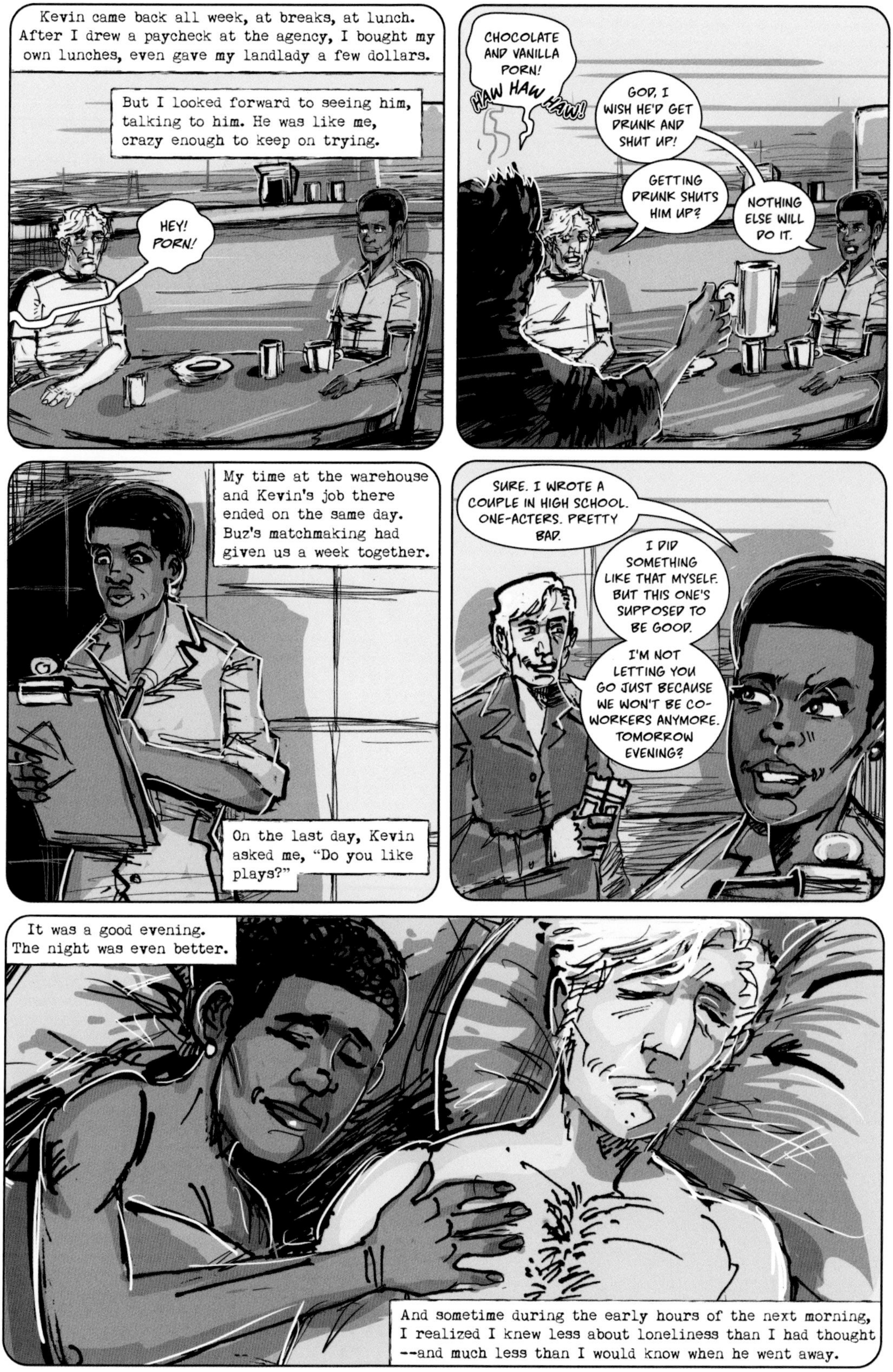
Kevin came back all week, at breaks, at lunch. After I drew a paycheck at the agency, I bought my own lunches, even gave my landlady a few dollars.
But I looked forward to seeing him, talking to him. He was like me, crazy enough to keep on trying.
HEY! PORN!
CHOCOLATE AND VANILLA PORN!
HAW HAW HAW!
GOD, I WISH HE'D GET DRUNK AND SHUT UP!
GETTING DRUNK SHUTS HIM UP?
NOTHING ELSE WILL DO IT.
My time at the warehouse and Kevin's job there ended on the same day. Buz's matchmaking had given us a week together.
On the last day, Kevin asked me, "Do you like plays?"
SURE. I WROTE A COUPLE IN HIGH SCHOOL. ONE-ACTERS. PRETTY BAD.
I DID SOMETHING LIKE THAT MYSELF. BUT THIS ONE'S SUPPOSED TO BE GOOD.
I'M NOT LETTING YOU GO JUST BECAUSE WE WON'T BE CO-WORKERS ANYMORE. TOMORROW EVENING?
It was a good evening. The night was even better.
And sometime during the early hours of the next morning, I realized I knew less about loneliness than I had thought --and much less than I would know when he went away.

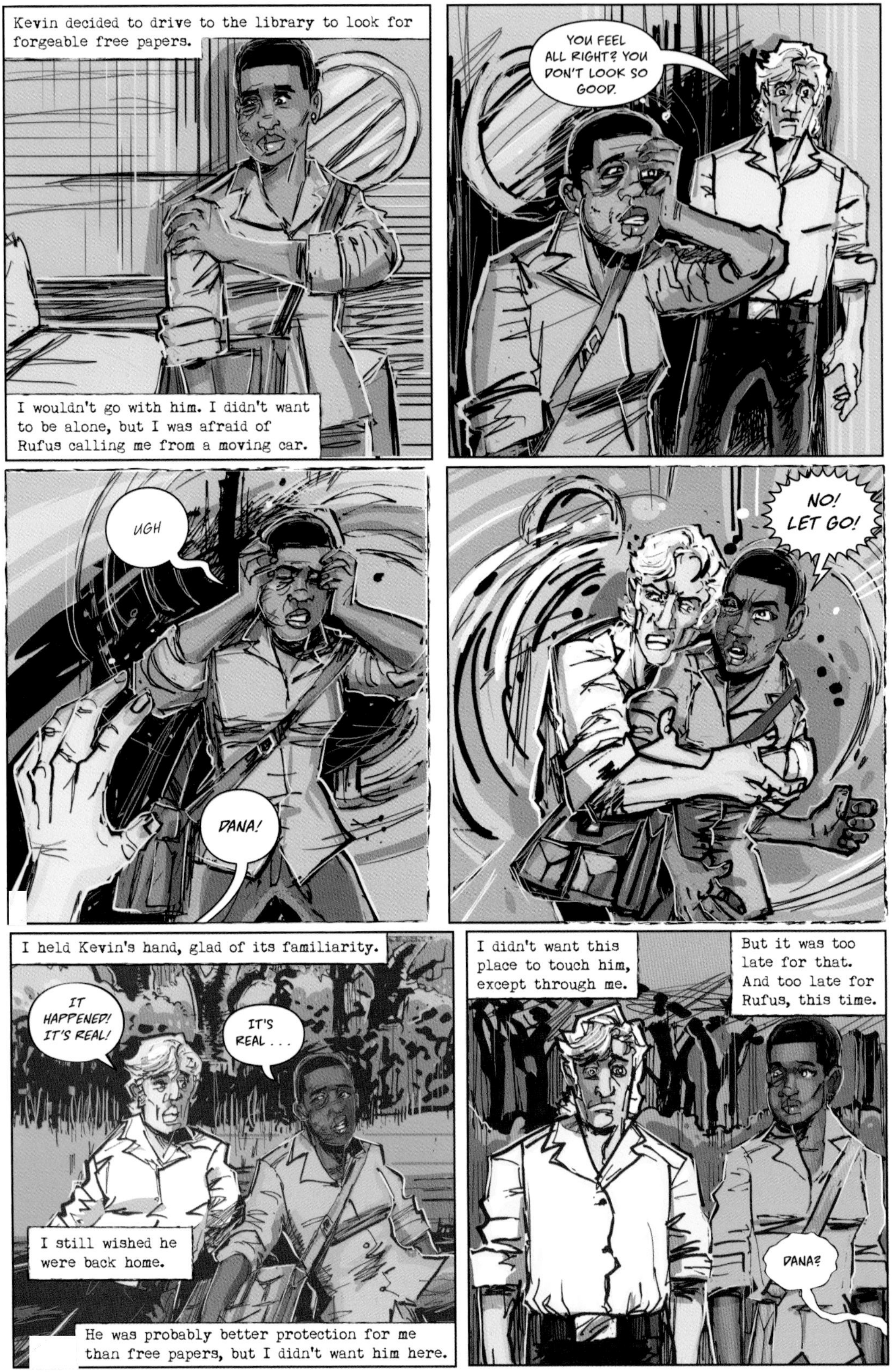
Kevin decided to drive to the library to look for forgeable free papers.
I wouldn't go with him. I didn't want to be alone, but I was afraid of Rufus calling me from a moving car.
YOU FEEL ALL RIGHT? YOU DON'T LOOK SO GOOD.
UGH
DANA!
NO! LET GO!
I held Kevin's hand, glad of its familiarity.
IT HAPPENED! IT'S REAL!
IT'S REAL . . .
I still wished he were back home.
He was probably better protection for me than free papers, but I didn't want him here.
I didn't want this place to touch him, except through me.
But it was too late for that. And too late for Rufus, this time.
DANA?

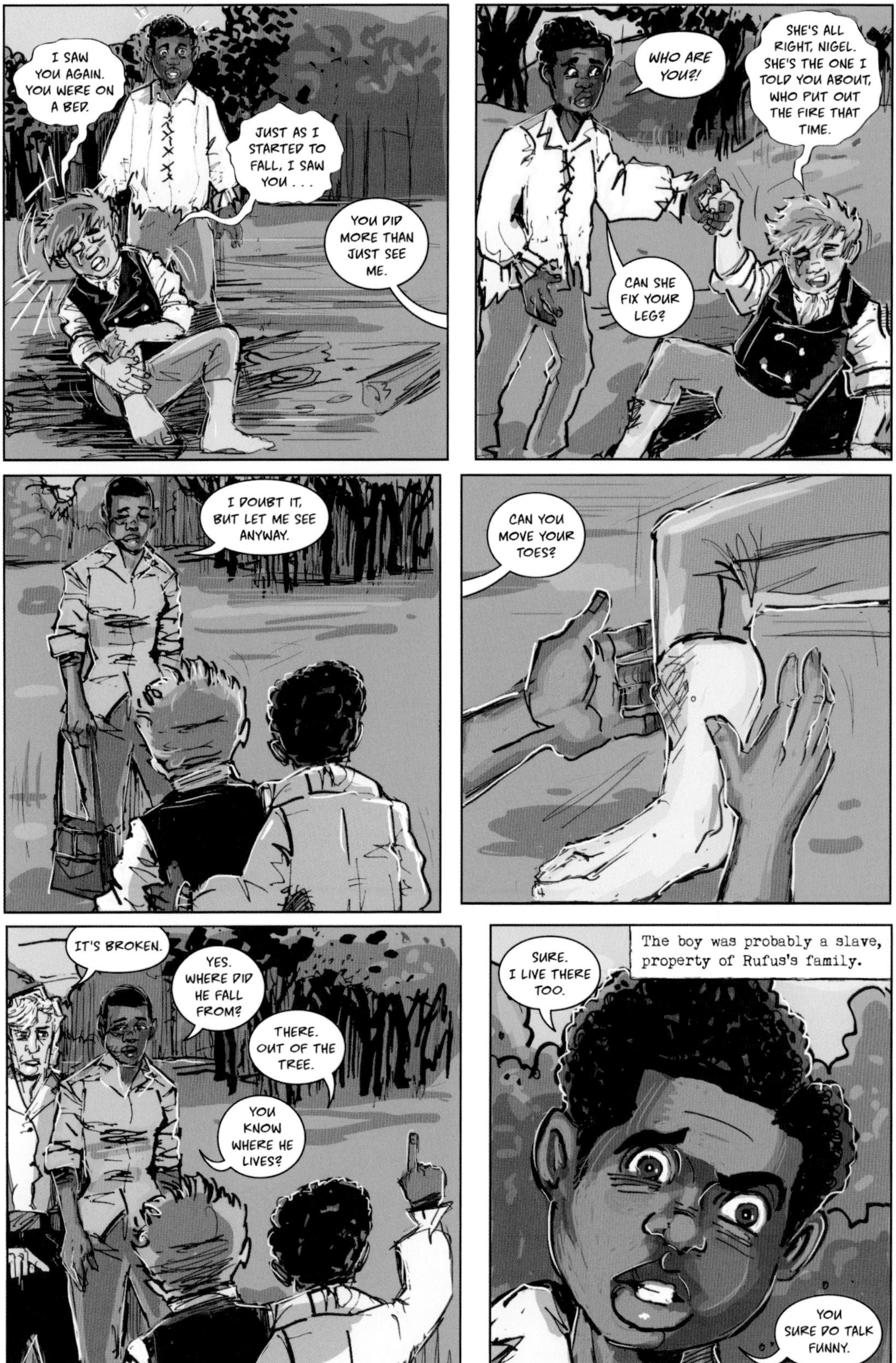
I SAW YOU AGAIN. YOU WERE ON A BED.
JUST AS I STARTED TO FALL, I SAW YOU . . .
YOU DID MORE THAN JUST SEE ME.
WHO ARE YOU?!
SHE'S ALL RIGHT, NIGEL. SHE'S THE ONE I TOLD YOU ABOUT, WHO PUT OUT THE FIRE THAT TIME.
CAN SHE FIX YOUR LEG?
I DOUBT IT, BUT LET ME SEE ANYWAY.
CAN YOU MOVE YOUR TOES?
IT'S BROKEN.
YES. WHERE DID HE FALL FROM?
THERE. OUT OF THE TREE.
YOU KNOW WHERE HE LIVES?
The boy was probably a slave, property of Rufus's family.
SURE. I LIVE THERE TOO.
YOU SURE DO TALK FUNNY.

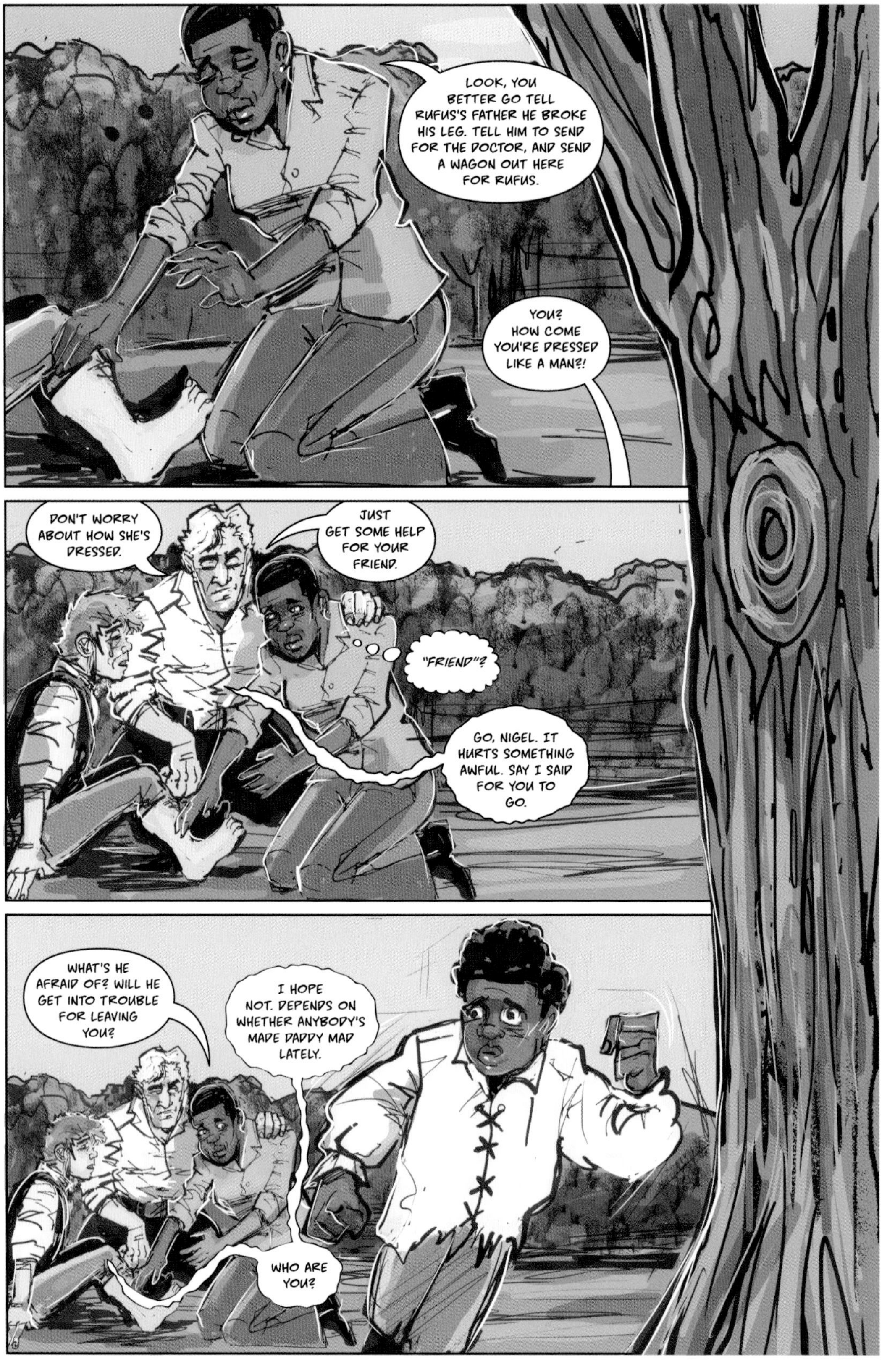
LOOK, YOU BETTER GO TELL RUFUS'S FATHER HE BROKE HIS LEG. TELL HIM TO SEND FOR THE DOCTOR, AND SEND A WAGON OUT HERE FOR RUFUS.
YOU? HOW COME YOU'RE DRESSED LIKE A MAN?!
DON'T WORRY ABOUT HOW SHE'S DRESSED.
JUST GET SOME HELP FOR YOUR FRIEND.
"FRIEND"?
GO, NIGEL. IT HURTS SOMETHING AWFUL. SAY I SAID FOR YOU TO GO.
WHAT'S HE AFRAID OF? WILL HE GET INTO TROUBLE FOR LEAVING YOU?
I HOPE NOT. DEPENDS ON WHETHER ANYBODY'S MADE DADDY MAD LATELY.
WHO ARE YOU?

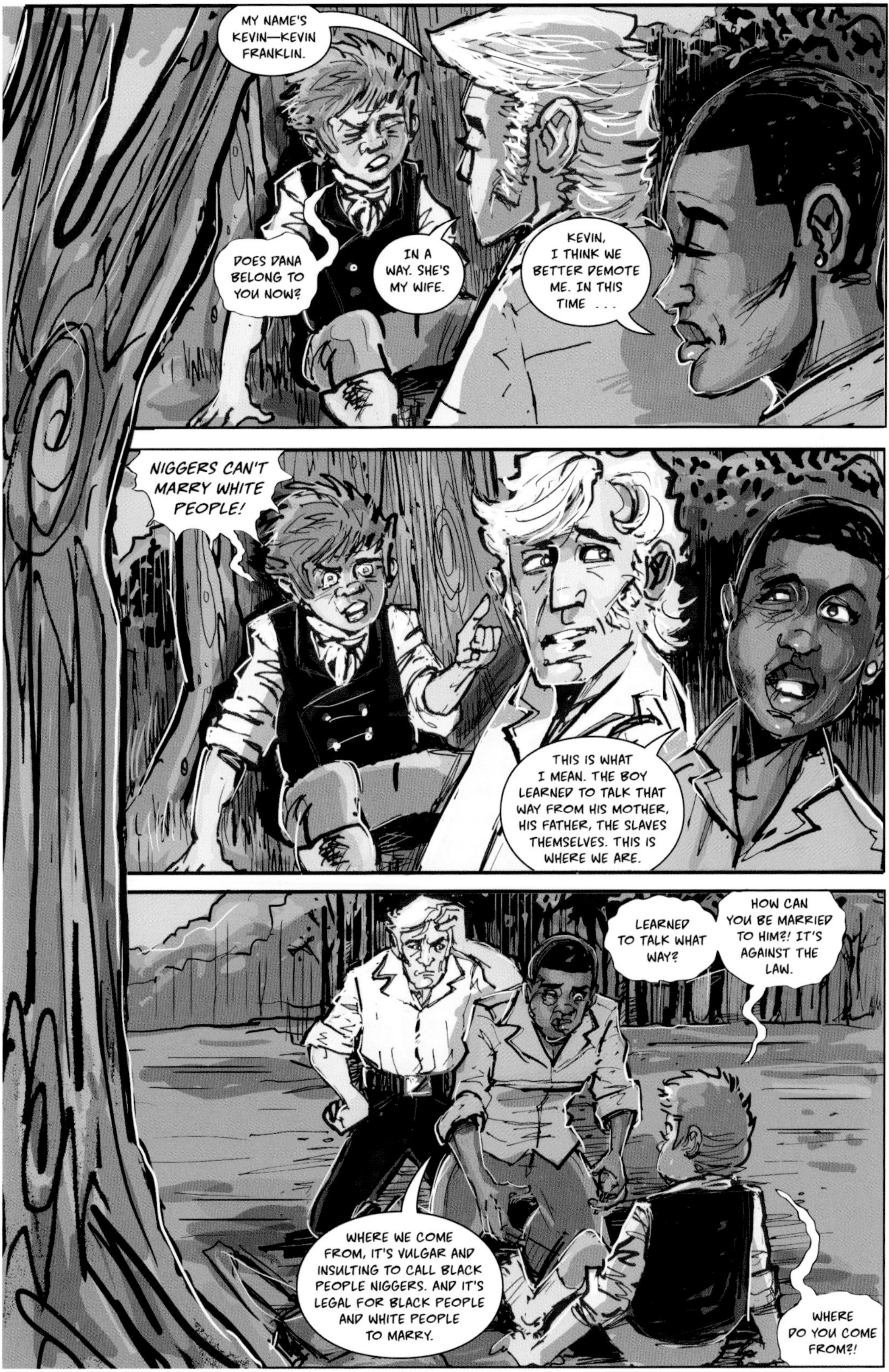
MY NAME'S KEVIN—KEVIN FRANKLIN.
DOES DANA BELONG TO YOU NOW?
IN A WAY. SHE'S MY WIFE.
KEVIN, I THINK WE BETTER DEMOTE ME. IN THIS TIME . . .
NIGGERS CAN'T MARRY WHITE PEOPLE!
THIS IS WHAT I MEAN. THE BOY LEARNED TO TALK THAT WAY FROM HIS MOTHER, HIS FATHER, THE SLAVES THEMSELVES. THIS IS WHERE WE ARE.
LEARNED TO TALK WHAT WAY?
HOW CAN YOU BE MARRIED TO HIM?! IT'S AGAINST THE LAW.
WHERE WE COME FROM, IT'S VULGAR AND INSULTING TO CALL BLACK PEOPLE NIGGERS. AND IT'S LEGAL FOR BLACK PEOPLE AND WHITE PEOPLE TO MARRY.
WHERE DO YOU COME FROM?!

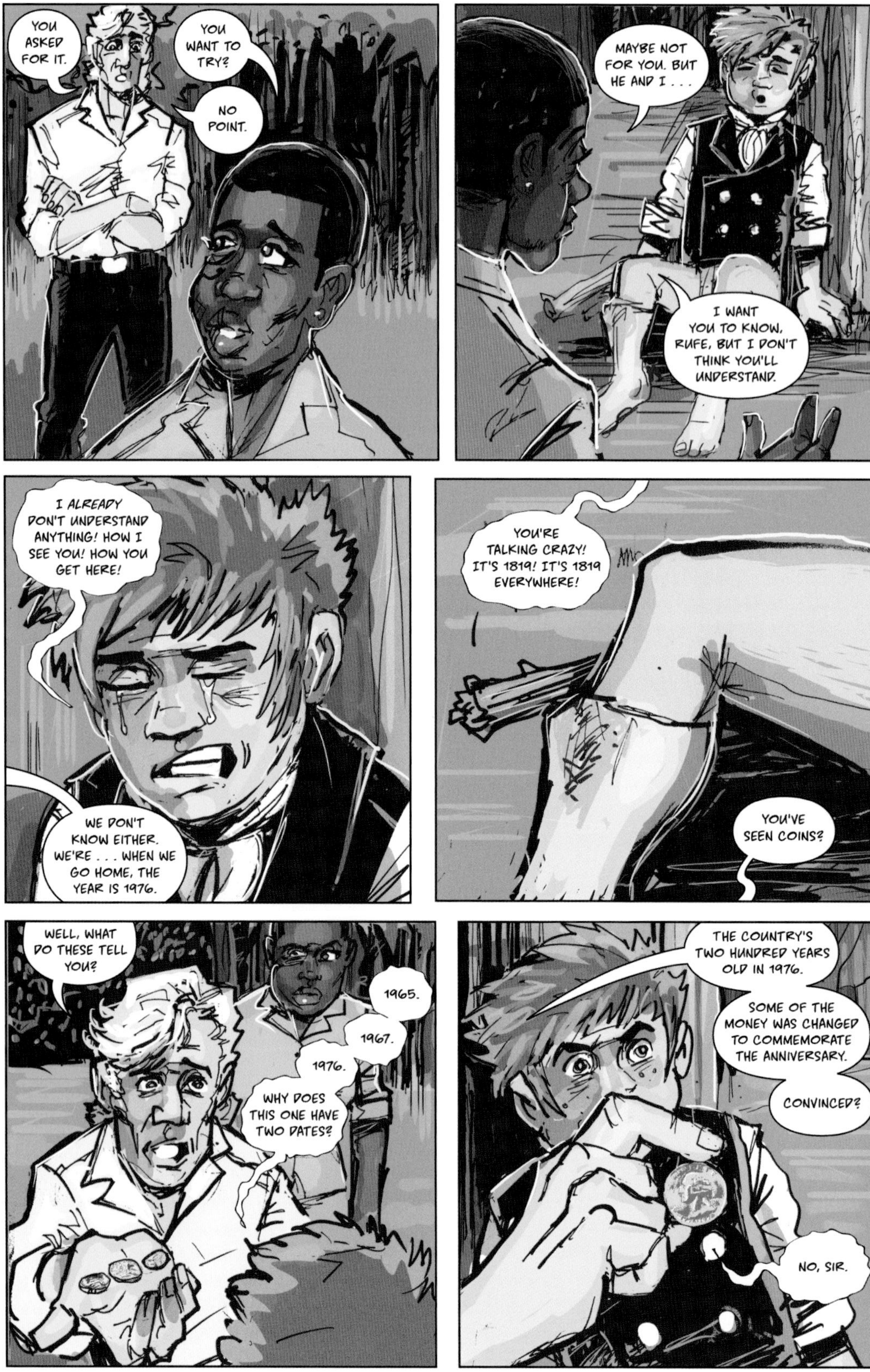

YOU ASKED FOR IT.
YOU WANT TO TRY?
NO POINT.
MAYBE NOT FOR YOU. BUT HE AND I . . .
I WANT YOU TO KNOW, RUFE, BUT I DON'T THINK YOU'LL UNDERSTAND.
I ALREADY DON'T UNDERSTAND ANYTHING! HOW I SEE YOU! HOW YOU GET HERE!
WE DON'T KNOW EITHER. WE'RE . . . WHEN WE GO HOME, THE YEAR IS 1976.
YOU'RE TALKING CRAZY! IT'S 1819! IT'S 1819 EVERYWHERE!
YOU'VE SEEN COINS?
WELL, WHAT DO THESE TELL YOU?
1965.
1967.
1976.
WHY DOES THIS ONE HAVE TWO DATES?
THE COUNTRY'S TWO HUNDRED YEARS OLD IN 1976.
SOME OF THE MONEY WAS CHANGED TO COMMEMORATE THE ANNIVERSARY.
CONVINCED?
NO, SIR.

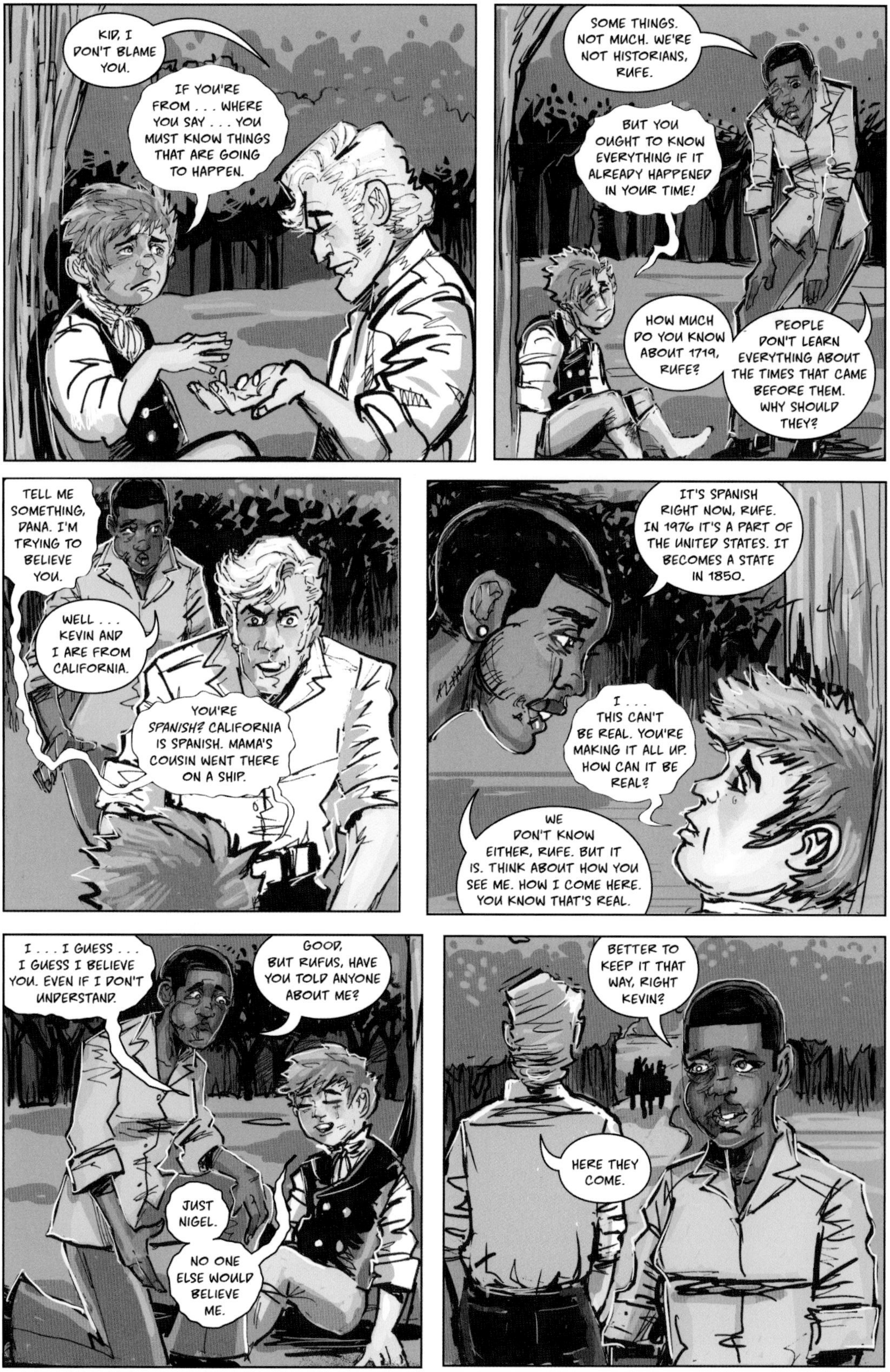
KID, I DON'T BLAME YOU.
IF YOU'RE FROM . . . WHERE YOU SAY . . . YOU MUST KNOW THINGS THAT ARE GOING TO HAPPEN.
SOME THINGS. NOT MUCH. WE'RE NOT HISTORIANS, RUFE.
BUT YOU OUGHT TO KNOW EVERYTHING IF IT ALREADY HAPPENED IN YOUR TIME!
HOW MUCH DO YOU KNOW ABOUT 1719, RUFE?
PEOPLE DON'T LEARN EVERYTHING ABOUT THE TIMES THAT CAME BEFORE THEM. WHY SHOULD THEY?
TELL ME SOMETHING, DANA. I'M TRYING TO BELIEVE YOU.
WELL . . . KEVIN AND I ARE FROM CALIFORNIA.
YOU'RE *SPANISH?* CALIFORNIA IS SPANISH. MAMA'S COUSIN WENT THERE ON A SHIP.
IT'S SPANISH RIGHT NOW, RUFE. IN 1976 IT'S A PART OF THE UNITED STATES. IT BECOMES A STATE IN 1850.
I . . . THIS CAN'T BE REAL. YOU'RE MAKING IT ALL UP. HOW CAN IT BE REAL?
WE DON'T KNOW EITHER, RUFE. BUT IT IS. THINK ABOUT HOW YOU SEE ME. HOW I COME HERE. YOU KNOW THAT'S REAL.
I . . . I GUESS . . . I GUESS I BELIEVE YOU. EVEN IF I DON'T UNDERSTAND.
GOOD, BUT RUFUS, HAVE YOU TOLD ANYONE ABOUT ME?
JUST NIGEL.
NO ONE ELSE WOULD BELIEVE ME.
BETTER TO KEEP IT THAT WAY, RIGHT KEVIN?
HERE THEY COME.

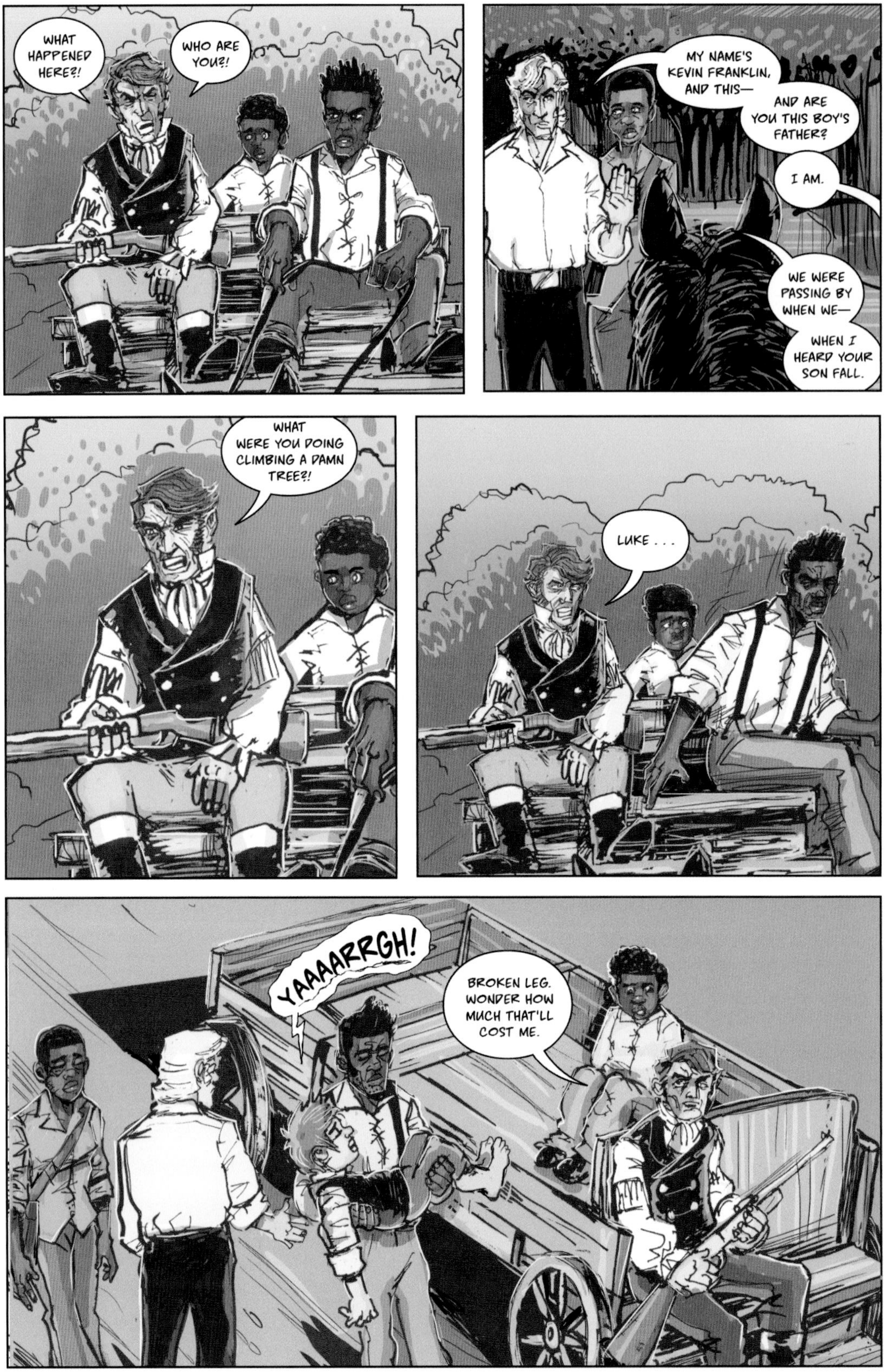
WHAT HAPPENED HERE?!
WHO ARE YOU?!
MY NAME'S KEVIN FRANKLIN, AND THIS—
AND ARE YOU THIS BOY'S FATHER?
I AM.
WE WERE PASSING BY WHEN WE—
WHEN I HEARD YOUR SON FALL.
WHAT WERE YOU DOING CLIMBING A DAMN TREE?!
LUKE . . .
YAAAARRGH!
BROKEN LEG. WONDER HOW MUCH THAT'LL COST ME.

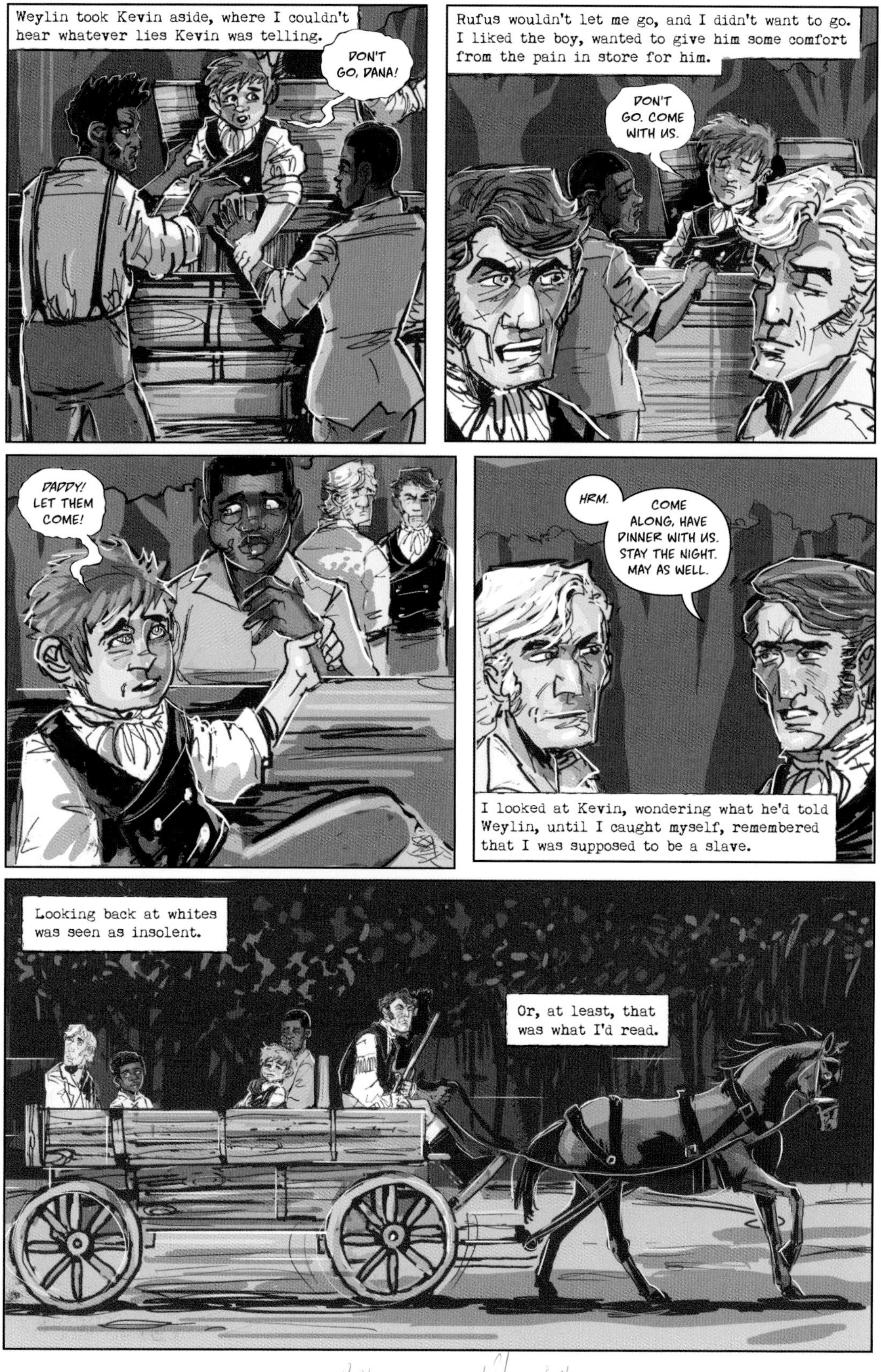
Weylin took Kevin aside, where I couldn't hear whatever lies Kevin was telling.
DON'T GO, DANA!
Rufus wouldn't let me go, and I didn't want to go. I liked the boy, wanted to give him some comfort from the pain in store for him.
DON'T GO. COME WITH US.
DADDY! LET THEM COME!
HRM.
COME ALONG, HAVE DINNER WITH US. STAY THE NIGHT. MAY AS WELL.
I looked at Kevin, wondering what he'd told Weylin, until I caught myself, remembered that I was supposed to be a slave.
Looking back at whites was seen as insolent.
Or, at least, that was what I'd read.

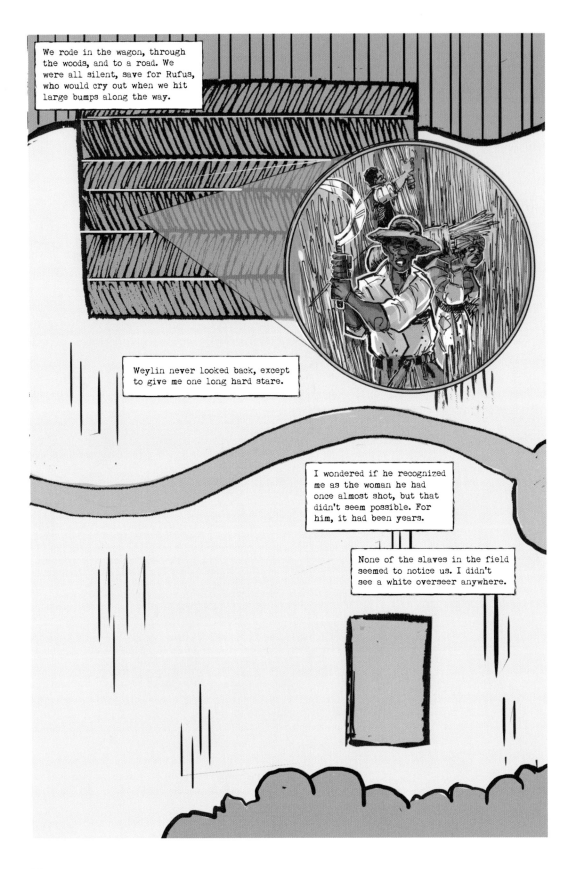

We rode in the wagon, through the woods, and to a road. We were all silent, save for Rufus, who would cry out when we hit large bumps along the way.

Weylin never looked back, except to give me one long hard stare.

I wondered if he recognized me as the woman he had once almost shot, but that didn't seem possible. For him, it had been years.

None of the slaves in the field seemed to notice us. I didn't see a white overseer anywhere.

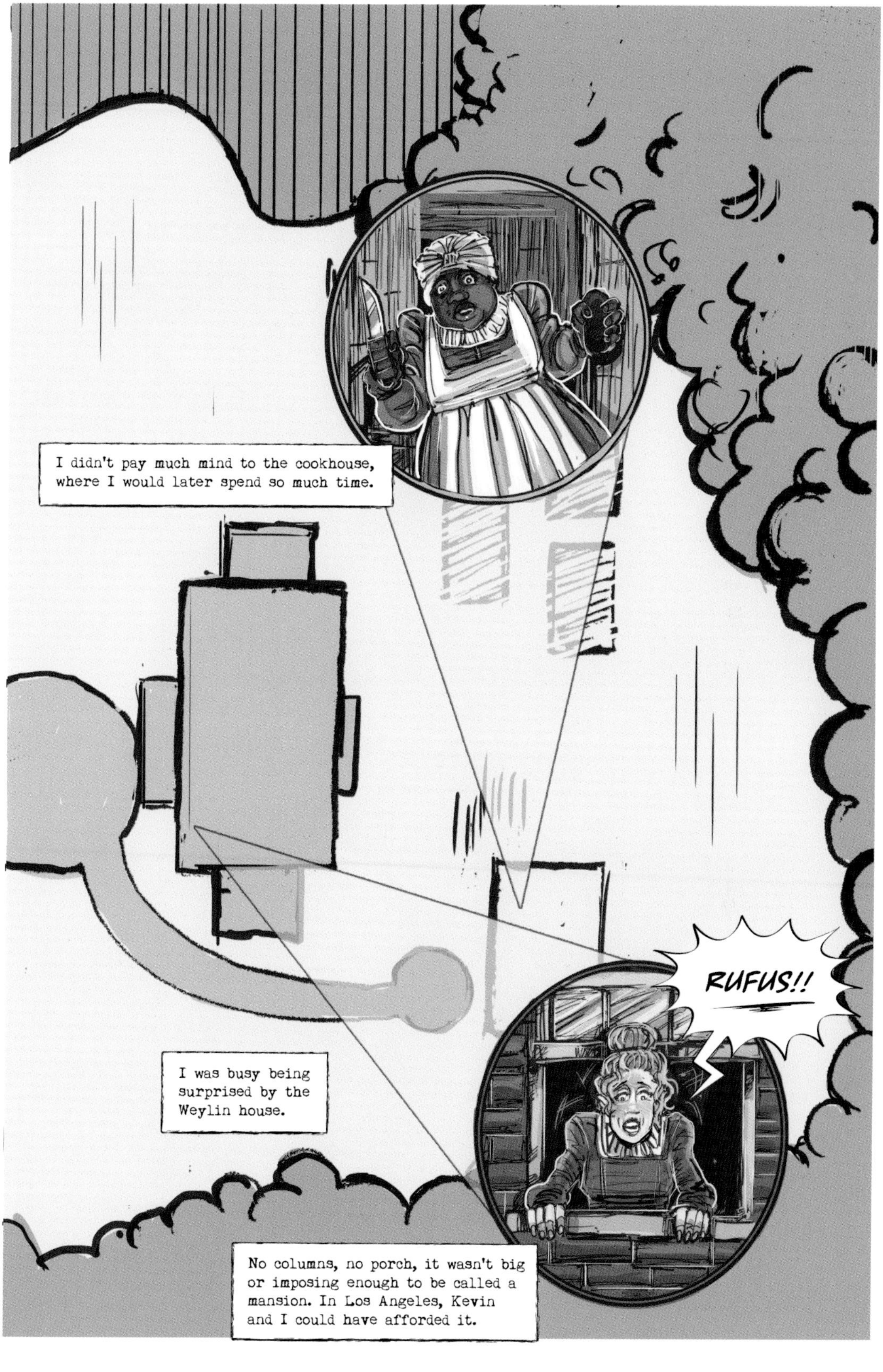
I didn't pay much mind to the cookhouse, where I would later spend so much time.
RUFUS!!
I was busy being surprised by the Weylin house.
No columns, no porch, it wasn't big or imposing enough to be called a mansion. In Los Angeles, Kevin and I could have afforded it.

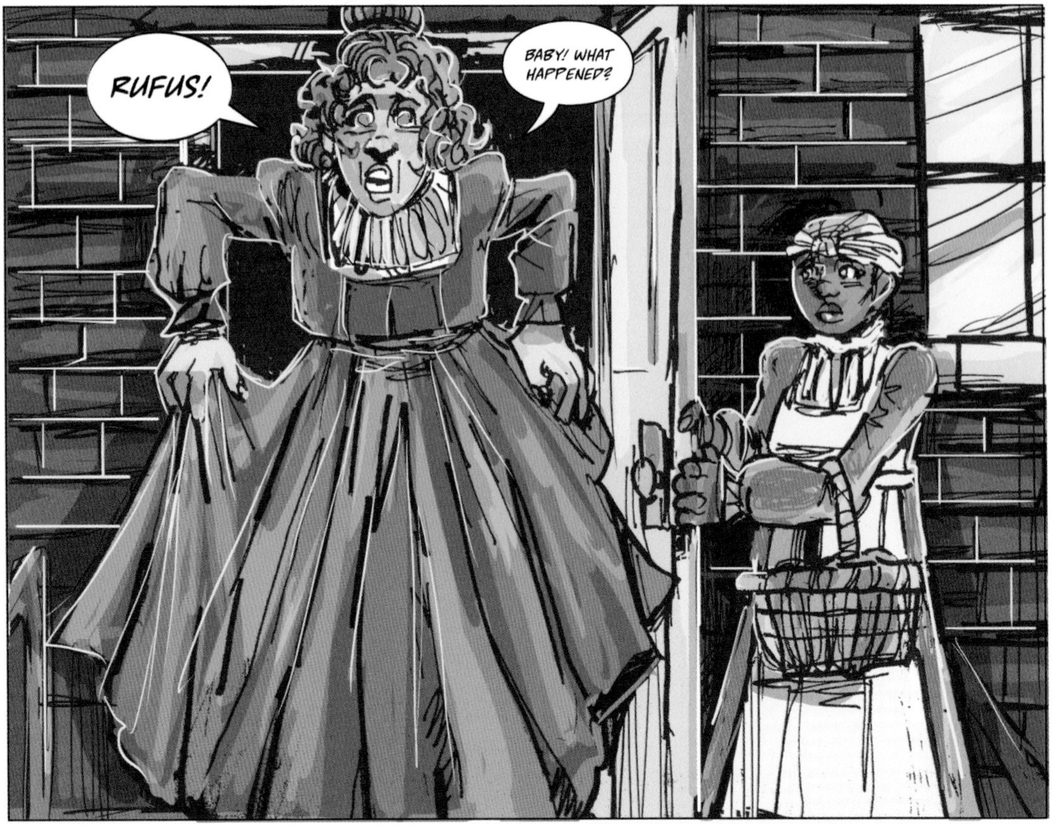
RUFUS!
BABY! WHAT HAPPENED?
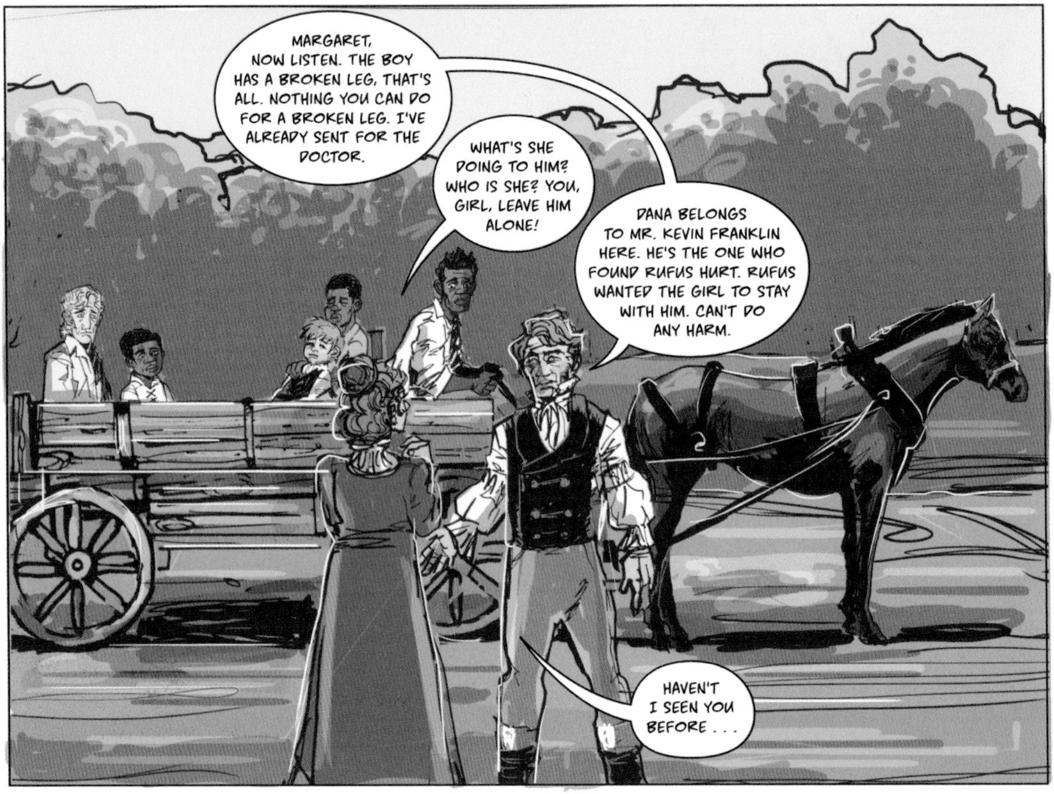
MARGARET, NOW LISTEN. THE BOY HAS A BROKEN LEG, THAT'S ALL. NOTHING YOU CAN DO FOR A BROKEN LEG. I'VE ALREADY SENT FOR THE DOCTOR.
WHAT'S SHE DOING TO HIM? WHO IS SHE? YOU, GIRL, LEAVE HIM ALONE!
DANA BELONGS TO MR. KEVIN FRANKLIN HERE. HE'S THE ONE WHO FOUND RUFUS HURT. RUFUS WANTED THE GIRL TO STAY WITH HIM. CAN'T DO ANY HARM.
HAVEN'T I SEEN YOU BEFORE . . .

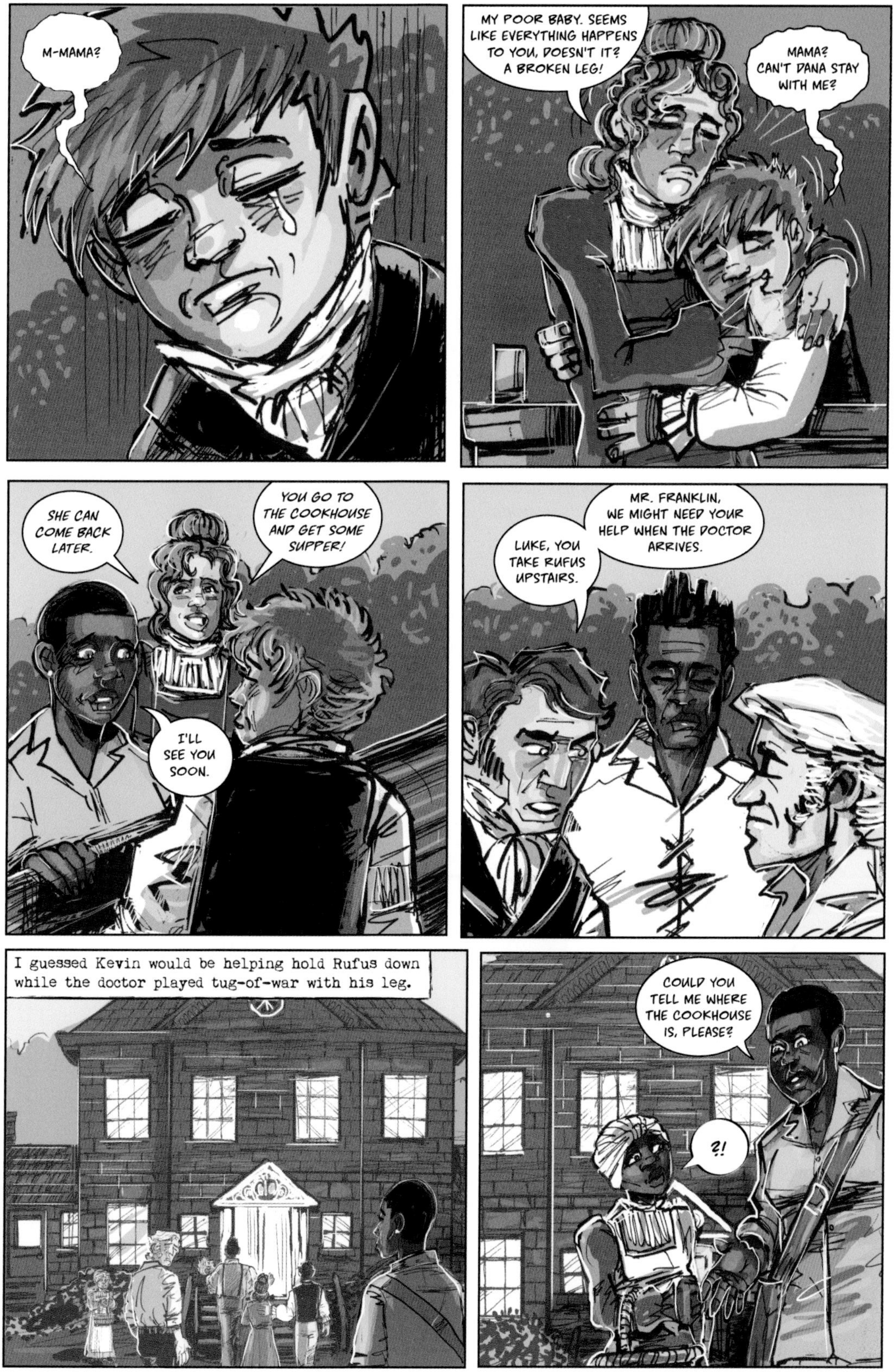
M-MAMA?
MY POOR BABY. SEEMS LIKE EVERYTHING HAPPENS TO YOU, DOESN'T IT? A BROKEN LEG!
MAMA? CAN'T DANA STAY WITH ME?
SHE CAN COME BACK LATER.
YOU GO TO THE COOKHOUSE AND GET SOME SUPPER!
I'LL SEE YOU SOON.
LUKE, YOU TAKE RUFUS UPSTAIRS.
MR. FRANKLIN, WE MIGHT NEED YOUR HELP WHEN THE DOCTOR ARRIVES.
I guessed Kevin would be helping hold Rufus down while the doctor played tug-of-war with his leg.
COULD YOU TELL ME WHERE THE COOKHOUSE IS, PLEASE?
?!

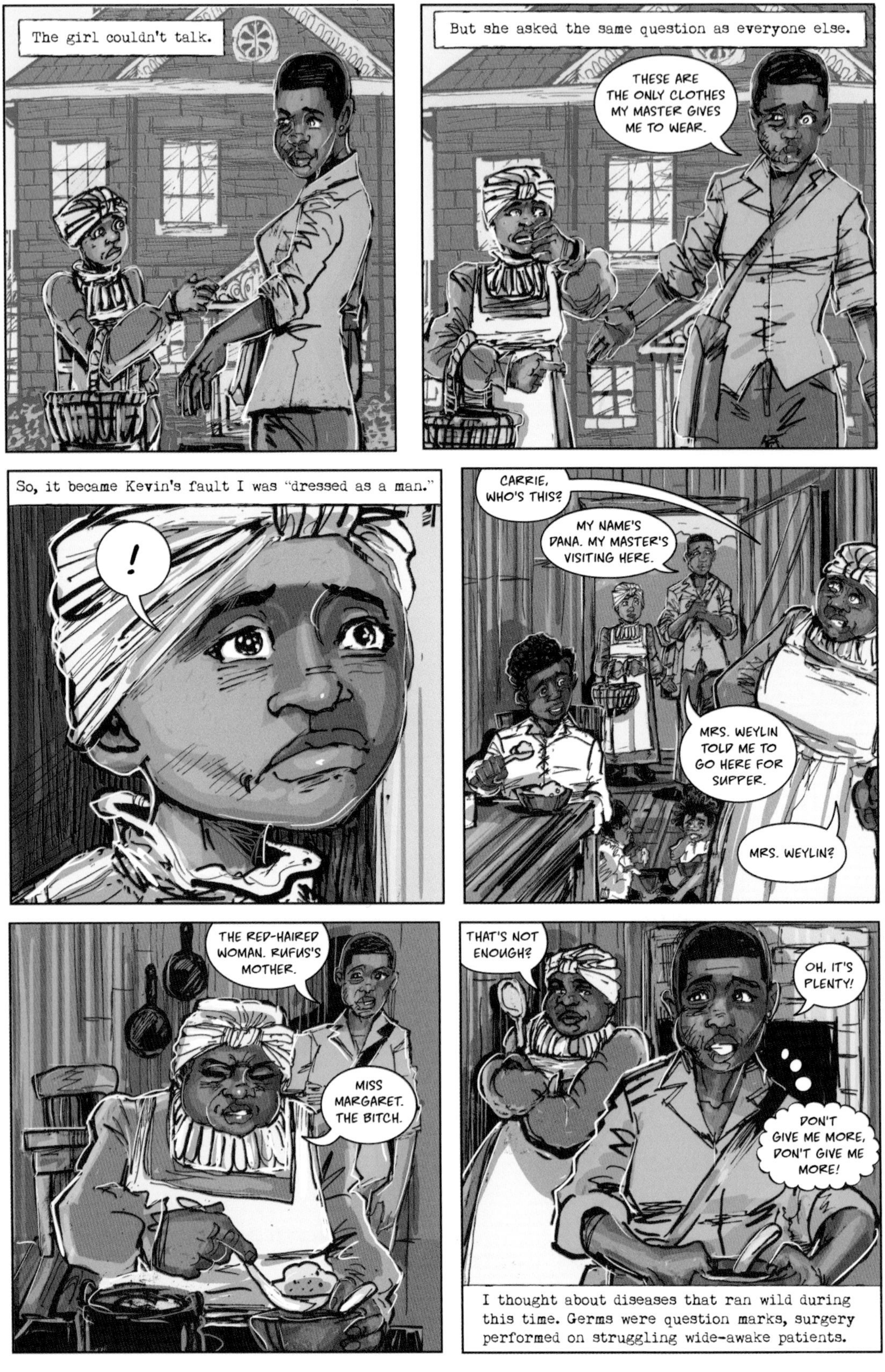
The girl couldn't talk.
But she asked the same question as everyone else.
THESE ARE THE ONLY CLOTHES MY MASTER GIVES ME TO WEAR.
So, it became Kevin's fault I was "dressed as a man."
!
CARRIE, WHO'S THIS?
MY NAME'S DANA. MY MASTER'S VISITING HERE.
MRS. WEYLIN TOLD ME TO GO HERE FOR SUPPER.
MRS. WEYLIN?
THE RED-HAIRED WOMAN. RUFUS'S MOTHER.
MISS MARGARET. THE BITCH.
THAT'S NOT ENOUGH?
OH, IT'S PLENTY!
DON'T GIVE ME MORE, DON'T GIVE ME MORE!
I thought about diseases that ran wild during this time. Germs were question marks, surgery performed on struggling wide-awake patients.

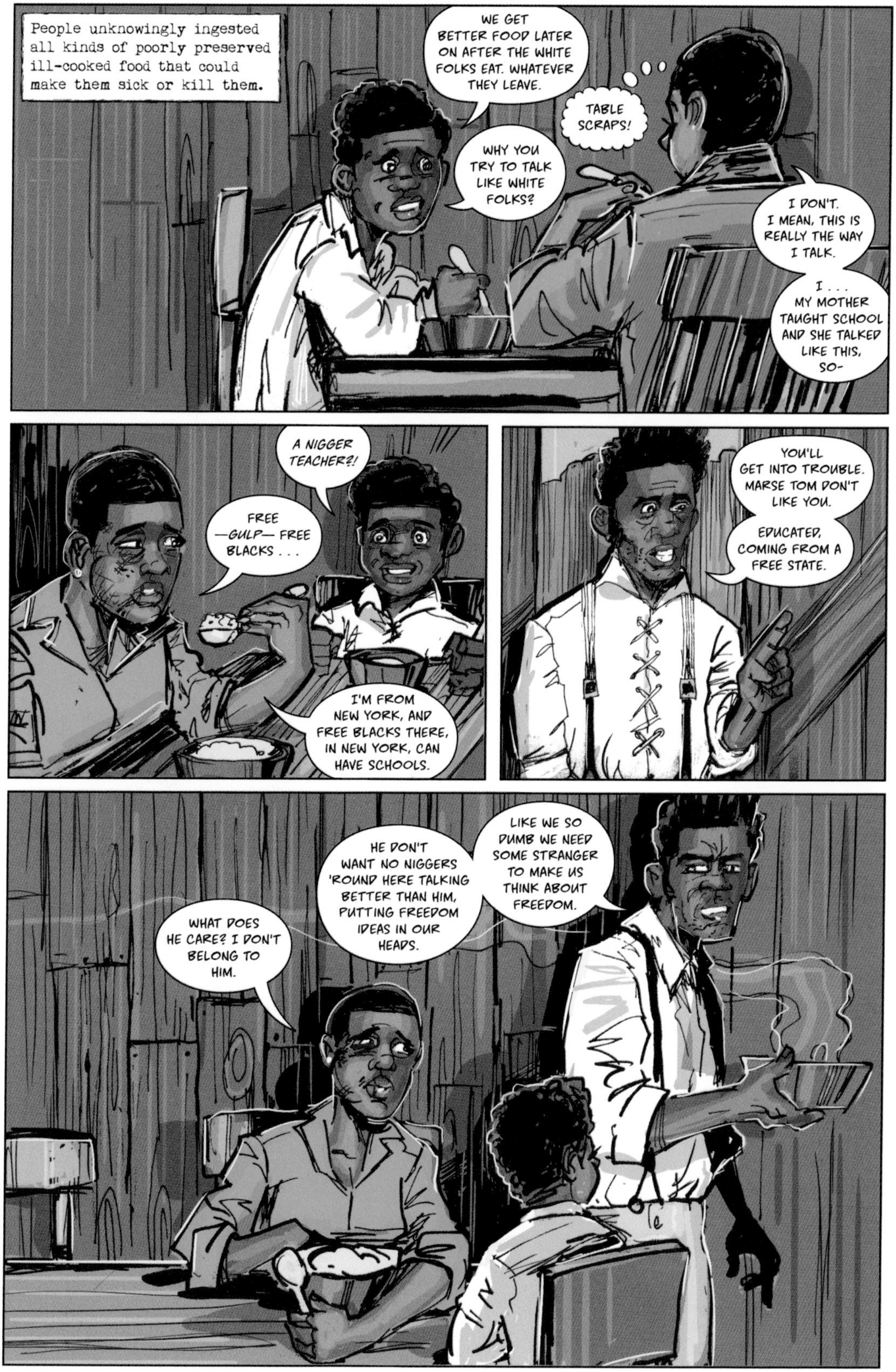
People unknowingly ingested all kinds of poorly preserved ill-cooked food that could make them sick or kill them.
WE GET BETTER FOOD LATER ON AFTER THE WHITE FOLKS EAT. WHATEVER THEY LEAVE.
TABLE SCRAPS!
WHY YOU TRY TO TALK LIKE WHITE FOLKS?
I DON'T. I MEAN, THIS IS REALLY THE WAY I TALK.
I . . . MY MOTHER TAUGHT SCHOOL AND SHE TALKED LIKE THIS, SO-
A NIGGER TEACHER?!
FREE —GULP— FREE BLACKS . . .
I'M FROM NEW YORK, AND FREE BLACKS THERE, IN NEW YORK, CAN HAVE SCHOOLS.
YOU'LL GET INTO TROUBLE. MARSE TOM DON'T LIKE YOU.
EDUCATED, COMING FROM A FREE STATE.
WHAT DOES HE CARE? I DON'T BELONG TO HIM.
HE DON'T WANT NO NIGGERS 'ROUND HERE TALKING BETTER THAN HIM, PUTTING FREEDOM IDEAS IN OUR HEADS.
LIKE WE SO DUMB WE NEED SOME STRANGER TO MAKE US THINK ABOUT FREEDOM.

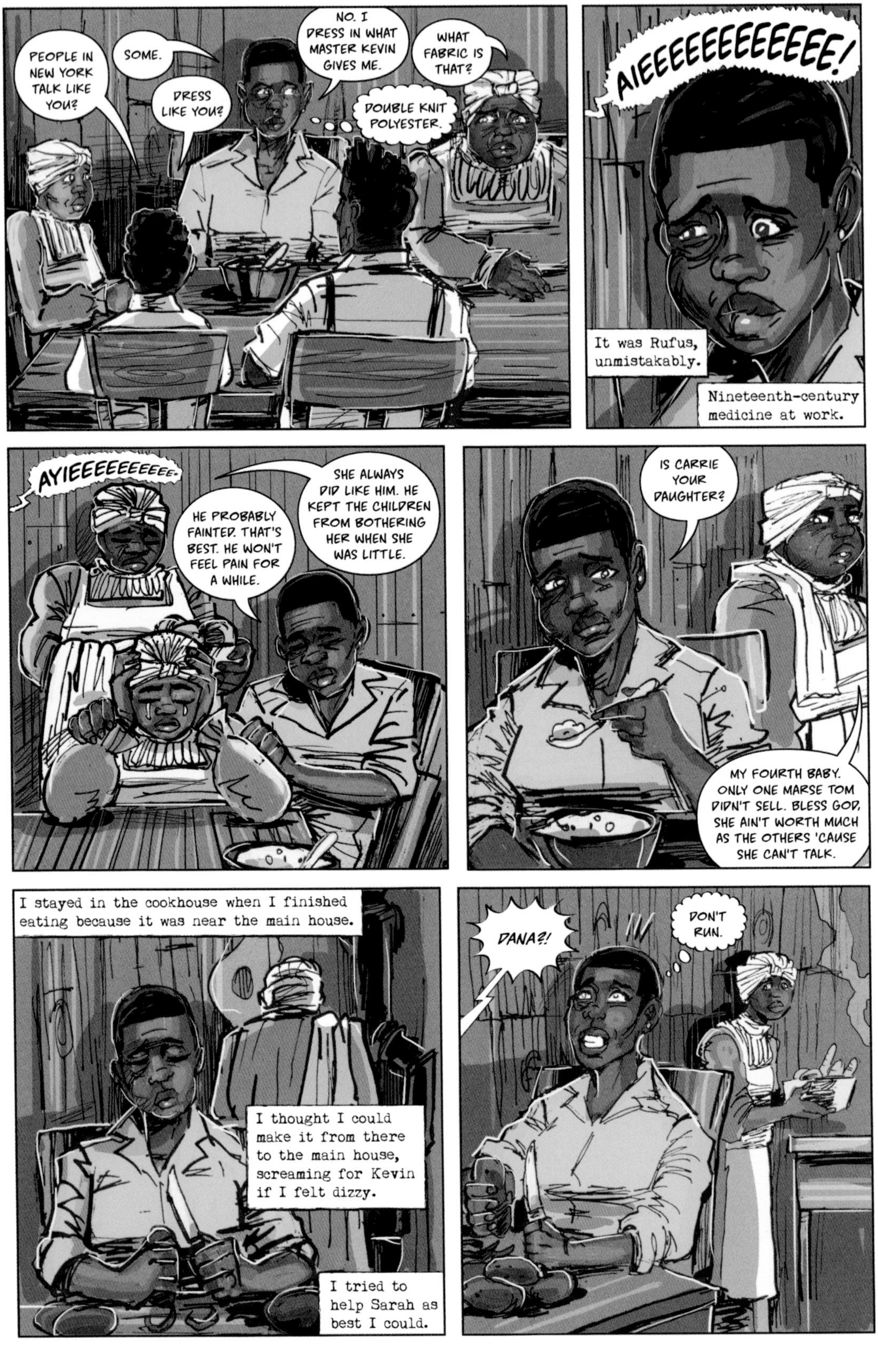
PEOPLE IN NEW YORK TALK LIKE YOU?
SOME.
DRESS LIKE YOU?
NO. I DRESS IN WHAT MASTER KEVIN GIVES ME.
WHAT FABRIC IS THAT?
DOUBLE KNIT POLYESTER.
AIEEEEEEEEEEEEE!
It was Rufus, unmistakably.
Nineteenth-century medicine at work.
AYIEEEEEEEEEEE.
HE PROBABLY FAINTED. THAT'S BEST. HE WON'T FEEL PAIN FOR A WHILE.
SHE ALWAYS DID LIKE HIM. HE KEPT THE CHILDREN FROM BOTHERING HER WHEN SHE WAS LITTLE.
IS CARRIE YOUR DAUGHTER?
MY FOURTH BABY. ONLY ONE MARSE TOM DIDN'T SELL. BLESS GOD, SHE AIN'T WORTH MUCH AS THE OTHERS 'CAUSE SHE CAN'T TALK.
I stayed in the cookhouse when I finished eating because it was near the main house.
I thought I could make it from there to the main house, screaming for Kevin if I felt dizzy.
I tried to help Sarah as best I could.
DANA?!
DON'T RUN.

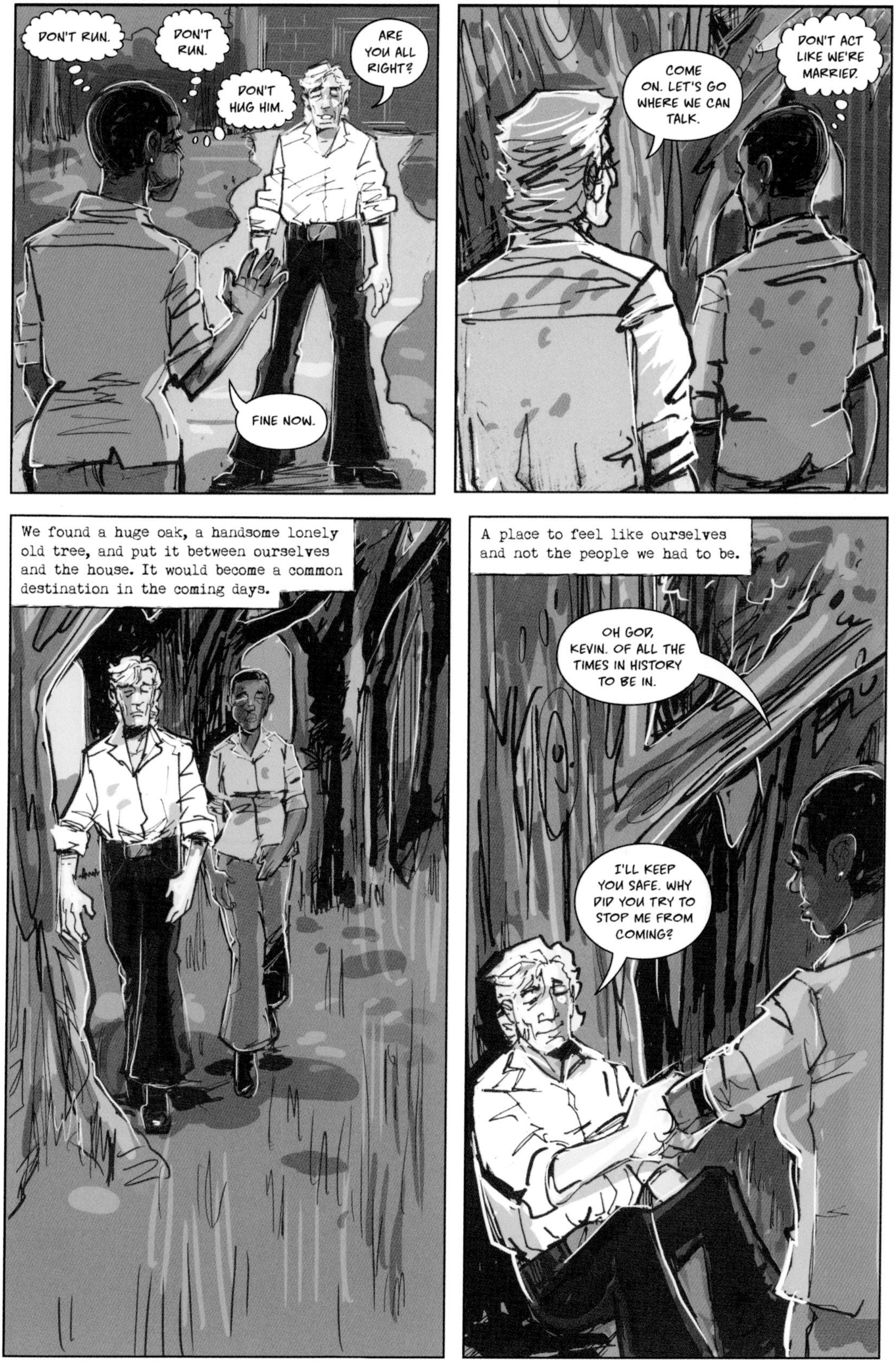
DON'T RUN.
DON'T RUN.
DON'T HUG HIM.
ARE YOU ALL RIGHT?
FINE NOW.
COME ON. LET'S GO WHERE WE CAN TALK.
DON'T ACT LIKE WE'RE MARRIED.
We found a huge oak, a handsome lonely old tree, and put it between ourselves and the house. It would become a common destination in the coming days.
A place to feel like ourselves and not the people we had to be.
OH GOD, KEVIN. OF ALL THE TIMES IN HISTORY TO BE IN.
I'LL KEEP YOU SAFE. WHY DID YOU TRY TO STOP ME FROM COMING?

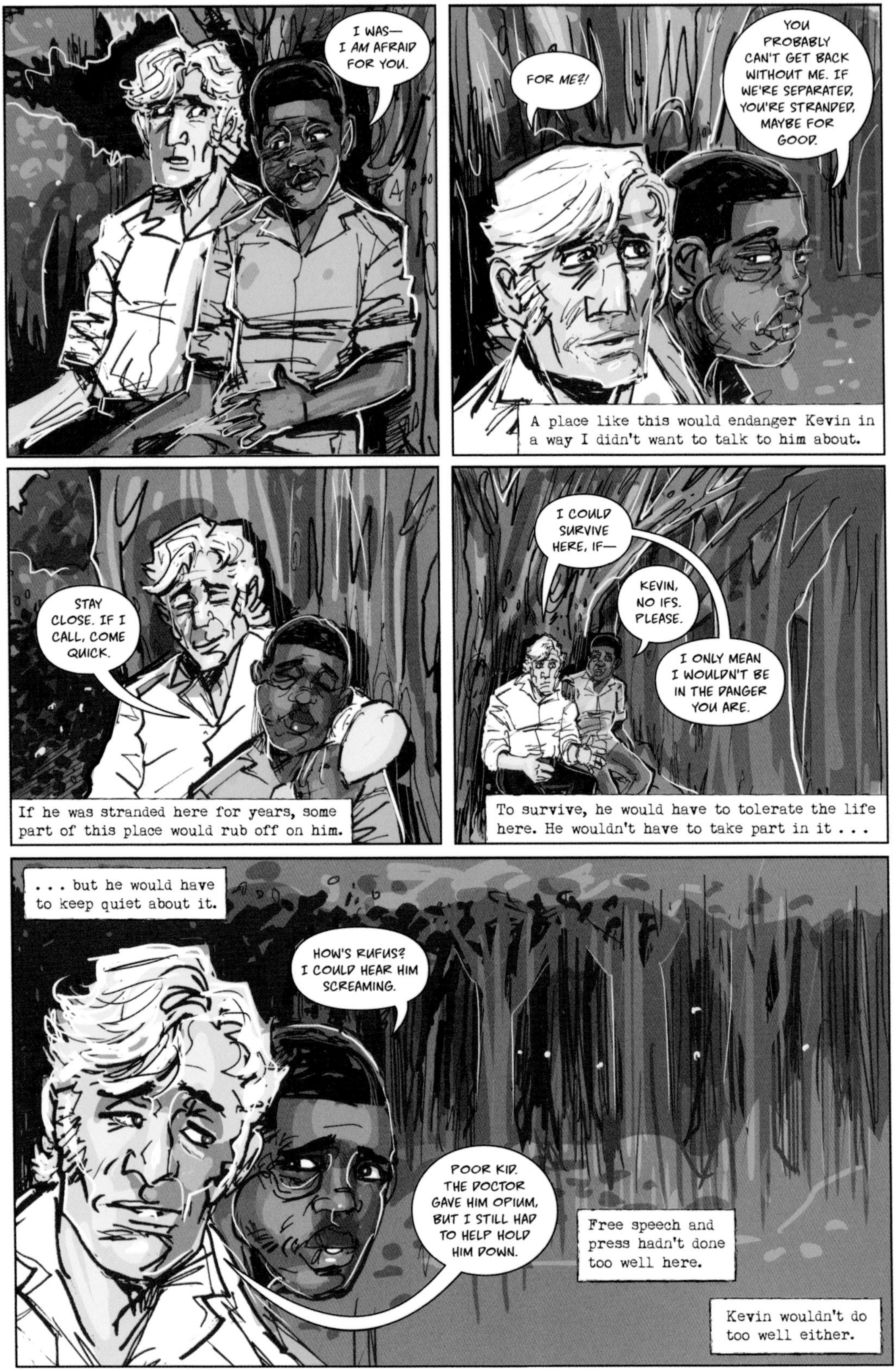
I WAS— I AM AFRAID FOR YOU.
FOR ME?!
YOU PROBABLY CAN'T GET BACK WITHOUT ME. IF WE'RE SEPARATED, YOU'RE STRANDED, MAYBE FOR GOOD.
A place like this would endanger Kevin in a way I didn't want to talk to him about.
STAY CLOSE. IF I CALL, COME QUICK.
If he was stranded here for years, some part of this place would rub off on him.
I COULD SURVIVE HERE, IF—
KEVIN, NO IFS. PLEASE.
I ONLY MEAN I WOULDN'T BE IN THE DANGER YOU ARE.
To survive, he would have to tolerate the life here. He wouldn't have to take part in it . . .
. . . but he would have to keep quiet about it.
HOW'S RUFUS? I COULD HEAR HIM SCREAMING.
POOR KID. THE DOCTOR GAVE HIM OPIUM, BUT I STILL HAD TO HELP HOLD HIM DOWN.
Free speech and press hadn't done too well here.
Kevin wouldn't do too well either.

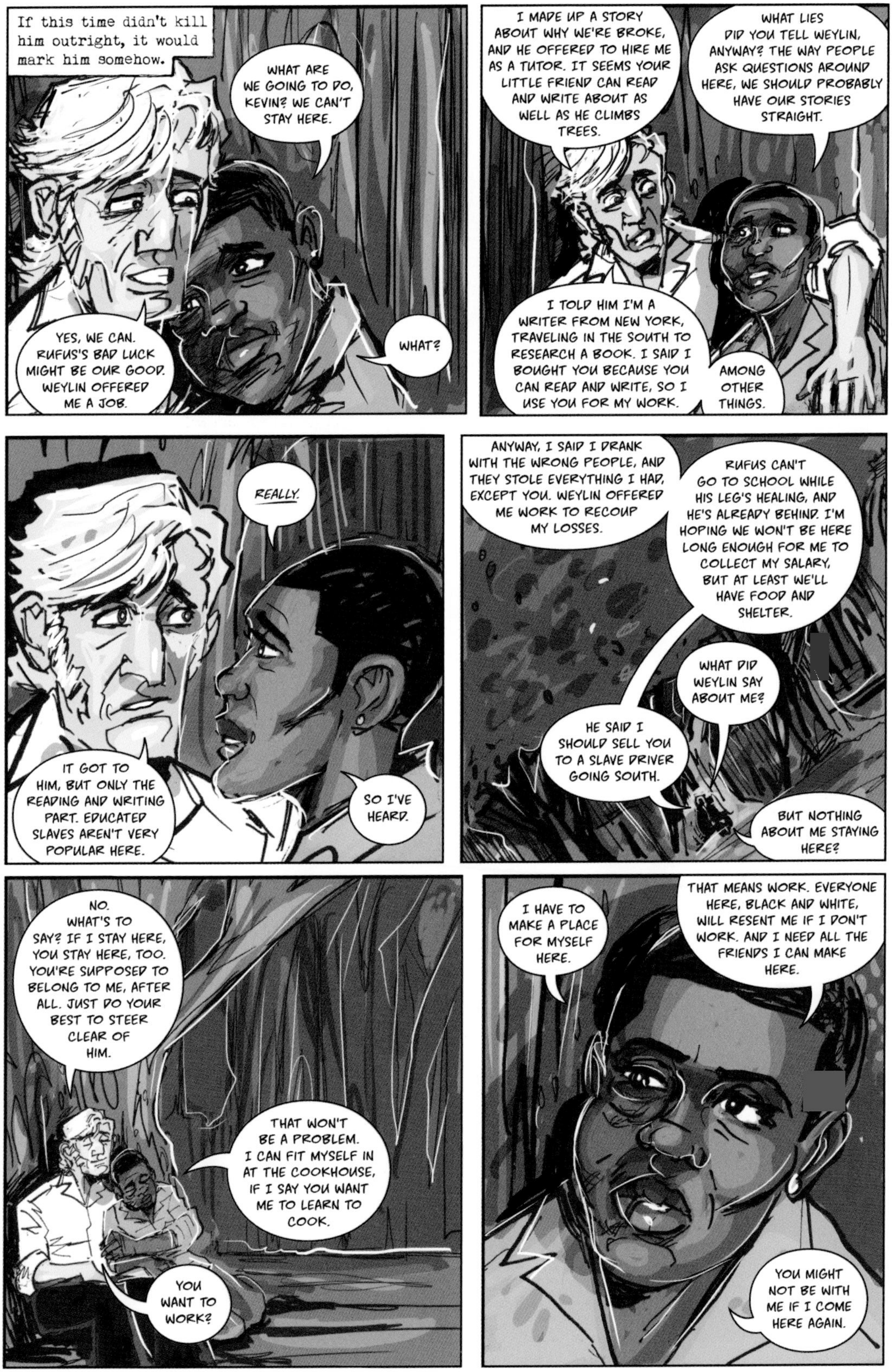

If this time didn't kill him outright, it would mark him somehow.
WHAT ARE WE GOING TO DO, KEVIN? WE CAN'T STAY HERE.
YES, WE CAN. RUFUS'S BAD LUCK MIGHT BE OUR GOOD. WEYLIN OFFERED ME A JOB.
WHAT?
I MADE UP A STORY ABOUT WHY WE'RE BROKE, AND HE OFFERED TO HIRE ME AS A TUTOR. IT SEEMS YOUR LITTLE FRIEND CAN READ AND WRITE ABOUT AS WELL AS HE CLIMBS TREES.
WHAT LIES DID YOU TELL WEYLIN, ANYWAY? THE WAY PEOPLE ASK QUESTIONS AROUND HERE, WE SHOULD PROBABLY HAVE OUR STORIES STRAIGHT.
I TOLD HIM I'M A WRITER FROM NEW YORK, TRAVELING IN THE SOUTH TO RESEARCH A BOOK. I SAID I BOUGHT YOU BECAUSE YOU CAN READ AND WRITE, SO I USE YOU FOR MY WORK.
AMONG OTHER THINGS.
REALLY.
IT GOT TO HIM, BUT ONLY THE READING AND WRITING PART. EDUCATED SLAVES AREN'T VERY POPULAR HERE.
SO I'VE HEARD.
ANYWAY, I SAID I DRANK WITH THE WRONG PEOPLE, AND THEY STOLE EVERYTHING I HAD, EXCEPT YOU. WEYLIN OFFERED ME WORK TO RECOUP MY LOSSES.
RUFUS CAN'T GO TO SCHOOL WHILE HIS LEG'S HEALING, AND HE'S ALREADY BEHIND. I'M HOPING WE WON'T BE HERE LONG ENOUGH FOR ME TO COLLECT MY SALARY, BUT AT LEAST WE'LL HAVE FOOD AND SHELTER.
WHAT DID WEYLIN SAY ABOUT ME?
HE SAID I SHOULD SELL YOU TO A SLAVE DRIVER GOING SOUTH.
BUT NOTHING ABOUT ME STAYING HERE?
NO. WHAT'S TO SAY? IF I STAY HERE, YOU STAY HERE, TOO. YOU'RE SUPPOSED TO BELONG TO ME, AFTER ALL. JUST DO YOUR BEST TO STEER CLEAR OF HIM.
THAT WON'T BE A PROBLEM. I CAN FIT MYSELF IN AT THE COOKHOUSE, IF I SAY YOU WANT ME TO LEARN TO COOK.
YOU WANT TO WORK?
I HAVE TO MAKE A PLACE FOR MYSELF HERE.
THAT MEANS WORK. EVERYONE HERE, BLACK AND WHITE, WILL RESENT ME IF I DON'T WORK. AND I NEED ALL THE FRIENDS I CAN MAKE HERE.
YOU MIGHT NOT BE WITH ME IF I COME HERE AGAIN.

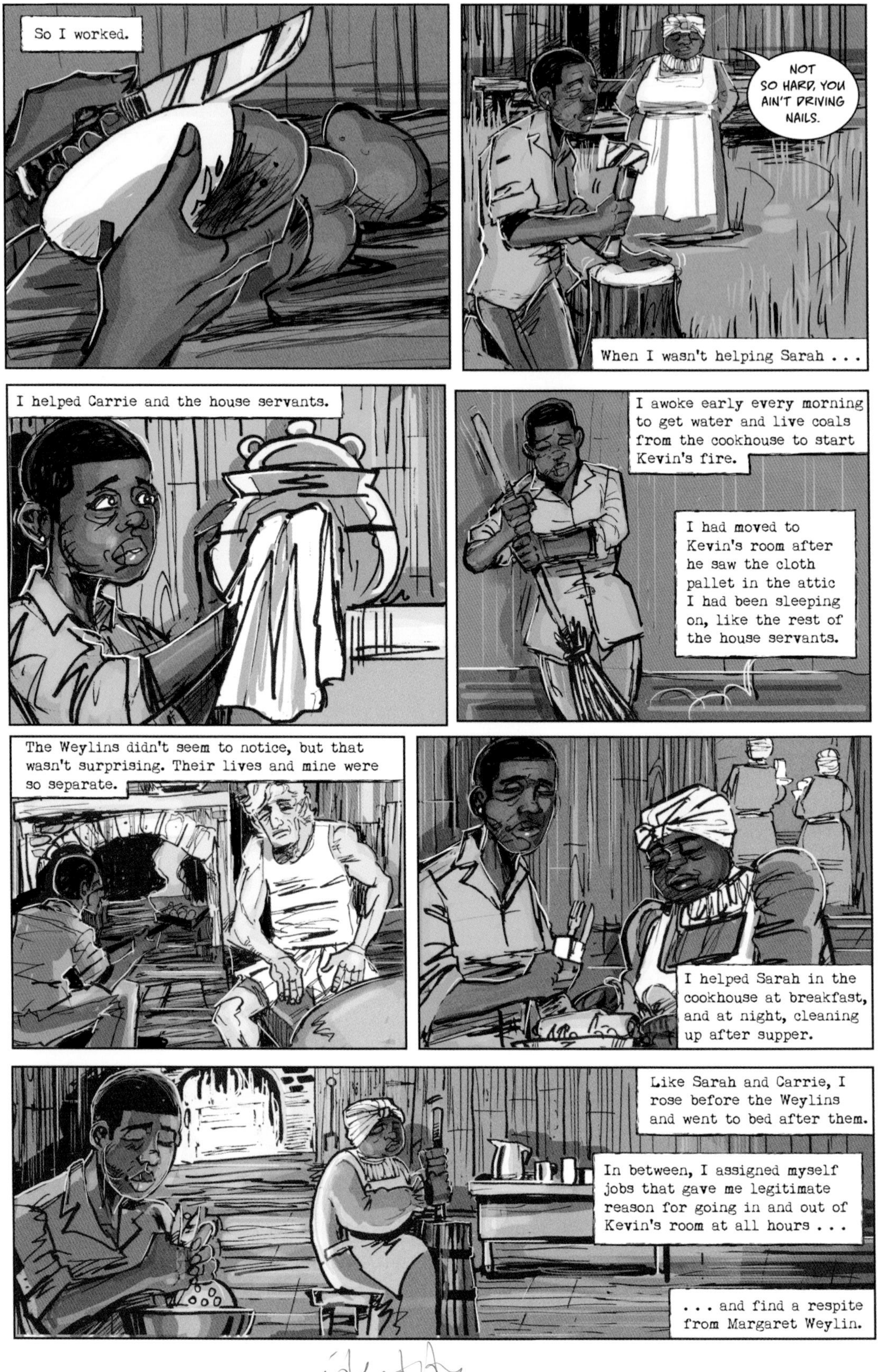

So I worked.
NOT SO HARD, YOU AIN'T DRIVING NAILS.
When I wasn't helping Sarah . . .
I helped Carrie and the house servants.
I awoke early every morning to get water and live coals from the cookhouse to start Kevin's fire.
I had moved to Kevin's room after he saw the cloth pallet in the attic I had been sleeping on, like the rest of the house servants.
The Weylins didn't seem to notice, but that wasn't surprising. Their lives and mine were so separate.
I helped Sarah in the cookhouse at breakfast, and at night, cleaning up after supper.
Like Sarah and Carrie, I rose before the Weylins and went to bed after them.
In between, I assigned myself jobs that gave me legitimate reason for going in and out of Kevin's room at all hours . . .
. . . and find a respite from Margaret Weylin.

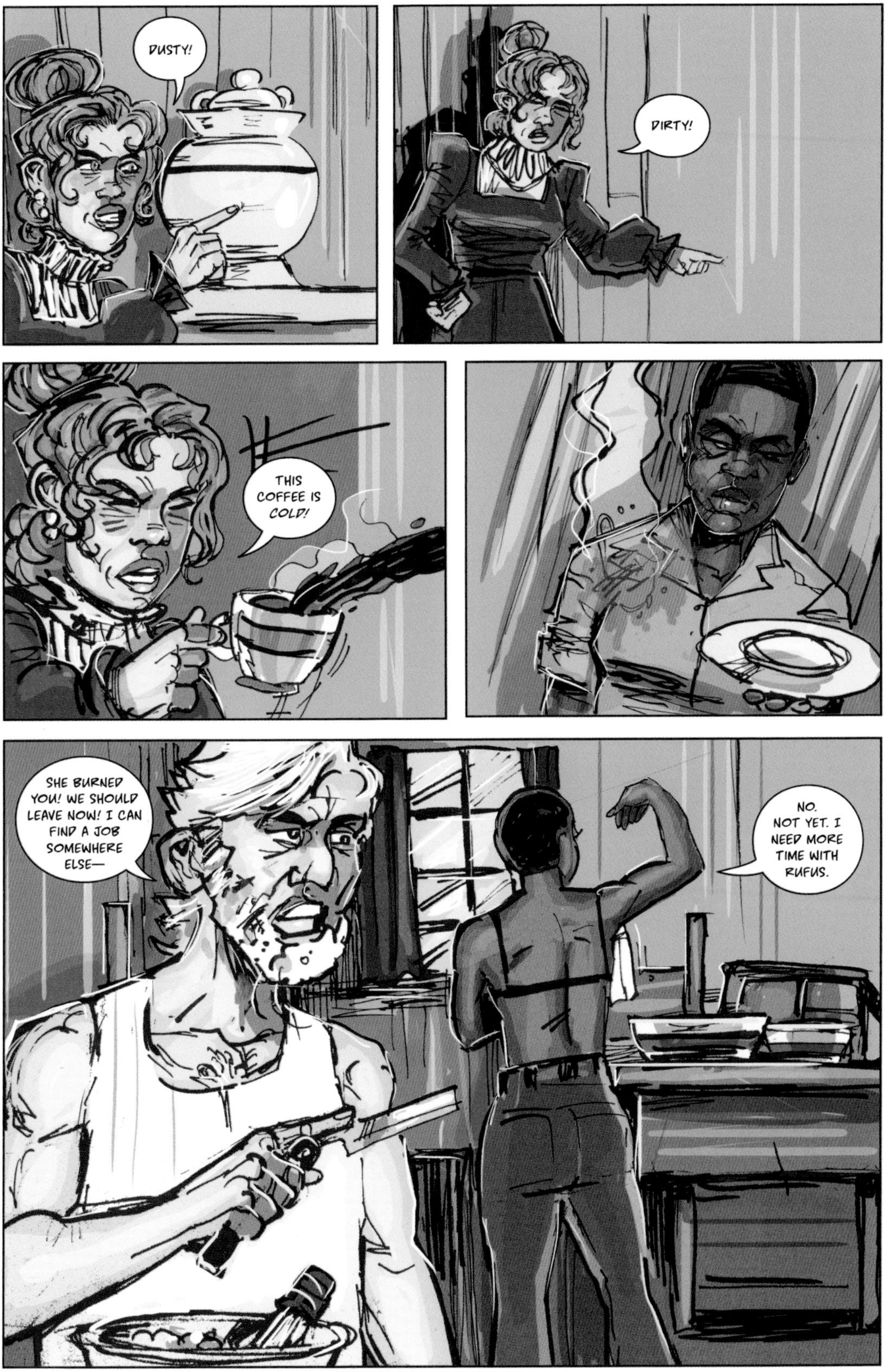
DUSTY!
DIRTY!
THIS COFFEE IS COLD!
SHE BURNED YOU! WE SHOULD LEAVE NOW! I CAN FIND A JOB SOMEWHERE ELSE—
NO. NOT YET. I NEED MORE TIME WITH RUFUS.

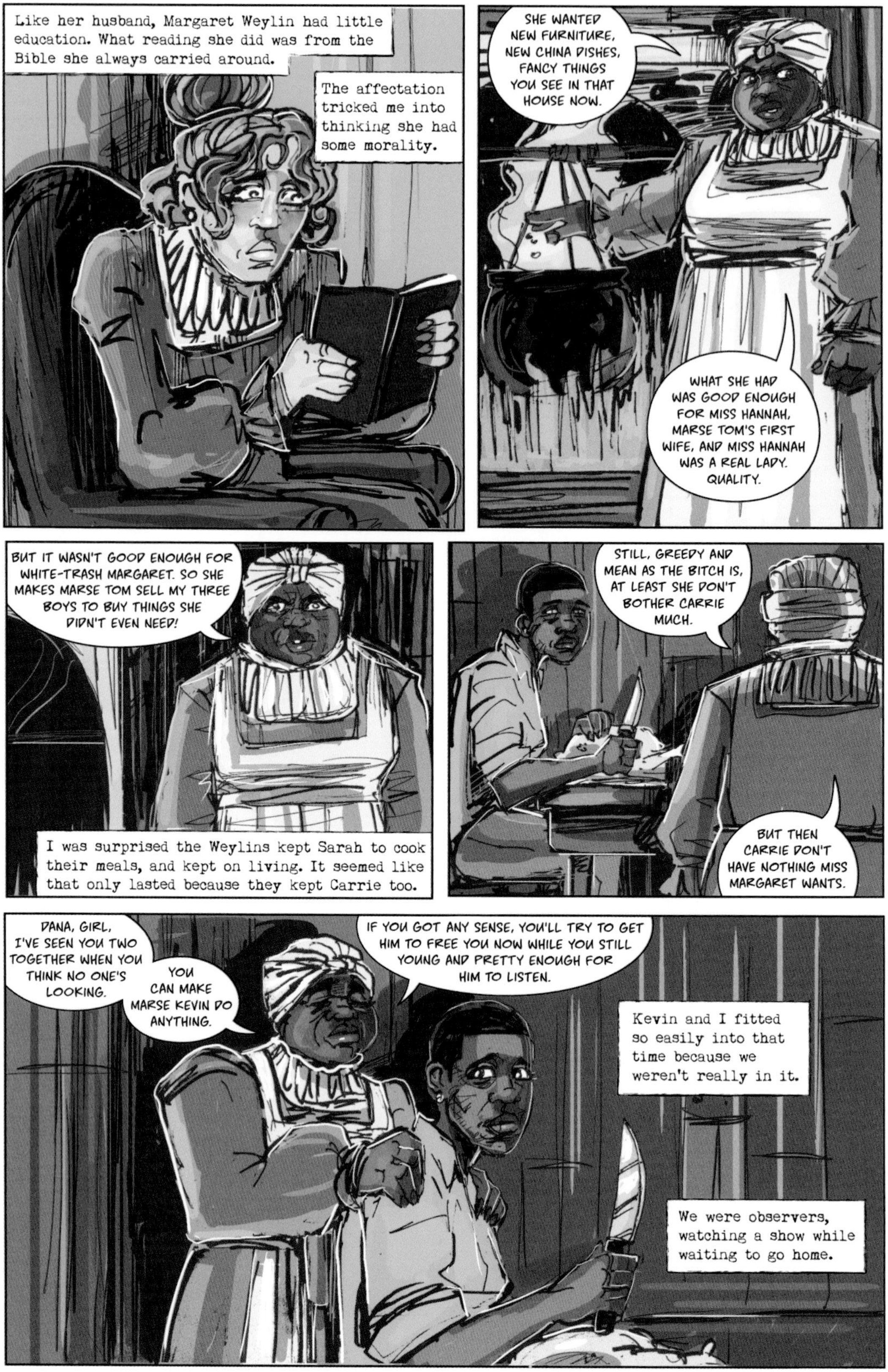
Like her husband, Margaret Weylin had little education. What reading she did was from the Bible she always carried around.
The affectation tricked me into thinking she had some morality.
SHE WANTED NEW FURNITURE, NEW CHINA DISHES, FANCY THINGS YOU SEE IN THAT HOUSE NOW.
WHAT SHE HAD WAS GOOD ENOUGH FOR MISS HANNAH, MARSE TOM'S FIRST WIFE, AND MISS HANNAH WAS A REAL LADY. QUALITY.
BUT IT WASN'T GOOD ENOUGH FOR WHITE-TRASH MARGARET. SO SHE MAKES MARSE TOM SELL MY THREE BOYS TO BUY THINGS SHE DIDN'T EVEN NEED!
I was surprised the Weylins kept Sarah to cook their meals, and kept on living. It seemed like that only lasted because they kept Carrie too.
STILL, GREEDY AND MEAN AS THE BITCH IS, AT LEAST SHE DON'T BOTHER CARRIE MUCH.
BUT THEN CARRIE DON'T HAVE NOTHING MISS MARGARET WANTS.
DANA, GIRL, I'VE SEEN YOU TWO TOGETHER WHEN YOU THINK NO ONE'S LOOKING.
YOU CAN MAKE MARSE KEVIN DO ANYTHING.
IF YOU GOT ANY SENSE, YOU'LL TRY TO GET HIM TO FREE YOU NOW WHILE YOU STILL YOUNG AND PRETTY ENOUGH FOR HIM TO LISTEN.
Kevin and I fitted so easily into that time because we weren't really in it.
We were observers, watching a show while waiting to go home.

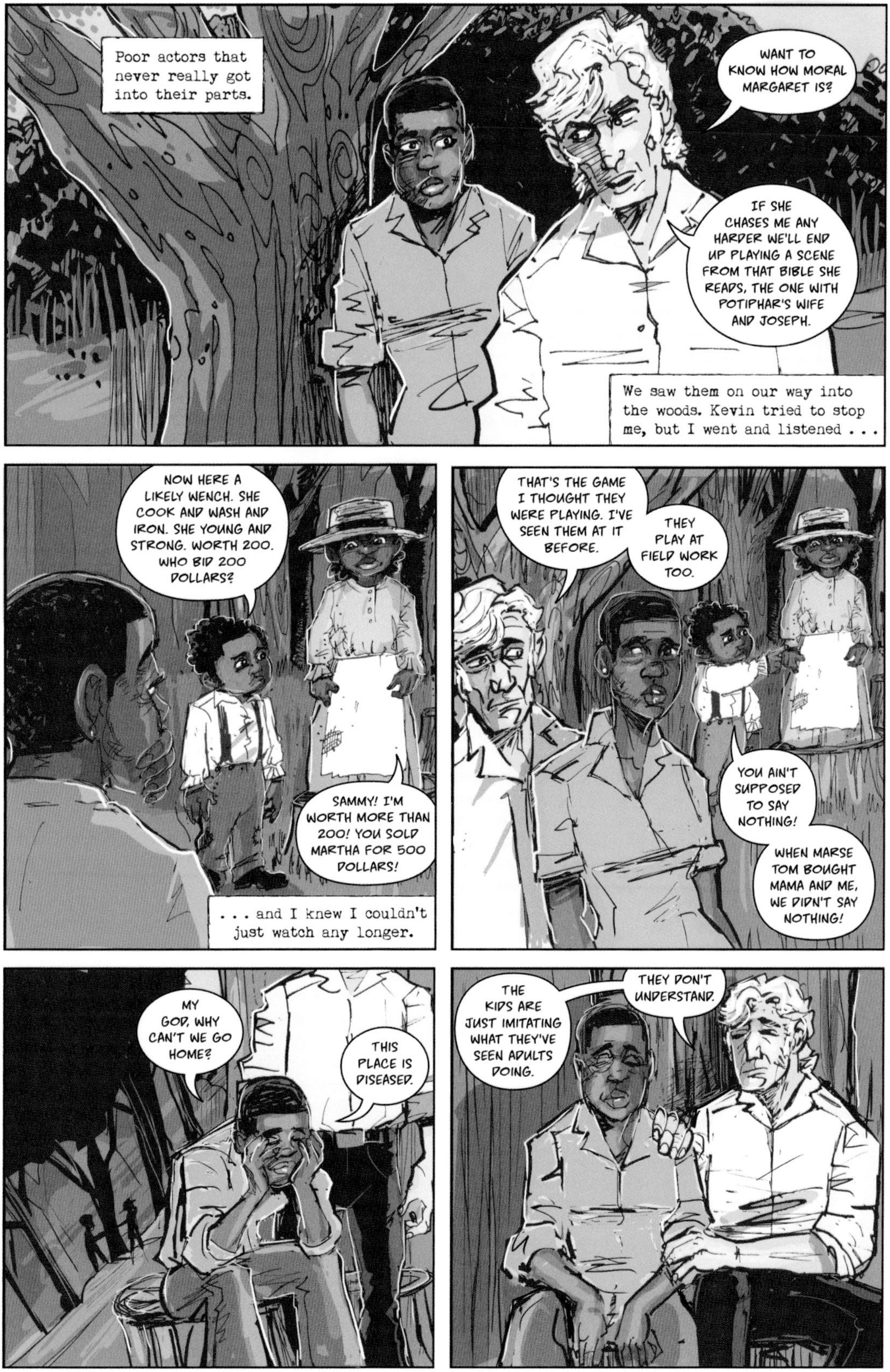
Poor actors that never really got into their parts.
WANT TO KNOW HOW MORAL MARGARET IS?
IF SHE CHASES ME ANY HARDER WE'LL END UP PLAYING A SCENE FROM THAT BIBLE SHE READS, THE ONE WITH POTIPHAR'S WIFE AND JOSEPH.
We saw them on our way into the woods. Kevin tried to stop me, but I went and listened . . .
NOW HERE A LIKELY WENCH. SHE COOK AND WASH AND IRON. SHE YOUNG AND STRONG. WORTH 200. WHO BID 200 DOLLARS?
SAMMY! I'M WORTH MORE THAN 200! YOU SOLD MARTHA FOR 500 DOLLARS!
. . . and I knew I couldn't just watch any longer.
THAT'S THE GAME I THOUGHT THEY WERE PLAYING. I'VE SEEN THEM AT IT BEFORE.
THEY PLAY AT FIELD WORK TOO.
YOU AIN'T SUPPOSED TO SAY NOTHING!
WHEN MARSE TOM BOUGHT MAMA AND ME, WE DIDN'T SAY NOTHING!
MY GOD, WHY CAN'T WE GO HOME?
THIS PLACE IS DISEASED.
THE KIDS ARE JUST IMITATING WHAT THEY'VE SEEN ADULTS DOING.
THEY DON'T UNDERSTAND.

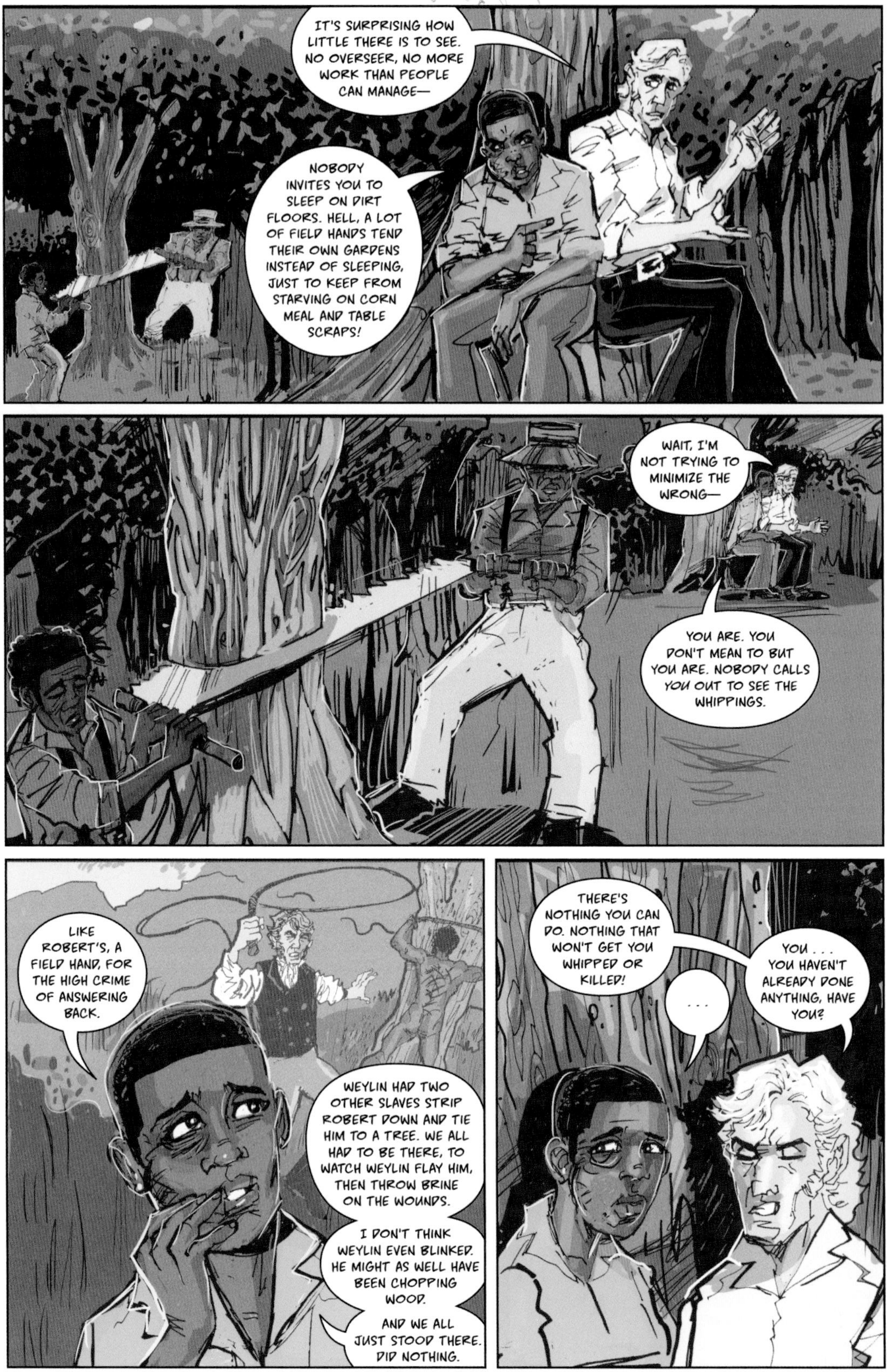
IT'S SURPRISING HOW LITTLE THERE IS TO SEE. NO OVERSEER, NO MORE WORK THAN PEOPLE CAN MANAGE—
NOBODY INVITES YOU TO SLEEP ON DIRT FLOORS. HELL, A LOT OF FIELD HANDS TEND THEIR OWN GARDENS INSTEAD OF SLEEPING, JUST TO KEEP FROM STARVING ON CORN MEAL AND TABLE SCRAPS!
WAIT, I'M NOT TRYING TO MINIMIZE THE WRONG—
YOU ARE. YOU DON'T MEAN TO BUT YOU ARE. NOBODY CALLS YOU OUT TO SEE THE WHIPPINGS.
LIKE ROBERT'S, A FIELD HAND, FOR THE HIGH CRIME OF ANSWERING BACK.
WEYLIN HAD TWO OTHER SLAVES STRIP ROBERT DOWN AND TIE HIM TO A TREE. WE ALL HAD TO BE THERE, TO WATCH WEYLIN FLAY HIM, THEN THROW BRINE ON THE WOUNDS.
I DON'T THINK WEYLIN EVEN BLINKED. HE MIGHT AS WELL HAVE BEEN CHOPPING WOOD.
AND WE ALL JUST STOOD THERE. DID NOTHING.
THERE'S NOTHING YOU CAN DO. NOTHING THAT WON'T GET YOU WHIPPED OR KILLED!
. . .
YOU . . . YOU HAVEN'T ALREADY DONE ANYTHING, HAVE YOU?

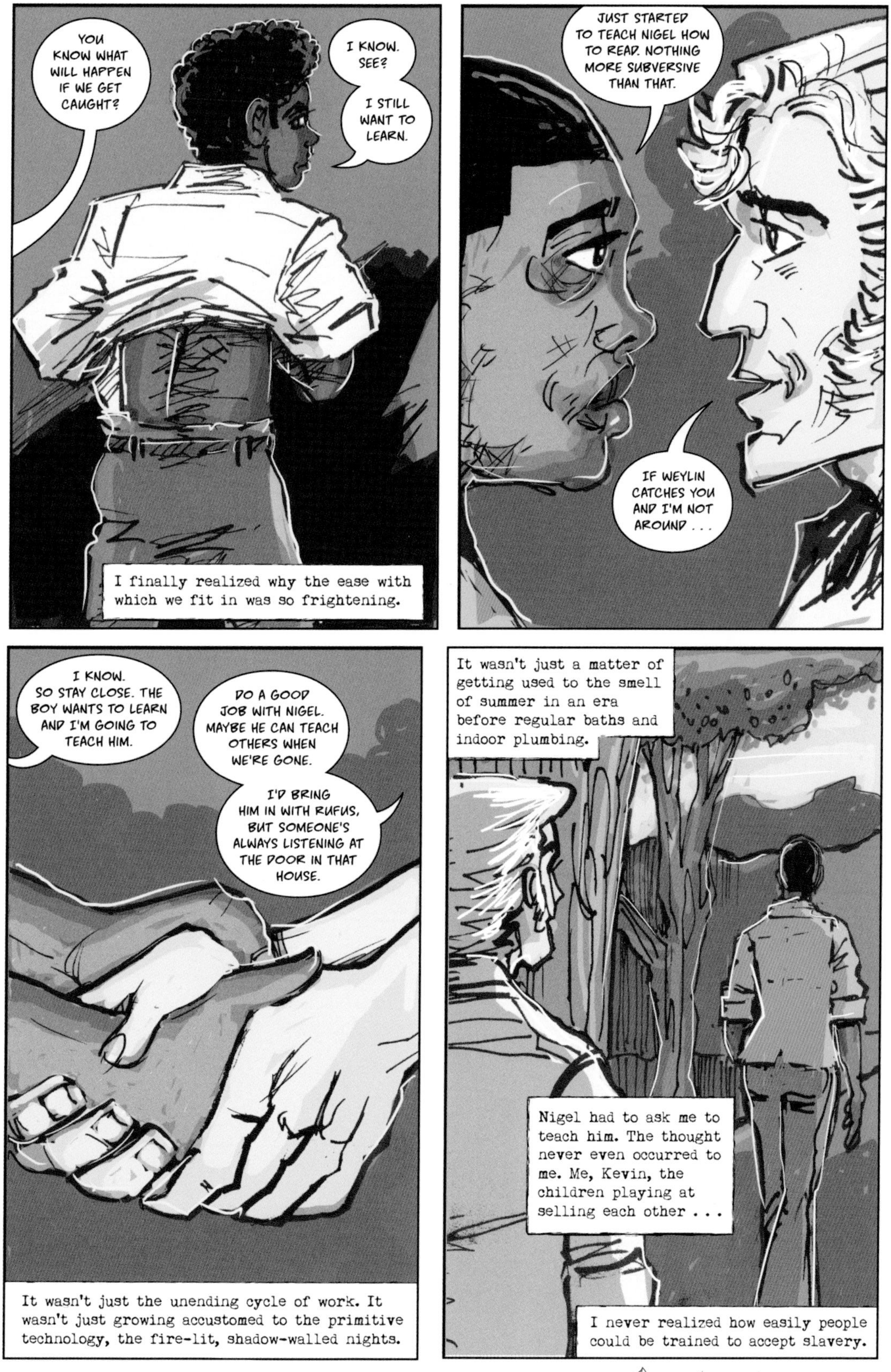
YOU KNOW WHAT WILL HAPPEN IF WE GET CAUGHT?
I KNOW. SEE?
I STILL WANT TO LEARN.
I finally realized why the ease with which we fit in was so frightening.
JUST STARTED TO TEACH NIGEL HOW TO READ. NOTHING MORE SUBVERSIVE THAN THAT.
IF WEYLIN CATCHES YOU AND I'M NOT AROUND . . .
I KNOW. SO STAY CLOSE. THE BOY WANTS TO LEARN AND I'M GOING TO TEACH HIM.
DO A GOOD JOB WITH NIGEL. MAYBE HE CAN TEACH OTHERS WHEN WE'RE GONE.
I'D BRING HIM IN WITH RUFUS, BUT SOMEONE'S ALWAYS LISTENING AT THE DOOR IN THAT HOUSE.
It wasn't just the unending cycle of work. It wasn't just growing accustomed to the primitive technology, the fire-lit, shadow-walled nights.
It wasn't just a matter of getting used to the smell of summer in an era before regular baths and indoor plumbing.
Nigel had to ask me to teach him. The thought never even occurred to me. Me, Kevin, the children playing at selling each other . . .
I never realized how easily people could be trained to accept slavery.

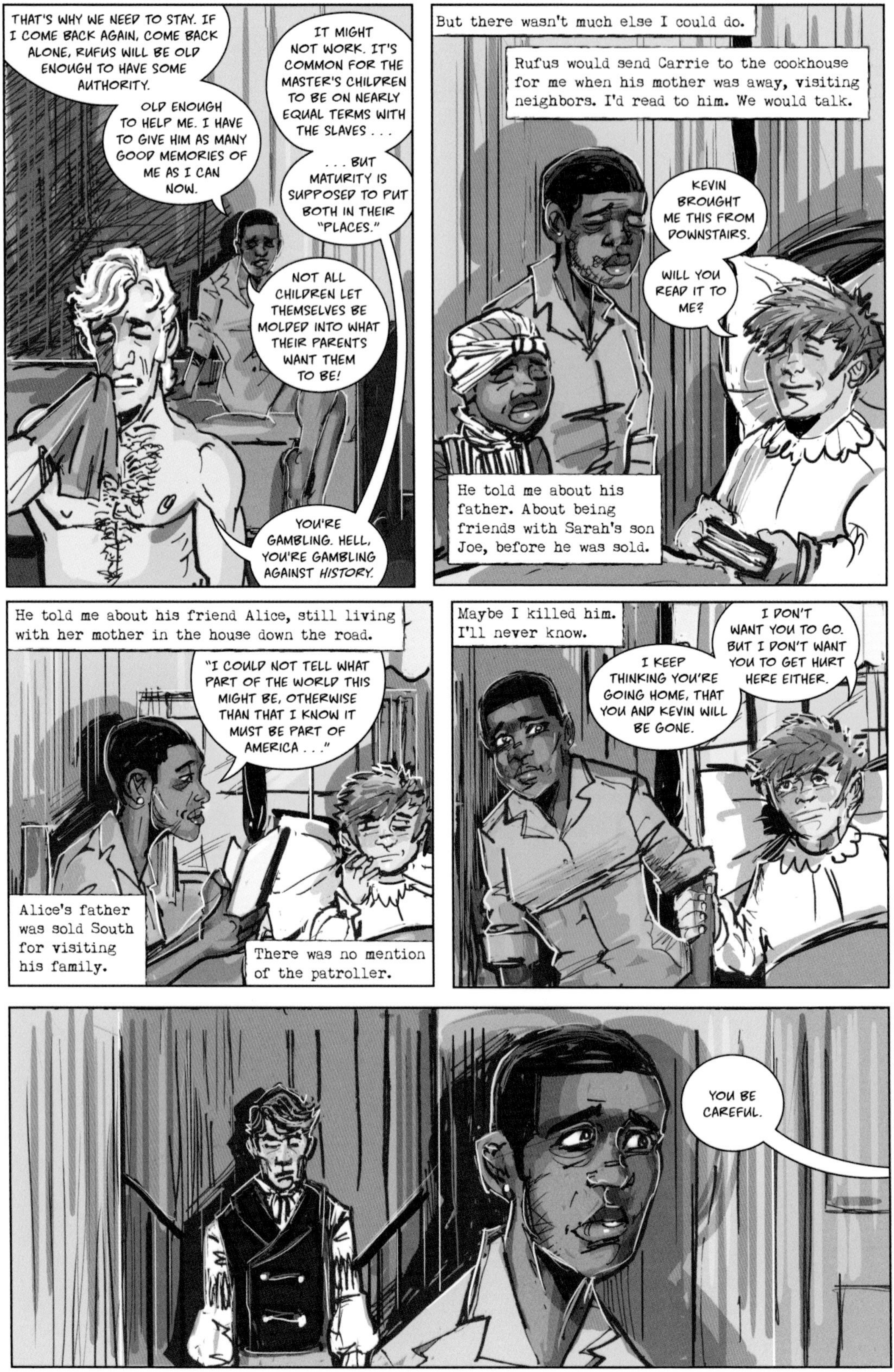
THAT'S WHY WE NEED TO STAY. IF I COME BACK AGAIN, COME BACK ALONE, RUFUS WILL BE OLD ENOUGH TO HAVE SOME AUTHORITY.
OLD ENOUGH TO HELP ME. I HAVE TO GIVE HIM AS MANY GOOD MEMORIES OF ME AS I CAN NOW.
IT MIGHT NOT WORK. IT'S COMMON FOR THE MASTER'S CHILDREN TO BE ON NEARLY EQUAL TERMS WITH THE SLAVES . . .
. . . BUT MATURITY IS SUPPOSED TO PUT BOTH IN THEIR "PLACES."
NOT ALL CHILDREN LET THEMSELVES BE MOLDED INTO WHAT THEIR PARENTS WANT THEM TO BE!
YOU'RE GAMBLING. HELL, YOU'RE GAMBLING AGAINST *HISTORY*.
But there wasn't much else I could do.
Rufus would send Carrie to the cookhouse for me when his mother was away, visiting neighbors. I'd read to him. We would talk.
KEVIN BROUGHT ME THIS FROM DOWNSTAIRS.
WILL YOU READ IT TO ME?
He told me about his father. About being friends with Sarah's son Joe, before he was sold.
He told me about his friend Alice, still living with her mother in the house down the road.
"I COULD NOT TELL WHAT PART OF THE WORLD THIS MIGHT BE, OTHERWISE THAN THAT I KNOW IT MUST BE PART OF AMERICA . . ."
Alice's father was sold South for visiting his family.
There was no mention of the patroller.
Maybe I killed him. I'll never know.
I DON'T WANT YOU TO GO. BUT I DON'T WANT YOU TO GET HURT HERE EITHER.
I KEEP THINKING YOU'RE GOING HOME, THAT YOU AND KEVIN WILL BE GONE.
YOU BE CAREFUL.

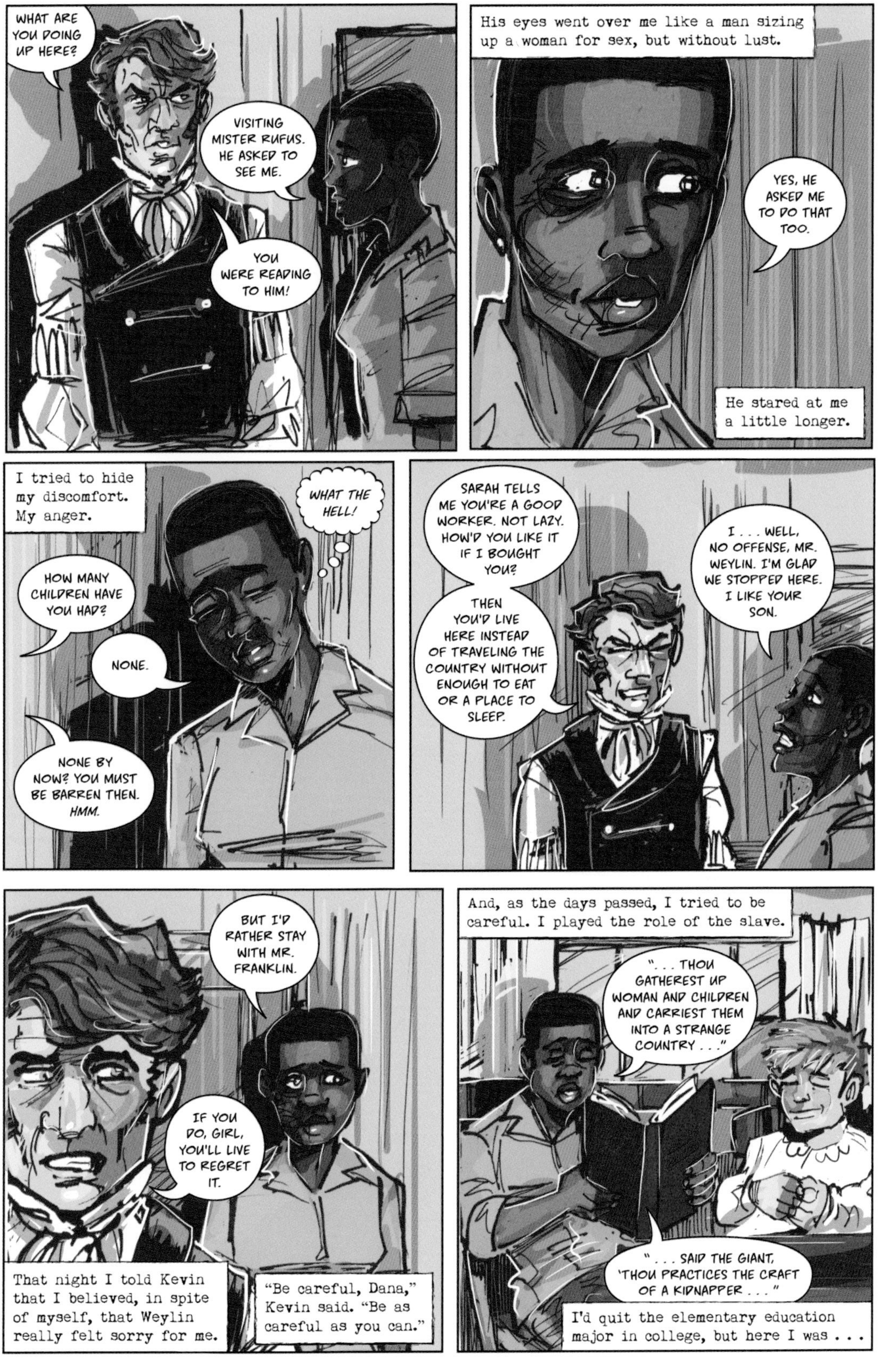
WHAT ARE YOU DOING UP HERE?
VISITING MISTER RUFUS. HE ASKED TO SEE ME.
YOU WERE READING TO HIM!
His eyes went over me like a man sizing up a woman for sex, but without lust.
YES, HE ASKED ME TO DO THAT TOO.
He stared at me a little longer.
I tried to hide my discomfort. My anger.
WHAT THE HELL!
HOW MANY CHILDREN HAVE YOU HAD?
NONE.
NONE BY NOW? YOU MUST BE BARREN THEN. HMM.
SARAH TELLS ME YOU'RE A GOOD WORKER. NOT LAZY. HOW'D YOU LIKE IT IF I BOUGHT YOU?
THEN YOU'D LIVE HERE INSTEAD OF TRAVELING THE COUNTRY WITHOUT ENOUGH TO EAT OR A PLACE TO SLEEP.
I . . . WELL, NO OFFENSE, MR. WEYLIN. I'M GLAD WE STOPPED HERE. I LIKE YOUR SON.
BUT I'D RATHER STAY WITH MR. FRANKLIN.
IF YOU DO, GIRL, YOU'LL LIVE TO REGRET IT.
That night I told Kevin that I believed, in spite of myself, that Weylin really felt sorry for me.
"Be careful, Dana," Kevin said. "Be as careful as you can."
And, as the days passed, I tried to be careful. I played the role of the slave.
". . . THOU GATHEREST UP WOMAN AND CHILDREN AND CARRIEST THEM INTO A STRANGE COUNTRY . . ."
" . . . SAID THE GIANT, 'THOU PRACTICES THE CRAFT OF A KIDNAPPER . . ."
I'd quit the elementary education major in college, but here I was . . .

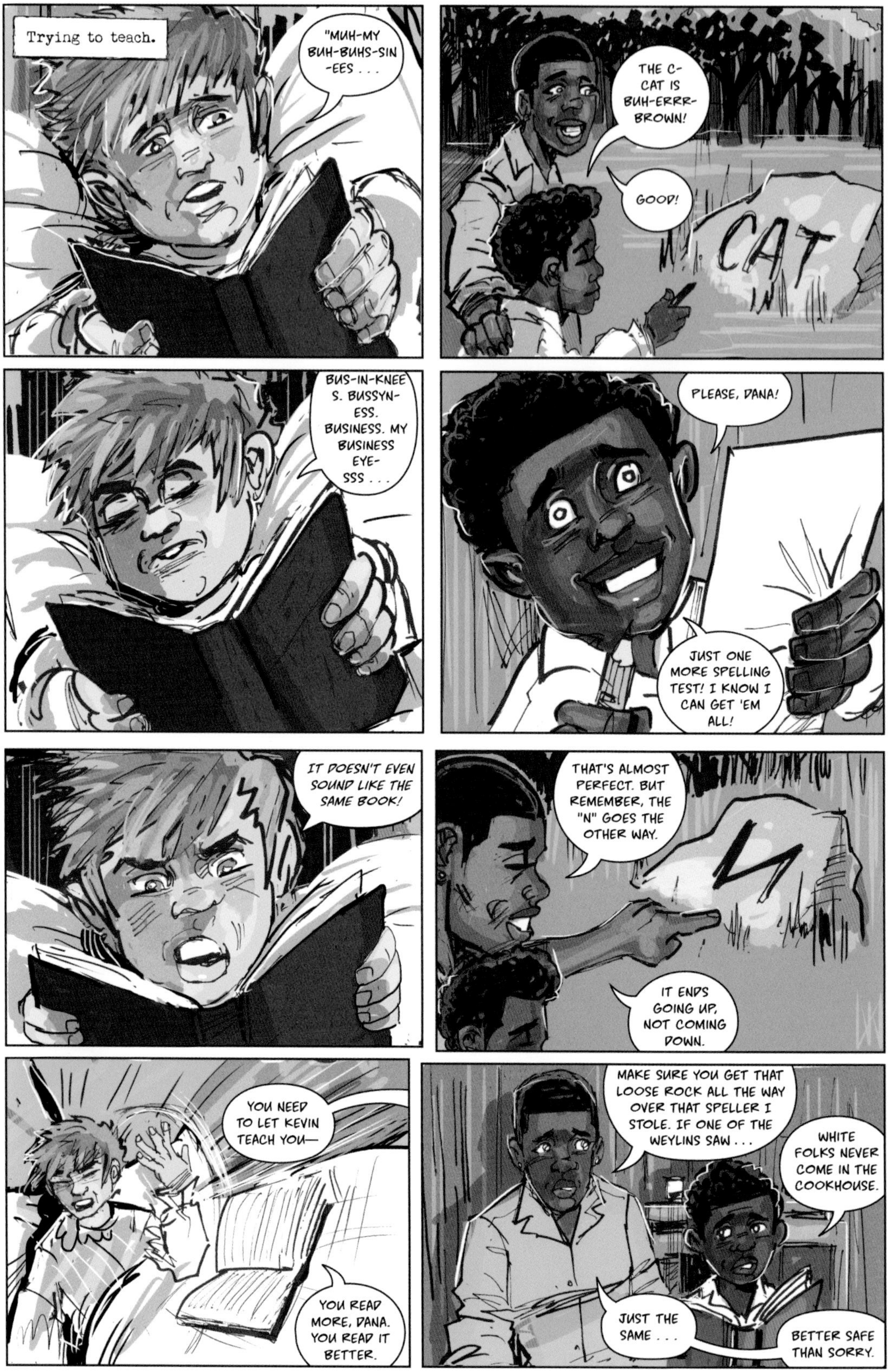
Trying to teach.
"MUH-MY BUH-BUHS-SIN -EES . . .
THE C-CAT IS BUH-ERRR-BROWN!
GOOD!
CAT
BUS-IN-KNEE S. BUSSYN-ESS. BUSINESS. MY BUSINESS EYE-SSS . . .
PLEASE, DANA!
JUST ONE MORE SPELLING TEST! I KNOW I CAN GET 'EM ALL!
IT DOESN'T EVEN SOUND LIKE THE SAME BOOK!
THAT'S ALMOST PERFECT. BUT REMEMBER, THE "N" GOES THE OTHER WAY.
IT ENDS GOING UP, NOT COMING DOWN.
YOU NEED TO LET KEVIN TEACH YOU—
YOU READ MORE, DANA. YOU READ IT BETTER.
MAKE SURE YOU GET THAT LOOSE ROCK ALL THE WAY OVER THAT SPELLER I STOLE. IF ONE OF THE WEYLINS SAW . . .
WHITE FOLKS NEVER COME IN THE COOKHOUSE.
JUST THE SAME . . .
BETTER SAFE THAN SORRY.

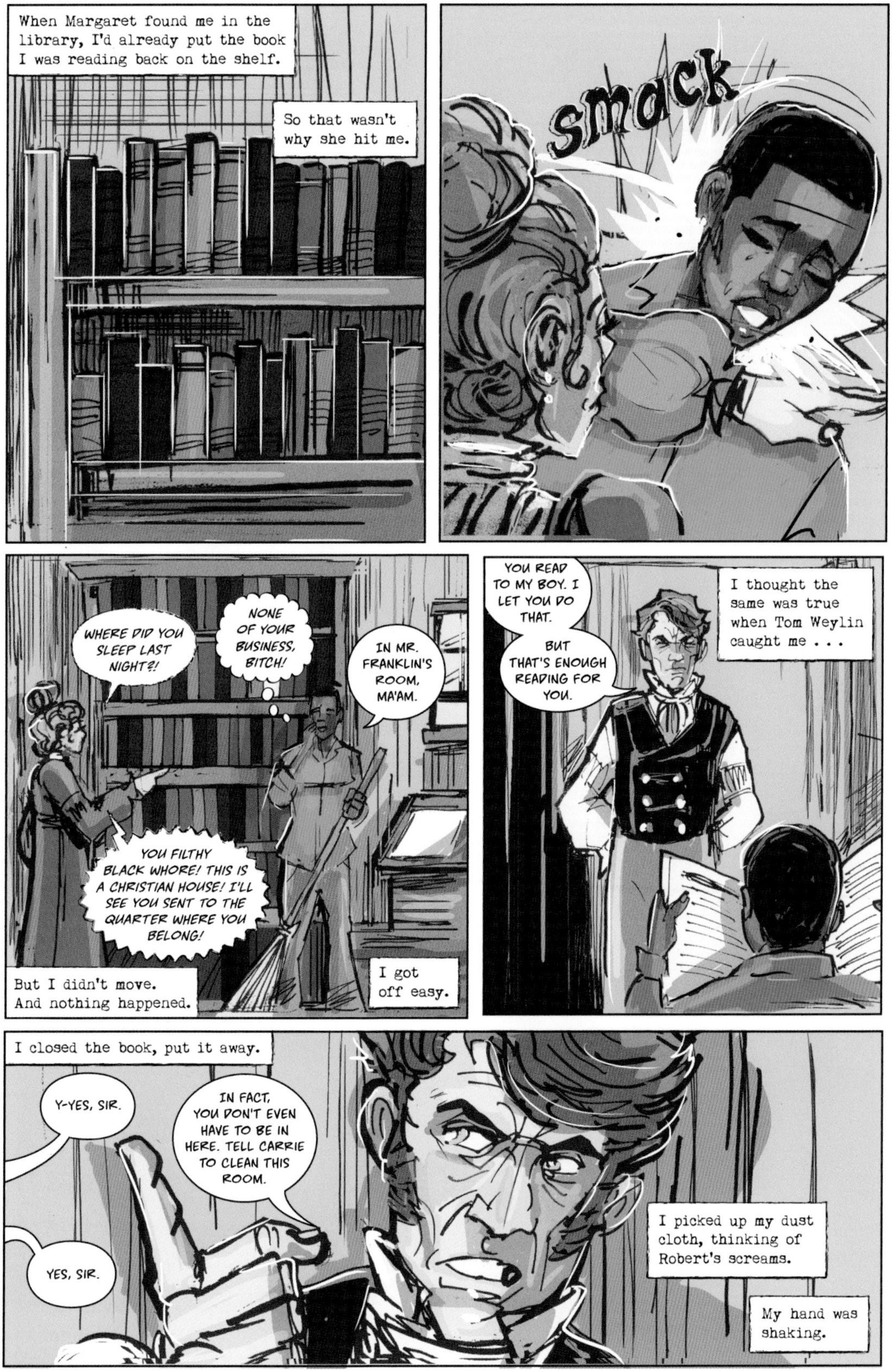
When Margaret found me in the library, I'd already put the book I was reading back on the shelf.
So that wasn't why she hit me.
SMACK
WHERE DID YOU SLEEP LAST NIGHT?!
NONE OF YOUR BUSINESS, BITCH!
IN MR. FRANKLIN'S ROOM, MA'AM.
YOU FILTHY BLACK WHORE! THIS IS A CHRISTIAN HOUSE! I'LL SEE YOU SENT TO THE QUARTER WHERE YOU BELONG!
But I didn't move. And nothing happened.
I got off easy.
YOU READ TO MY BOY. I LET YOU DO THAT.
I thought the same was true when Tom Weylin caught me . . .
BUT THAT'S ENOUGH READING FOR YOU.
I closed the book, put it away.
Y-YES, SIR.
IN FACT, YOU DON'T EVEN HAVE TO BE IN HERE. TELL CARRIE TO CLEAN THIS ROOM.
YES, SIR.
I picked up my dust cloth, thinking of Robert's screams.
My hand was shaking.

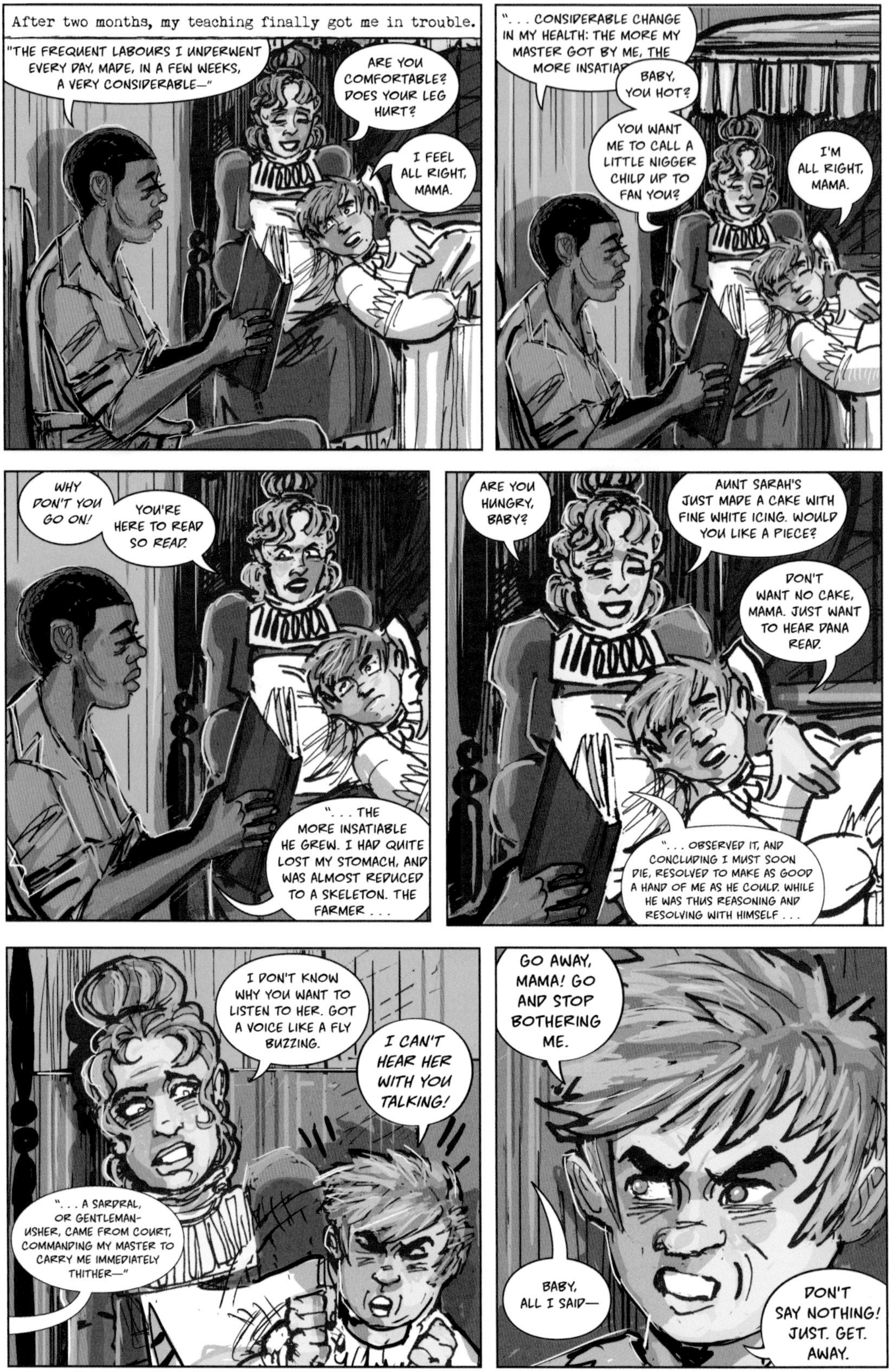
After two months, my teaching finally got me in trouble.
"THE FREQUENT LABOURS I UNDERWENT EVERY DAY, MADE, IN A FEW WEEKS, A VERY CONSIDERABLE—"
ARE YOU COMFORTABLE? DOES YOUR LEG HURT?
I FEEL ALL RIGHT, MAMA.
". . . CONSIDERABLE CHANGE IN MY HEALTH: THE MORE MY MASTER GOT BY ME, THE MORE INSATIA
BABY, YOU HOT?
YOU WANT ME TO CALL A LITTLE NIGGER CHILD UP TO FAN YOU?
I'M ALL RIGHT, MAMA.
WHY DON'T YOU GO ON!
YOU'RE HERE TO READ SO READ.
". . . THE MORE INSATIABLE HE GREW. I HAD QUITE LOST MY STOMACH, AND WAS ALMOST REDUCED TO A SKELETON. THE FARMER . . .
ARE YOU HUNGRY, BABY?
AUNT SARAH'S JUST MADE A CAKE WITH FINE WHITE ICING. WOULD YOU LIKE A PIECE?
DON'T WANT NO CAKE, MAMA. JUST WANT TO HEAR DANA READ.
". . . OBSERVED IT, AND CONCLUDING I MUST SOON DIE, RESOLVED TO MAKE AS GOOD A HAND OF ME AS HE COULD. WHILE HE WAS THUS REASONING AND RESOLVING WITH HIMSELF . . .
I DON'T KNOW WHY YOU WANT TO LISTEN TO HER. GOT A VOICE LIKE A FLY BUZZING.
I CAN'T HEAR HER WITH YOU TALKING!
". . . A SARDRAL, OR GENTLEMAN-USHER, CAME FROM COURT, COMMANDING MY MASTER TO CARRY ME IMMEDIATELY THITHER—"
GO AWAY, MAMA! GO AND STOP BOTHERING ME.
BABY, ALL I SAID—
DON'T SAY NOTHING! JUST. GET. AWAY.

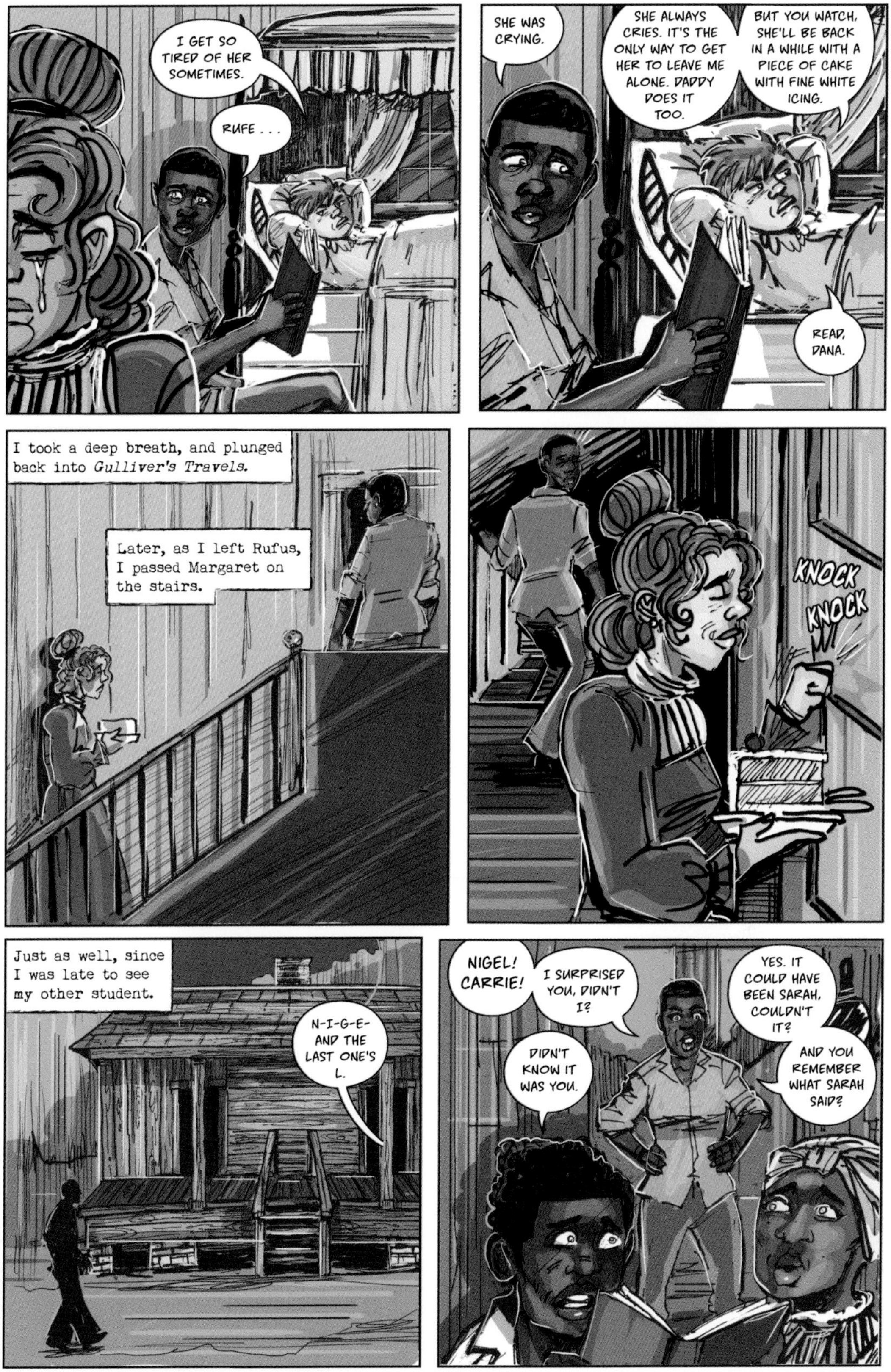
I GET SO TIRED OF HER SOMETIMES.
RUFE . . .
SHE WAS CRYING.
SHE ALWAYS CRIES. IT'S THE ONLY WAY TO GET HER TO LEAVE ME ALONE. DADDY DOES IT TOO.
BUT YOU WATCH, SHE'LL BE BACK IN A WHILE WITH A PIECE OF CAKE WITH FINE WHITE ICING.
READ, DANA.
I took a deep breath, and plunged back into *Gulliver's Travels.*
Later, as I left Rufus, I passed Margaret on the stairs.
KNOCK
KNOCK
Just as well, since I was late to see my other student.
N-I-G-E- AND THE LAST ONE'S L.
NIGEL! CARRIE!
I SURPRISED YOU, DIDN'T I?
DIDN'T KNOW IT WAS YOU.
YES. IT COULD HAVE BEEN SARAH, COULDN'T IT?
AND YOU REMEMBER WHAT SARAH SAID?

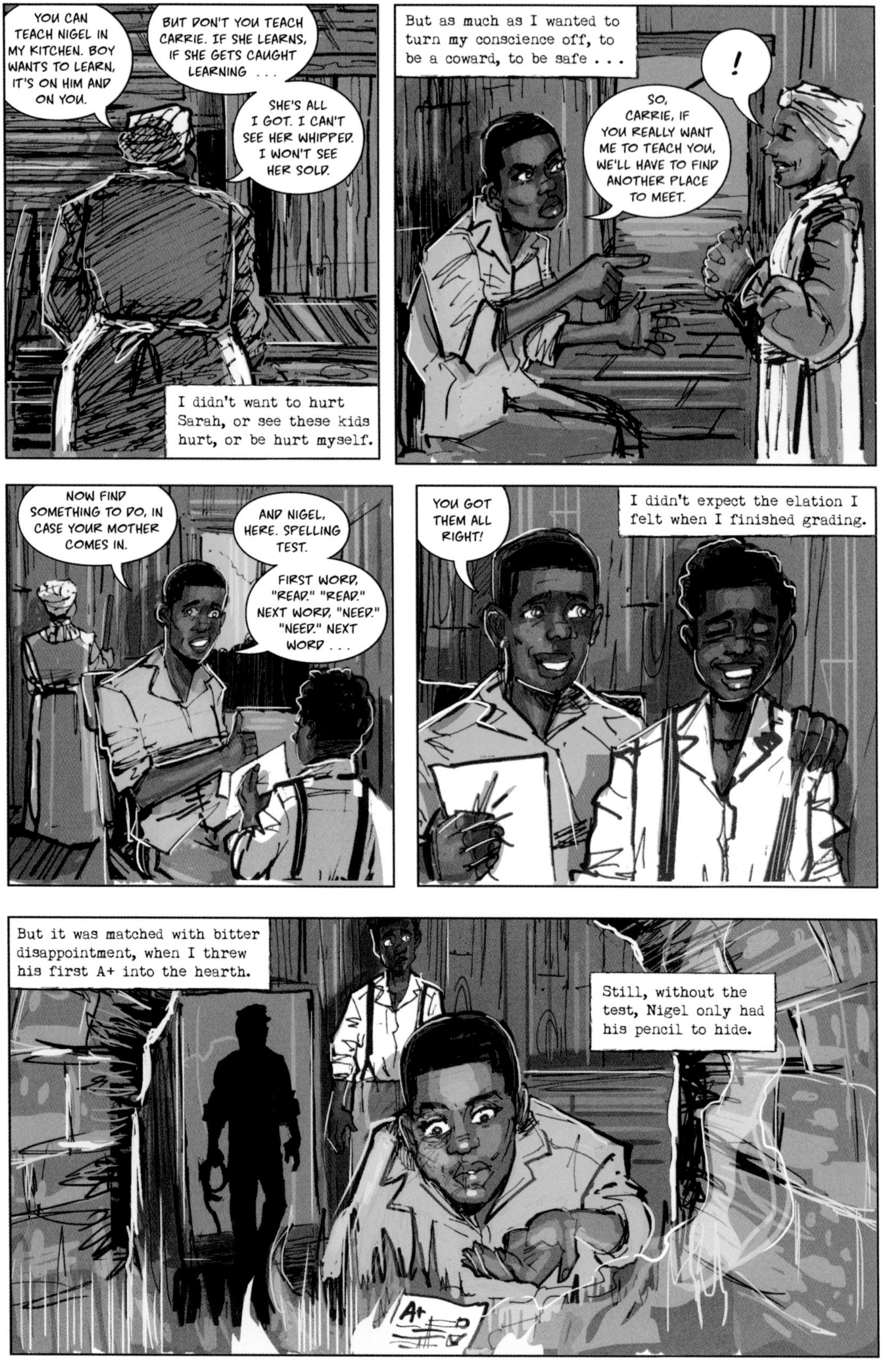

YOU CAN TEACH NIGEL IN MY KITCHEN. BOY WANTS TO LEARN, IT'S ON HIM AND ON YOU.
BUT DON'T YOU TEACH CARRIE. IF SHE LEARNS, IF SHE GETS CAUGHT LEARNING . . .
SHE'S ALL I GOT. I CAN'T SEE HER WHIPPED. I WON'T SEE HER SOLD.
I didn't want to hurt Sarah, or see these kids hurt, or be hurt myself.
But as much as I wanted to turn my conscience off, to be a coward, to be safe . . .
SO, CARRIE, IF YOU REALLY WANT ME TO TEACH YOU, WE'LL HAVE TO FIND ANOTHER PLACE TO MEET.
!
NOW FIND SOMETHING TO DO, IN CASE YOUR MOTHER COMES IN.
AND NIGEL, HERE. SPELLING TEST.
FIRST WORD, "READ." "READ." NEXT WORD, "NEED." "NEED." NEXT WORD . . .
YOU GOT THEM ALL RIGHT!
I didn't expect the elation I felt when I finished grading.
But it was matched with bitter disappointment, when I threw his first A+ into the hearth.
Still, without the test, Nigel only had his pencil to hide.
A+

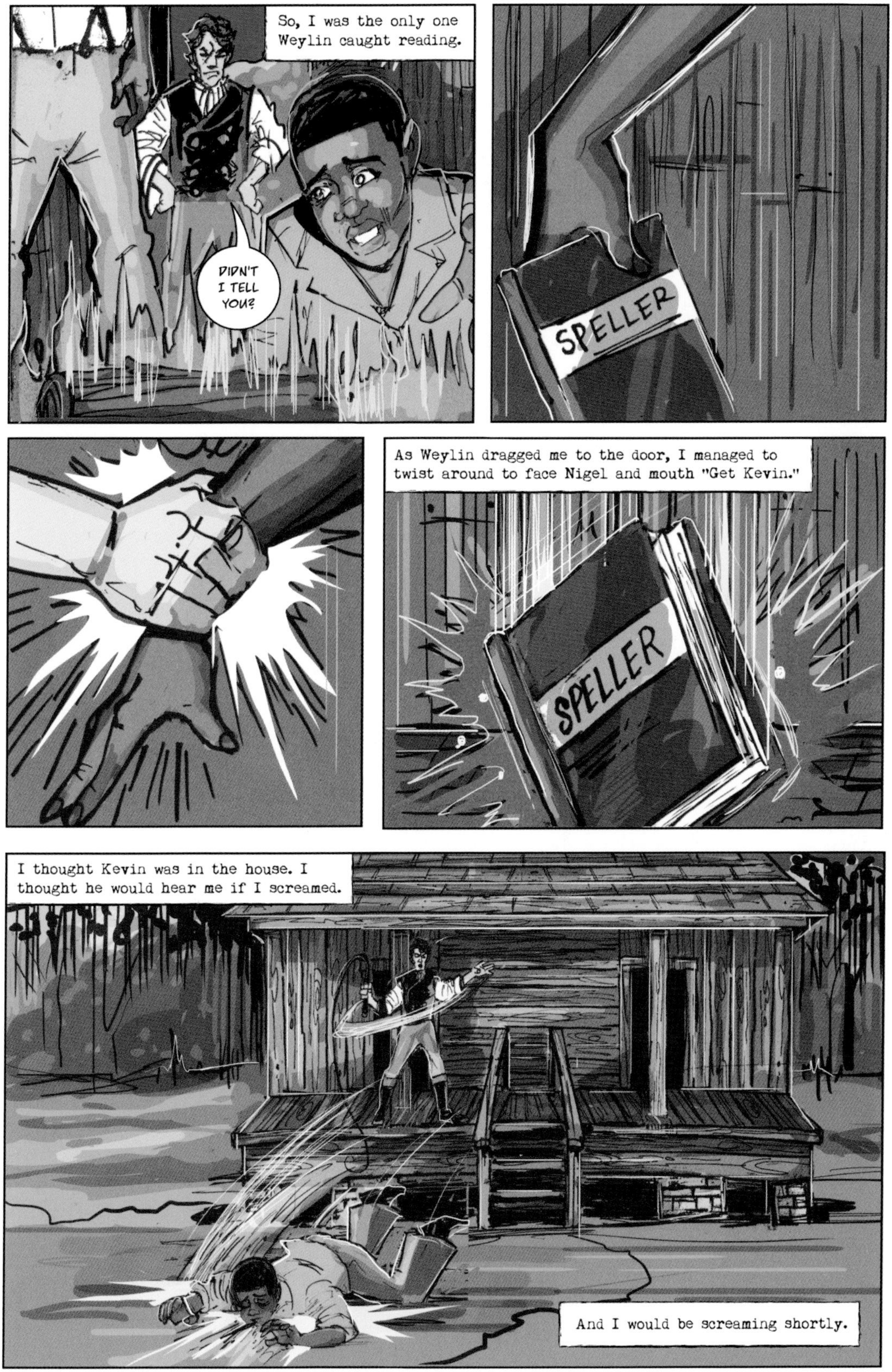
So, I was the only one Weylin caught reading.
DIDN'T I TELL YOU?
SPELLER
As Weylin dragged me to the door, I managed to twist around to face Nigel and mouth "Get Kevin."
SPELLER
I thought Kevin was in the house. I thought he would hear me if I screamed.
And I would be screaming shortly.

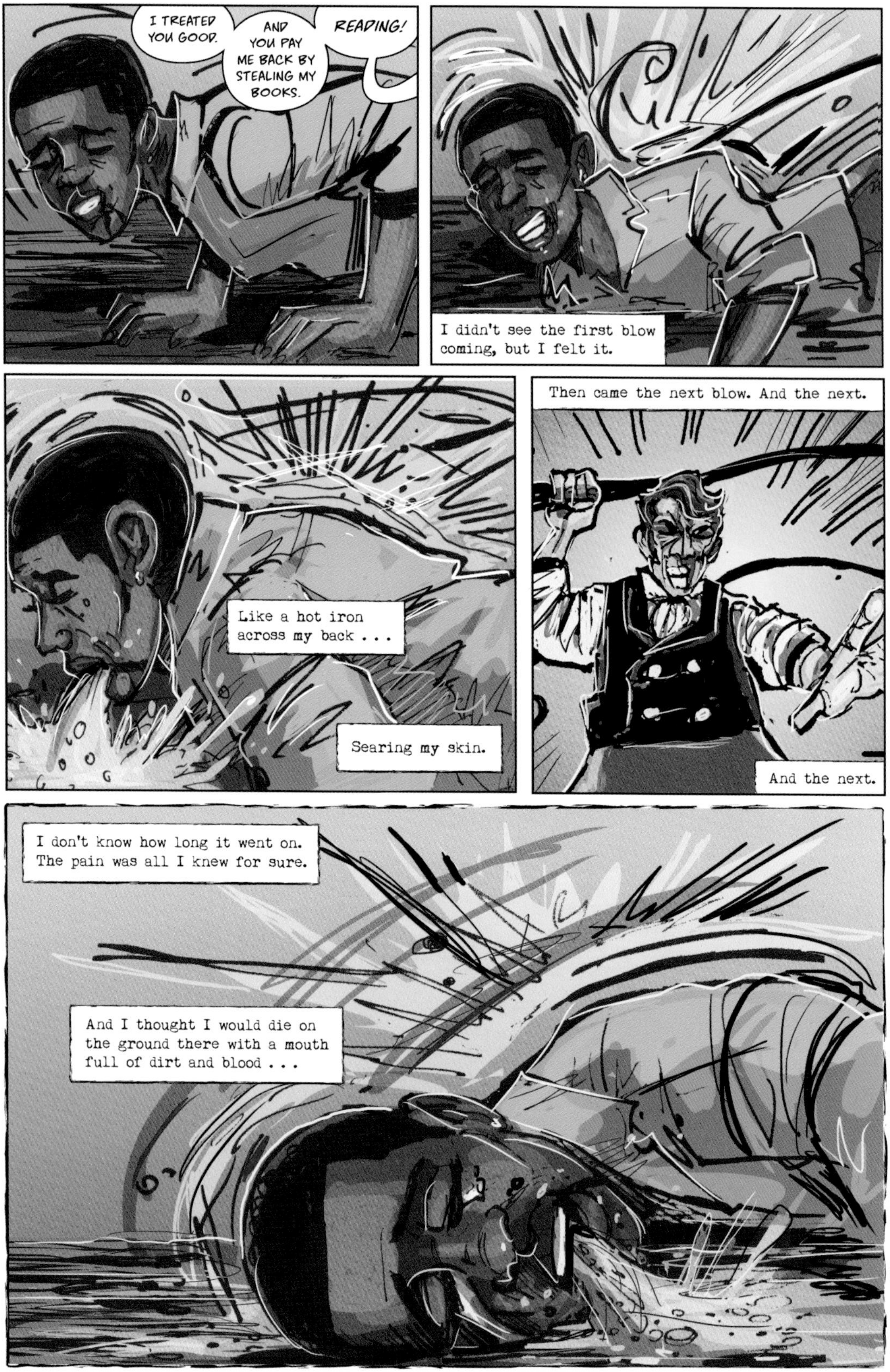

I TREATED YOU GOOD.
AND YOU PAY ME BACK BY STEALING MY BOOKS.
READING!
I didn't see the first blow coming, but I felt it.
Like a hot iron across my back . . .
Searing my skin.
Then came the next blow. And the next.
And the next.
I don't know how long it went on. The pain was all I knew for sure.
And I thought I would die on the ground there with a mouth full of dirt and blood . . .

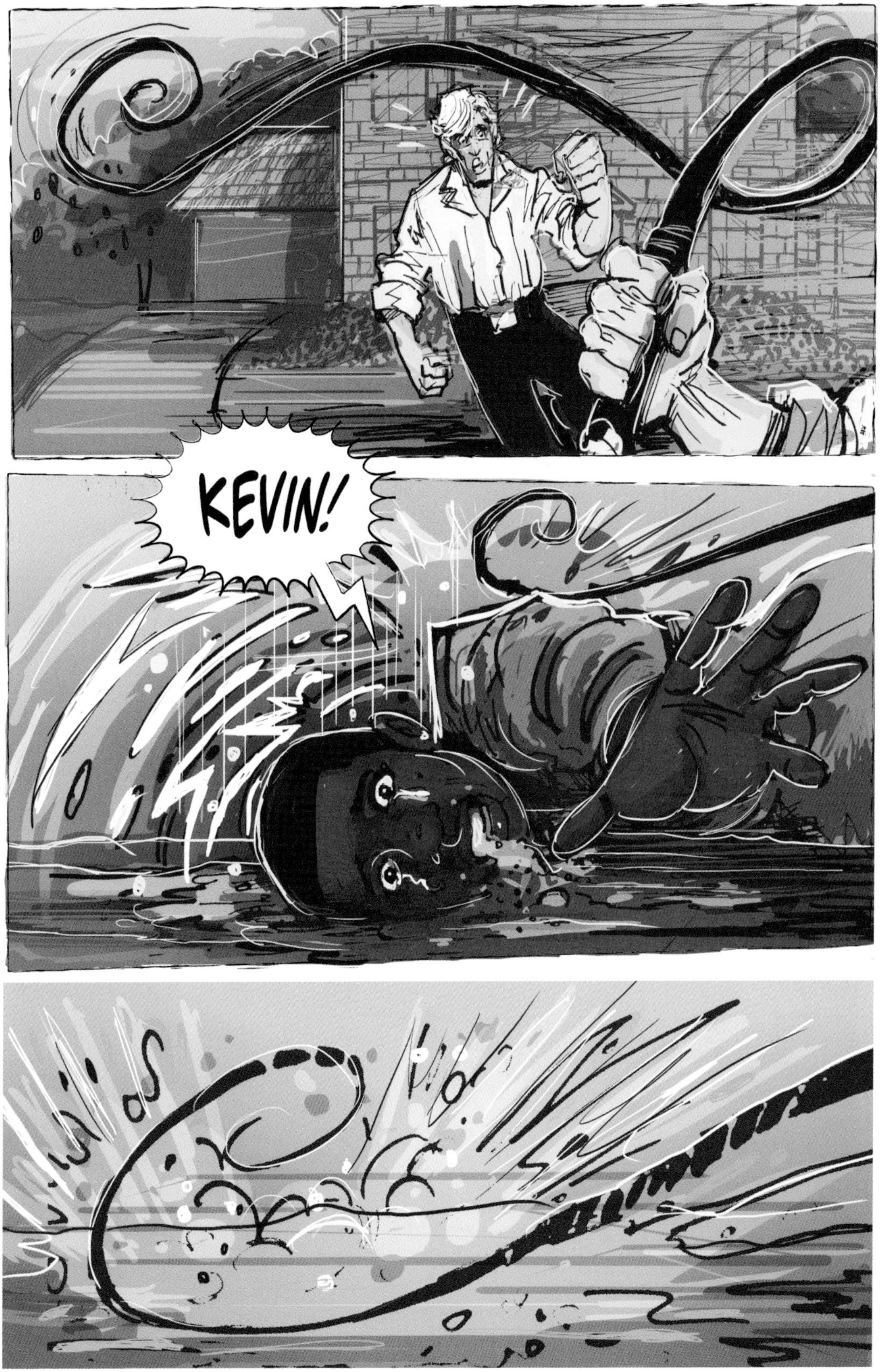
KEVIN!

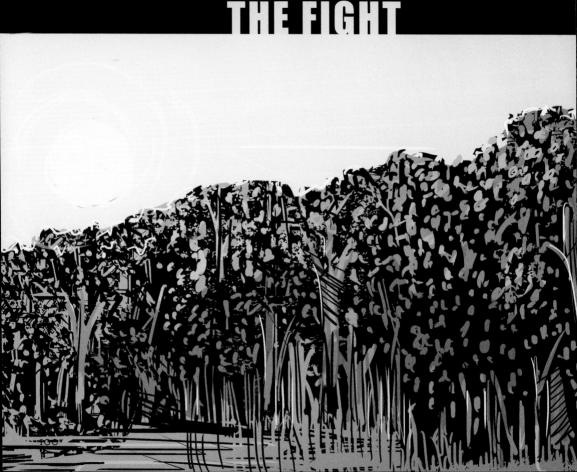

THE FIGHT

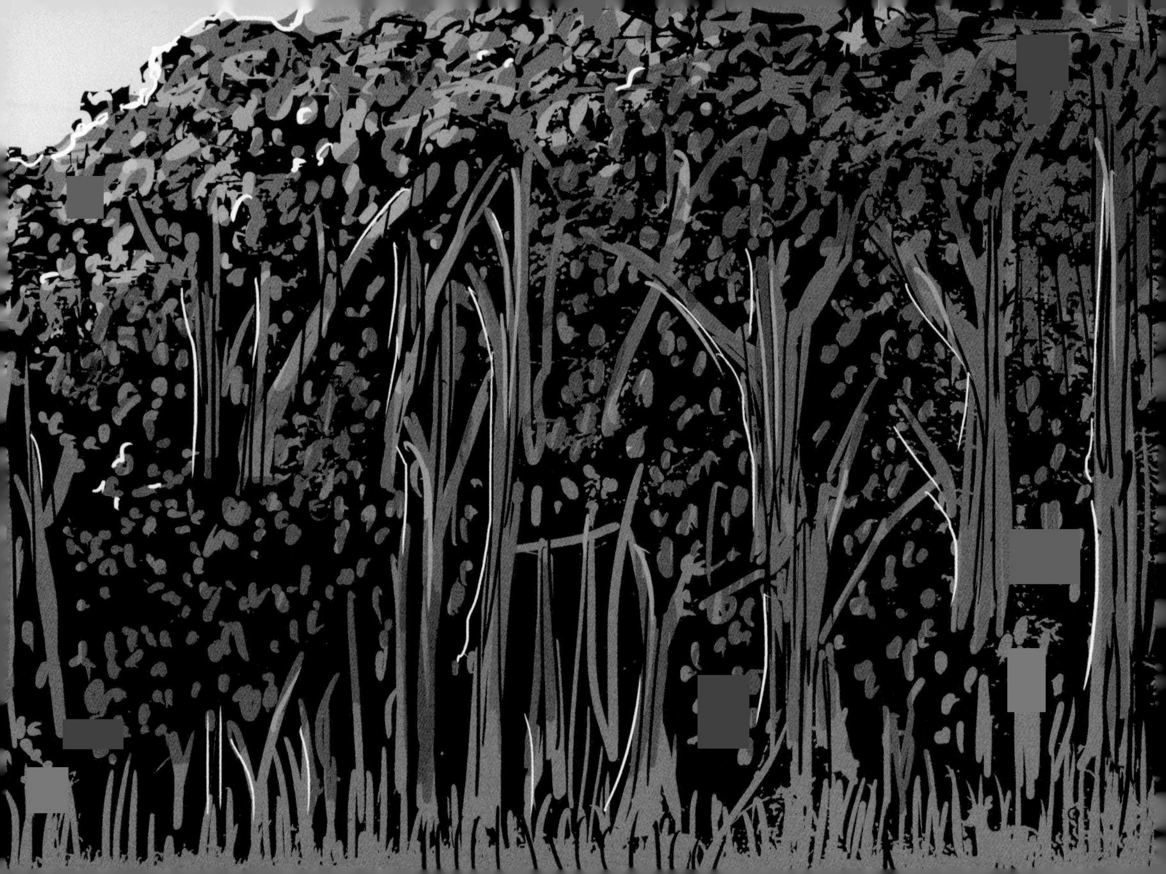

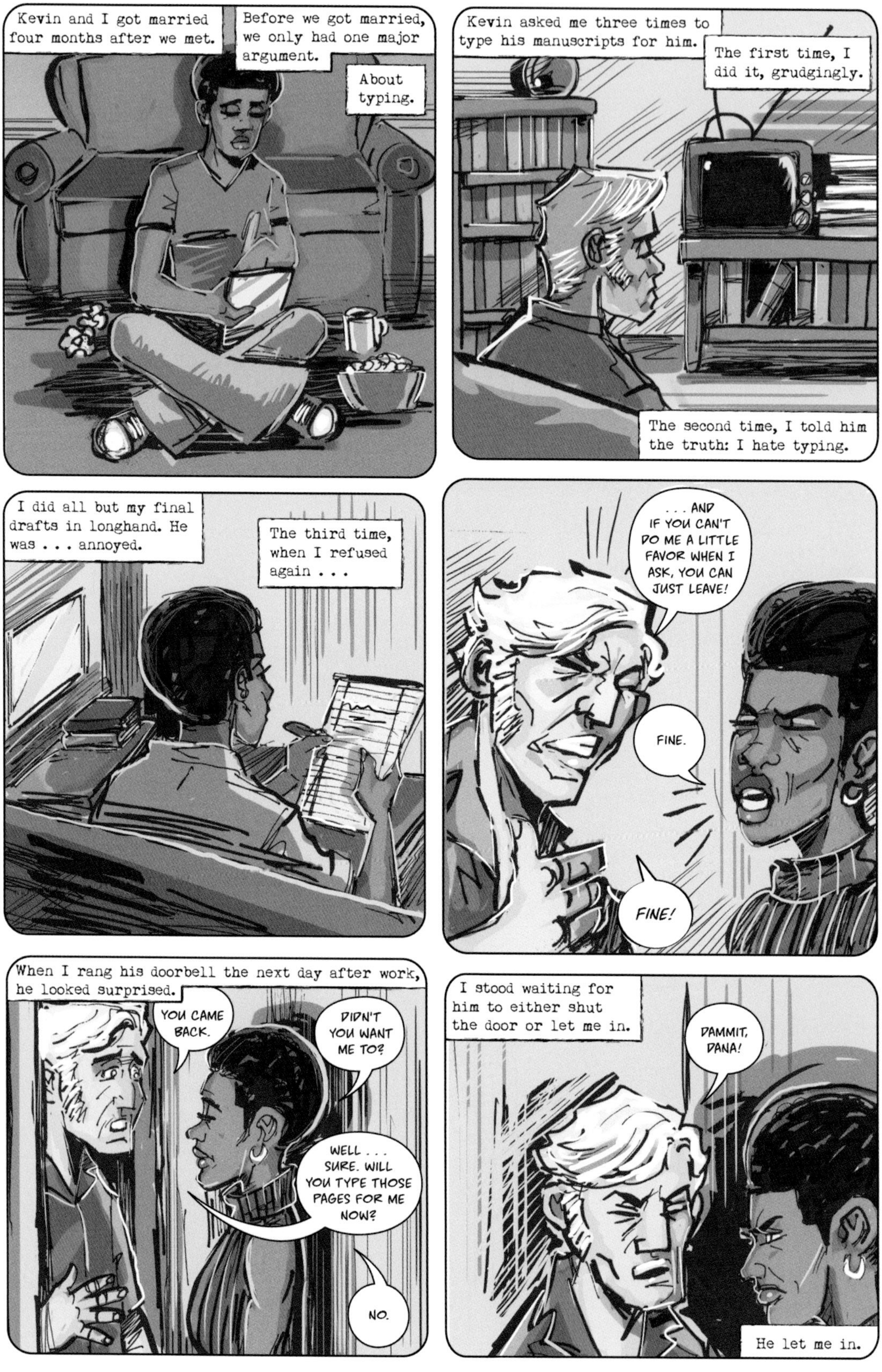
Kevin and I got married four months after we met.
Before we got married, we only had one major argument.
About typing.
Kevin asked me three times to type his manuscripts for him.
The first time, I did it, grudgingly.
The second time, I told him the truth: I hate typing.
I did all but my final drafts in longhand. He was . . . annoyed.
The third time, when I refused again . . .
. . . AND IF YOU CAN'T DO ME A LITTLE FAVOR WHEN I ASK, YOU CAN JUST LEAVE!
FINE.
FINE!
When I rang his doorbell the next day after work, he looked surprised.
YOU CAME BACK.
DIDN'T YOU WANT ME TO?
WELL . . . SURE. WILL YOU TYPE THOSE PAGES FOR ME NOW?
NO.
I stood waiting for him to either shut the door or let me in.
DAMMIT, DANA!
He let me in.

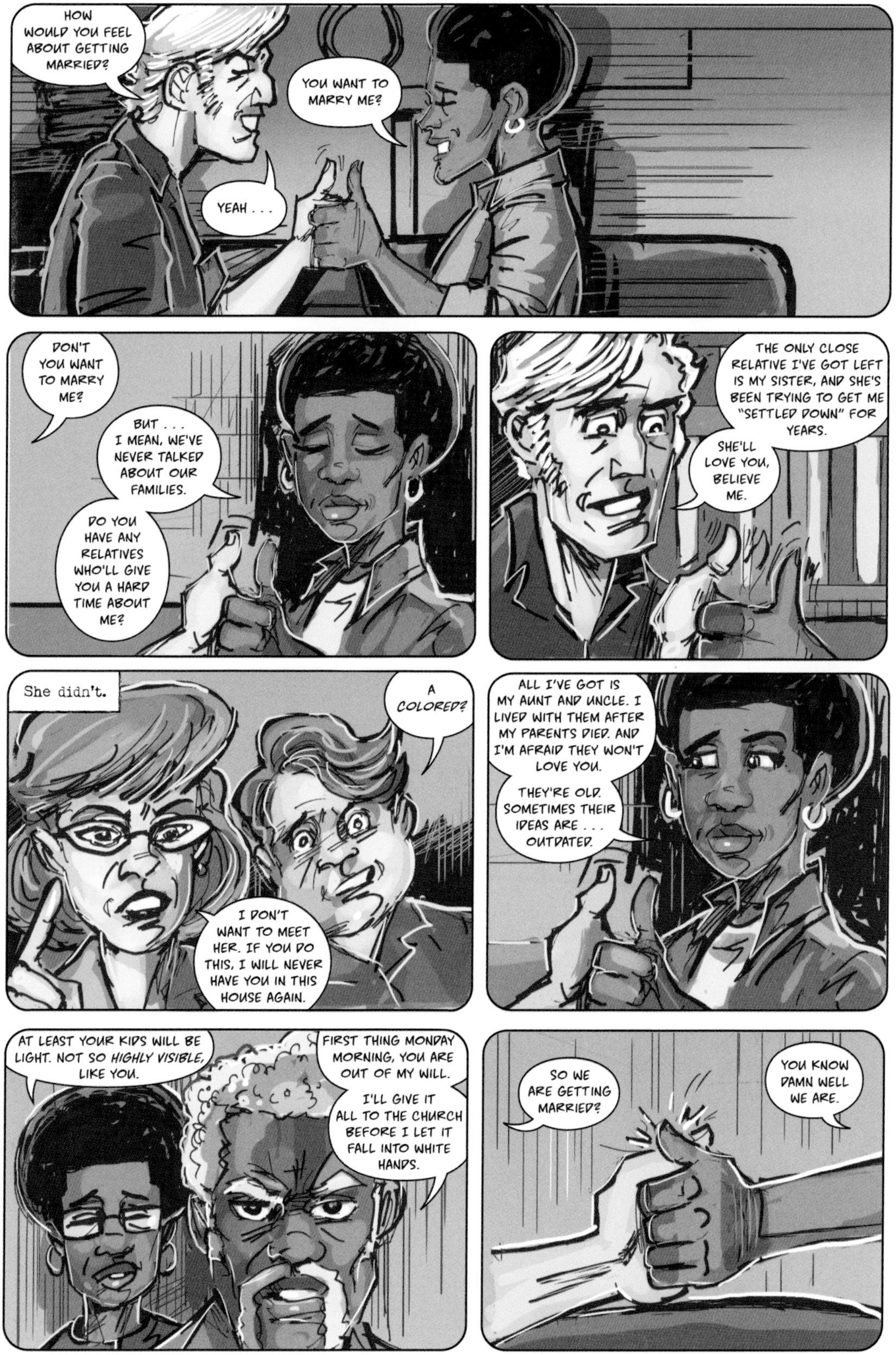
HOW WOULD YOU FEEL ABOUT GETTING MARRIED?
YOU WANT TO MARRY ME?
YEAH . . .
DON'T YOU WANT TO MARRY ME?
BUT . . . I MEAN, WE'VE NEVER TALKED ABOUT OUR FAMILIES.
DO YOU HAVE ANY RELATIVES WHO'LL GIVE YOU A HARD TIME ABOUT ME?
THE ONLY CLOSE RELATIVE I'VE GOT LEFT IS MY SISTER, AND SHE'S BEEN TRYING TO GET ME "SETTLED DOWN" FOR YEARS.
SHE'LL LOVE YOU, BELIEVE ME.
She didn't.
A COLORED?
I DON'T WANT TO MEET HER. IF YOU DO THIS, I WILL NEVER HAVE YOU IN THIS HOUSE AGAIN.
ALL I'VE GOT IS MY AUNT AND UNCLE. I LIVED WITH THEM AFTER MY PARENTS DIED. AND I'M AFRAID THEY WON'T LOVE YOU.
THEY'RE OLD. SOMETIMES THEIR IDEAS ARE . . . OUTDATED.
AT LEAST YOUR KIDS WILL BE LIGHT. NOT SO *HIGHLY VISIBLE*, LIKE YOU.
FIRST THING MONDAY MORNING, YOU ARE OUT OF MY WILL.
I'LL GIVE IT ALL TO THE CHURCH BEFORE I LET IT FALL INTO WHITE HANDS.
SO WE ARE GETTING MARRIED?
YOU KNOW DAMN WELL WE ARE.

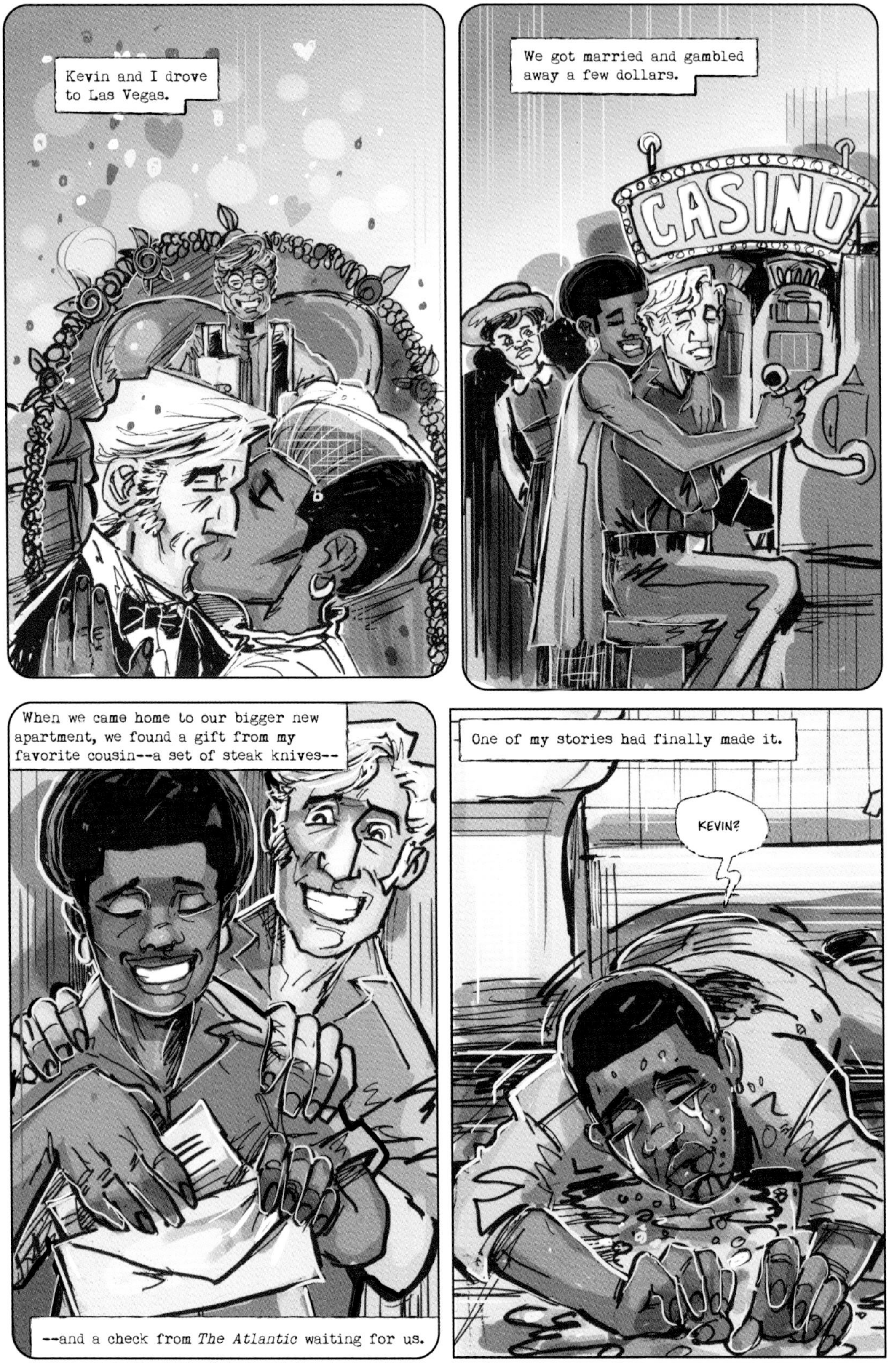
Kevin and I drove to Las Vegas.
We got married and gambled away a few dollars.
CASINO
When we came home to our bigger new apartment, we found a gift from my favorite cousin--a set of steak knives--
--and a check from The Atlantic waiting for us.
One of my stories had finally made it.
KEVIN?

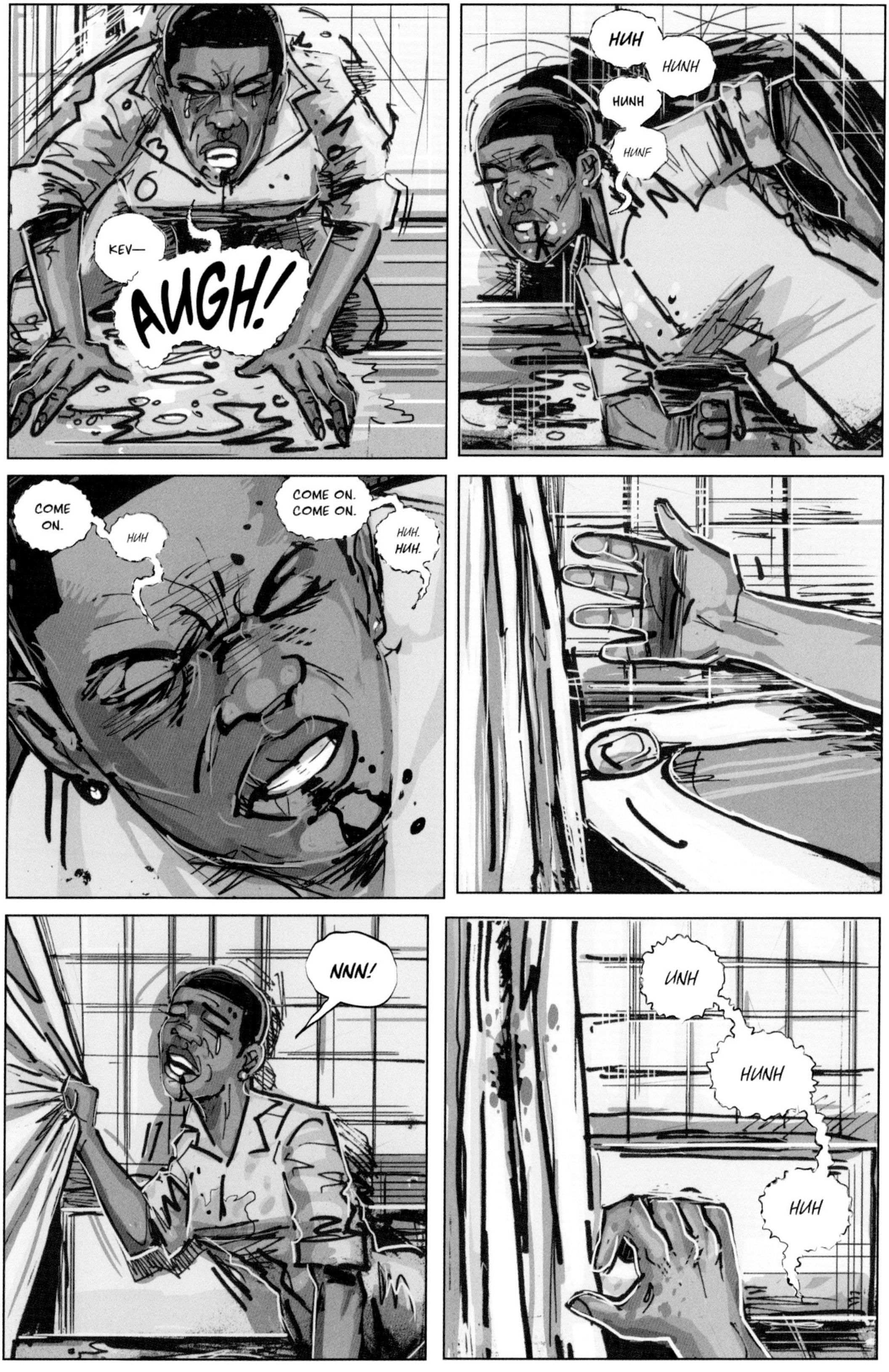
KEV—
AUGH!
HUH
HUNH
HUNH
HUNF
COME ON.
HUH
COME ON. COME ON.
HUH. HUH.
NNN!
UNH
HUNH
HUH

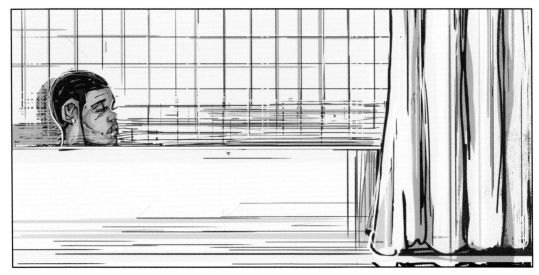

Every move only managed to stretch the skin on my back.

Pain had never been a friend to me before, but now it forced reality on me.

Kept me sane.

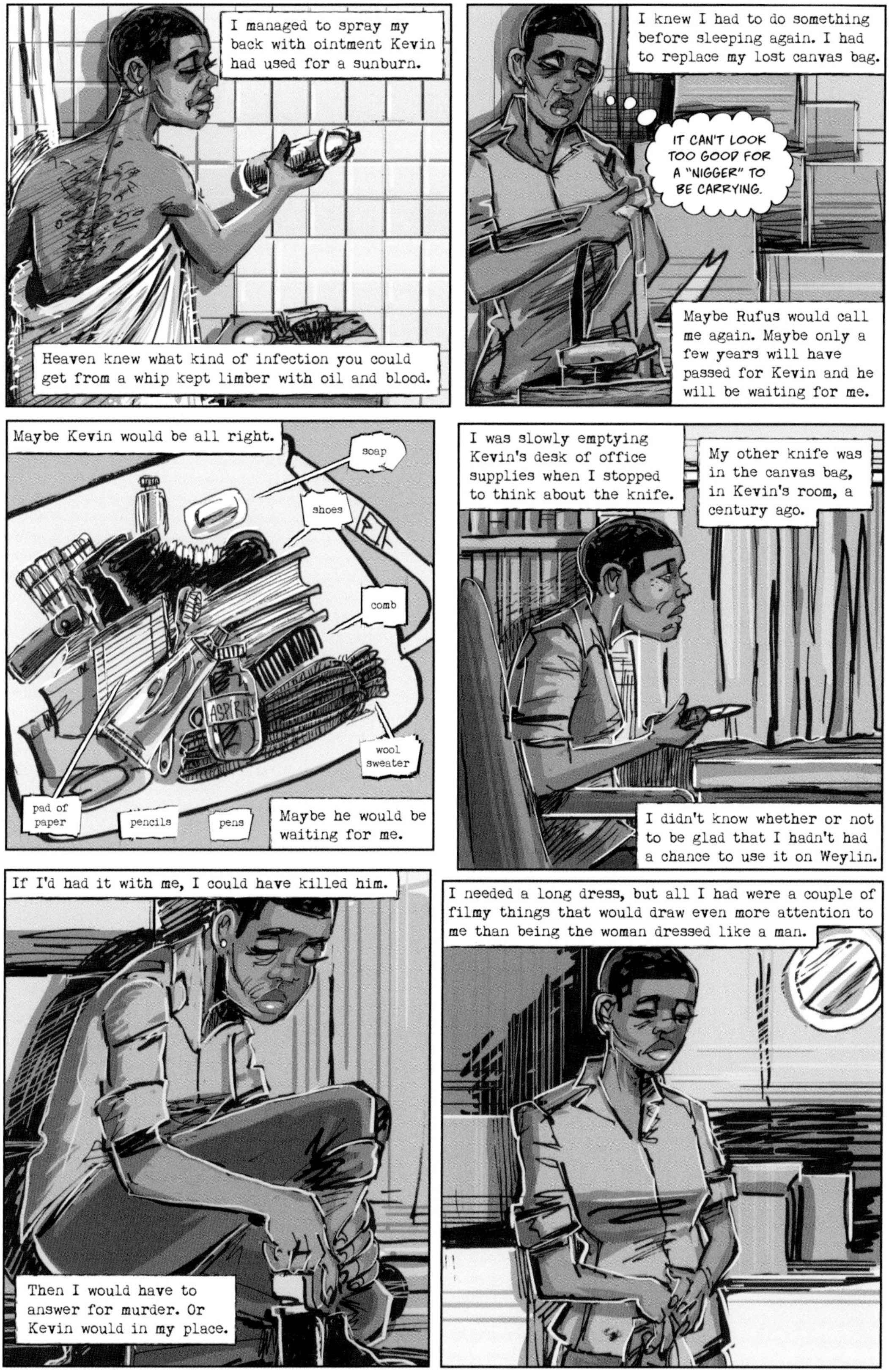
I managed to spray my back with ointment Kevin had used for a sunburn.
Heaven knew what kind of infection you could get from a whip kept limber with oil and blood.
I knew I had to do something before sleeping again. I had to replace my lost canvas bag.
IT CAN'T LOOK TOO GOOD FOR A "NIGGER" TO BE CARRYING.
Maybe Rufus would call me again. Maybe only a few years will have passed for Kevin and he will be waiting for me.
Maybe Kevin would be all right.
soap
shoes
comb
ASPIRIN
wool sweater
pad of paper
pencils
pens
Maybe he would be waiting for me.
I was slowly emptying Kevin's desk of office supplies when I stopped to think about the knife.
My other knife was in the canvas bag, in Kevin's room, a century ago.
I didn't know whether or not to be glad that I hadn't had a chance to use it on Weylin.
If I'd had it with me, I could have killed him.
Then I would have to answer for murder. Or Kevin would in my place.
I needed a long dress, but all I had were a couple of filmy things that would draw even more attention to me than being the woman dressed like a man.

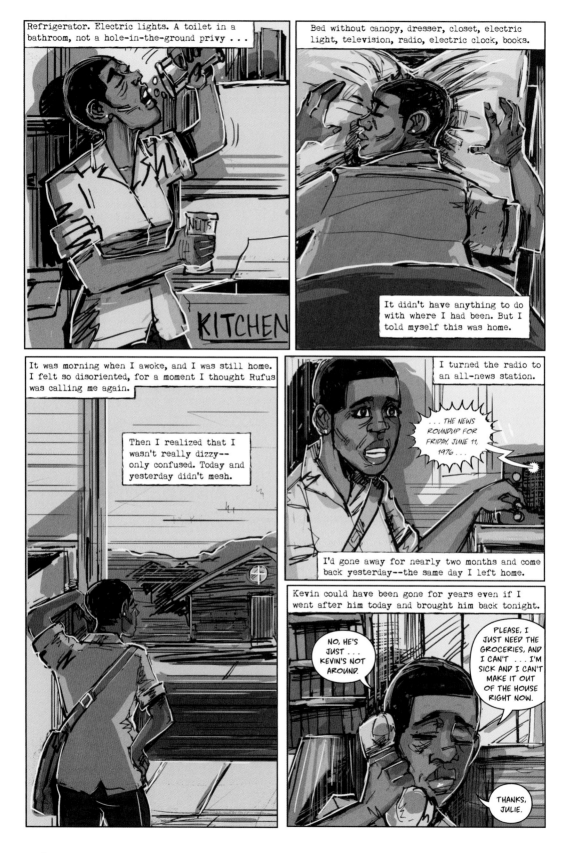

Refrigerator. Electric lights. A toilet in a bathroom, not a hole-in-the-ground privy . . .

KITCHEN

Bed without canopy, dresser, closet, electric light, television, radio, electric clock, books.

It didn't have anything to do with where I had been. But I told myself this was home.

It was morning when I awoke, and I was still home. I felt so disoriented, for a moment I thought Rufus was calling me again.

Then I realized that I wasn't really dizzy-- only confused. Today and yesterday didn't mesh.

I turned the radio to an all-news station.

. . . THE NEWS ROUNDUP FOR FRIDAY, JUNE 11, 1976 . . .

I'd gone away for nearly two months and come back yesterday--the same day I left home.

Kevin could have been gone for years even if I went after him today and brought him back tonight.

NO, HE'S JUST . . . KEVIN'S NOT AROUND.

PLEASE, I JUST NEED THE GROCERIES, AND I CAN'T . . . I'M SICK AND I CAN'T MAKE IT OUT OF THE HOUSE RIGHT NOW.

THANKS, JULIE.

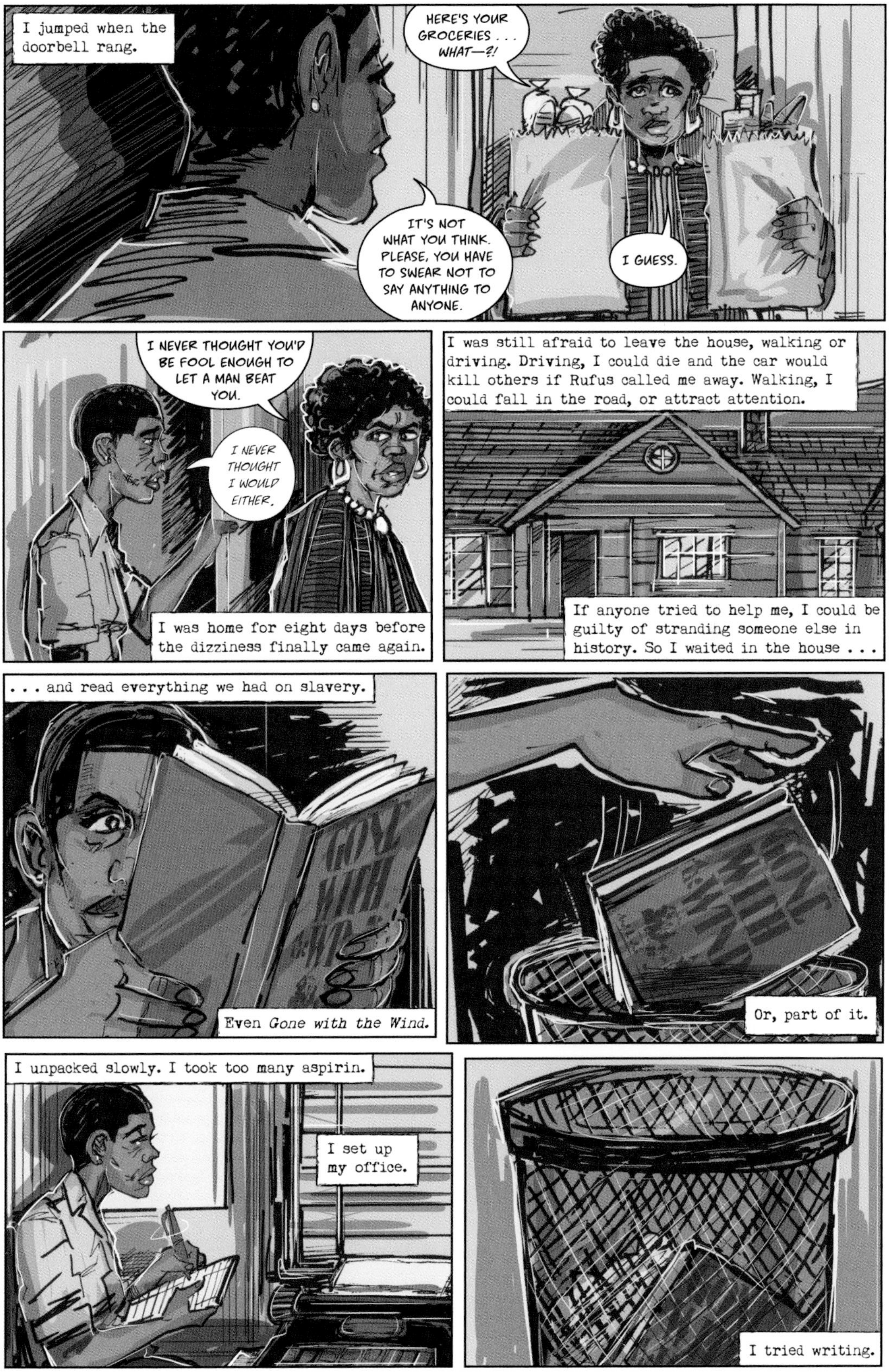
I jumped when the doorbell rang.
HERE'S YOUR GROCERIES . . . WHAT—?!
IT'S NOT WHAT YOU THINK. PLEASE, YOU HAVE TO SWEAR NOT TO SAY ANYTHING TO ANYONE.
I GUESS.
I NEVER THOUGHT YOU'D BE FOOL ENOUGH TO LET A MAN BEAT YOU.
I NEVER THOUGHT I WOULD EITHER.
I was home for eight days before the dizziness finally came again.
I was still afraid to leave the house, walking or driving. Driving, I could die and the car would kill others if Rufus called me away. Walking, I could fall in the road, or attract attention.
If anyone tried to help me, I could be guilty of stranding someone else in history. So I waited in the house . . .
. . . and read everything we had on slavery.
Even *Gone with the Wind*.
Or, part of it.
I unpacked slowly. I took too many aspirin.
I set up my office.
I tried writing.

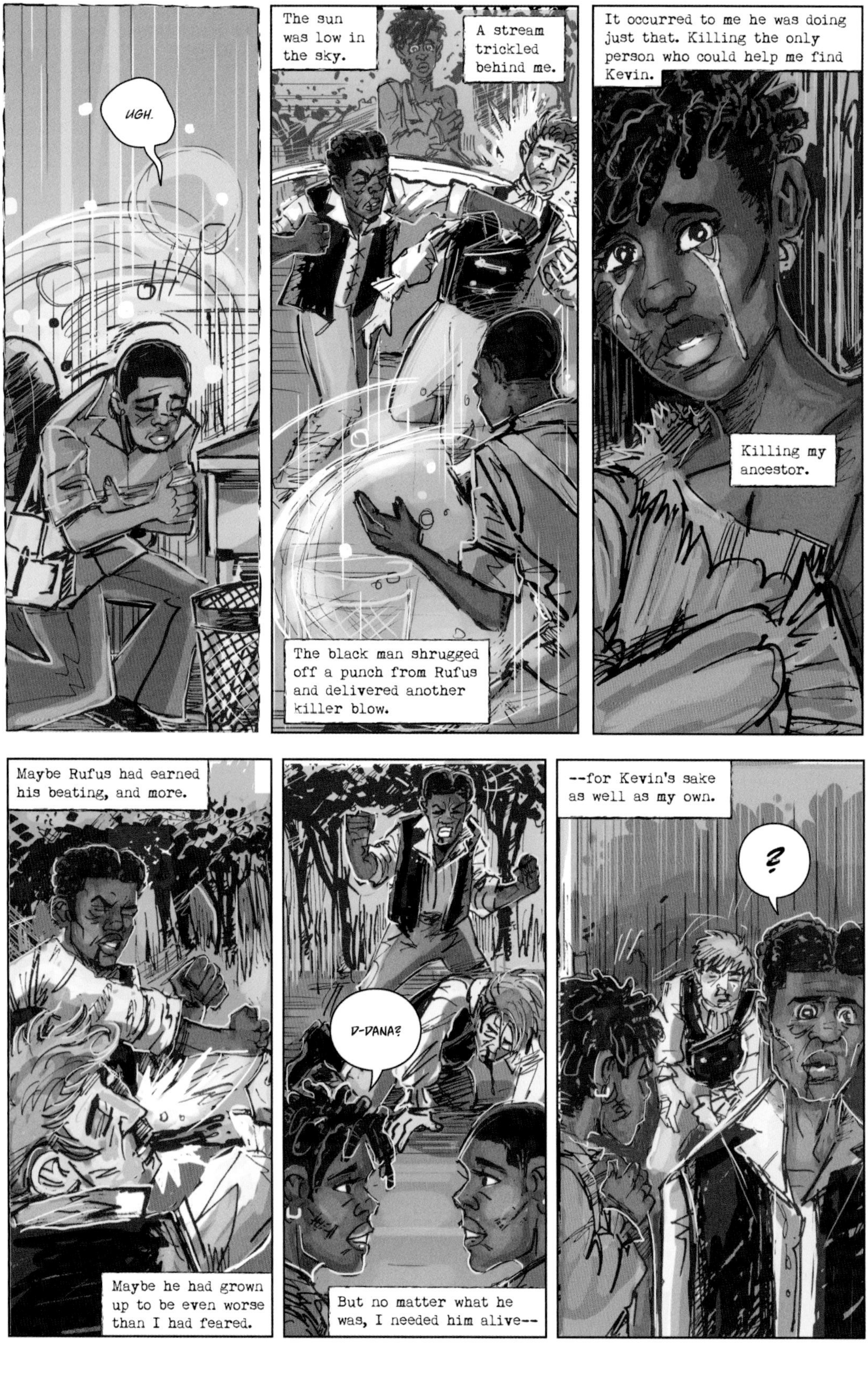

UGH.
The sun was low in the sky.
A stream trickled behind me.
The black man shrugged off a punch from Rufus and delivered another killer blow.
It occurred to me he was doing just that. Killing the only person who could help me find Kevin.
Killing my ancestor.
Maybe Rufus had earned his beating, and more.
Maybe he had grown up to be even worse than I had feared.
D-DANA?
But no matter what he was, I needed him alive--
--for Kevin's sake as well as my own.
?

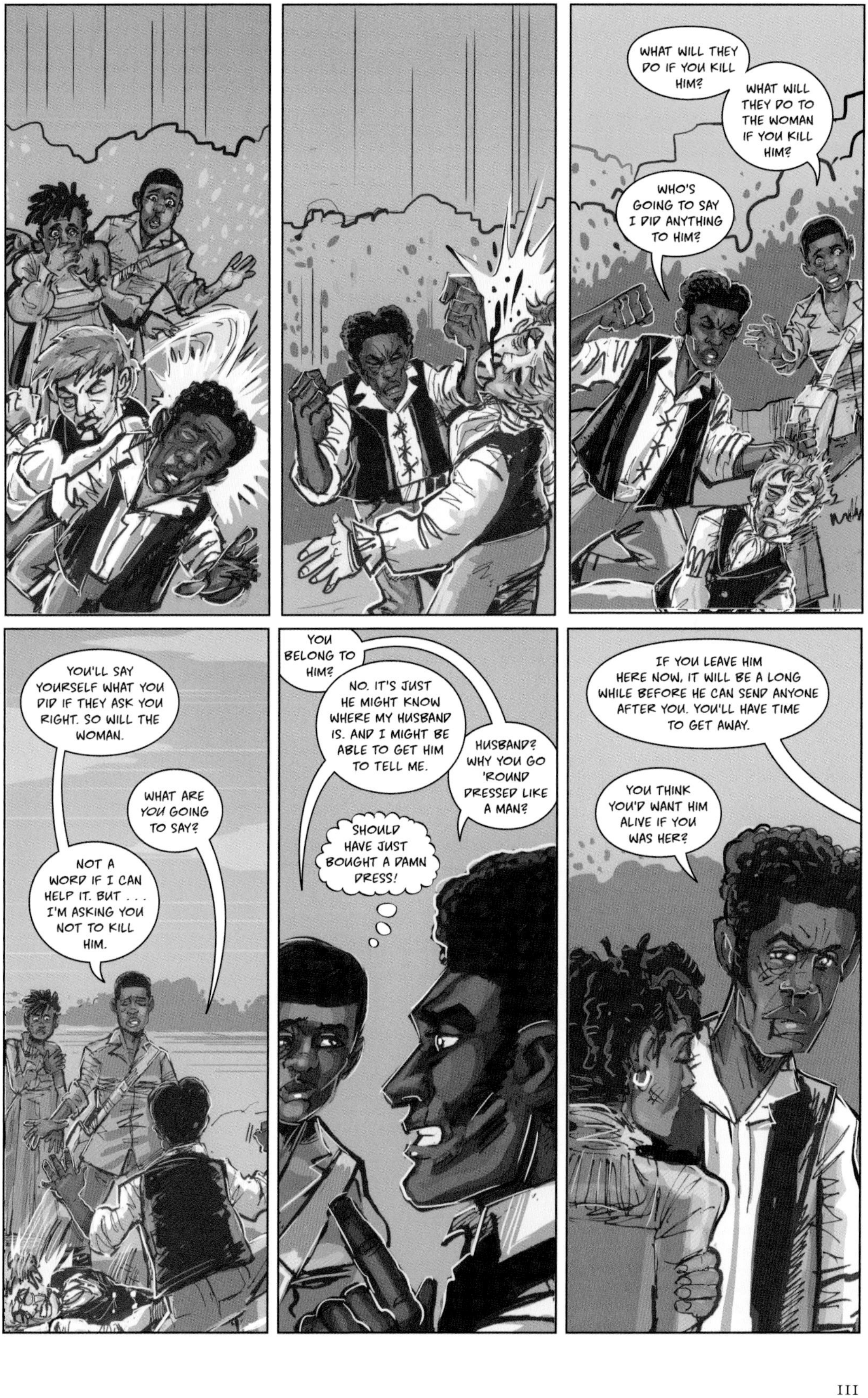
WHAT WILL THEY DO IF YOU KILL HIM?
WHAT WILL THEY DO TO THE WOMAN IF YOU KILL HIM?
WHO'S GOING TO SAY I DID ANYTHING TO HIM?
YOU'LL SAY YOURSELF WHAT YOU DID IF THEY ASK YOU RIGHT. SO WILL THE WOMAN.
WHAT ARE YOU GOING TO SAY?
NOT A WORD IF I CAN HELP IT. BUT . . . I'M ASKING YOU NOT TO KILL HIM.
YOU BELONG TO HIM?
NO. IT'S JUST HE MIGHT KNOW WHERE MY HUSBAND IS. AND I MIGHT BE ABLE TO GET HIM TO TELL ME.
HUSBAND? WHY YOU GO 'ROUND DRESSED LIKE A MAN?
SHOULD HAVE JUST BOUGHT A DAMN DRESS!
IF YOU LEAVE HIM HERE NOW, IT WILL BE A LONG WHILE BEFORE HE CAN SEND ANYONE AFTER YOU. YOU'LL HAVE TIME TO GET AWAY.
YOU THINK YOU'D WANT HIM ALIVE IF YOU WAS HER?

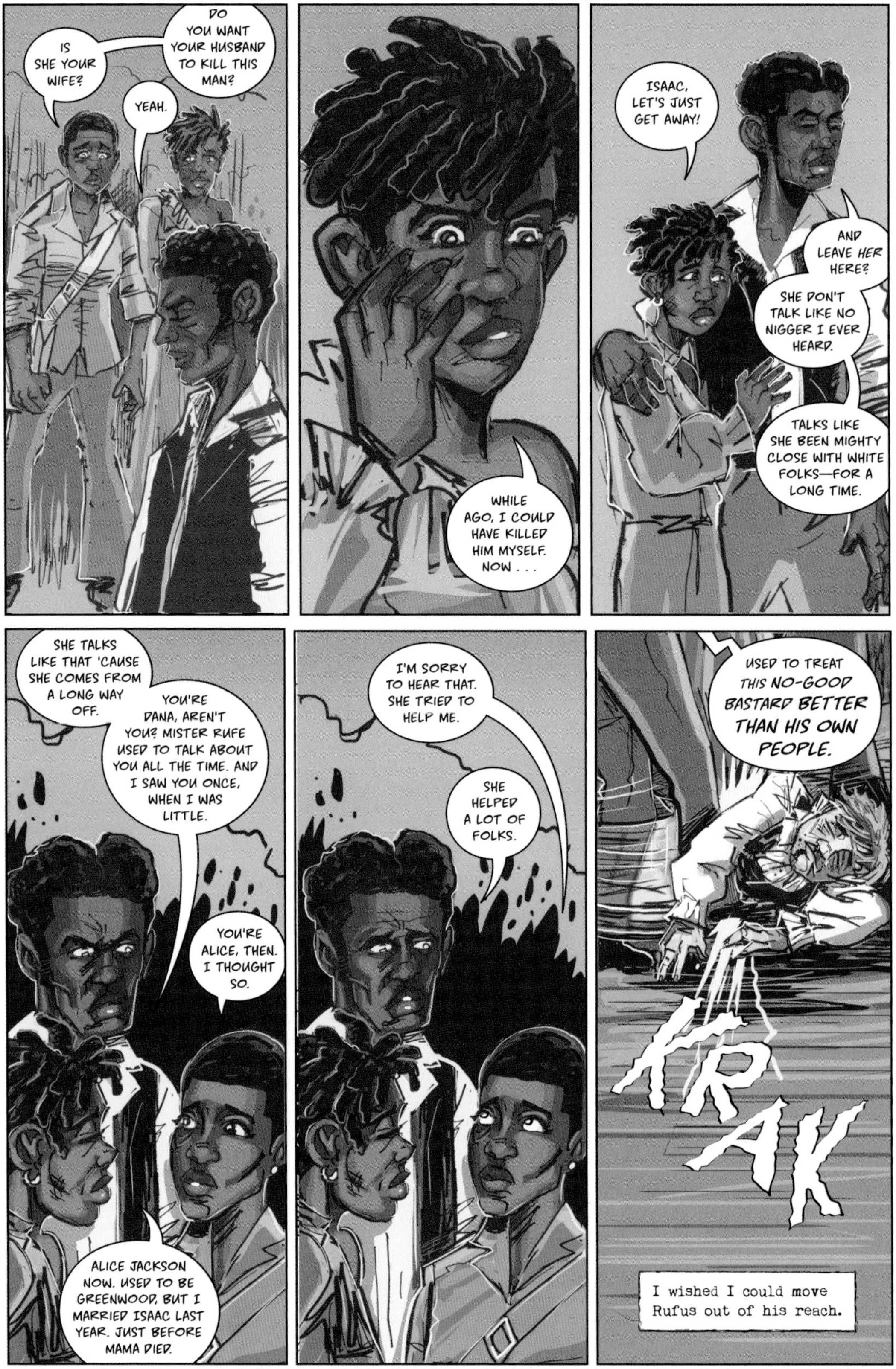
IS SHE YOUR WIFE?
YEAH.
DO YOU WANT YOUR HUSBAND TO KILL THIS MAN?
WHILE AGO, I COULD HAVE KILLED HIM MYSELF. NOW . . .
ISAAC, LET'S JUST GET AWAY!
AND LEAVE HER HERE?
SHE DON'T TALK LIKE NO NIGGER I EVER HEARD.
TALKS LIKE SHE BEEN MIGHTY CLOSE WITH WHITE FOLKS—FOR A LONG TIME.
SHE TALKS LIKE THAT 'CAUSE SHE COMES FROM A LONG WAY OFF.
YOU'RE DANA, AREN'T YOU? MISTER RUFE USED TO TALK ABOUT YOU ALL THE TIME. AND I SAW YOU ONCE, WHEN I WAS LITTLE.
YOU'RE ALICE, THEN. I THOUGHT SO.
ALICE JACKSON NOW. USED TO BE GREENWOOD, BUT I MARRIED ISAAC LAST YEAR. JUST BEFORE MAMA DIED.
I'M SORRY TO HEAR THAT. SHE TRIED TO HELP ME.
SHE HELPED A LOT OF FOLKS.
USED TO TREAT *THIS* NO-GOOD BASTARD BETTER THAN HIS OWN PEOPLE.
KRAK
I wished I could move Rufus out of his reach.

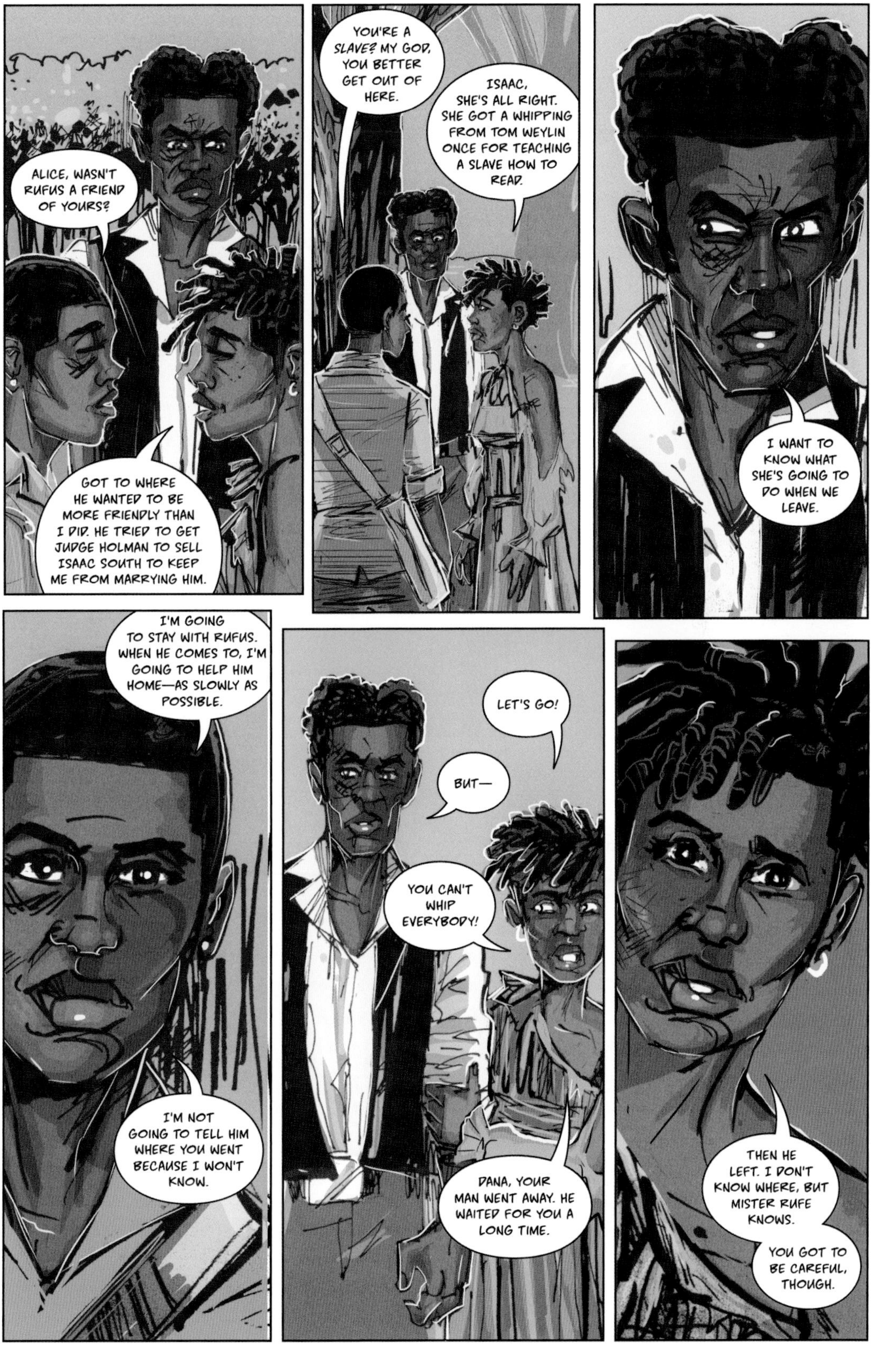
ALICE, WASN'T RUFUS A FRIEND OF YOURS?
GOT TO WHERE HE WANTED TO BE MORE FRIENDLY THAN I DID. HE TRIED TO GET JUDGE HOLMAN TO SELL ISAAC SOUTH TO KEEP ME FROM MARRYING HIM.
YOU'RE A SLAVE? MY GOD, YOU BETTER GET OUT OF HERE.
ISAAC, SHE'S ALL RIGHT. SHE GOT A WHIPPING FROM TOM WEYLIN ONCE FOR TEACHING A SLAVE HOW TO READ.
I WANT TO KNOW WHAT SHE'S GOING TO DO WHEN WE LEAVE.
I'M GOING TO STAY WITH RUFUS. WHEN HE COMES TO, I'M GOING TO HELP HIM HOME—AS SLOWLY AS POSSIBLE.
I'M NOT GOING TO TELL HIM WHERE YOU WENT BECAUSE I WON'T KNOW.
LET'S GO!
BUT—
YOU CAN'T WHIP EVERYBODY!
DANA, YOUR MAN WENT AWAY. HE WAITED FOR YOU A LONG TIME.
THEN HE LEFT. I DON'T KNOW WHERE, BUT MISTER RUFE KNOWS.
YOU GOT TO BE CAREFUL, THOUGH.

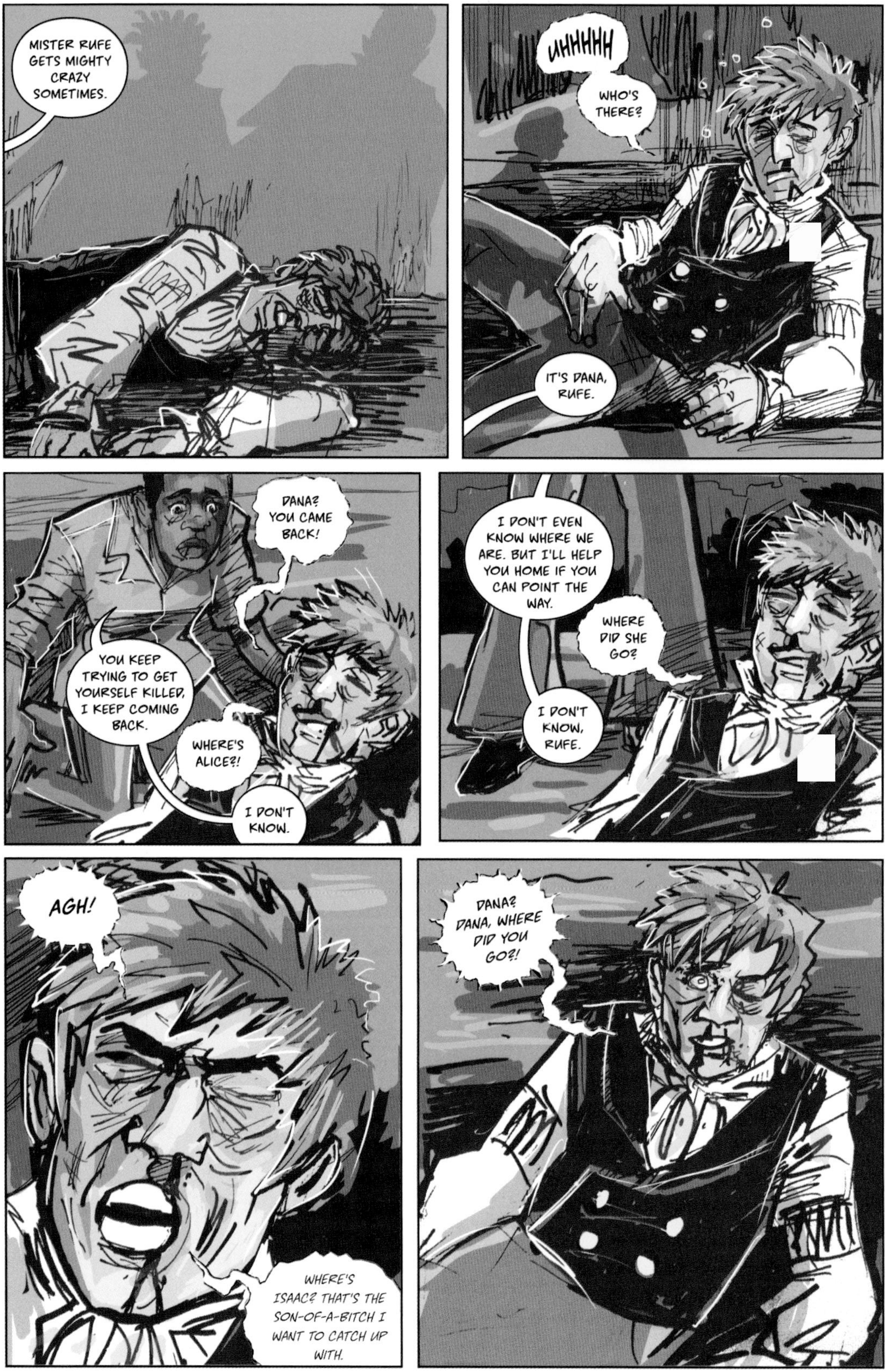
MISTER RUFE GETS MIGHTY CRAZY SOMETIMES.
UHHHHH
WHO'S THERE?
IT'S DANA, RUFE.
DANA? YOU CAME BACK!
YOU KEEP TRYING TO GET YOURSELF KILLED, I KEEP COMING BACK.
WHERE'S ALICE?!
I DON'T KNOW.
I DON'T EVEN KNOW WHERE WE ARE. BUT I'LL HELP YOU HOME IF YOU CAN POINT THE WAY.
WHERE DID SHE GO?
I DON'T KNOW, RUFE.
AGH!
WHERE'S ISAAC? THAT'S THE SON-OF-A-BITCH I WANT TO CATCH UP WITH.
DANA? DANA, WHERE DID YOU GO?!

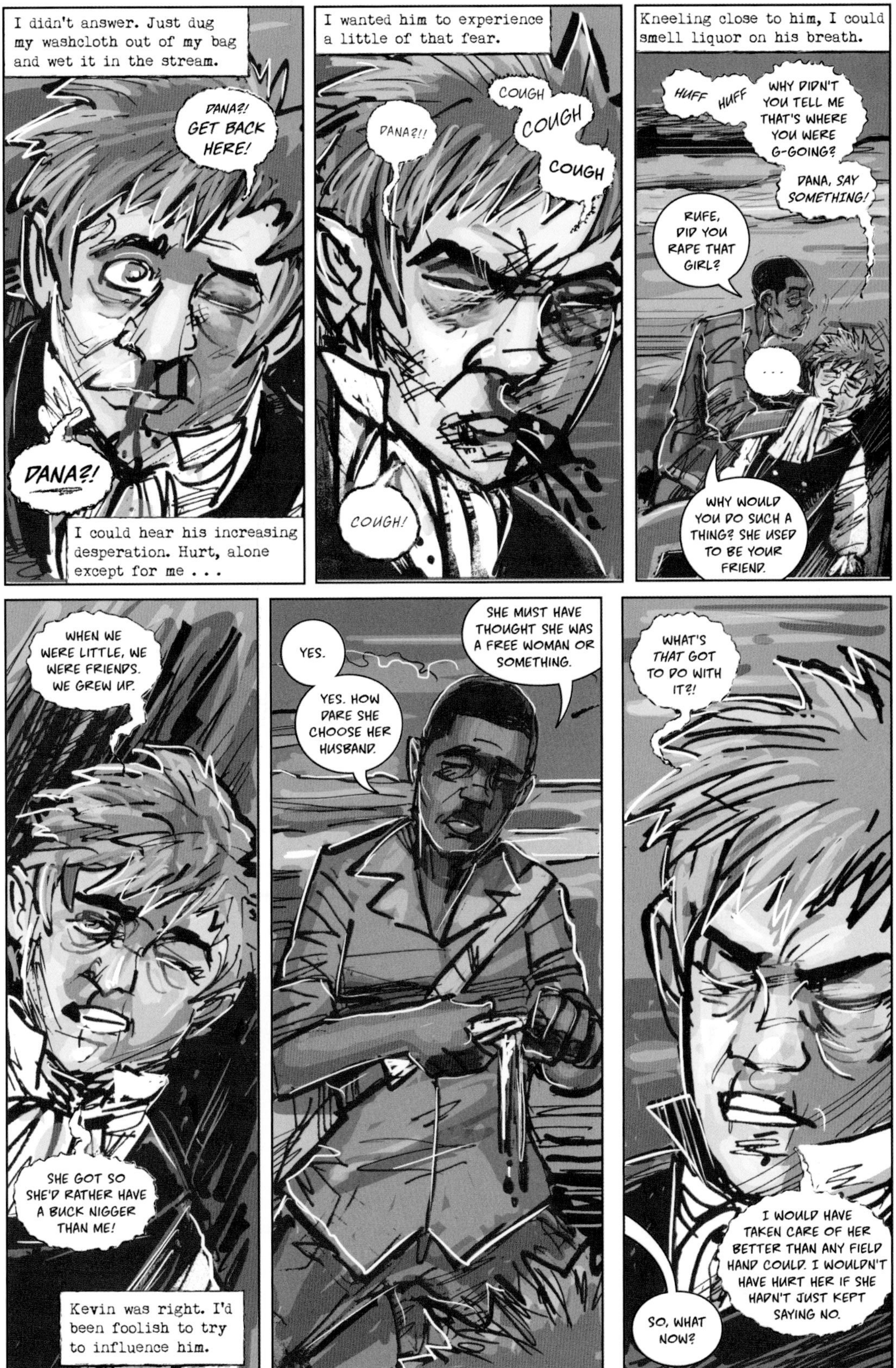

I didn't answer. Just dug my washcloth out of my bag and wet it in the stream.
DANA?! GET BACK HERE!
DANA?!
I could hear his increasing desperation. Hurt, alone except for me . . .
I wanted him to experience a little of that fear.
DANA?!!
COUGH
COUGH
COUGH
COUGH!
Kneeling close to him, I could smell liquor on his breath.
HUFF HUFF
WHY DIDN'T YOU TELL ME THAT'S WHERE YOU WERE G-GOING?
DANA, SAY SOMETHING!
RUFE, DID YOU RAPE THAT GIRL?
. . .
WHY WOULD YOU DO SUCH A THING? SHE USED TO BE YOUR FRIEND.
WHEN WE WERE LITTLE, WE WERE FRIENDS. WE GREW UP.
SHE GOT SO SHE'D RATHER HAVE A BUCK NIGGER THAN ME!
Kevin was right. I'd been foolish to try to influence him.
YES.
SHE MUST HAVE THOUGHT SHE WAS A FREE WOMAN OR SOMETHING.
YES. HOW DARE SHE CHOOSE HER HUSBAND.
WHAT'S THAT GOT TO DO WITH IT?!
I WOULD HAVE TAKEN CARE OF HER BETTER THAN ANY FIELD HAND COULD. I WOULDN'T HAVE HURT HER IF SHE HADN'T JUST KEPT SAYING NO.
SO, WHAT NOW?

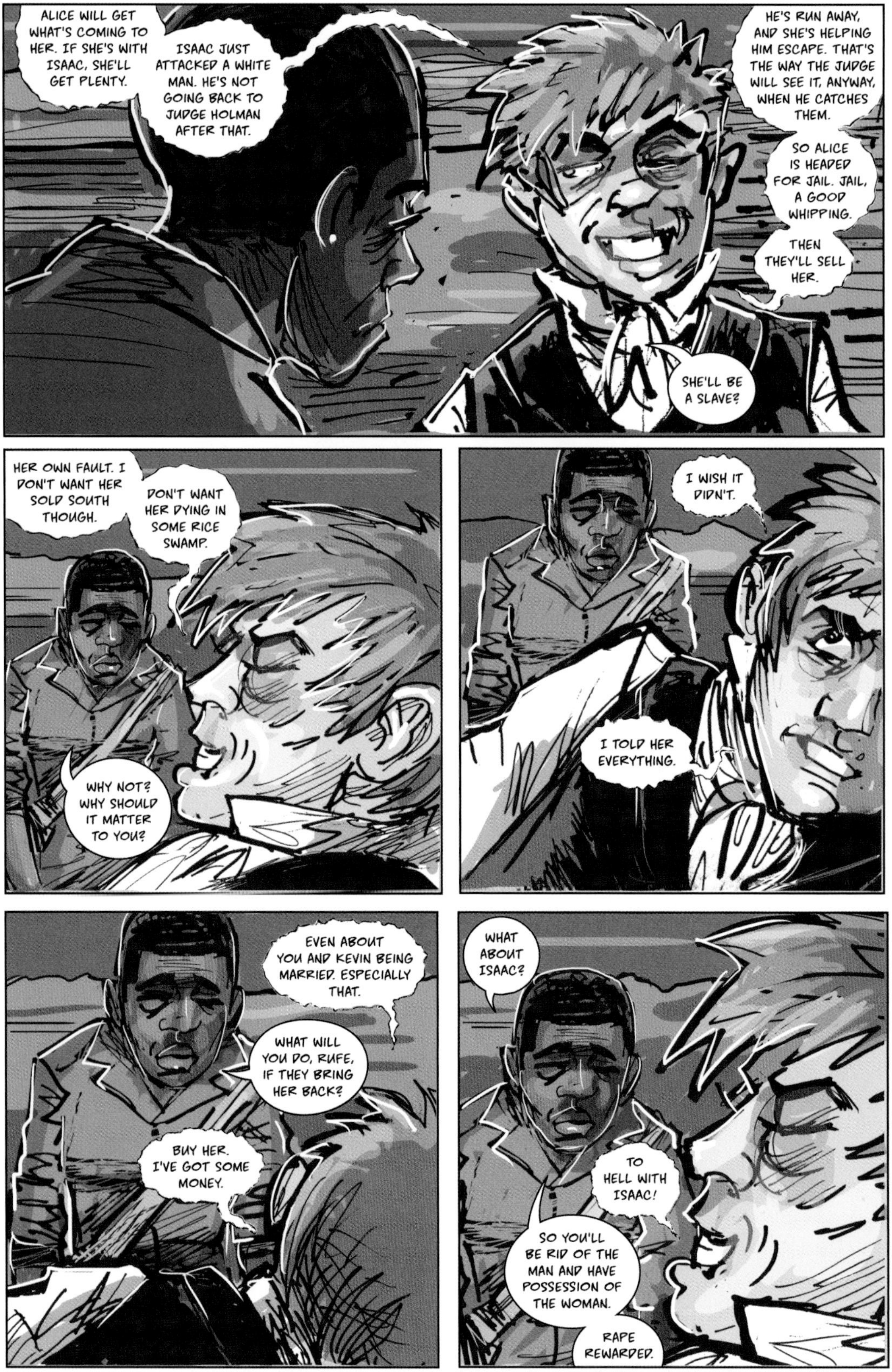
ALICE WILL GET WHAT'S COMING TO HER. IF SHE'S WITH ISAAC, SHE'LL GET PLENTY.
ISAAC JUST ATTACKED A WHITE MAN. HE'S NOT GOING BACK TO JUDGE HOLMAN AFTER THAT.
HE'S RUN AWAY, AND SHE'S HELPING HIM ESCAPE. THAT'S THE WAY THE JUDGE WILL SEE IT, ANYWAY, WHEN HE CATCHES THEM.
SO ALICE IS HEADED FOR JAIL. JAIL, A GOOD WHIPPING.
THEN THEY'LL SELL HER.
SHE'LL BE A SLAVE?
HER OWN FAULT. I DON'T WANT HER SOLD SOUTH THOUGH.
DON'T WANT HER DYING IN SOME RICE SWAMP.
WHY NOT? WHY SHOULD IT MATTER TO YOU?
I WISH IT DIDN'T.
I TOLD HER EVERYTHING.
EVEN ABOUT YOU AND KEVIN BEING MARRIED. ESPECIALLY THAT.
WHAT WILL YOU DO, RUFE, IF THEY BRING HER BACK?
BUY HER. I'VE GOT SOME MONEY.
WHAT ABOUT ISAAC?
TO HELL WITH ISAAC!
SO YOU'LL BE RID OF THE MAN AND HAVE POSSESSION OF THE WOMAN.
RAPE REWARDED.

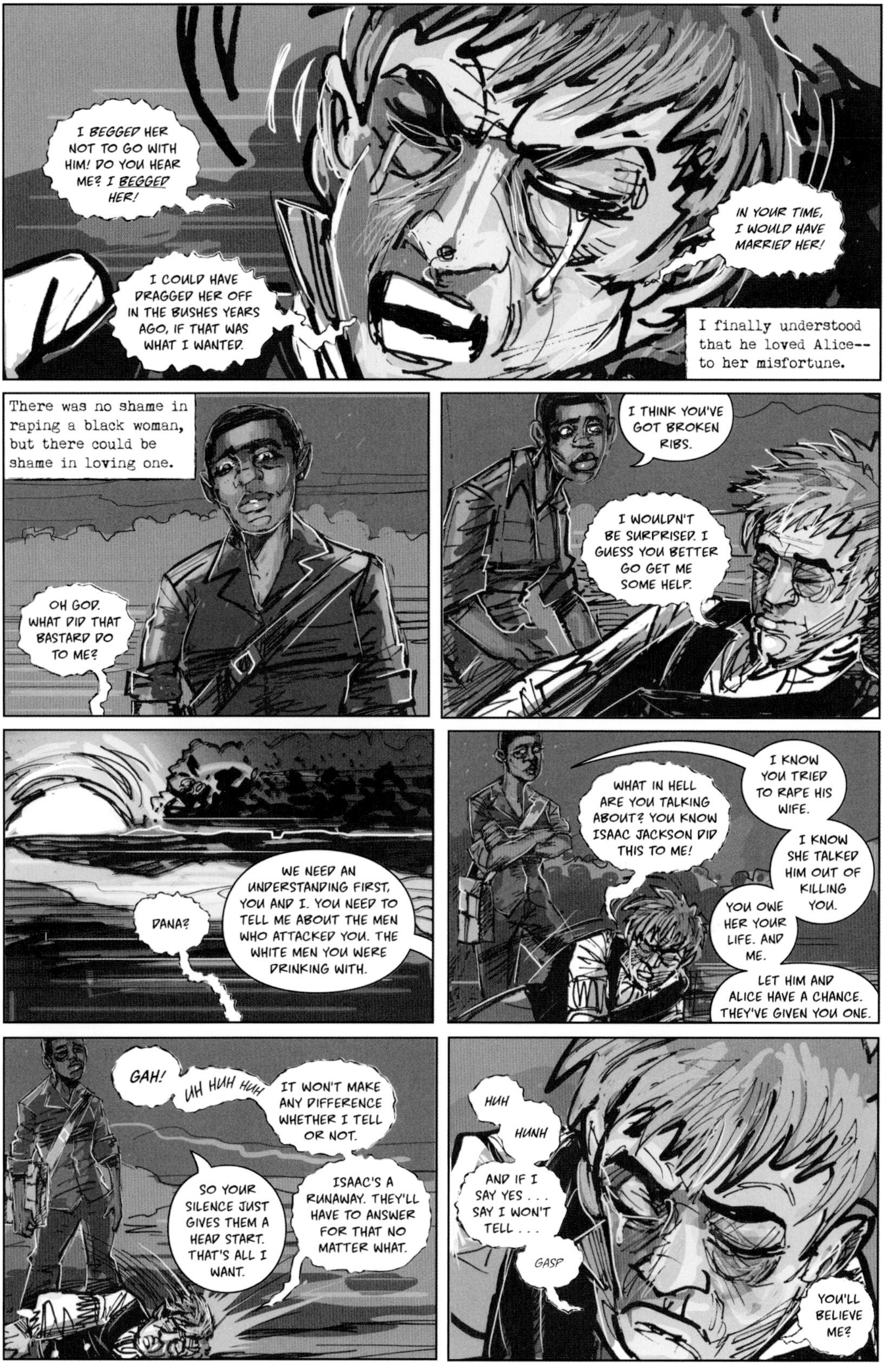
I BEGGED HER NOT TO GO WITH HIM! DO YOU HEAR ME? I BEGGED HER!
I COULD HAVE DRAGGED HER OFF IN THE BUSHES YEARS AGO, IF THAT WAS WHAT I WANTED.
IN YOUR TIME, I WOULD HAVE MARRIED HER!
I finally understood that he loved Alice-- to her misfortune.
There was no shame in raping a black woman, but there could be shame in loving one.
OH GOD. WHAT DID THAT BASTARD DO TO ME?
I THINK YOU'VE GOT BROKEN RIBS.
I WOULDN'T BE SURPRISED. I GUESS YOU BETTER GO GET ME SOME HELP.
DANA?
WE NEED AN UNDERSTANDING FIRST, YOU AND I. YOU NEED TO TELL ME ABOUT THE MEN WHO ATTACKED YOU. THE WHITE MEN YOU WERE DRINKING WITH.
WHAT IN HELL ARE YOU TALKING ABOUT? YOU KNOW ISAAC JACKSON DID THIS TO ME!
I KNOW YOU TRIED TO RAPE HIS WIFE.
I KNOW SHE TALKED HIM OUT OF KILLING YOU.
YOU OWE HER YOUR LIFE. AND ME.
LET HIM AND ALICE HAVE A CHANCE. THEY'VE GIVEN YOU ONE.
GAH!
UH HUH HUH
IT WON'T MAKE ANY DIFFERENCE WHETHER I TELL OR NOT.
ISAAC'S A RUNAWAY. THEY'LL HAVE TO ANSWER FOR THAT NO MATTER WHAT.
SO YOUR SILENCE JUST GIVES THEM A HEAD START. THAT'S ALL I WANT.
HUH
HUNH
AND IF I SAY YES . . . SAY I WON'T TELL . . .
GASP
YOU'LL BELIEVE ME?

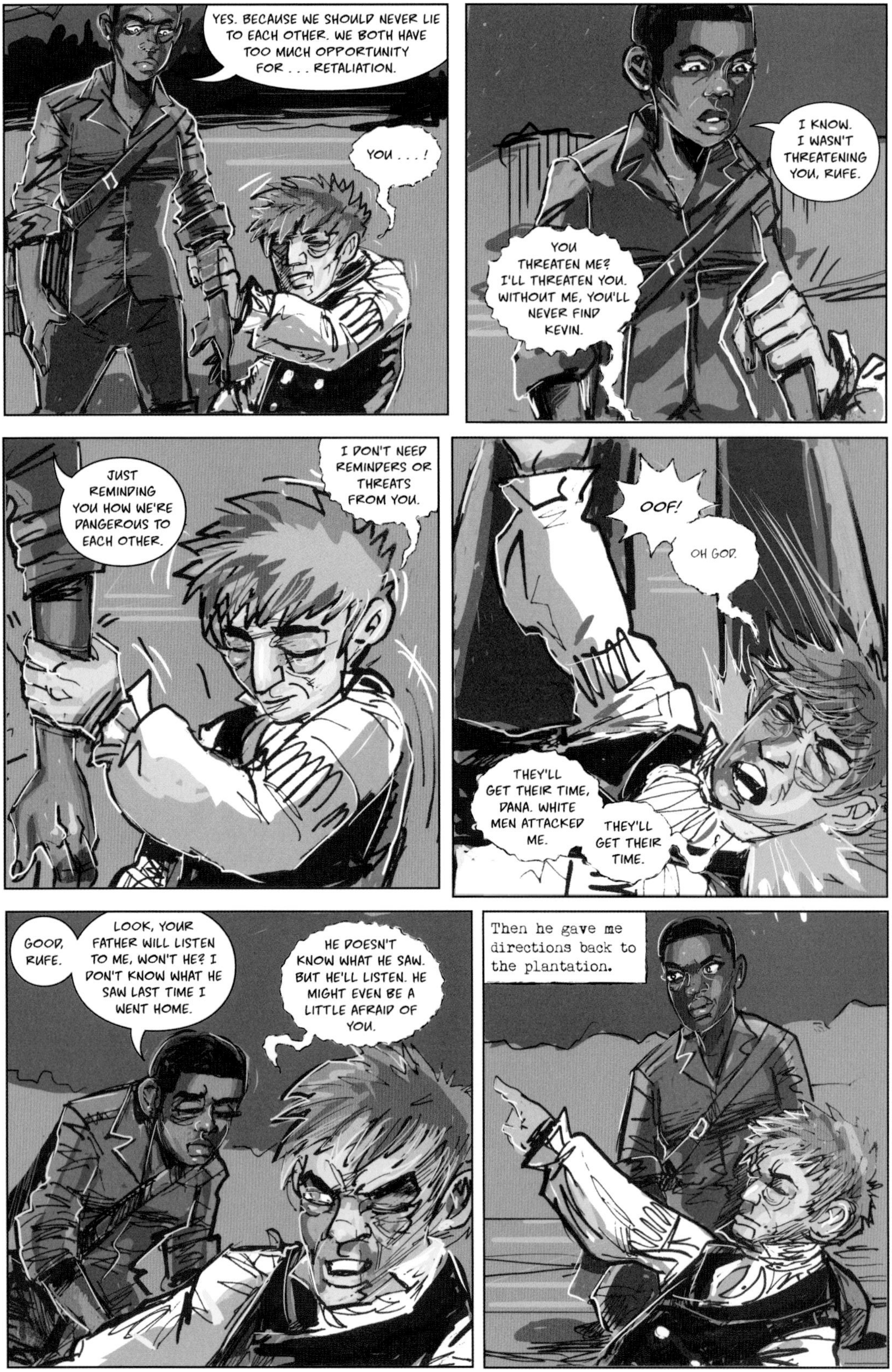
YES. BECAUSE WE SHOULD NEVER LIE TO EACH OTHER. WE BOTH HAVE TOO MUCH OPPORTUNITY FOR . . . RETALIATION.
YOU . . . !
I KNOW. I WASN'T THREATENING YOU, RUFE.
YOU THREATEN ME? I'LL THREATEN YOU. WITHOUT ME, YOU'LL NEVER FIND KEVIN.
JUST REMINDING YOU HOW WE'RE DANGEROUS TO EACH OTHER.
I DON'T NEED REMINDERS OR THREATS FROM YOU.
OOF!
OH GOD.
THEY'LL GET THEIR TIME, DANA. WHITE MEN ATTACKED ME.
THEY'LL GET THEIR TIME.
GOOD, RUFE.
LOOK, YOUR FATHER WILL LISTEN TO ME, WON'T HE? I DON'T KNOW WHAT HE SAW LAST TIME I WENT HOME.
HE DOESN'T KNOW WHAT HE SAW. BUT HE'LL LISTEN. HE MIGHT EVEN BE A LITTLE AFRAID OF YOU.
Then he gave me directions back to the plantation.

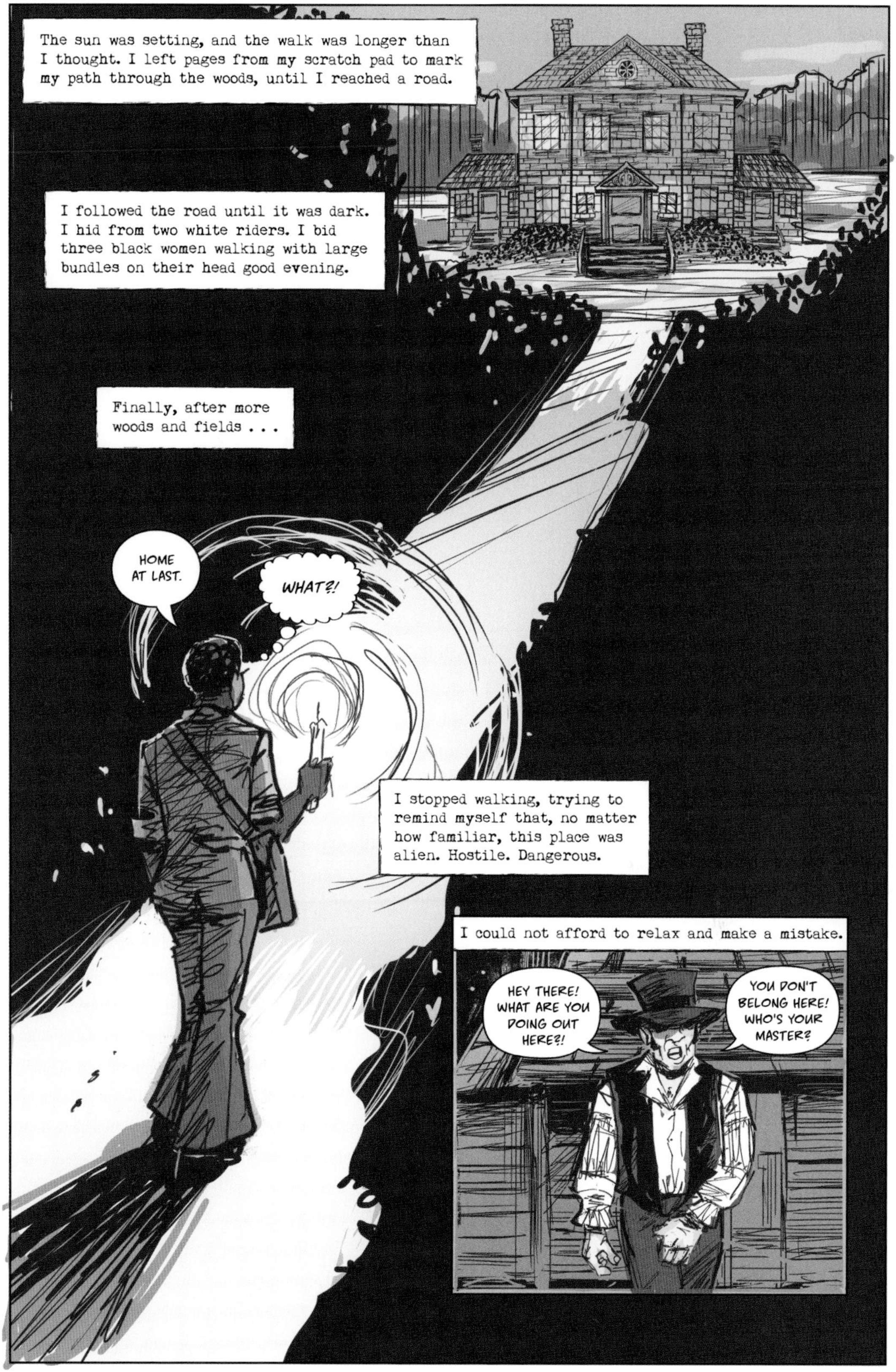
The sun was setting, and the walk was longer than I thought. I left pages from my scratch pad to mark my path through the woods, until I reached a road.
I followed the road until it was dark. I hid from two white riders. I bid three black women walking with large bundles on their head good evening.
Finally, after more woods and fields . . .
HOME AT LAST.
WHAT?!
I stopped walking, trying to remind myself that, no matter how familiar, this place was alien. Hostile. Dangerous.
I could not afford to relax and make a mistake.
HEY THERE! WHAT ARE YOU DOING OUT HERE?!
YOU DON'T BELONG HERE! WHO'S YOUR MASTER?

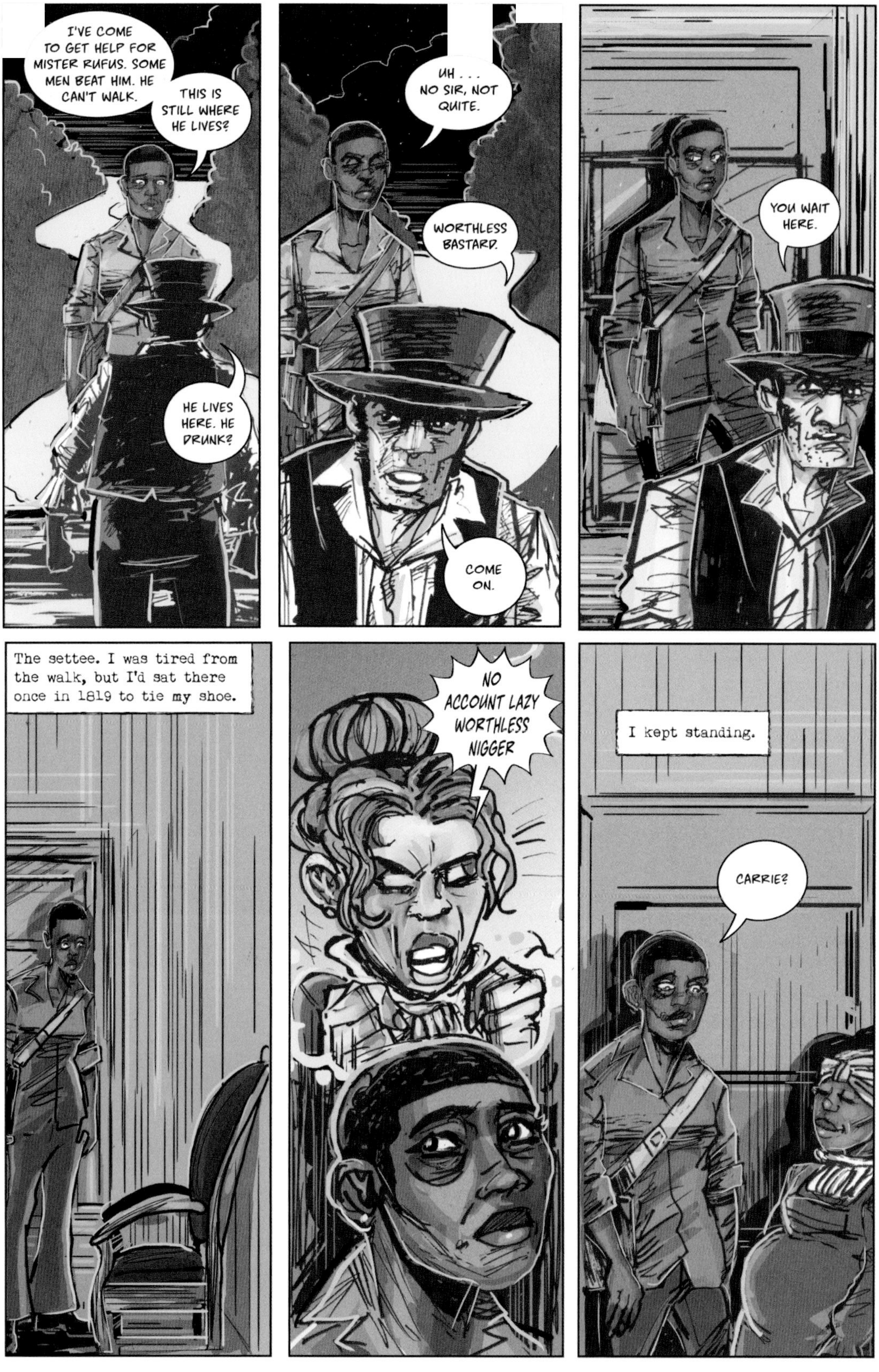
I'VE COME TO GET HELP FOR MISTER RUFUS. SOME MEN BEAT HIM. HE CAN'T WALK.
THIS IS STILL WHERE HE LIVES?
HE LIVES HERE. HE DRUNK?
UH . . . NO SIR, NOT QUITE.
WORTHLESS BASTARD.
COME ON.
YOU WAIT HERE.
The settee. I was tired from the walk, but I'd sat there once in 1819 to tie my shoe.
NO ACCOUNT LAZY WORTHLESS NIGGER
I kept standing.
CARRIE?

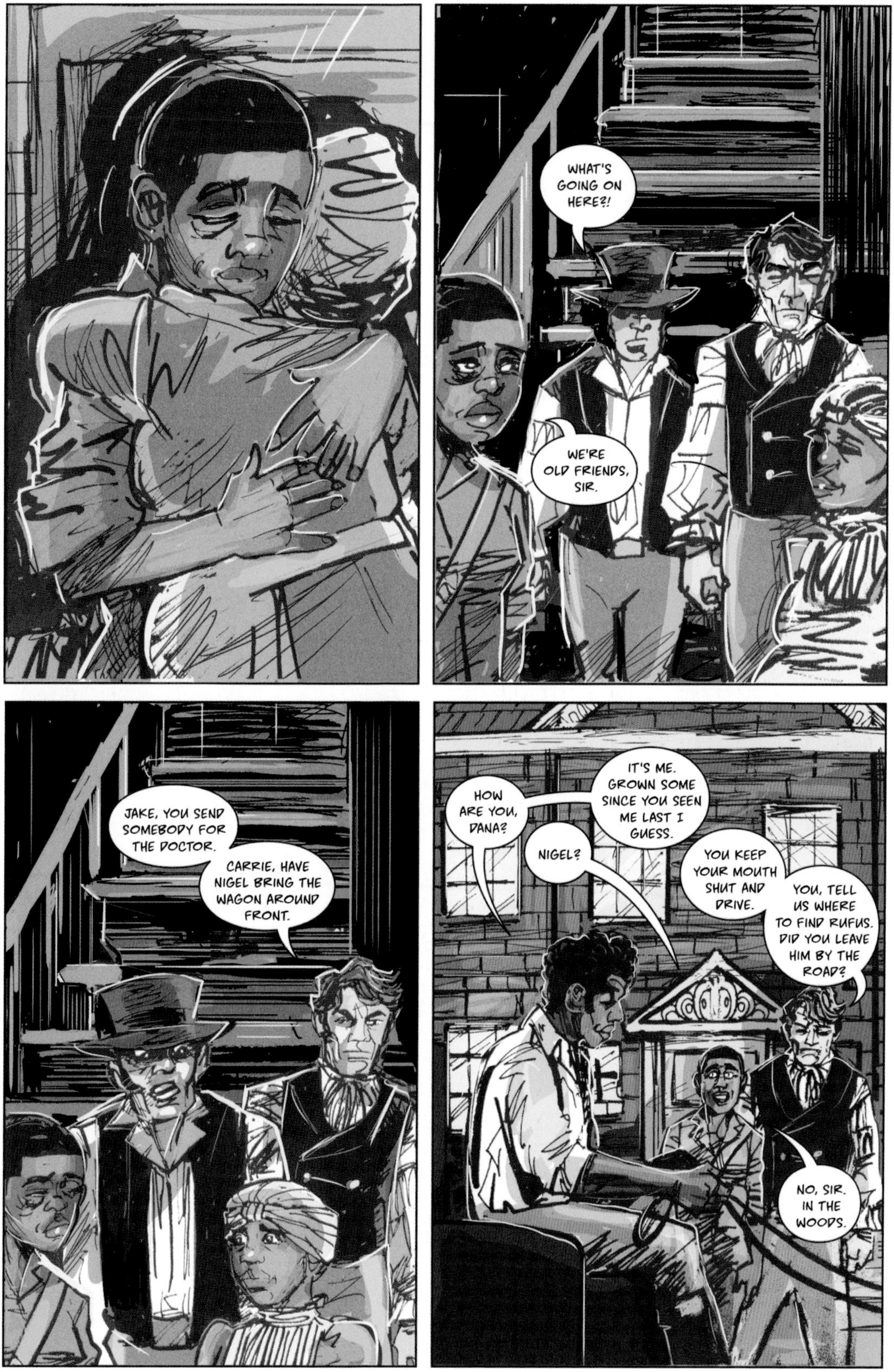
WHAT'S GOING ON HERE?!
WE'RE OLD FRIENDS, SIR.
JAKE, YOU SEND SOMEBODY FOR THE DOCTOR.
CARRIE, HAVE NIGEL BRING THE WAGON AROUND FRONT.
HOW ARE YOU, DANA?
IT'S ME. GROWN SOME SINCE YOU SEEN ME LAST I GUESS.
NIGEL?
YOU KEEP YOUR MOUTH SHUT AND DRIVE.
YOU, TELL US WHERE TO FIND RUFUS. DID YOU LEAVE HIM BY THE ROAD?
NO, SIR. IN THE WOODS.

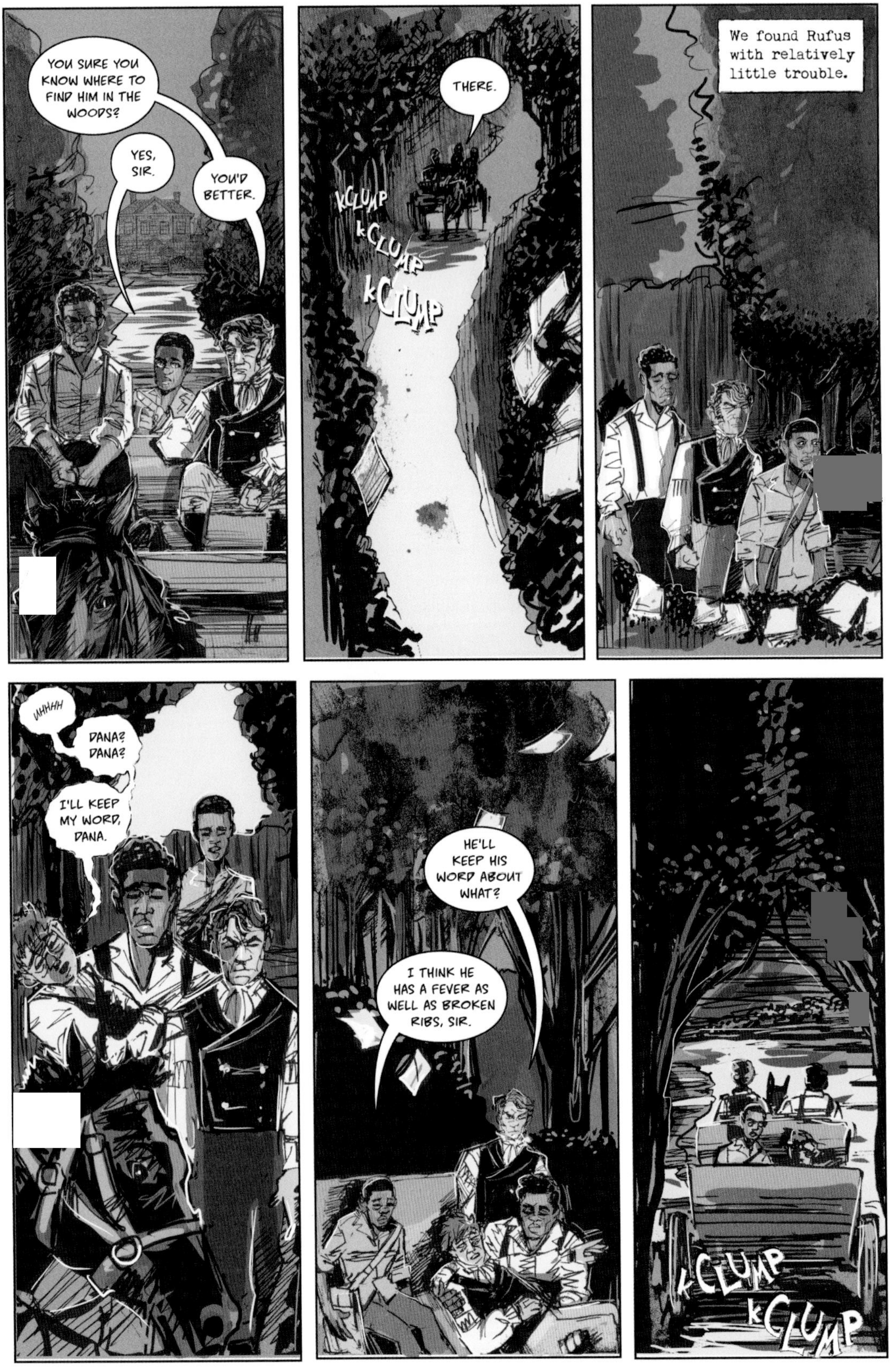
YOU SURE YOU KNOW WHERE TO FIND HIM IN THE WOODS?
YES, SIR.
YOU'D BETTER.
THERE.
kCLUMP
kCLUMP
kCLUMP
We found Rufus with relatively little trouble.
UHHHH
DANA? DANA?
I'LL KEEP MY WORD, DANA.
HE'LL KEEP HIS WORD ABOUT WHAT?
I THINK HE HAS A FEVER AS WELL AS BROKEN RIBS, SIR.
kCLUMP
kCLUMP

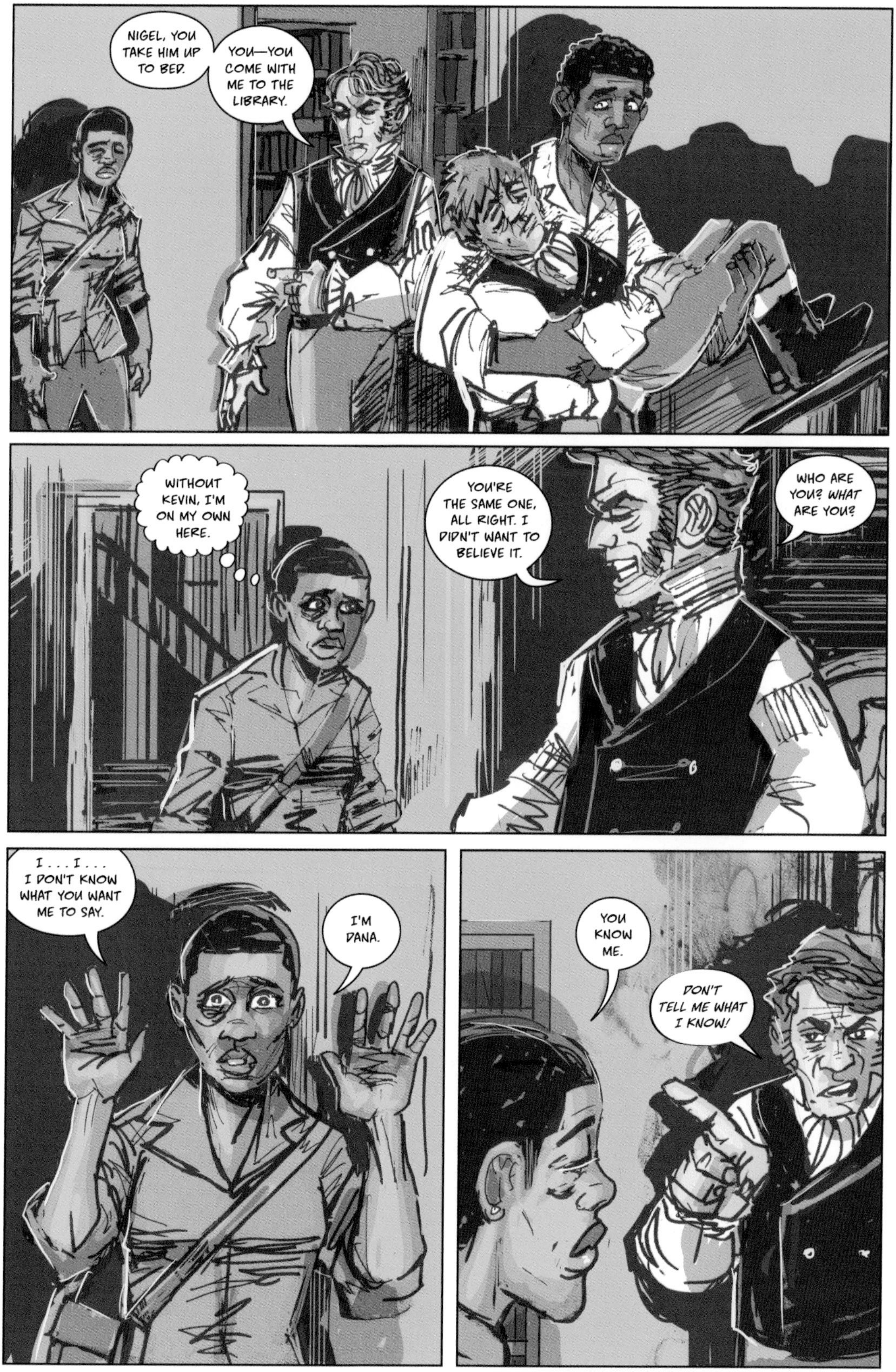
NIGEL, YOU TAKE HIM UP TO BED.
YOU—YOU COME WITH ME TO THE LIBRARY.
WITHOUT KEVIN, I'M ON MY OWN HERE.
YOU'RE THE SAME ONE, ALL RIGHT. I DIDN'T WANT TO BELIEVE IT.
WHO ARE YOU? WHAT ARE YOU?
I . . . I . . . I DON'T KNOW WHAT YOU WANT ME TO SAY.
I'M DANA.
YOU KNOW ME.
DON'T TELL ME WHAT I KNOW!

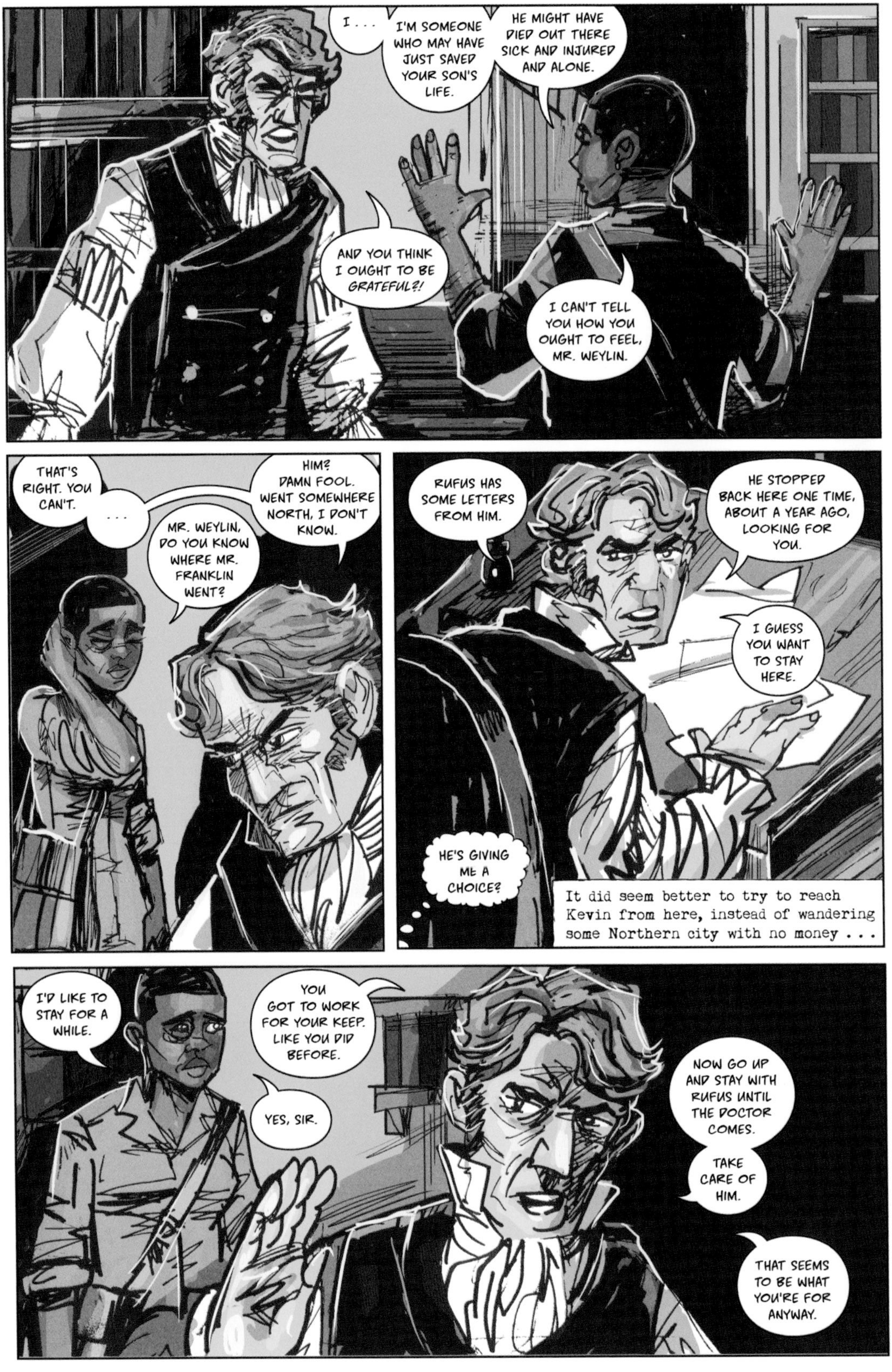
I . . .
I'M SOMEONE WHO MAY HAVE JUST SAVED YOUR SON'S LIFE.
HE MIGHT HAVE DIED OUT THERE SICK AND INJURED AND ALONE.
AND YOU THINK I OUGHT TO BE GRATEFUL?!
I CAN'T TELL YOU HOW YOU OUGHT TO FEEL, MR. WEYLIN.
THAT'S RIGHT. YOU CAN'T.
. . .
MR. WEYLIN, DO YOU KNOW WHERE MR. FRANKLIN WENT?
HIM? DAMN FOOL. WENT SOMEWHERE NORTH, I DON'T KNOW.
RUFUS HAS SOME LETTERS FROM HIM.
HE STOPPED BACK HERE ONE TIME, ABOUT A YEAR AGO, LOOKING FOR YOU.
I GUESS YOU WANT TO STAY HERE.
HE'S GIVING ME A CHOICE?
It did seem better to try to reach Kevin from here, instead of wandering some Northern city with no money . . .
I'D LIKE TO STAY FOR A WHILE.
YOU GOT TO WORK FOR YOUR KEEP. LIKE YOU DID BEFORE.
YES, SIR.
NOW GO UP AND STAY WITH RUFUS UNTIL THE DOCTOR COMES.
TAKE CARE OF HIM.
THAT SEEMS TO BE WHAT YOU'RE FOR ANYWAY.

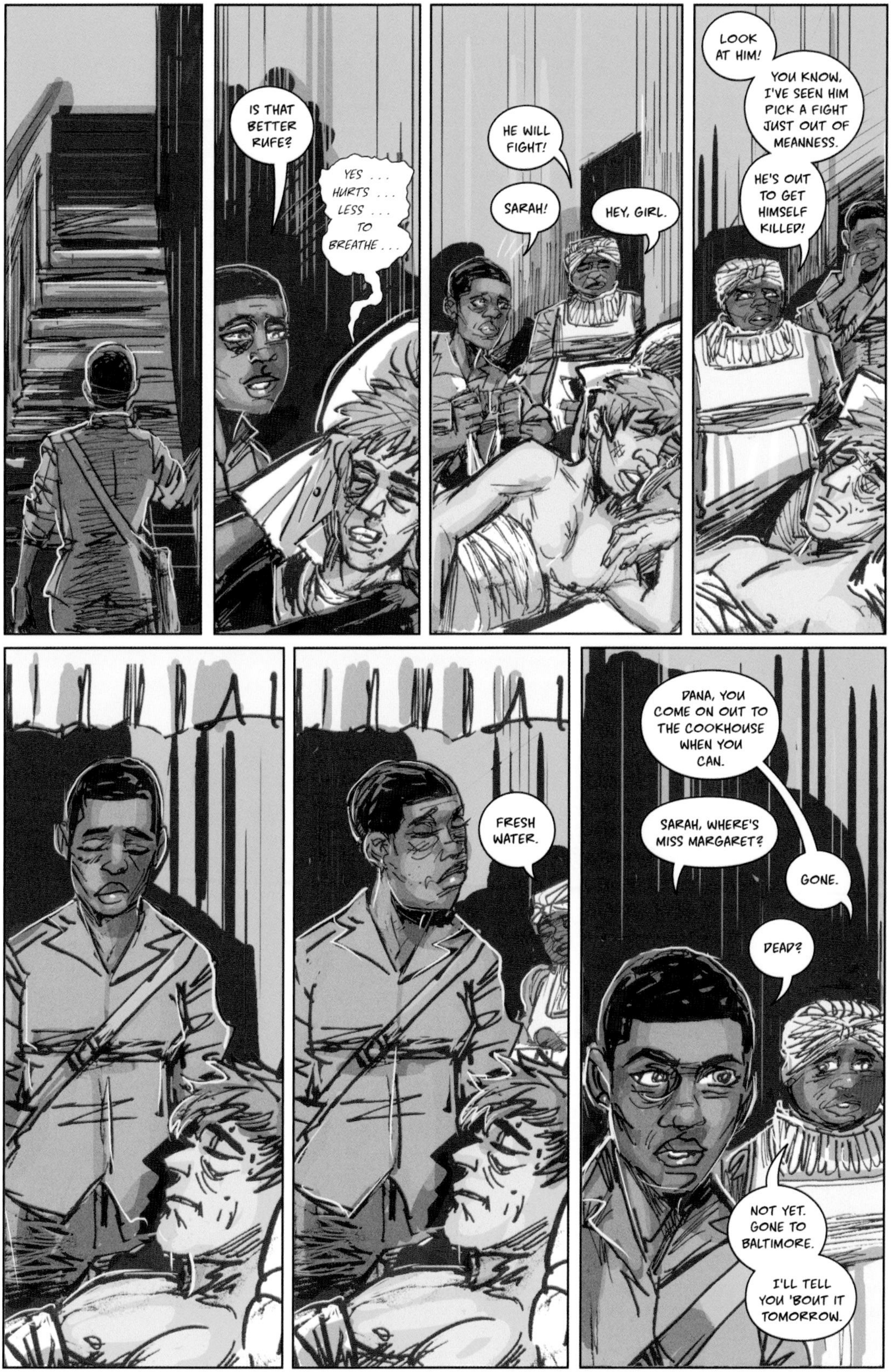
IS THAT BETTER RUFE?
YES . . . HURTS . . . LESS . . . TO BREATHE . . .
HE WILL FIGHT!
SARAH!
HEY, GIRL.
LOOK AT HIM!
YOU KNOW, I'VE SEEN HIM PICK A FIGHT JUST OUT OF MEANNESS.
HE'S OUT TO GET HIMSELF KILLED!
FRESH WATER.
DANA, YOU COME ON OUT TO THE COOKHOUSE WHEN YOU CAN.
SARAH, WHERE'S MISS MARGARET?
GONE.
DEAD?
NOT YET. GONE TO BALTIMORE.
I'LL TELL YOU 'BOUT IT TOMORROW.

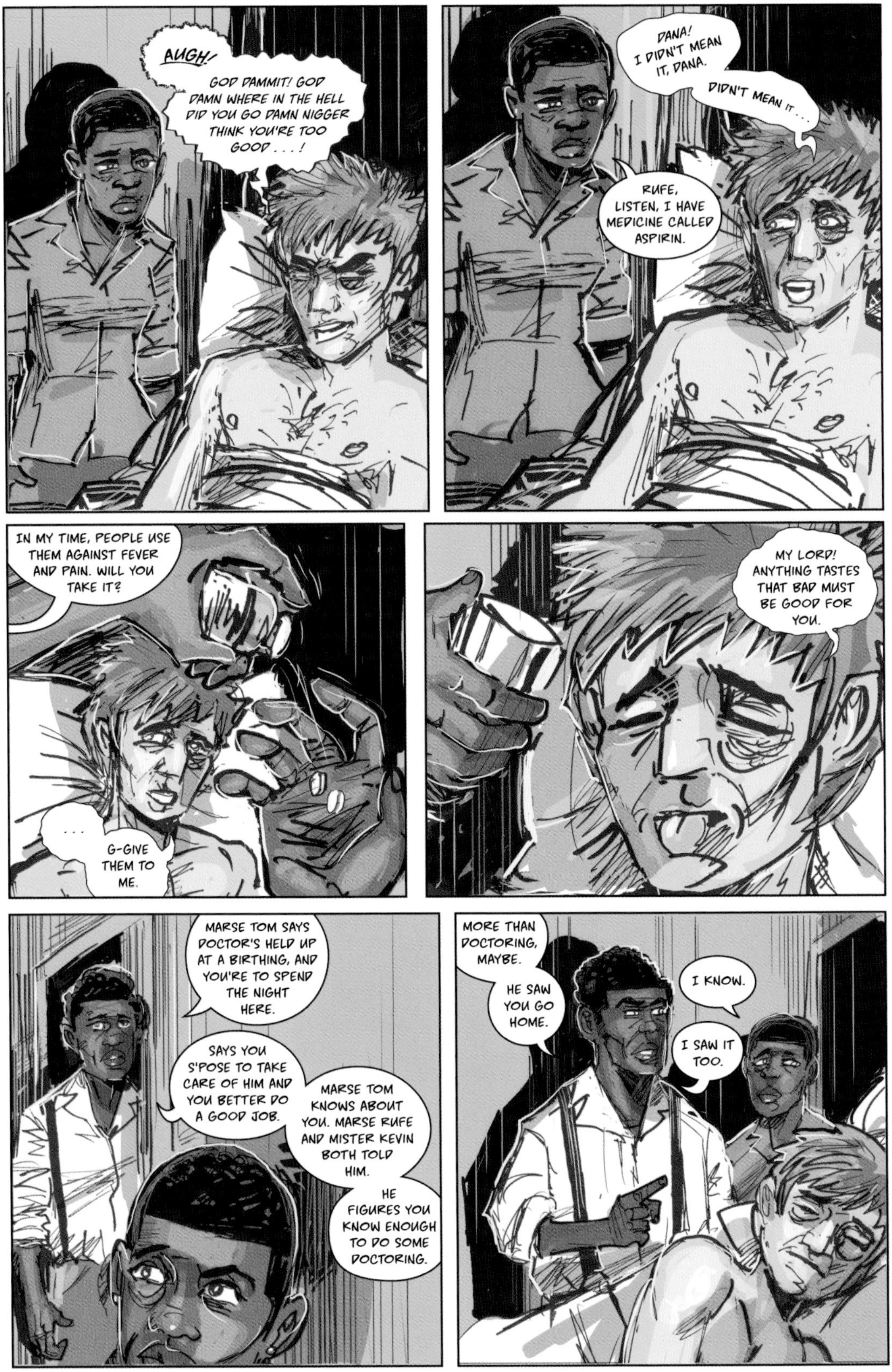
AUGH!
GOD DAMMIT! GOD DAMN WHERE IN THE HELL DID YOU GO DAMN NIGGER THINK YOU'RE TOO GOOD . . . !
DANA! I DIDN'T MEAN IT, DANA.
DIDN'T MEAN IT . . .
RUFE, LISTEN, I HAVE MEDICINE CALLED ASPIRIN.
IN MY TIME, PEOPLE USE THEM AGAINST FEVER AND PAIN. WILL YOU TAKE IT?
. . .
G-GIVE THEM TO ME.
MY LORD! ANYTHING TASTES THAT BAD MUST BE GOOD FOR YOU.
MARSE TOM SAYS DOCTOR'S HELD UP AT A BIRTHING, AND YOU'RE TO SPEND THE NIGHT HERE.
SAYS YOU S'POSE TO TAKE CARE OF HIM AND YOU BETTER DO A GOOD JOB.
MARSE TOM KNOWS ABOUT YOU. MARSE RUFE AND MISTER KEVIN BOTH TOLD HIM.
HE FIGURES YOU KNOW ENOUGH TO DO SOME DOCTORING.
MORE THAN DOCTORING, MAYBE.
HE SAW YOU GO HOME.
I KNOW.
I SAW IT TOO.

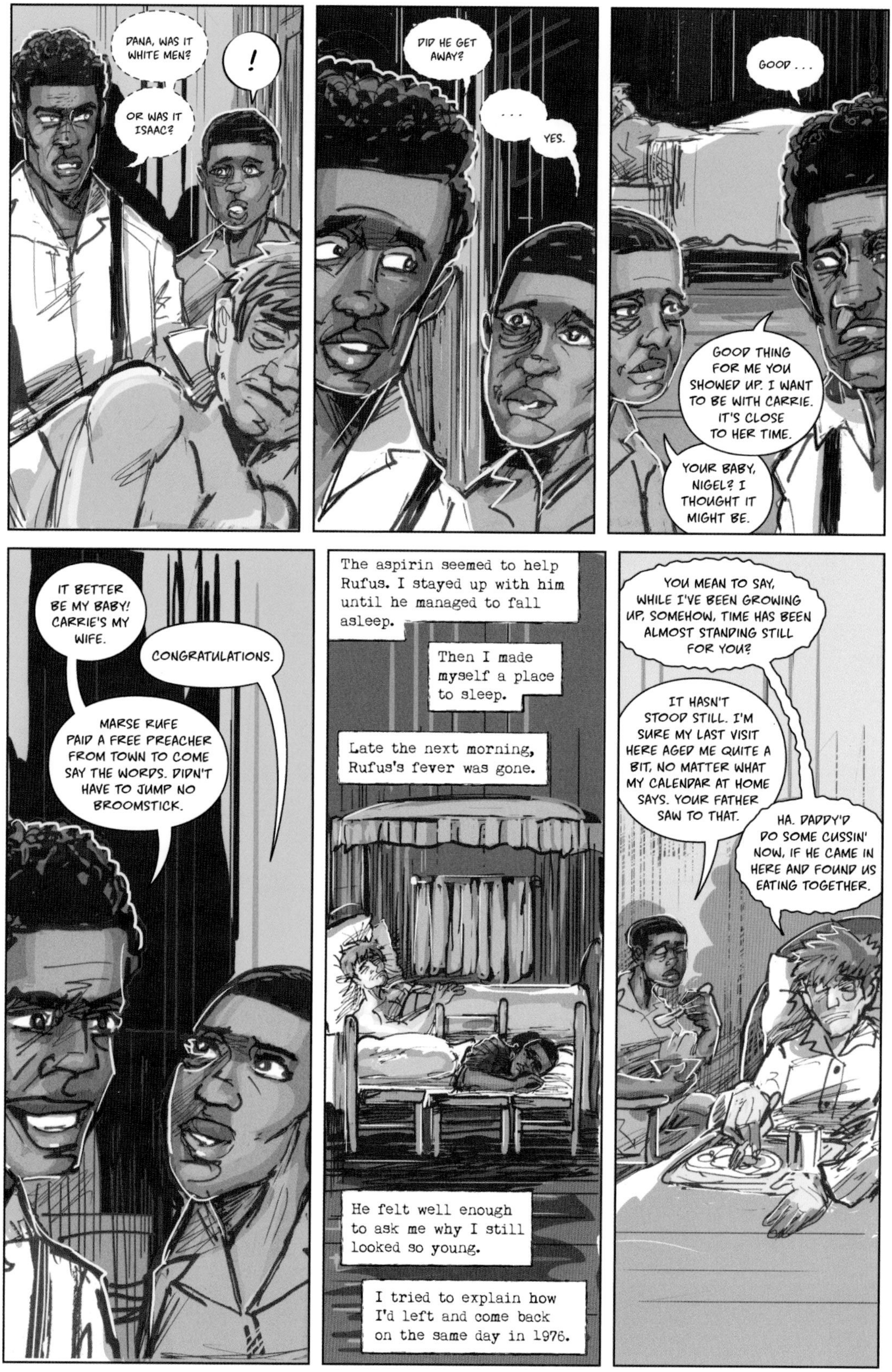
DANA, WAS IT WHITE MEN?
OR WAS IT ISAAC?
!
DID HE GET AWAY?
. . .
YES.
GOOD . . .
GOOD THING FOR ME YOU SHOWED UP. I WANT TO BE WITH CARRIE. IT'S CLOSE TO HER TIME.
YOUR BABY, NIGEL? I THOUGHT IT MIGHT BE.
IT BETTER BE MY BABY! CARRIE'S MY WIFE.
CONGRATULATIONS.
MARSE RUFE PAID A FREE PREACHER FROM TOWN TO COME SAY THE WORDS. DIDN'T HAVE TO JUMP NO BROOMSTICK.
The aspirin seemed to help Rufus. I stayed up with him until he managed to fall asleep.
Then I made myself a place to sleep.
Late the next morning, Rufus's fever was gone.
He felt well enough to ask me why I still looked so young.
I tried to explain how I'd left and come back on the same day in 1976.
YOU MEAN TO SAY, WHILE I'VE BEEN GROWING UP, SOMEHOW, TIME HAS BEEN ALMOST STANDING STILL FOR YOU?
IT HASN'T STOOD STILL. I'M SURE MY LAST VISIT HERE AGED ME QUITE A BIT, NO MATTER WHAT MY CALENDAR AT HOME SAYS. YOUR FATHER SAW TO THAT.
HA. DADDY'D DO SOME CUSSIN' NOW, IF HE CAME IN HERE AND FOUND US EATING TOGETHER.

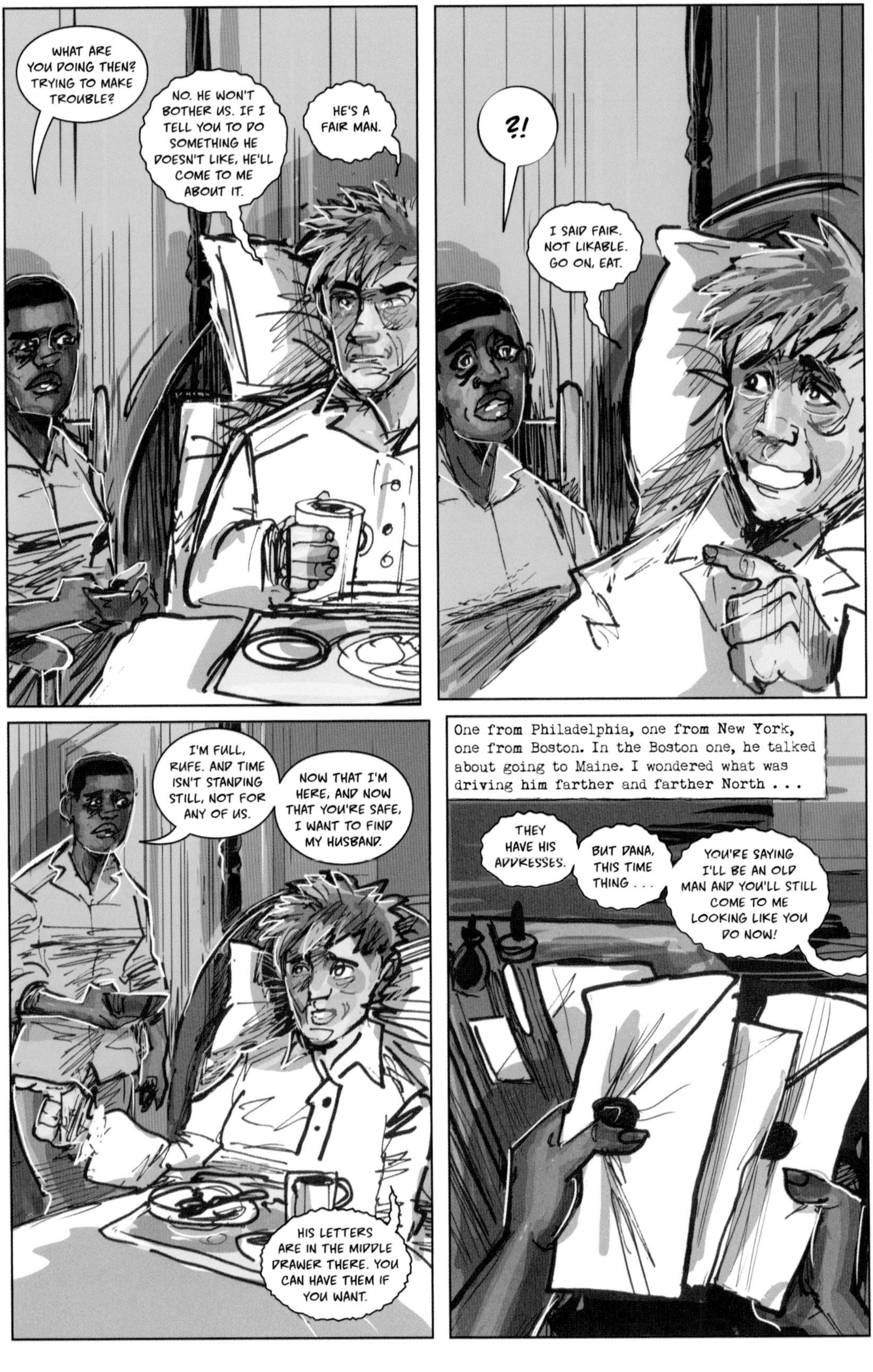
WHAT ARE YOU DOING THEN? TRYING TO MAKE TROUBLE?
NO. HE WON'T BOTHER US. IF I TELL YOU TO DO SOMETHING HE DOESN'T LIKE, HE'LL COME TO ME ABOUT IT.
HE'S A FAIR MAN.
?!
I SAID FAIR. NOT LIKABLE. GO ON, EAT.
I'M FULL, RUFE. AND TIME ISN'T STANDING STILL, NOT FOR ANY OF US.
NOW THAT I'M HERE, AND NOW THAT YOU'RE SAFE, I WANT TO FIND MY HUSBAND.
HIS LETTERS ARE IN THE MIDDLE DRAWER THERE. YOU CAN HAVE THEM IF YOU WANT.
One from Philadelphia, one from New York, one from Boston. In the Boston one, he talked about going to Maine. I wondered what was driving him farther and farther North . . .
THEY HAVE HIS ADDRESSES.
BUT DANA, THIS TIME THING . . .
YOU'RE SAYING I'LL BE AN OLD MAN AND YOU'LL STILL COME TO ME LOOKING LIKE YOU DO NOW!

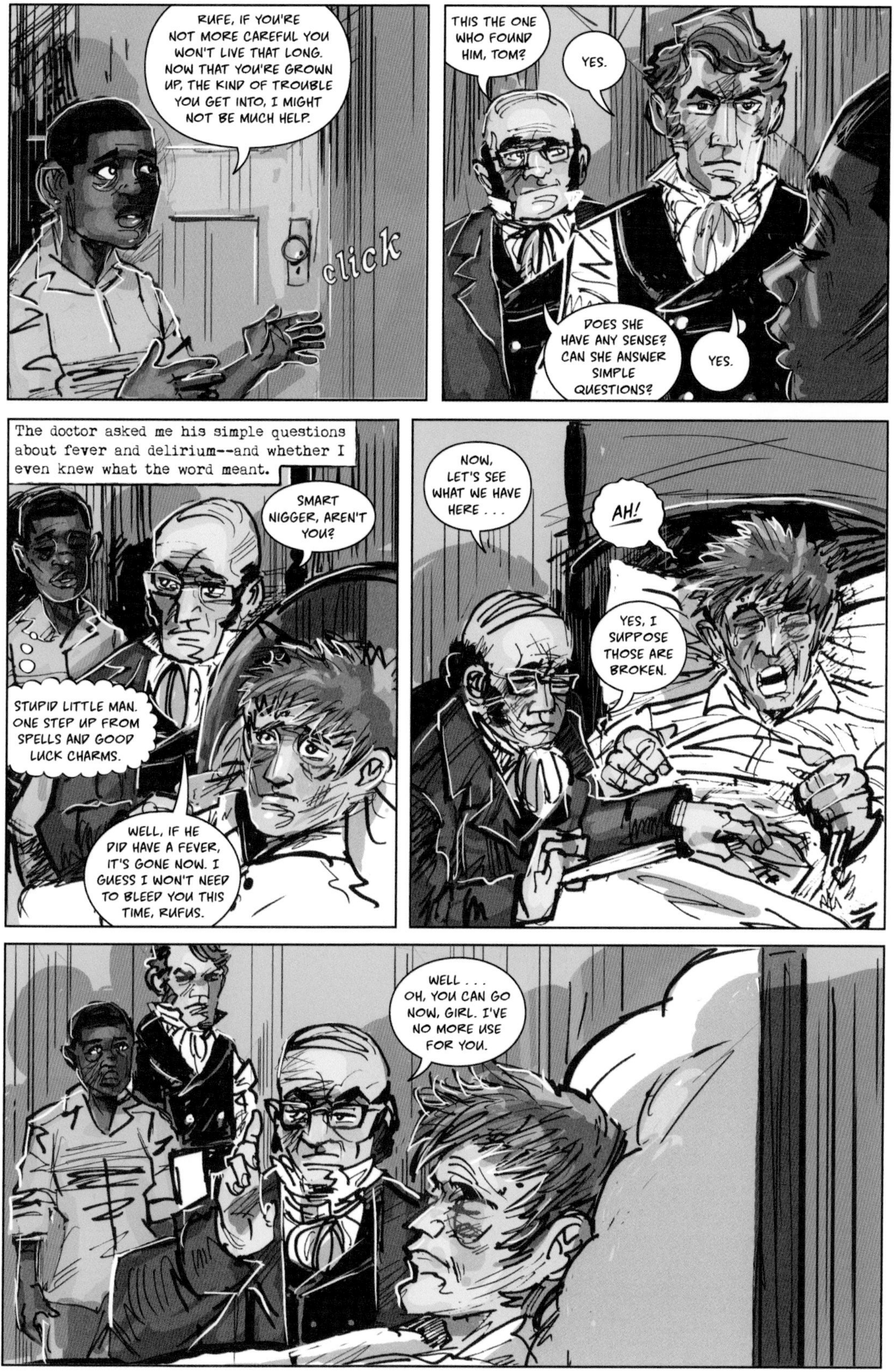
RUFE, IF YOU'RE NOT MORE CAREFUL YOU WON'T LIVE THAT LONG. NOW THAT YOU'RE GROWN UP, THE KIND OF TROUBLE YOU GET INTO, I MIGHT NOT BE MUCH HELP.
click
THIS THE ONE WHO FOUND HIM, TOM?
YES.
DOES SHE HAVE ANY SENSE? CAN SHE ANSWER SIMPLE QUESTIONS?
YES.
The doctor asked me his simple questions about fever and delirium--and whether I even knew what the word meant.
SMART NIGGER, AREN'T YOU?
STUPID LITTLE MAN. ONE STEP UP FROM SPELLS AND GOOD LUCK CHARMS.
WELL, IF HE DID HAVE A FEVER, IT'S GONE NOW. I GUESS I WON'T NEED TO BLEED YOU THIS TIME, RUFUS.
NOW, LET'S SEE WHAT WE HAVE HERE . . .
AH!
YES, I SUPPOSE THOSE ARE BROKEN.
WELL . . . OH, YOU CAN GO NOW, GIRL. I'VE NO MORE USE FOR YOU.

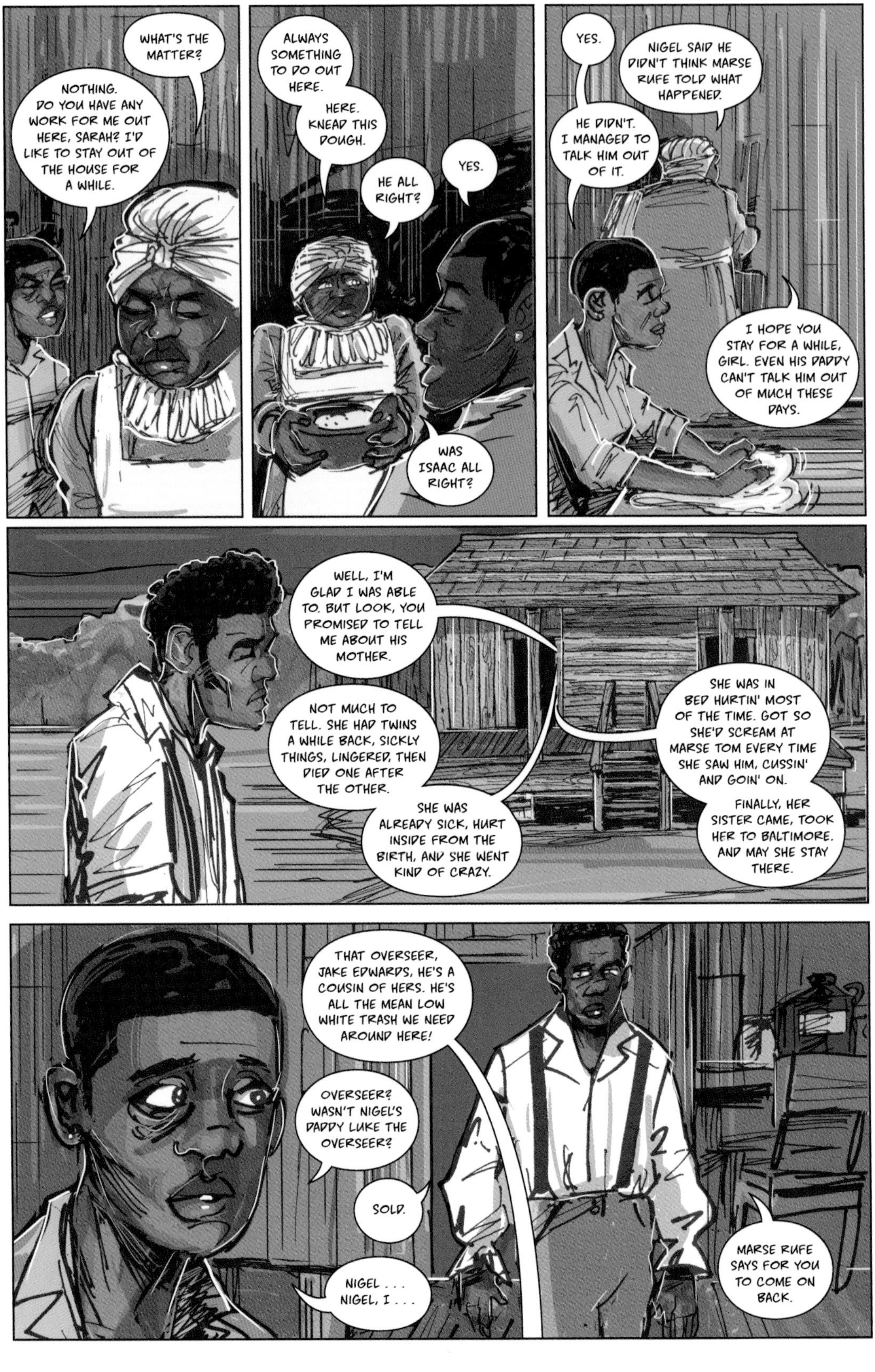

WHAT'S THE MATTER?
NOTHING. DO YOU HAVE ANY WORK FOR ME OUT HERE, SARAH? I'D LIKE TO STAY OUT OF THE HOUSE FOR A WHILE.
ALWAYS SOMETHING TO DO OUT HERE.
HERE. KNEAD THIS DOUGH.
HE ALL RIGHT?
YES.
WAS ISAAC ALL RIGHT?
YES.
NIGEL SAID HE DIDN'T THINK MARSE RUFE TOLD WHAT HAPPENED.
HE DIDN'T. I MANAGED TO TALK HIM OUT OF IT.
I HOPE YOU STAY FOR A WHILE, GIRL. EVEN HIS DADDY CAN'T TALK HIM OUT OF MUCH THESE DAYS.
WELL, I'M GLAD I WAS ABLE TO. BUT LOOK, YOU PROMISED TO TELL ME ABOUT HIS MOTHER.
NOT MUCH TO TELL. SHE HAD TWINS A WHILE BACK, SICKLY THINGS, LINGERED, THEN DIED ONE AFTER THE OTHER.
SHE WAS ALREADY SICK, HURT INSIDE FROM THE BIRTH, AND SHE WENT KIND OF CRAZY.
SHE WAS IN BED HURTIN' MOST OF THE TIME. GOT SO SHE'D SCREAM AT MARSE TOM EVERY TIME SHE SAW HIM, CUSSIN' AND GOIN' ON.
FINALLY, HER SISTER CAME, TOOK HER TO BALTIMORE. AND MAY SHE STAY THERE.
THAT OVERSEER, JAKE EDWARDS, HE'S A COUSIN OF HERS. HE'S ALL THE MEAN LOW WHITE TRASH WE NEED AROUND HERE!
OVERSEER? WASN'T NIGEL'S DADDY LUKE THE OVERSEER?
SOLD.
NIGEL . . . NIGEL, I . . .
MARSE RUFE SAYS FOR YOU TO COME ON BACK.

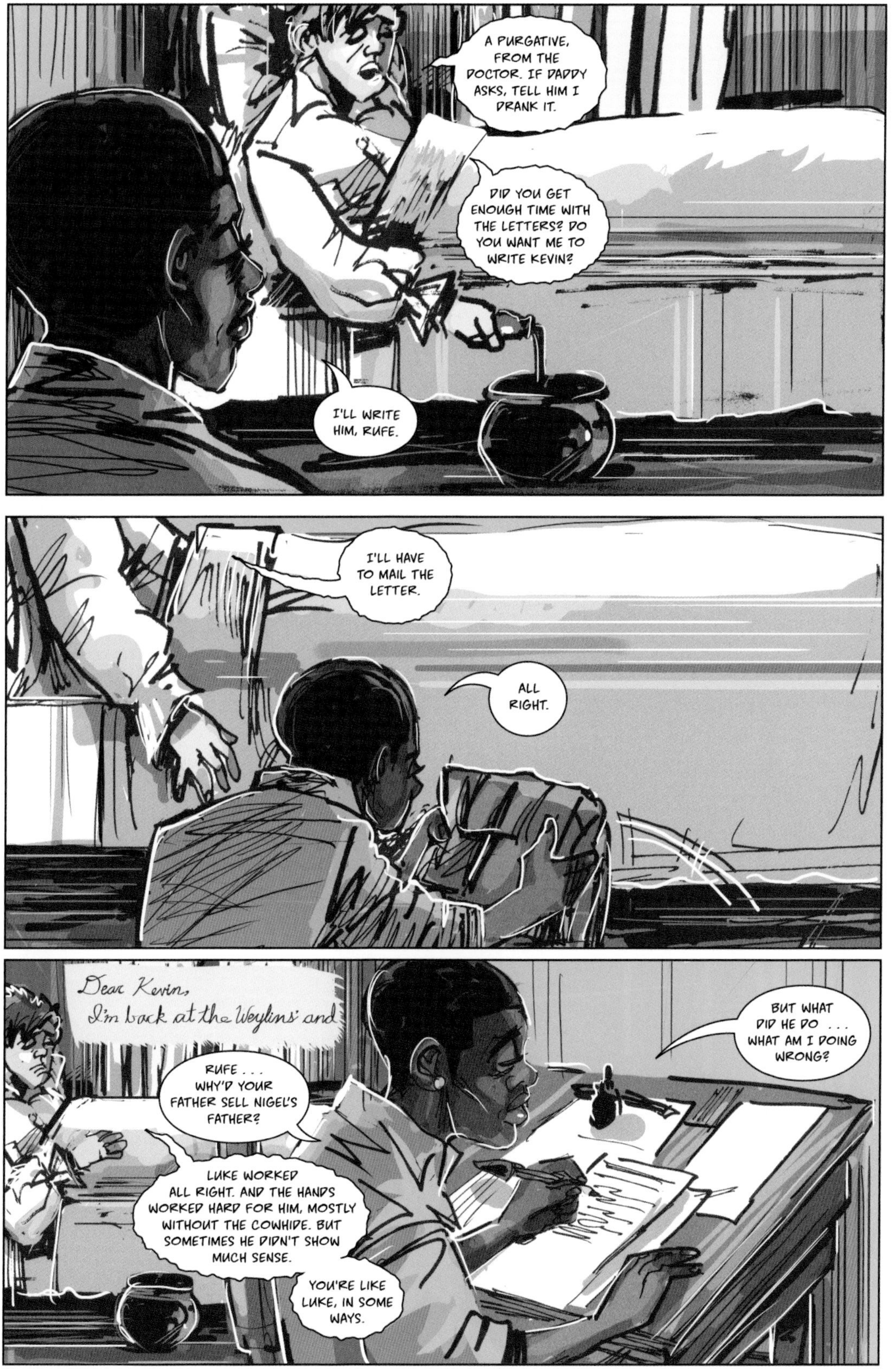
A PURGATIVE, FROM THE DOCTOR. IF DADDY ASKS, TELL HIM I DRANK IT.
DID YOU GET ENOUGH TIME WITH THE LETTERS? DO YOU WANT ME TO WRITE KEVIN?
I'LL WRITE HIM, RUFE.
I'LL HAVE TO MAIL THE LETTER.
ALL RIGHT.
Dear Kevin,
I'm back at the Weylins' and
BUT WHAT DID HE DO . . . WHAT AM I DOING WRONG?
RUFE . . . WHY'D YOUR FATHER SELL NIGEL'S FATHER?
LUKE WORKED ALL RIGHT. AND THE HANDS WORKED HARD FOR HIM, MOSTLY WITHOUT THE COWHIDE. BUT SOMETIMES HE DIDN'T SHOW MUCH SENSE.
YOU'RE LIKE LUKE, IN SOME WAYS.

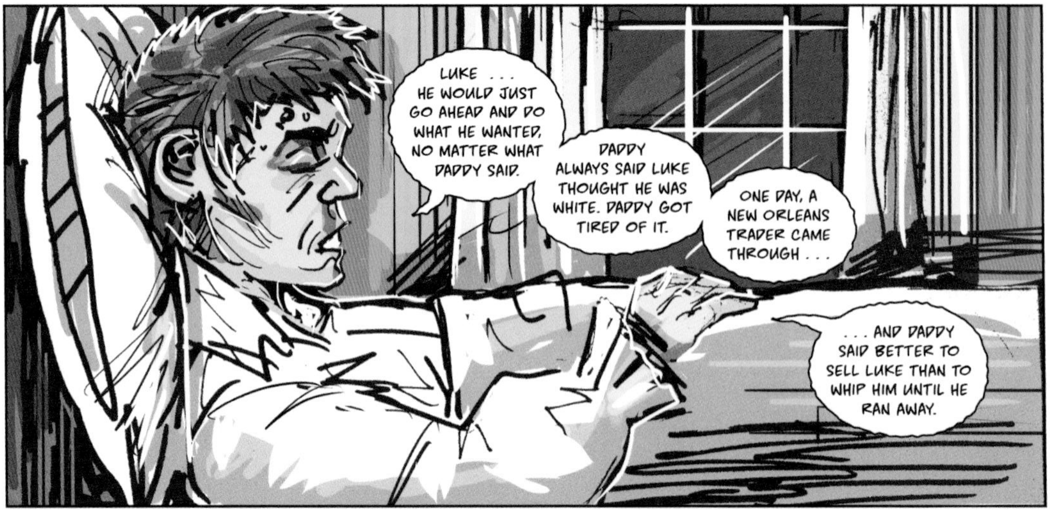
LUKE . . . HE WOULD JUST GO AHEAD AND DO WHAT HE WANTED, NO MATTER WHAT DADDY SAID.
DADDY ALWAYS SAID LUKE THOUGHT HE WAS WHITE. DADDY GOT TIRED OF IT.
ONE DAY, A NEW ORLEANS TRADER CAME THROUGH . . .
. . . AND DADDY SAID BETTER TO SELL LUKE THAN TO WHIP HIM UNTIL HE RAN AWAY.

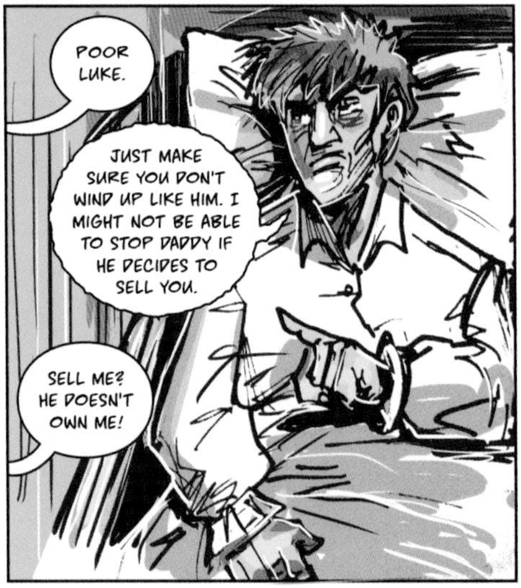
POOR LUKE.
JUST MAKE SURE YOU DON'T WIND UP LIKE HIM. I MIGHT NOT BE ABLE TO STOP DADDY IF HE DECIDES TO SELL YOU.
SELL ME? HE DOESN'T OWN ME!

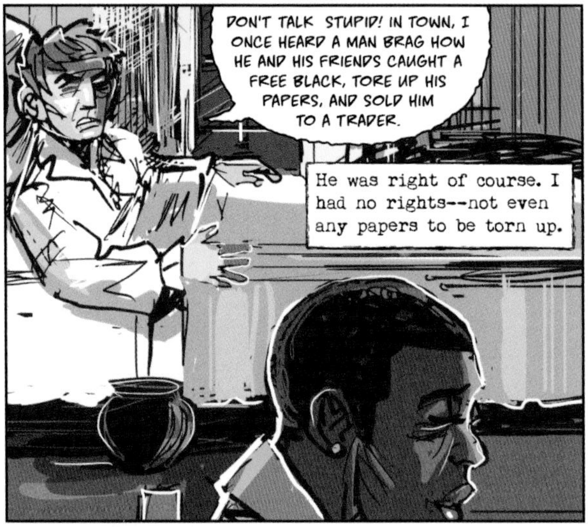
DON'T TALK STUPID! IN TOWN, I ONCE HEARD A MAN BRAG HOW HE AND HIS FRIENDS CAUGHT A FREE BLACK, TORE UP HIS PAPERS, AND SOLD HIM TO A TRADER.
He was right of course. I had no rights--not even any papers to be torn up.

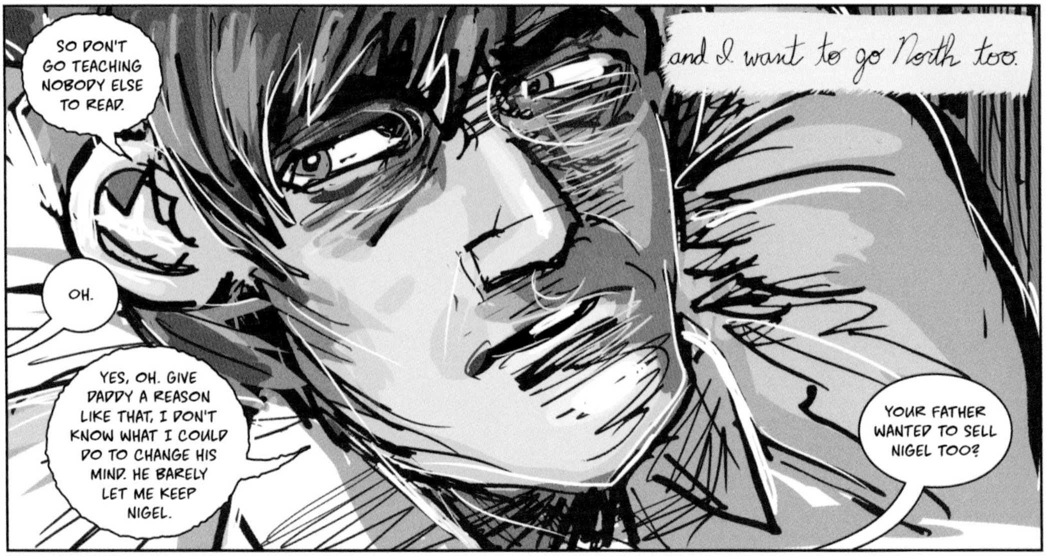
SO DON'T GO TEACHING NOBODY ELSE TO READ.
and I want to go North too.
OH.
YES, OH. GIVE DADDY A REASON LIKE THAT, I DON'T KNOW WHAT I COULD DO TO CHANGE HIS MIND. HE BARELY LET ME KEEP NIGEL.
YOUR FATHER WANTED TO SELL NIGEL TOO?

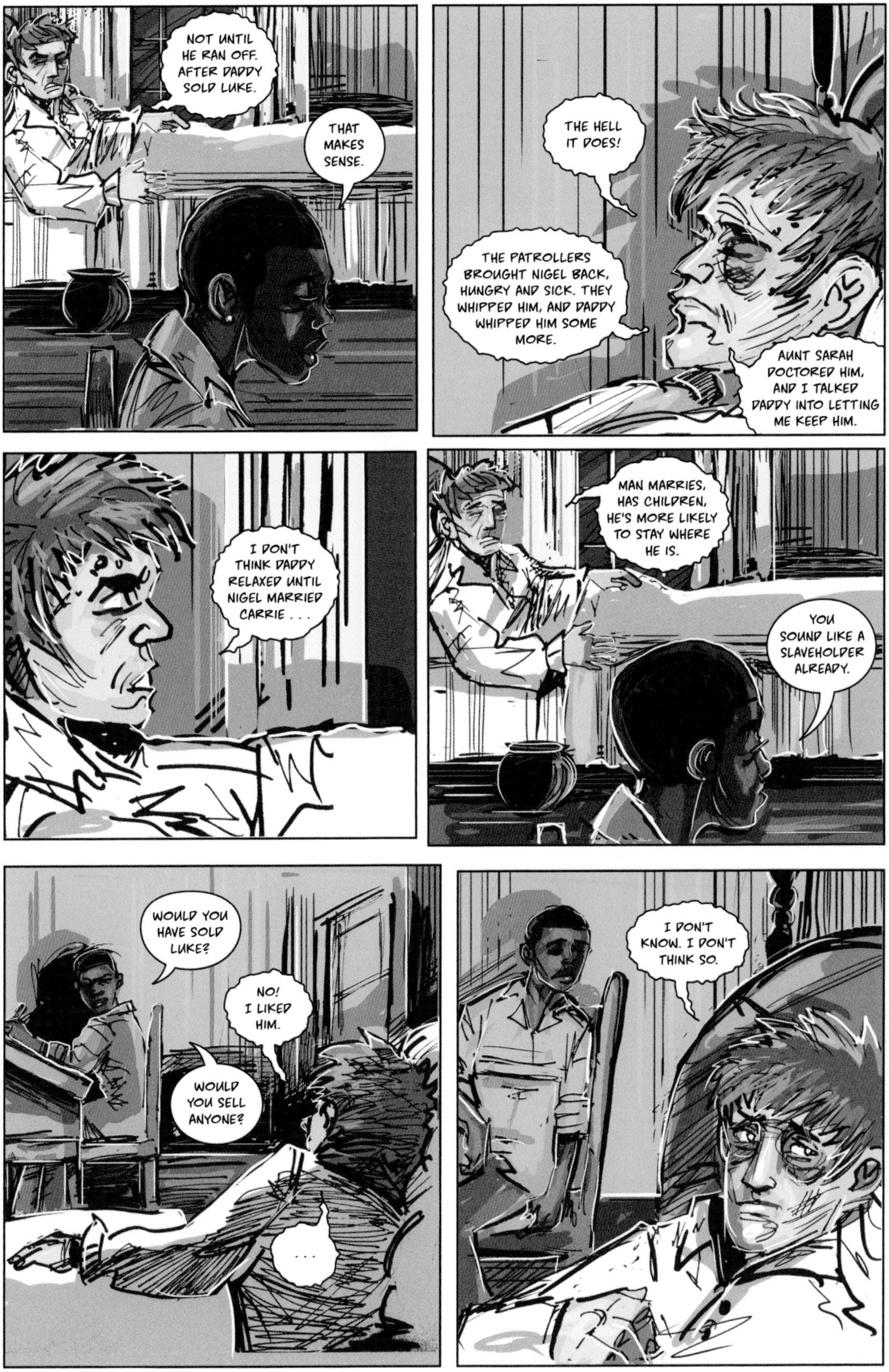

NOT UNTIL HE RAN OFF. AFTER DADDY SOLD LUKE.
THAT MAKES SENSE.
THE HELL IT DOES!
THE PATROLLERS BROUGHT NIGEL BACK, HUNGRY AND SICK. THEY WHIPPED HIM, AND DADDY WHIPPED HIM SOME MORE.
AUNT SARAH DOCTORED HIM, AND I TALKED DADDY INTO LETTING ME KEEP HIM.
I DON'T THINK DADDY RELAXED UNTIL NIGEL MARRIED CARRIE . . .
MAN MARRIES, HAS CHILDREN, HE'S MORE LIKELY TO STAY WHERE HE IS.
YOU SOUND LIKE A SLAVEHOLDER ALREADY.
WOULD YOU HAVE SOLD LUKE?
NO! I LIKED HIM.
WOULD YOU SELL ANYONE?
. . .
I DON'T KNOW. I DON'T THINK SO.

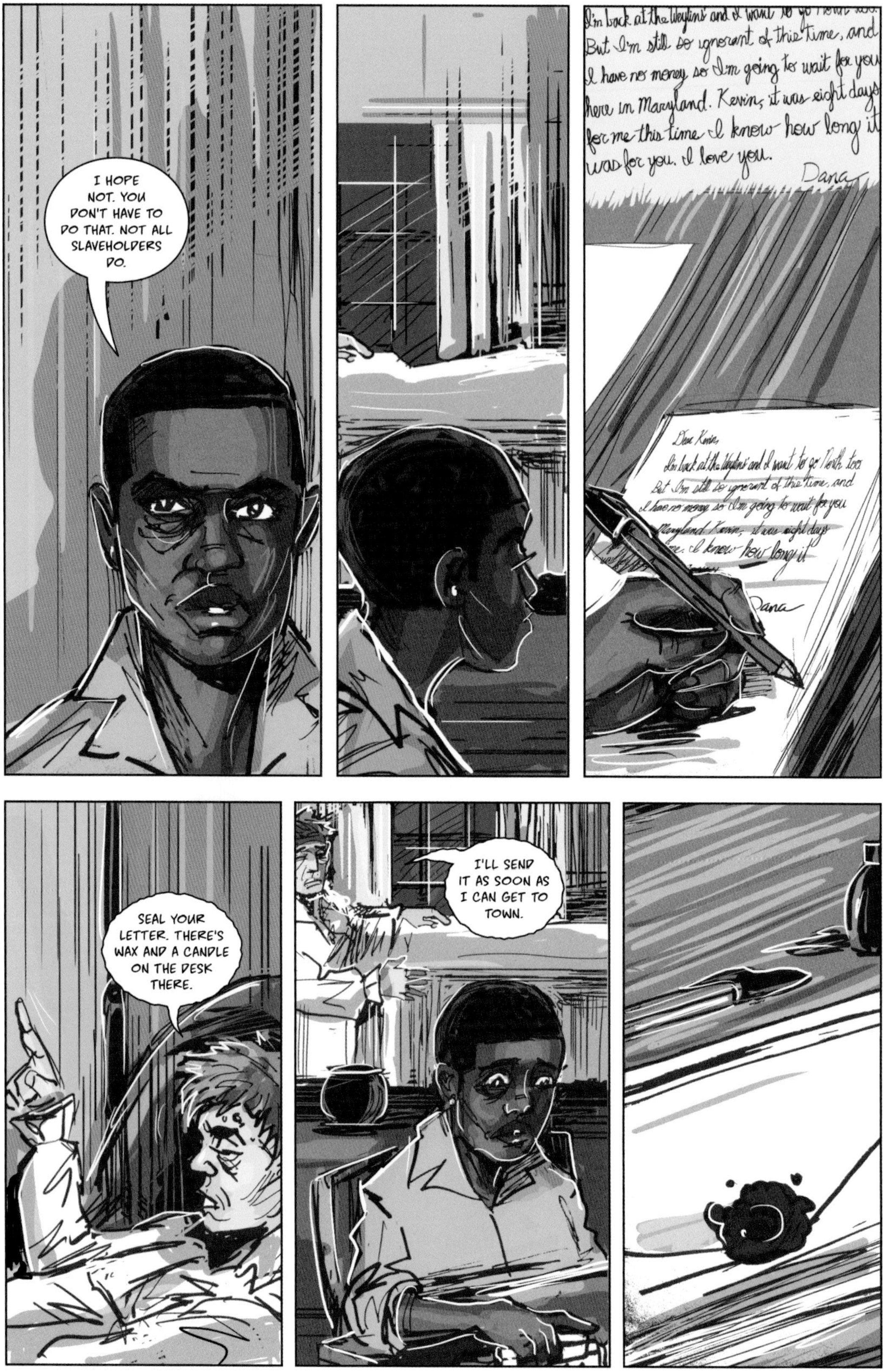
I HOPE NOT. YOU DON'T HAVE TO DO THAT. NOT ALL SLAVEHOLDERS DO.
I'm back at the Weylins' and I want to go North
But I'm still so ignorant of this time, and I have no money so I'm going to wait for you here in Maryland. Kevin, it was eight days for me this time I know how long it was for you. I love you.
Dana
SEAL YOUR LETTER. THERE'S WAX AND A CANDLE ON THE DESK THERE.
I'LL SEND IT AS SOON AS I CAN GET TO TOWN.

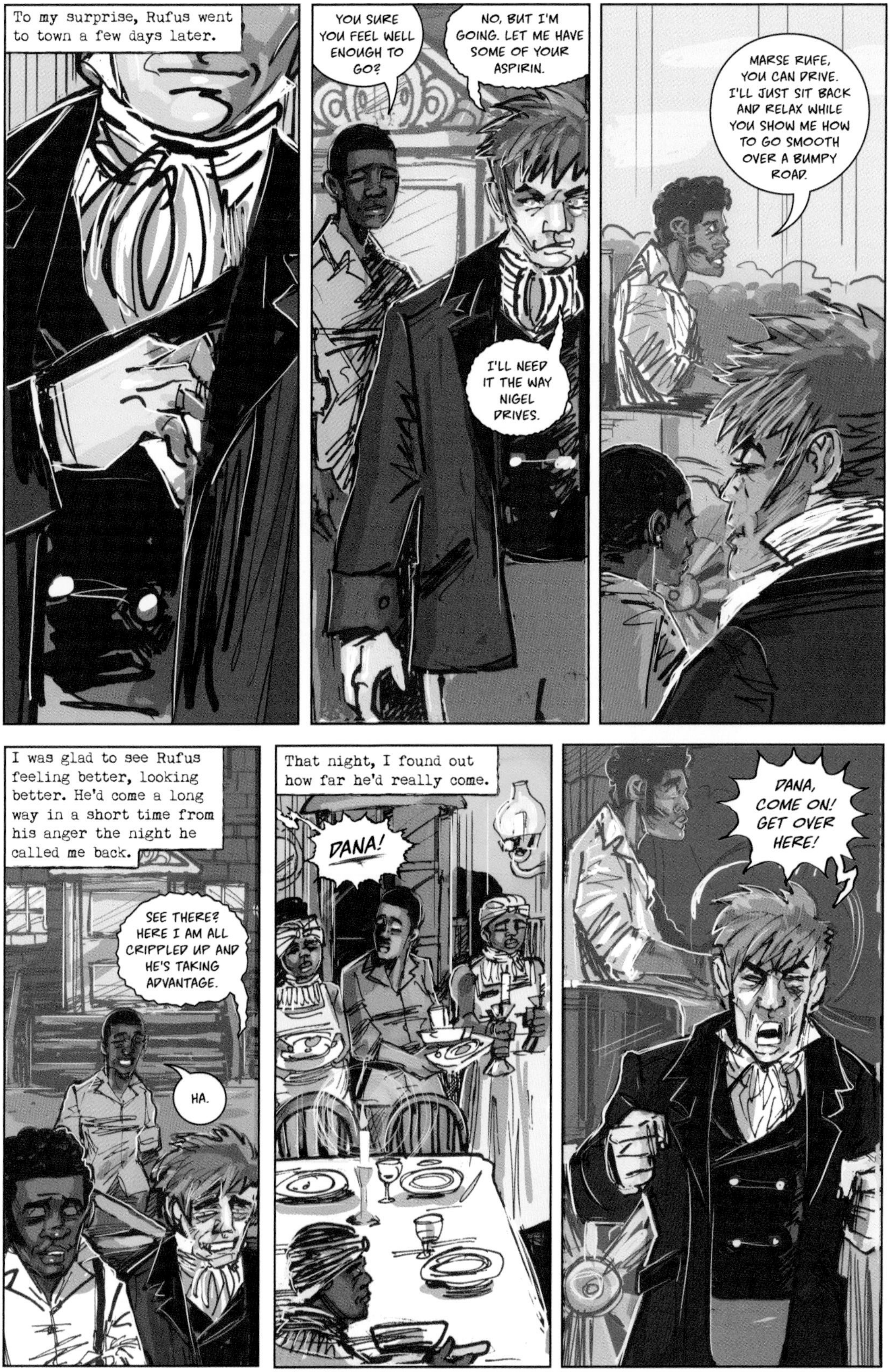
To my surprise, Rufus went to town a few days later.
YOU SURE YOU FEEL WELL ENOUGH TO GO?
NO, BUT I'M GOING. LET ME HAVE SOME OF YOUR ASPIRIN.
I'LL NEED IT THE WAY NIGEL DRIVES.
MARSE RUFE, YOU CAN DRIVE. I'LL JUST SIT BACK AND RELAX WHILE YOU SHOW ME HOW TO GO SMOOTH OVER A BUMPY ROAD.
I was glad to see Rufus feeling better, looking better. He'd come a long way in a short time from his anger the night he called me back.
SEE THERE? HERE I AM ALL CRIPPLED UP AND HE'S TAKING ADVANTAGE.
HA.
That night, I found out how far he'd really come.
DANA!
DANA, COME ON! GET OVER HERE!

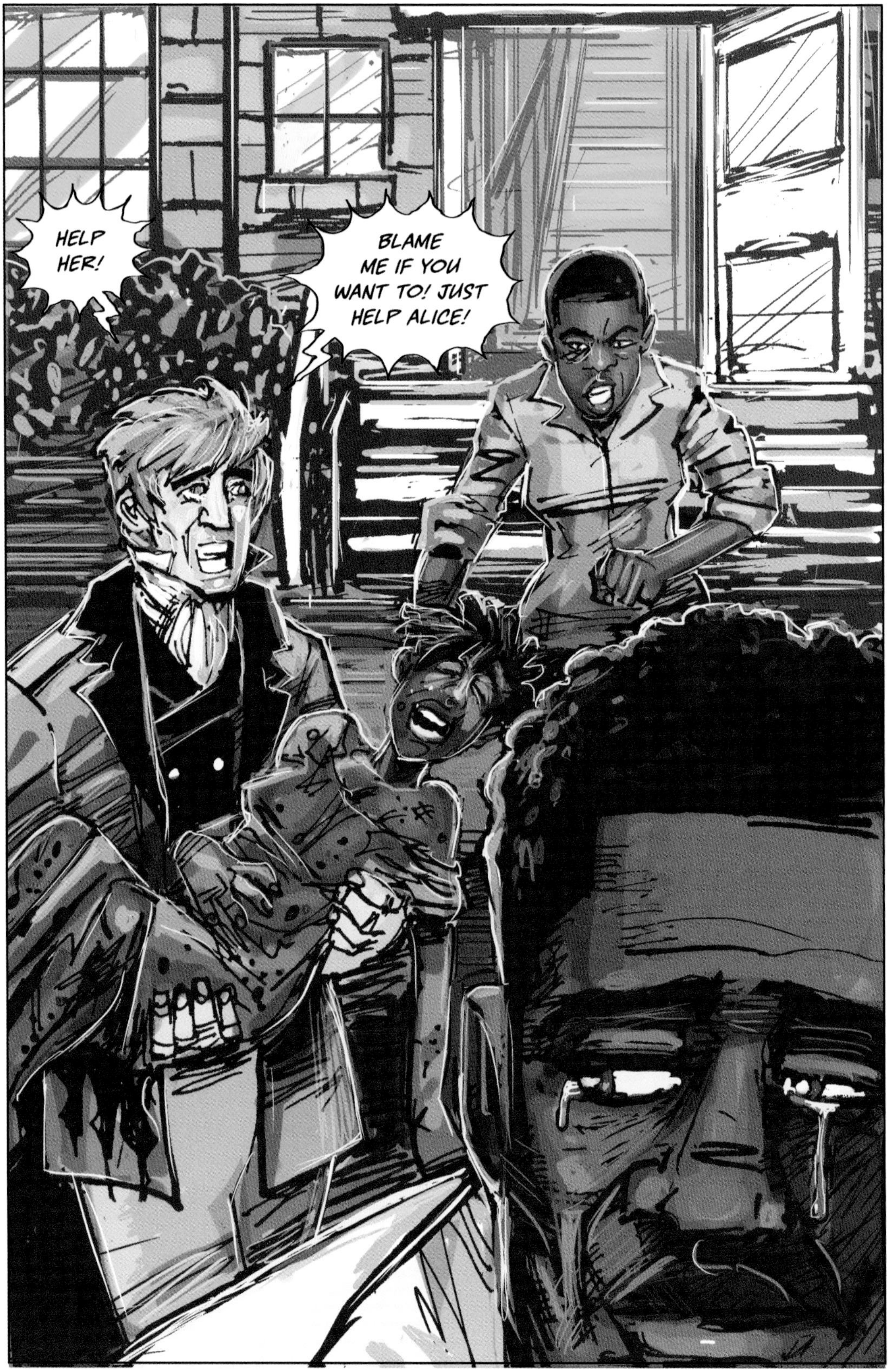
HELP HER!
BLAME ME IF YOU WANT TO! JUST HELP ALICE!

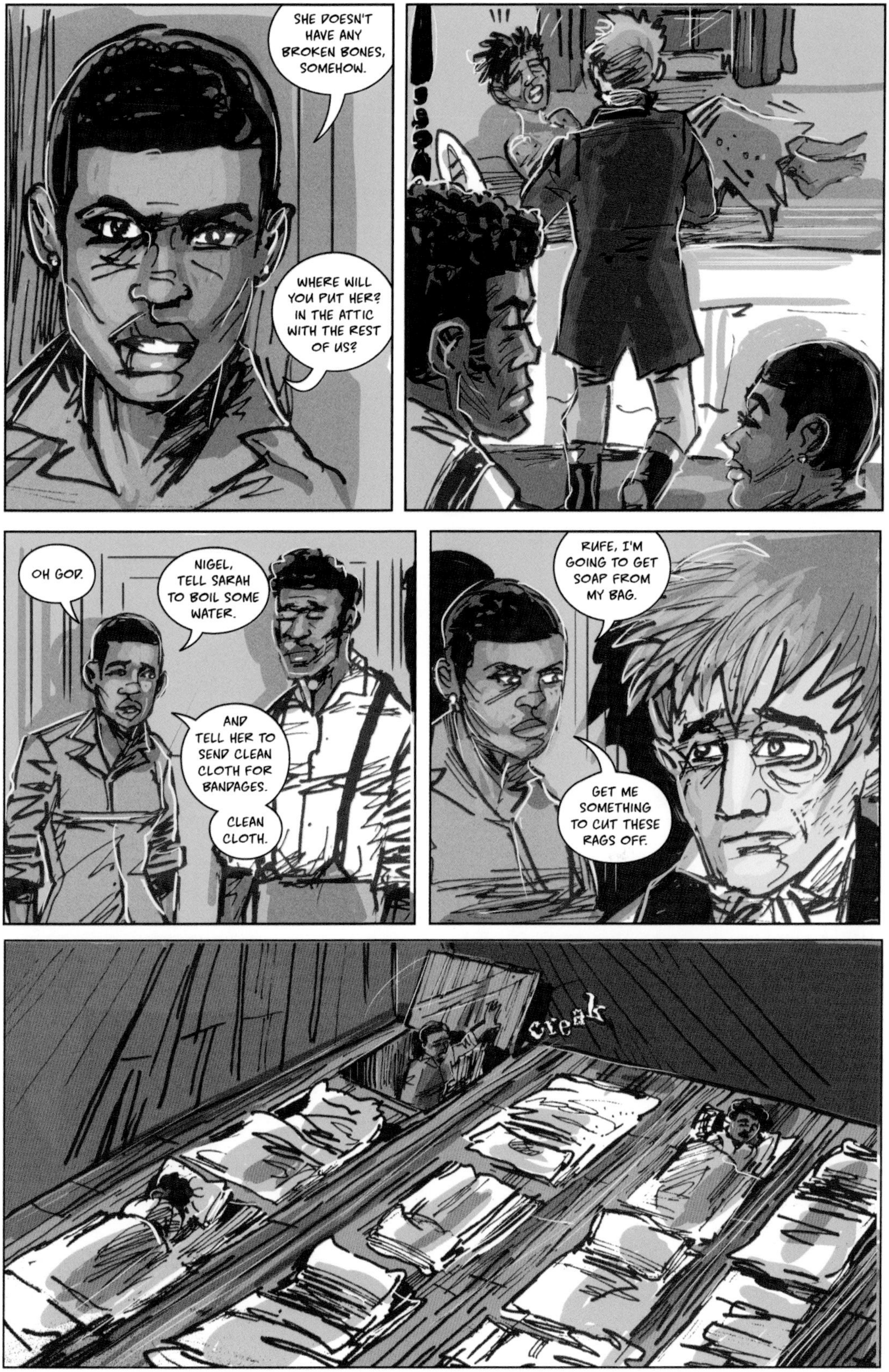
SHE DOESN'T HAVE ANY BROKEN BONES, SOMEHOW.
WHERE WILL YOU PUT HER? IN THE ATTIC WITH THE REST OF US?
OH GOD.
NIGEL, TELL SARAH TO BOIL SOME WATER.
AND TELL HER TO SEND CLEAN CLOTH FOR BANDAGES.
CLEAN CLOTH.
RUFE, I'M GOING TO GET SOAP FROM MY BAG.
GET ME SOMETHING TO CUT THESE RAGS OFF.
creak

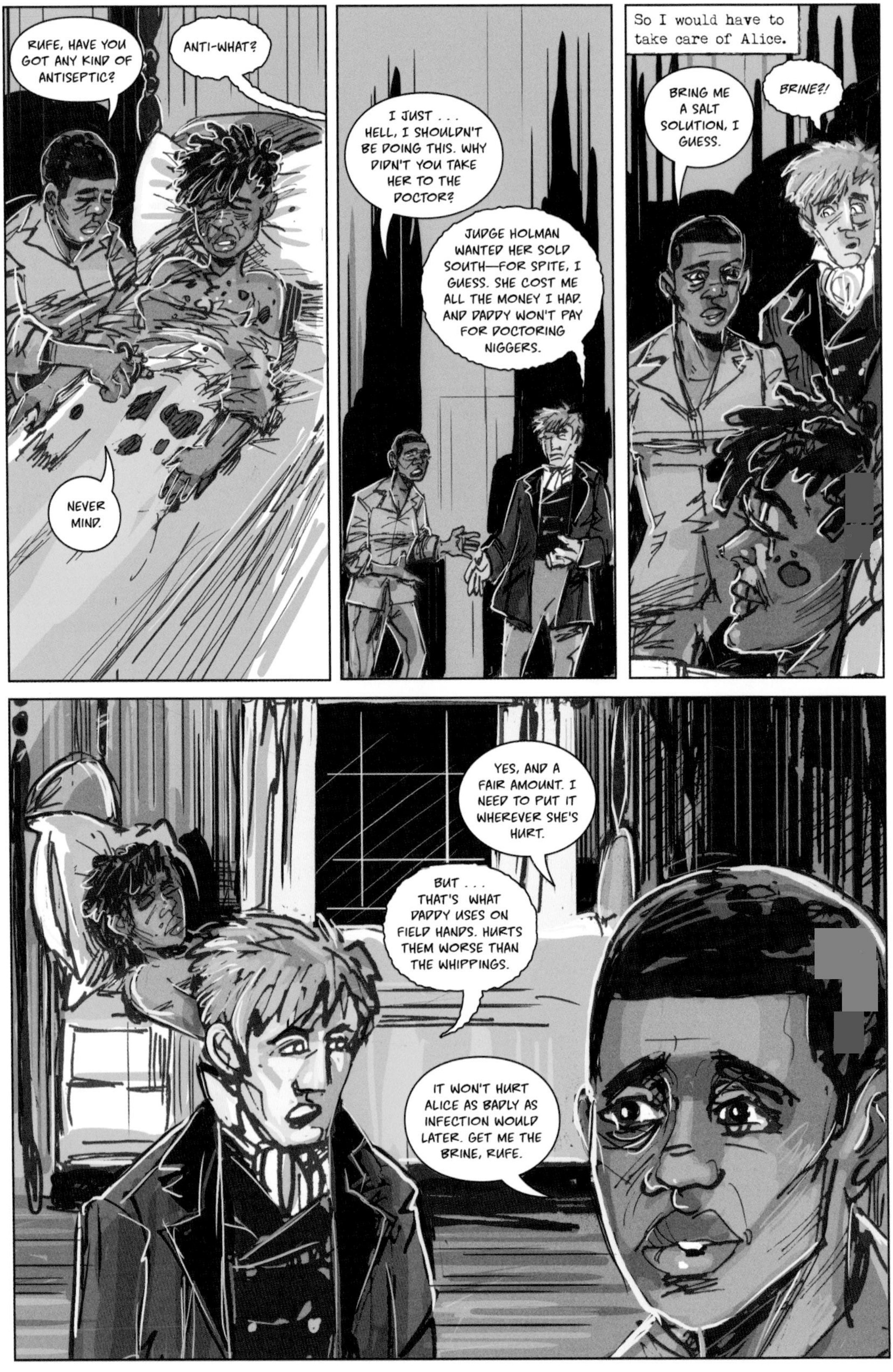
RUFE, HAVE YOU GOT ANY KIND OF ANTISEPTIC?
ANTI-WHAT?
NEVER MIND.
I JUST . . . HELL, I SHOULDN'T BE DOING THIS. WHY DIDN'T YOU TAKE HER TO THE DOCTOR?
JUDGE HOLMAN WANTED HER SOLD SOUTH—FOR SPITE, I GUESS. SHE COST ME ALL THE MONEY I HAD. AND DADDY WON'T PAY FOR DOCTORING NIGGERS.
So I would have to take care of Alice.
BRING ME A SALT SOLUTION, I GUESS.
BRINE?!
YES, AND A FAIR AMOUNT. I NEED TO PUT IT WHEREVER SHE'S HURT.
BUT . . . THAT'S WHAT DADDY USES ON FIELD HANDS. HURTS THEM WORSE THAN THE WHIPPINGS.
IT WON'T HURT ALICE AS BADLY AS INFECTION WOULD LATER. GET ME THE BRINE, RUFE.

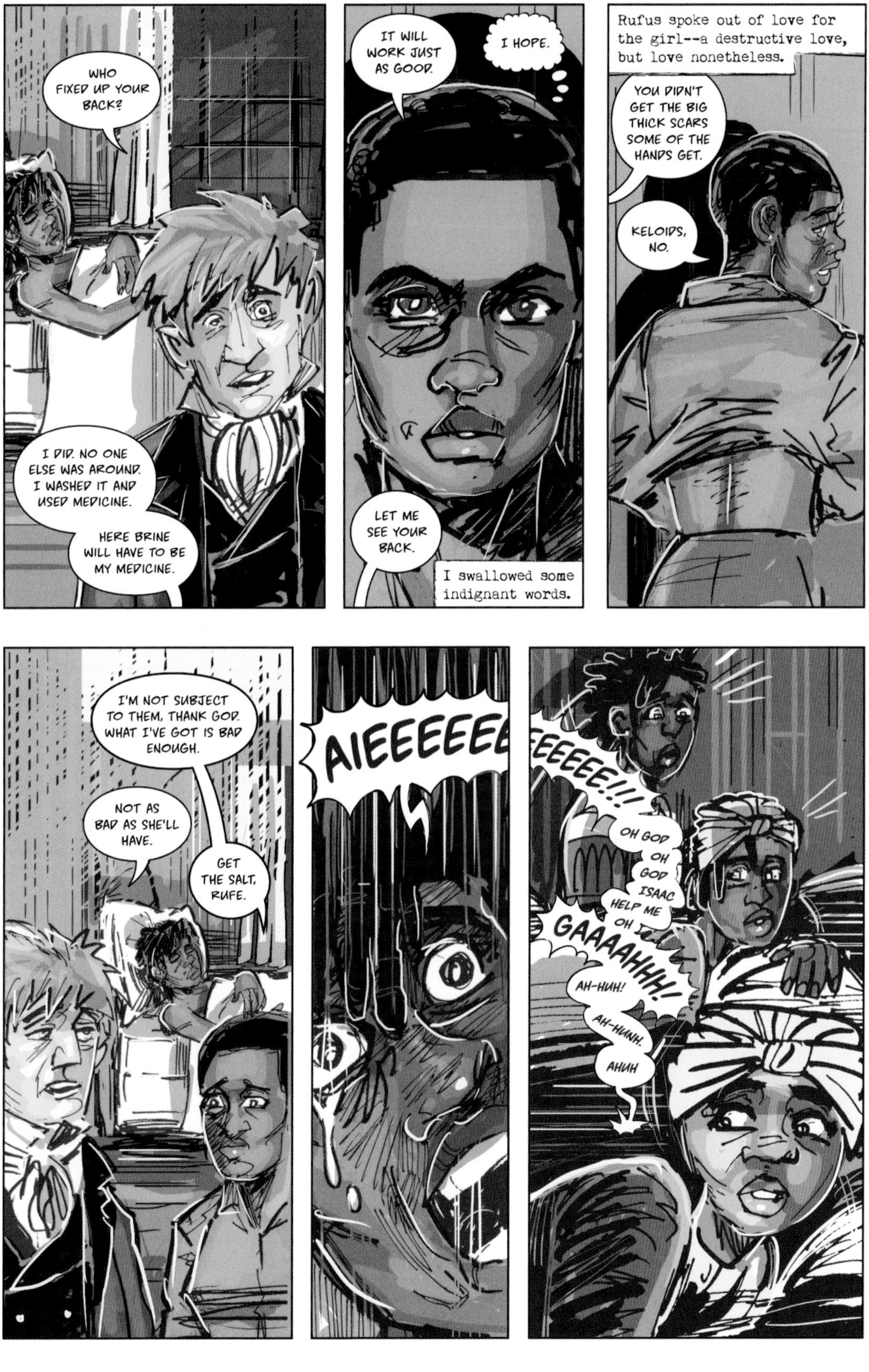

WHO FIXED UP YOUR BACK?
I DID. NO ONE ELSE WAS AROUND. I WASHED IT AND USED MEDICINE.
HERE BRINE WILL HAVE TO BE MY MEDICINE.
IT WILL WORK JUST AS GOOD.
I HOPE.
LET ME SEE YOUR BACK.
I swallowed some indignant words.
Rufus spoke out of love for the girl--a destructive love, but love nonetheless.
YOU DIDN'T GET THE BIG THICK SCARS SOME OF THE HANDS GET.
KELOIDS, NO.
I'M NOT SUBJECT TO THEM, THANK GOD. WHAT I'VE GOT IS BAD ENOUGH.
NOT AS BAD AS SHE'LL HAVE.
GET THE SALT, RUFE.
AIEEEEEEEEEEEEE!!!!
OH GOD OH GOD ISAAC HELP ME OH
GAAAAHHH!
AH-HUH!
AH-HUNH.
AHUH

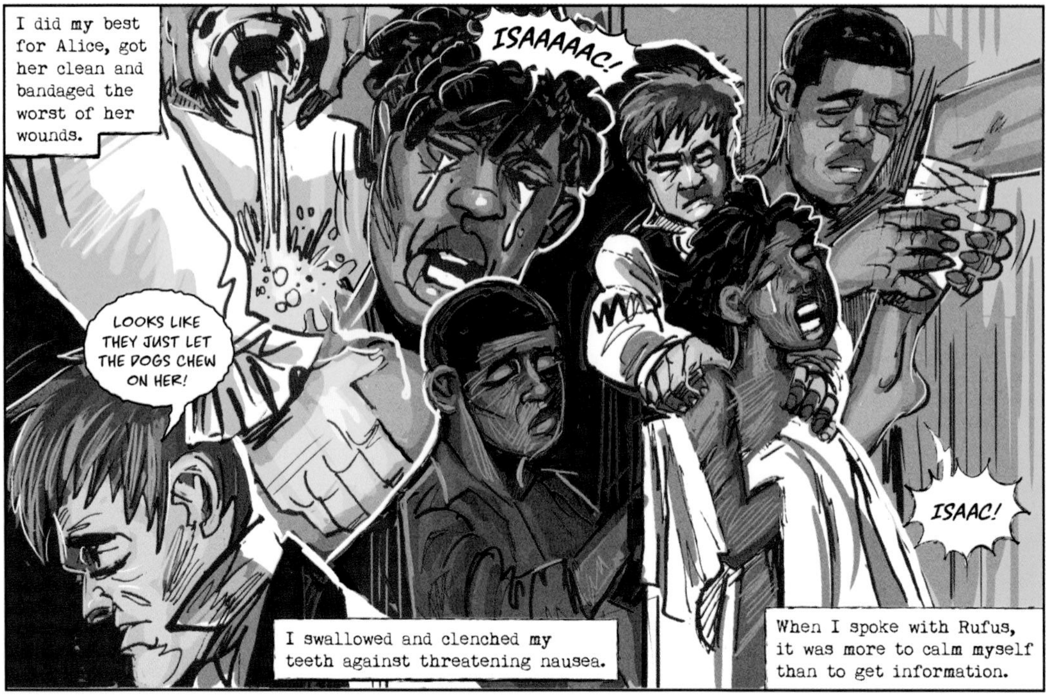
I did my best for Alice, got her clean and bandaged the worst of her wounds.
ISAAAAAC!
LOOKS LIKE THEY JUST LET THE DOGS CHEW ON HER!
ISAAC!
I swallowed and clenched my teeth against threatening nausea.
When I spoke with Rufus, it was more to calm myself than to get information.

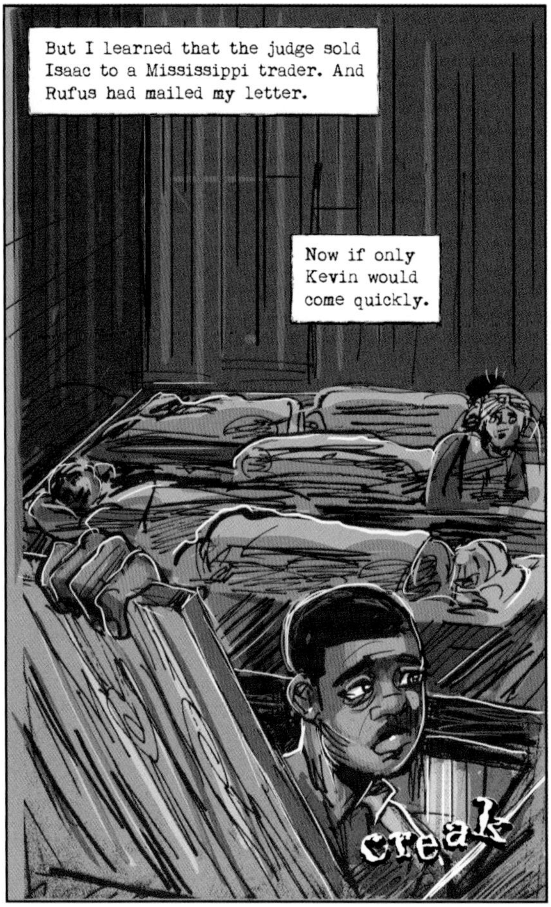
But I learned that the judge sold Isaac to a Mississippi trader. And Rufus had mailed my letter.
Now if only Kevin would come quickly.
creak

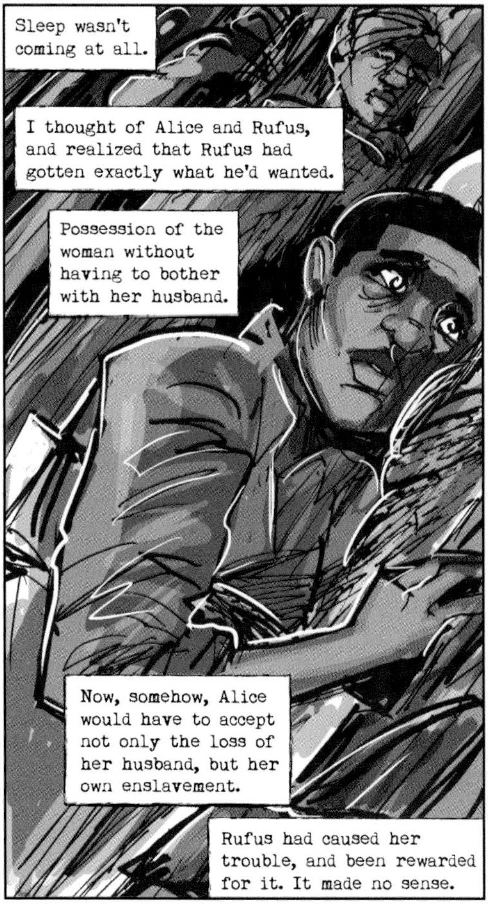
Sleep wasn't coming at all.
I thought of Alice and Rufus, and realized that Rufus had gotten exactly what he'd wanted.
Possession of the woman without having to bother with her husband.
Now, somehow, Alice would have to accept not only the loss of her husband, but her own enslavement.
Rufus had caused her trouble, and been rewarded for it. It made no sense.

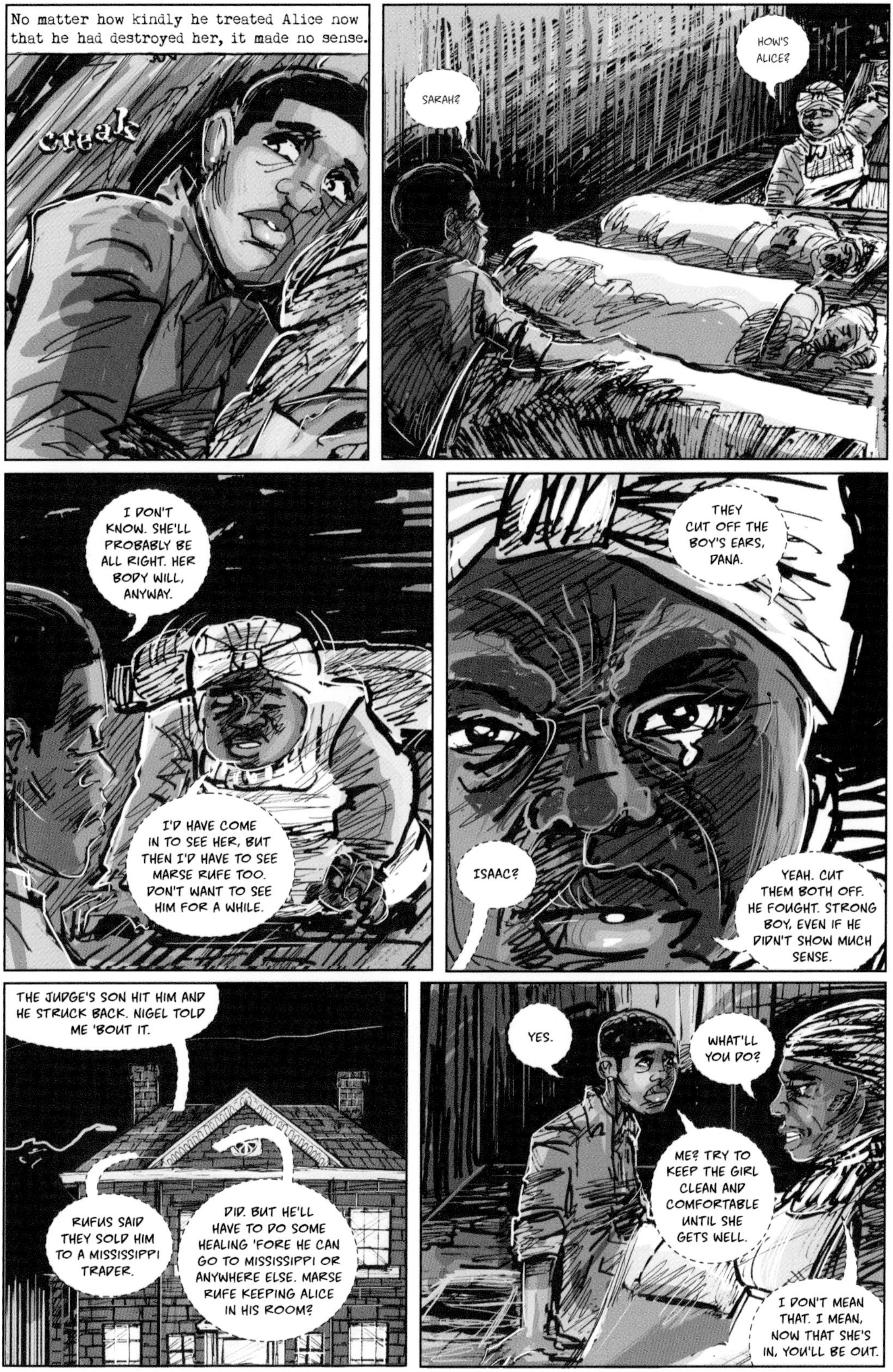
No matter how kindly he treated Alice now that he had destroyed her, it made no sense.
creak
SARAH?
HOW'S ALICE?
I DON'T KNOW. SHE'LL PROBABLY BE ALL RIGHT. HER BODY WILL, ANYWAY.
I'D HAVE COME IN TO SEE HER, BUT THEN I'D HAVE TO SEE MARSE RUFE TOO. DON'T WANT TO SEE HIM FOR A WHILE.
THEY CUT OFF THE BOY'S EARS, DANA.
ISAAC?
YEAH. CUT THEM BOTH OFF. HE FOUGHT. STRONG BOY, EVEN IF HE DIDN'T SHOW MUCH SENSE.
THE JUDGE'S SON HIT HIM AND HE STRUCK BACK. NIGEL TOLD ME 'BOUT IT.
RUFUS SAID THEY SOLD HIM TO A MISSISSIPPI TRADER.
DID. BUT HE'LL HAVE TO DO SOME HEALING 'FORE HE CAN GO TO MISSISSIPPI OR ANYWHERE ELSE. MARSE RUFE KEEPING ALICE IN HIS ROOM?
YES.
WHAT'LL YOU DO?
ME? TRY TO KEEP THE GIRL CLEAN AND COMFORTABLE UNTIL SHE GETS WELL.
I DON'T MEAN THAT. I MEAN, NOW THAT SHE'S IN, YOU'LL BE OUT.

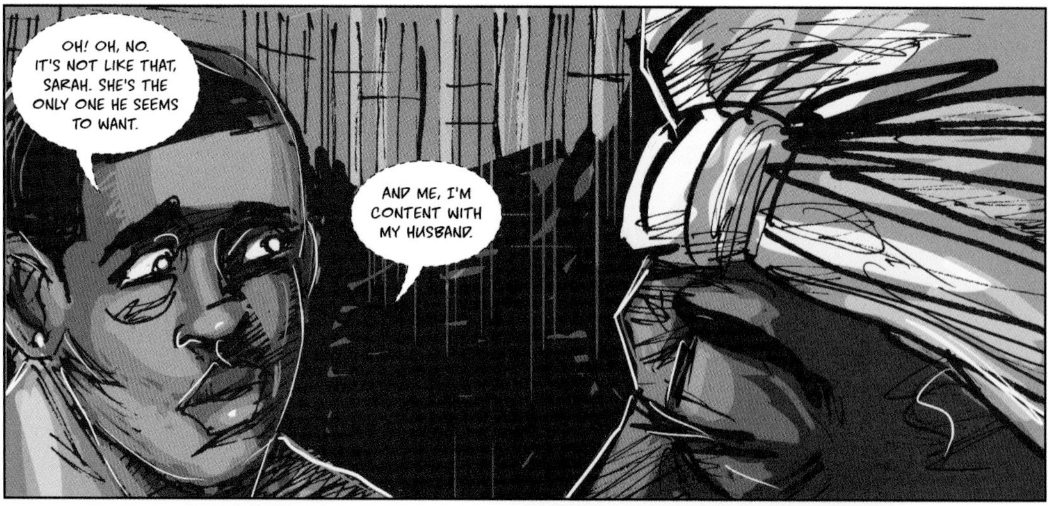
OH! OH, NO. IT'S NOT LIKE THAT, SARAH. SHE'S THE ONLY ONE HE SEEMS TO WANT.
AND ME, I'M CONTENT WITH MY HUSBAND.

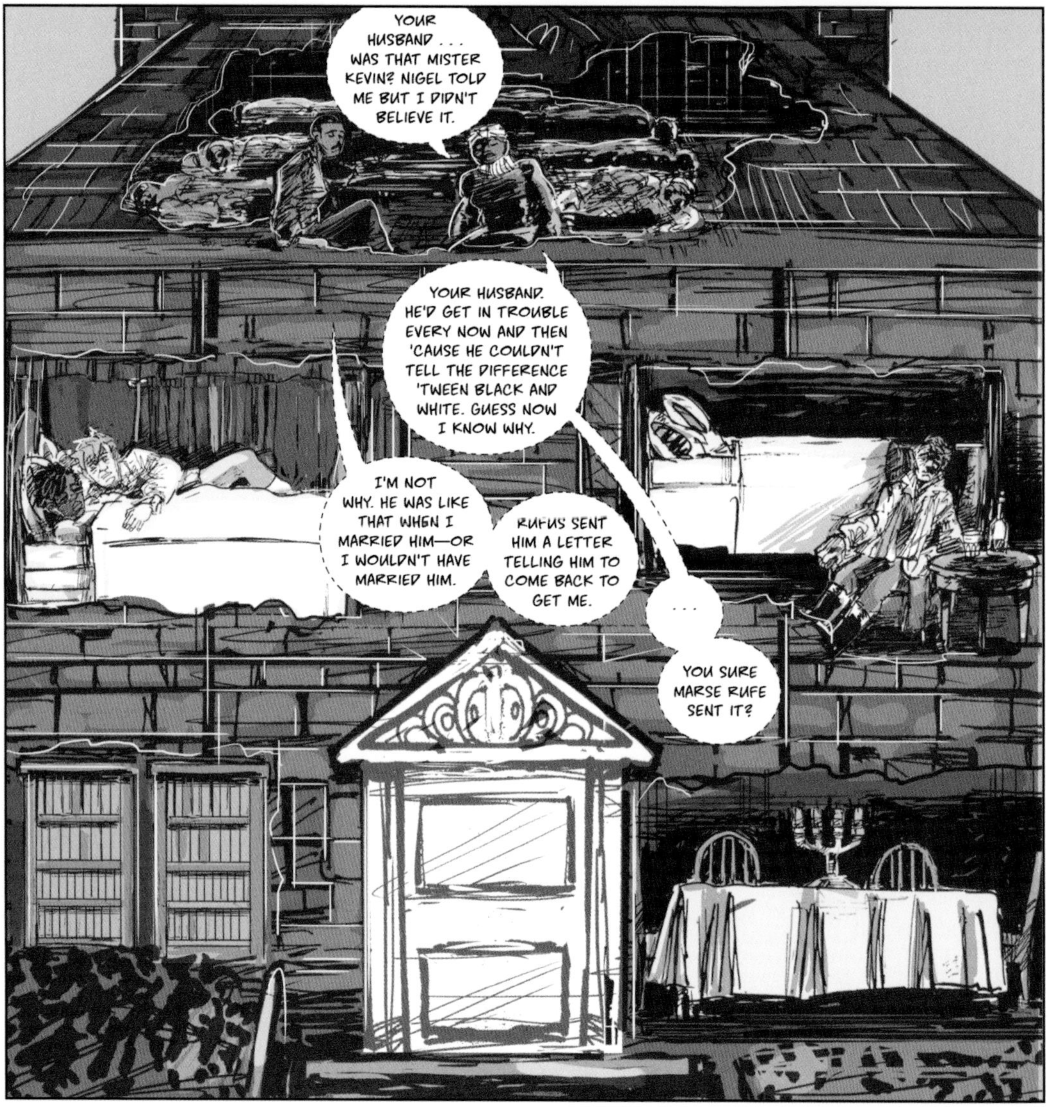
YOUR HUSBAND . . . WAS THAT MISTER KEVIN? NIGEL TOLD ME BUT I DIDN'T BELIEVE IT.
YOUR HUSBAND. HE'D GET IN TROUBLE EVERY NOW AND THEN 'CAUSE HE COULDN'T TELL THE DIFFERENCE 'TWEEN BLACK AND WHITE. GUESS NOW I KNOW WHY.
I'M NOT WHY. HE WAS LIKE THAT WHEN I MARRIED HIM—OR I WOULDN'T HAVE MARRIED HIM.
RUFUS SENT HIM A LETTER TELLING HIM TO COME BACK TO GET ME.
. . .
YOU SURE MARSE RUFE SENT IT?

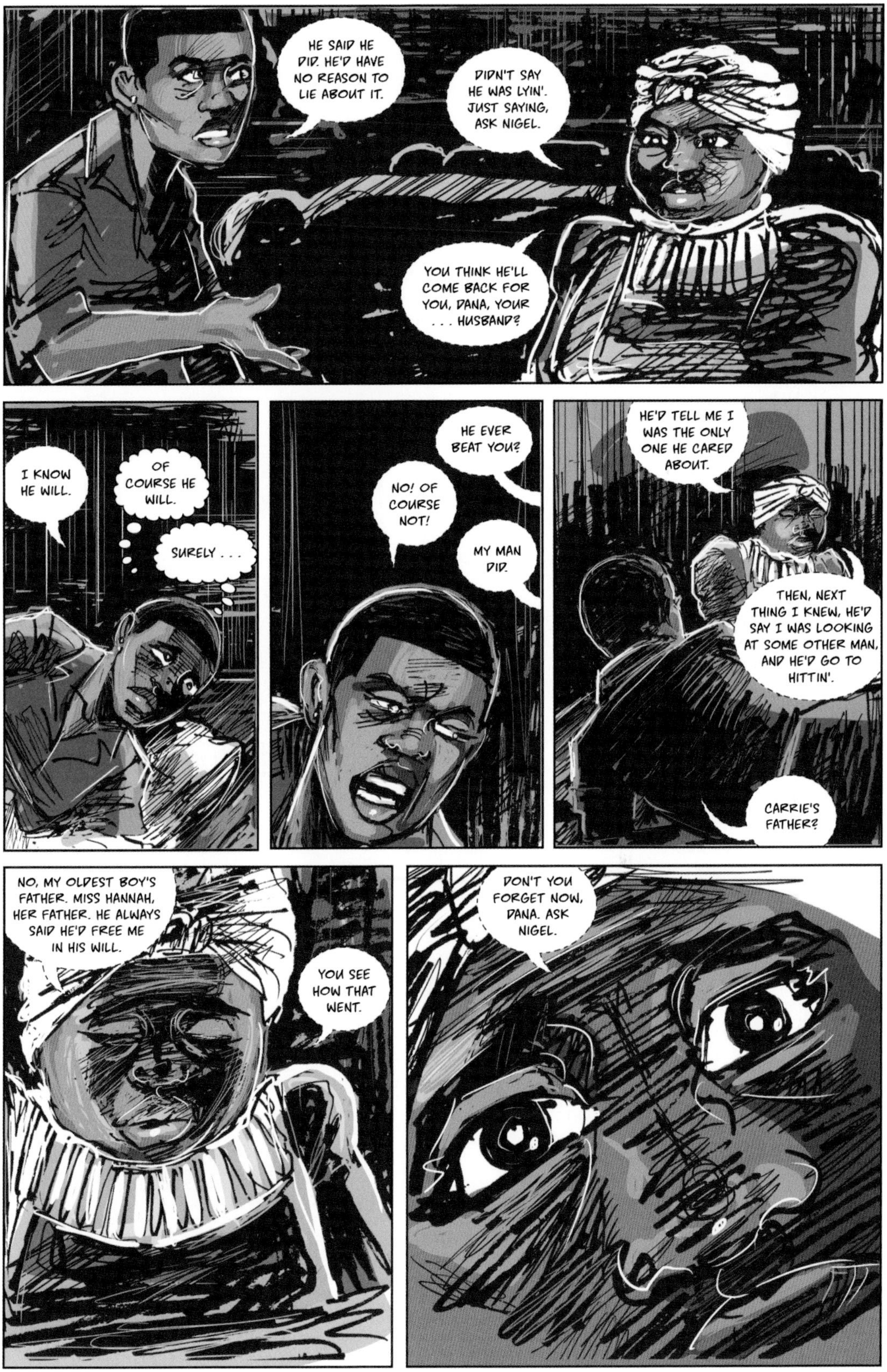
HE SAID HE DID. HE'D HAVE NO REASON TO LIE ABOUT IT.
DIDN'T SAY HE WAS LYIN'. JUST SAYING, ASK NIGEL.
YOU THINK HE'LL COME BACK FOR YOU, DANA, YOUR . . . HUSBAND?
I KNOW HE WILL.
OF COURSE HE WILL.
SURELY . . .
HE EVER BEAT YOU?
NO! OF COURSE NOT!
MY MAN DID.
HE'D TELL ME I WAS THE ONLY ONE HE CARED ABOUT.
THEN, NEXT THING I KNEW, HE'D SAY I WAS LOOKING AT SOME OTHER MAN, AND HE'D GO TO HITTIN'.
CARRIE'S FATHER?
NO, MY OLDEST BOY'S FATHER. MISS HANNAH, HER FATHER. HE ALWAYS SAID HE'D FREE ME IN HIS WILL.
YOU SEE HOW THAT WENT.
DON'T YOU FORGET NOW, DANA. ASK NIGEL.

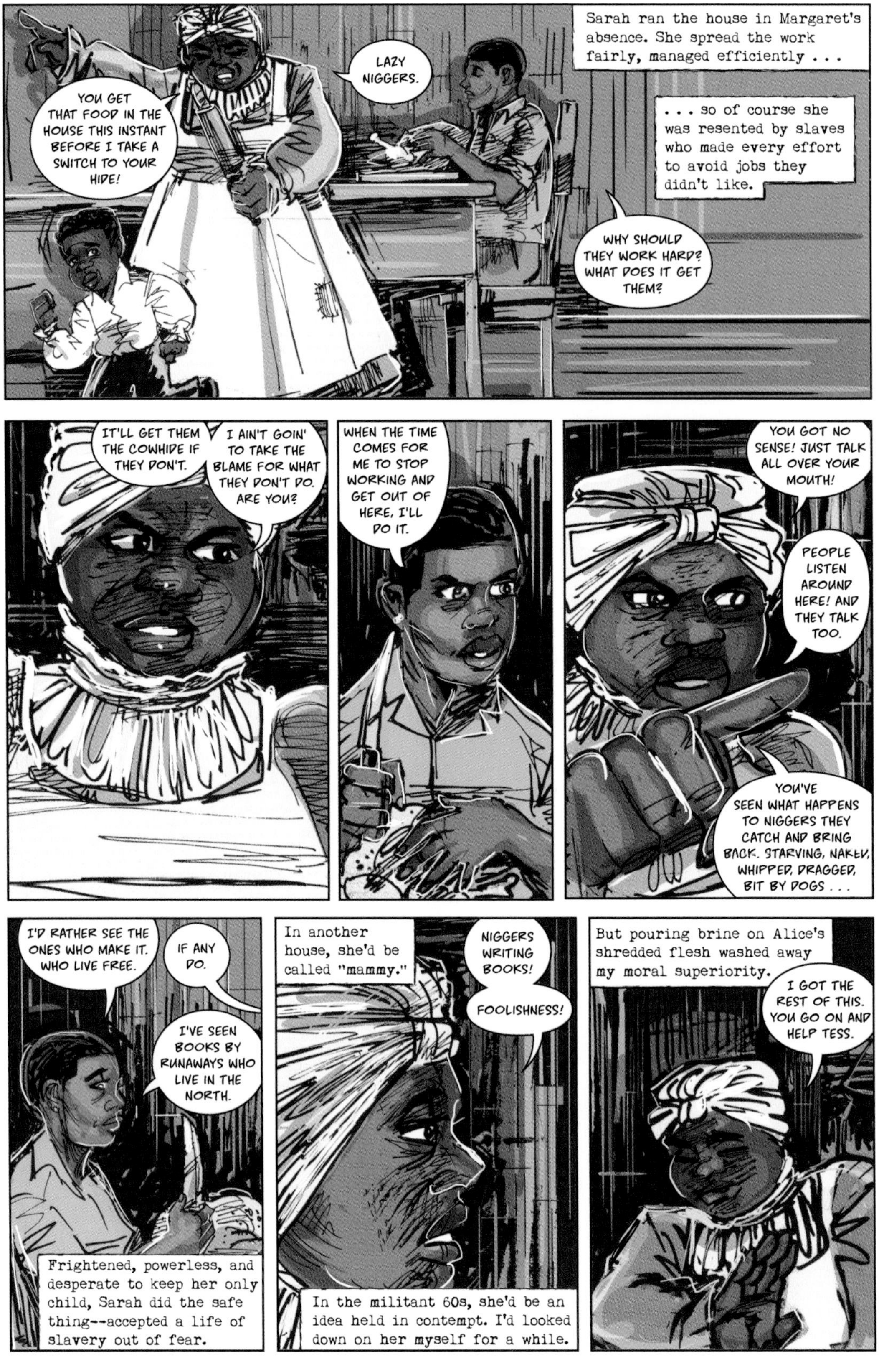
Sarah ran the house in Margaret's absence. She spread the work fairly, managed efficiently . . .
YOU GET THAT FOOD IN THE HOUSE THIS INSTANT BEFORE I TAKE A SWITCH TO YOUR HIDE!
LAZY NIGGERS.
. . . so of course she was resented by slaves who made every effort to avoid jobs they didn't like.
WHY SHOULD THEY WORK HARD? WHAT DOES IT GET THEM?
IT'LL GET THEM THE COWHIDE IF THEY DON'T.
I AIN'T GOIN' TO TAKE THE BLAME FOR WHAT THEY DON'T DO. ARE YOU?
WHEN THE TIME COMES FOR ME TO STOP WORKING AND GET OUT OF HERE, I'LL DO IT.
YOU GOT NO SENSE! JUST TALK ALL OVER YOUR MOUTH!
PEOPLE LISTEN AROUND HERE! AND THEY TALK TOO.
YOU'VE SEEN WHAT HAPPENS TO NIGGERS THEY CATCH AND BRING BACK. STARVING, NAKED, WHIPPED, DRAGGED, BIT BY DOGS . . .
I'D RATHER SEE THE ONES WHO MAKE IT. WHO LIVE FREE.
IF ANY DO.
I'VE SEEN BOOKS BY RUNAWAYS WHO LIVE IN THE NORTH.
Frightened, powerless, and desperate to keep her only child, Sarah did the safe thing--accepted a life of slavery out of fear.
In another house, she'd be called "mammy."
NIGGERS WRITING BOOKS!
FOOLISHNESS!
In the militant 60s, she'd be an idea held in contempt. I'd looked down on her myself for a while.
But pouring brine on Alice's shredded flesh washed away my moral superiority.
I GOT THE REST OF THIS. YOU GO ON AND HELP TESS.

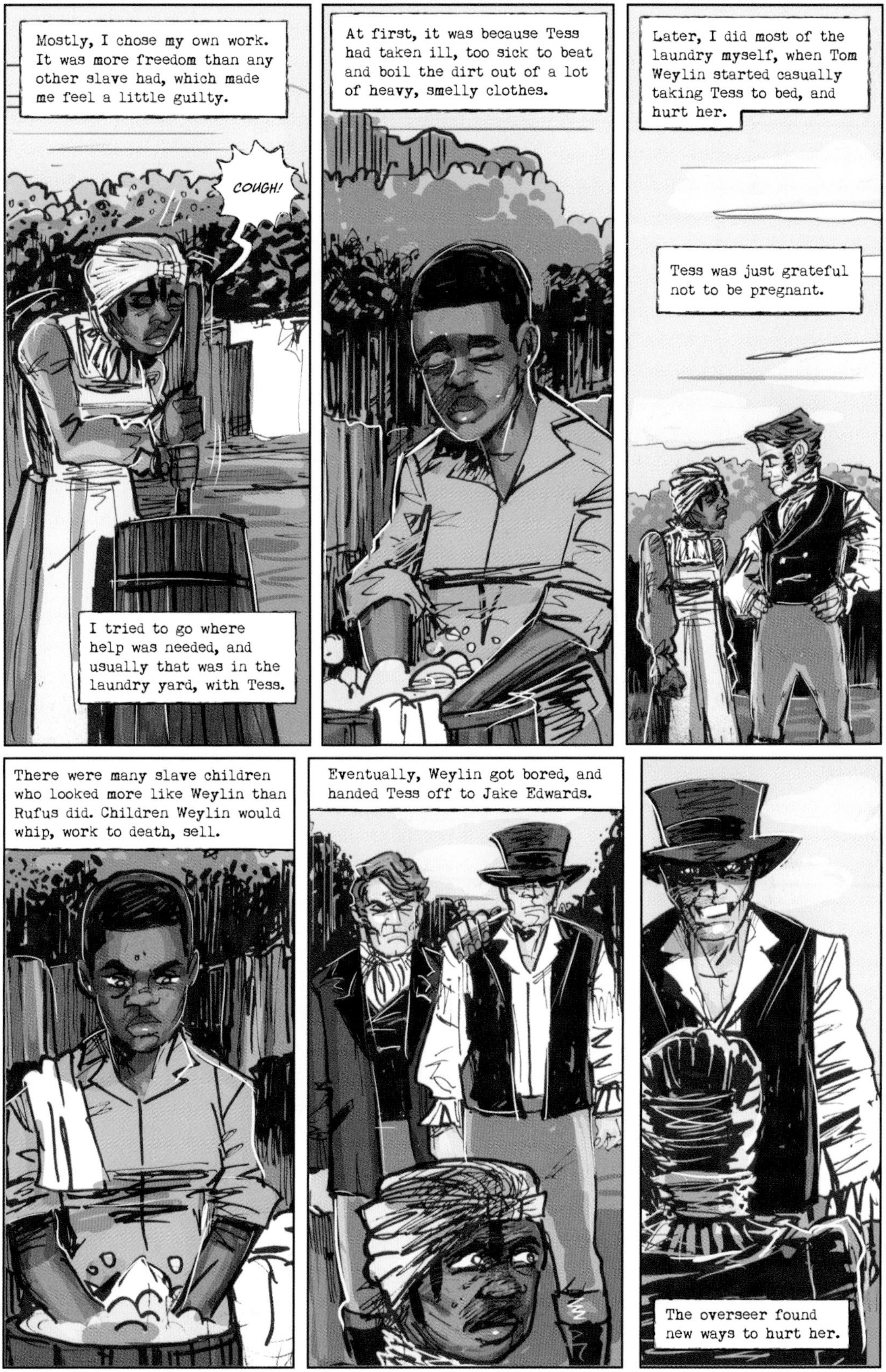

Mostly, I chose my own work. It was more freedom than any other slave had, which made me feel a little guilty.
COUGH!
I tried to go where help was needed, and usually that was in the laundry yard, with Tess.
At first, it was because Tess had taken ill, too sick to beat and boil the dirt out of a lot of heavy, smelly clothes.
Later, I did most of the laundry myself, when Tom Weylin started casually taking Tess to bed, and hurt her.
Tess was just grateful not to be pregnant.
There were many slave children who looked more like Weylin than Rufus did. Children Weylin would whip, work to death, sell.
Eventually, Weylin got bored, and handed Tess off to Jake Edwards.
The overseer found new ways to hurt her.

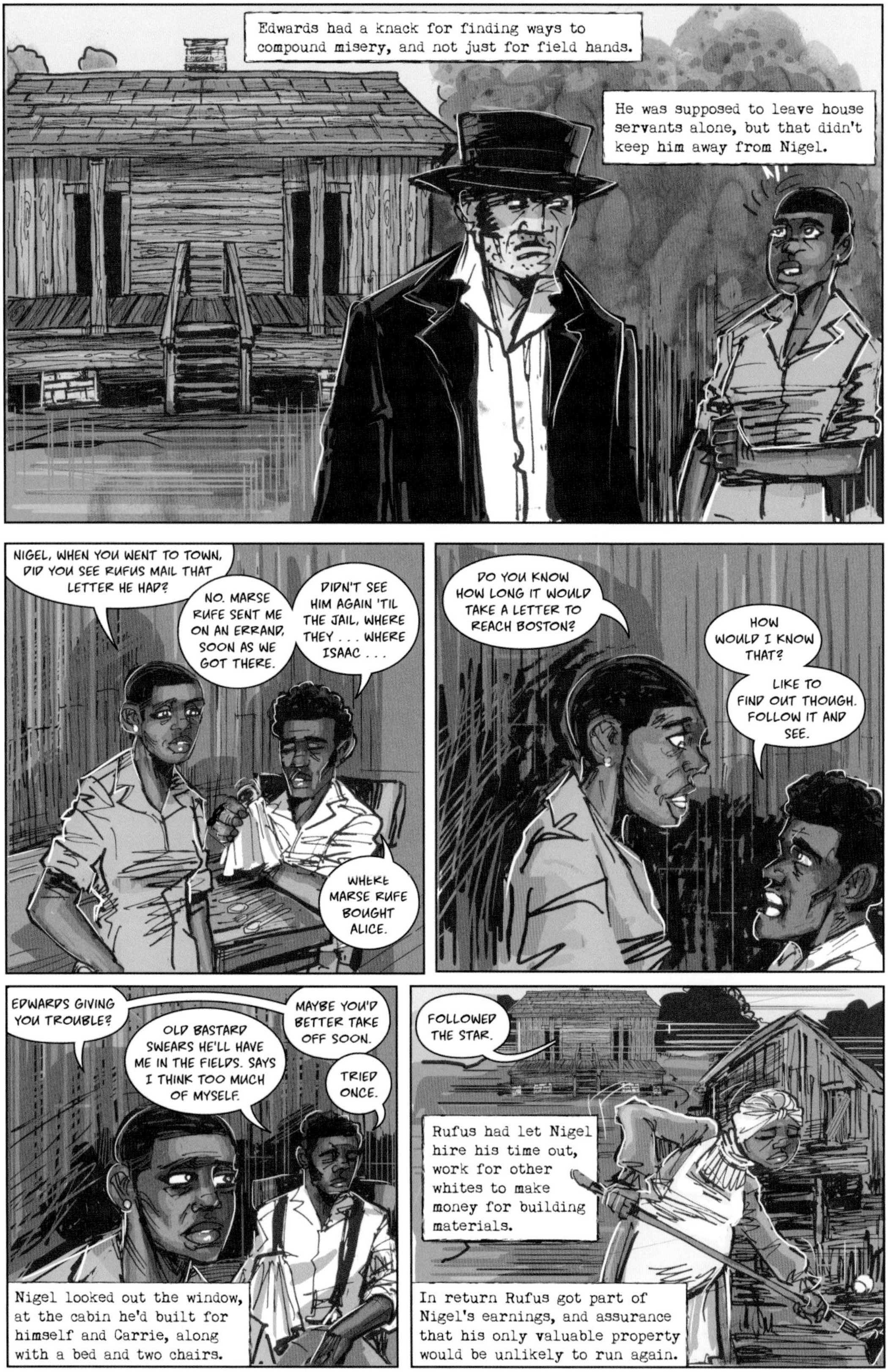

Edwards had a knack for finding ways to compound misery, and not just for field hands.
He was supposed to leave house servants alone, but that didn't keep him away from Nigel.
NIGEL, WHEN YOU WENT TO TOWN, DID YOU SEE RUFUS MAIL THAT LETTER HE HAD?
NO. MARSE RUFE SENT ME ON AN ERRAND, SOON AS WE GOT THERE.
DIDN'T SEE HIM AGAIN 'TIL THE JAIL, WHERE THEY . . . WHERE ISAAC . . .
WHERE MARSE RUFE BOUGHT ALICE.
DO YOU KNOW HOW LONG IT WOULD TAKE A LETTER TO REACH BOSTON?
HOW WOULD I KNOW THAT?
LIKE TO FIND OUT THOUGH. FOLLOW IT AND SEE.
EDWARDS GIVING YOU TROUBLE?
OLD BASTARD SWEARS HE'LL HAVE ME IN THE FIELDS. SAYS I THINK TOO MUCH OF MYSELF.
MAYBE YOU'D BETTER TAKE OFF SOON.
TRIED ONCE.
Nigel looked out the window, at the cabin he'd built for himself and Carrie, along with a bed and two chairs.
FOLLOWED THE STAR.
Rufus had let Nigel hire his time out, work for other whites to make money for building materials.
In return Rufus got part of Nigel's earnings, and assurance that his only valuable property would be unlikely to run again.

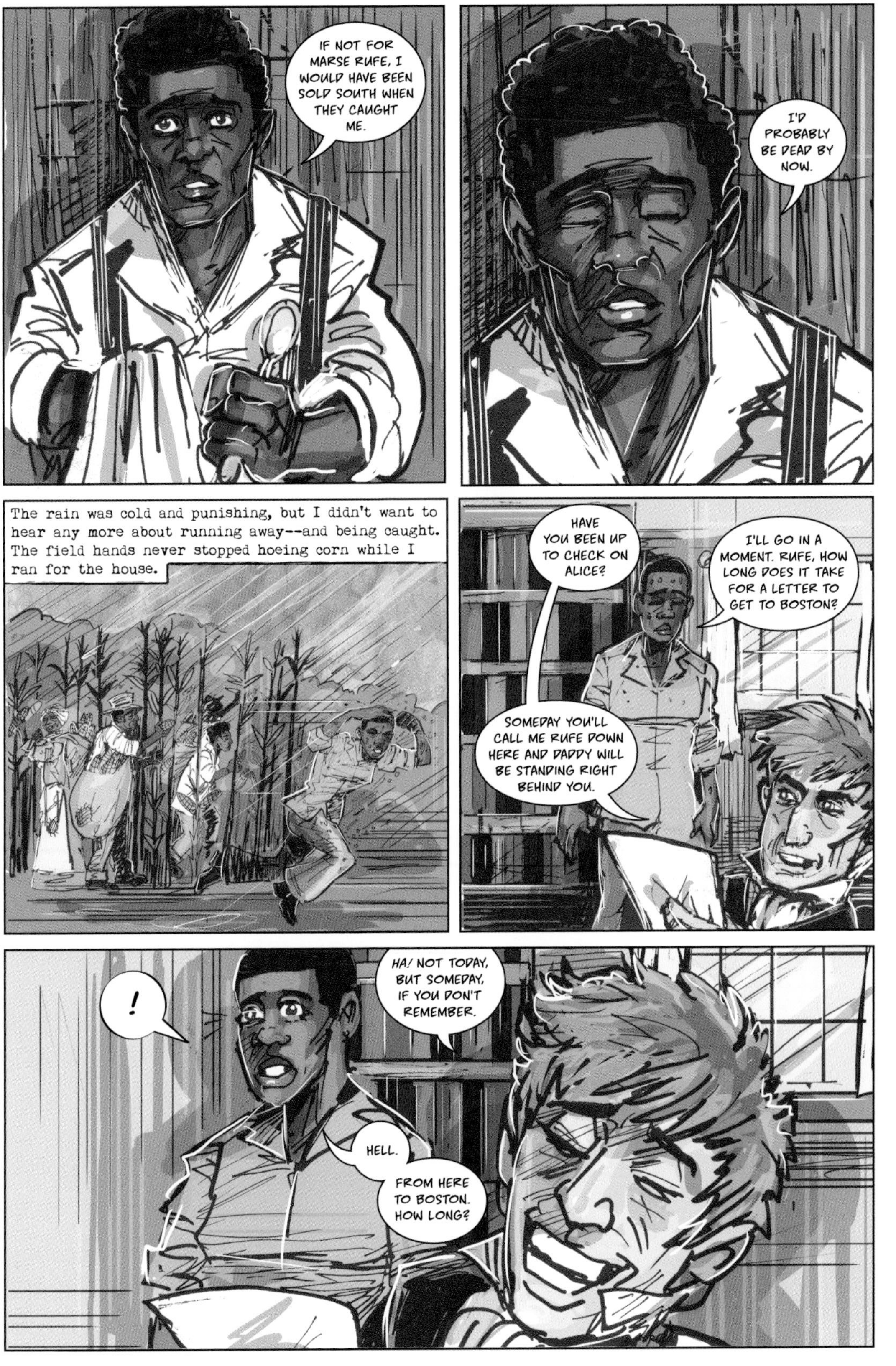

IF NOT FOR MARSE RUFE, I WOULD HAVE BEEN SOLD SOUTH WHEN THEY CAUGHT ME.
I'D PROBABLY BE DEAD BY NOW.
The rain was cold and punishing, but I didn't want to hear any more about running away--and being caught. The field hands never stopped hoeing corn while I ran for the house.
HAVE YOU BEEN UP TO CHECK ON ALICE?
I'LL GO IN A MOMENT. RUFE, HOW LONG DOES IT TAKE FOR A LETTER TO GET TO BOSTON?
SOMEDAY YOU'LL CALL ME RUFE DOWN HERE AND DADDY WILL BE STANDING RIGHT BEHIND YOU.
!
HA! NOT TODAY, BUT SOMEDAY, IF YOU DON'T REMEMBER.
HELL.
FROM HERE TO BOSTON. HOW LONG?

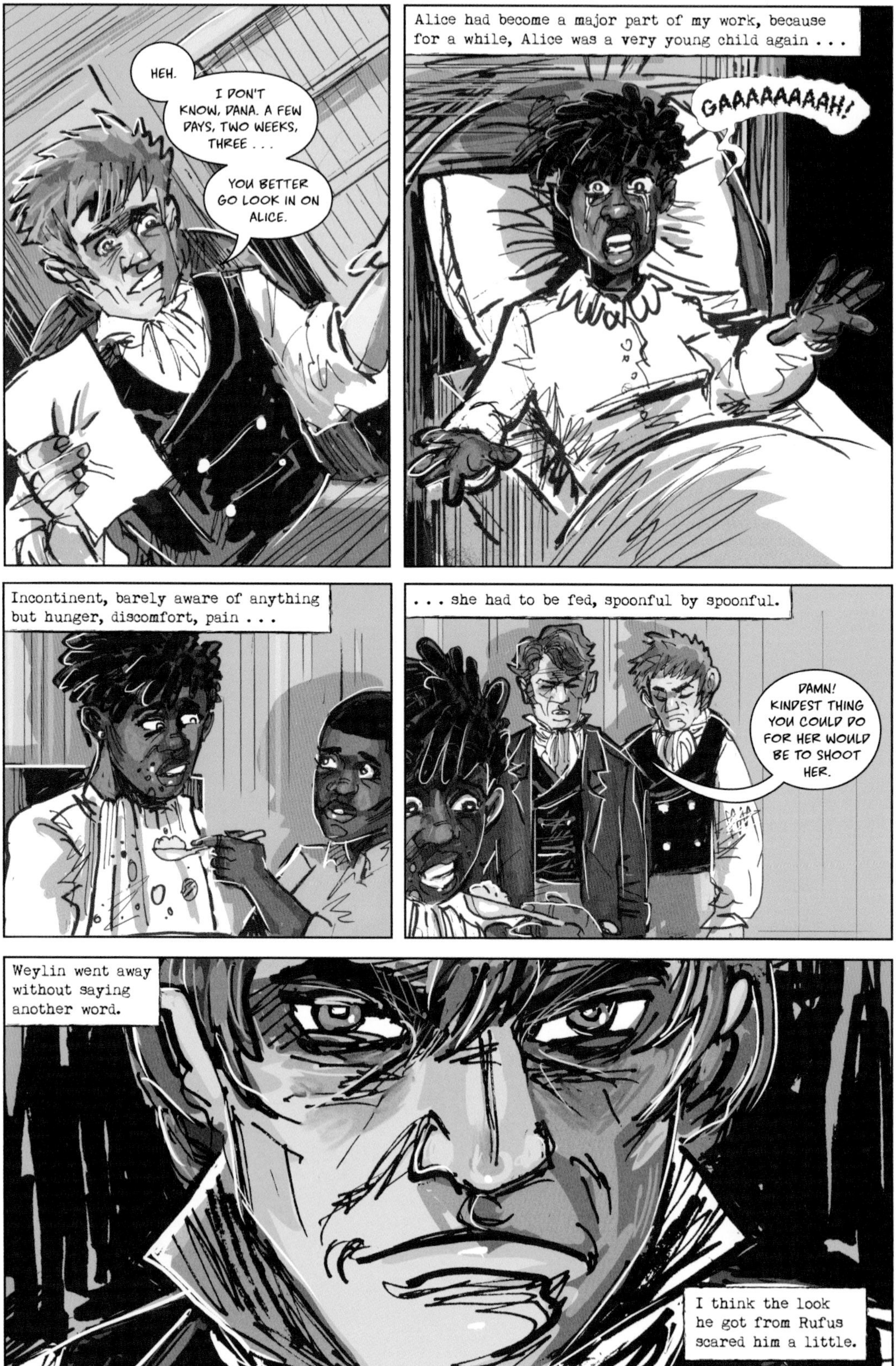
HEH.
I DON'T KNOW, DANA. A FEW DAYS, TWO WEEKS, THREE . . .
YOU BETTER GO LOOK IN ON ALICE.
Alice had become a major part of my work, because for a while, Alice was a very young child again . . .
GAAAAAAAAH!
Incontinent, barely aware of anything but hunger, discomfort, pain . . .
. . . she had to be fed, spoonful by spoonful.
DAMN! KINDEST THING YOU COULD DO FOR HER WOULD BE TO SHOOT HER.
Weylin went away without saying another word.
I think the look he got from Rufus scared him a little.

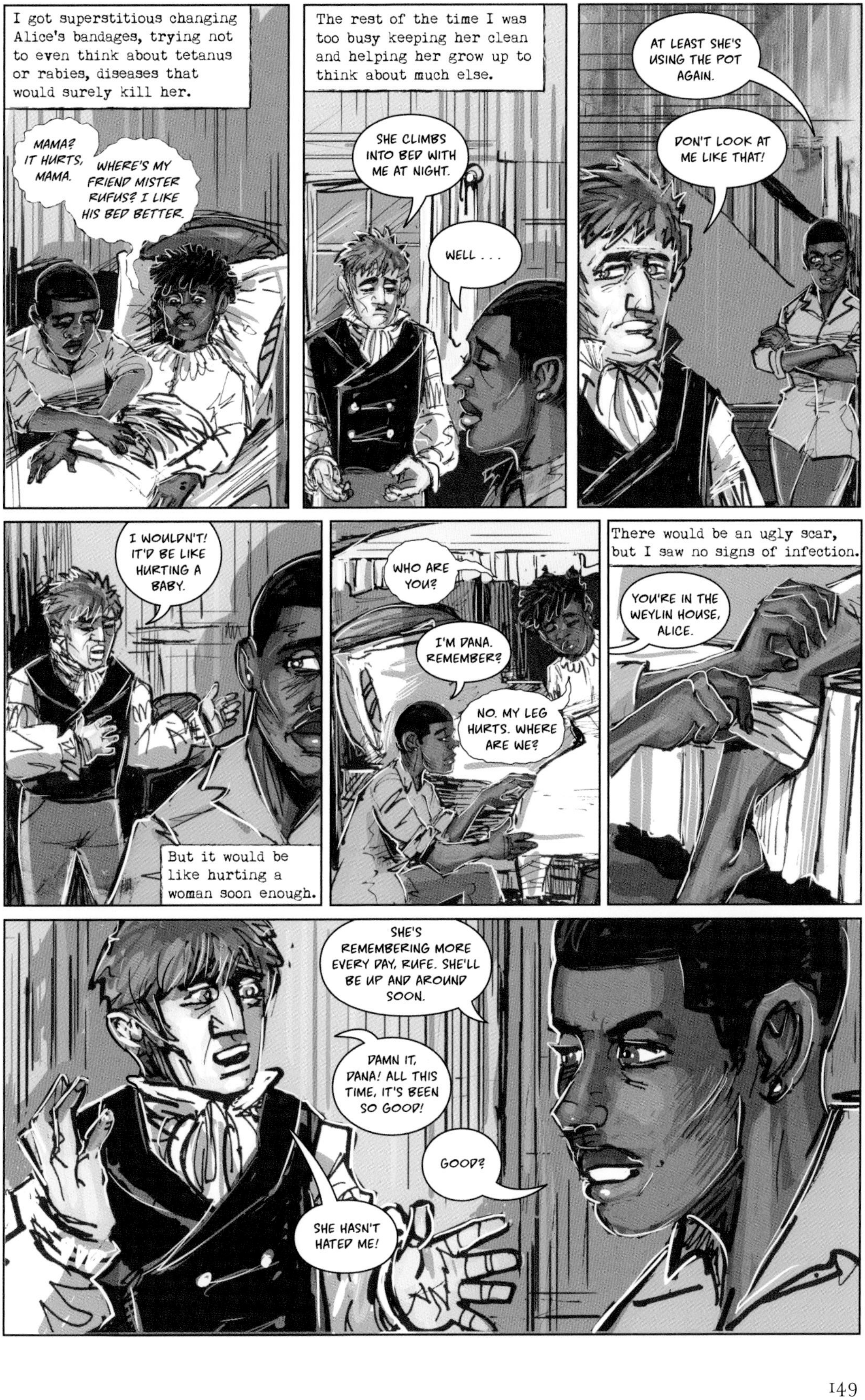
I got superstitious changing Alice's bandages, trying not to even think about tetanus or rabies, diseases that would surely kill her.
MAMA? IT HURTS, MAMA.
WHERE'S MY FRIEND MISTER RUFUS? I LIKE HIS BED BETTER.
The rest of the time I was too busy keeping her clean and helping her grow up to think about much else.
SHE CLIMBS INTO BED WITH ME AT NIGHT.
WELL . . .
AT LEAST SHE'S USING THE POT AGAIN.
DON'T LOOK AT ME LIKE THAT!
I WOULDN'T! IT'D BE LIKE HURTING A BABY.
But it would be like hurting a woman soon enough.
WHO ARE YOU?
I'M DANA. REMEMBER?
NO. MY LEG HURTS. WHERE ARE WE?
There would be an ugly scar, but I saw no signs of infection.
YOU'RE IN THE WEYLIN HOUSE, ALICE.
SHE'S REMEMBERING MORE EVERY DAY, RUFE. SHE'LL BE UP AND AROUND SOON.
DAMN IT, DANA! ALL THIS TIME, IT'S BEEN SO GOOD!
GOOD?
SHE HASN'T HATED ME!

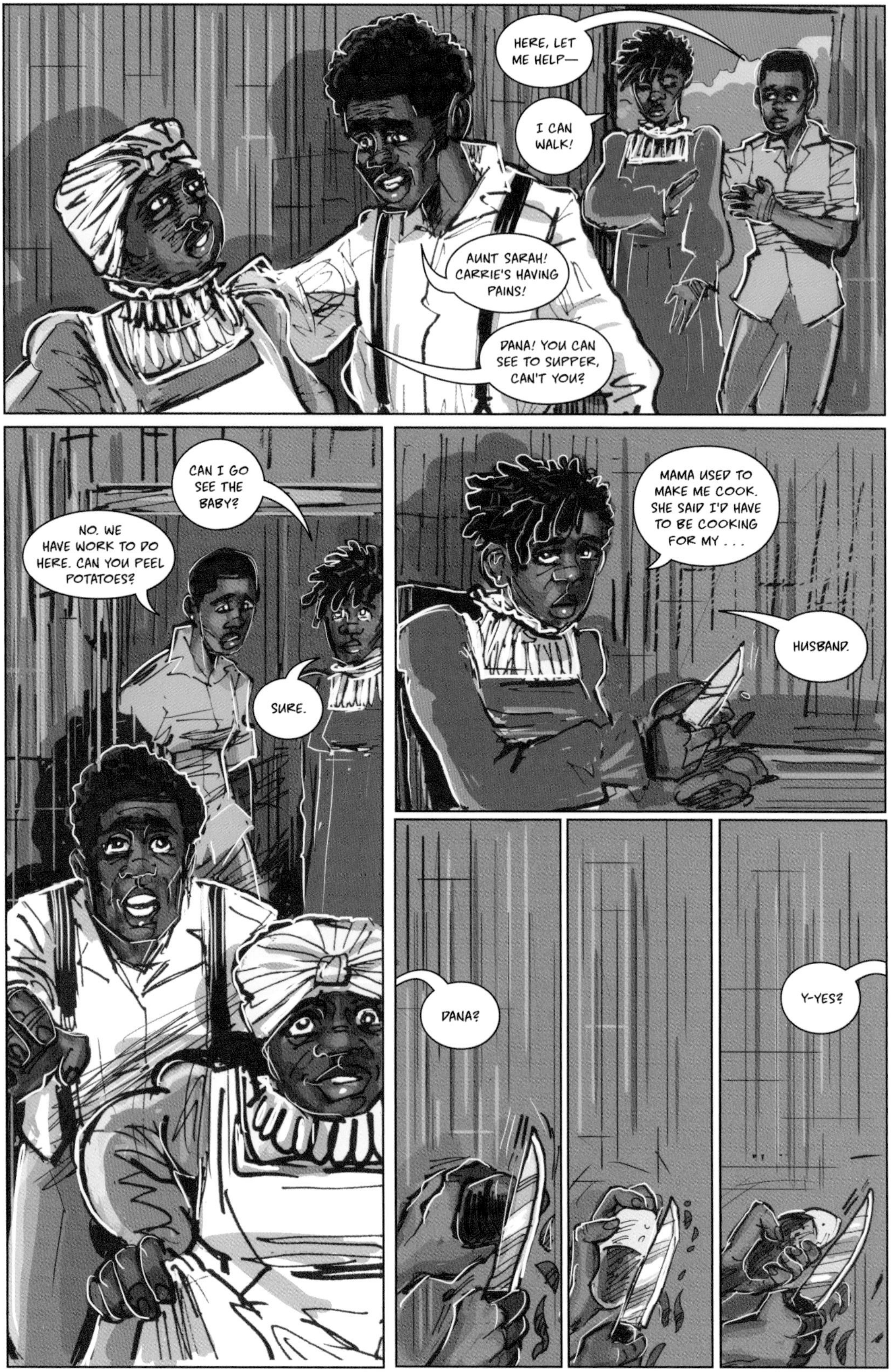
HERE, LET ME HELP—
I CAN WALK!
AUNT SARAH! CARRIE'S HAVING PAINS!
DANA! YOU CAN SEE TO SUPPER, CAN'T YOU?
CAN I GO SEE THE BABY?
NO. WE HAVE WORK TO DO HERE. CAN YOU PEEL POTATOES?
SURE.
MAMA USED TO MAKE ME COOK. SHE SAID I'D HAVE TO BE COOKING FOR MY . . .
HUSBAND.
DANA?
Y-YES?

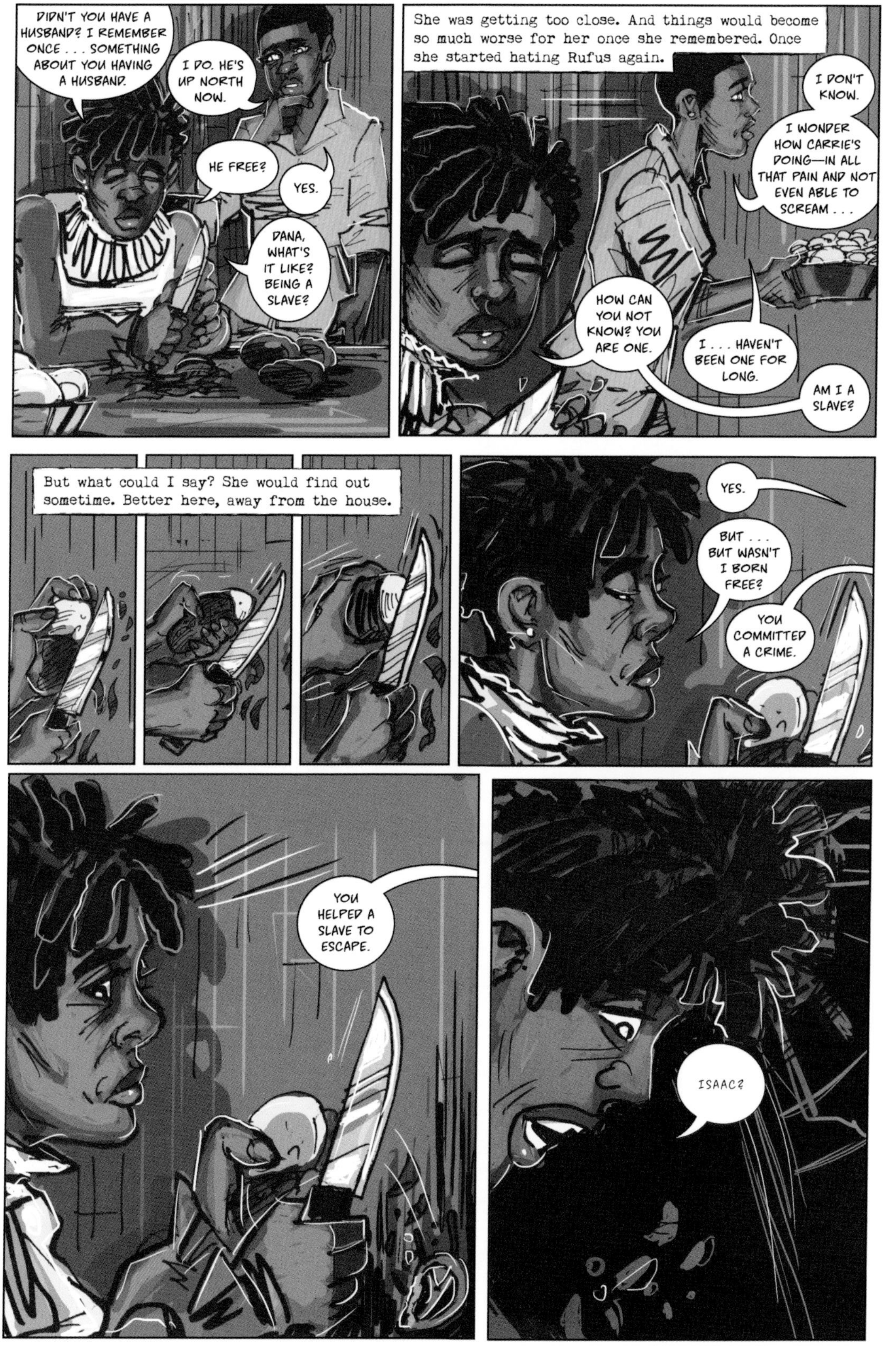
DIDN'T YOU HAVE A HUSBAND? I REMEMBER ONCE . . . SOMETHING ABOUT YOU HAVING A HUSBAND.
I DO. HE'S UP NORTH NOW.
HE FREE?
YES.
DANA, WHAT'S IT LIKE? BEING A SLAVE?
She was getting too close. And things would become so much worse for her once she remembered. Once she started hating Rufus again.
I DON'T KNOW.
I WONDER HOW CARRIE'S DOING—IN ALL THAT PAIN AND NOT EVEN ABLE TO SCREAM . . .
HOW CAN YOU NOT KNOW? YOU ARE ONE.
I . . . HAVEN'T BEEN ONE FOR LONG.
AM I A SLAVE?
But what could I say? She would find out sometime. Better here, away from the house.
YES.
BUT . . . BUT WASN'T I BORN FREE?
YOU COMMITTED A CRIME.
YOU HELPED A SLAVE TO ESCAPE.
ISAAC?

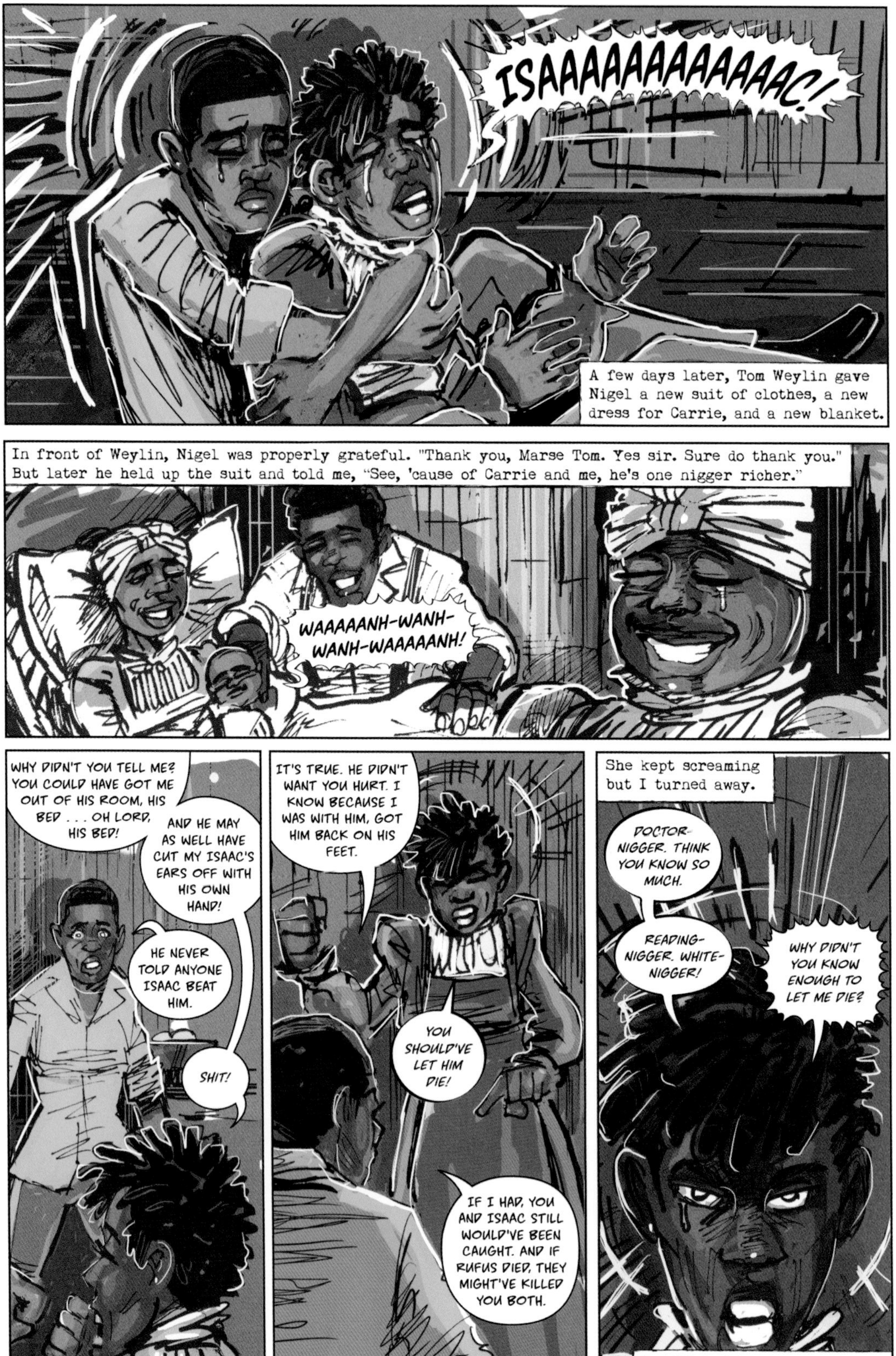
ISAAAAAAAAAAAC!
A few days later, Tom Weylin gave Nigel a new suit of clothes, a new dress for Carrie, and a new blanket.
In front of Weylin, Nigel was properly grateful. "Thank you, Marse Tom. Yes sir. Sure do thank you." But later he held up the suit and told me, "See, 'cause of Carrie and me, he's one nigger richer."
WAAAAANH-WANH-WANH-WAAAAANH!
WHY DIDN'T YOU TELL ME? YOU COULD HAVE GOT ME OUT OF HIS ROOM, HIS BED . . . OH LORD, HIS BED!
AND HE MAY AS WELL HAVE CUT MY ISAAC'S EARS OFF WITH HIS OWN HAND!
HE NEVER TOLD ANYONE ISAAC BEAT HIM.
SHIT!
IT'S TRUE. HE DIDN'T WANT YOU HURT. I KNOW BECAUSE I WAS WITH HIM, GOT HIM BACK ON HIS FEET.
YOU SHOULD'VE LET HIM DIE!
IF I HAD, YOU AND ISAAC STILL WOULD'VE BEEN CAUGHT. AND IF RUFUS DIED, THEY MIGHT'VE KILLED YOU BOTH.
She kept screaming but I turned away.
DOCTOR-NIGGER. THINK YOU KNOW SO MUCH.
READING-NIGGER. WHITE-NIGGER!
WHY DIDN'T YOU KNOW ENOUGH TO LET ME DIE?
I still had to prepare dinner.

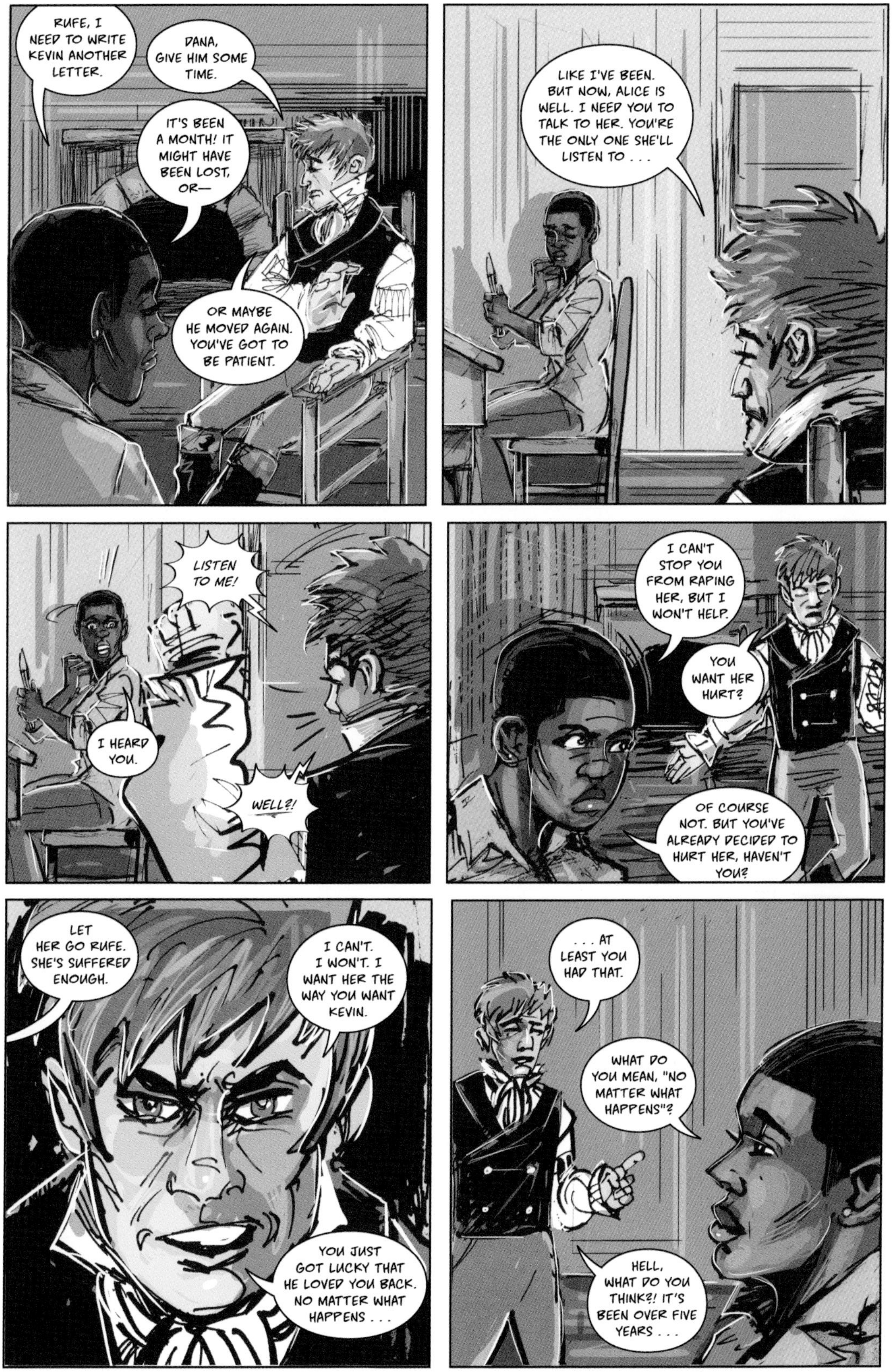
RUFE, I NEED TO WRITE KEVIN ANOTHER LETTER.
DANA, GIVE HIM SOME TIME.
IT'S BEEN A MONTH! IT MIGHT HAVE BEEN LOST, OR—
OR MAYBE HE MOVED AGAIN. YOU'VE GOT TO BE PATIENT.
LIKE I'VE BEEN. BUT NOW, ALICE IS WELL. I NEED YOU TO TALK TO HER. YOU'RE THE ONLY ONE SHE'LL LISTEN TO . . .
LISTEN TO ME!
I HEARD YOU.
WELL?!
I CAN'T STOP YOU FROM RAPING HER, BUT I WON'T HELP.
YOU WANT HER HURT?
OF COURSE NOT. BUT YOU'VE ALREADY DECIDED TO HURT HER, HAVEN'T YOU?
LET HER GO RUFE. SHE'S SUFFERED ENOUGH.
I CAN'T. I WON'T. I WANT HER THE WAY YOU WANT KEVIN.
YOU JUST GOT LUCKY THAT HE LOVED YOU BACK. NO MATTER WHAT HAPPENS . . .
. . . AT LEAST YOU HAD THAT.
WHAT DO YOU MEAN, "NO MATTER WHAT HAPPENS"?
HELL, WHAT DO YOU THINK?! IT'S BEEN OVER FIVE YEARS . . .

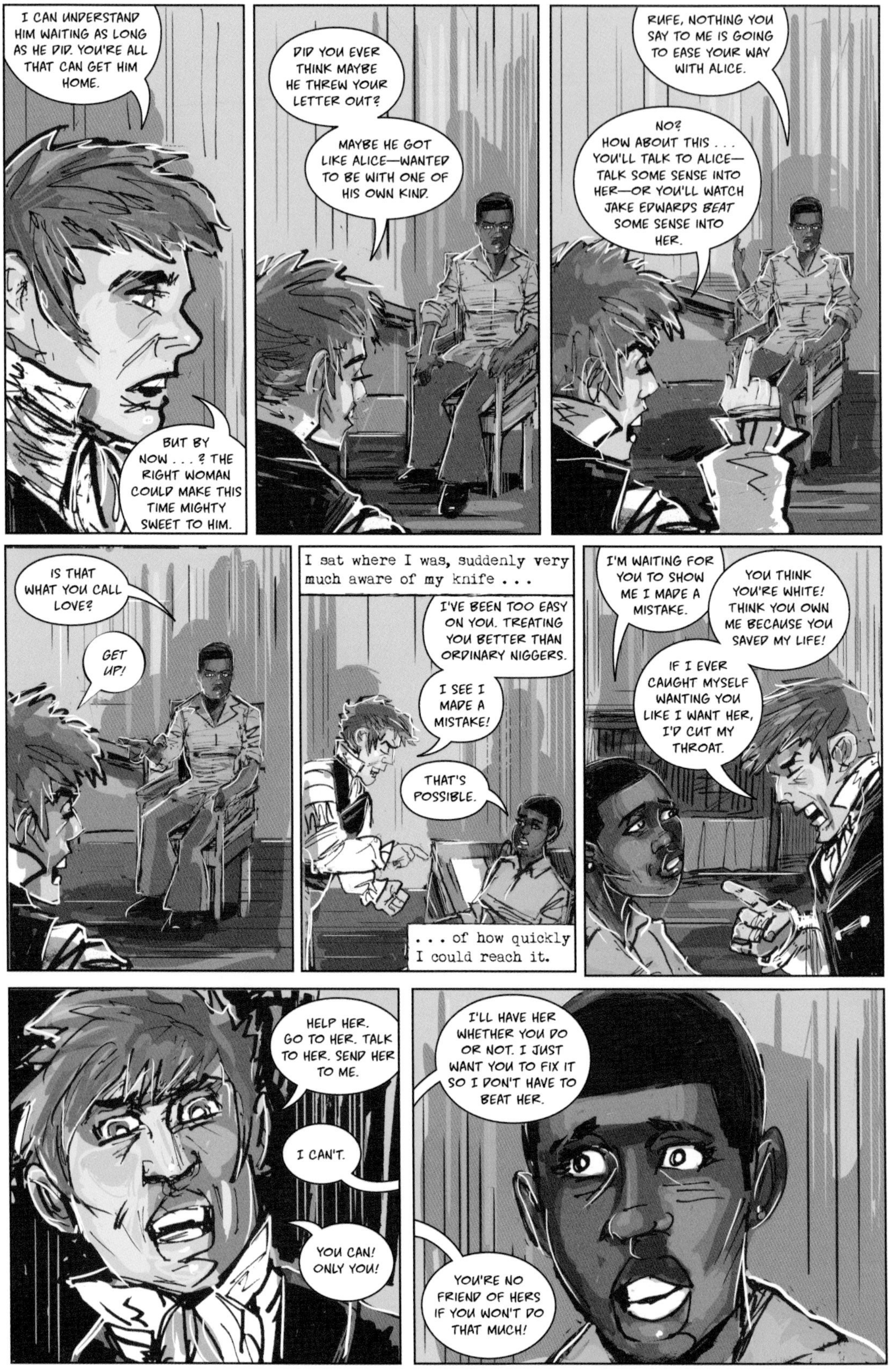
I CAN UNDERSTAND HIM WAITING AS LONG AS HE DID. YOU'RE ALL THAT CAN GET HIM HOME.
BUT BY NOW . . . ? THE RIGHT WOMAN COULD MAKE THIS TIME MIGHTY SWEET TO HIM.
DID YOU EVER THINK MAYBE HE THREW YOUR LETTER OUT?
MAYBE HE GOT LIKE ALICE—WANTED TO BE WITH ONE OF HIS OWN KIND.
RUFE, NOTHING YOU SAY TO ME IS GOING TO EASE YOUR WAY WITH ALICE.
NO? HOW ABOUT THIS . . . YOU'LL TALK TO ALICE—TALK SOME SENSE INTO HER—OR YOU'LL WATCH JAKE EDWARDS *BEAT* SOME SENSE INTO HER.
IS THAT WHAT YOU CALL LOVE?
GET UP!
I sat where I was, suddenly very much aware of my knife . . .
I'VE BEEN TOO EASY ON YOU. TREATING YOU BETTER THAN ORDINARY NIGGERS.
I SEE I MADE A MISTAKE!
THAT'S POSSIBLE.
. . . of how quickly I could reach it.
I'M WAITING FOR YOU TO SHOW ME I MADE A MISTAKE.
YOU THINK YOU'RE WHITE! THINK YOU OWN ME BECAUSE YOU SAVED MY LIFE!
IF I EVER CAUGHT MYSELF WANTING YOU LIKE I WANT HER, I'D CUT MY THROAT.
HELP HER. GO TO HER. TALK TO HER. SEND HER TO ME.
I CAN'T.
YOU CAN! ONLY YOU!
I'LL HAVE HER WHETHER YOU DO OR NOT. I JUST WANT YOU TO FIX IT SO I DON'T HAVE TO BEAT HER.
YOU'RE NO FRIEND OF HERS IF YOU WON'T DO THAT MUCH!

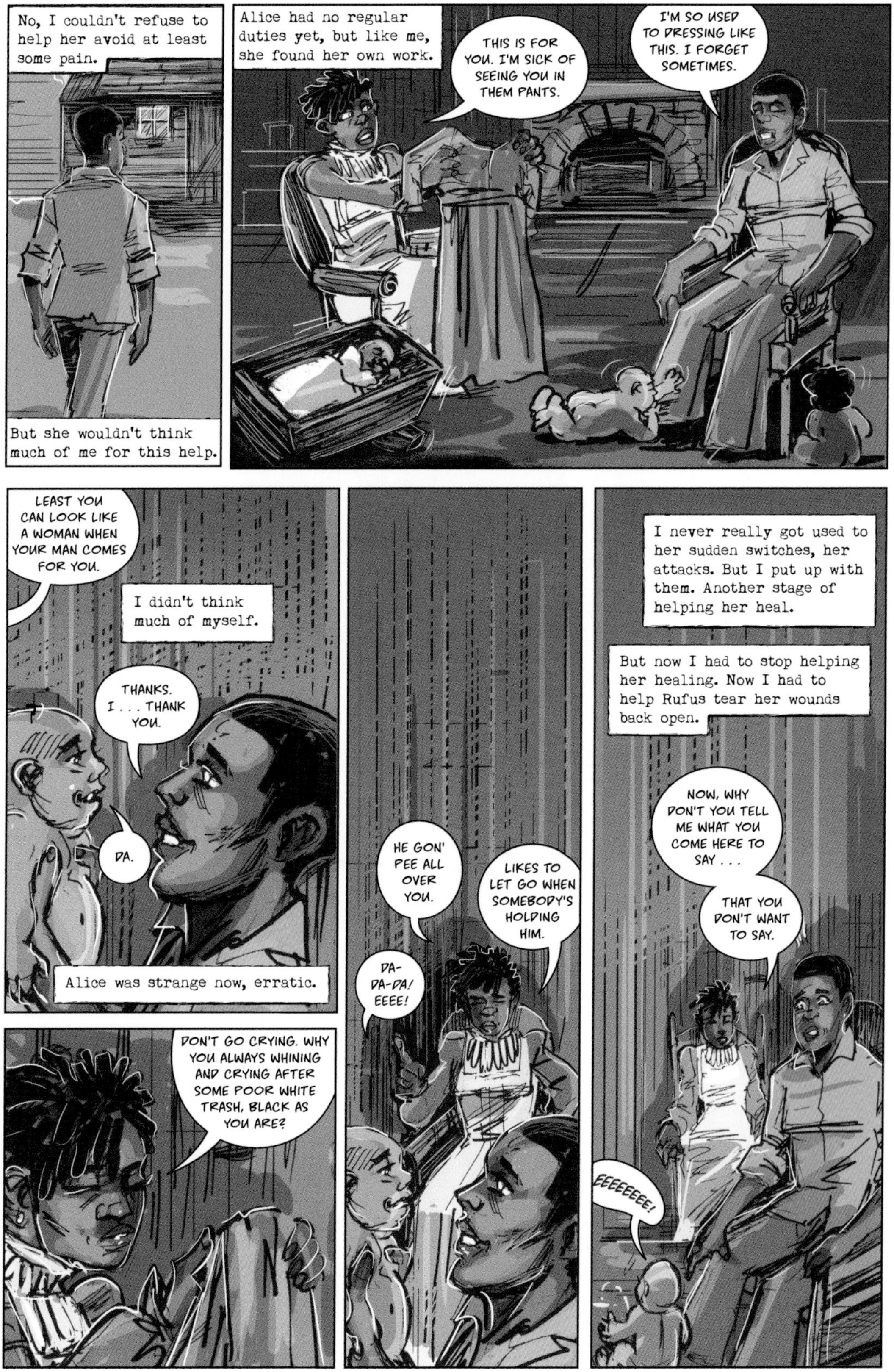

No, I couldn't refuse to help her avoid at least some pain.
But she wouldn't think much of me for this help.
Alice had no regular duties yet, but like me, she found her own work.
THIS IS FOR YOU. I'M SICK OF SEEING YOU IN THEM PANTS.
I'M SO USED TO DRESSING LIKE THIS. I FORGET SOMETIMES.
LEAST YOU CAN LOOK LIKE A WOMAN WHEN YOUR MAN COMES FOR YOU.
I didn't think much of myself.
THANKS. I . . . THANK YOU.
DA.
Alice was strange now, erratic.
HE GON' PEE ALL OVER YOU.
LIKES TO LET GO WHEN SOMEBODY'S HOLDING HIM.
DA-DA-DA! EEEE!
I never really got used to her sudden switches, her attacks. But I put up with them. Another stage of helping her heal.
But now I had to stop helping her healing. Now I had to help Rufus tear her wounds back open.
NOW, WHY DON'T YOU TELL ME WHAT YOU COME HERE TO SAY . . .
THAT YOU DON'T WANT TO SAY.
EEEEEEE!
DON'T GO CRYING. WHY YOU ALWAYS WHINING AND CRYING AFTER SOME POOR WHITE TRASH, BLACK AS YOU ARE?

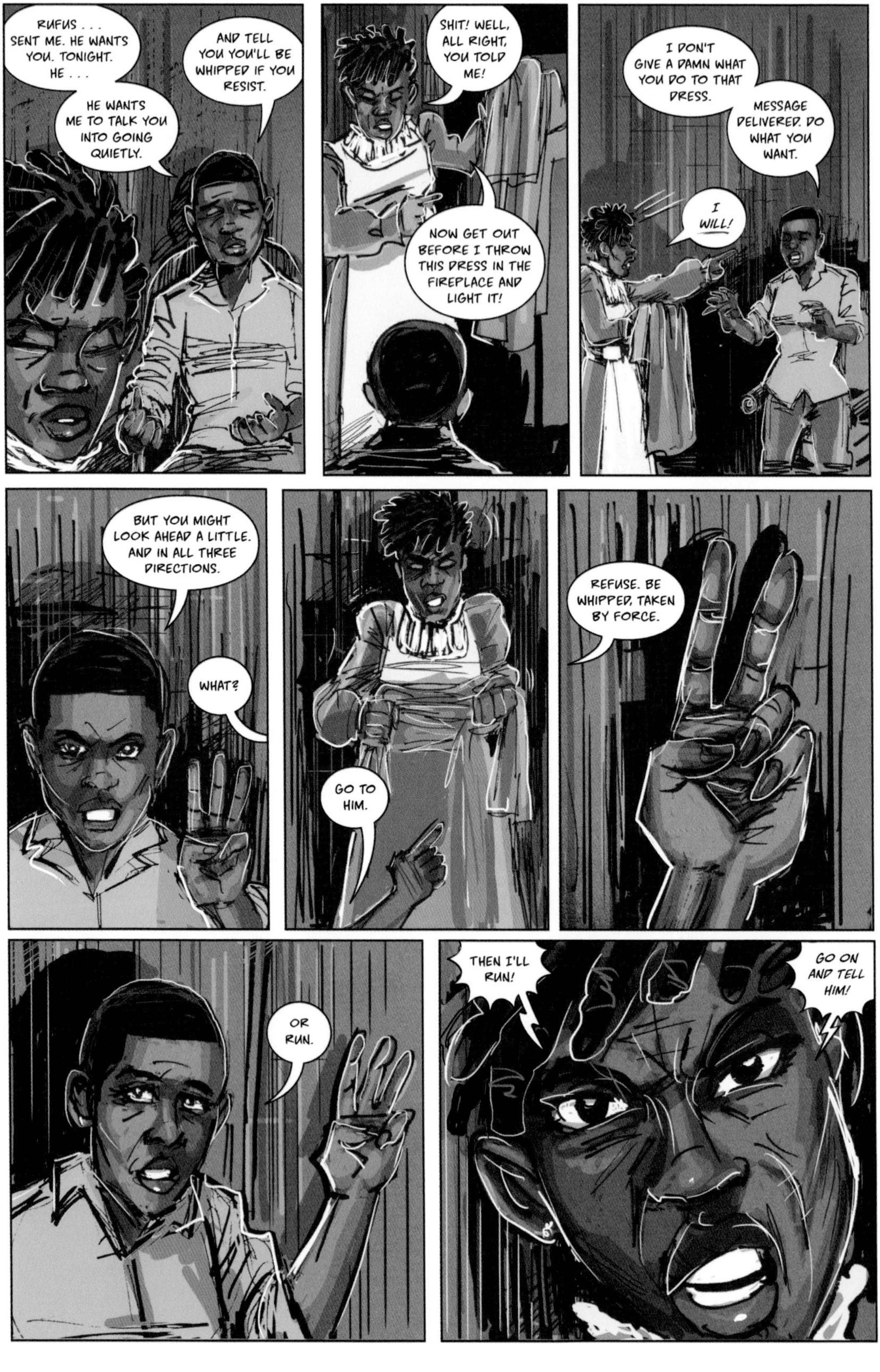
RUFUS . . . SENT ME. HE WANTS YOU. TONIGHT. HE . . .
HE WANTS ME TO TALK YOU INTO GOING QUIETLY.
AND TELL YOU YOU'LL BE WHIPPED IF YOU RESIST.
SHIT! WELL, ALL RIGHT, YOU TOLD ME!
NOW GET OUT BEFORE I THROW THIS DRESS IN THE FIREPLACE AND LIGHT IT!
I DON'T GIVE A DAMN WHAT YOU DO TO THAT DRESS.
MESSAGE DELIVERED. DO WHAT YOU WANT.
I WILL!
BUT YOU MIGHT LOOK AHEAD A LITTLE. AND IN ALL THREE DIRECTIONS.
WHAT?
GO TO HIM.
REFUSE. BE WHIPPED, TAKEN BY FORCE.
OR RUN.
THEN I'LL RUN!
GO ON AND TELL HIM!

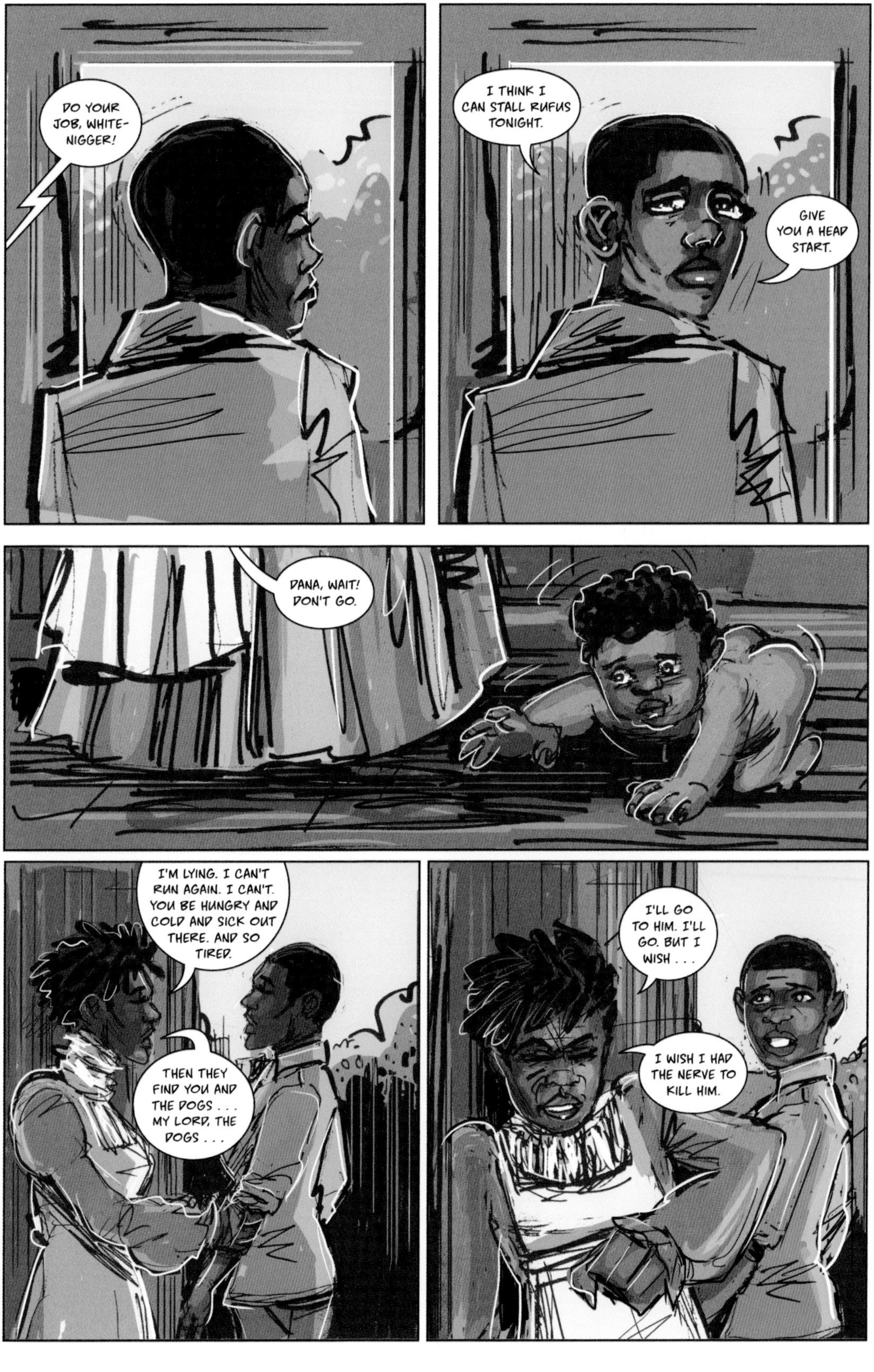
DO YOUR JOB, WHITE-NIGGER!
I THINK I CAN STALL RUFUS TONIGHT.
GIVE YOU A HEAD START.
DANA, WAIT! DON'T GO.
I'M LYING. I CAN'T RUN AGAIN. I CAN'T. YOU BE HUNGRY AND COLD AND SICK OUT THERE. AND SO TIRED.
THEN THEY FIND YOU AND THE DOGS . . . MY LORD, THE DOGS . . .
I'LL GO TO HIM. I'LL GO. BUT I WISH . . .
I WISH I HAD THE NERVE TO KILL HIM.

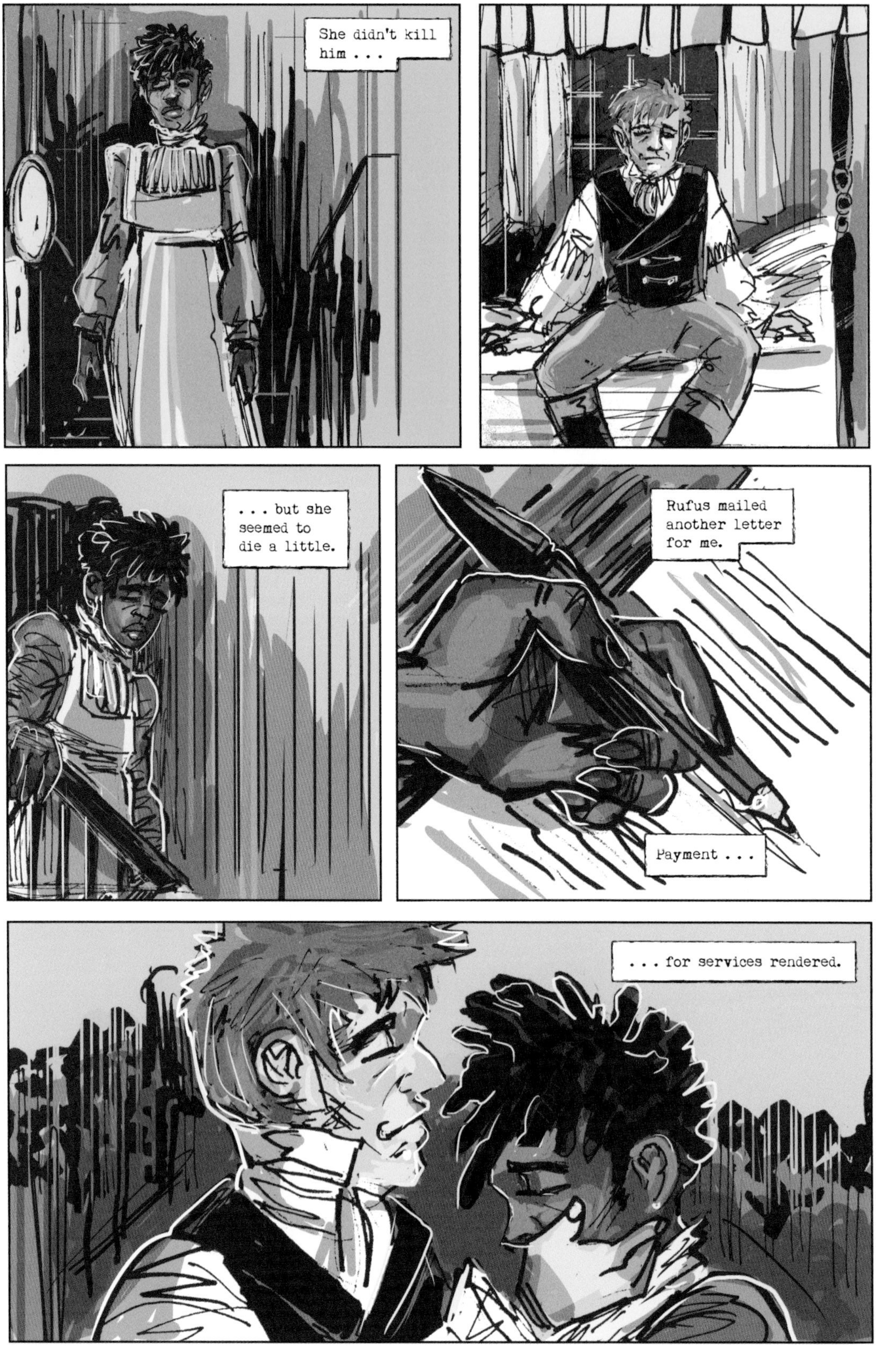
She didn't kill him . . .
. . . but she seemed to die a little.
Rufus mailed another letter for me.
Payment . . .
. . . for services rendered.

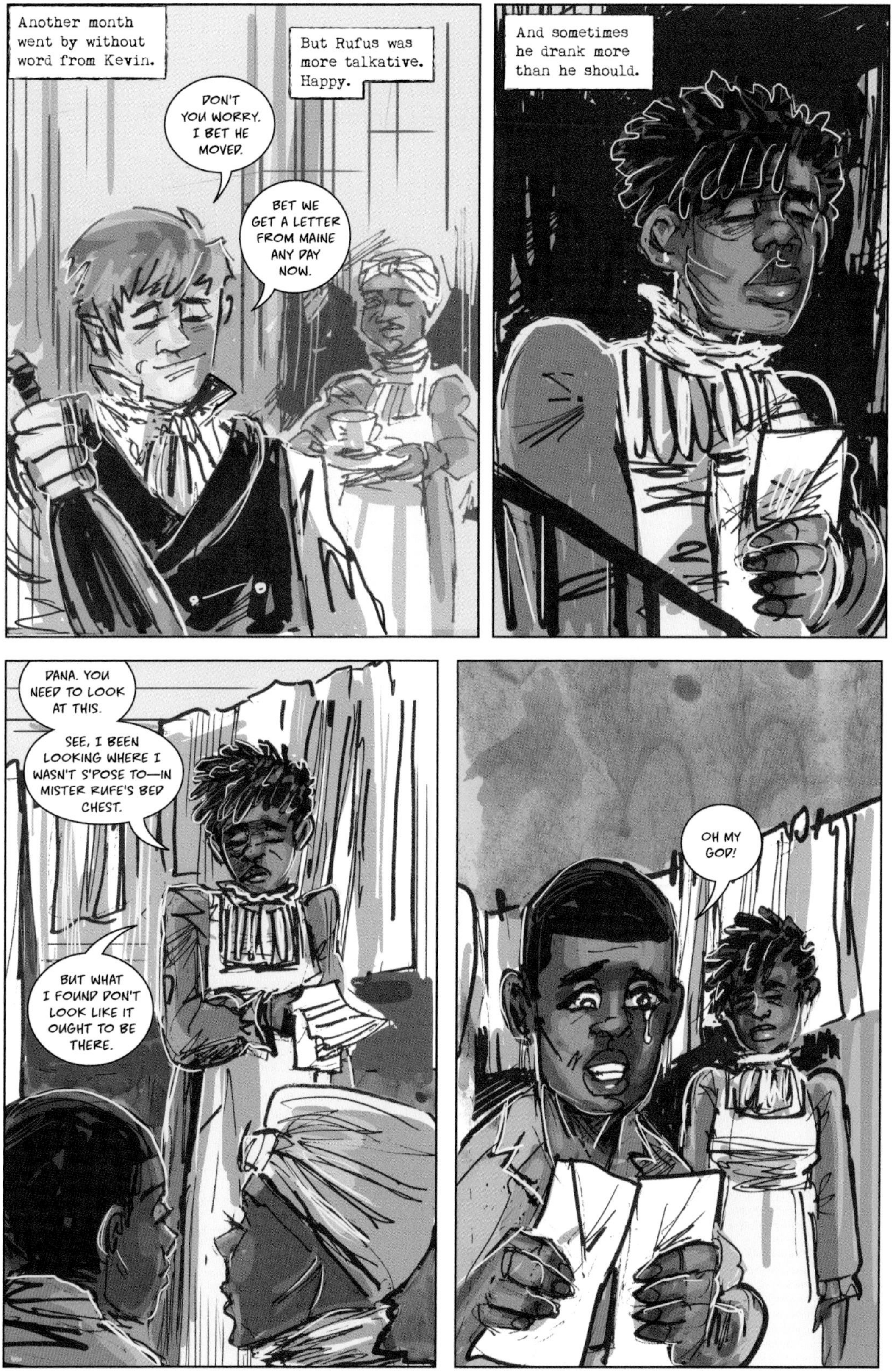

Another month went by without word from Kevin.
But Rufus was more talkative. Happy.
DON'T YOU WORRY. I BET HE MOVED.
BET WE GET A LETTER FROM MAINE ANY DAY NOW.
And sometimes he drank more than he should.
DANA. YOU NEED TO LOOK AT THIS.
SEE, I BEEN LOOKING WHERE I WASN'T S'POSE TO—IN MISTER RUFE'S BED CHEST.
BUT WHAT I FOUND DON'T LOOK LIKE IT OUGHT TO BE THERE.
OH MY GOD!

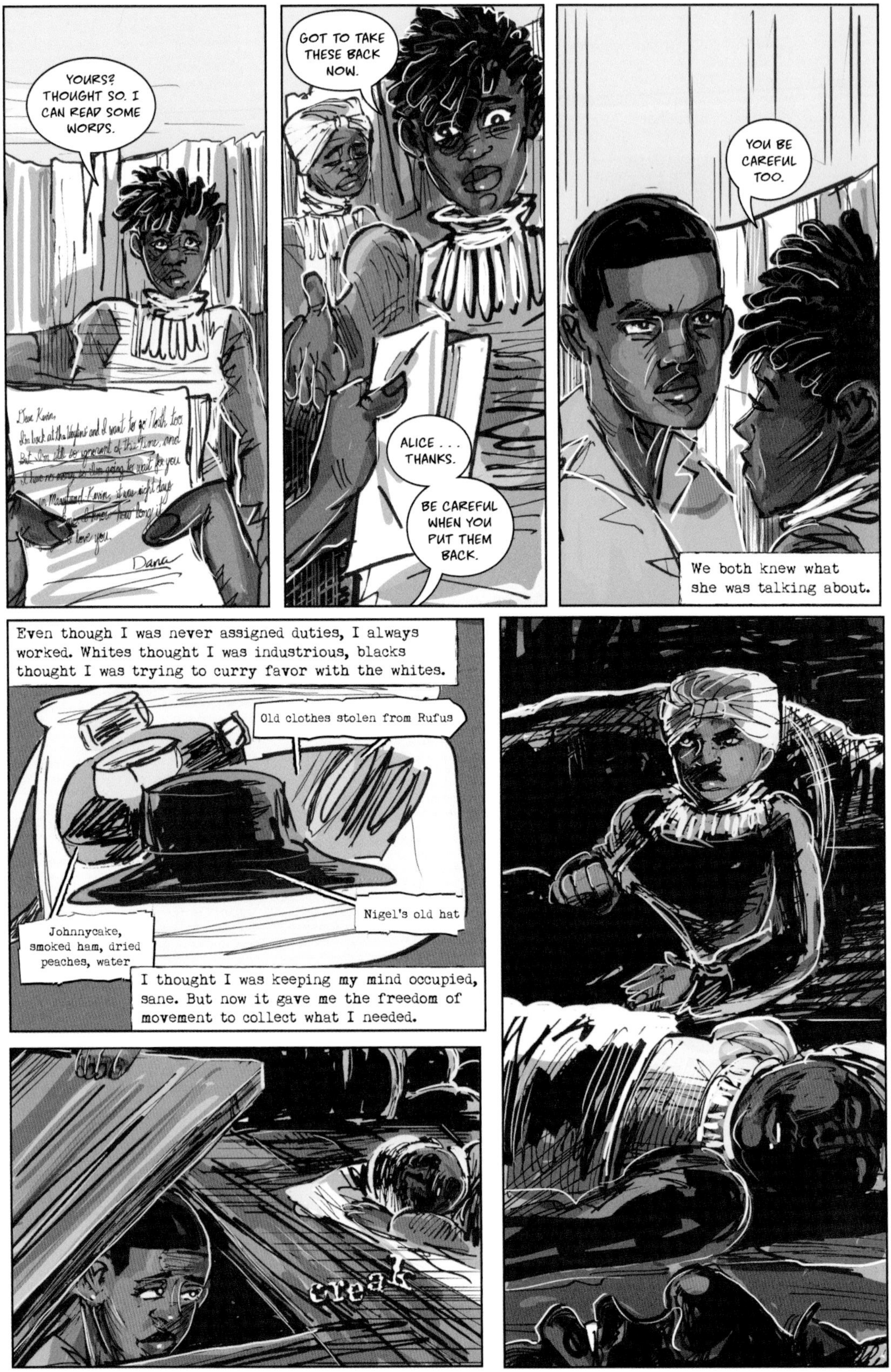
YOURS? THOUGHT SO. I CAN READ SOME WORDS.
Dear Kevin,
I'm back at the Weylins' and I want to go North too
Dana
GOT TO TAKE THESE BACK NOW.
ALICE . . . THANKS.
BE CAREFUL WHEN YOU PUT THEM BACK.
YOU BE CAREFUL TOO.
We both knew what she was talking about.
Even though I was never assigned duties, I always worked. Whites thought I was industrious, blacks thought I was trying to curry favor with the whites.
Old clothes stolen from Rufus
Nigel's old hat
Johnnycake, smoked ham, dried peaches, water
I thought I was keeping my mind occupied, sane. But now it gave me the freedom of movement to collect what I needed.
creak

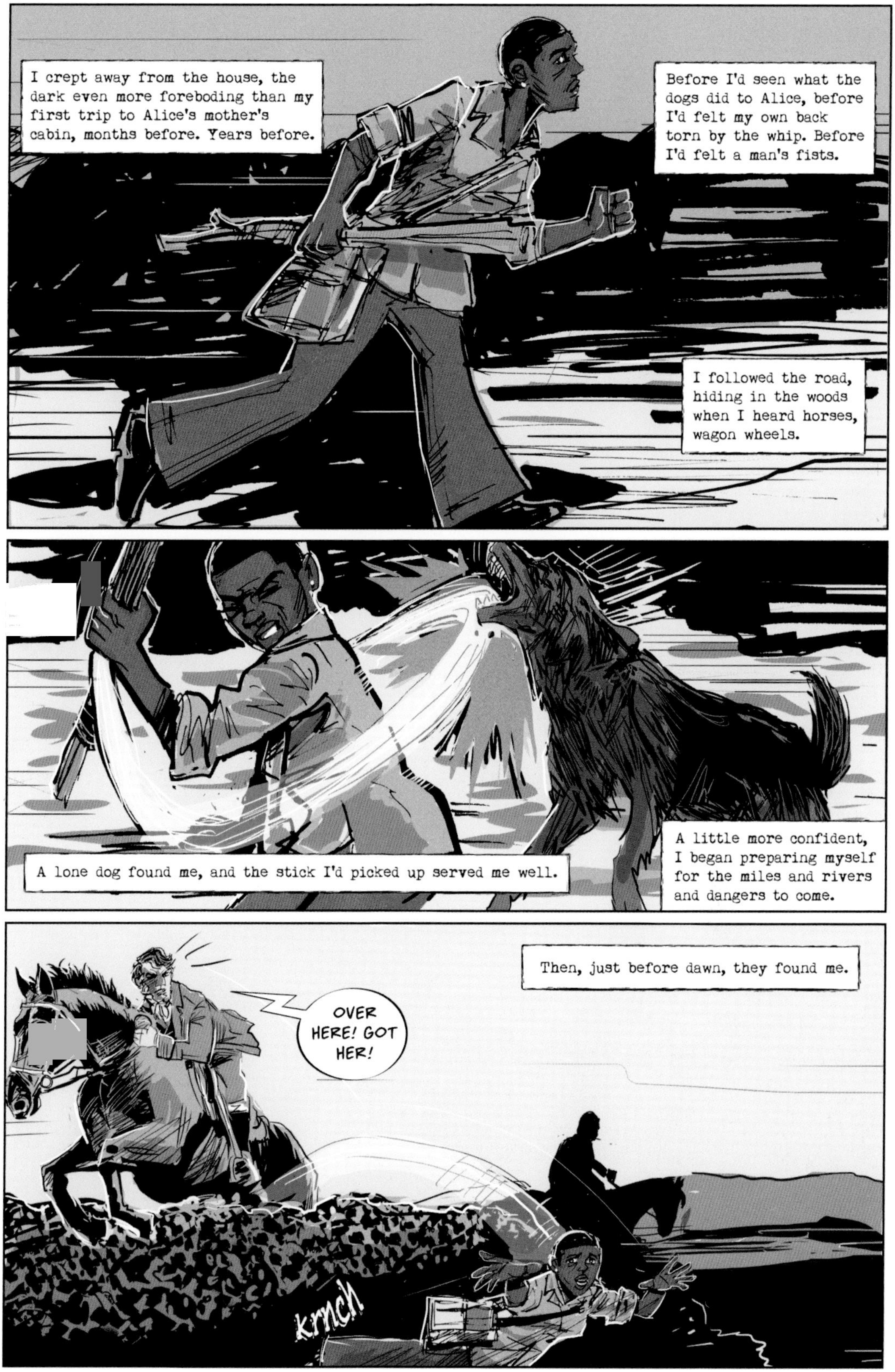
I crept away from the house, the dark even more foreboding than my first trip to Alice's mother's cabin, months before. Years before.
Before I'd seen what the dogs did to Alice, before I'd felt my own back torn by the whip. Before I'd felt a man's fists.
I followed the road, hiding in the woods when I heard horses, wagon wheels.
A lone dog found me, and the stick I'd picked up served me well.
A little more confident, I began preparing myself for the miles and rivers and dangers to come.
Then, just before dawn, they found me.
OVER HERE! GOT HER!
krnch

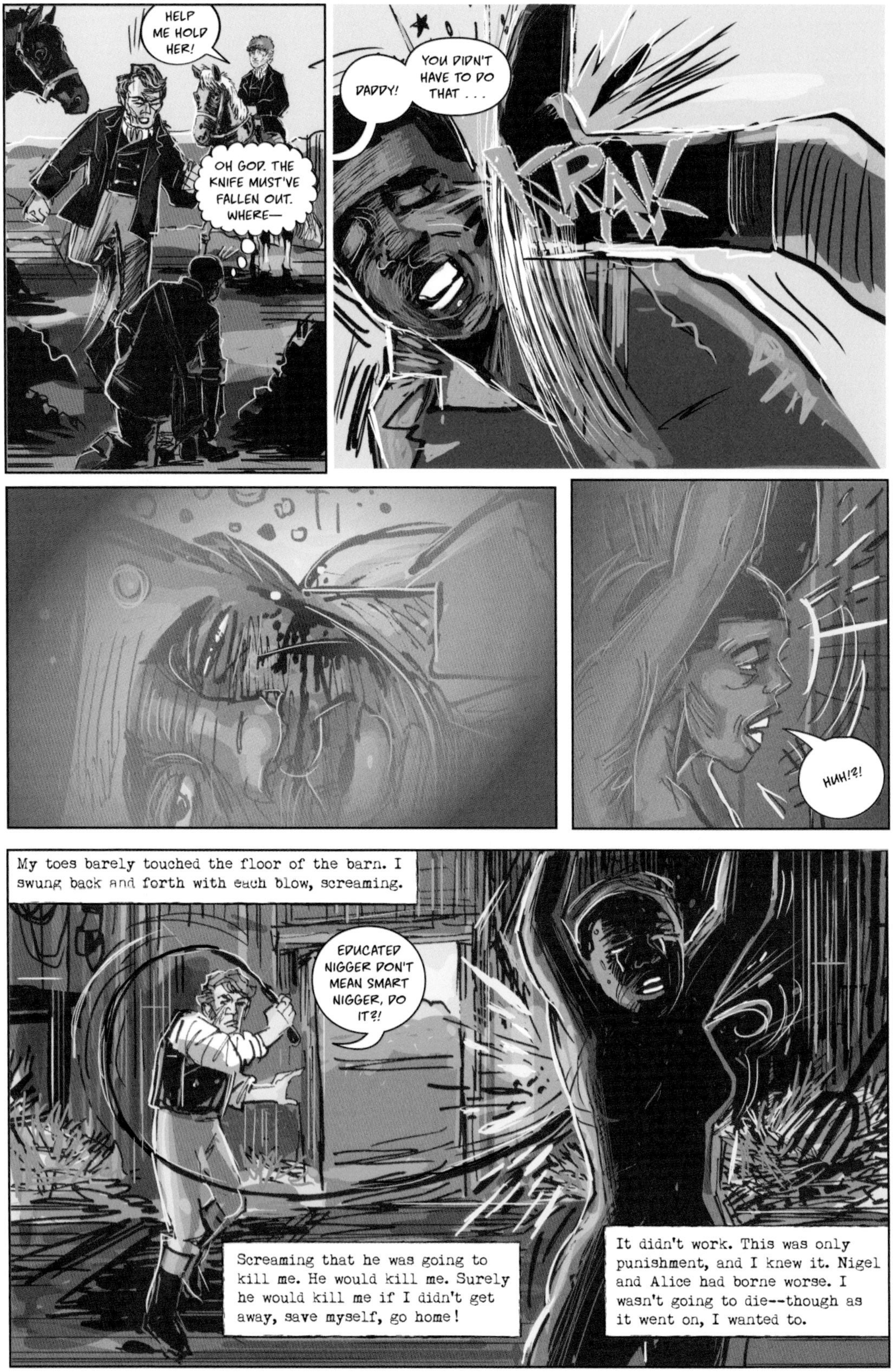
HELP ME HOLD HER!
OH GOD. THE KNIFE MUST'VE FALLEN OUT. WHERE—
DADDY!
YOU DIDN'T HAVE TO DO THAT . . .
KRAK
HUH!?!
My toes barely touched the floor of the barn. I swung back and forth with each blow, screaming.
EDUCATED NIGGER DON'T MEAN SMART NIGGER, DO IT?!
Screaming that he was going to kill me. He would kill me. Surely he would kill me if I didn't get away, save myself, go home!
It didn't work. This was only punishment, and I knew it. Nigel and Alice had borne worse. I wasn't going to die--though as it went on, I wanted to.

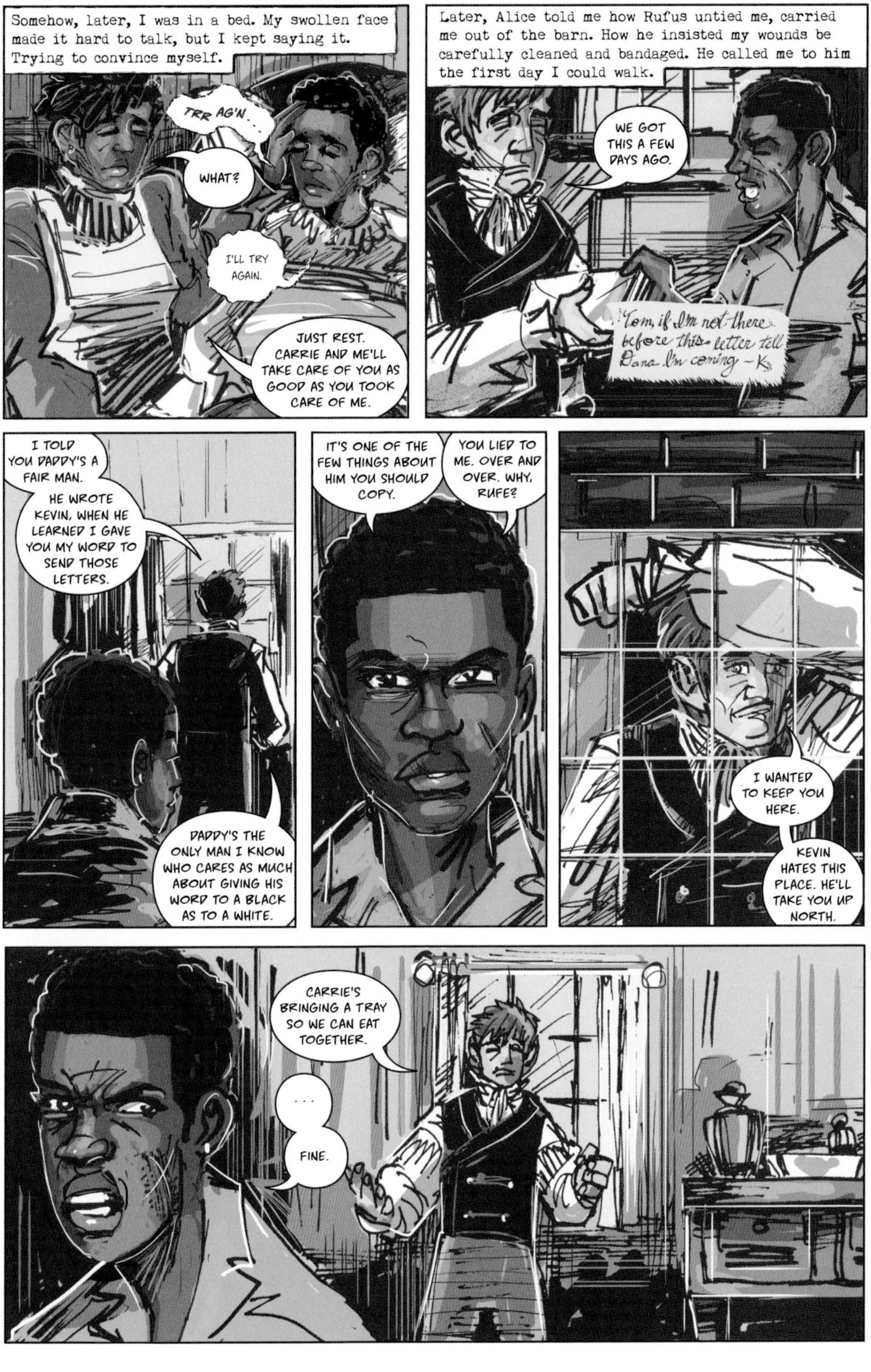
Somehow, later, I was in a bed. My swollen face made it hard to talk, but I kept saying it. Trying to convince myself.
TRR AG'N...
WHAT?
I'LL TRY AGAIN.
JUST REST. CARRIE AND ME'LL TAKE CARE OF YOU AS GOOD AS YOU TOOK CARE OF ME.
Later, Alice told me how Rufus untied me, carried me out of the barn. How he insisted my wounds be carefully cleaned and bandaged. He called me to him the first day I could walk.
WE GOT THIS A FEW DAYS AGO.
Tom, if I'm not there before this letter tell Dana I'm coming —K
I TOLD YOU DADDY'S A FAIR MAN.
HE WROTE KEVIN, WHEN HE LEARNED I GAVE YOU MY WORD TO SEND THOSE LETTERS.
DADDY'S THE ONLY MAN I KNOW WHO CARES AS MUCH ABOUT GIVING HIS WORD TO A BLACK AS TO A WHITE.
IT'S ONE OF THE FEW THINGS ABOUT HIM YOU SHOULD COPY.
YOU LIED TO ME. OVER AND OVER. WHY, RUFE?
I WANTED TO KEEP YOU HERE.
KEVIN HATES THIS PLACE. HE'LL TAKE YOU UP NORTH.
CARRIE'S BRINGING A TRAY SO WE CAN EAT TOGETHER.
...
FINE.

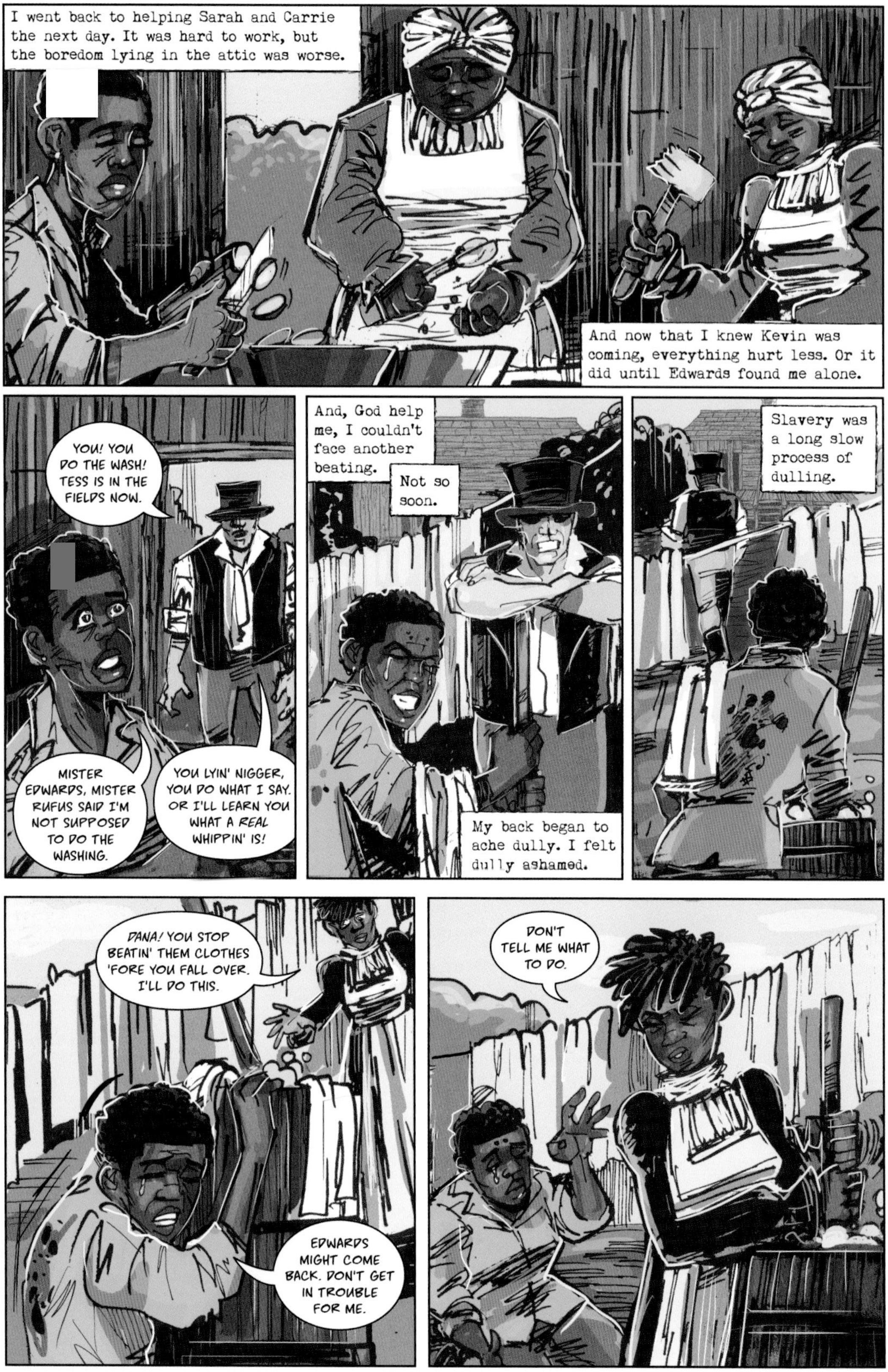
I went back to helping Sarah and Carrie the next day. It was hard to work, but the boredom lying in the attic was worse.
And now that I knew Kevin was coming, everything hurt less. Or it did until Edwards found me alone.
YOU! YOU DO THE WASH! TESS IS IN THE FIELDS NOW.
MISTER EDWARDS, MISTER RUFUS SAID I'M NOT SUPPOSED TO DO THE WASHING.
YOU LYIN' NIGGER, YOU DO WHAT I SAY. OR I'LL LEARN YOU WHAT A *REAL* WHIPPIN' IS!
And, God help me, I couldn't face another beating.
Not so soon.
My back began to ache dully. I felt dully ashamed.
Slavery was a long slow process of dulling.
DANA! YOU STOP BEATIN' THEM CLOTHES 'FORE YOU FALL OVER. I'LL DO THIS.
EDWARDS MIGHT COME BACK. DON'T GET IN TROUBLE FOR ME.
DON'T TELL ME WHAT TO DO.

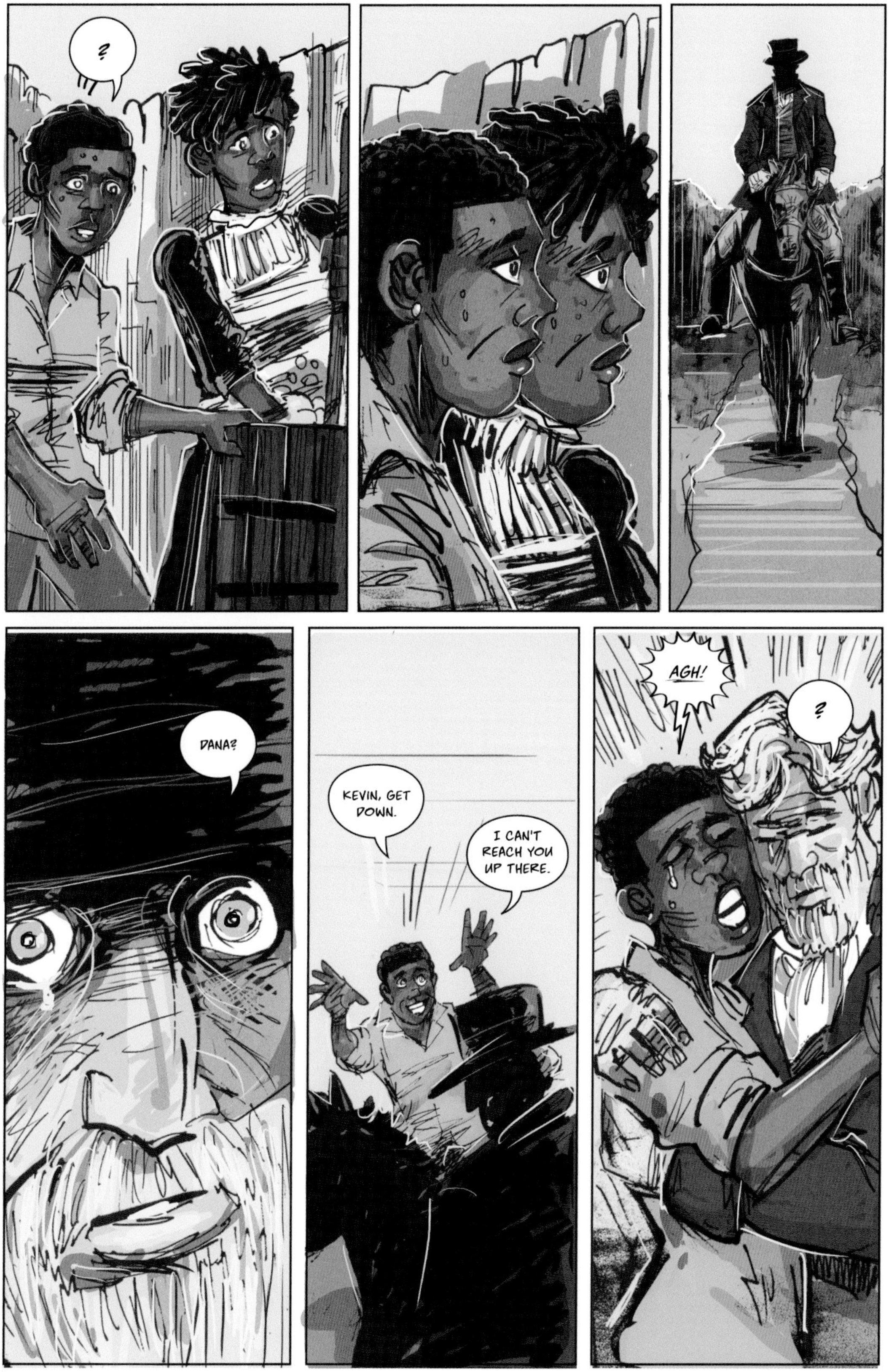
?
DANA?
KEVIN, GET DOWN.
I CAN'T REACH YOU UP THERE.
AGH!
?

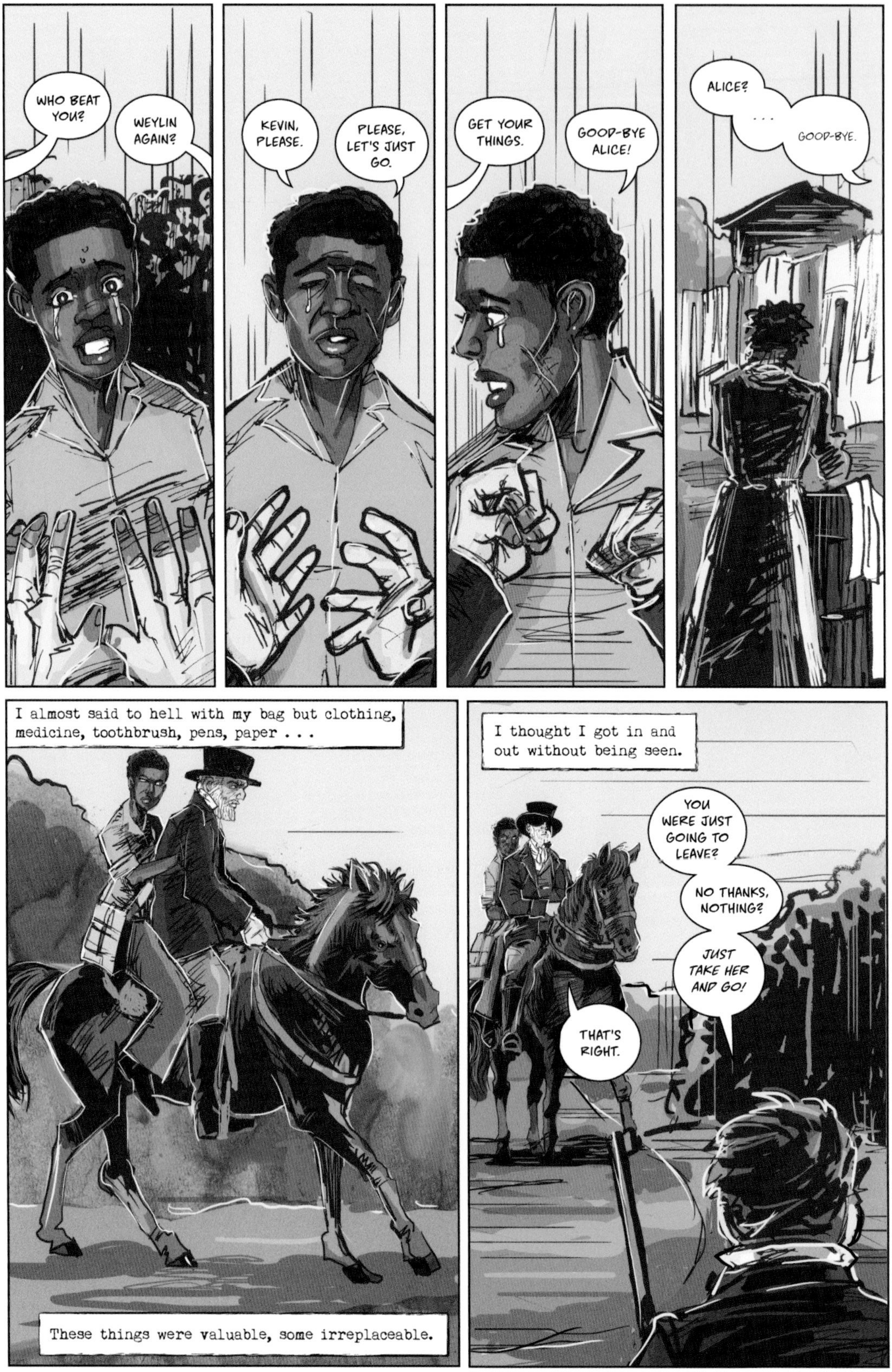
WHO BEAT YOU?
WEYLIN AGAIN?
KEVIN, PLEASE.
PLEASE, LET'S JUST GO.
GET YOUR THINGS.
GOOD-BYE ALICE!
ALICE?
. . .
GOOD-BYE.
I almost said to hell with my bag but clothing, medicine, toothbrush, pens, paper . . .
These things were valuable, some irreplaceable.
I thought I got in and out without being seen.
YOU WERE JUST GOING TO LEAVE?
NO THANKS, NOTHING?
JUST TAKE HER AND GO!
THAT'S RIGHT.

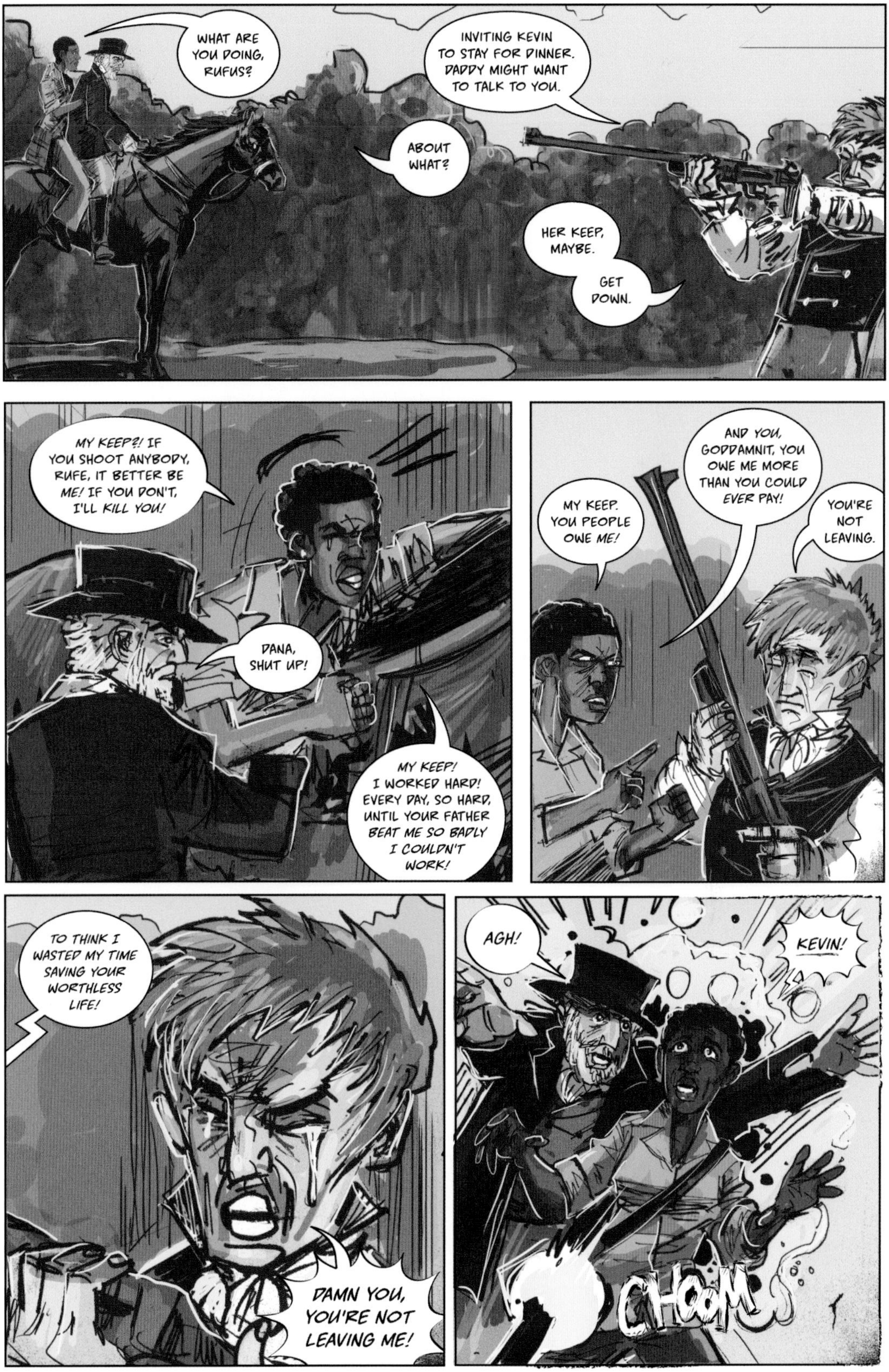
WHAT ARE YOU DOING, RUFUS?
INVITING KEVIN TO STAY FOR DINNER. DADDY MIGHT WANT TO TALK TO YOU.
ABOUT WHAT?
HER KEEP, MAYBE.
GET DOWN.
MY KEEP?! IF YOU SHOOT ANYBODY, RUFE, IT BETTER BE ME! IF YOU DON'T, I'LL KILL YOU!
DANA, SHUT UP!
MY KEEP! I WORKED HARD! EVERY DAY, SO HARD, UNTIL YOUR FATHER BEAT ME SO BADLY I COULDN'T WORK!
MY KEEP. YOU PEOPLE OWE ME!
AND YOU, GODDAMNIT, YOU OWE ME MORE THAN YOU COULD EVER PAY!
YOU'RE NOT LEAVING.
TO THINK I WASTED MY TIME SAVING YOUR WORTHLESS LIFE!
DAMN YOU, YOU'RE NOT LEAVING ME!
AGH!
KEVIN!
CHOOM

THE STORM

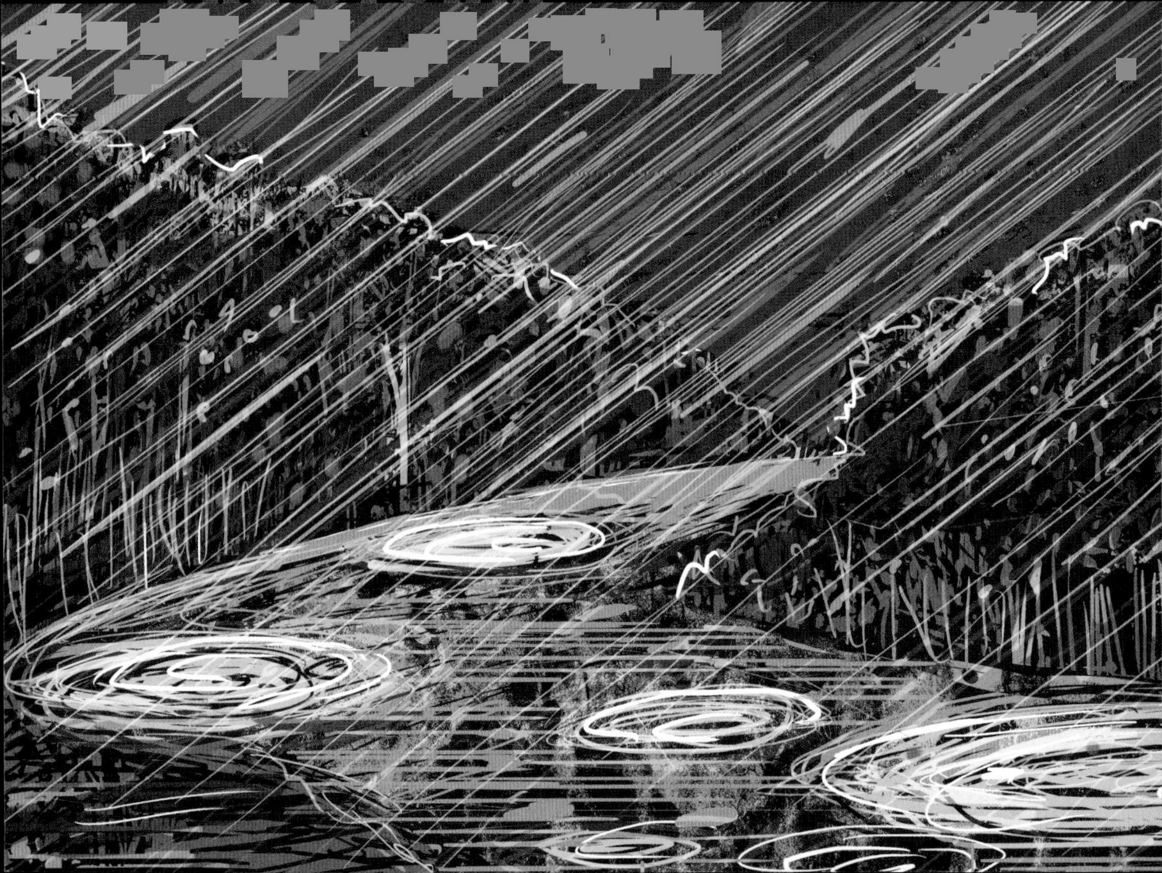

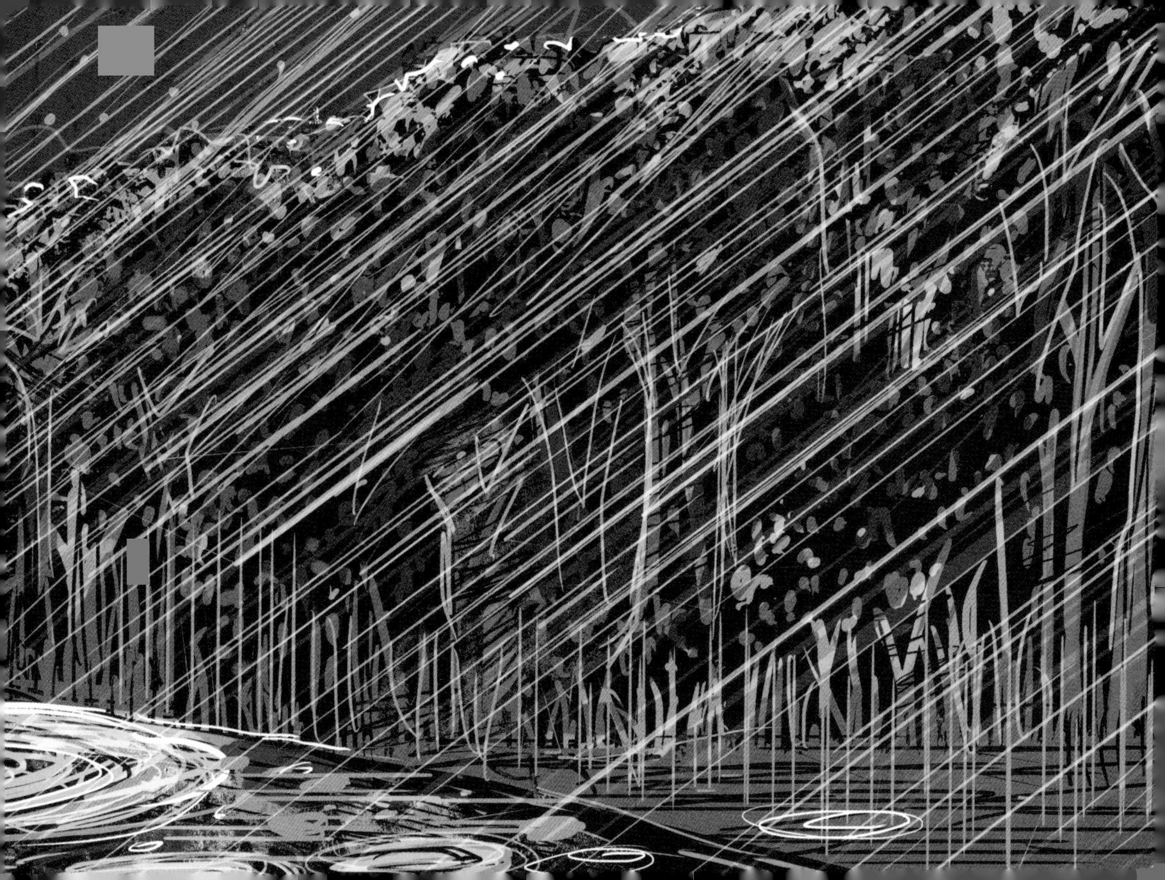

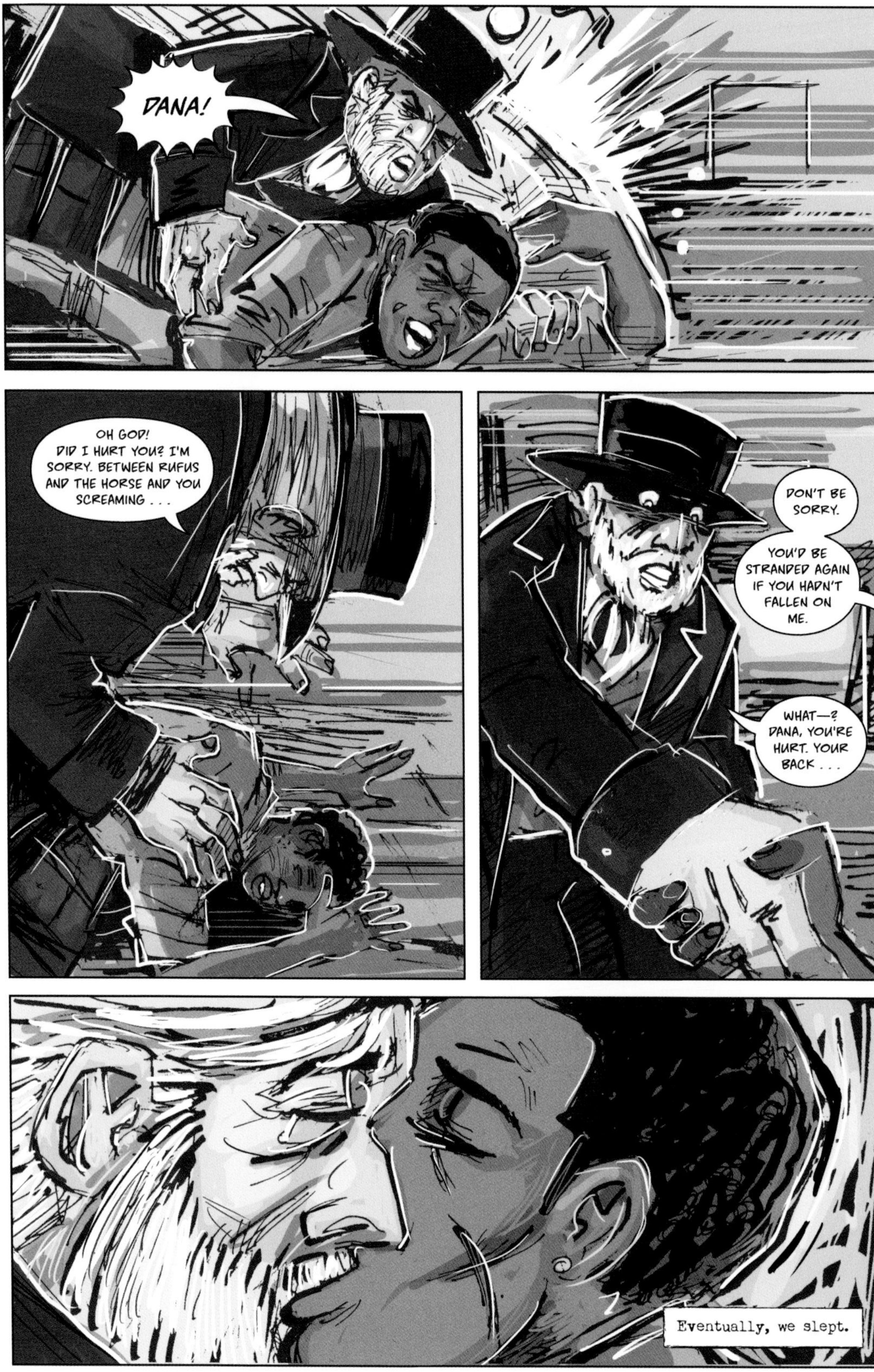
DANA!
OH GOD! DID I HURT YOU? I'M SORRY. BETWEEN RUFUS AND THE HORSE AND YOU SCREAMING . . .
DON'T BE SORRY.
YOU'D BE STRANDED AGAIN IF YOU HADN'T FALLEN ON ME.
WHAT—? DANA, YOU'RE HURT. YOUR BACK . . .
Eventually, we slept.

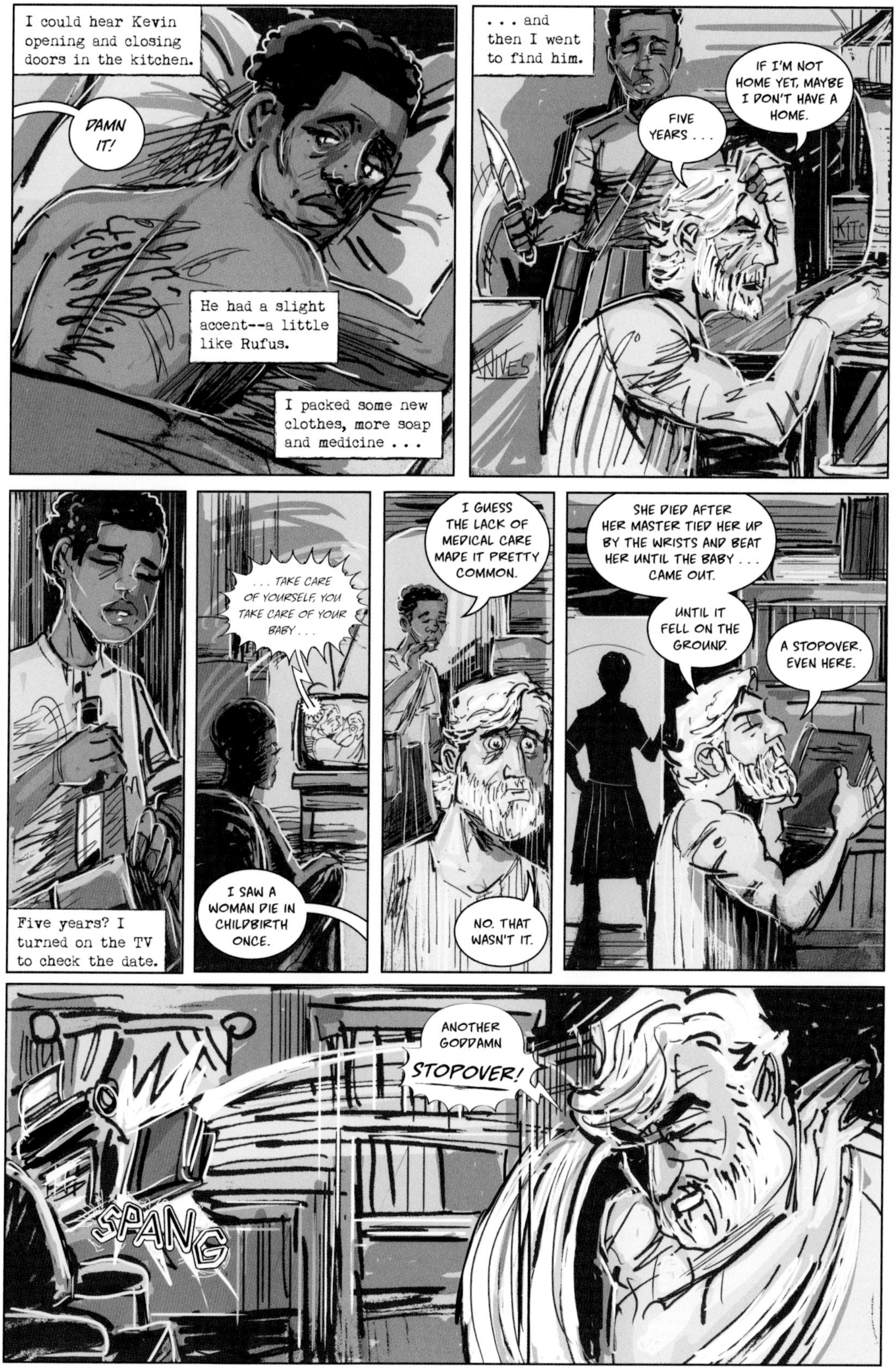
I could hear Kevin opening and closing doors in the kitchen.
DAMN IT!
He had a slight accent--a little like Rufus.
I packed some new clothes, more soap and medicine . . .
. . . and then I went to find him.
FIVE YEARS . . .
IF I'M NOT HOME YET, MAYBE I DON'T HAVE A HOME.
Five years? I turned on the TV to check the date.
. . . TAKE CARE OF YOURSELF, YOU TAKE CARE OF YOUR BABY . . .
I SAW A WOMAN DIE IN CHILDBIRTH ONCE.
I GUESS THE LACK OF MEDICAL CARE MADE IT PRETTY COMMON.
NO. THAT WASN'T IT.
SHE DIED AFTER HER MASTER TIED HER UP BY THE WRISTS AND BEAT HER UNTIL THE BABY . . . CAME OUT.
UNTIL IT FELL ON THE GROUND.
A STOPOVER. EVEN HERE.
ANOTHER GODDAMN STOPOVER!
SPANG

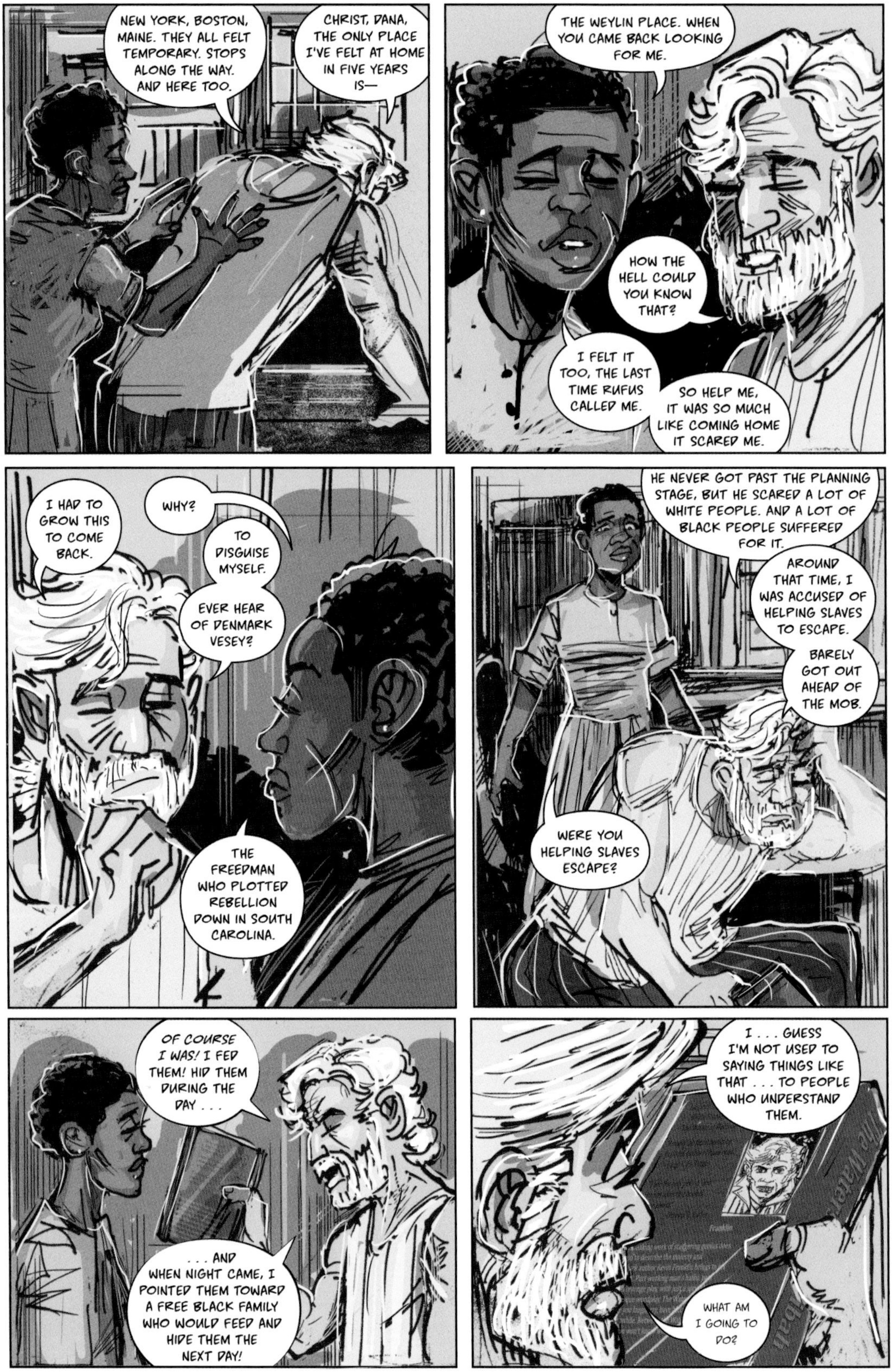
NEW YORK, BOSTON, MAINE. THEY ALL FELT TEMPORARY. STOPS ALONG THE WAY. AND HERE TOO.
CHRIST, DANA, THE ONLY PLACE I'VE FELT AT HOME IN FIVE YEARS IS—
THE WEYLIN PLACE. WHEN YOU CAME BACK LOOKING FOR ME.
HOW THE HELL COULD YOU KNOW THAT?
I FELT IT TOO, THE LAST TIME RUFUS CALLED ME.
SO HELP ME, IT WAS SO MUCH LIKE COMING HOME IT SCARED ME.
I HAD TO GROW THIS TO COME BACK.
WHY?
TO DISGUISE MYSELF.
EVER HEAR OF DENMARK VESEY?
THE FREEDMAN WHO PLOTTED REBELLION DOWN IN SOUTH CAROLINA.
HE NEVER GOT PAST THE PLANNING STAGE, BUT HE SCARED A LOT OF WHITE PEOPLE. AND A LOT OF BLACK PEOPLE SUFFERED FOR IT.
AROUND THAT TIME, I WAS ACCUSED OF HELPING SLAVES TO ESCAPE.
BARELY GOT OUT AHEAD OF THE MOB.
WERE YOU HELPING SLAVES ESCAPE?
OF COURSE I WAS! I FED THEM! HID THEM DURING THE DAY . . .
. . . AND WHEN NIGHT CAME, I POINTED THEM TOWARD A FREE BLACK FAMILY WHO WOULD FEED AND HIDE THEM THE NEXT DAY!
I . . . GUESS I'M NOT USED TO SAYING THINGS LIKE THAT . . . TO PEOPLE WHO UNDERSTAND THEM.
WHAT AM I GOING TO DO?

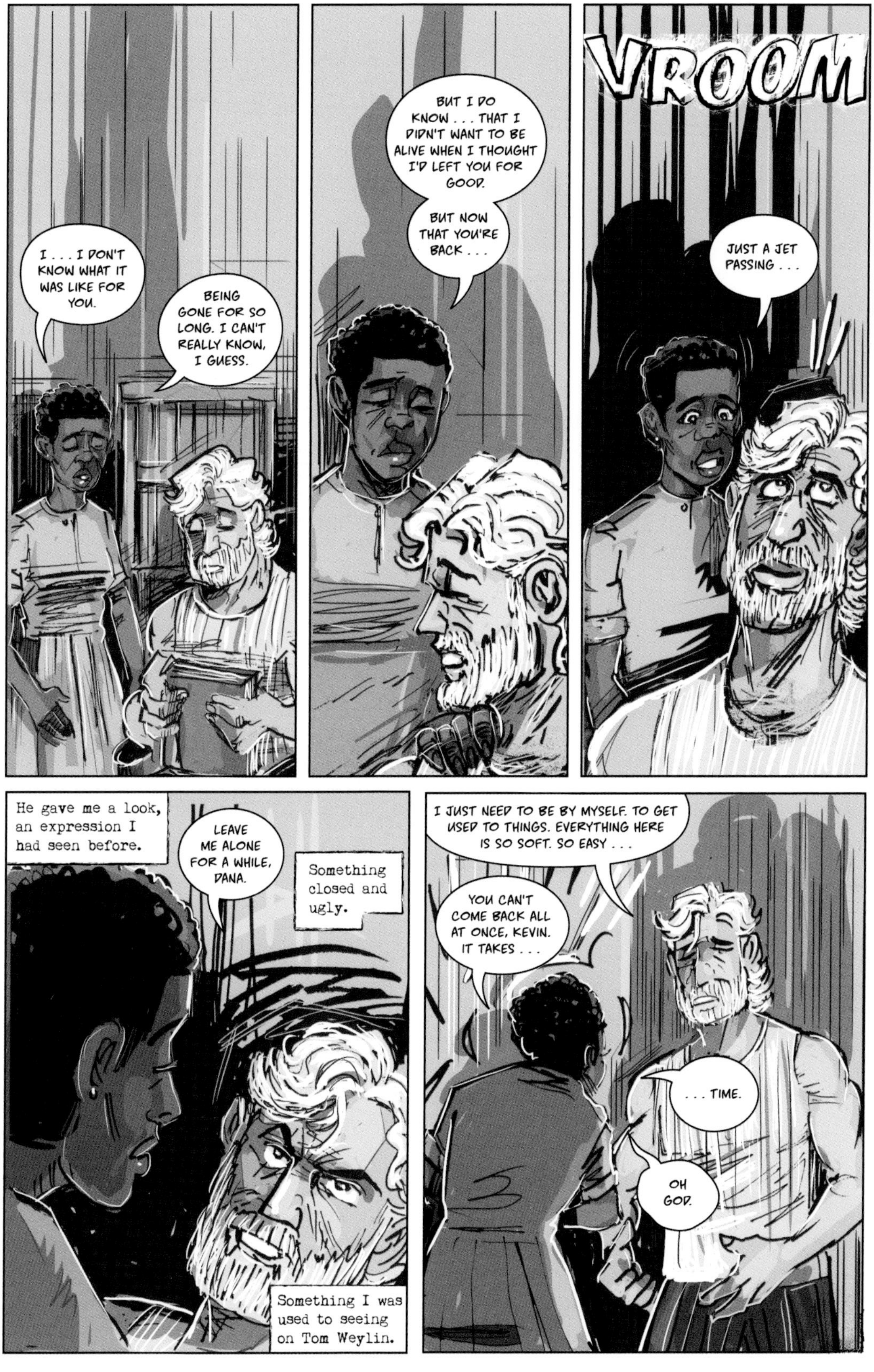
I . . . I DON'T KNOW WHAT IT WAS LIKE FOR YOU.
BEING GONE FOR SO LONG. I CAN'T REALLY KNOW, I GUESS.
BUT I DO KNOW . . . THAT I DIDN'T WANT TO BE ALIVE WHEN I THOUGHT I'D LEFT YOU FOR GOOD.
BUT NOW THAT YOU'RE BACK . . .
VROOM
JUST A JET PASSING . . .
He gave me a look, an expression I had seen before.
LEAVE ME ALONE FOR A WHILE, DANA.
Something closed and ugly.
Something I was used to seeing on Tom Weylin.
I JUST NEED TO BE BY MYSELF. TO GET USED TO THINGS. EVERYTHING HERE IS SO SOFT. SO EASY . . .
YOU CAN'T COME BACK ALL AT ONCE, KEVIN. IT TAKES . . .
. . . TIME.
OH GOD.

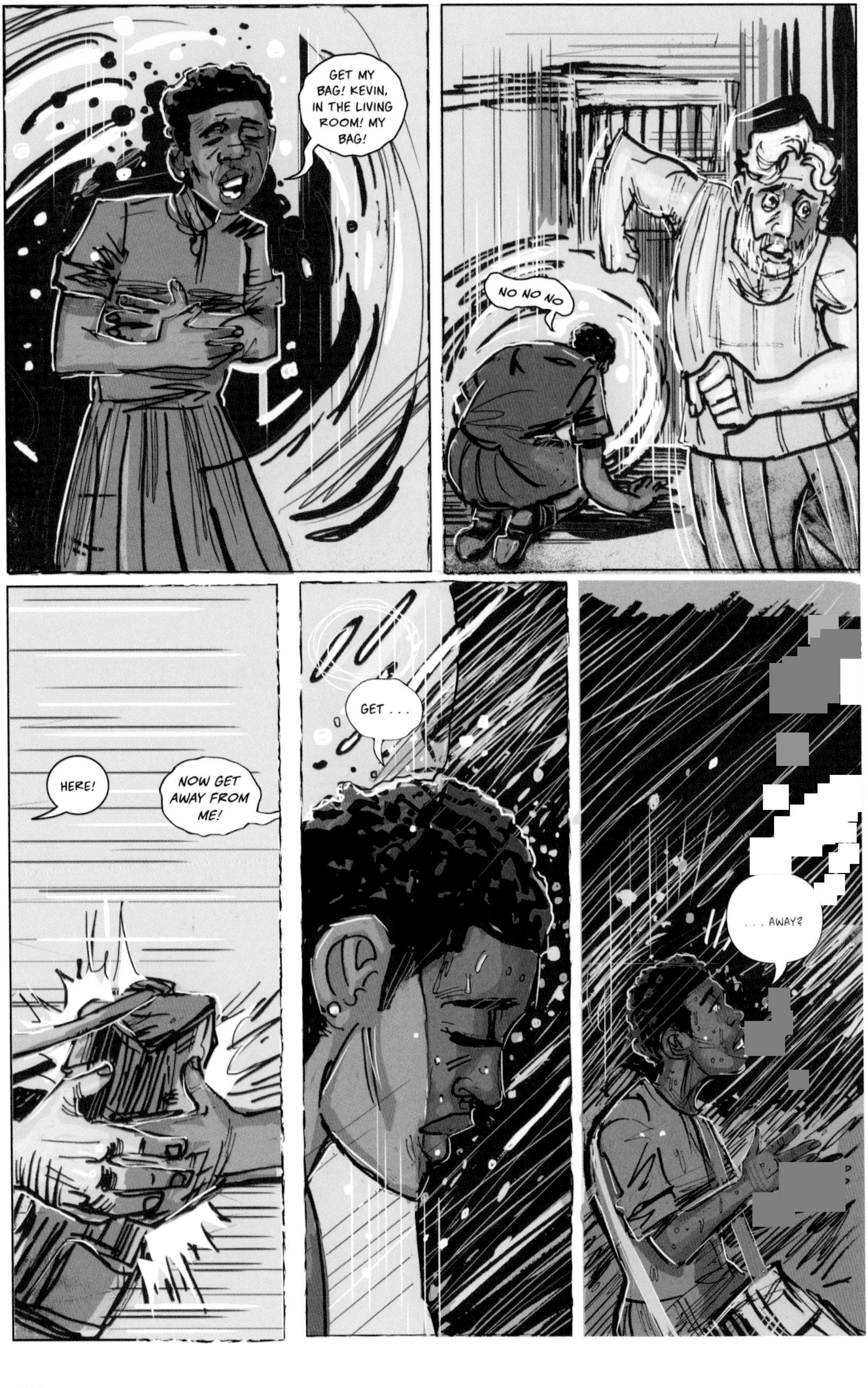
GET MY BAG! KEVIN, IN THE LIVING ROOM! MY BAG!
NO NO NO
HERE!
NOW GET AWAY FROM ME!
GET . . .
. . . AWAY?

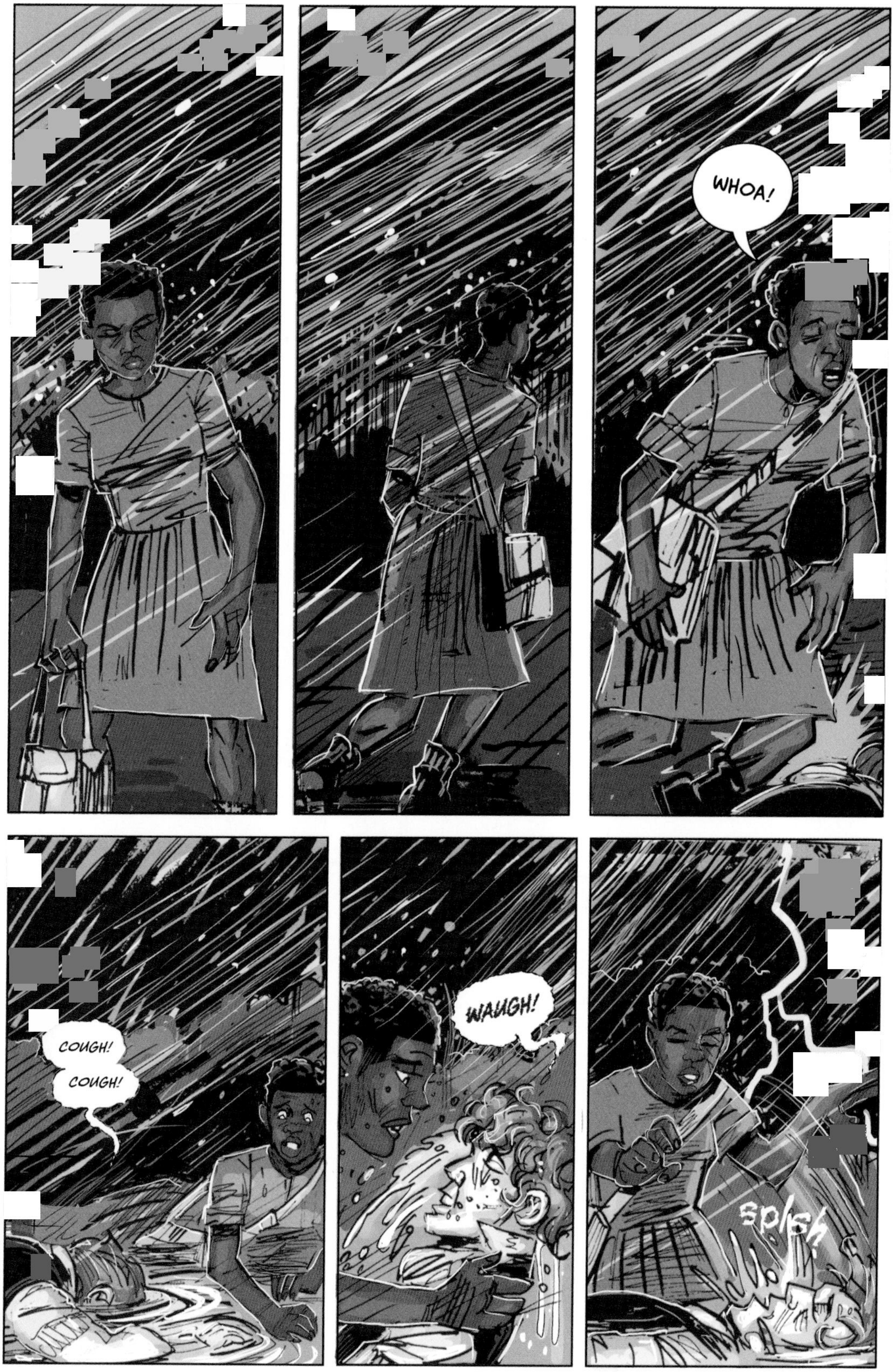
WHOA!
COUGH!
COUGH!
WAUGH!
splsh

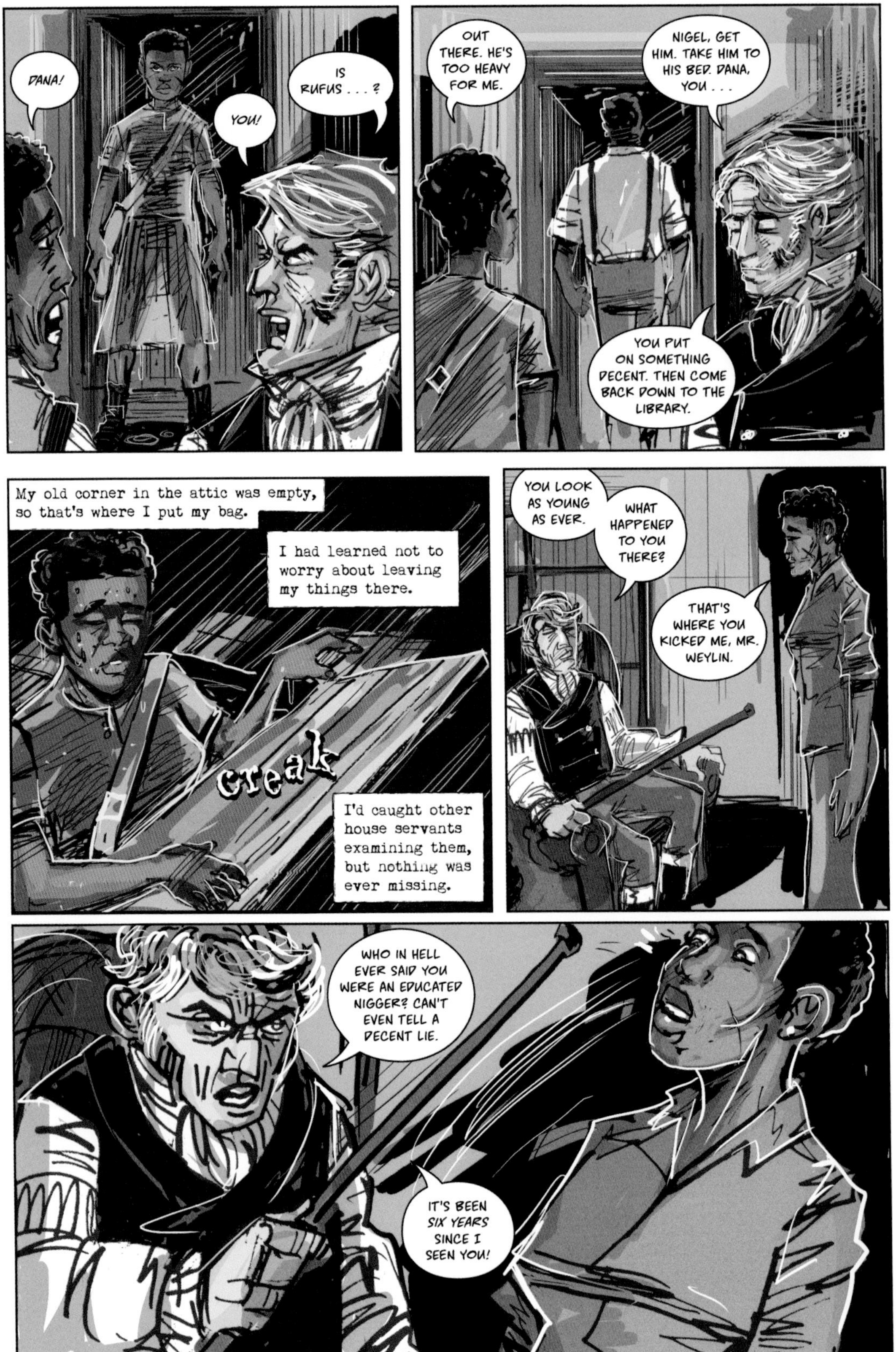
DANA!
YOU!
IS RUFUS . . . ?
OUT THERE. HE'S TOO HEAVY FOR ME.
NIGEL, GET HIM. TAKE HIM TO HIS BED. DANA, YOU . . .
YOU PUT ON SOMETHING DECENT. THEN COME BACK DOWN TO THE LIBRARY.
My old corner in the attic was empty, so that's where I put my bag.
I had learned not to worry about leaving my things there.
creak
I'd caught other house servants examining them, but nothing was ever missing.
YOU LOOK AS YOUNG AS EVER.
WHAT HAPPENED TO YOU THERE?
THAT'S WHERE YOU KICKED ME, MR. WEYLIN.
WHO IN HELL EVER SAID YOU WERE AN EDUCATED NIGGER? CAN'T EVEN TELL A DECENT LIE.
IT'S BEEN SIX YEARS SINCE I SEEN YOU!

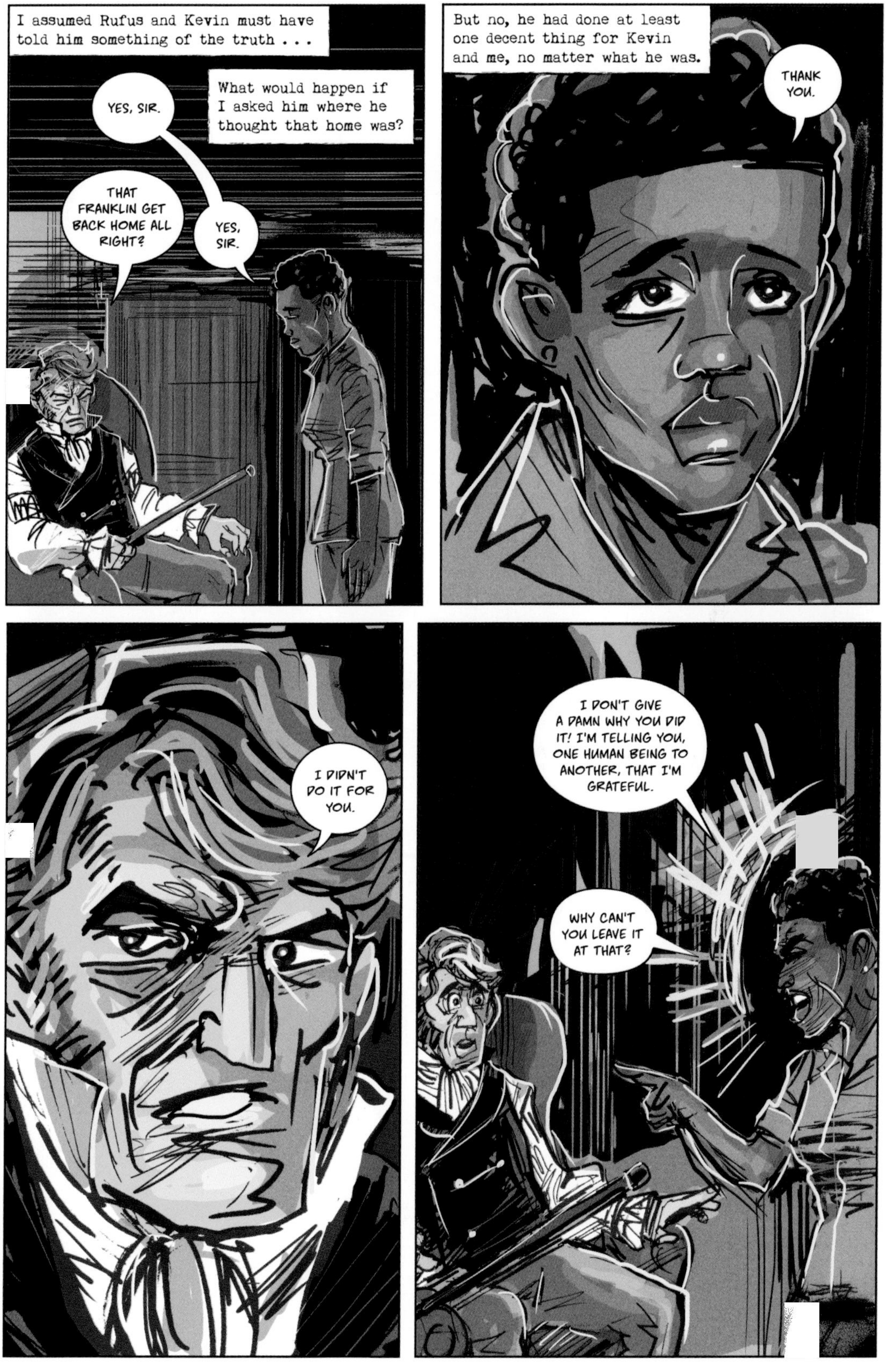

I assumed Rufus and Kevin must have told him something of the truth . . .
What would happen if I asked him where he thought that home was?
YES, SIR.
THAT FRANKLIN GET BACK HOME ALL RIGHT?
YES, SIR.
But no, he had done at least one decent thing for Kevin and me, no matter what he was.
THANK YOU.
I DIDN'T DO IT FOR YOU.
I DON'T GIVE A DAMN WHY YOU DID IT! I'M TELLING YOU, ONE HUMAN BEING TO ANOTHER, THAT I'M GRATEFUL.
WHY CAN'T YOU LEAVE IT AT THAT?

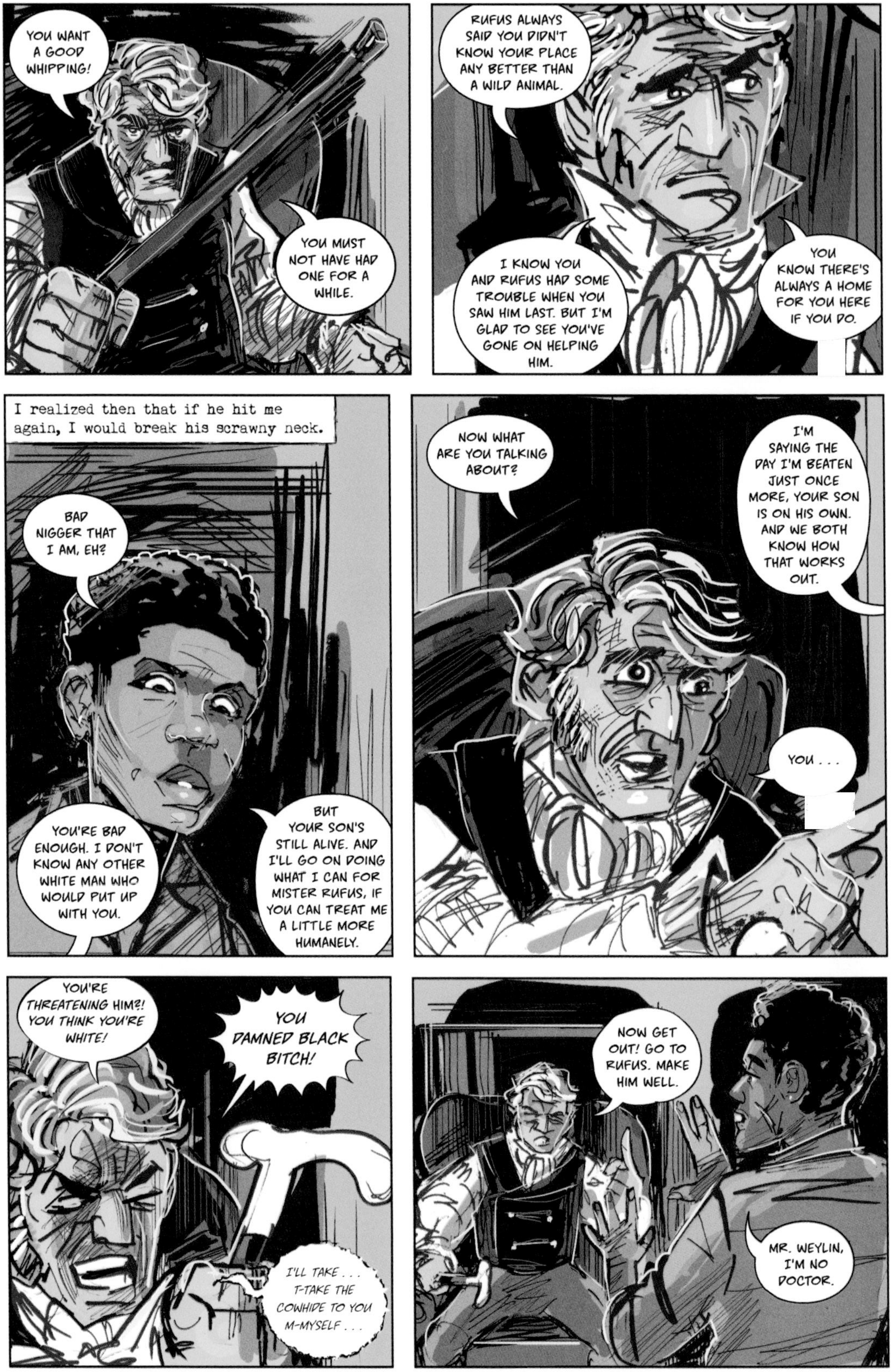
YOU WANT A GOOD WHIPPING!
YOU MUST NOT HAVE HAD ONE FOR A WHILE.
RUFUS ALWAYS SAID YOU DIDN'T KNOW YOUR PLACE ANY BETTER THAN A WILD ANIMAL.
I KNOW YOU AND RUFUS HAD SOME TROUBLE WHEN YOU SAW HIM LAST. BUT I'M GLAD TO SEE YOU'VE GONE ON HELPING HIM.
YOU KNOW THERE'S ALWAYS A HOME FOR YOU HERE IF YOU DO.
I realized then that if he hit me again, I would break his scrawny neck.
BAD NIGGER THAT I AM, EH?
YOU'RE BAD ENOUGH. I DON'T KNOW ANY OTHER WHITE MAN WHO WOULD PUT UP WITH YOU.
BUT YOUR SON'S STILL ALIVE. AND I'LL GO ON DOING WHAT I CAN FOR MISTER RUFUS, IF YOU CAN TREAT ME A LITTLE MORE HUMANELY.
NOW WHAT ARE YOU TALKING ABOUT?
I'M SAYING THE DAY I'M BEATEN JUST ONCE MORE, YOUR SON IS ON HIS OWN. AND WE BOTH KNOW HOW THAT WORKS OUT.
YOU . . .
YOU'RE THREATENING HIM?! YOU THINK YOU'RE WHITE!
YOU DAMNED BLACK BITCH!
I'LL TAKE . . . T-TAKE THE COWHIDE TO YOU M-MYSELF . . .
NOW GET OUT! GO TO RUFUS. MAKE HIM WELL.
MR. WEYLIN, I'M NO DOCTOR.

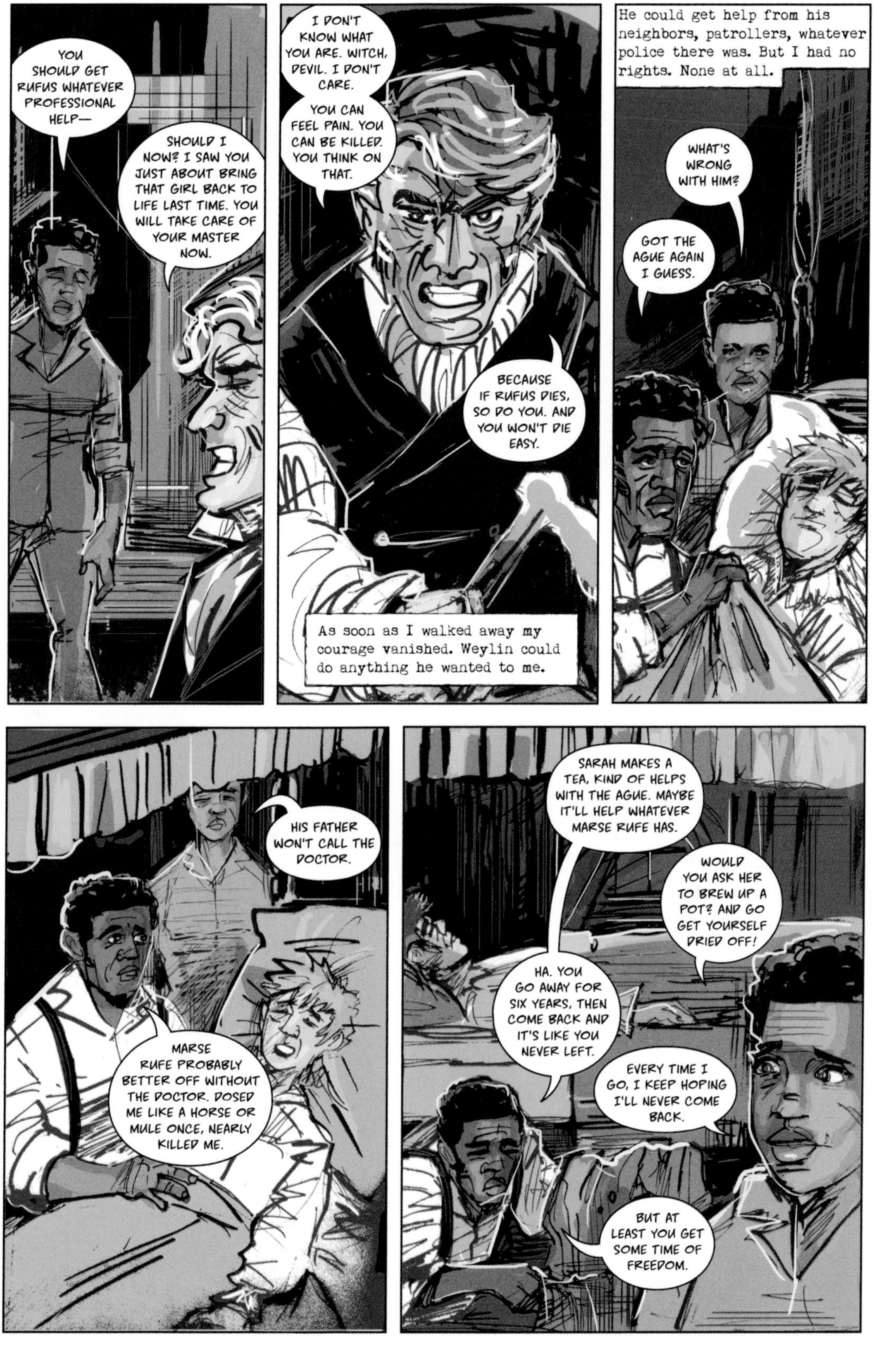
YOU SHOULD GET RUFUS WHATEVER PROFESSIONAL HELP—
SHOULD I NOW? I SAW YOU JUST ABOUT BRING THAT GIRL BACK TO LIFE LAST TIME. YOU WILL TAKE CARE OF YOUR MASTER NOW.
I DON'T KNOW WHAT YOU ARE. WITCH, DEVIL. I DON'T CARE.
YOU CAN FEEL PAIN. YOU CAN BE KILLED. YOU THINK ON THAT.
BECAUSE IF RUFUS DIES, SO DO YOU. AND YOU WON'T DIE EASY.
As soon as I walked away my courage vanished. Weylin could do anything he wanted to me.
He could get help from his neighbors, patrollers, whatever police there was. But I had no rights. None at all.
WHAT'S WRONG WITH HIM?
GOT THE AGUE AGAIN I GUESS.
HIS FATHER WON'T CALL THE DOCTOR.
MARSE RUFE PROBABLY BETTER OFF WITHOUT THE DOCTOR. DOSED ME LIKE A HORSE OR MULE ONCE, NEARLY KILLED ME.
SARAH MAKES A TEA, KIND OF HELPS WITH THE AGUE. MAYBE IT'LL HELP WHATEVER MARSE RUFE HAS.
WOULD YOU ASK HER TO BREW UP A POT? AND GO GET YOURSELF DRIED OFF!
HA. YOU GO AWAY FOR SIX YEARS, THEN COME BACK AND IT'S LIKE YOU NEVER LEFT.
EVERY TIME I GO, I KEEP HOPING I'LL NEVER COME BACK.
BUT AT LEAST YOU GET SOME TIME OF FREEDOM.

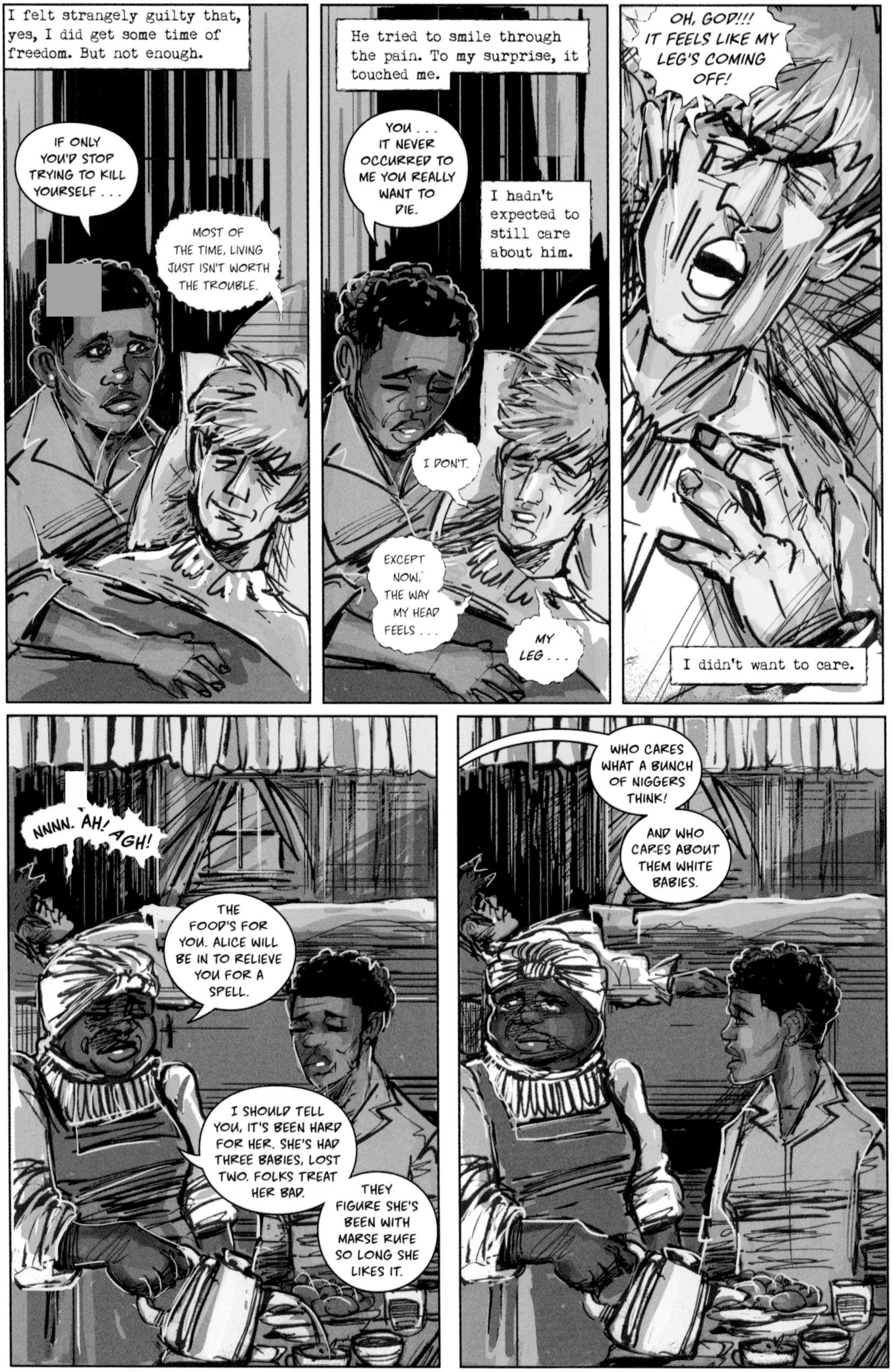
I felt strangely guilty that, yes, I did get some time of freedom. But not enough.
IF ONLY YOU'D STOP TRYING TO KILL YOURSELF . . .
MOST OF THE TIME, LIVING JUST ISN'T WORTH THE TROUBLE.
He tried to smile through the pain. To my surprise, it touched me.
YOU . . . IT NEVER OCCURRED TO ME YOU REALLY WANT TO DIE.
I hadn't expected to still care about him.
I DON'T.
EXCEPT NOW, THE WAY MY HEAD FEELS . . .
MY LEG . . .
OH, GOD!!! IT FEELS LIKE MY LEG'S COMING OFF!
I didn't want to care.
NNNN. AH! AGH!
THE FOOD'S FOR YOU. ALICE WILL BE IN TO RELIEVE YOU FOR A SPELL.
I SHOULD TELL YOU, IT'S BEEN HARD FOR HER. SHE'S HAD THREE BABIES, LOST TWO. FOLKS TREAT HER BAD.
THEY FIGURE SHE'S BEEN WITH MARSE RUFE SO LONG SHE LIKES IT.
WHO CARES WHAT A BUNCH OF NIGGERS THINK!
AND WHO CARES ABOUT THEM WHITE BABIES.

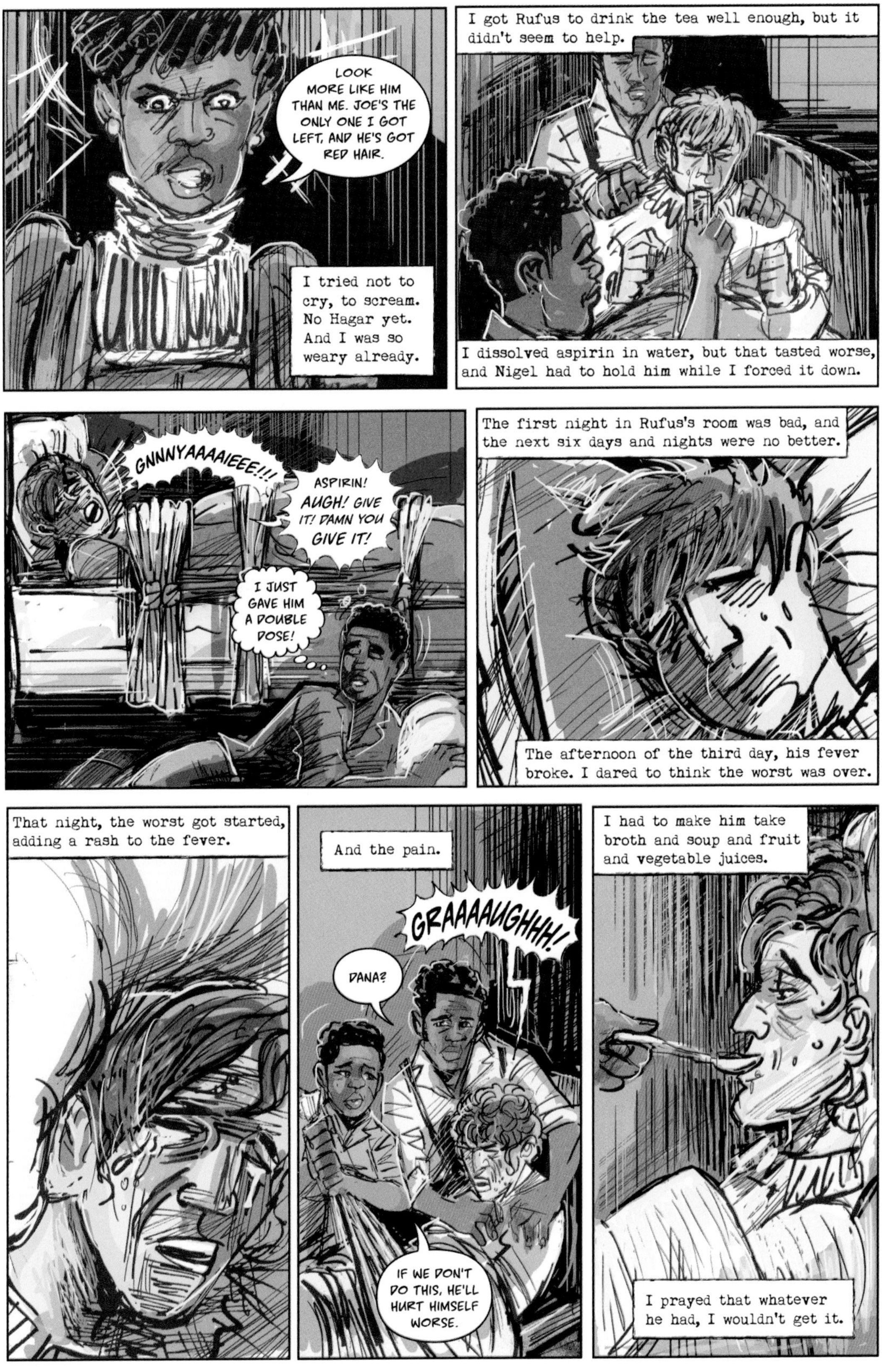

LOOK MORE LIKE HIM THAN ME. JOE'S THE ONLY ONE I GOT LEFT, AND HE'S GOT RED HAIR.
I tried not to cry, to scream. No Hagar yet. And I was so weary already.
I got Rufus to drink the tea well enough, but it didn't seem to help.
I dissolved aspirin in water, but that tasted worse, and Nigel had to hold him while I forced it down.
GNNNYAAAAIEEE!!!
ASPIRIN! AUGH! GIVE IT! DAMN YOU GIVE IT!
I JUST GAVE HIM A DOUBLE DOSE!
The first night in Rufus's room was bad, and the next six days and nights were no better.
The afternoon of the third day, his fever broke. I dared to think the worst was over.
That night, the worst got started, adding a rash to the fever.
And the pain.
GRAAAAUGHHH!
DANA?
IF WE DON'T DO THIS, HE'LL HURT HIMSELF WORSE.
I had to make him take broth and soup and fruit and vegetable juices.
I prayed that whatever he had, I wouldn't get it.

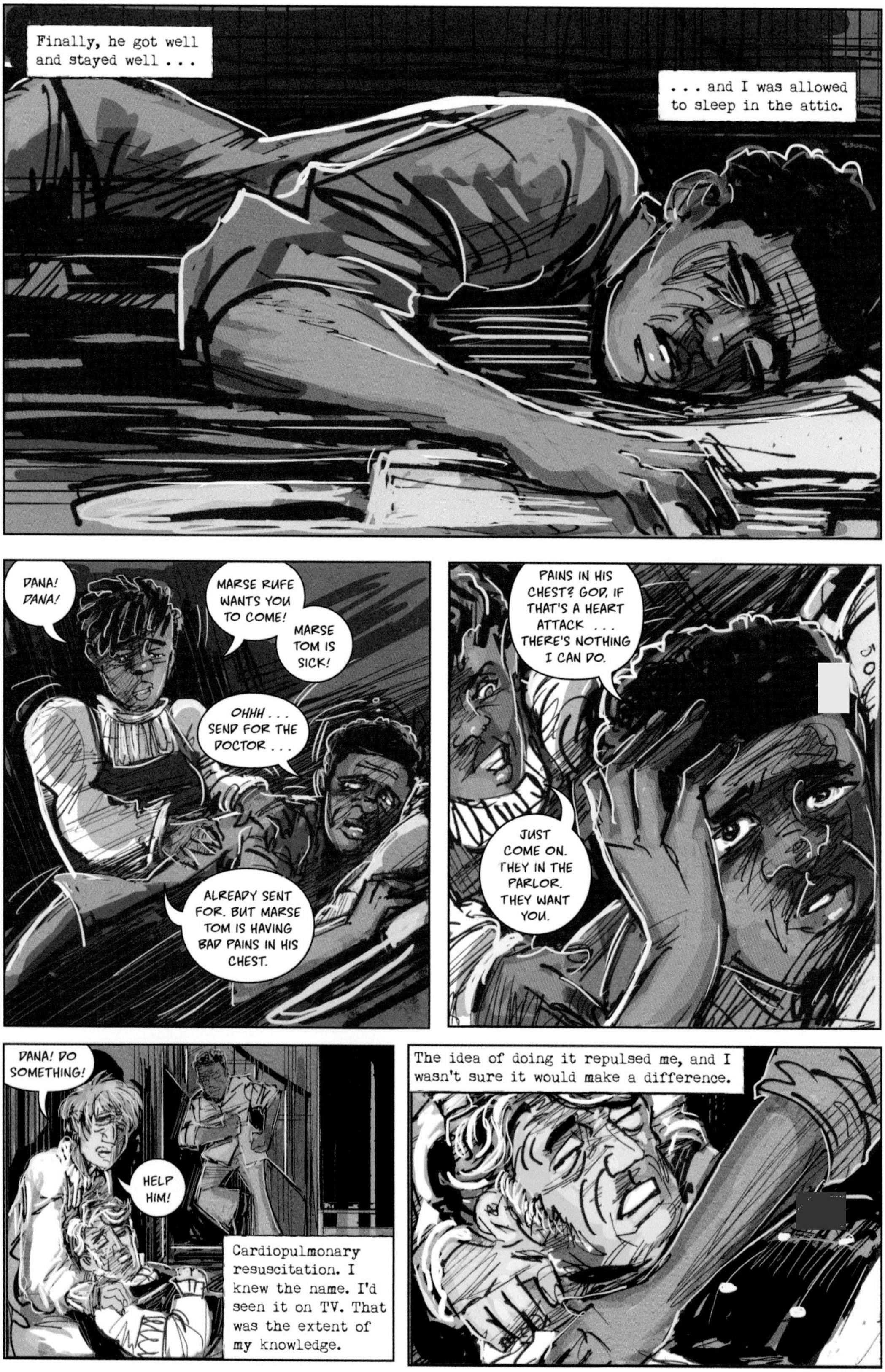
Finally, he got well and stayed well . . .
. . . and I was allowed to sleep in the attic.
DANA! DANA!
MARSE RUFE WANTS YOU TO COME!
MARSE TOM IS SICK!
OHHH . . . SEND FOR THE DOCTOR . . .
ALREADY SENT FOR. BUT MARSE TOM IS HAVING BAD PAINS IN HIS CHEST.
PAINS IN HIS CHEST? GOD, IF THAT'S A HEART ATTACK . . . THERE'S NOTHING I CAN DO.
JUST COME ON. THEY IN THE PARLOR. THEY WANT YOU.
DANA! DO SOMETHING!
HELP HIM!
Cardiopulmonary resuscitation. I knew the name. I'd seen it on TV. That was the extent of my knowledge.
The idea of doing it repulsed me, and I wasn't sure it would make a difference.

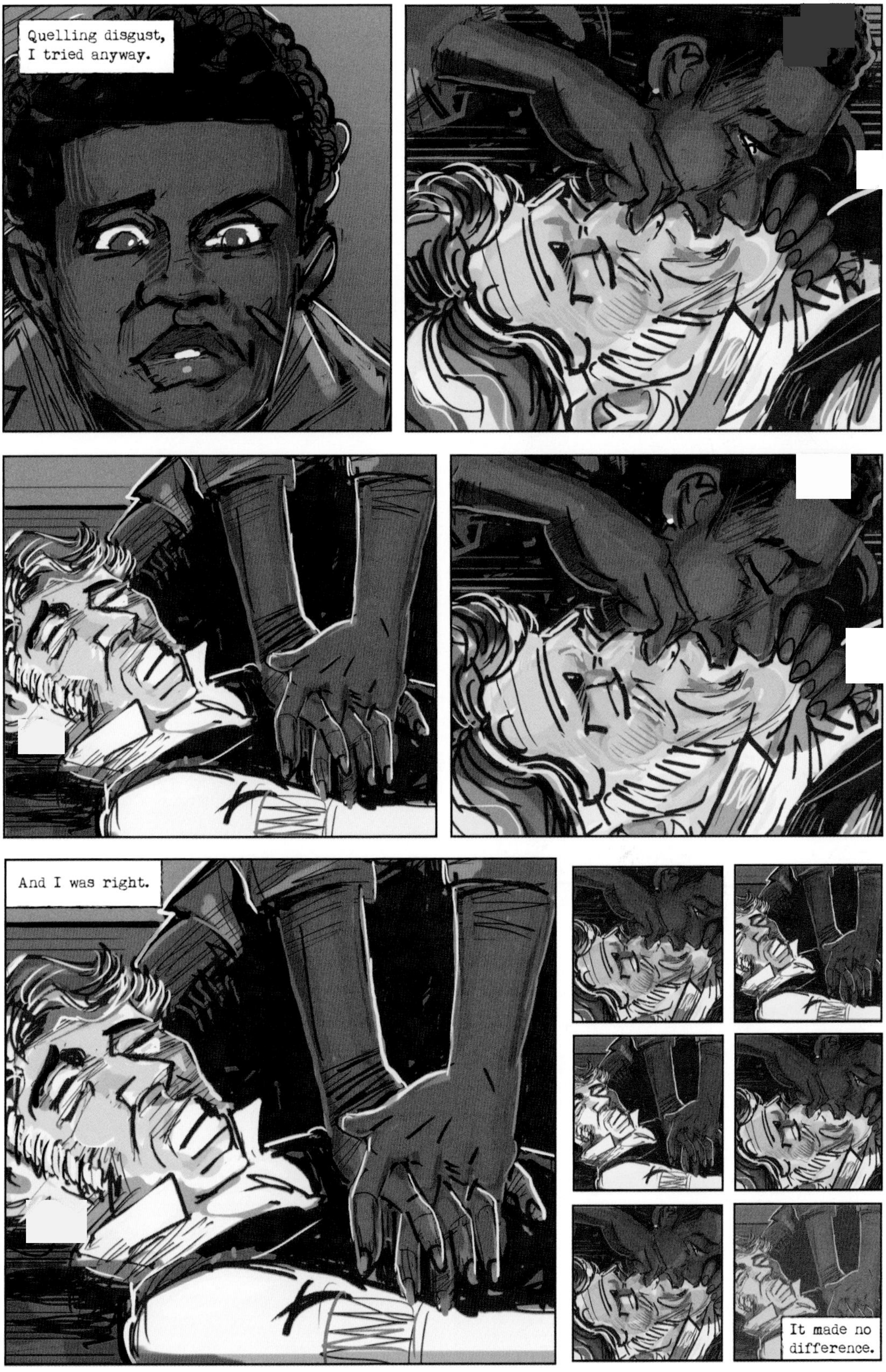
Quelling disgust,
I tried anyway.
And I was right.
It made no
difference.

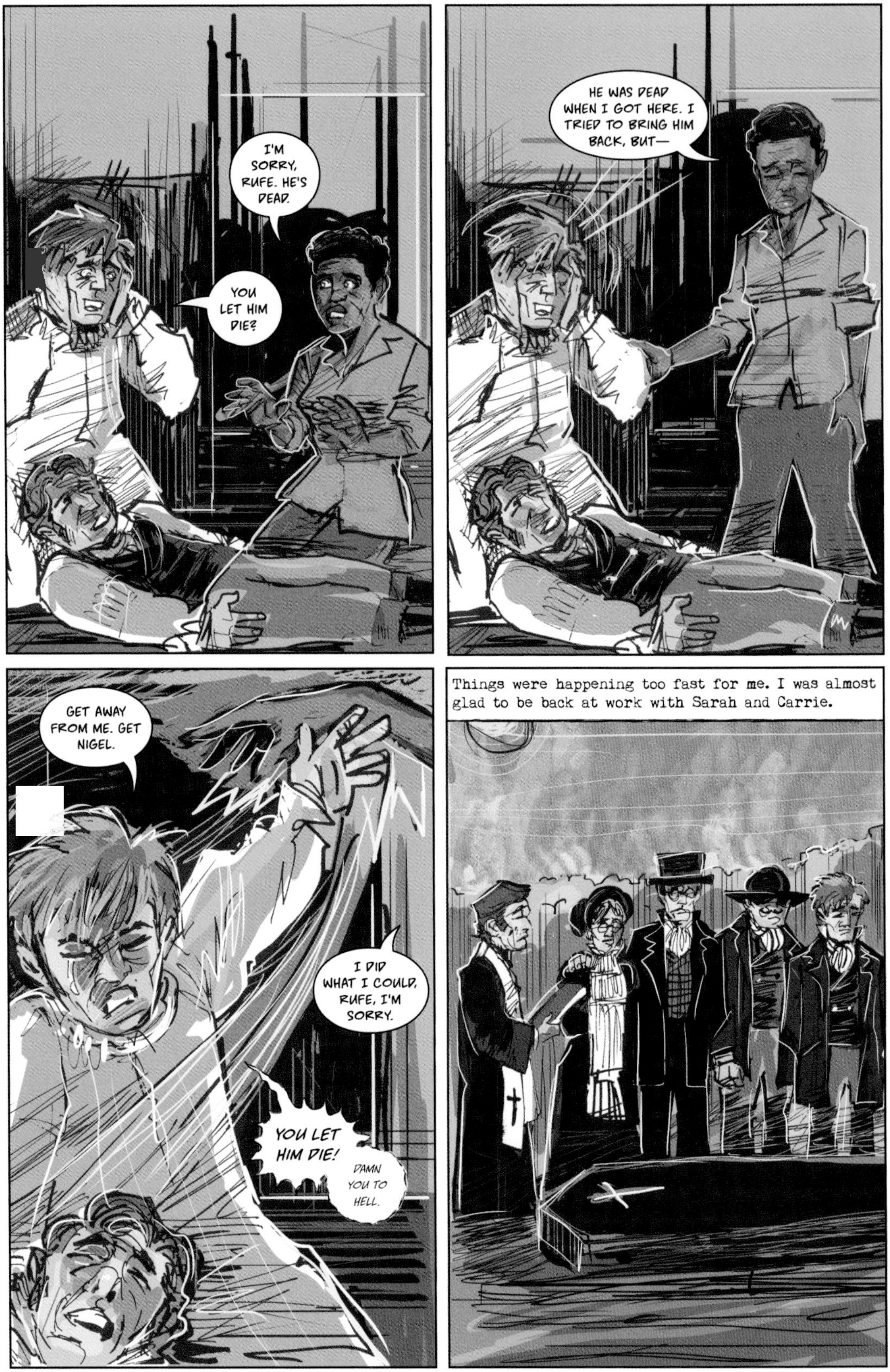
I'M SORRY, RUFE. HE'S DEAD.
YOU LET HIM DIE?
HE WAS DEAD WHEN I GOT HERE. I TRIED TO BRING HIM BACK, BUT—
GET AWAY FROM ME. GET NIGEL.
I DID WHAT I COULD, RUFE, I'M SORRY.
YOU LET HIM DIE!
DAMN YOU TO HELL.
Things were happening too fast for me. I was almost glad to be back at work with Sarah and Carrie.

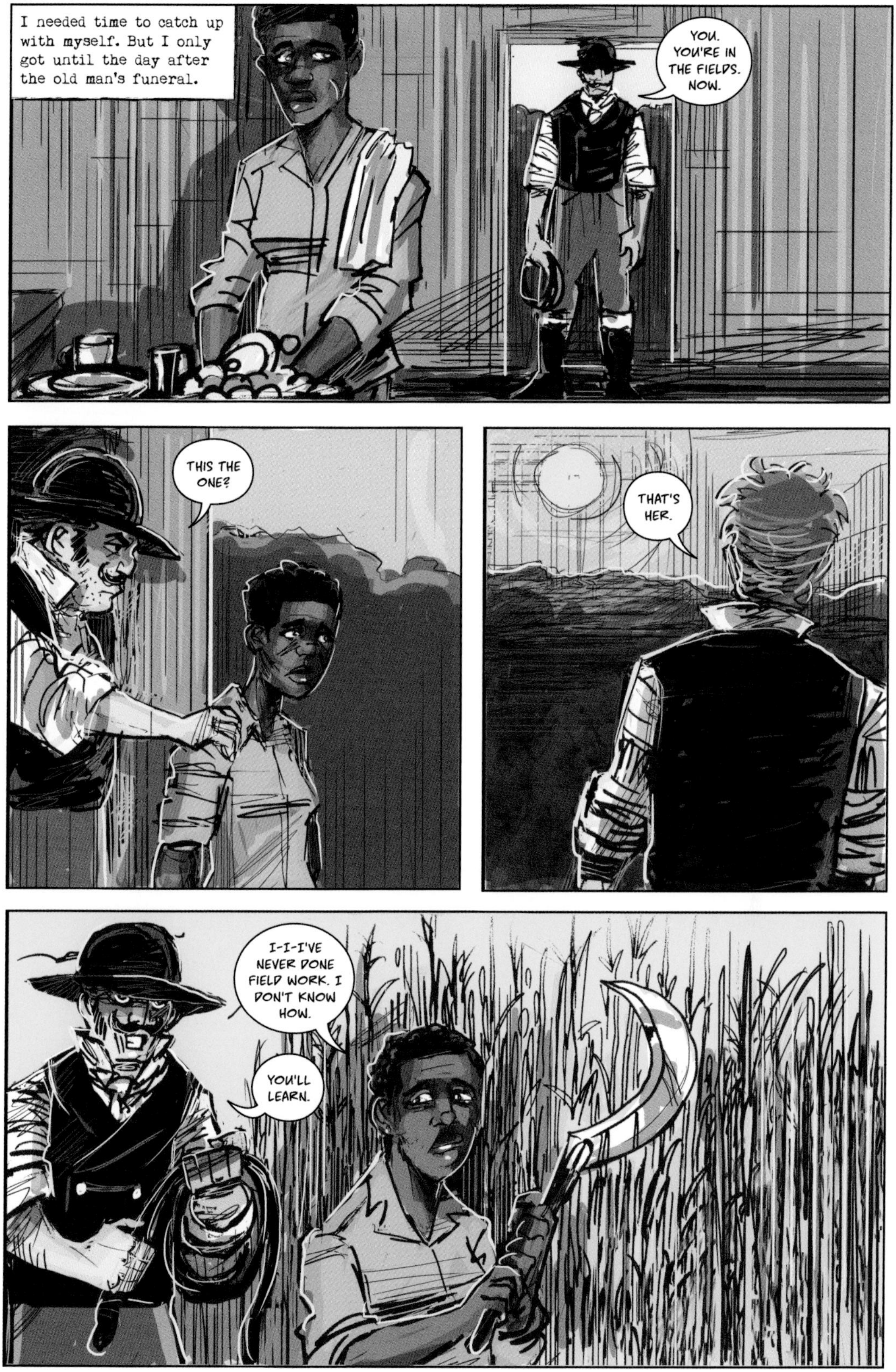
I needed time to catch up with myself. But I only got until the day after the old man's funeral.
YOU. YOU'RE IN THE FIELDS. NOW.
THIS THE ONE?
THAT'S HER.
I-I-I'VE NEVER DONE FIELD WORK. I DON'T KNOW HOW.
YOU'LL LEARN.

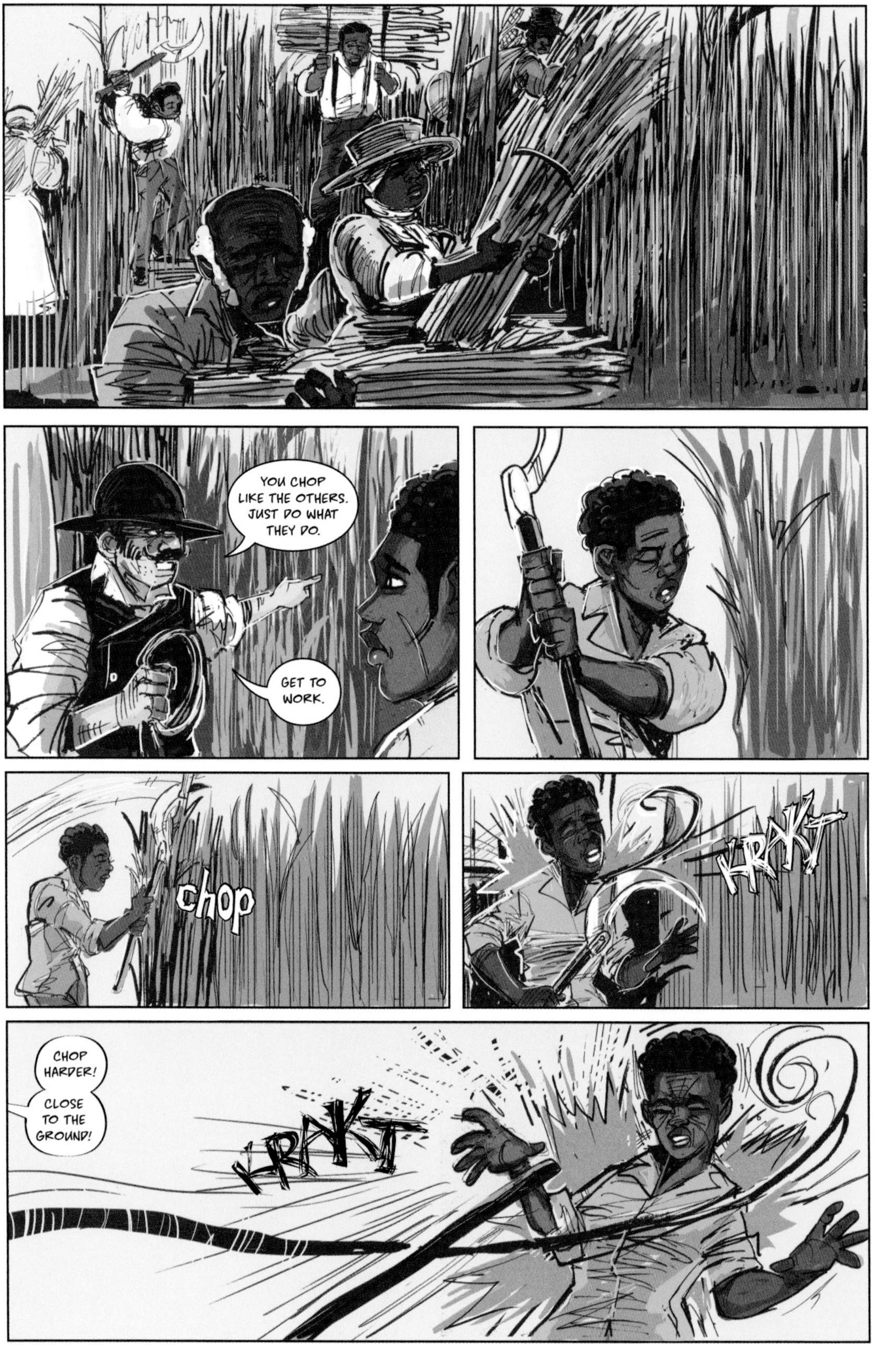
YOU CHOP LIKE THE OTHERS. JUST DO WHAT THEY DO.
GET TO WORK.
chop
KRAKT
CHOP HARDER!
CLOSE TO THE GROUND!
KRAKT

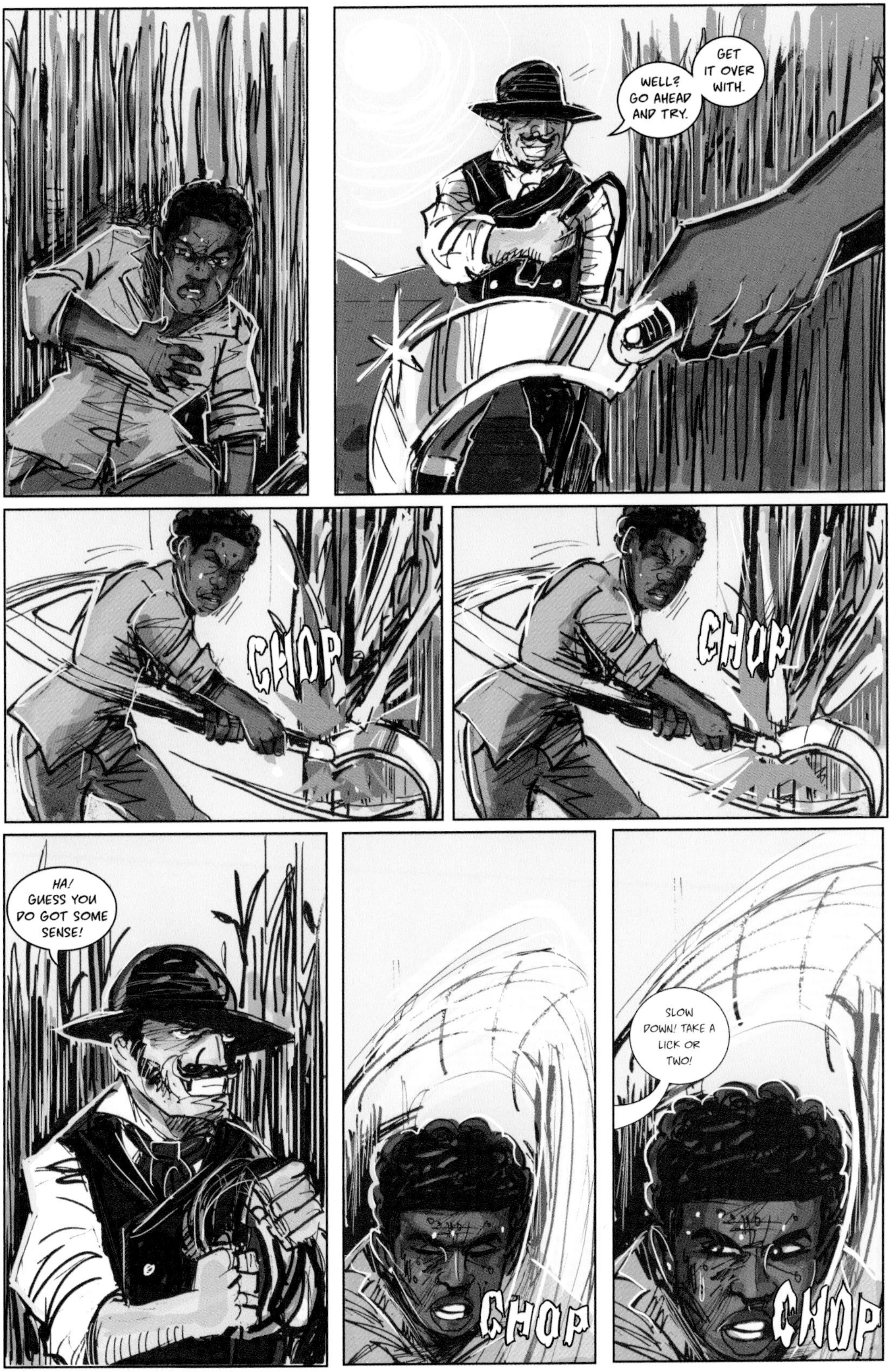
WELL? GO AHEAD AND TRY.
GET IT OVER WITH.
CHOP
CHOP
HA! GUESS YOU DO GOT SOME SENSE!
CHOP
SLOW DOWN! TAKE A LICK OR TWO!
CHOP

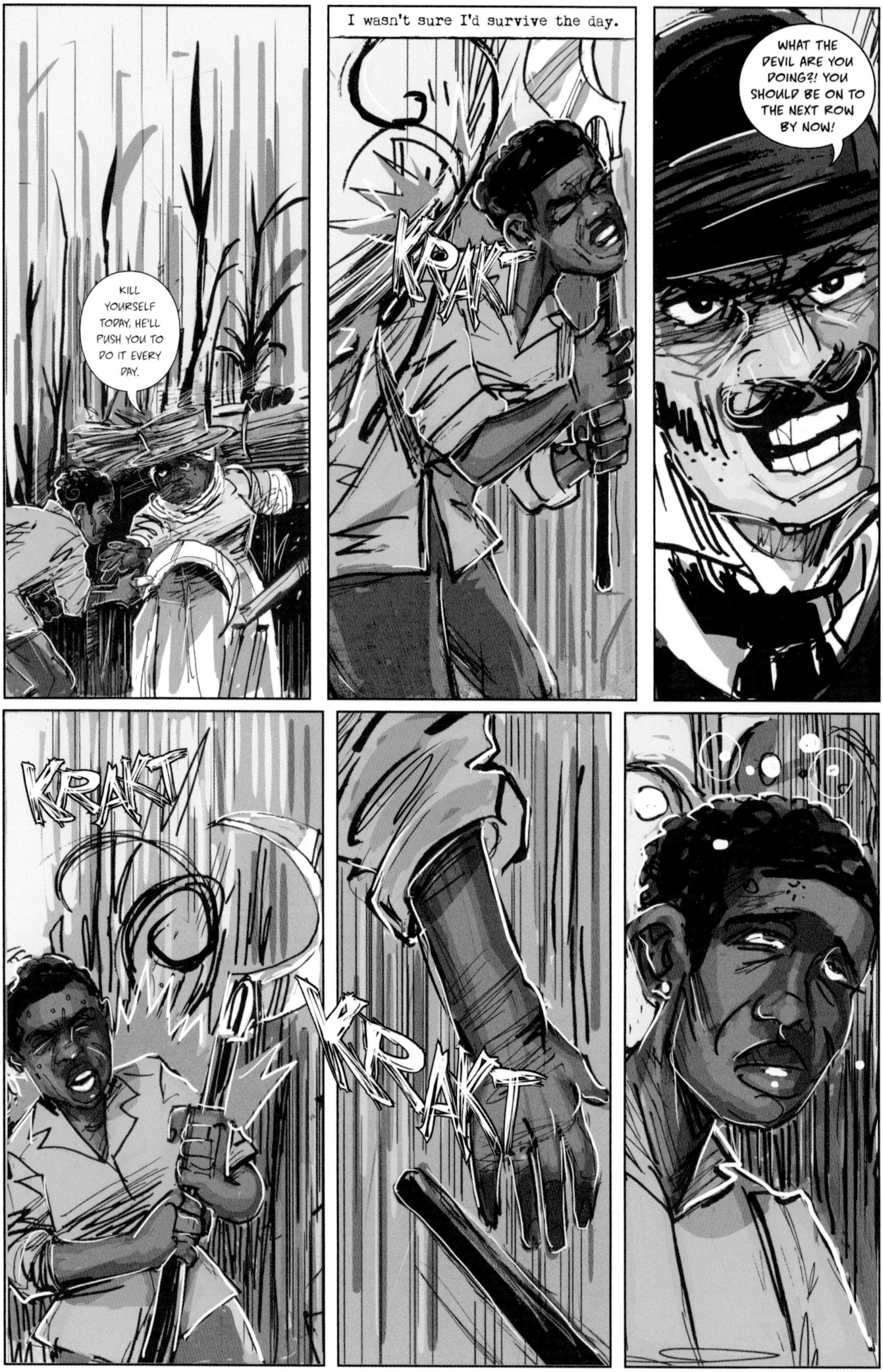
KILL YOURSELF TODAY, HE'LL PUSH YOU TO DO IT EVERY DAY.
I wasn't sure I'd survive the day.
KRAKT
WHAT THE DEVIL ARE YOU DOING?! YOU SHOULD BE ON TO THE NEXT ROW BY NOW!
KRAKT
KRAKT

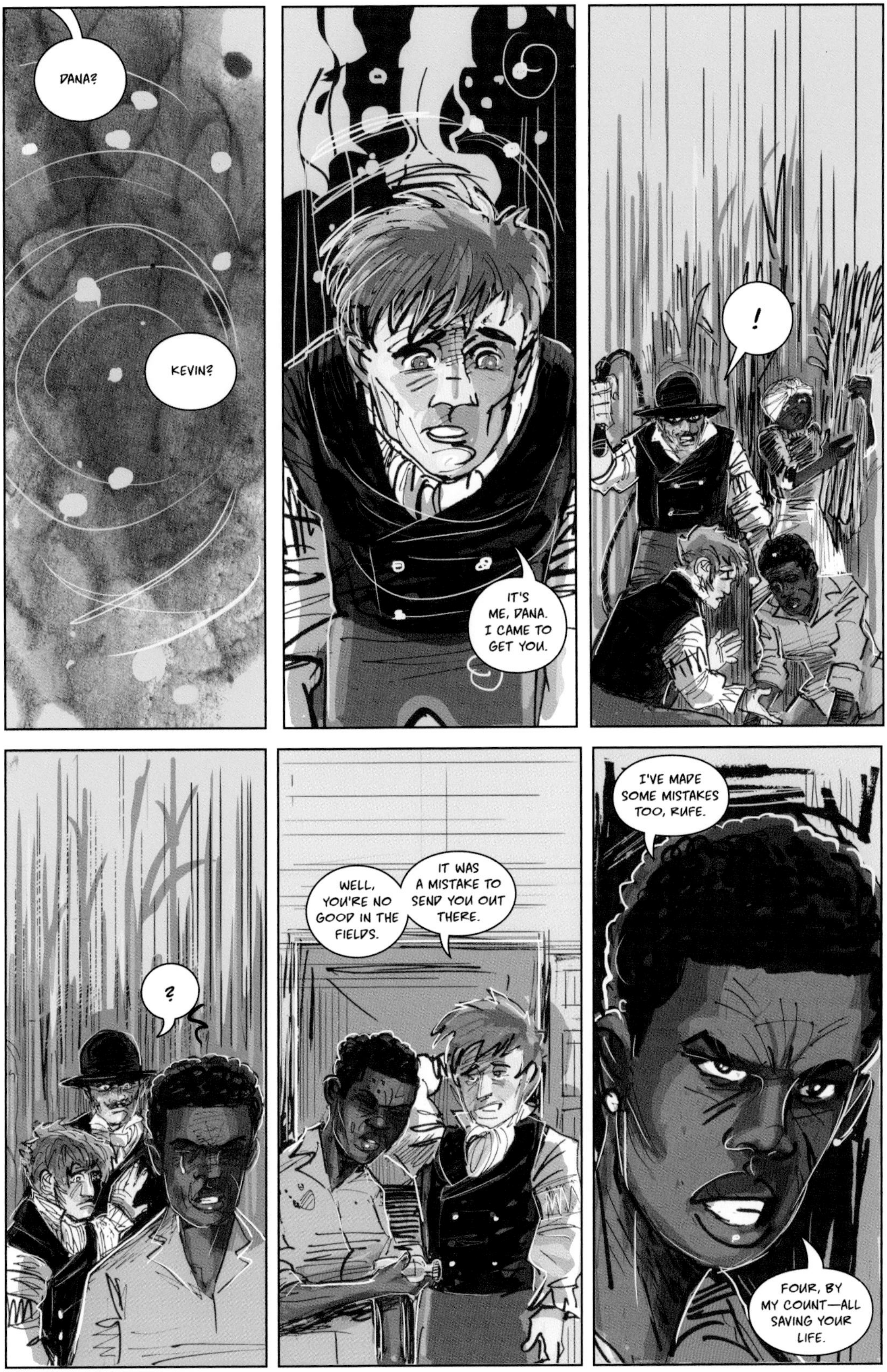
DANA?
KEVIN?
IT'S ME, DANA. I CAME TO GET YOU.
!
?
WELL, YOU'RE NO GOOD IN THE FIELDS.
IT WAS A MISTAKE TO SEND YOU OUT THERE.
I'VE MADE SOME MISTAKES TOO, RUFE.
FOUR, BY MY COUNT—ALL SAVING YOUR LIFE.

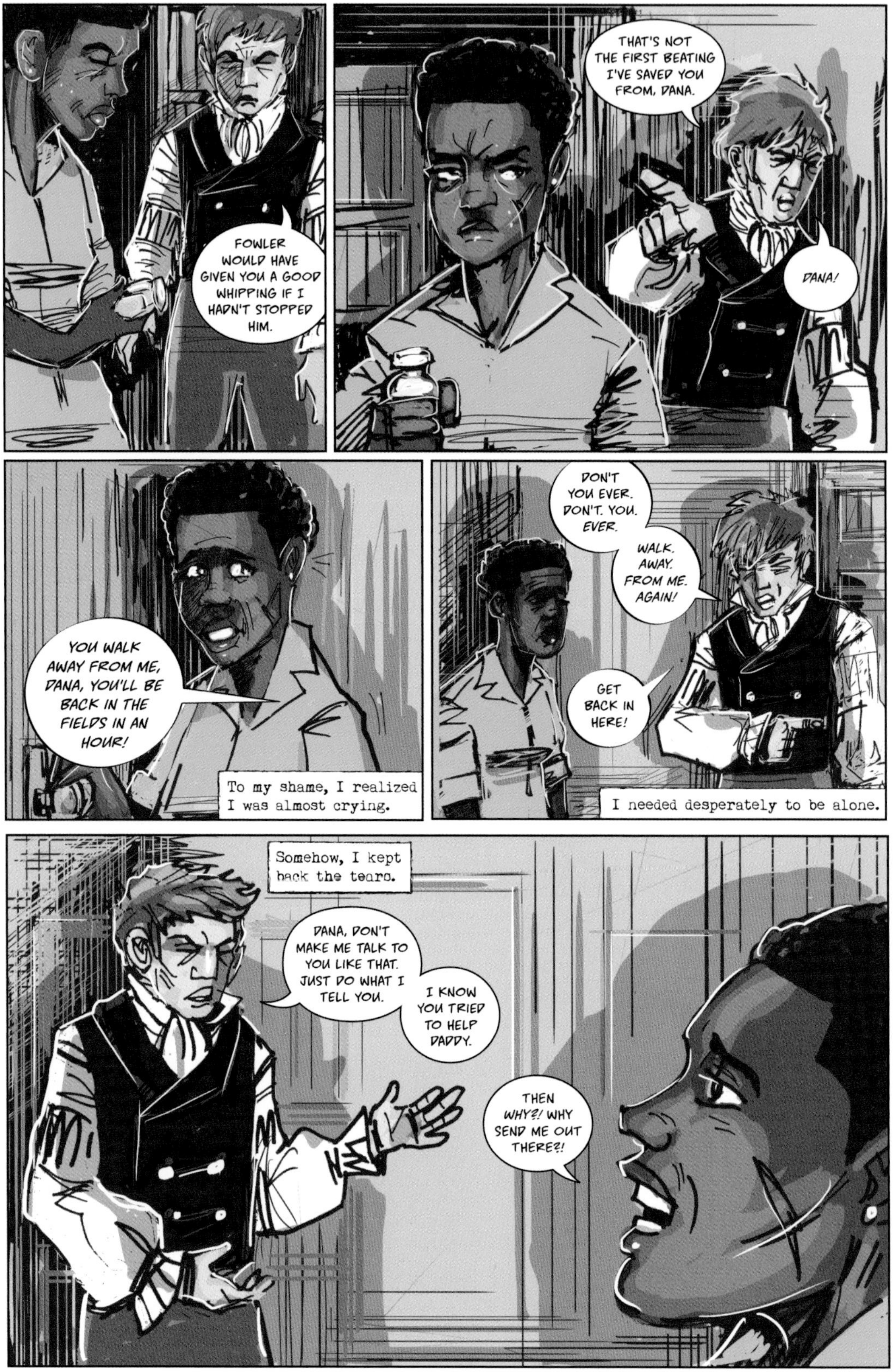
FOWLER WOULD HAVE GIVEN YOU A GOOD WHIPPING IF I HADN'T STOPPED HIM.
THAT'S NOT THE FIRST BEATING I'VE SAVED YOU FROM, DANA.
DANA!
YOU WALK AWAY FROM ME, DANA, YOU'LL BE BACK IN THE FIELDS IN AN HOUR!
To my shame, I realized I was almost crying.
DON'T YOU EVER. DON'T. YOU. EVER.
WALK. AWAY. FROM ME. AGAIN!
GET BACK IN HERE!
I needed desperately to be alone.
Somehow, I kept back the tears.
DANA, DON'T MAKE ME TALK TO YOU LIKE THAT. JUST DO WHAT I TELL YOU.
I KNOW YOU TRIED TO HELP DADDY.
THEN WHY?! WHY SEND ME OUT THERE?!

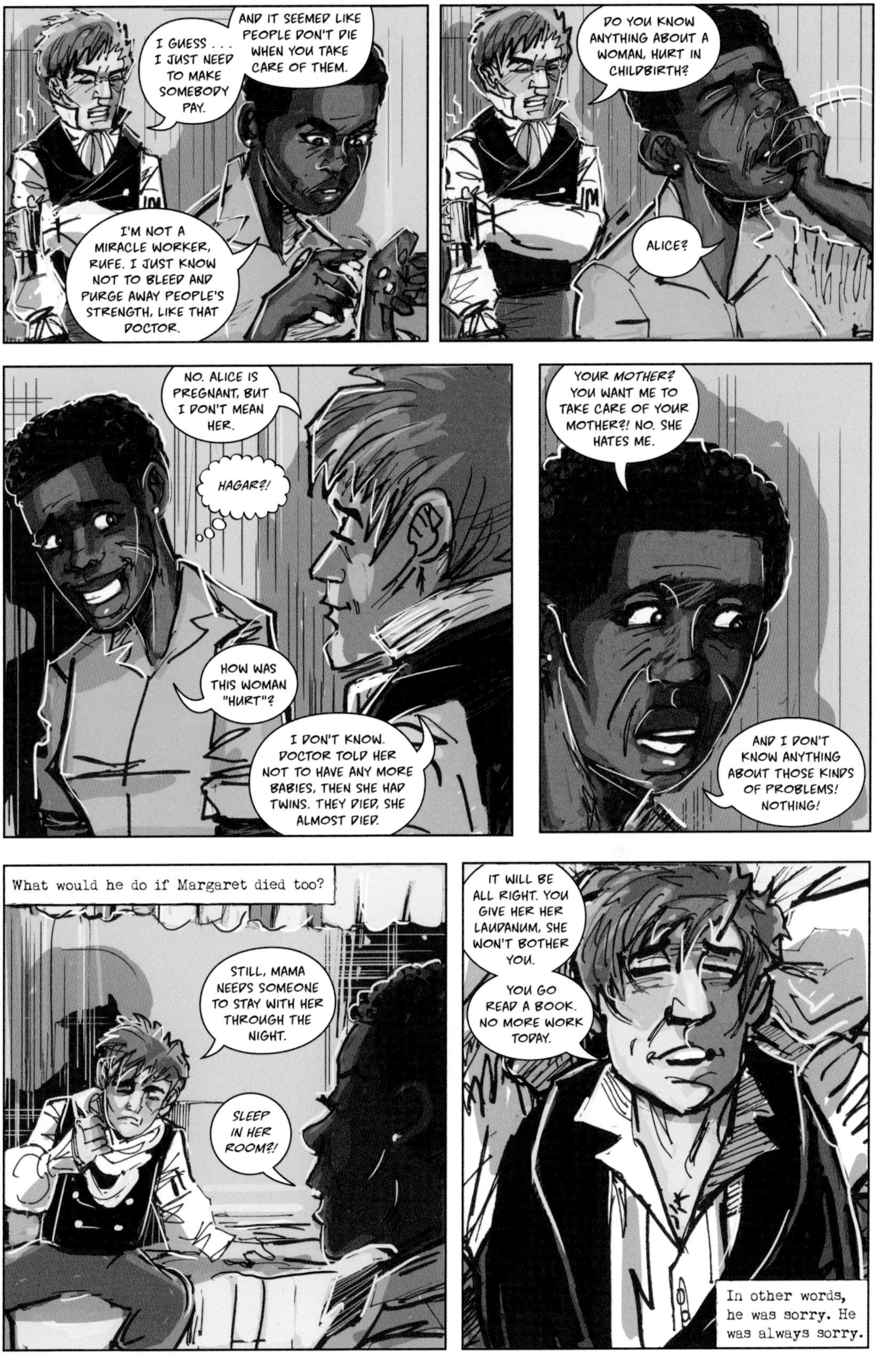
I GUESS . . . I JUST NEED TO MAKE SOMEBODY PAY.
AND IT SEEMED LIKE PEOPLE DON'T DIE WHEN YOU TAKE CARE OF THEM.
I'M NOT A MIRACLE WORKER, RUFE. I JUST KNOW NOT TO BLEED AND PURGE AWAY PEOPLE'S STRENGTH, LIKE THAT DOCTOR.
DO YOU KNOW ANYTHING ABOUT A WOMAN, HURT IN CHILDBIRTH?
ALICE?
NO. ALICE IS PREGNANT, BUT I DON'T MEAN HER.
HAGAR?!
HOW WAS THIS WOMAN "HURT"?
I DON'T KNOW. DOCTOR TOLD HER NOT TO HAVE ANY MORE BABIES, THEN SHE HAD TWINS. THEY DIED, SHE ALMOST DIED.
YOUR MOTHER? YOU WANT ME TO TAKE CARE OF YOUR MOTHER?! NO. SHE HATES ME.
AND I DON'T KNOW ANYTHING ABOUT THOSE KINDS OF PROBLEMS! NOTHING!
What would he do if Margaret died too?
STILL, MAMA NEEDS SOMEONE TO STAY WITH HER THROUGH THE NIGHT.
SLEEP IN HER ROOM?!
IT WILL BE ALL RIGHT. YOU GIVE HER HER LAUDANUM, SHE WON'T BOTHER YOU.
YOU GO READ A BOOK. NO MORE WORK TODAY.
In other words, he was sorry. He was always sorry.

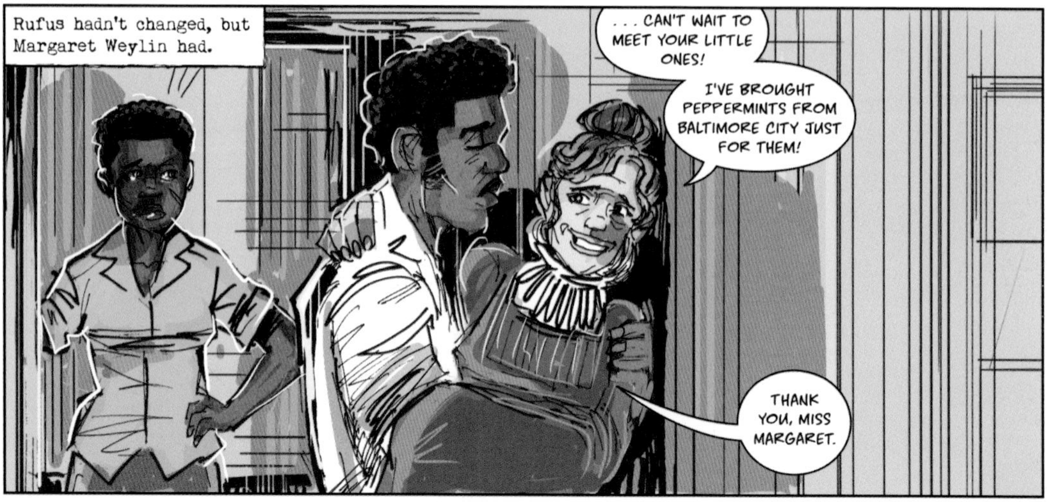
Rufus hadn't changed, but Margaret Weylin had.
. . . CAN'T WAIT TO MEET YOUR LITTLE ONES!
I'VE BROUGHT PEPPERMINTS FROM BALTIMORE CITY JUST FOR THEM!
THANK YOU, MISS MARGARET.

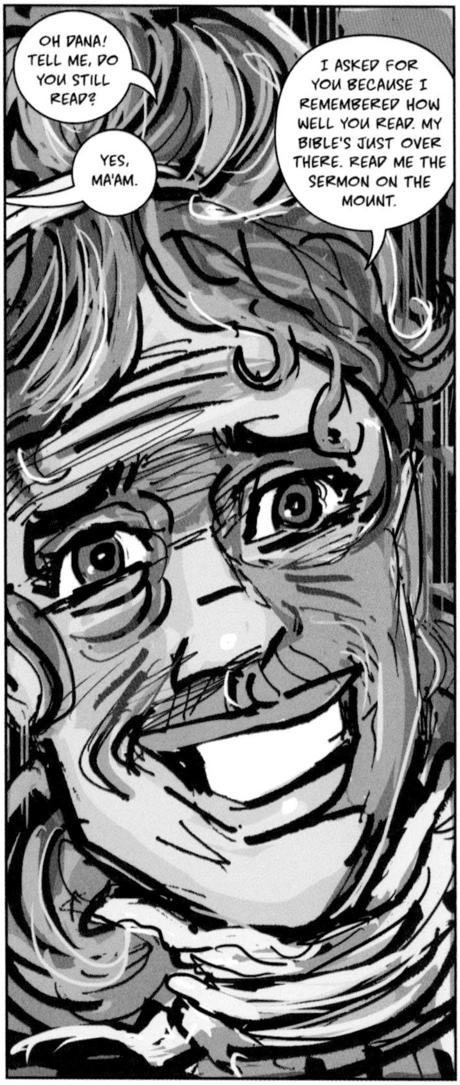
OH DANA! TELL ME, DO YOU STILL READ?
YES, MA'AM.
I ASKED FOR YOU BECAUSE I REMEMBERED HOW WELL YOU READ. MY BIBLE'S JUST OVER THERE. READ ME THE SERMON ON THE MOUNT.

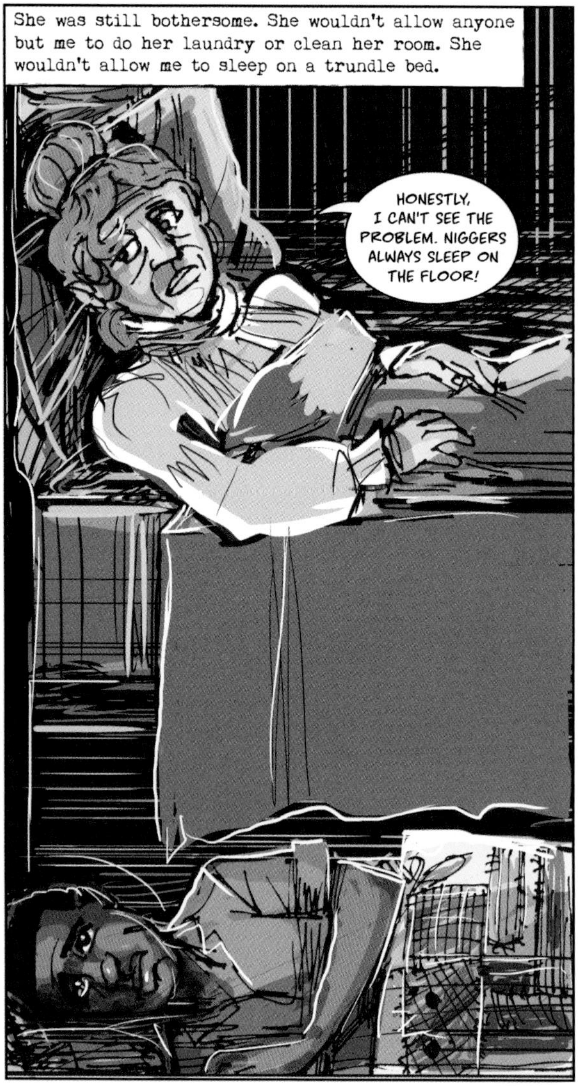
She was still bothersome. She wouldn't allow anyone but me to do her laundry or clean her room. She wouldn't allow me to sleep on a trundle bed.
HONESTLY, I CAN'T SEE THE PROBLEM. NIGGERS ALWAYS SLEEP ON THE FLOOR!

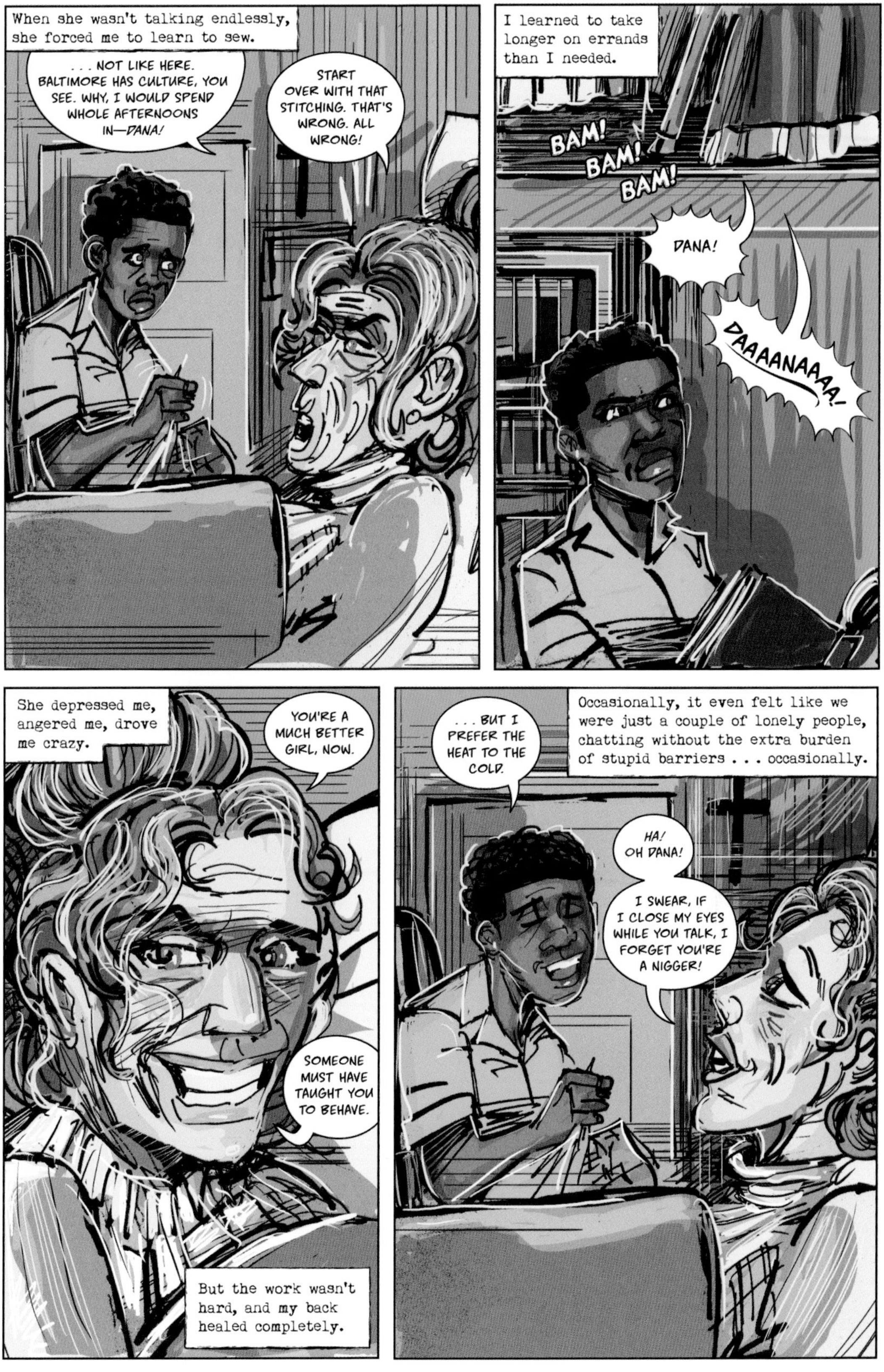
When she wasn't talking endlessly, she forced me to learn to sew.
. . . NOT LIKE HERE. BALTIMORE HAS CULTURE, YOU SEE. WHY, I WOULD SPEND WHOLE AFTERNOONS IN—DANA!
START OVER WITH THAT STITCHING. THAT'S WRONG. ALL WRONG!
I learned to take longer on errands than I needed.
BAM!
BAM!
BAM!
DANA!
DAAAANAAAA!
She depressed me, angered me, drove me crazy.
YOU'RE A MUCH BETTER GIRL, NOW.
SOMEONE MUST HAVE TAUGHT YOU TO BEHAVE.
But the work wasn't hard, and my back healed completely.
Occasionally, it even felt like we were just a couple of lonely people, chatting without the extra burden of stupid barriers . . . occasionally.
. . . BUT I PREFER THE HEAT TO THE COLD.
HA! OH DANA!
I SWEAR, IF I CLOSE MY EYES WHILE YOU TALK, I FORGET YOU'RE A NIGGER!

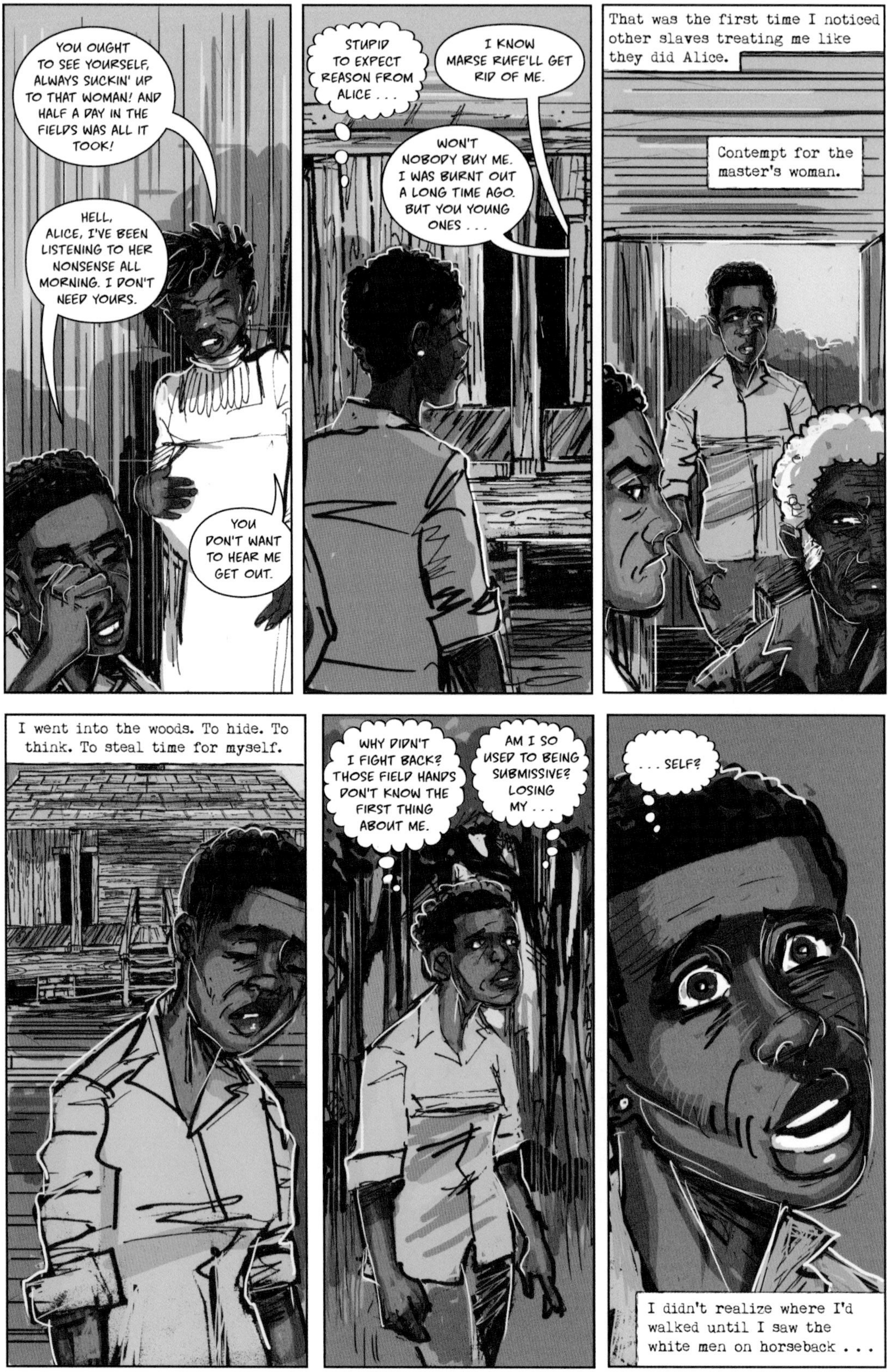
YOU OUGHT TO SEE YOURSELF, ALWAYS SUCKIN' UP TO THAT WOMAN! AND HALF A DAY IN THE FIELDS WAS ALL IT TOOK!
HELL, ALICE, I'VE BEEN LISTENING TO HER NONSENSE ALL MORNING. I DON'T NEED YOURS.
YOU DON'T WANT TO HEAR ME GET OUT.
STUPID TO EXPECT REASON FROM ALICE . . .
I KNOW MARSE RUFE'LL GET RID OF ME.
WON'T NOBODY BUY ME. I WAS BURNT OUT A LONG TIME AGO. BUT YOU YOUNG ONES . . .
That was the first time I noticed other slaves treating me like they did Alice.
Contempt for the master's woman.
I went into the woods. To hide. To think. To steal time for myself.
WHY DIDN'T I FIGHT BACK? THOSE FIELD HANDS DON'T KNOW THE FIRST THING ABOUT ME.
AM I SO USED TO BEING SUBMISSIVE? LOSING MY . . .
. . . SELF?
I didn't realize where I'd walked until I saw the white men on horseback . . .

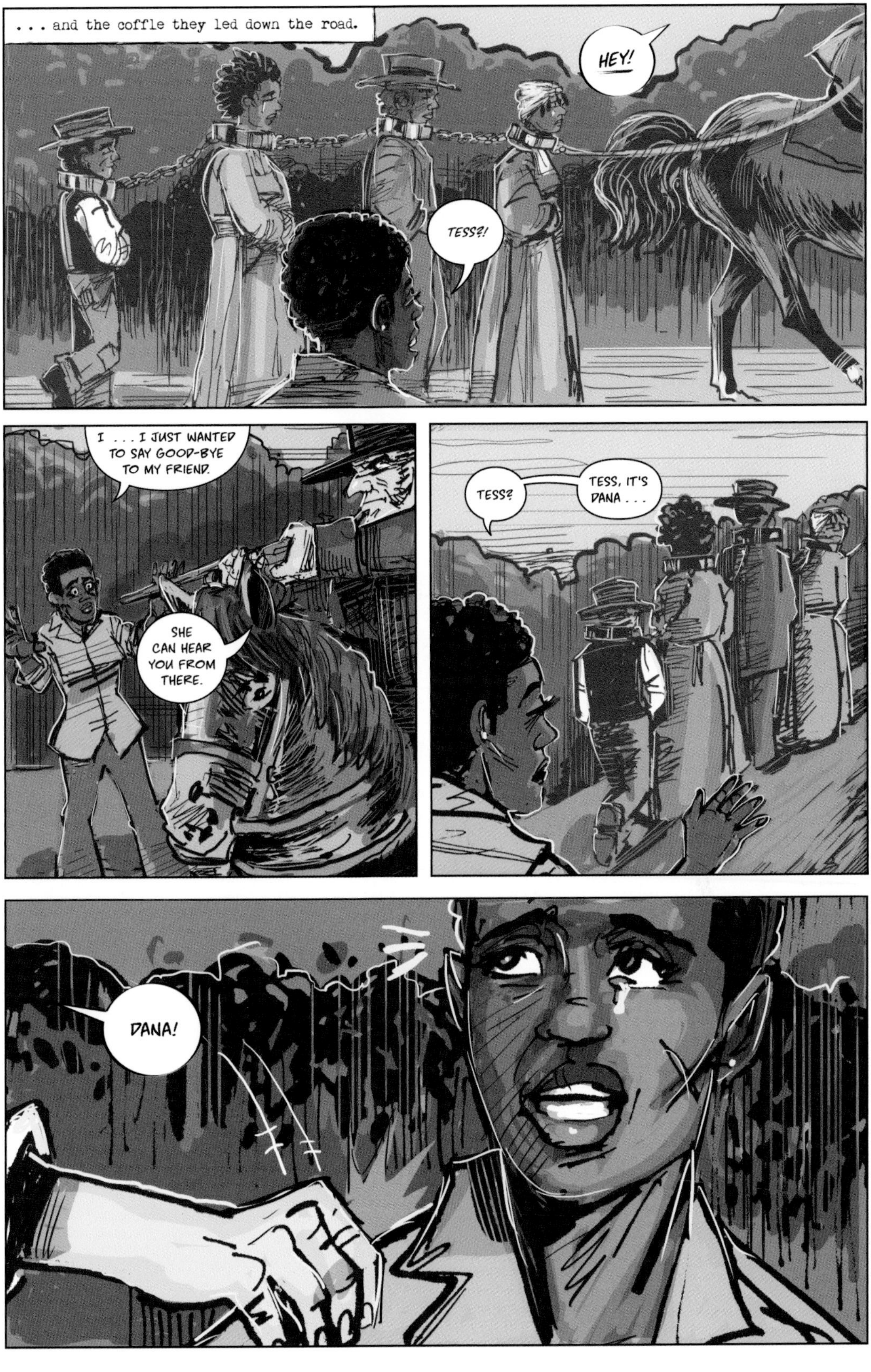
. . . and the coffle they led down the road.
HEY!
TESS?!
I . . . I JUST WANTED TO SAY GOOD-BYE TO MY FRIEND.
SHE CAN HEAR YOU FROM THERE.
TESS?
TESS, IT'S DANA . . .
DANA!

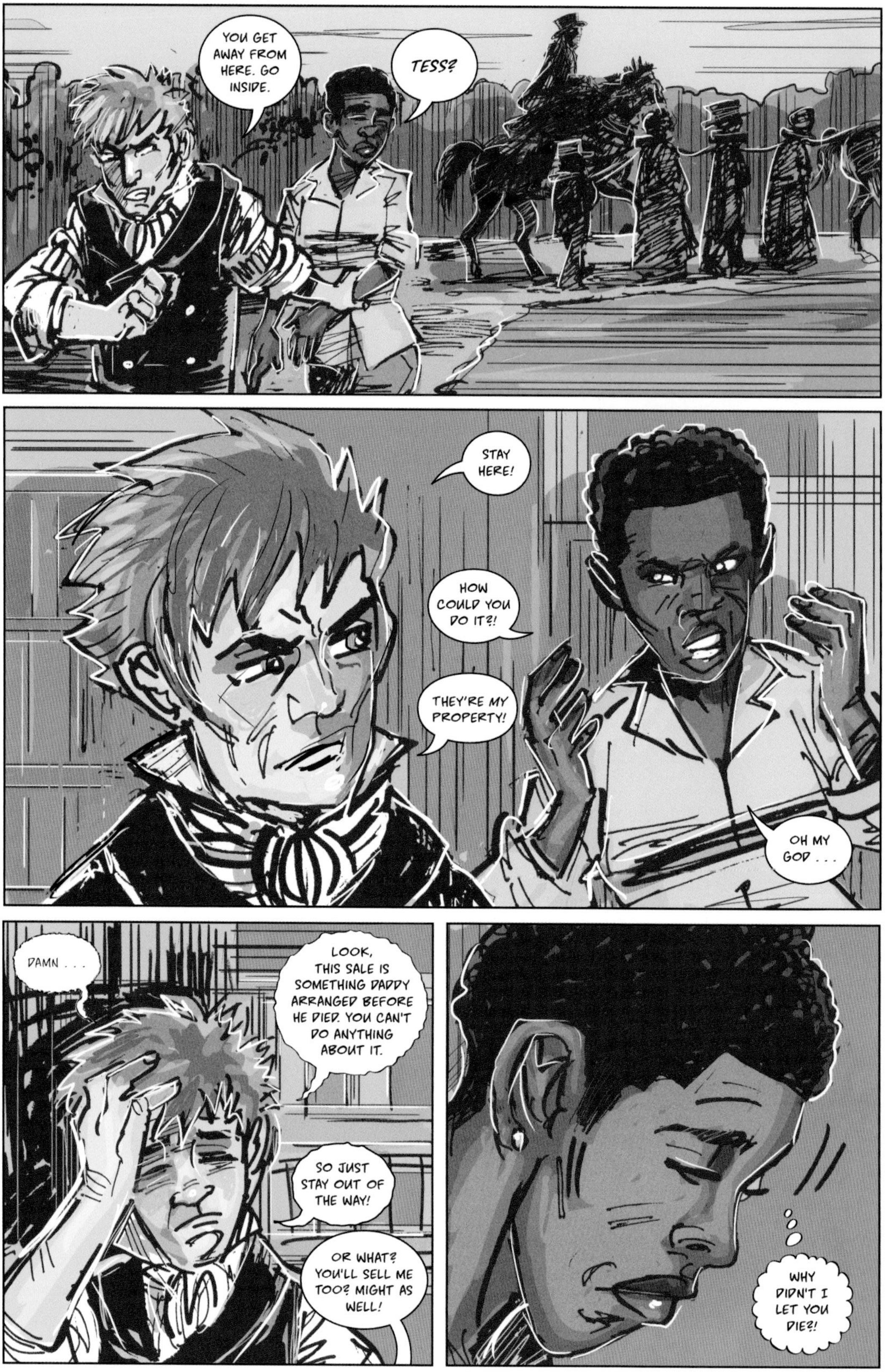
YOU GET AWAY FROM HERE. GO INSIDE.
TESS?
STAY HERE!
HOW COULD YOU DO IT?!
THEY'RE MY PROPERTY!
OH MY GOD . . .
DAMN . . .
LOOK, THIS SALE IS SOMETHING DADDY ARRANGED BEFORE HE DIED. YOU CAN'T DO ANYTHING ABOUT IT.
SO JUST STAY OUT OF THE WAY!
OR WHAT? YOU'LL SELL ME TOO? MIGHT AS WELL!
WHY DIDN'T I LET YOU DIE?!

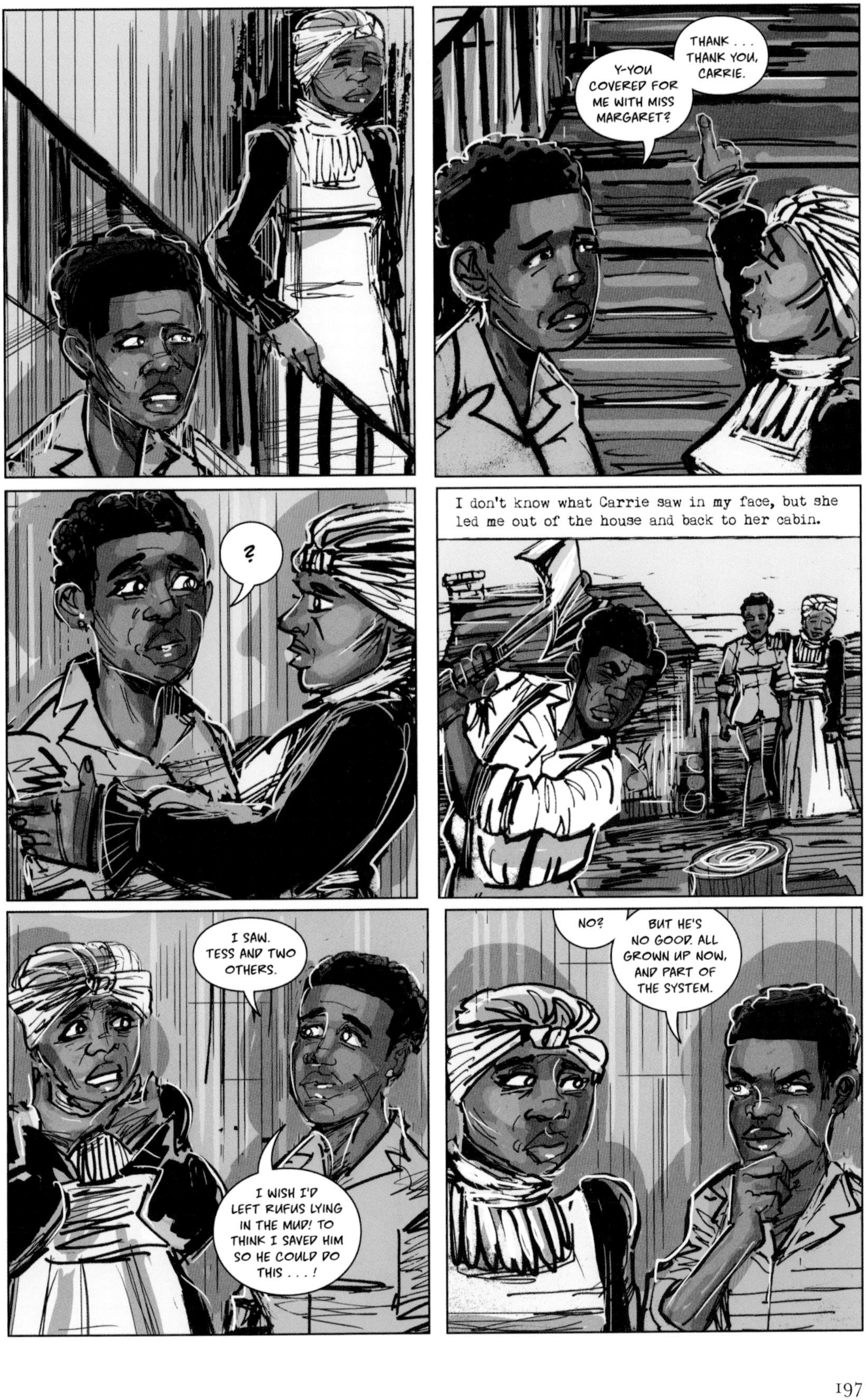
Y-YOU COVERED FOR ME WITH MISS MARGARET?
THANK . . . THANK YOU, CARRIE.
?
I don't know what Carrie saw in my face, but she led me out of the house and back to her cabin.
I SAW. TESS AND TWO OTHERS.
I WISH I'D LEFT RUFUS LYING IN THE MUD! TO THINK I SAVED HIM SO HE COULD DO THIS . . . !
NO?
BUT HE'S NO GOOD. ALL GROWN UP NOW, AND PART OF THE SYSTEM.

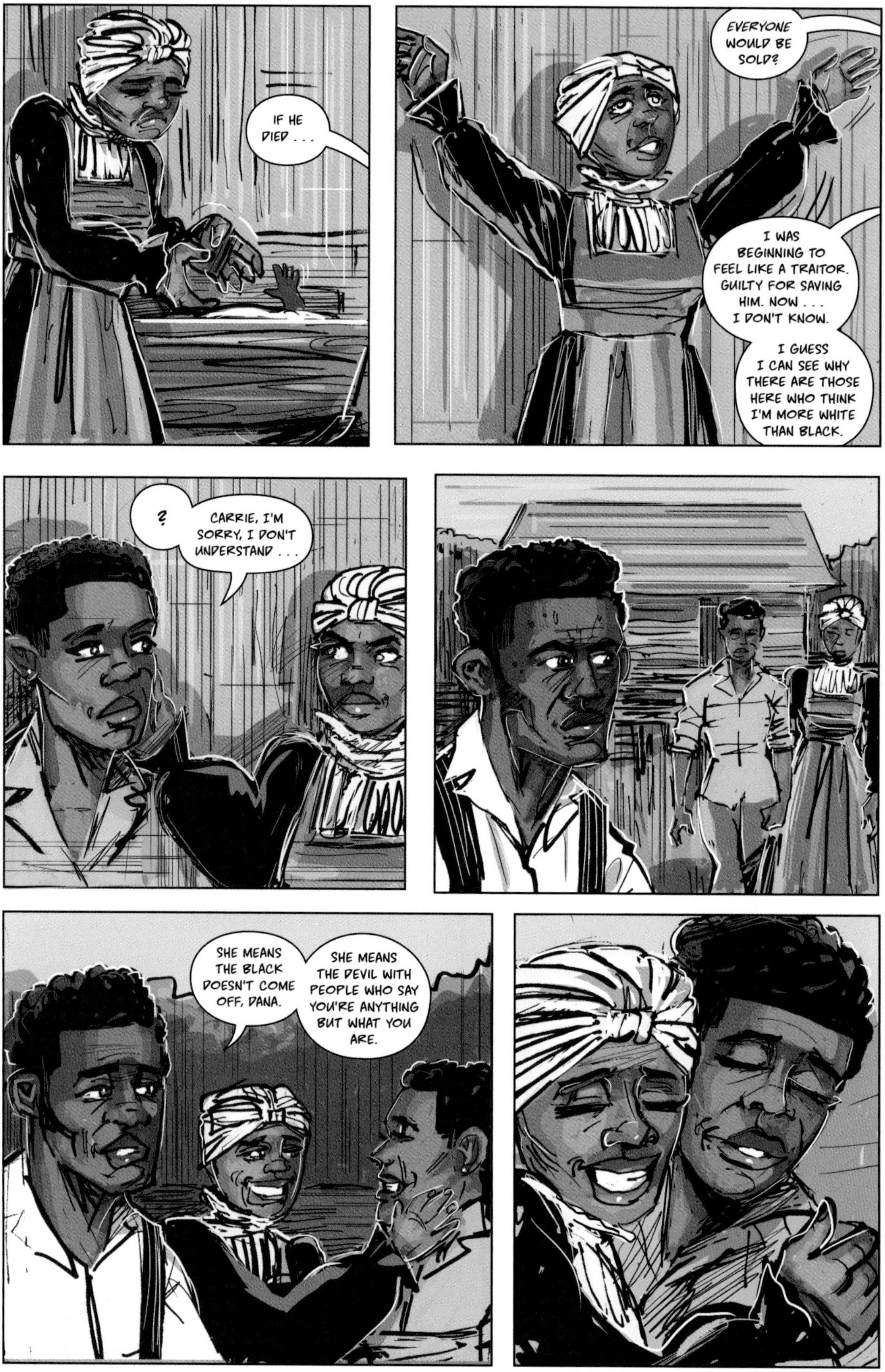
IF HE DIED . . .
EVERYONE WOULD BE SOLD?
I WAS BEGINNING TO FEEL LIKE A TRAITOR. GUILTY FOR SAVING HIM. NOW . . . I DON'T KNOW.
I GUESS I CAN SEE WHY THERE ARE THOSE HERE WHO THINK I'M MORE WHITE THAN BLACK.
?
CARRIE, I'M SORRY, I DON'T UNDERSTAND . . .
SHE MEANS THE BLACK DOESN'T COME OFF, DANA.
SHE MEANS THE DEVIL WITH PEOPLE WHO SAY YOU'RE ANYTHING BUT WHAT YOU ARE.

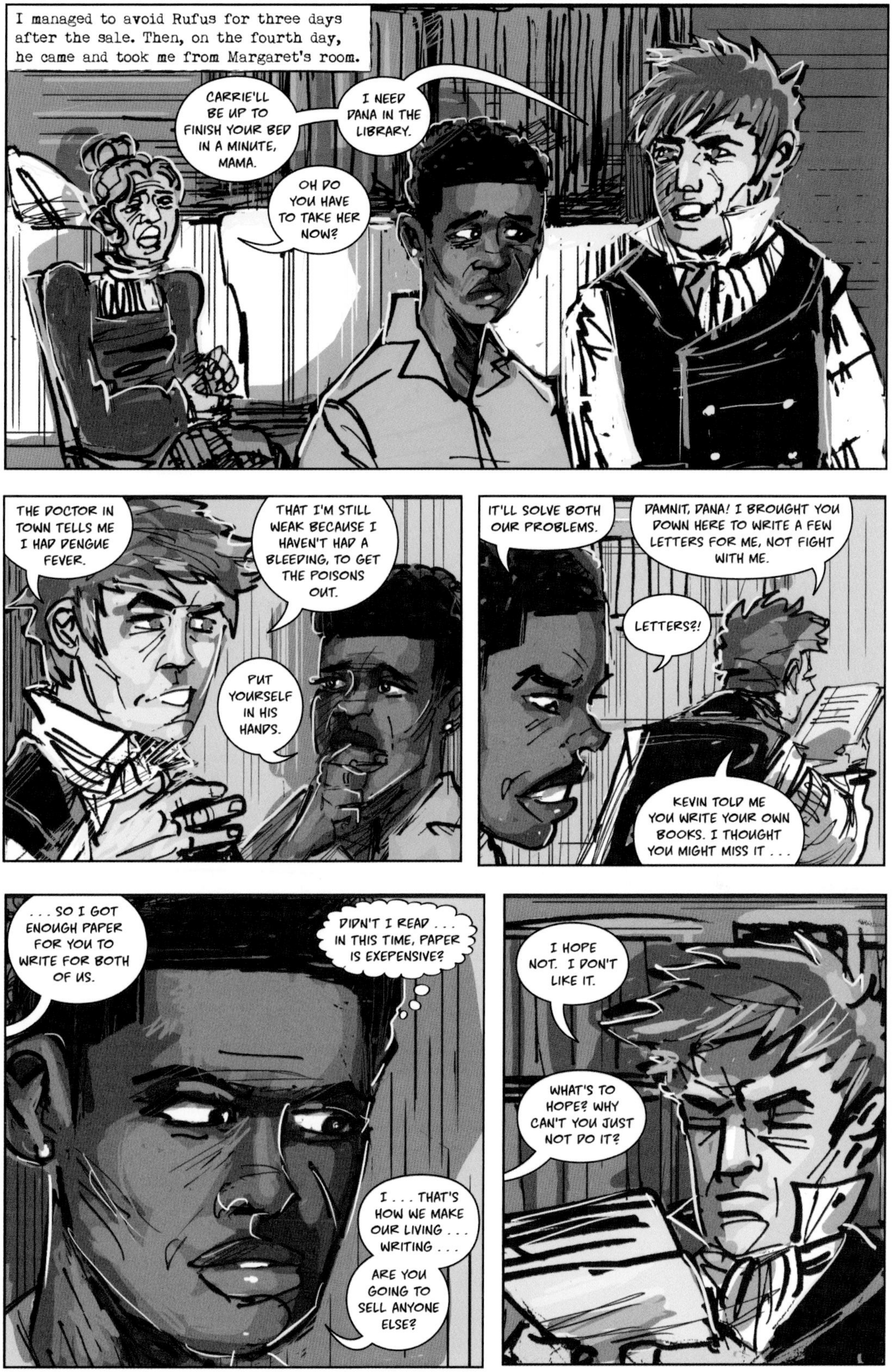
I managed to avoid Rufus for three days after the sale. Then, on the fourth day, he came and took me from Margaret's room.
CARRIE'LL BE UP TO FINISH YOUR BED IN A MINUTE, MAMA.
I NEED DANA IN THE LIBRARY.
OH DO YOU HAVE TO TAKE HER NOW?
THE DOCTOR IN TOWN TELLS ME I HAD DENGUE FEVER.
THAT I'M STILL WEAK BECAUSE I HAVEN'T HAD A BLEEDING, TO GET THE POISONS OUT.
PUT YOURSELF IN HIS HANDS.
IT'LL SOLVE BOTH OUR PROBLEMS.
DAMNIT, DANA! I BROUGHT YOU DOWN HERE TO WRITE A FEW LETTERS FOR ME, NOT FIGHT WITH ME.
LETTERS?!
KEVIN TOLD ME YOU WRITE YOUR OWN BOOKS. I THOUGHT YOU MIGHT MISS IT . . .
. . . SO I GOT ENOUGH PAPER FOR YOU TO WRITE FOR BOTH OF US.
DIDN'T I READ . . . IN THIS TIME, PAPER IS EXEPENSIVE?
I . . . THAT'S HOW WE MAKE OUR LIVING . . . WRITING . . .
ARE YOU GOING TO SELL ANYONE ELSE?
I HOPE NOT. I DON'T LIKE IT.
WHAT'S TO HOPE? WHY CAN'T YOU JUST NOT DO IT?

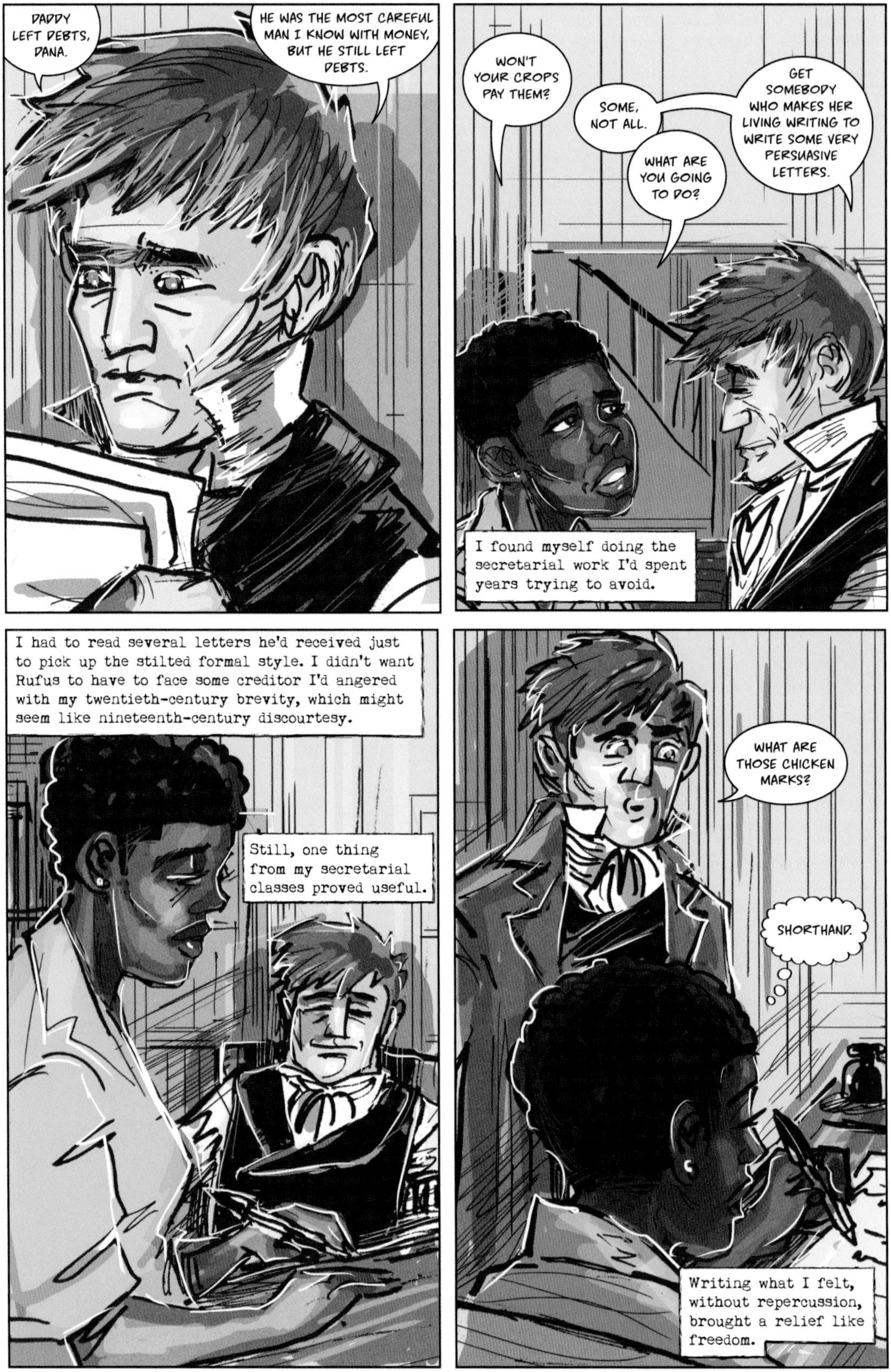
DADDY LEFT DEBTS, DANA.
HE WAS THE MOST CAREFUL MAN I KNOW WITH MONEY, BUT HE STILL LEFT DEBTS.
WON'T YOUR CROPS PAY THEM?
SOME, NOT ALL.
WHAT ARE YOU GOING TO DO?
GET SOMEBODY WHO MAKES HER LIVING WRITING TO WRITE SOME VERY PERSUASIVE LETTERS.
I found myself doing the secretarial work I'd spent years trying to avoid.
I had to read several letters he'd received just to pick up the stilted formal style. I didn't want Rufus to have to face some creditor I'd angered with my twentieth-century brevity, which might seem like nineteenth-century discourtesy.
Still, one thing from my secretarial classes proved useful.
WHAT ARE THOSE CHICKEN MARKS?
SHORTHAND.
Writing what I felt, without repercussion, brought a relief like freedom.

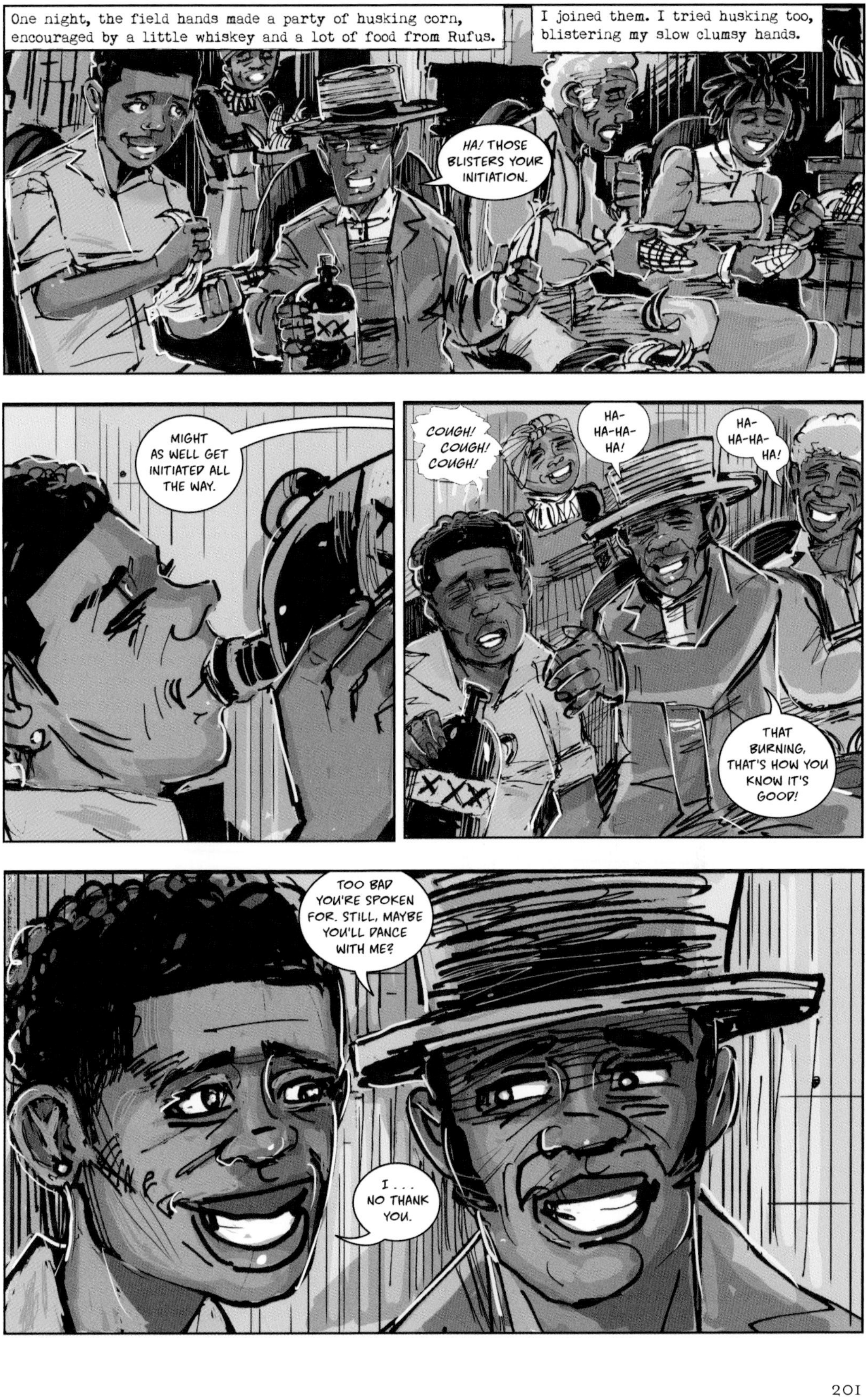
One night, the field hands made a party of husking corn, encouraged by a little whiskey and a lot of food from Rufus.
I joined them. I tried husking too, blistering my slow clumsy hands.
HA! THOSE BLISTERS YOUR INITIATION.
MIGHT AS WELL GET INITIATED ALL THE WAY.
COUGH! COUGH! COUGH!
HA-HA-HA-HA!
HA-HA-HA-HA!
THAT BURNING, THAT'S HOW YOU KNOW IT'S GOOD!
TOO BAD YOU'RE SPOKEN FOR. STILL, MAYBE YOU'LL DANCE WITH ME?
I . . . NO THANK YOU.

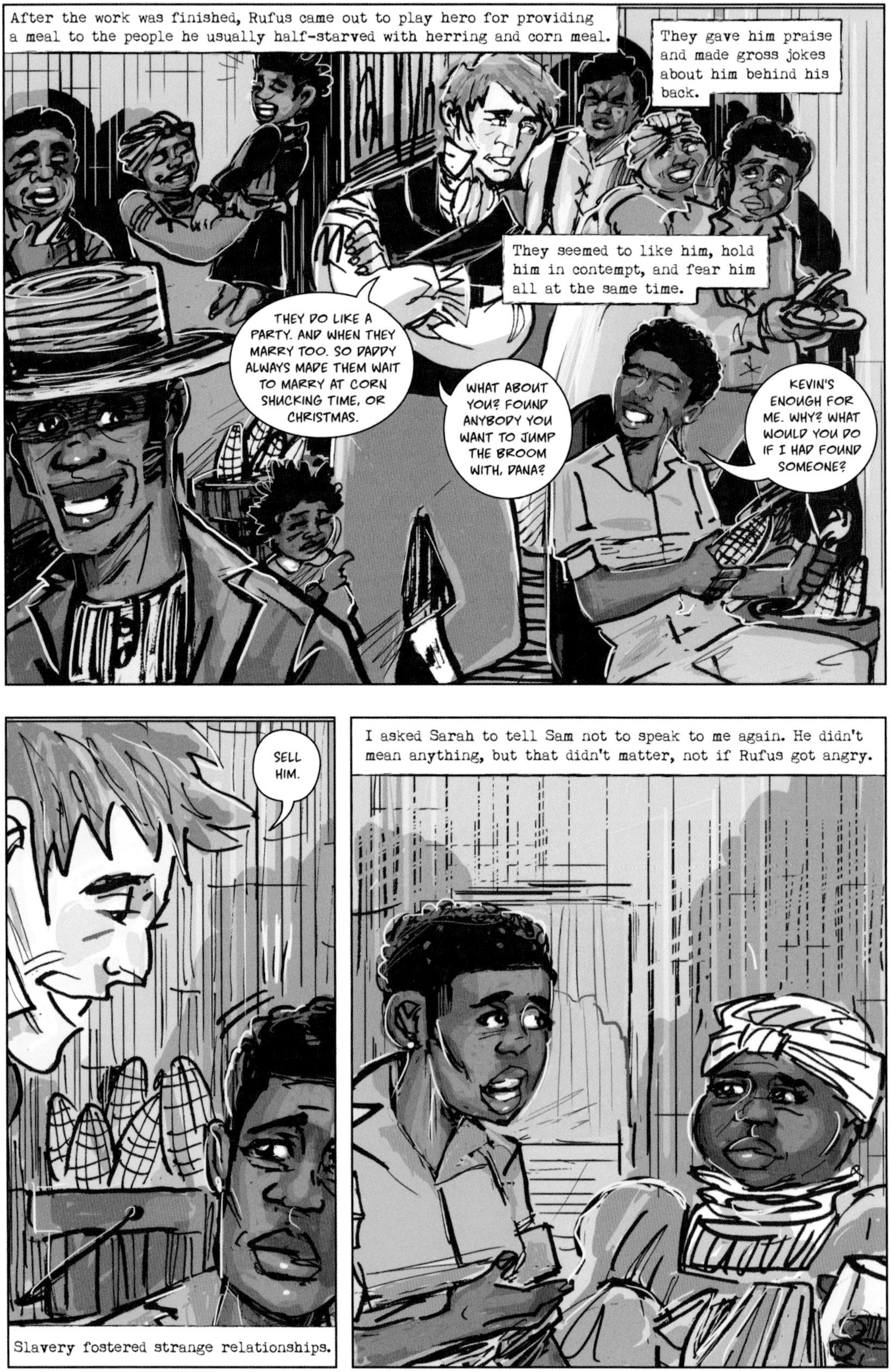
After the work was finished, Rufus came out to play hero for providing a meal to the people he usually half-starved with herring and corn meal.
They gave him praise and made gross jokes about him behind his back.
They seemed to like him, hold him in contempt, and fear him all at the same time.
THEY DO LIKE A PARTY. AND WHEN THEY MARRY TOO. SO DADDY ALWAYS MADE THEM WAIT TO MARRY AT CORN SHUCKING TIME, OR CHRISTMAS.
WHAT ABOUT YOU? FOUND ANYBODY YOU WANT TO JUMP THE BROOM WITH, DANA?
KEVIN'S ENOUGH FOR ME. WHY? WHAT WOULD YOU DO IF I HAD FOUND SOMEONE?
SELL HIM.
Slavery fostered strange relationships.
I asked Sarah to tell Sam not to speak to me again. He didn't mean anything, but that didn't matter, not if Rufus got angry.

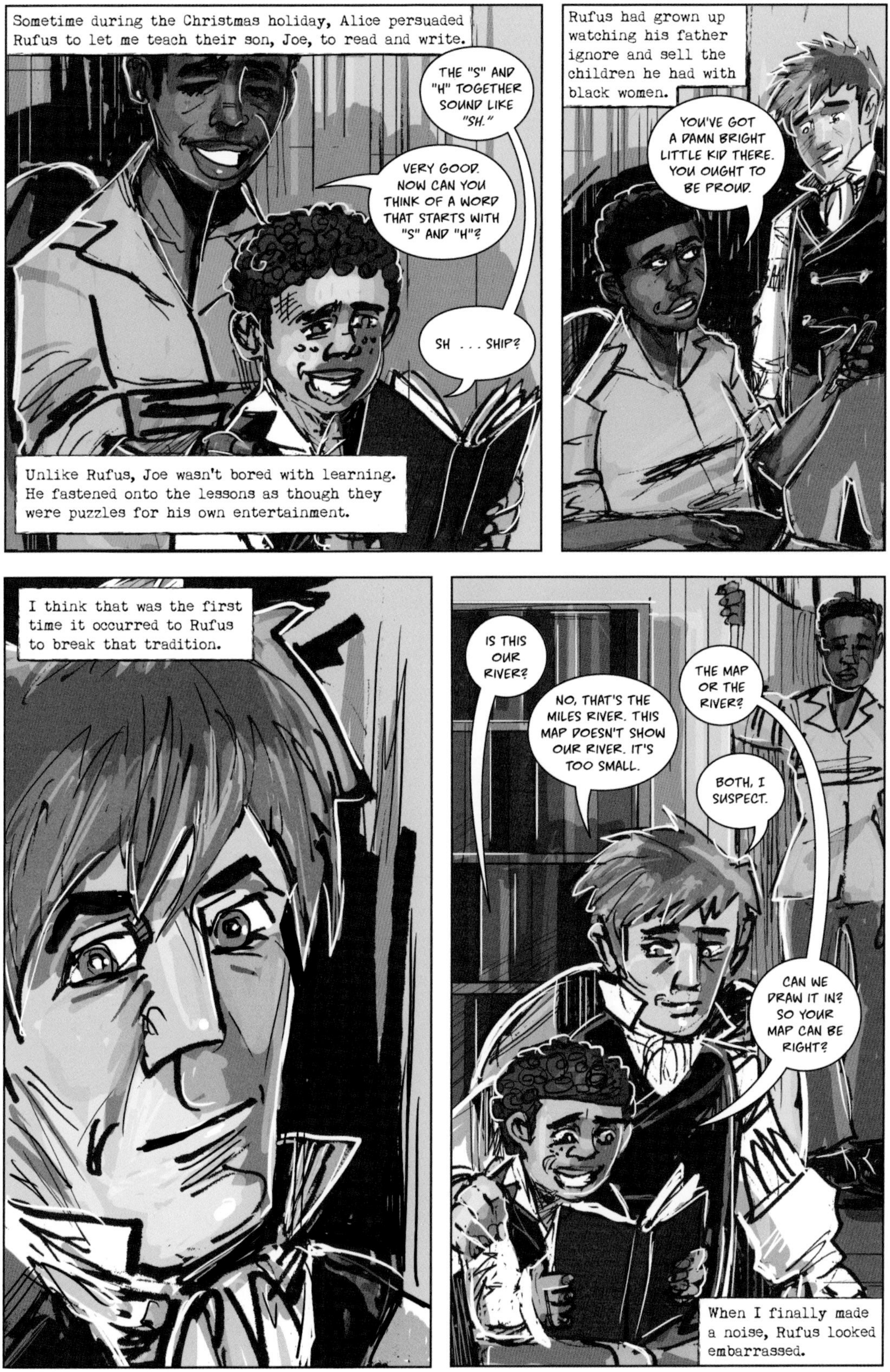
Sometime during the Christmas holiday, Alice persuaded Rufus to let me teach their son, Joe, to read and write.
THE "S" AND "H" TOGETHER SOUND LIKE "SH."
VERY GOOD. NOW CAN YOU THINK OF A WORD THAT STARTS WITH "S" AND "H"?
SH . . . SHIP?
Unlike Rufus, Joe wasn't bored with learning. He fastened onto the lessons as though they were puzzles for his own entertainment.
Rufus had grown up watching his father ignore and sell the children he had with black women.
YOU'VE GOT A DAMN BRIGHT LITTLE KID THERE. YOU OUGHT TO BE PROUD.
I think that was the first time it occurred to Rufus to break that tradition.
IS THIS OUR RIVER?
NO, THAT'S THE MILES RIVER. THIS MAP DOESN'T SHOW OUR RIVER. IT'S TOO SMALL.
THE MAP OR THE RIVER?
BOTH, I SUSPECT.
CAN WE DRAW IT IN? SO YOUR MAP CAN BE RIGHT?
When I finally made a noise, Rufus looked embarrassed.

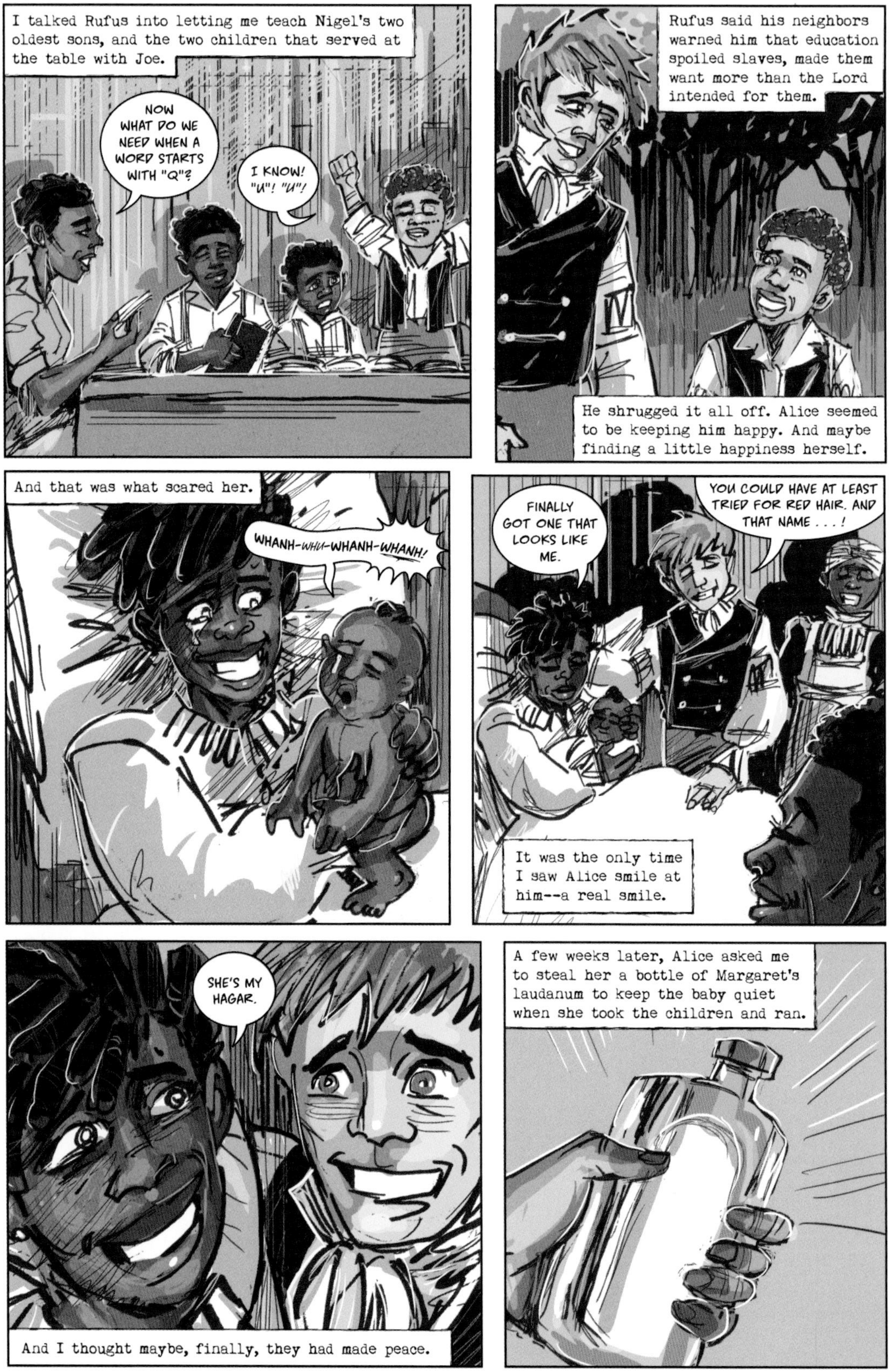
I talked Rufus into letting me teach Nigel's two oldest sons, and the two children that served at the table with Joe.
NOW WHAT DO WE NEED WHEN A WORD STARTS WITH "Q"?
I KNOW! "U"! "U"!
Rufus said his neighbors warned him that education spoiled slaves, made them want more than the Lord intended for them.
He shrugged it all off. Alice seemed to be keeping him happy. And maybe finding a little happiness herself.
And that was what scared her.
WHANH-WHU-WHANH-WHANH!
FINALLY GOT ONE THAT LOOKS LIKE ME.
YOU COULD HAVE AT LEAST TRIED FOR RED HAIR. AND THAT NAME . . . !
It was the only time I saw Alice smile at him--a real smile.
SHE'S MY HAGAR.
And I thought maybe, finally, they had made peace.
A few weeks later, Alice asked me to steal her a bottle of Margaret's laudanum to keep the baby quiet when she took the children and ran.

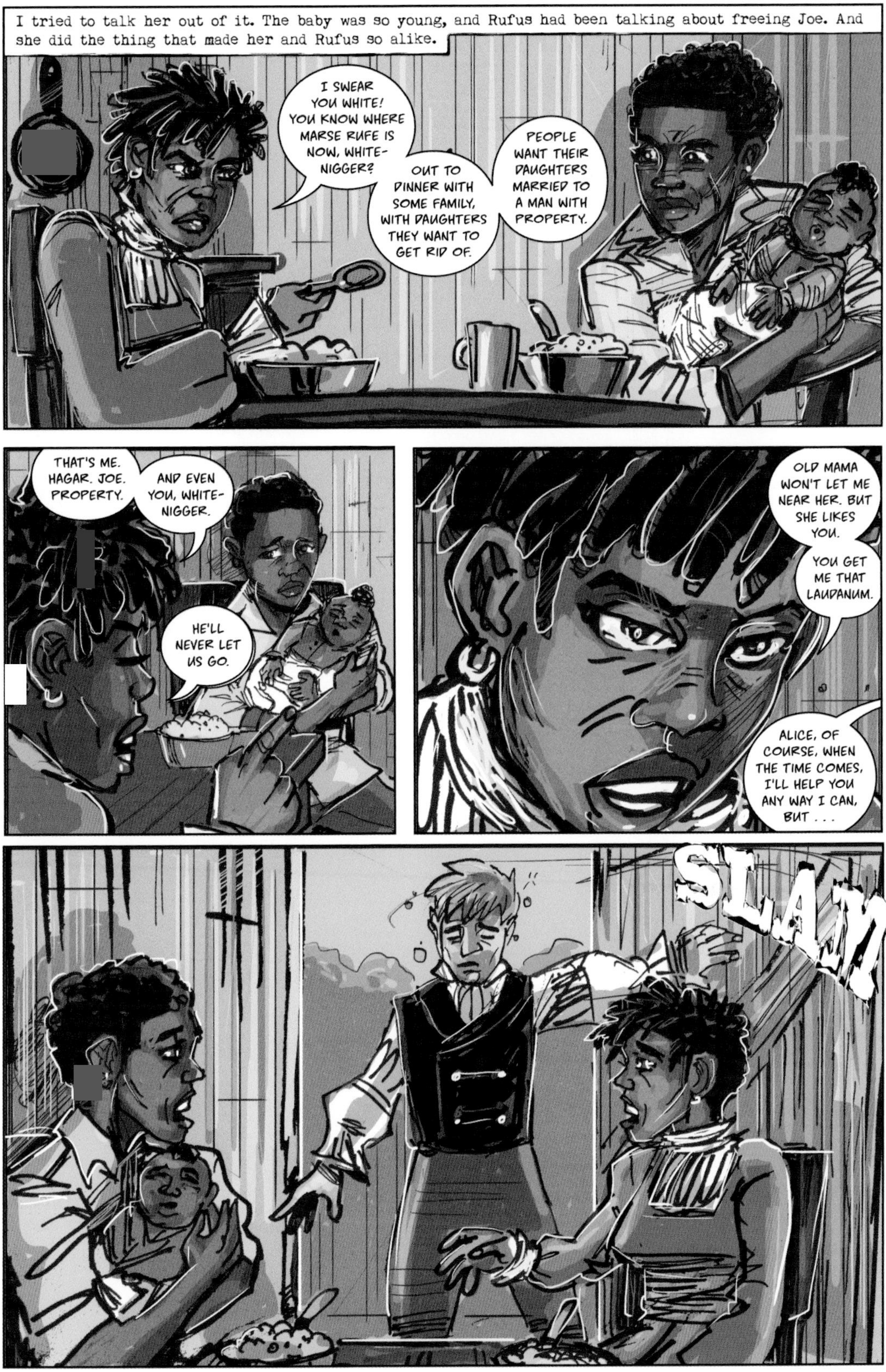
I tried to talk her out of it. The baby was so young, and Rufus had been talking about freeing Joe. And she did the thing that made her and Rufus so alike.
I SWEAR YOU WHITE! YOU KNOW WHERE MARSE RUFE IS NOW, WHITE-NIGGER?
OUT TO DINNER WITH SOME FAMILY, WITH DAUGHTERS THEY WANT TO GET RID OF.
PEOPLE WANT THEIR DAUGHTERS MARRIED TO A MAN WITH PROPERTY.
THAT'S ME. HAGAR. JOE. PROPERTY.
AND EVEN YOU, WHITE-NIGGER.
HE'LL NEVER LET US GO.
OLD MAMA WON'T LET ME NEAR HER. BUT SHE LIKES YOU.
YOU GET ME THAT LAUDANUM.
ALICE, OF COURSE, WHEN THE TIME COMES, I'LL HELP YOU ANY WAY I CAN, BUT . . .
SLAM

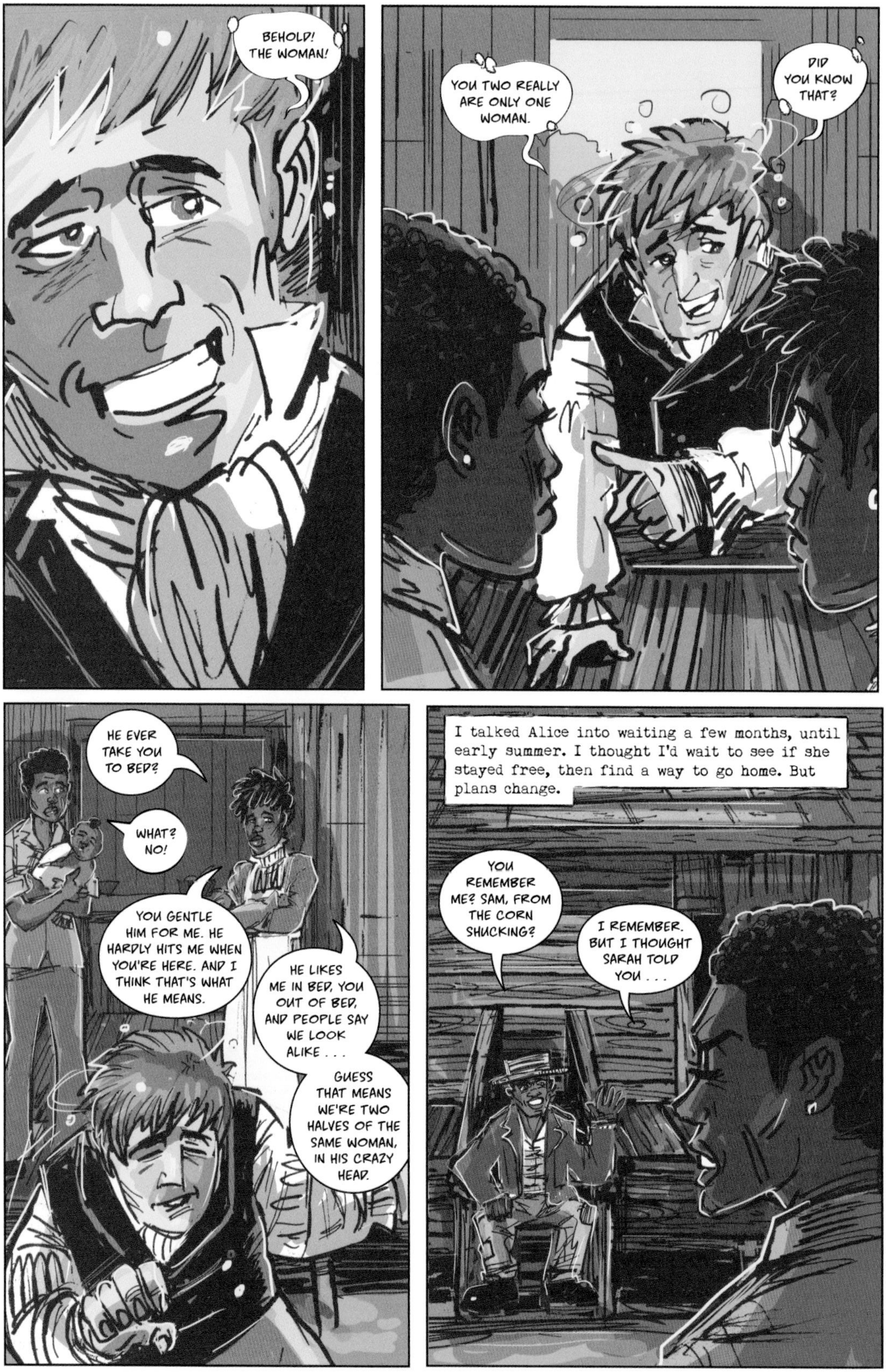
BEHOLD! THE WOMAN!
YOU TWO REALLY ARE ONLY ONE WOMAN.
DID YOU KNOW THAT?
HE EVER TAKE YOU TO BED?
WHAT? NO!
YOU GENTLE HIM FOR ME. HE HARDLY HITS ME WHEN YOU'RE HERE. AND I THINK THAT'S WHAT HE MEANS.
HE LIKES ME IN BED, YOU OUT OF BED, AND PEOPLE SAY WE LOOK ALIKE . . .
GUESS THAT MEANS WE'RE TWO HALVES OF THE SAME WOMAN, IN HIS CRAZY HEAD.
I talked Alice into waiting a few months, until early summer. I thought I'd wait to see if she stayed free, then find a way to go home. But plans change.
YOU REMEMBER ME? SAM, FROM THE CORN SHUCKING?
I REMEMBER. BUT I THOUGHT SARAH TOLD YOU . . .

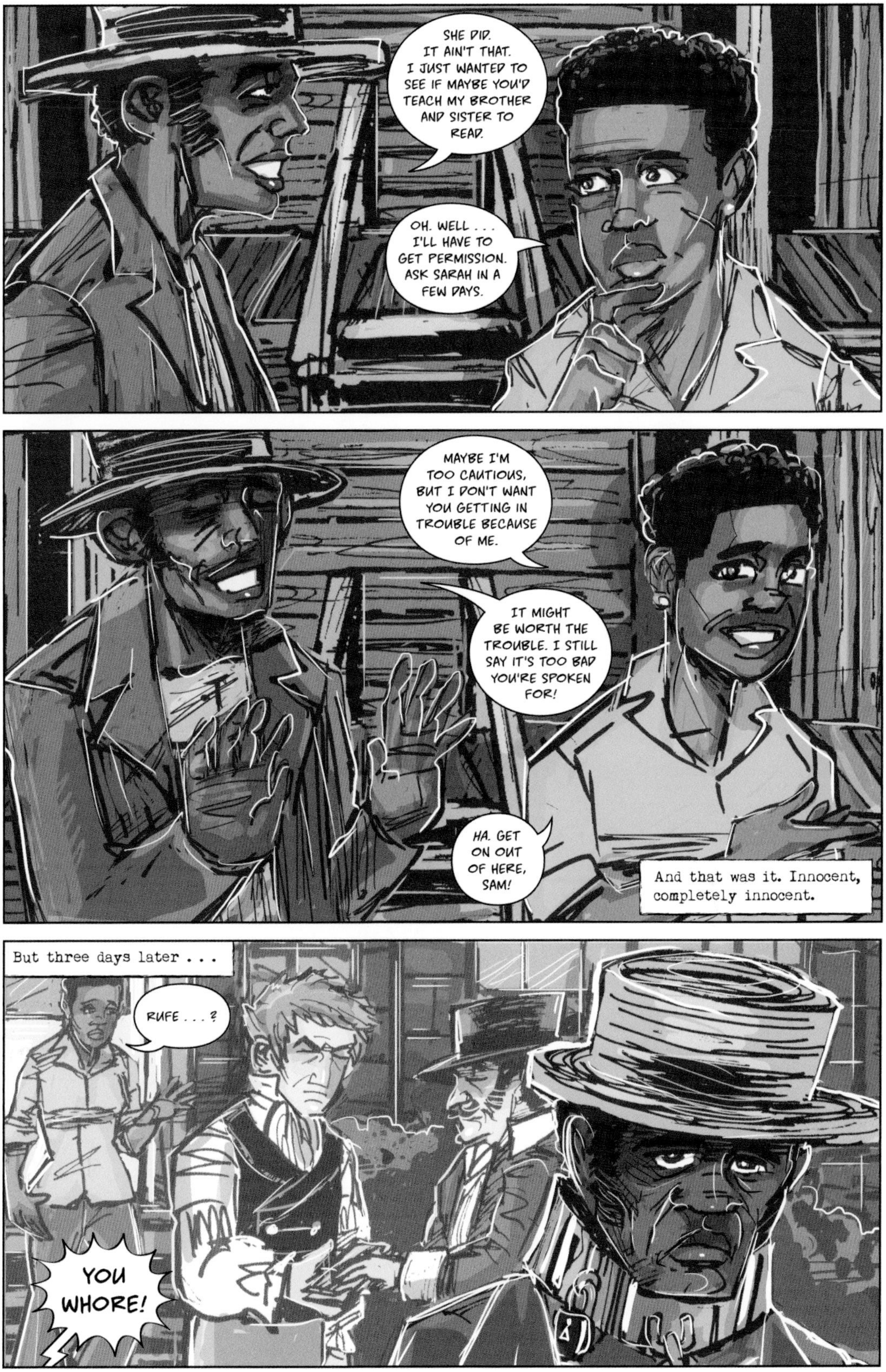
SHE DID. IT AIN'T THAT. I JUST WANTED TO SEE IF MAYBE YOU'D TEACH MY BROTHER AND SISTER TO READ.
OH. WELL . . . I'LL HAVE TO GET PERMISSION. ASK SARAH IN A FEW DAYS.
MAYBE I'M TOO CAUTIOUS, BUT I DON'T WANT YOU GETTING IN TROUBLE BECAUSE OF ME.
IT MIGHT BE WORTH THE TROUBLE. I STILL SAY IT'S TOO BAD YOU'RE SPOKEN FOR!
HA. GET ON OUT OF HERE, SAM!
And that was it. Innocent, completely innocent.
But three days later . . .
RUFE . . . ?
YOU WHORE!

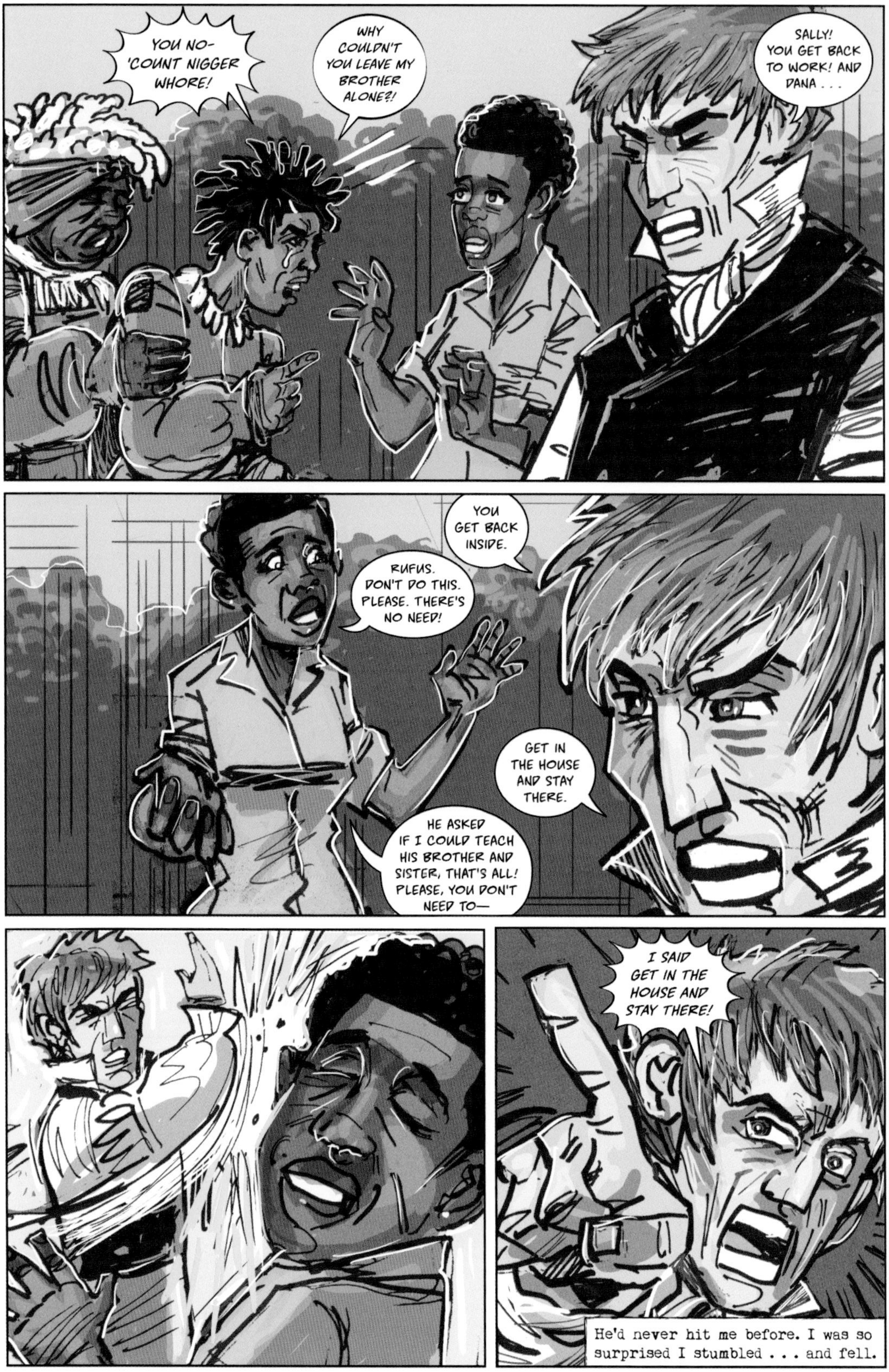
YOU NO-'COUNT NIGGER WHORE!
WHY COULDN'T YOU LEAVE MY BROTHER ALONE?!
SALLY! YOU GET BACK TO WORK! AND DANA . . .
YOU GET BACK INSIDE.
RUFUS. DON'T DO THIS. PLEASE. THERE'S NO NEED!
GET IN THE HOUSE AND STAY THERE.
HE ASKED IF I COULD TEACH HIS BROTHER AND SISTER, THAT'S ALL! PLEASE, YOU DON'T NEED TO—
I SAID GET IN THE HOUSE AND STAY THERE!
He'd never hit me before. I was so surprised I stumbled . . . and fell.

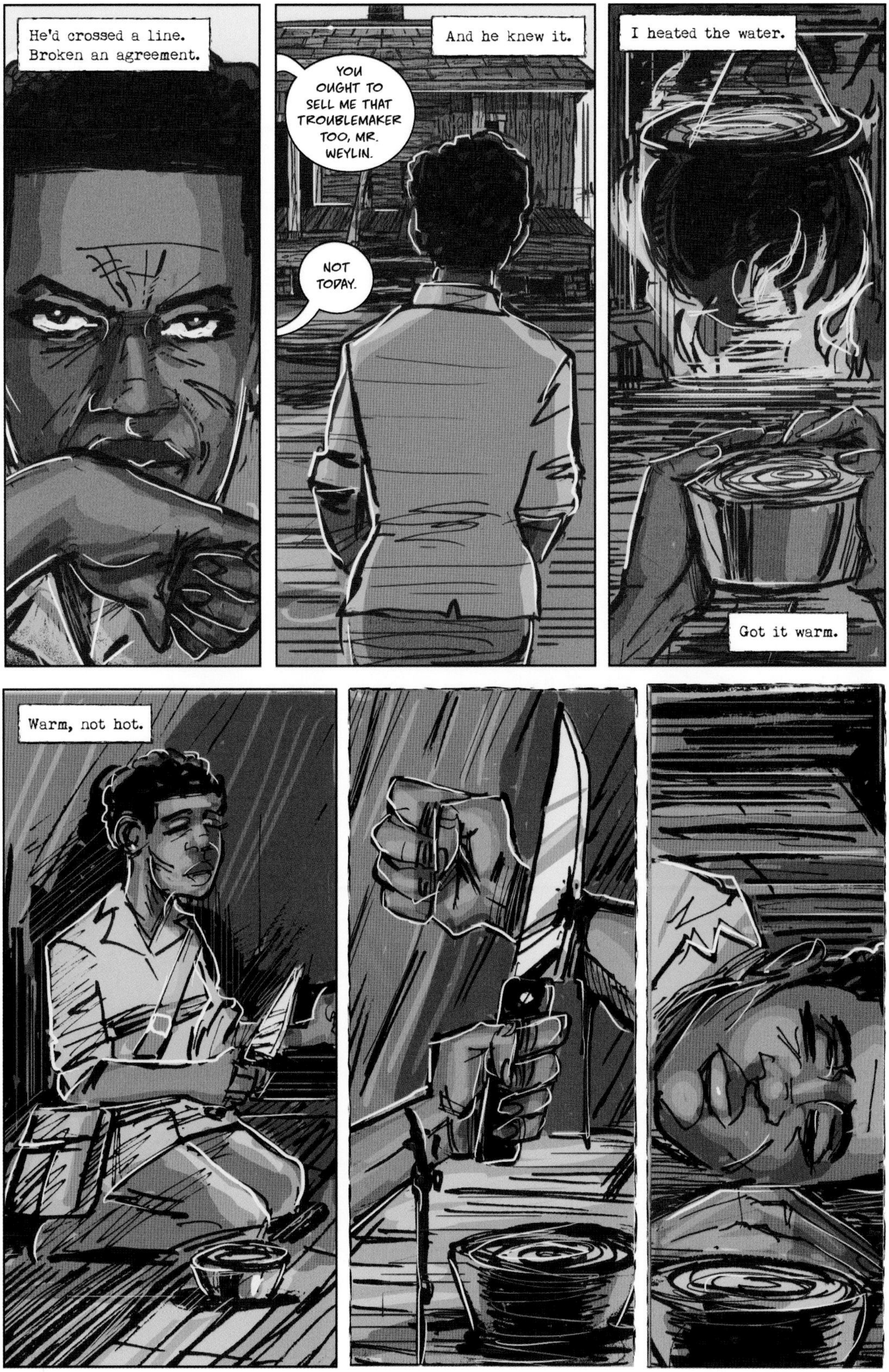
He'd crossed a line.
Broken an agreement.
And he knew it.
YOU OUGHT TO SELL ME THAT TROUBLEMAKER TOO, MR. WEYLIN.
NOT TODAY.
I heated the water.
Got it warm.
Warm, not hot.

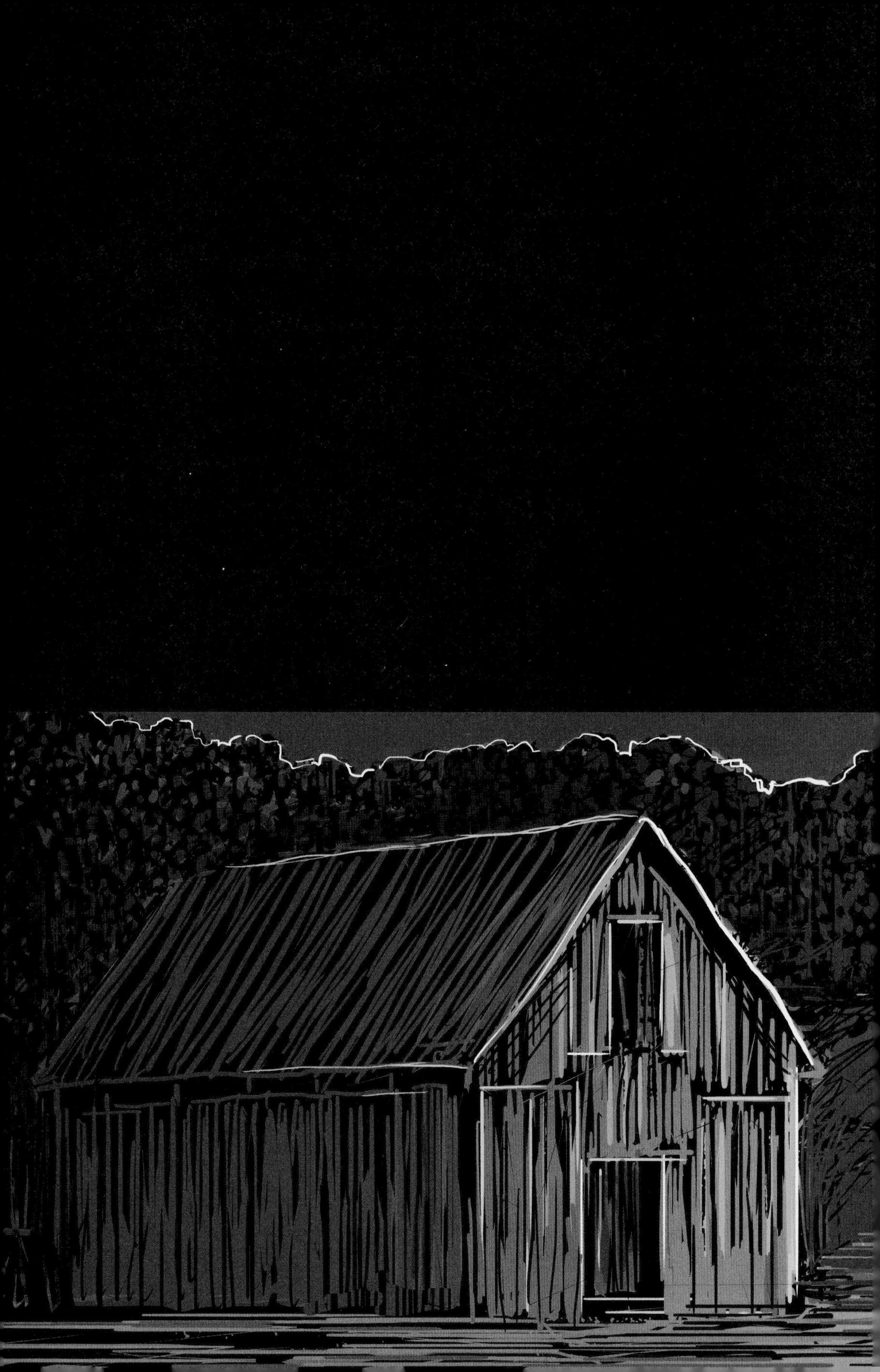

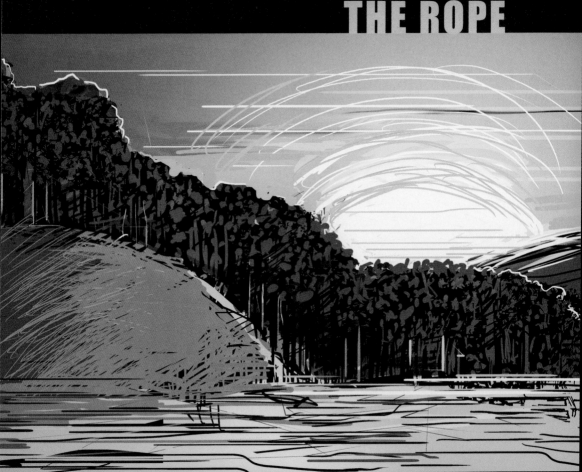

THE ROPE

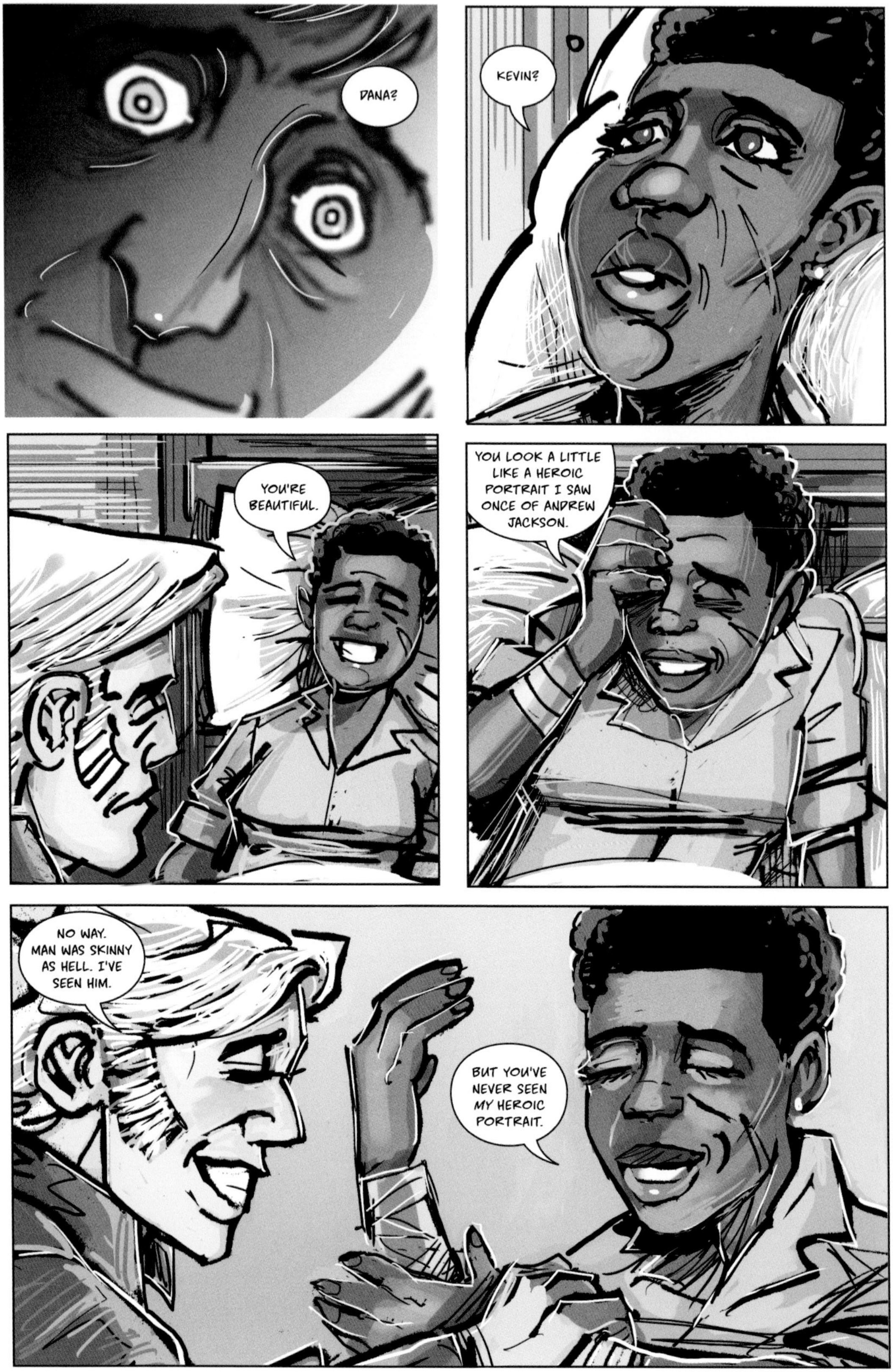
DANA?
KEVIN?
YOU'RE BEAUTIFUL.
YOU LOOK A LITTLE LIKE A HEROIC PORTRAIT I SAW ONCE OF ANDREW JACKSON.
NO WAY. MAN WAS SKINNY AS HELL. I'VE SEEN HIM.
BUT YOU'VE NEVER SEEN MY HEROIC PORTRAIT.

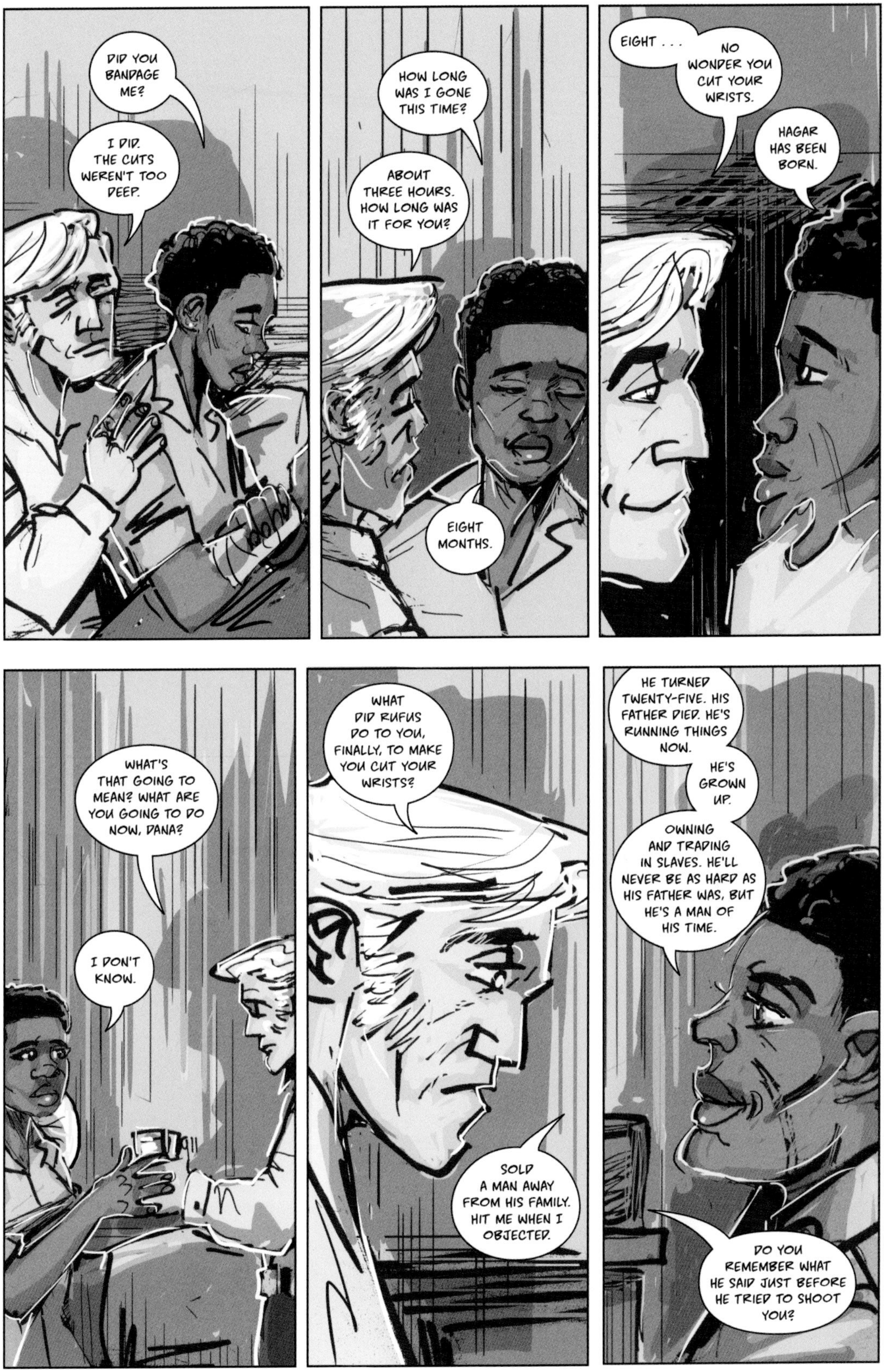
DID YOU BANDAGE ME?
I DID. THE CUTS WEREN'T TOO DEEP.
HOW LONG WAS I GONE THIS TIME?
ABOUT THREE HOURS. HOW LONG WAS IT FOR YOU?
EIGHT MONTHS.
EIGHT . . .
NO WONDER YOU CUT YOUR WRISTS.
HAGAR HAS BEEN BORN.
WHAT'S THAT GOING TO MEAN? WHAT ARE YOU GOING TO DO NOW, DANA?
I DON'T KNOW.
WHAT DID RUFUS DO TO YOU, FINALLY, TO MAKE YOU CUT YOUR WRISTS?
SOLD A MAN AWAY FROM HIS FAMILY. HIT ME WHEN I OBJECTED.
HE TURNED TWENTY-FIVE. HIS FATHER DIED. HE'S RUNNING THINGS NOW.
HE'S GROWN UP.
OWNING AND TRADING IN SLAVES. HE'LL NEVER BE AS HARD AS HIS FATHER WAS, BUT HE'S A MAN OF HIS TIME.
DO YOU REMEMBER WHAT HE SAID JUST BEFORE HE TRIED TO SHOOT YOU?

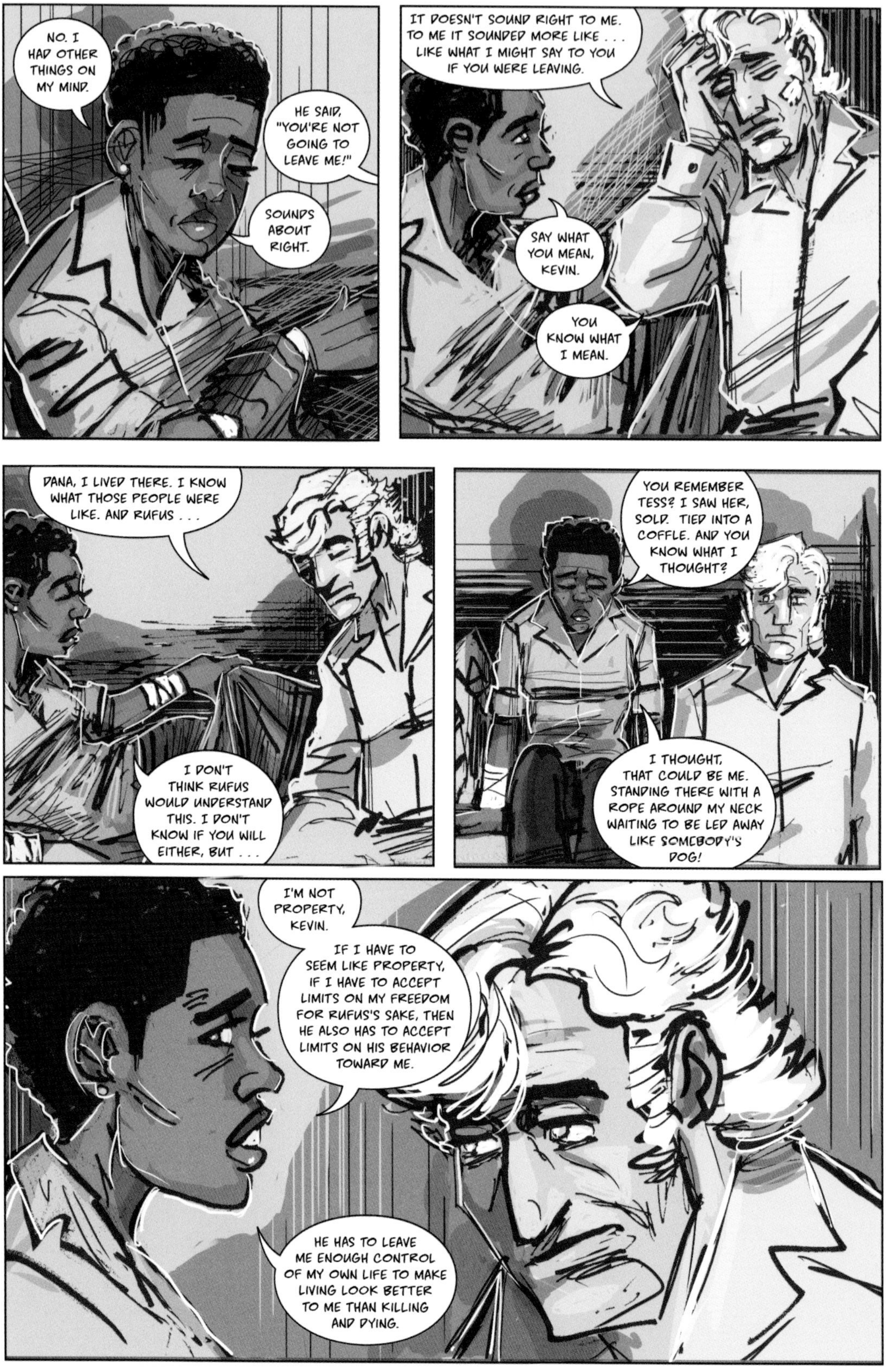
NO. I HAD OTHER THINGS ON MY MIND.
HE SAID, "YOU'RE NOT GOING TO LEAVE ME!"
SOUNDS ABOUT RIGHT.
IT DOESN'T SOUND RIGHT TO ME. TO ME IT SOUNDED MORE LIKE . . . LIKE WHAT I MIGHT SAY TO YOU IF YOU WERE LEAVING.
SAY WHAT YOU MEAN, KEVIN.
YOU KNOW WHAT I MEAN.
DANA, I LIVED THERE. I KNOW WHAT THOSE PEOPLE WERE LIKE. AND RUFUS . . .
I DON'T THINK RUFUS WOULD UNDERSTAND THIS. I DON'T KNOW IF YOU WILL EITHER, BUT . . .
YOU REMEMBER TESS? I SAW HER, SOLD. TIED INTO A COFFLE. AND YOU KNOW WHAT I THOUGHT?
I THOUGHT, THAT COULD BE ME. STANDING THERE WITH A ROPE AROUND MY NECK WAITING TO BE LED AWAY LIKE SOMEBODY'S DOG!
I'M NOT PROPERTY, KEVIN.
IF I HAVE TO SEEM LIKE PROPERTY, IF I HAVE TO ACCEPT LIMITS ON MY FREEDOM FOR RUFUS'S SAKE, THEN HE ALSO HAS TO ACCEPT LIMITS ON HIS BEHAVIOR TOWARD ME.
HE HAS TO LEAVE ME ENOUGH CONTROL OF MY OWN LIFE TO MAKE LIVING LOOK BETTER TO ME THAN KILLING AND DYING.

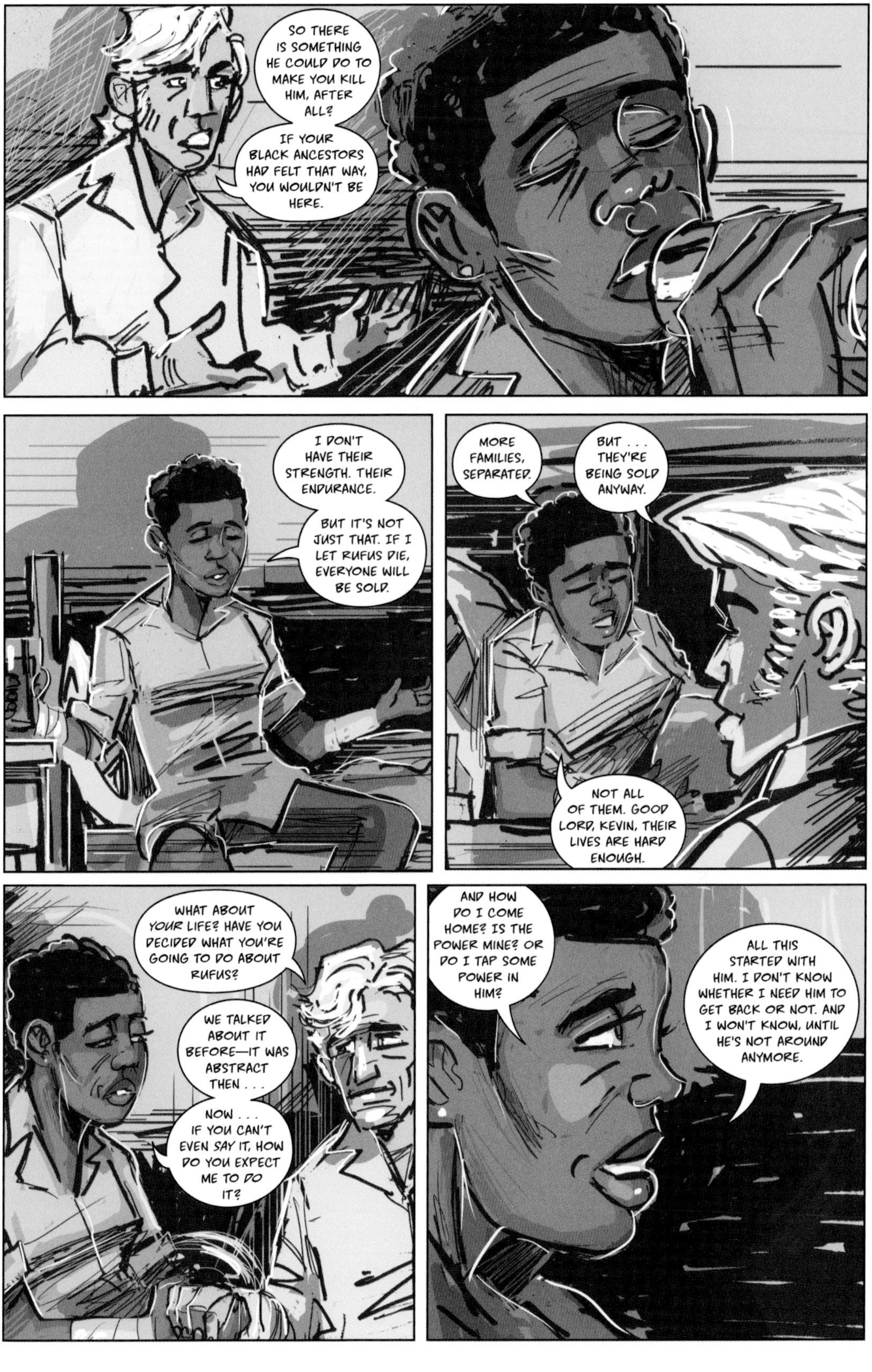
SO THERE IS SOMETHING HE COULD DO TO MAKE YOU KILL HIM, AFTER ALL?
IF YOUR BLACK ANCESTORS HAD FELT THAT WAY, YOU WOULDN'T BE HERE.
I DON'T HAVE THEIR STRENGTH. THEIR ENDURANCE.
BUT IT'S NOT JUST THAT. IF I LET RUFUS DIE, EVERYONE WILL BE SOLD.
MORE FAMILIES, SEPARATED.
BUT . . . THEY'RE BEING SOLD ANYWAY.
NOT ALL OF THEM. GOOD LORD, KEVIN, THEIR LIVES ARE HARD ENOUGH.
WHAT ABOUT YOUR LIFE? HAVE YOU DECIDED WHAT YOU'RE GOING TO DO ABOUT RUFUS?
WE TALKED ABOUT IT BEFORE—IT WAS ABSTRACT THEN . . .
NOW . . . IF YOU CAN'T EVEN SAY IT, HOW DO YOU EXPECT ME TO DO IT?
AND HOW DO I COME HOME? IS THE POWER MINE? OR DO I TAP SOME POWER IN HIM?
ALL THIS STARTED WITH HIM. I DON'T KNOW WHETHER I NEED HIM TO GET BACK OR NOT. AND I WON'T KNOW, UNTIL HE'S NOT AROUND ANYMORE.

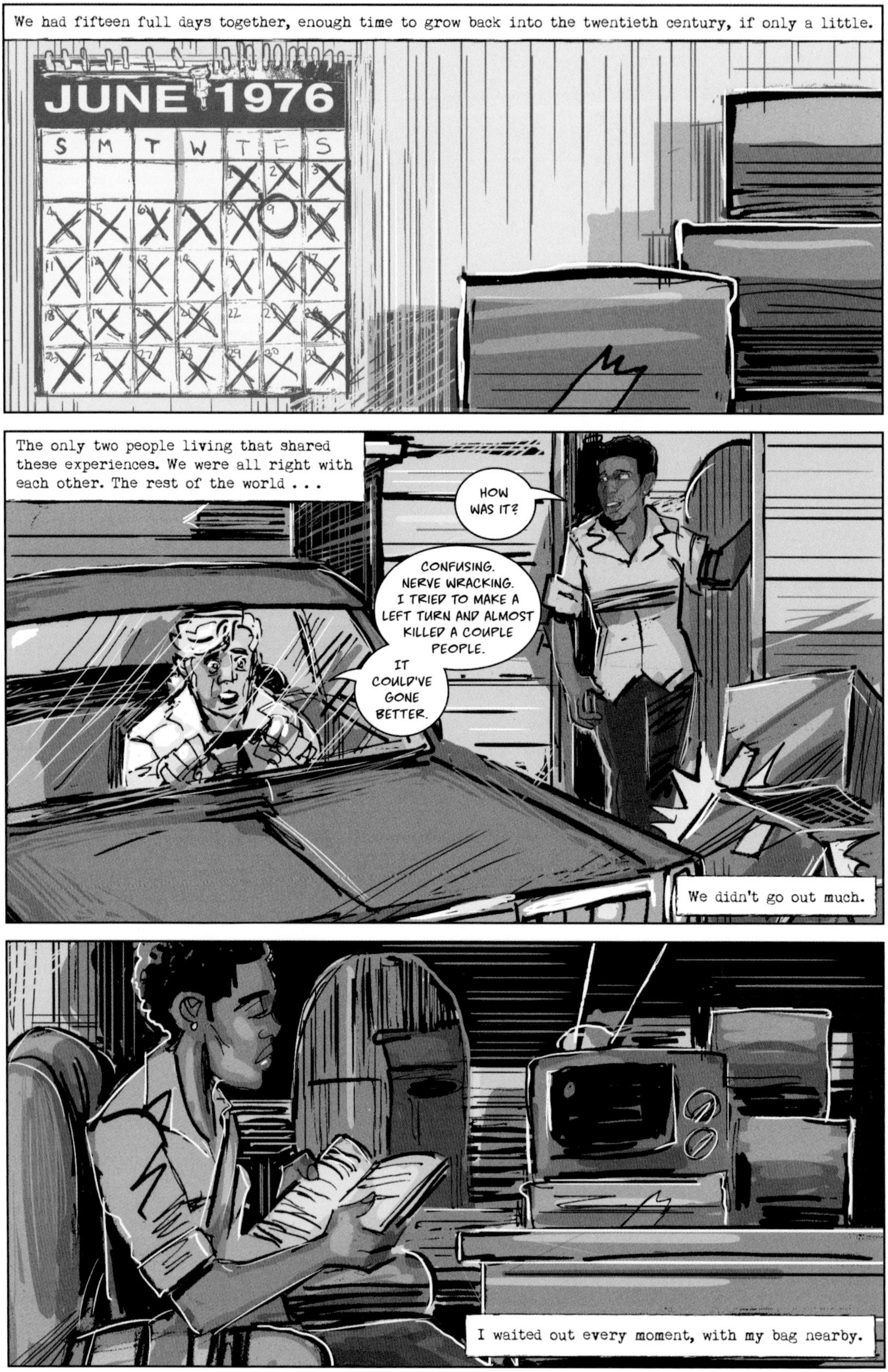
We had fifteen full days together, enough time to grow back into the twentieth century, if only a little.
JUNE 1976
S M T W T F S
The only two people living that shared these experiences. We were all right with each other. The rest of the world . . .
HOW WAS IT?
CONFUSING. NERVE WRACKING. I TRIED TO MAKE A LEFT TURN AND ALMOST KILLED A COUPLE PEOPLE.
IT COULD'VE GONE BETTER.
We didn't go out much.
I waited out every moment, with my bag nearby.

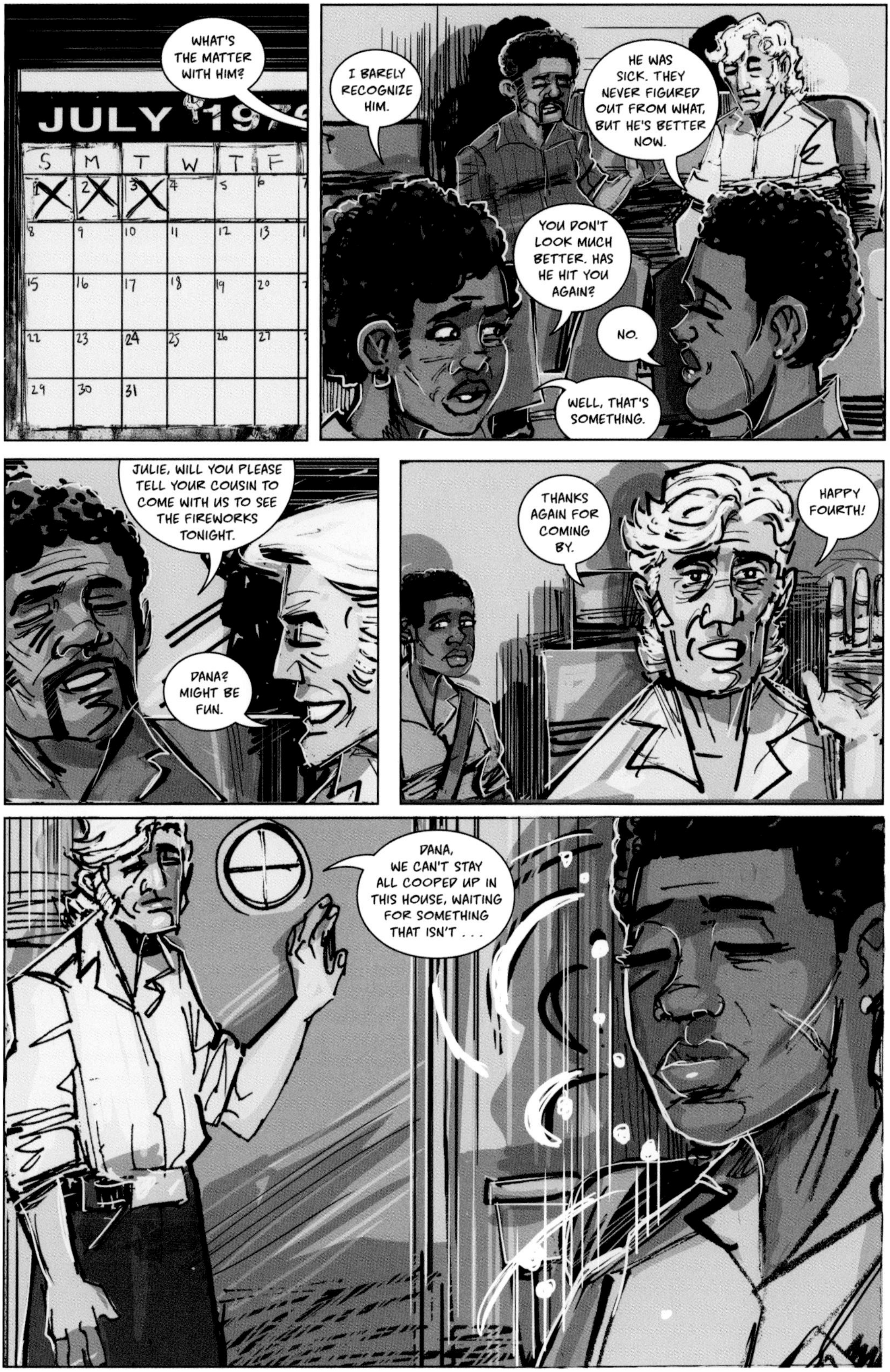
JULY 197
S M T W T F
1 2 3 4 5 6 7
8 9 10 11 12 13
15 16 17 18 19 20
22 23 24 25 26 27
29 30 31
WHAT'S THE MATTER WITH HIM?
I BARELY RECOGNIZE HIM.
HE WAS SICK. THEY NEVER FIGURED OUT FROM WHAT, BUT HE'S BETTER NOW.
YOU DON'T LOOK MUCH BETTER. HAS HE HIT YOU AGAIN?
NO.
WELL, THAT'S SOMETHING.
JULIE, WILL YOU PLEASE TELL YOUR COUSIN TO COME WITH US TO SEE THE FIREWORKS TONIGHT.
DANA? MIGHT BE FUN.
THANKS AGAIN FOR COMING BY.
HAPPY FOURTH!
DANA, WE CAN'T STAY ALL COOPED UP IN THIS HOUSE, WAITING FOR SOMETHING THAT ISN'T . . .

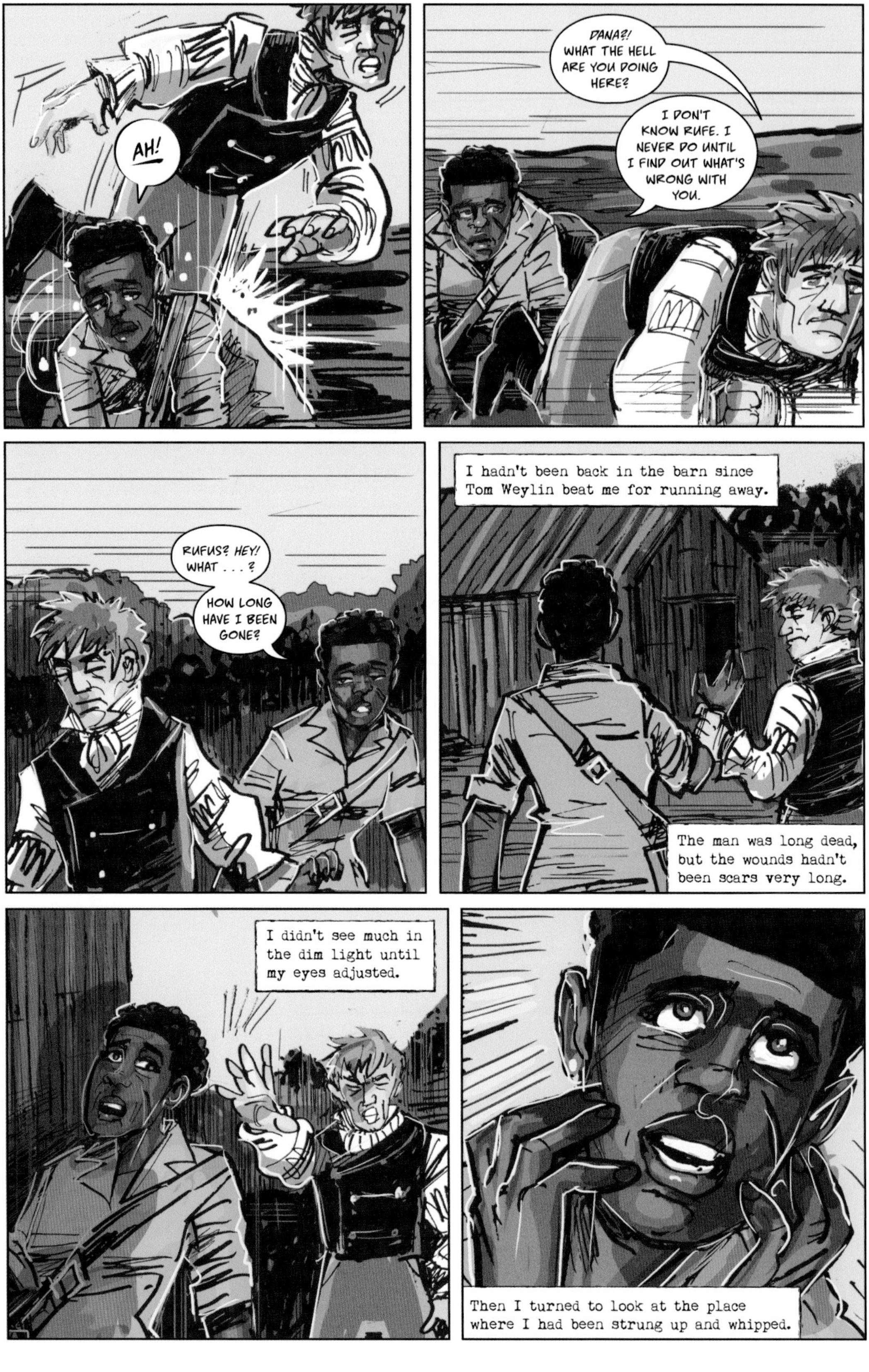

AH!
DANA?! WHAT THE HELL ARE YOU DOING HERE?
I DON'T KNOW RUFE. I NEVER DO UNTIL I FIND OUT WHAT'S WRONG WITH YOU.
RUFUS? HEY! WHAT . . . ?
HOW LONG HAVE I BEEN GONE?
I hadn't been back in the barn since Tom Weylin beat me for running away.
The man was long dead, but the wounds hadn't been scars very long.
I didn't see much in the dim light until my eyes adjusted.
Then I turned to look at the place where I had been strung up and whipped.

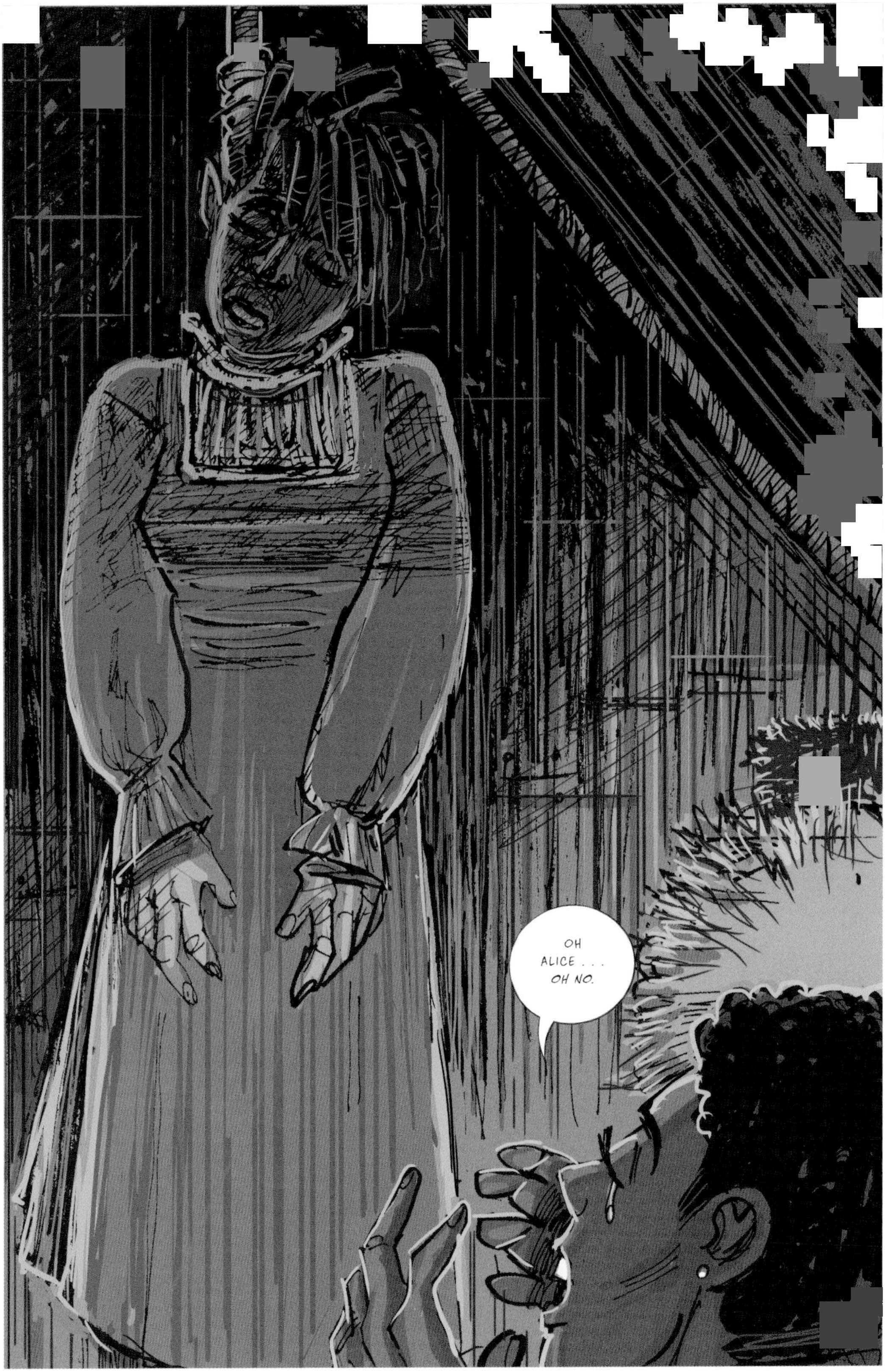
OH ALICE . . . OH NO.

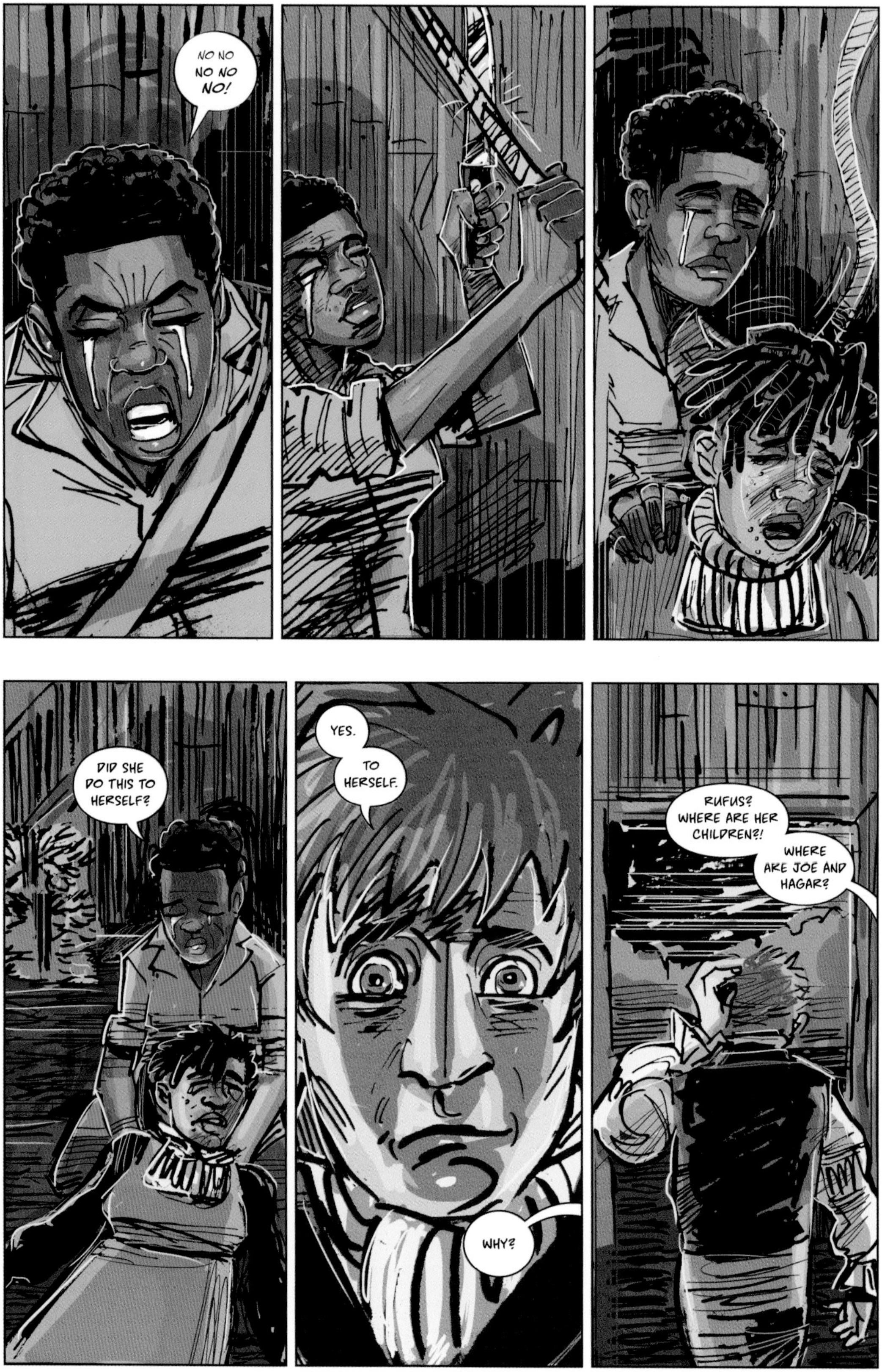
NO NO
NO NO
NO!
DID SHE DO THIS TO HERSELF?
YES.
TO HERSELF.
WHY?
RUFUS? WHERE ARE HER CHILDREN?!
WHERE ARE JOE AND HAGAR?

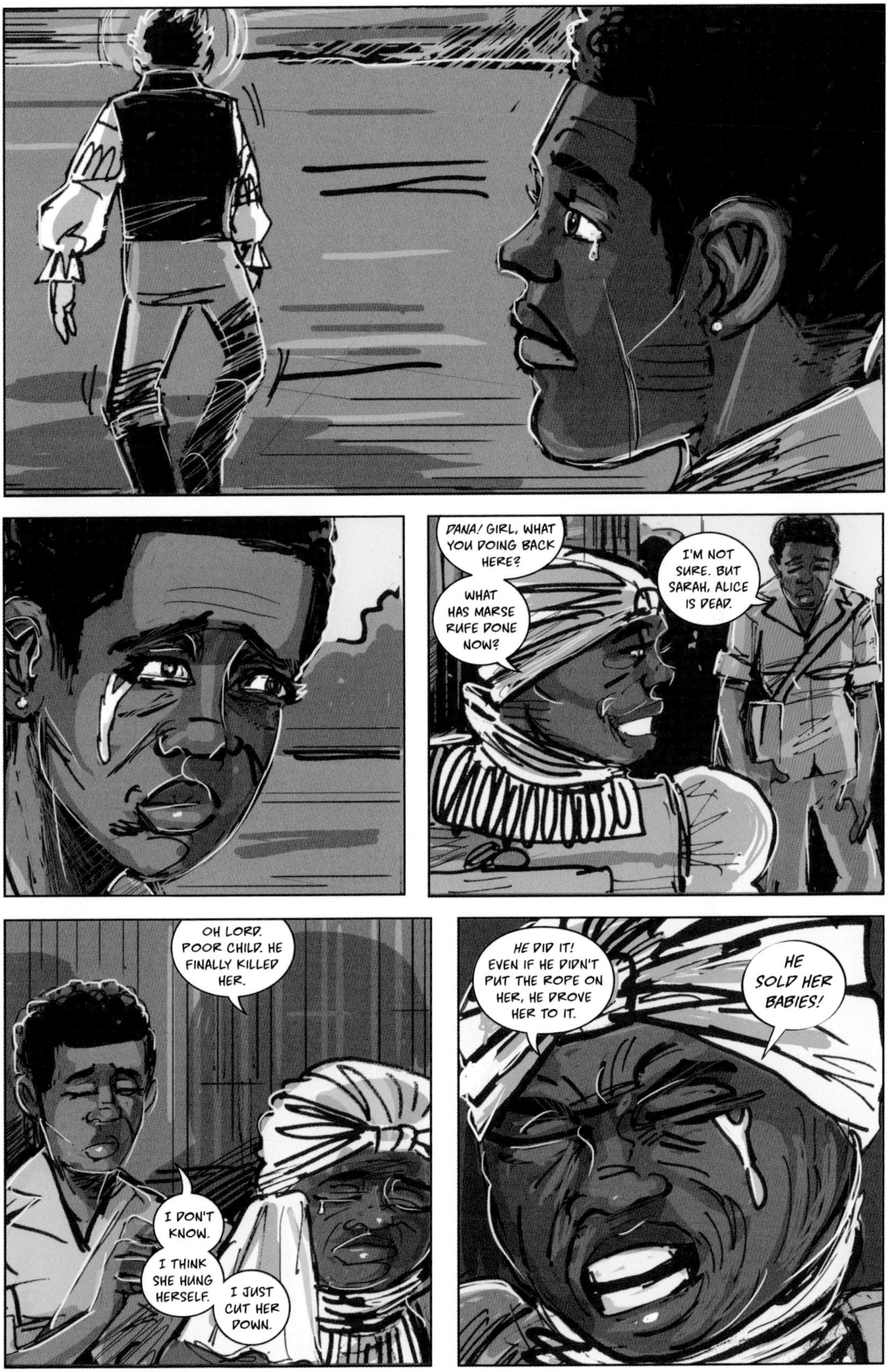
DANA! GIRL, WHAT YOU DOING BACK HERE?
WHAT HAS MARSE RUFE DONE NOW?
I'M NOT SURE. BUT SARAH, ALICE IS DEAD.
OH LORD. POOR CHILD. HE FINALLY KILLED HER.
I DON'T KNOW.
I THINK SHE HUNG HERSELF.
I JUST CUT HER DOWN.
HE DID IT! EVEN IF HE DIDN'T PUT THE ROPE ON HER, HE DROVE HER TO IT.
HE SOLD HER BABIES!

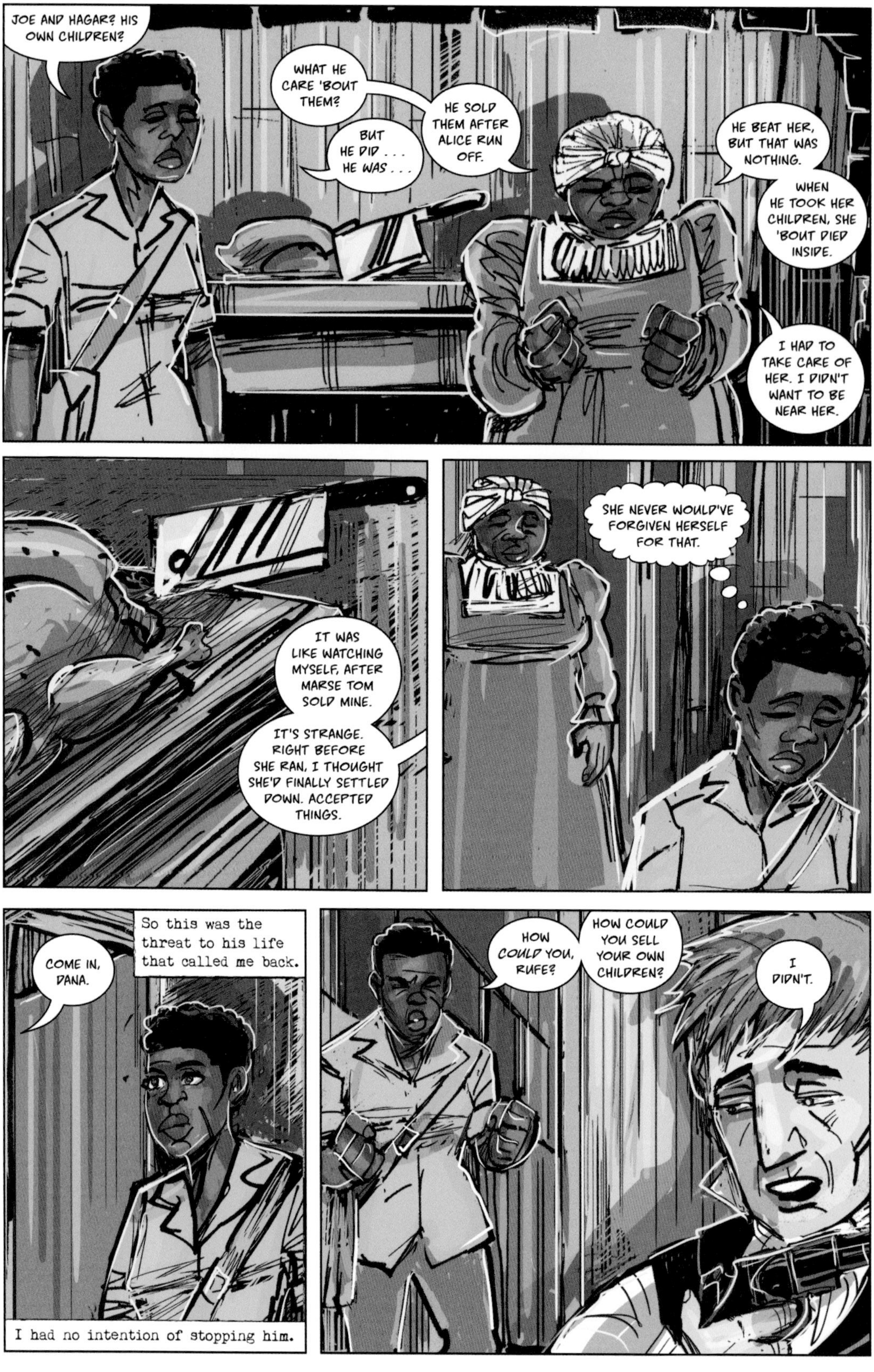
JOE AND HAGAR? HIS OWN CHILDREN?
WHAT HE CARE 'BOUT THEM?
BUT HE DID . . . HE WAS . . .
HE SOLD THEM AFTER ALICE RUN OFF.
HE BEAT HER, BUT THAT WAS NOTHING.
WHEN HE TOOK HER CHILDREN, SHE 'BOUT DIED INSIDE.
I HAD TO TAKE CARE OF HER. I DIDN'T WANT TO BE NEAR HER.
IT WAS LIKE WATCHING MYSELF, AFTER MARSE TOM SOLD MINE.
IT'S STRANGE. RIGHT BEFORE SHE RAN, I THOUGHT SHE'D FINALLY SETTLED DOWN. ACCEPTED THINGS.
SHE NEVER WOULD'VE FORGIVEN HERSELF FOR THAT.
So this was the threat to his life that called me back.
COME IN, DANA.
I had no intention of stopping him.
HOW COULD YOU, RUFE?
HOW COULD YOU SELL YOUR OWN CHILDREN?
I DIDN'T.

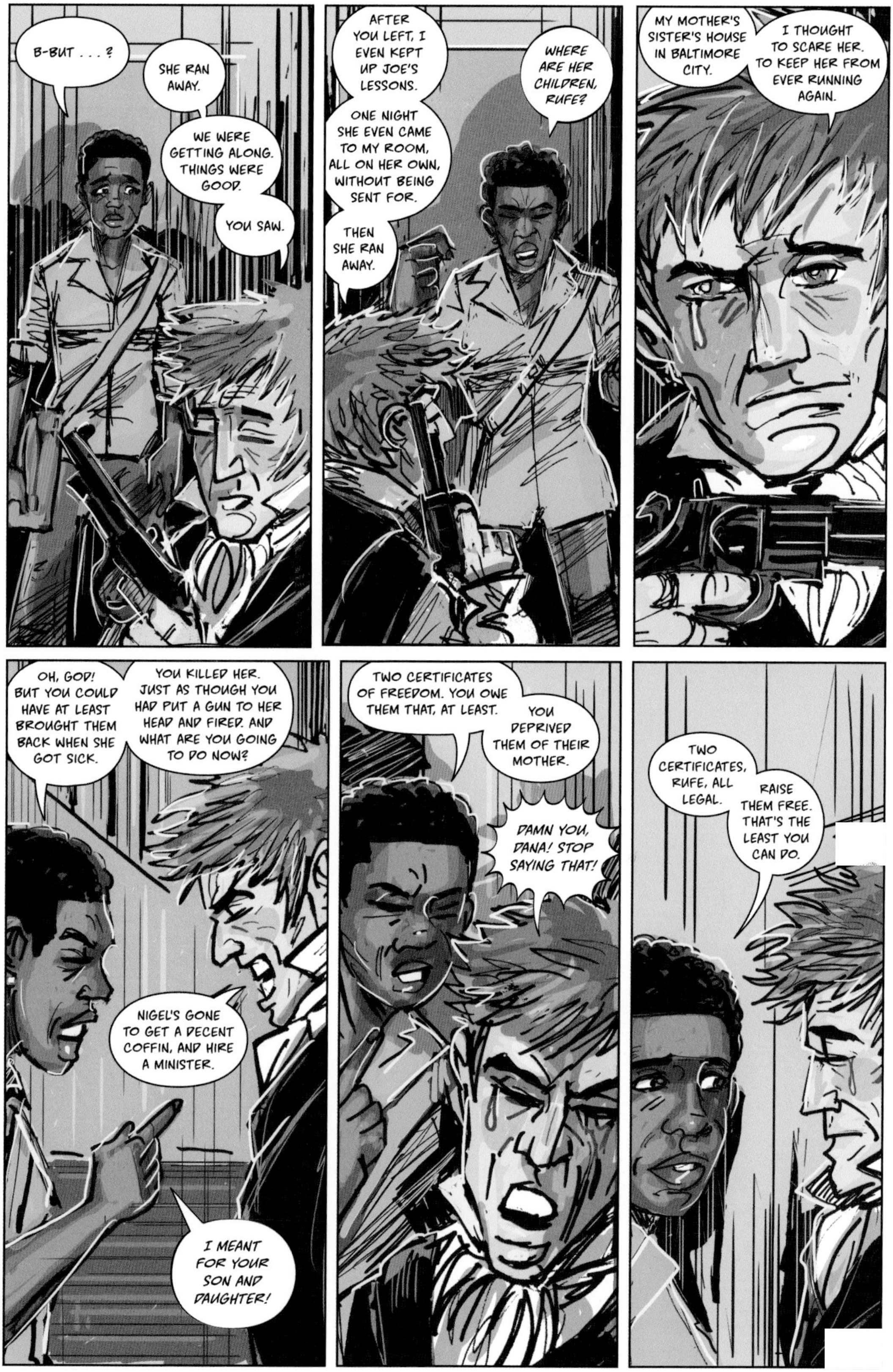
B-BUT . . . ?
SHE RAN AWAY.
WE WERE GETTING ALONG. THINGS WERE GOOD.
YOU SAW.
AFTER YOU LEFT, I EVEN KEPT UP JOE'S LESSONS.
ONE NIGHT SHE EVEN CAME TO MY ROOM, ALL ON HER OWN, WITHOUT BEING SENT FOR.
THEN SHE RAN AWAY.
WHERE ARE HER CHILDREN, RUFE?
MY MOTHER'S SISTER'S HOUSE IN BALTIMORE CITY.
I THOUGHT TO SCARE HER. TO KEEP HER FROM EVER RUNNING AGAIN.
OH, GOD! BUT YOU COULD HAVE AT LEAST BROUGHT THEM BACK WHEN SHE GOT SICK.
YOU KILLED HER. JUST AS THOUGH YOU HAD PUT A GUN TO HER HEAD AND FIRED. AND WHAT ARE YOU GOING TO DO NOW?
NIGEL'S GONE TO GET A DECENT COFFIN, AND HIRE A MINISTER.
I MEANT FOR YOUR SON AND DAUGHTER!
TWO CERTIFICATES OF FREEDOM. YOU OWE THEM THAT, AT LEAST.
YOU DEPRIVED THEM OF THEIR MOTHER.
DAMN YOU, DANA! STOP SAYING THAT!
TWO CERTIFICATES, RUFE, ALL LEGAL.
RAISE THEM FREE. THAT'S THE LEAST YOU CAN DO.

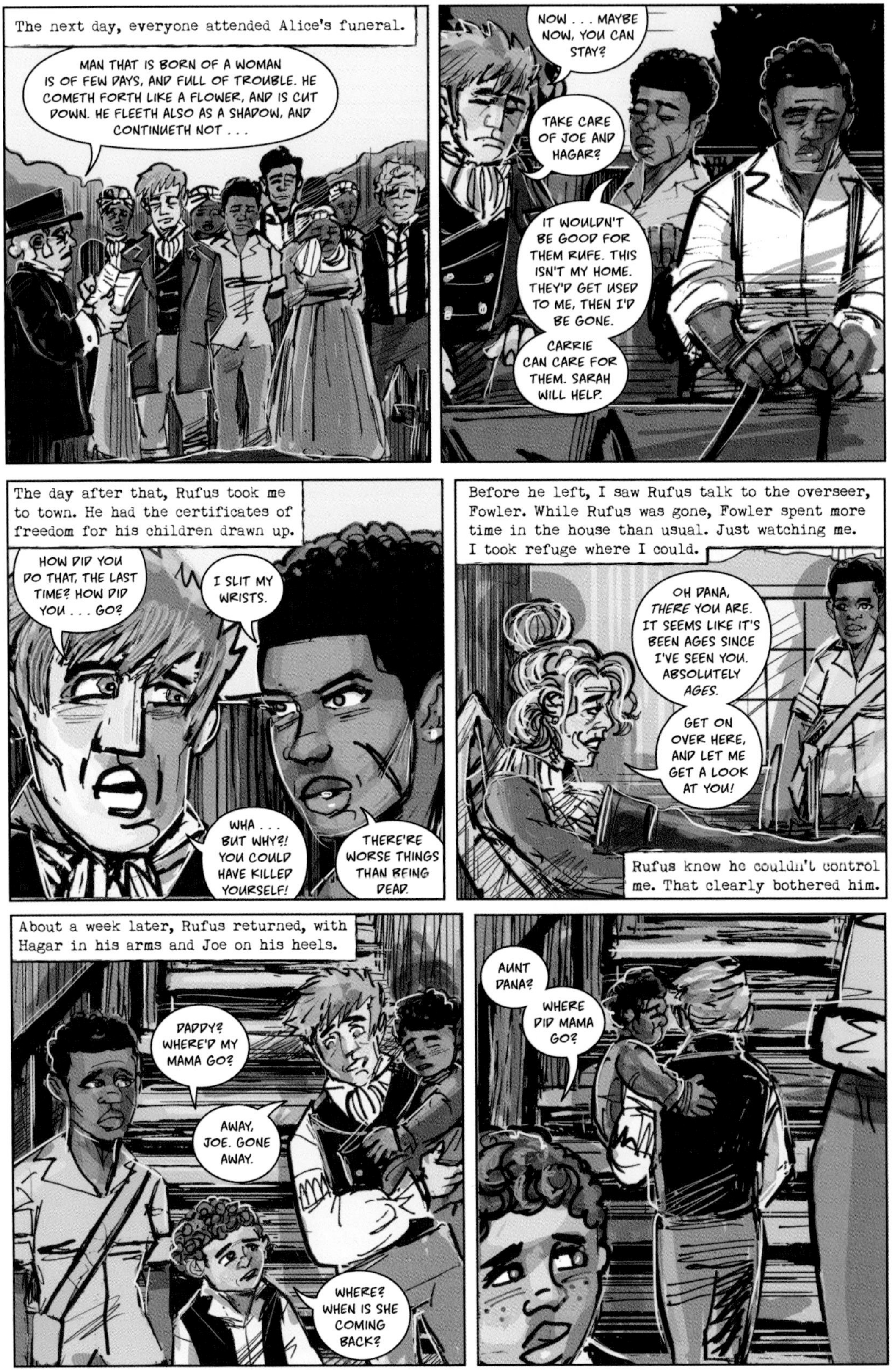
The next day, everyone attended Alice's funeral.
MAN THAT IS BORN OF A WOMAN IS OF FEW DAYS, AND FULL OF TROUBLE. HE COMETH FORTH LIKE A FLOWER, AND IS CUT DOWN. HE FLEETH ALSO AS A SHADOW, AND CONTINUETH NOT . . .
NOW . . . MAYBE NOW, YOU CAN STAY?
TAKE CARE OF JOE AND HAGAR?
IT WOULDN'T BE GOOD FOR THEM RUFE. THIS ISN'T MY HOME. THEY'D GET USED TO ME, THEN I'D BE GONE.
CARRIE CAN CARE FOR THEM. SARAH WILL HELP.
The day after that, Rufus took me to town. He had the certificates of freedom for his children drawn up.
HOW DID YOU DO THAT, THE LAST TIME? HOW DID YOU . . . GO?
I SLIT MY WRISTS.
WHA . . . BUT WHY?! YOU COULD HAVE KILLED YOURSELF!
THERE'RE WORSE THINGS THAN BEING DEAD.
Before he left, I saw Rufus talk to the overseer, Fowler. While Rufus was gone, Fowler spent more time in the house than usual. Just watching me. I took refuge where I could.
OH DANA, THERE YOU ARE. IT SEEMS LIKE IT'S BEEN AGES SINCE I'VE SEEN YOU. ABSOLUTELY AGES.
GET ON OVER HERE, AND LET ME GET A LOOK AT YOU!
Rufus knew he couldn't control me. That clearly bothered him.
About a week later, Rufus returned, with Hagar in his arms and Joe on his heels.
DADDY? WHERE'D MY MAMA GO?
AWAY, JOE. GONE AWAY.
WHERE? WHEN IS SHE COMING BACK?
AUNT DANA?
WHERE DID MAMA GO?

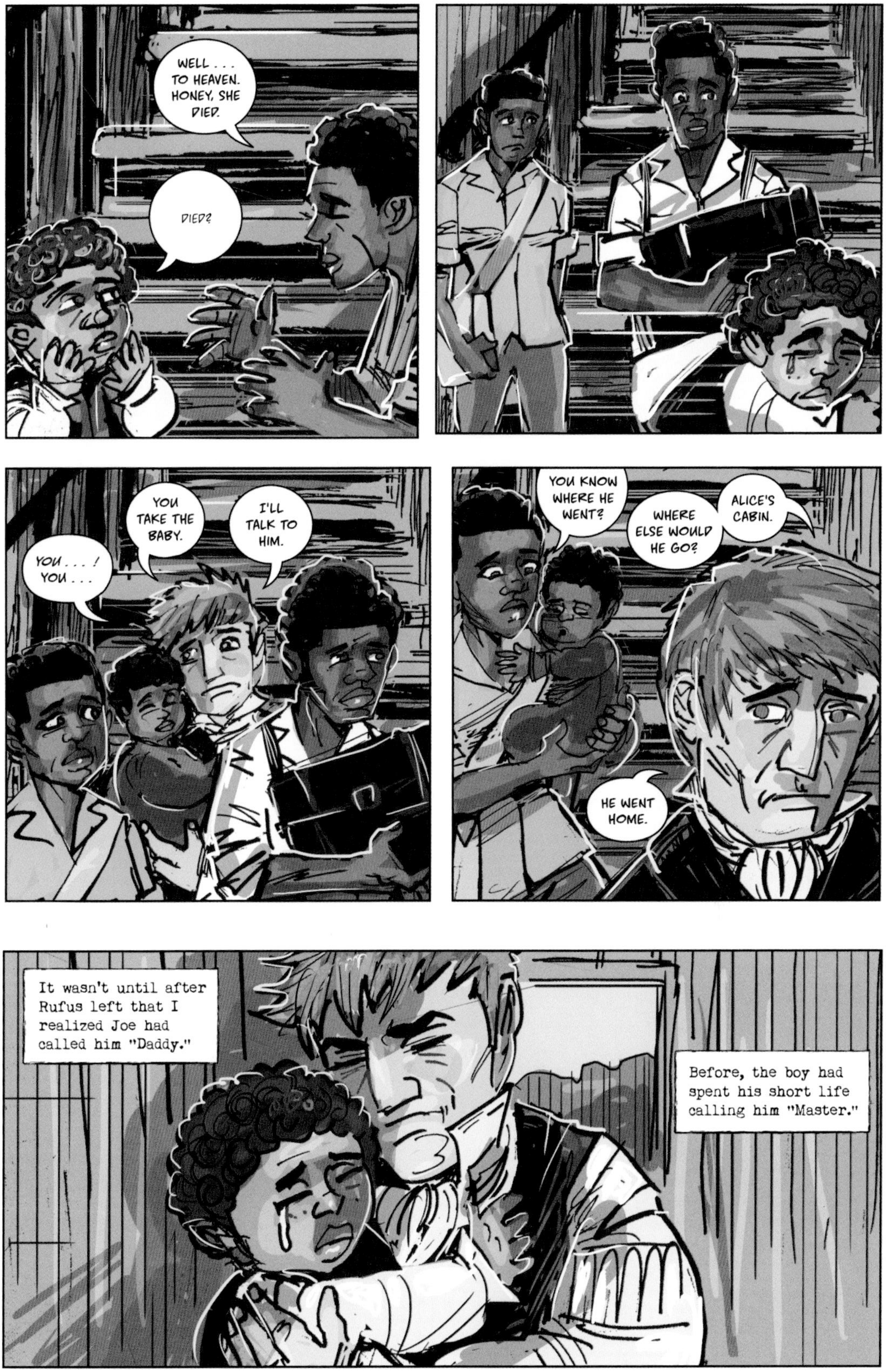
WELL . . . TO HEAVEN. HONEY, SHE DIED.
DIED?
YOU . . . ! YOU . . .
YOU TAKE THE BABY.
I'LL TALK TO HIM.
YOU KNOW WHERE HE WENT?
WHERE ELSE WOULD HE GO?
ALICE'S CABIN.
HE WENT HOME.
It wasn't until after Rufus left that I realized Joe had called him "Daddy."
Before, the boy had spent his short life calling him "Master."

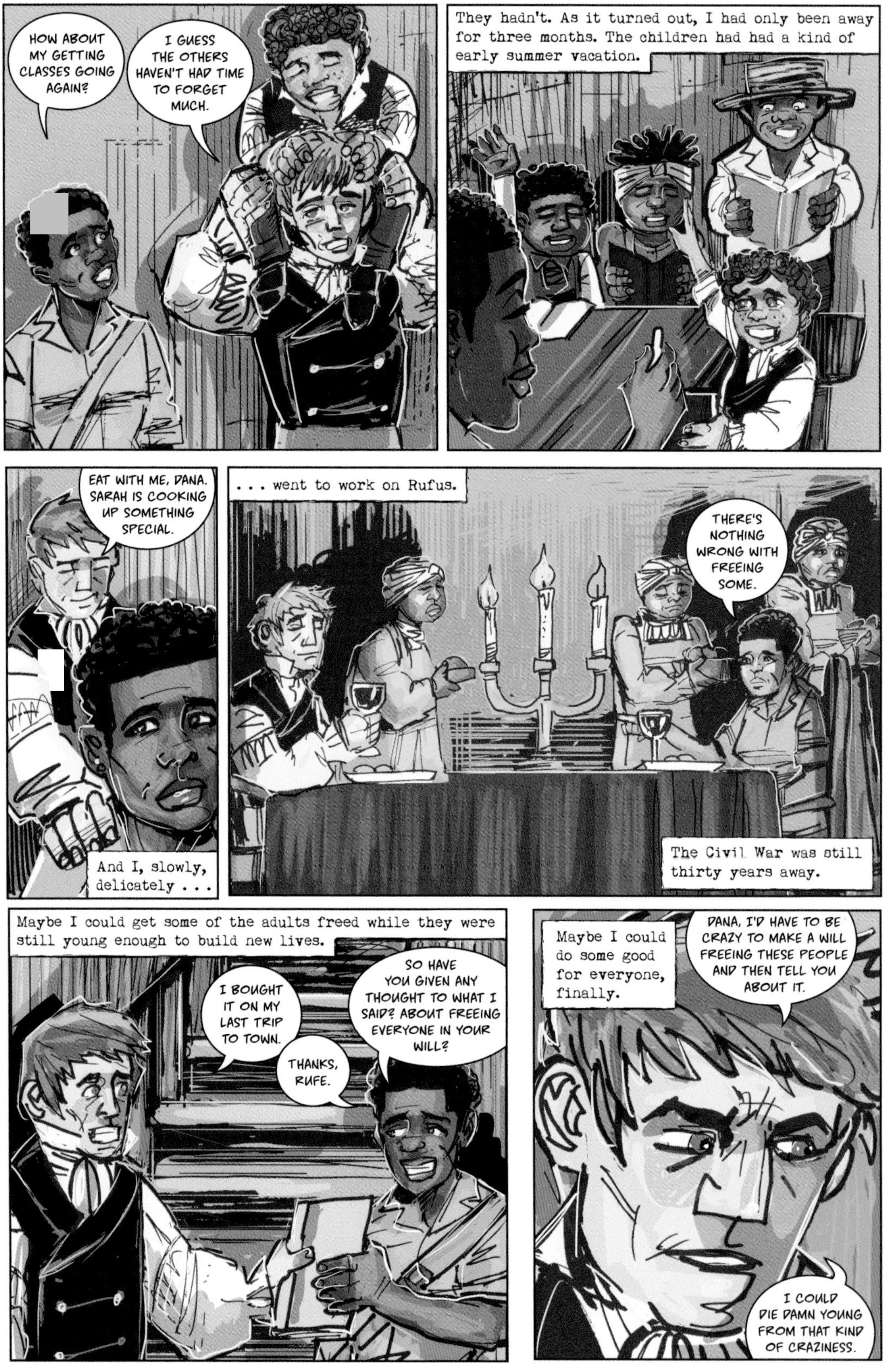
HOW ABOUT MY GETTING CLASSES GOING AGAIN?
I GUESS THE OTHERS HAVEN'T HAD TIME TO FORGET MUCH.
They hadn't. As it turned out, I had only been away for three months. The children had had a kind of early summer vacation.
EAT WITH ME, DANA. SARAH IS COOKING UP SOMETHING SPECIAL.
And I, slowly, delicately . . .
. . . went to work on Rufus.
THERE'S NOTHING WRONG WITH FREEING SOME.
The Civil War was still thirty years away.
Maybe I could get some of the adults freed while they were still young enough to build new lives.
I BOUGHT IT ON MY LAST TRIP TO TOWN.
THANKS, RUFE.
SO HAVE YOU GIVEN ANY THOUGHT TO WHAT I SAID? ABOUT FREEING EVERYONE IN YOUR WILL?
Maybe I could do some good for everyone, finally.
DANA, I'D HAVE TO BE CRAZY TO MAKE A WILL FREEING THESE PEOPLE AND THEN TELL YOU ABOUT IT.
I COULD DIE DAMN YOUNG FROM THAT KIND OF CRAZINESS.

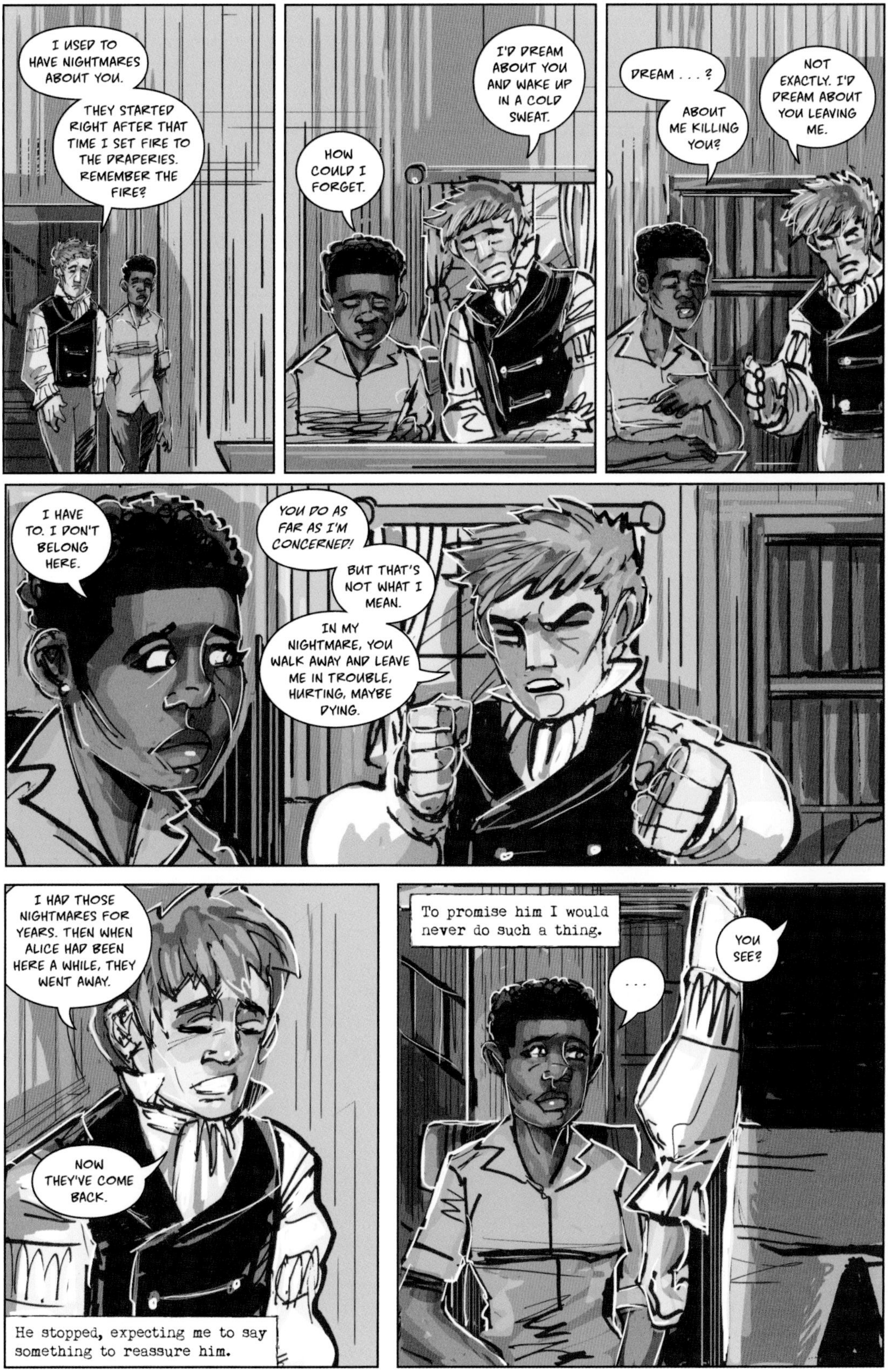
I USED TO HAVE NIGHTMARES ABOUT YOU.
THEY STARTED RIGHT AFTER THAT TIME I SET FIRE TO THE DRAPERIES. REMEMBER THE FIRE?
HOW COULD I FORGET.
I'D DREAM ABOUT YOU AND WAKE UP IN A COLD SWEAT.
DREAM . . . ?
ABOUT ME KILLING YOU?
NOT EXACTLY. I'D DREAM ABOUT YOU LEAVING ME.
I HAVE TO. I DON'T BELONG HERE.
YOU DO AS FAR AS I'M CONCERNED!
BUT THAT'S NOT WHAT I MEAN.
IN MY NIGHTMARE, YOU WALK AWAY AND LEAVE ME IN TROUBLE, HURTING, MAYBE DYING.
I HAD THOSE NIGHTMARES FOR YEARS. THEN WHEN ALICE HAD BEEN HERE A WHILE, THEY WENT AWAY.
NOW THEY'VE COME BACK.
He stopped, expecting me to say something to reassure him.
To promise him I would never do such a thing.
. . .
YOU SEE?

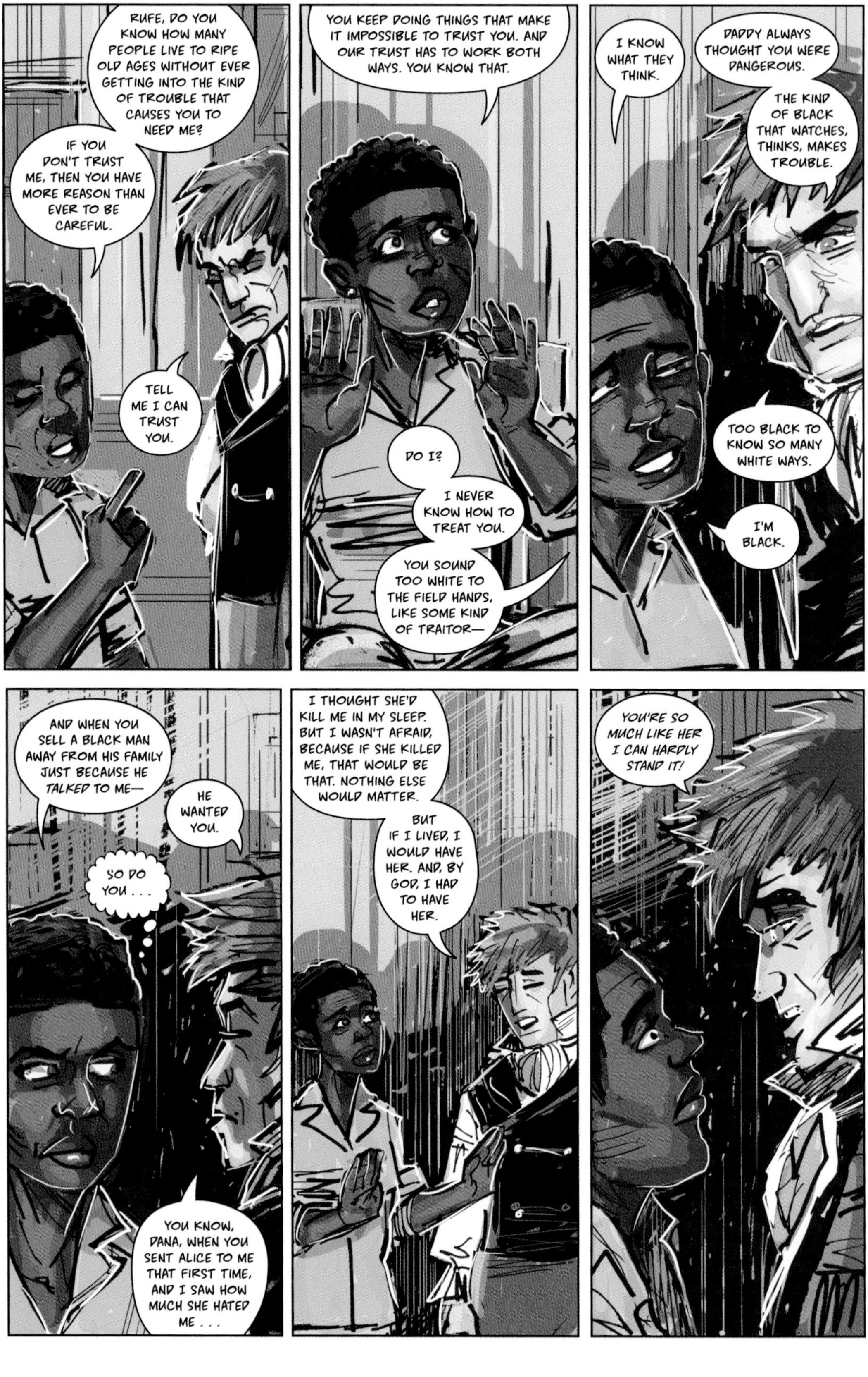
RUFE, DO YOU KNOW HOW MANY PEOPLE LIVE TO RIPE OLD AGES WITHOUT EVER GETTING INTO THE KIND OF TROUBLE THAT CAUSES YOU TO NEED ME?
IF YOU DON'T TRUST ME, THEN YOU HAVE MORE REASON THAN EVER TO BE CAREFUL.
TELL ME I CAN TRUST YOU.
YOU KEEP DOING THINGS THAT MAKE IT IMPOSSIBLE TO TRUST YOU. AND OUR TRUST HAS TO WORK BOTH WAYS. YOU KNOW THAT.
DO I?
I NEVER KNOW HOW TO TREAT YOU.
YOU SOUND TOO WHITE TO THE FIELD HANDS, LIKE SOME KIND OF TRAITOR—
I KNOW WHAT THEY THINK.
DADDY ALWAYS THOUGHT YOU WERE DANGEROUS.
THE KIND OF BLACK THAT WATCHES, THINKS, MAKES TROUBLE.
TOO BLACK TO KNOW SO MANY WHITE WAYS.
I'M BLACK.
AND WHEN YOU SELL A BLACK MAN AWAY FROM HIS FAMILY JUST BECAUSE HE *TALKED* TO ME—
HE WANTED YOU.
SO DO YOU . . .
YOU KNOW, DANA, WHEN YOU SENT ALICE TO ME THAT FIRST TIME, AND I SAW HOW MUCH SHE HATED ME . . .
I THOUGHT SHE'D KILL ME IN MY SLEEP. BUT I WASN'T AFRAID, BECAUSE IF SHE KILLED ME, THAT WOULD BE THAT. NOTHING ELSE WOULD MATTER.
BUT IF I LIVED, I WOULD HAVE HER. AND, BY GOD, I HAD TO HAVE HER.
YOU'RE SO MUCH LIKE HER I CAN HARDLY STAND IT!

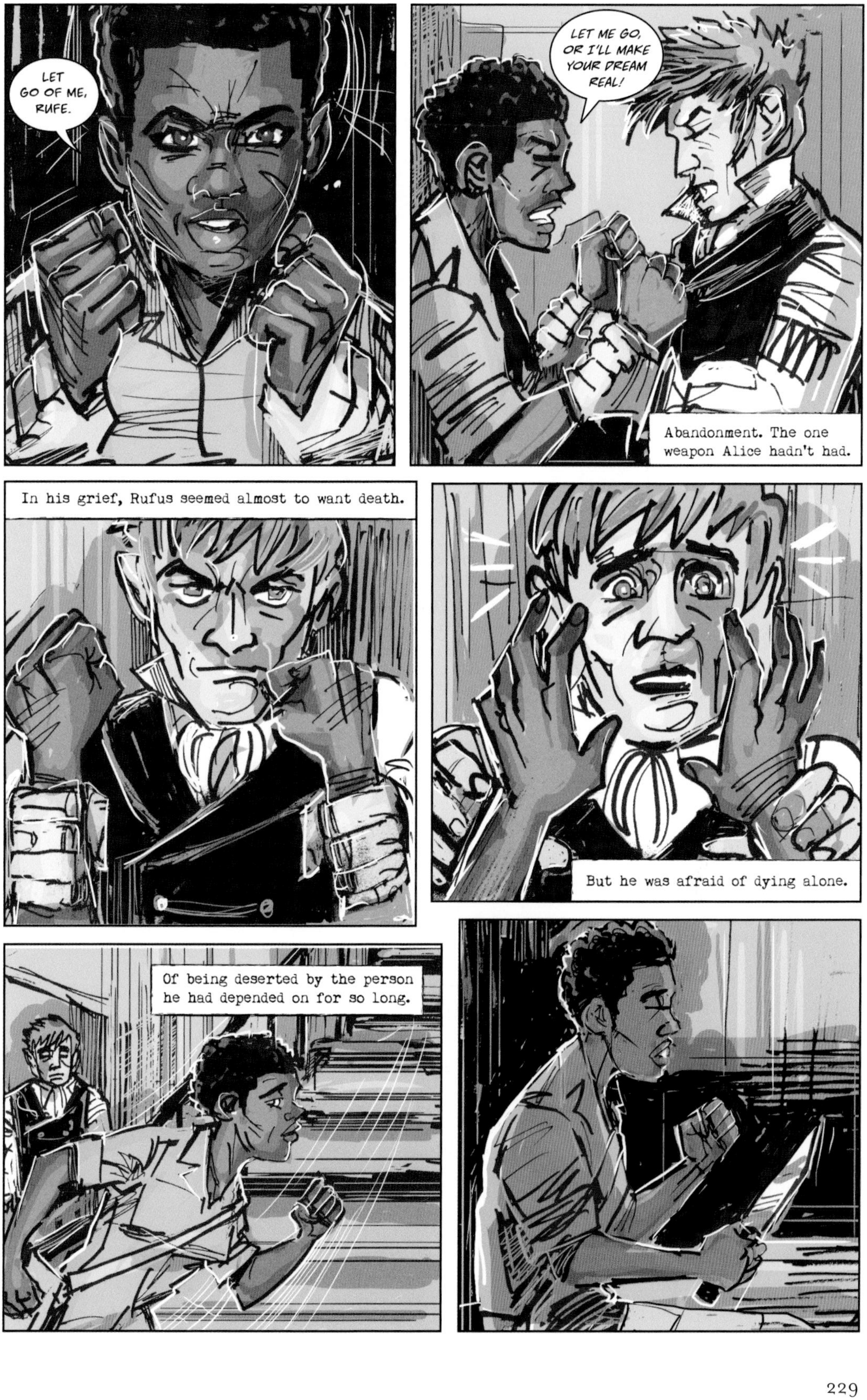
LET GO OF ME, RUFE.
LET ME GO, OR I'LL MAKE YOUR DREAM REAL!
Abandonment. The one weapon Alice hadn't had.
In his grief, Rufus seemed almost to want death.
But he was afraid of dying alone.
Of being deserted by the person he had depended on for so long.

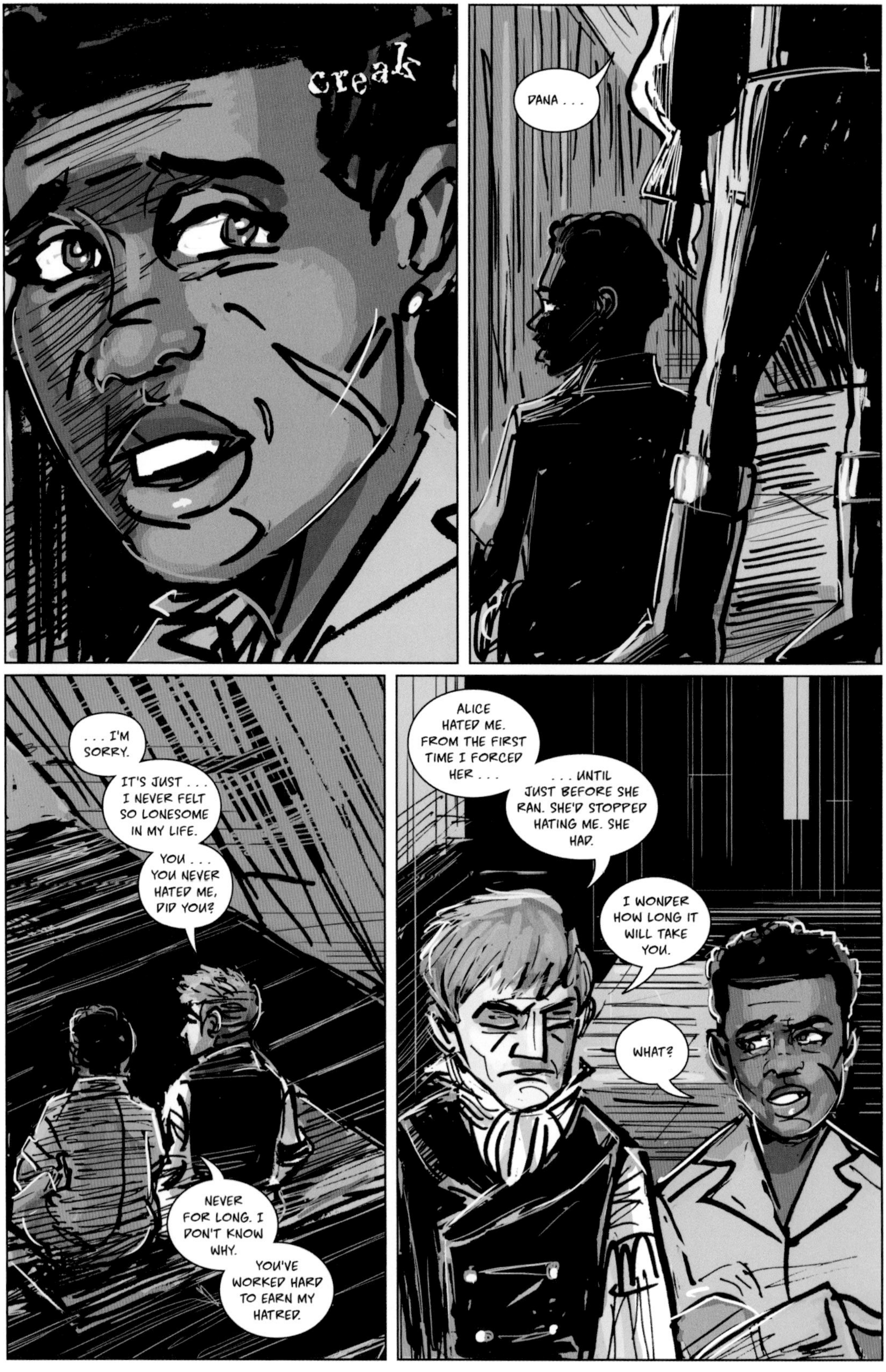
creak
DANA . . .
. . . I'M SORRY.
IT'S JUST . . . I NEVER FELT SO LONESOME IN MY LIFE.
YOU . . . YOU NEVER HATED ME, DID YOU?
NEVER FOR LONG. I DON'T KNOW WHY.
YOU'VE WORKED HARD TO EARN MY HATRED.
ALICE HATED ME. FROM THE FIRST TIME I FORCED HER . . .
. . . UNTIL JUST BEFORE SHE RAN. SHE'D STOPPED HATING ME. SHE HAD.
I WONDER HOW LONG IT WILL TAKE YOU.
WHAT?

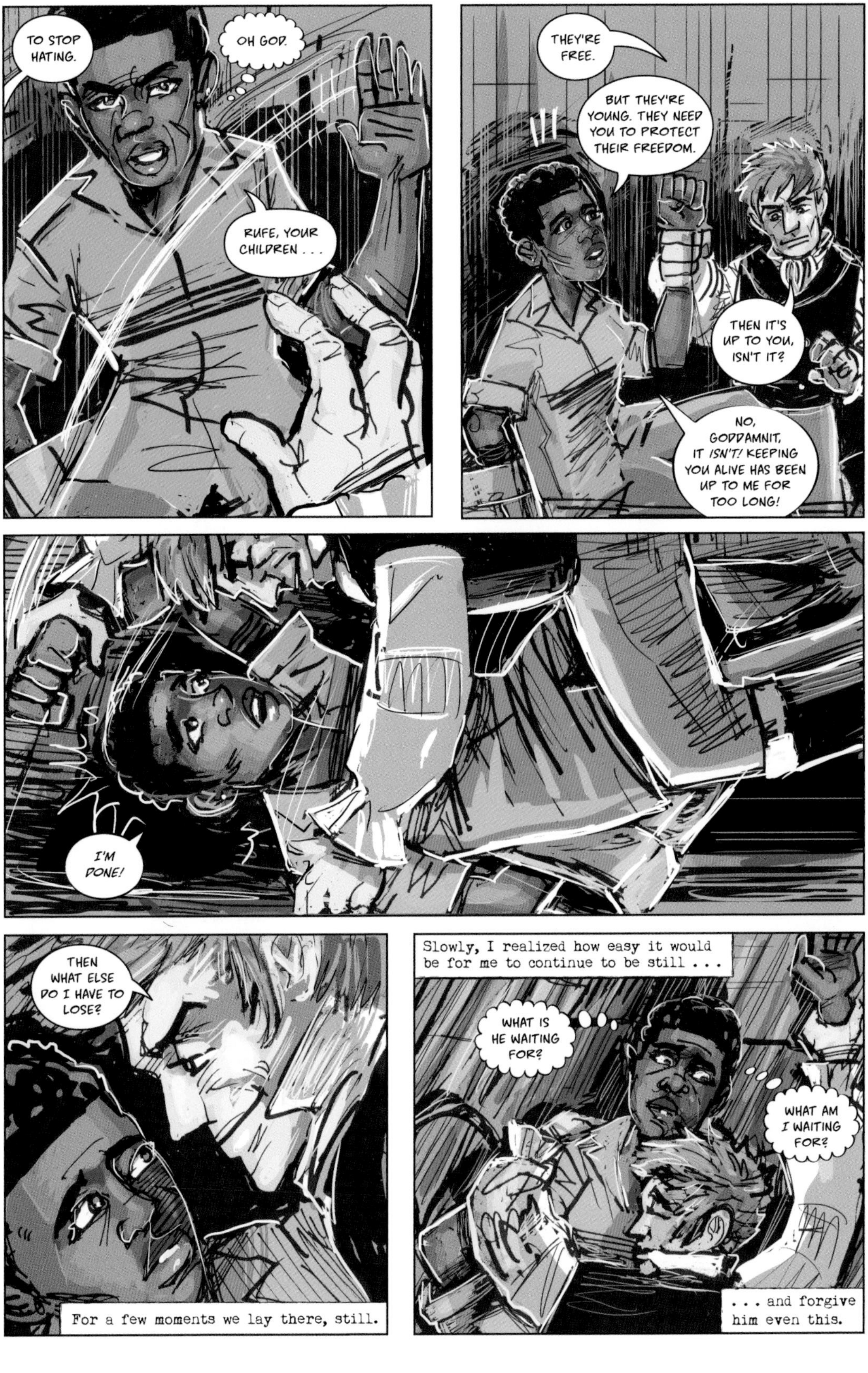
TO STOP HATING.
OH GOD.
RUFE, YOUR CHILDREN . . .
THEY'RE FREE.
BUT THEY'RE YOUNG. THEY NEED YOU TO PROTECT THEIR FREEDOM.
THEN IT'S UP TO YOU, ISN'T IT?
NO, GODDAMNIT, IT *ISN'T!* KEEPING YOU ALIVE HAS BEEN UP TO ME FOR TOO LONG!
I'M DONE!
THEN WHAT ELSE DO I HAVE TO LOSE?
For a few moments we lay there, still.
Slowly, I realized how easy it would be for me to continue to be still . . .
WHAT IS HE WAITING FOR?
WHAT AM I WAITING FOR?
. . . and forgive him even this.

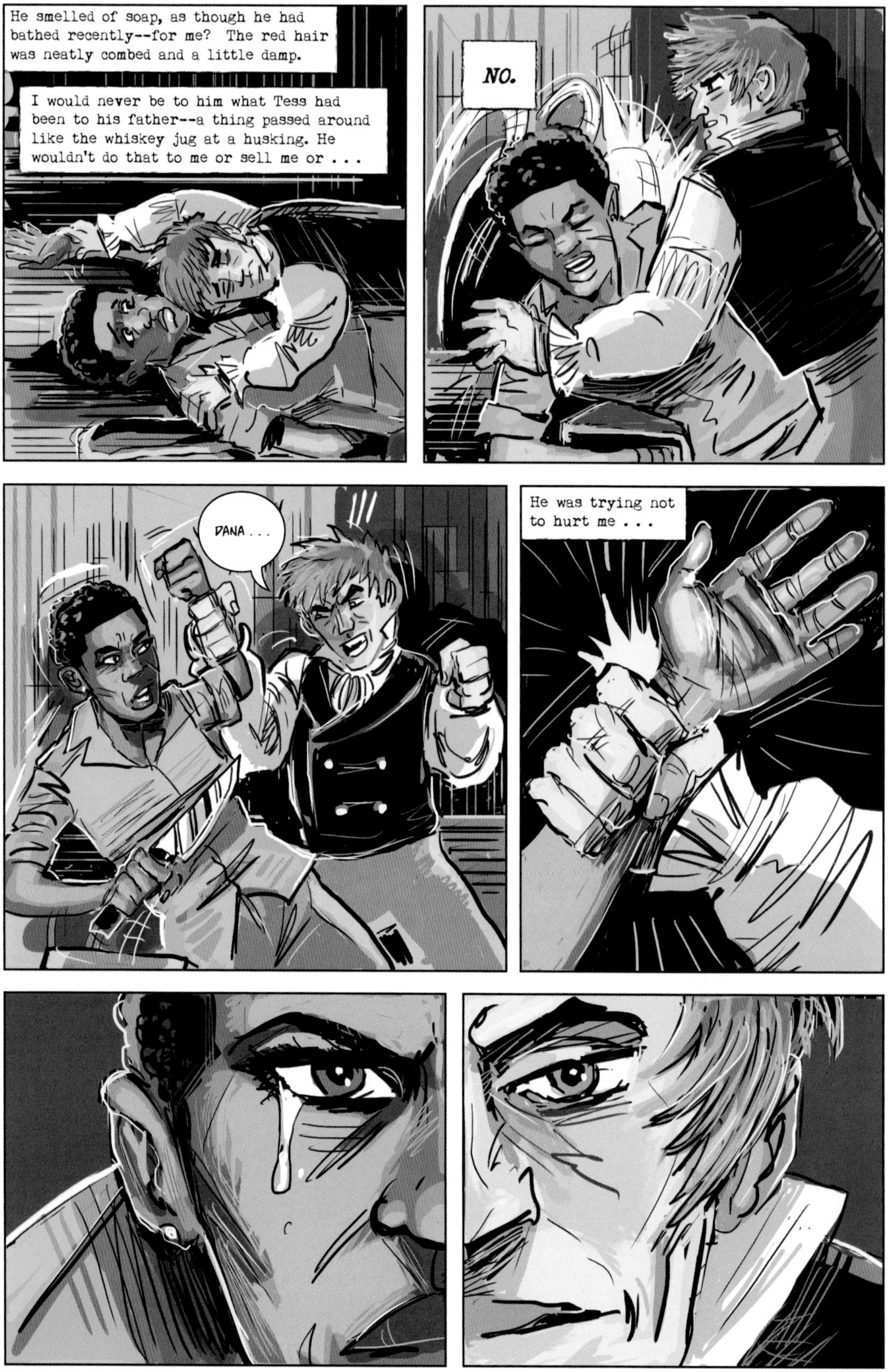
He smelled of soap, as though he had bathed recently--for me? The red hair was neatly combed and a little damp.
I would never be to him what Tess had been to his father--a thing passed around like the whiskey jug at a husking. He wouldn't do that to me or sell me or . . .
NO.
DANA . . .
He was trying not to hurt me . . .

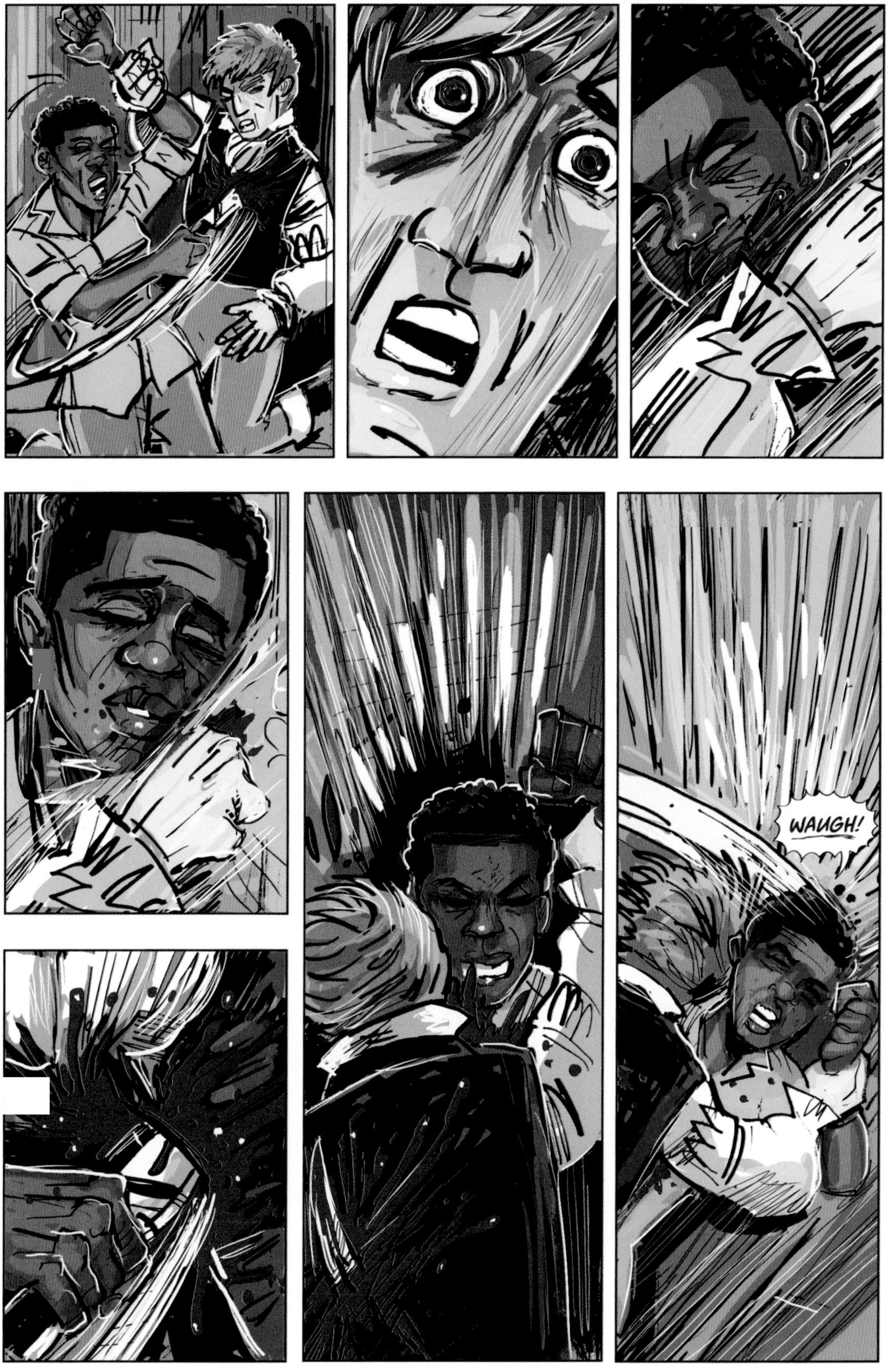
WAUGH!

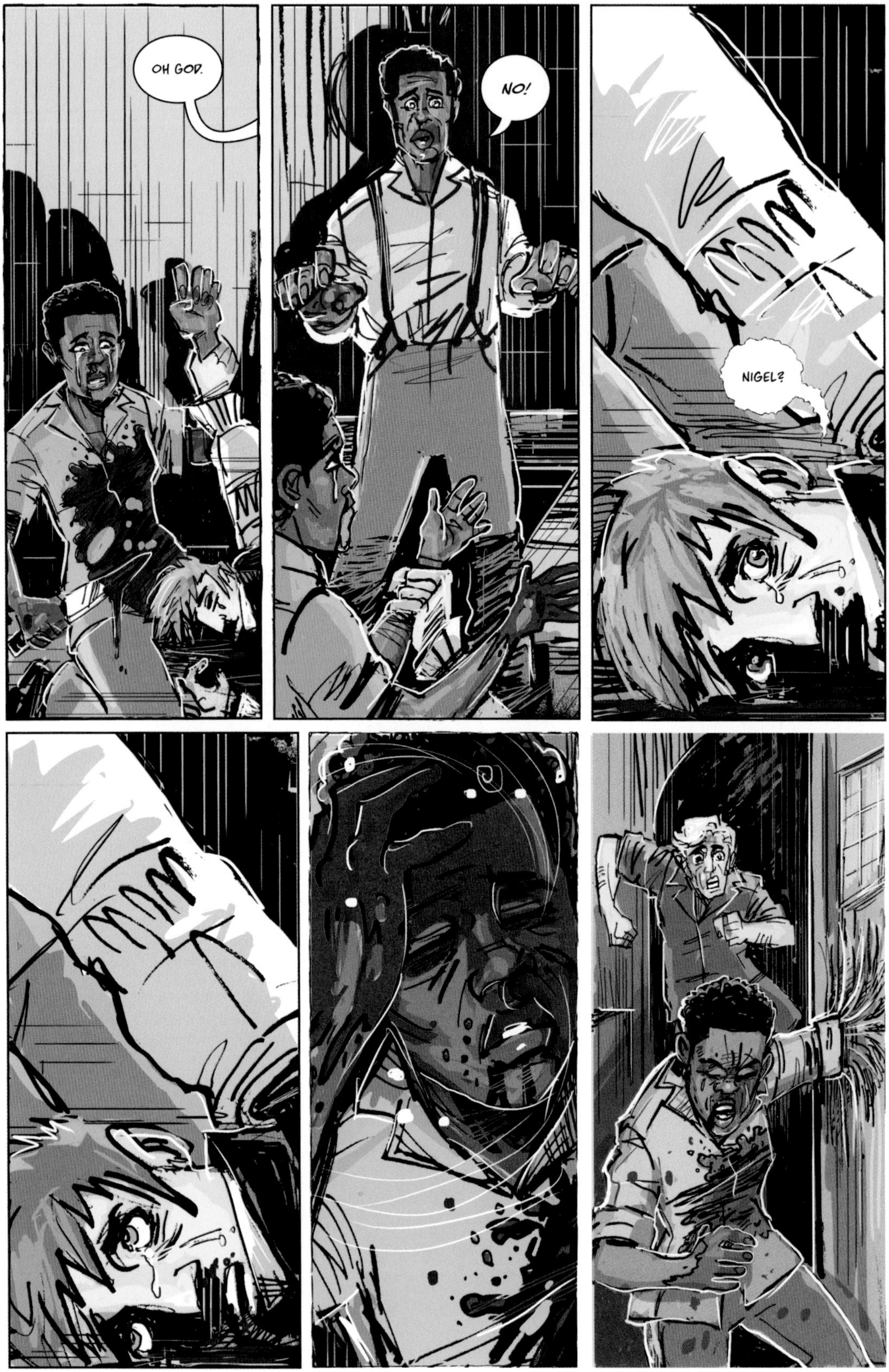
OH GOD.
NO!
NIGEL?

EPILOGUE

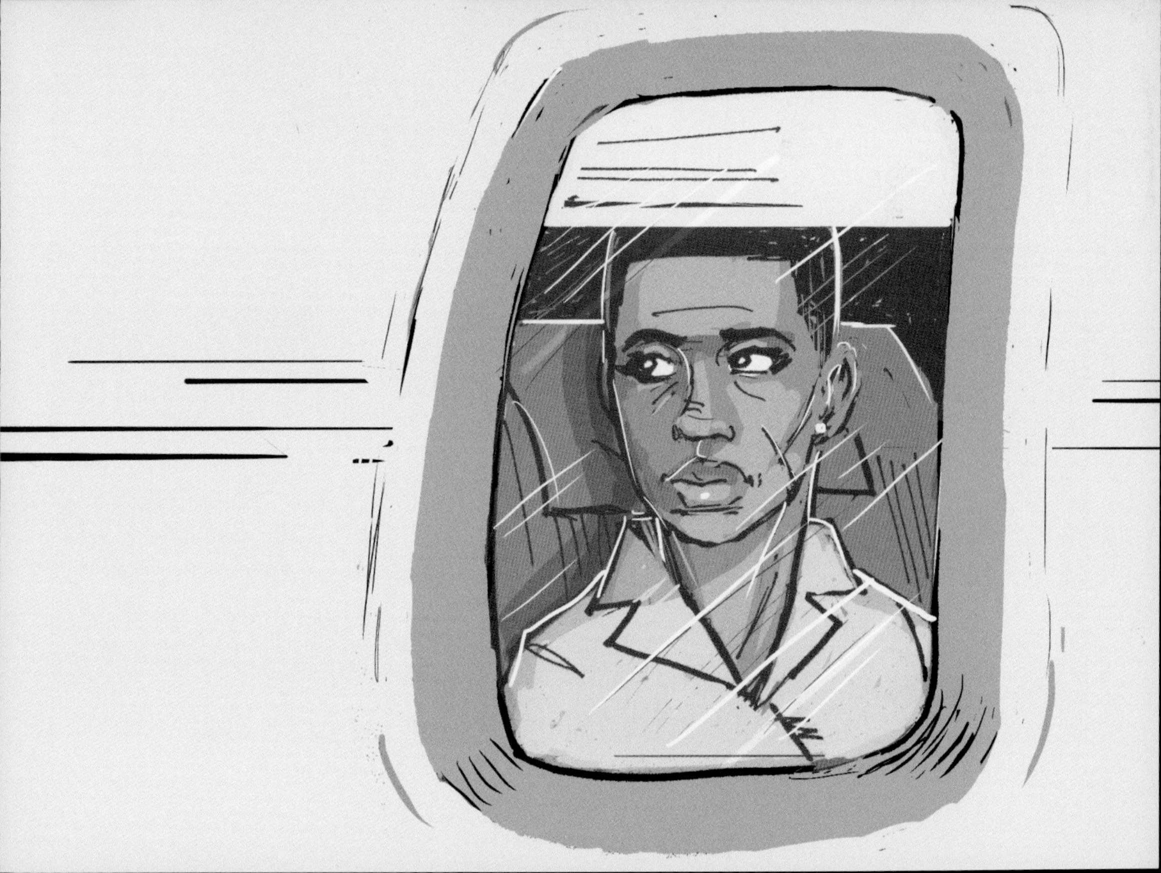

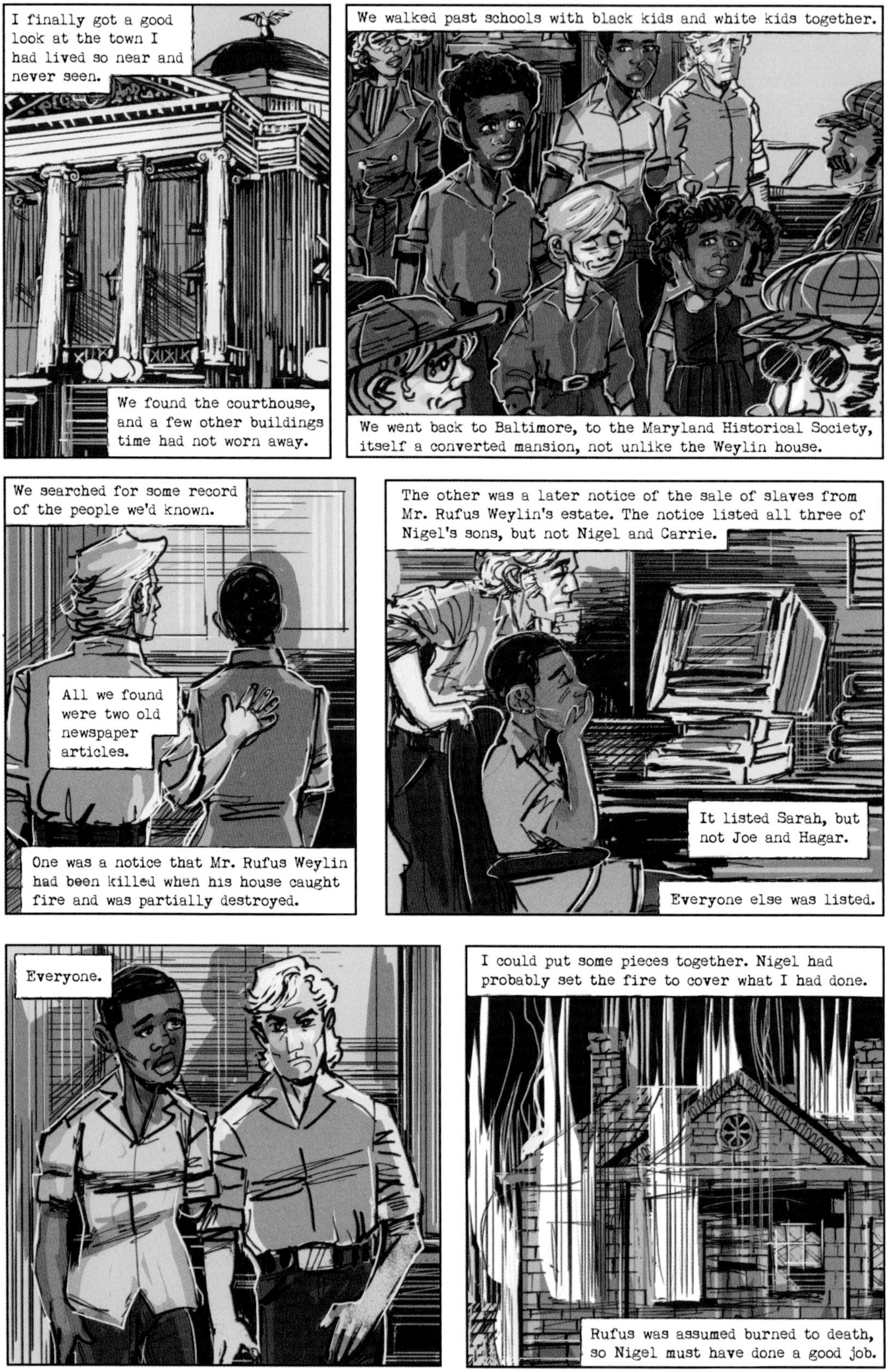
I finally got a good look at the town I had lived so near and never seen.
We found the courthouse, and a few other buildings time had not worn away.
We walked past schools with black kids and white kids together.
We went back to Baltimore, to the Maryland Historical Society, itself a converted mansion, not unlike the Weylin house.
We searched for some record of the people we'd known.
All we found were two old newspaper articles.
One was a notice that Mr. Rufus Weylin had been killed when his house caught fire and was partially destroyed.
The other was a later notice of the sale of slaves from Mr. Rufus Weylin's estate. The notice listed all three of Nigel's sons, but not Nigel and Carrie.
It listed Sarah, but not Joe and Hagar.
Everyone else was listed.
Everyone.
I could put some pieces together. Nigel had probably set the fire to cover what I had done.
Rufus was assumed burned to death, so Nigel must have done a good job.

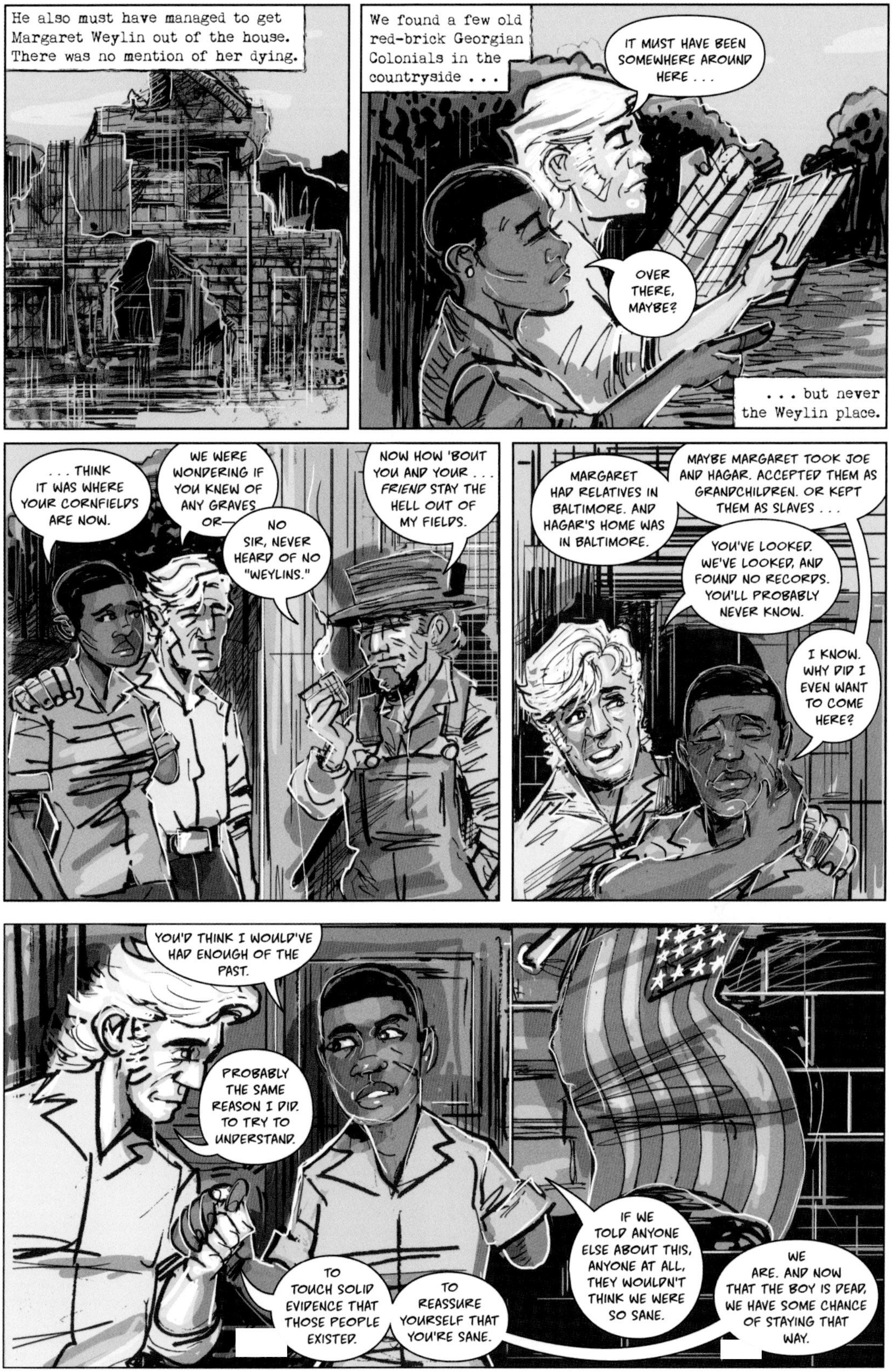

He also must have managed to get Margaret Weylin out of the house. There was no mention of her dying.
We found a few old red-brick Georgian Colonials in the countryside . . .
IT MUST HAVE BEEN SOMEWHERE AROUND HERE . . .
OVER THERE, MAYBE?
. . . but never the Weylin place.
. . . THINK IT WAS WHERE YOUR CORNFIELDS ARE NOW.
WE WERE WONDERING IF YOU KNEW OF ANY GRAVES OR—
NO SIR, NEVER HEARD OF NO "WEYLINS."
NOW HOW 'BOUT YOU AND YOUR . . . FRIEND STAY THE HELL OUT OF MY FIELDS.
MARGARET HAD RELATIVES IN BALTIMORE. AND HAGAR'S HOME WAS IN BALTIMORE.
MAYBE MARGARET TOOK JOE AND HAGAR. ACCEPTED THEM AS GRANDCHILDREN. OR KEPT THEM AS SLAVES . . .
YOU'VE LOOKED. WE'VE LOOKED, AND FOUND NO RECORDS. YOU'LL PROBABLY NEVER KNOW.
I KNOW. WHY DID I EVEN WANT TO COME HERE?
YOU'D THINK I WOULD'VE HAD ENOUGH OF THE PAST.
PROBABLY THE SAME REASON I DID. TO TRY TO UNDERSTAND.
TO TOUCH SOLID EVIDENCE THAT THOSE PEOPLE EXISTED.
TO REASSURE YOURSELF THAT YOU'RE SANE.
IF WE TOLD ANYONE ELSE ABOUT THIS, ANYONE AT ALL, THEY WOULDN'T THINK WE WERE SO SANE.
WE ARE. AND NOW THAT THE BOY IS DEAD, WE HAVE SOME CHANCE OF STAYING THAT WAY.

ABOUT OCTAVIA E. BUTLER

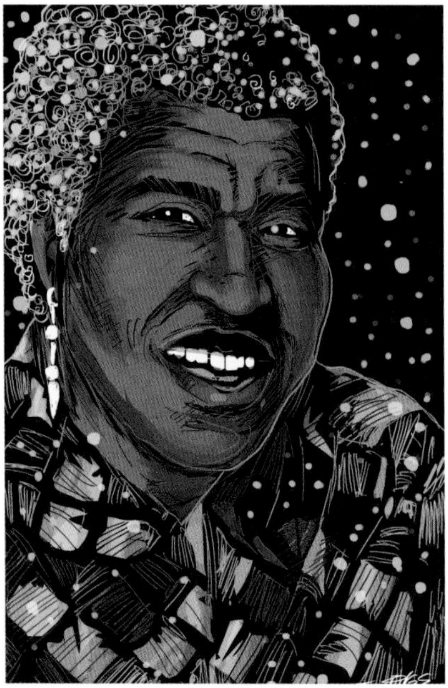

She described herself as, "I'm black, I'm solitary, I've always been an outsider"—but she left off "extraordinary."

Octavia Estelle Butler was indeed a most extraordinary writer. Often referred to as the "grande dame of science fiction," she is the author of a short story collection and more than a dozen novels, which have been translated into ten languages. Her work garnered two Hugo Awards, two Nebula Awards, and the PEN Lifetime Achievement Award. She was the first science fiction writer to win a MacArthur "Genius" Fellowship.

Butler was born in Pasadena, California, on June 22, 1947. A graduate of Pasadena Community College, she also attended California State University and UCLA. When she participated in the Clarion Science Fiction Writing Workshop, she attracted the attention of the famous science fiction writer and editor Harlan Ellison, who gave her a typewriter and bought Butler's first professional story.

Butler began writing as a child and was an avid reader of science fiction—which she couldn't help but notice never included characters like herself. Many of her novels, such as *Kindred*, feature strong, black, female protagonists struggling with complicated issues of survival. She was a master of powerful, realistic prose that supported inventive genre narratives, and most important explored the deepest, often disturbing possibilities of human relationships.

A list of Octavia Butler's books can be found on page 240.

ABOUT THE ADAPTOR

Damian Duffy is a cartoonist, writer, and letterer, and the co-editor of *Black Comix: African American Independent Comics Art & Culture*. He holds a PhD in Library and Information Science from the University of Illinois at Urbana-Champaign.

ABOUT THE ARTIST

John Jennings co-edited the Eisner Award–winning anthology *The Blacker the Ink: Constructions of Black Identity in Comics and Sequential Art*. He is professor of media and cultural studies at the University of California at Riverside and was awarded the Nasir Jones HipHop Fellowship at Harvard's Hutchins Center for African & African American Research.

ACKNOWLEDGMENTS

All encompassing thanks to Sheila Keenan for making this book exist.
More thanks to Charlie Kochman, Susan Van Metre, Pamela Notarantonio,
Chad W. Beckerman, Michael Clark, Kathy Lovisolo, Melissa Esner,
and Maya Bradford.

Further thanks to Alex Batchelor, Anthony Moncada, Stacey Robinson,
Solomon Robinson, and Tim Fielder. Thank you again to the Octavia E.
Butler estate, and thank you always to Octavia E. Butler.

FOR FURTHER READING BY OCTAVIA E. BUTLER

Patternist Series

Patternmaster

Mind of My Mind

Survivor

Wild Seed

Clay's Ark

Seed to Harvest (omnibus)

Xenogenesis Series

Dawn

Adulthood Rites

Imago

Xenogenesis (omnibus)

Lilith's Brood (omnibus)

Parable Series

Parable of the Sower

Parable of the Talents

Stand-Alone Novels

Kindred

Fledgling

Short Story Collections

Bloodchild and Other Stories

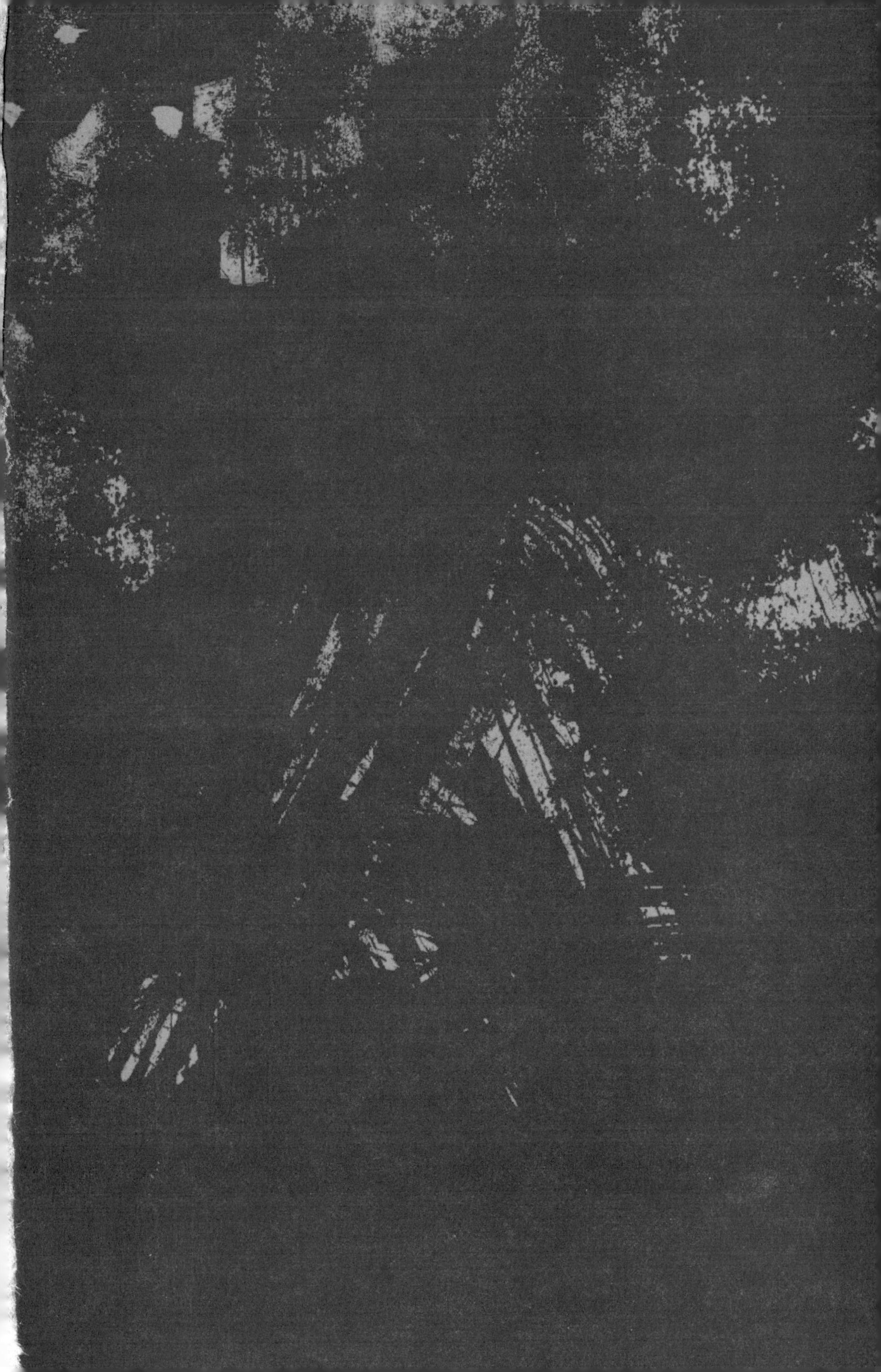